The Collector's Book of Science Fiction by H.G. WELLS

H.G. WELLS
as he appeared in *The Graphic*
of January 7, 1899

The Collector's Book of Science Fiction by H.G. WELLS

From Rare, Original, Illustrated Magazines

Including the complete novels

THE WAR OF THE WORLDS

THE FIRST MEN IN THE MOON

WHEN THE SLEEPER WAKES

. . . the short stories

THE COUNTRY OF THE BLIND

THE EMPIRE OF THE ANTS

THE VALLEY OF SPIDERS

THE MAN WHO COULD WORK MIRACLES

. . . and many more

Selected by ALAN K. RUSSELL

CASTLE BOOKS

BIBLIOGRAPHIC SOURCES

IN THE ABYSS   *Pearson's Magazine*, August 1896

THE WAR OF THE WORLDS   *Pearson's Magazine*, April-December 1897

STORIES OF THE STONE AGE   *The Idler*, May-November 1897

THE MAN WHO COULD WORK MIRACLES   *The Illustrated London News*, July 1898

WHEN THE SLEEPER WAKES   *The Graphic*, 1898-1899

THE FIRST MEN IN THE MOON   *The Strand Magazine*, December 1900-August 1901

THE STORY OF THE INEXPERIENCED GHOST   *The Strand Magazine*, March 1902

THE VALLEY OF SPIDERS   *Pearson's Magazine*, March 1903

THE LAND IRONCLADS   *The Strand Magazine*, December 1903

THE COUNTRY OF THE BLIND   *The Strand Magazine*, April 1904

AEPYORNIS ISLAND   *Pearson's Magazine*, February 1905

THE DIAMOND MAKER   *Pearson's Magazine*, March 1905

THE FLOWERING OF THE STRANGE ORCHID   *Pearson's Magazine*, April 1905

THE STOLEN BACILLUS   *Pearson's Magazine*, June 1905

THE EMPIRE OF THE ANTS   *The Strand Magazine*, December 1905

©Copyright 1978 by CASTLE BOOKS
A division of Book Sales, Inc., Secaucus, New Jersey

ISBN 0-89009-208-7   November—1978

Manufactured in the United States of America

© Selection and Compilation by Alan K. Russell 1978

CONTENTS

(Complete books appear in capitals)

Portrait of H.G. Wells   *Frontispiece*

H.G. Wells: A Biographical Note   *vii*

1
THE WAR OF THE WORLDS   1

2
The Country of the Blind   105

3
The Flowering of the Strange Orchid   123

4
Aepyornis Island   131

5
THE FIRST MEN IN THE MOON   141

6
The Diamond Maker   249

7
The Story of the Inexperienced Ghost   257

8
The Empire of the Ants   269

9
STORIES OF THE STONE AGE   281
    Ugh-Lomi and Uya
    Ugh-Lomi and the Cave Bear
    The First Horseman
    The Reign of Uya the Lion
    The Fight in the Lion's Thicket

10
The Stolen Bacillus   329

11
In the Abyss   337

12
The Valley of Spiders   351

13
WHEN THE SLEEPER WAKES   361

14
The Man Who Could Work Miracles   479

15
The Land Ironclads   499

Bibliographic Note   515

HERBERT GEORGE WELLS:
A BIOGRAPHICAL NOTE

H.G. WELLS was born on September 21, 1866, the third son of a shop-keeper in Bromley, a southern suburb of London.

After leaving school, he served for two unhappy periods as a draper's apprentice and a further period as a chemist's assistant. He then won a scholarship to the Normal School of Science in South Kensington (today the Imperial College of Science) and studied biology under the famous Thomas Henry Huxley. He went on to teach at a small school, where he sustained a serious kidney injury and was forced to return home for a period of convalescence, during which time he tutored and also enjoyed sporadic success in journalism. The publication of his first novel in 1895 met with widespread acclaim, and he embarked upon the rapid production of further scientific romances, collections of journalism, and short stories.

After moving to the seaside resort of Folkestone, where both his sons were born, Wells visited the United States and interviewed President Theodore Roosevelt. His literary career continued with a further output of novels and scientific romances until the outbreak of the first World War, when he became a leading advocate of the establishment of a strong League of Nations. He was in charge of British propaganda against Germany, and visited Lenin in the Kremlin. After the war, he traveled widely in a crusade for a new world order, and stood unsuccessfully for Parliament.

Wells' writings continued over the years. He had meetings with Joseph Stalin and Franklin D. Roosevelt, and—during World War II—organized the Sankey Committee for a new Declaration of the Rights of Man.

H.G. Wells wrote hundreds of stories and articles and 156 books. Apart from his science fiction (rare original magazine appearances of which are presented in this volume), he wrote best-selling novels and non-fiction. His novels include *Love and Mr. Lewisham*, *Kipps*, and *Mr. Britling Sees It Through* (which was on the best-seller lists for two years). Among his many works of non-fiction and social comment is *The Outline of History*, which sold over two million copies and remained on the best-seller lists for four years.

—1—

THE WAR OF THE WORLDS

Originally published in *Pearson's Magazine*
April-December 1897

THE WAR OF THE WORLDS

H. G. WELLS

"But who shall dwell in these Worlds if they be inhabited? . . . Are we or they Lords of the World? . . . And how are all things made for man?"—(Kepler: quoted in *The Anatomy of Melancholy*.)

I.—THE EVE OF THE WAR.

No one would have believed in the last years of the nineteenth century that human affairs were being watched keenly and closely by intelligences greater than man's and yet as mortal as his own; that as men busied themselves about their affairs they were scrutinised and studied perhaps almost as closely as a man with a microscope might scrutinise the transient creatures that swarm and multiply in a drop of water.

With infinite complacency men went to and fro over this little globe about their affairs, dreaming themselves the highest creatures in the whole vast universe, and serene in their assurance of their empire over matter. It is just possible that the infusoria under the microscope do the same.

No one gave a thought to the Older Worlds of Space, or thought of them only to dismiss the idea of life upon them as impossible or improbable. At most, terrestrial men fancied there might be other men upon Mars, probably inferior to themselves and ready to welcome a missionary enterprise. Yet across the gulf of space minds that are to our minds as ours are to those of the beasts that perish, intellects vast and cool and unsympathetic, regarded this earth with envious eyes, and slowly and surely drew up their plans against us. And early in the twentieth century came the great disillusionment.

The planet Mars, I may remind the reader, revolves about the sun at a mean distance of 140,000,000 miles, and the light and heat it receives from the sun is scarcely half of that received by this world. It must be, if the nebular hypothesis has any truth, older than

3

our world, and long before this earth ceased to be molten, life upon its surface must have begun its course. The fact that it is scarcely one seventh of the volume of the earth must have accelerated its cooling to the temperature at which life could begin. It has air and water, and all that is necessary for the support of animated existence.

Yet so vain is man, and so blinded by his vanity, that no writer up to the very end of the nineteenth century expressed any idea that intelligent life might have developed there, far, or indeed at all, beyond its earthly level. Nor was it generally understood that since Mars is older than our earth, with scarcely a quarter of the superficial area, and remoter from the sun, it necessarily followed that it was not only more distant from life's beginning there but nearer its end.

The secular cooling that must some day overtake our planet has already gone far indeed with our neighbour. Its physical condition is still largely a mystery, but we know now that even in its equatorial region the midday temperature barely approaches that of our coolest winter. Its air is much more attenuated than ours, its oceans have shrunk until they cover but a third of its surface, huge snowcaps gather and melt about either pole as its slow seasons change, and periodically inundate its temperate zones. That last stage of exhaustion which to us is still incredibly remote, has become a present-day problem for the inhabitants of Mars.

The immediate pressure of necessity has brightened their intellects, enlarged their powers, and hardened their hearts. And looking across space, with instruments and intelligences such as we can only dream of vaguely, they see at its nearest distance, only 35,000,000 of miles sunward of them, a morning star of hope, our own warmer planet, green with vegetation and grey with water, with a cloudy atmosphere eloquent of fertility, with glimpses through its drifting cloud wisps, of broad stretches of populous country and narrow navy-crowded seas.

And we men, the creatures who inhabit this earth, must be to them at least as alien and as lowly as are the monkeys and lemurs to us. The intellectual side of man already admits that life is an incessant struggle for existence, and it would seem that in the final issue the same is the belief of the minds upon Mars.

Their world is far gone in its cooling, and this world is still palpitating and crowded with life, but crowded only with what they regard as inferior animals. To carry warfare sunward is their only escape from the destruction that generation by generation creeps upon them.

And before we judge of them too harshly in their invasion we must remember what ruthless and utter destruction our own species has wrought not only upon animals, such as the vanished bison and the dodo, but upon its own inferior races. The Tasmanians, in spite of their human likeness, were entirely swept out of existence in a war of extermination waged by European immigrants in the space of fifty years. Are we such apostles of mercy as to complain if the Martians turned against us ?

The Martians seemed to have calculated their descent with amazing subtlety — their mathematical learning is evidently far in excess of ours—and to have carried out their preparations with a well-nigh perfect unanimity. Had our instruments only permitted it we might have seen the gathering trouble far back in the nineteenth century. Men like Schiaparelli watched the red planet—it is odd, by the bye, that for countless centuries Mars has been the star of War—but failed to interpret the fluctuating appearances of the markings they mapped so well. All that time the Martians must have been getting ready.

During the opposition of 1894 a great light was seen on the illuminated part of the disc, first by Perrotin, of the Nice observatory, and then by other observers. English readers heard of it first in the issue of *Nature* dated August 2nd. I am inclined to think that the appearance may have been the casting of the huge gun, the vast pit sunk into their planet, from which their shots were fired at us. Peculiar markings, as yet unexplained, were seen near the site of that outbreak during the next two oppositions.

The storm burst upon us six years ago now. As Mars approached opposition, Lavelle of Java set the wires of the astronomical exchange palpitating with the amazing intelligence of a huge outbreak of incandescent gas upon the planet. It had occurred towards midnight of the twelfth, and the spectroscope to which he had at once resorted indicated a mass of flaming gas, chiefly hydrogen, moving at an enormous velocity towards this earth. This jet of fire had become invisible about a quarter-past twelve. He compared it to a colossal puff of flame, suddenly and violently squirted out of the planet, "as flaming gas rushes out of a gun."

A singularly appropriate phrase it proved. Yet the next day there was nothing of this in the papers, except a little note in the *Daily Telegraph*, and the world went in ignorance of one of the gravest dangers that ever threatened the human race. I might not have heard of the eruption at all had I not met Ogilvy, the well known astronomer of Ottershaw. He was immensely excited at the news, and in the excess of his feelings invited me up to take a turn with him that night in a scrutiny of the red planet.

In spite of all that has happened since, I still remember that vigil very distinctly, the black and silent observatory, the shadowed lantern, throwing a feeble glow upon the floor in the corner, the steady ticking of the clockwork of the telescope, the little slit in

I still remember that vigil
very distinctly.

the roof, an oblong of blue profundity with the star dust streaked across it. Ogilvy moved about, invisible but audible. Looking through the telescope, one saw a circle of deep blue and the little round planet swimming in the field. It seemed such a little thing, so bright and small and still, faintly marked with transverse stripes, and slightly flattened from the perfect round. But so little it was, so silvery warm, a pin's head of light. It was as if it quivered a little, but really this was the telescope vibrating with the activity of the clock-work that kept the planet in view.

As I watched, the little star seemed to grow larger and smaller and to advance and recede, but that was simply that my eye was tired. Forty millions of miles it was from us, more than forty millions of miles of void. Few people realise the immensity of vacancy in which the dust of the material universe swims.

Near it in the field, I remember, were three little points of light, three telescopic stars infinitely remote, and all around it was the unfathomable darkness of empty space. You know how that blackness looks on a frosty starlight night. In a telescope it seems far profounder. And invisible to me because it was so remote and small, flying swiftly and steadily towards me across that incredible distance, drawing nearer every minute by so many thousands of miles, came the Thing they were sending us, the Thing that was to bring so much struggle and calamity and death to the earth. I never dreamt of it then as I watched; no one on earth dreamt of that unerring missile.

That night, too, there was another jetting out of gas from the distant planet. I saw it. A reddish flash at the edge, the slightest projection of the outline, just as the chronometer struck midnight, and at that I told Ogilvy and he took my place. I went, stretching my legs clumsily, and feeling my way in the darkness, to the little table where the syphon stood, for the night was warm and I was thirsty, while Ogilvy exclaimed at the streamer of gas that came out towards us.

That night another invisible missile started on its way to the earth from Mars, just a second or so under twenty-four hours after the first one. I remember how I sat on the table there in the blackness, with patches of green and crimson swimming before my eyes. I wished I had a light to smoke by, little suspecting the meaning of the minute gleam I had seen and all that it would presently bring me. Ogilvy watched until one, and then gave it up, and we lit the lanterns and walked over to his house. Down below in the darkness were Ottershaw and Chertsey and all their hundreds of people, sleeping in peace.

He was full of speculation that night about the condition of Mars, and scoffed at the vulgar idea of its having inhabitants who were signalling us. His idea was that meteorites might be falling in a heavy shower upon the planet, or that a huge volcanic explosion was in progress. He pointed out to me how unlikely it was that organic evolution had taken the same direction in the two adjacent planets—the chances against anything man-like on Mars are a million to one, he said.

Hundreds of observers saw the flame that night and the night after about midnight, and again the night after, and so for ten nights, a flame each night. Why the shots ceased after the tenth no one on earth has attempted to explain. Dense clouds of smoke or dust, too, visible through a powerful telescope on

earth as little, grey, fluctuating patches, spread through the clearness of the planet's atmosphere and obscured its more familiar features.

Even the daily papers woke up to the disturbances at last, and popular notes appeared here, there, and everywhere concerning the volcanoes upon Mars. The serio-comic periodical *Punch*, I remember, made a happy use of it in the political cartoon. And, all unsuspected, those missiles the Martians had fired at us drew earthward, rushing now at a pace of many miles a second through the empty gulf of space, hour by hour and day by day, nearer and nearer.

It seems to me now almost incredibly wonderful that with that swift fate hanging over us men could go about their petty concerns as they did. I remember how jubilant Markham was at securing a new photograph of the planet for the illustrated paper he edited in those days.

People in these latter times scarcely realise the abundance and enterprise of our nineteenth century papers. For my own part I was much occupied in learning to ride the bicycle, and busy upon a series of papers discussing the probable developments of moral ideas as civilisation progressed.

One night (the Thing then could scarcely have been ten million miles away) I went for a walk with my wife. It was starlight, and I explained the Signs of the Zodiac to her, and pointed out Mars, a bright dot of light creeping zenith-ward, towards which so many telescopes were pointed. For in those days there was no terror for men among the stars.

It was a warm night. Coming home, a party of excursionists from Chertsey or Isleworth passed us singing and playing music. There were lights in the upper windows of the houses as the people went to bed. From the railway station in the distance came the sound of shunting trains, ringing and rumbling, softened almost into melody by the distance. My wife pointed out to me the brightness of the red, green and yellow signal lights, hanging in a framework against the sky. It had all seemed so safe and tranquil.

II.—THE FALLING STAR.

THEN came the night of the first falling star. It was seen early in the morning rushing over

Winchester eastward, a line of flame, high in the atmosphere. Hundreds must have seen it and taken it for an ordinary falling star. Albin described it as leaving a greenish streak behind it that glowed for some seconds. Denning, our greatest authority on meteorites, stated that the height of its first appearance was about 90 or 100 miles. It seemed to him that it fell to earth about a hundred miles east of him.

I was at home at that hour and writing in my study, and although my French windows face towards Ottershaw and the blind was up (for I loved in those days to look up at the night sky), I saw nothing of it. Yet this strangest of all things that ever came to earth from outer space must have fallen while I was sitting there, visible to me had I only looked up as it passed. Some of those who saw its flight say it travelled with a hissing sound. I myself heard nothing of that. Many people in Berkshire, Surrey, and Middlesex must have seen the fall of it, and, at most, have thought that another meteorite had descended. No one seems to have troubled to look for the fallen mass that night.

But very early in the morning poor Ogilvy, who had seen the shooting star, and who was persuaded that a meteorite lay somewhere on the common between Horsell, Ottershaw and Woking, rose early with the idea of finding it. Find it he did soon after dawn and not far from the sand-pits. An enormous hole had been made by the impact of the projectile, and the sand and gravel had been flung violently in every direction over the heath and heather. They formed heaps visible a mile and a half away. The heather was on fire eastward, and a thin blue smoke arose against the dawn.

The Thing itself lay almost entirely buried in sand, amidst the scattered splinters of a fir tree it had shivered to fragments in its descent. The uncovered part had the appearance of a huge cylinder, caked over and its outline softened by a thick scaly dun-coloured incrustation. It had a diameter of about thirty yards. He approached the mass, surprised at the size and more so at the shape,

Find it he did soon after dawn.

since most meteorites are rounded more or less completely. It was, however, still so hot from its flight through the air as to forbid his near approach. A stirring noise within the cylinder he ascribed to the unequal cooling of its substance. For at that time it had not occurred to him that it might be hollow.

He remained standing at the edge of the pit that the Thing had made for itself, staring at its strange appearance, astonished chiefly at its unusual shape and colour, and dimly perceiving even then some evidence of design in its arrival. The early morning was wonderfully still, and the sun, just clearing the pine trees towards Weybridge, was already warm. He did not remember hearing any birds that morning, there was certainly no breeze stirring, and the only sounds were the faint movements from within the cindery cylinder. He was all alone on the common.

The dull radiation arrested him.

Then suddenly he noticed with a start that some of the grey clinker, the ashy incrustation that covered the meteorite, was falling off the circular edge of the end. It was dropping off in flakes, and raining down upon the sand. A large piece suddenly came off and fell with a sharp noise that brought his heart into his mouth.

For a minute he scarcely realised what this meant, and, although the heat was excessive, he clambered down into the pit close to the bulk to see the thing more clearly. He fancied even then that the cooling of the body might account for this, but what disturbed that idea was the fact that the ash was falling only from the end of the cylinder.

And then he perceived that very slowly the circular top of the cylinder was rotating on its body. It was such a gradual movement, that he saw that it was so only through noticing that a black mark that had been near him five minutes ago, was now at the other side of the circumference. Even then, he scarcely understood what this indicated until he heard a muffled grating sound and saw the black mark jerk forward an inch or so. Then the thing came upon him in a flash. The cylinder was artificial—hollow—with an end that screwed out! Something within the cylinder was unscrewing the top!

"Good Heavens!" said Ogilvy. "There's a man in it—men in it! Half roasted to death! Trying to escape!"

At once with a quick mental leap he linked the thing with the flash upon Mars!

The thought of the confined creature was so dreadful to him that he forgot the heat, and went forward to the cylinder to help turn. But luckily the dull radiation arrested him before he could burn his hands on the still glowing metal. At that, he stood irresolute for a moment, then turned, scrambled out of the pit, and set off running wildly into Woking. The time then must have been somewhere about six o'clock. He met a waggoner and tried to make him understand, but the tale he told and his appearance were so wild—his hat had fallen off in the pit— that the man simply drove on. He was equally unsuccessful with the potman who was just unlocking the doors of the public house by Horsell Bridge. The fellow thought he was a lunatic at large, and made an unsuccessful attempt to shut him into the tap-room. That sobered him a little, and when he saw Henderson, the London journalist, in his garden, he called over the palings and made himself understood.

"Henderson," he called; "you saw that shooting star last night?"

"Well?" said Henderson.

"It's out on Horsell Common now."

"Good Lord!" said Henderson. "Fallen meteorite! That's good."

"But it's something more than a meteorite. It's a cylinder—an artificial cylinder, man! And there's something inside."

Henderson stood up with his spade in his hand. "What's that?" he said. He is deaf in one ear. Ogilvy told him all that he had seen. Henderson was a minute or so taking it in. Then he dropped his spade, snatched at his jacket and came out into the road. The two men hurried back at once to the common, and found the cylinder still lying in the same position. But now the sounds inside had ceased, and a thin circle of bright metal showed between the top and the body of the cylinder. Air was either entering or escaping at the rim with a thin, sizzling sound.

They listened, rapped on the scale with a stick, and meeting with no response, they both concluded the man or men inside must be insensible or dead.

Of course the two were quite unable to do anything. They shouted consolation and promises, and went off back to the town again to get help. One can imagine them, covered with sand, excited and disordered, running up the little street in the bright sunlight, just as the shop folks were taking down their shutters, and people were opening their bedroom windows. Henderson went into the railway station at once, in order to persuade the officials to telegraph the news to London. The newspaper articles had prepared men's minds for the reception of the idea.

By eight o'clock, a number of boys and unemployed men had already started for the common to see the "dead men from Mars." That was the form the story took. I heard of it first from my newspaper boy, about a quarter to nine, when I went out to get my *Daily News.* I was naturally startled, and lost no time in going out and across the Ottershaw bridge to the sand-pits.

III.—ON HORSELL COMMON.

I found a little crowd of perhaps twenty people surrounding the huge hole in which the cylinder lay. I have already described the appearance of that colossal bulk, imbedded in the ground. The turf and gravel about it seemed charred as if by a sudden explosion. No doubt its impact had caused a flash of fire. Henderson and Ogilvy were not there. I think they perceived that nothing was to be done for the present, and had gone away to breakfast at Henderson's house.

There were four or five boys sitting on the edge of the pit with their feet dangling, and amusing themselves—until I stopped them— by throwing stones at the giant mass. After I had spoken to them about it, they began playing at "touch" in and out of the group of bystanders.

Among these were a couple of cyclists, a jobbing gardener I employed sometimes, a girl carrying a baby, Gregg the butcher and his little boy, and two or three loafers and golf caddies who were accustomed to hang about the railway station. There was very little talking. Few of the common people in England had anything but the vaguest astronomical ideas in those days. Most of them were staring quietly at the big table-like end of the cylinder, which was still as Henderson and Ogilvy had left it. I fancy the popular expectation of a heap of charred corpses was disappointed by this inanimate bulk. Some went away while I was there, and other people came. I clambered into the pit and fancied I heard a faint movement under my feet. The top had certainly ceased to rotate.

It was only when I got thus close to it that the strangeness of this object was at all evident to me. At the first glance it was really no more exciting than an overturned carriage or a tree blown across the road. Not so much so, indeed. It looked like a rusty gas float half buried, more than anything else in the world. It required a certain amount of scientific education to perceive that the grey scale on the thing was no common oxide, that the yellowish white metal that gleamed in the crack between the lid and the cylinder had an unfamiliar hue. "Extra-terrestrial" had no meaning for most of the onlookers.

At that time it was quite clear in my own mind that the Thing had come from the planet Mars, but I judged it improbable that it contained any living creature. I thought the unscrewing might be automatic. In spite of Ogilvy I still believed that there were men in Mars. My mind ran fancifully on the possibilites of its containing manuscript, on the difficulties in translation that might arise, whether we should find coins and models in it, and so forth. Yet it was a little too large for assurance on this idea. I felt an impatience to see it opened. About eleven, as nothing seemed happening, I walked back, full of such thoughts, to my home in Maybury. But I found it difficult to get to work upon my abstract investigations.

In the afternoon the appearance of the common had altered very much. The early editions of the evening papers had startled London with enormous headlines: "A MESSAGE RECEIVED FROM MARS," "Remarkable Story from Woking," and so forth. In addition, Ogilvy's wire to the Astronomical Exchange had roused every observatory in the three kingdoms.

There were half-a-dozen flys or more from the Woking station standing in the road by the sand-pits, a basket chaise from Chobham and a rather lordly carriage. Besides that there was quite a heap of bicycles. In addition a large number of people must have walked, in spite of the heat of the day, from Woking and Chertsey. So that there was altogether quite a considerable crowd—one or two gaily dressed ladies among the others.

It was glaringly hot, not a cloud in the sky, nor a breath of wind, and the only shadow was that of the few scattered pine trees. The burning heather had been extinguished, but the level ground towards Ottershaw was blackened as far as one could see, and still giving off vertical streamers of smoke. An enterprising sweet-stuff dealer in the Chobham road had sent up his son with a barrow-load of green apples and ginger beer.

Going to the edge of the pit I found it occupied by a group of about half-a-dozen men, Henderson, Ogilvy, and a tall fair-haired man, that I afterwards learnt was Stent, the Astronomer Royal, with several workmen wielding spades and pickaxes. Stent was giving directions in a clear, high-pitched voice. He was standing on the cylinder, which was now evidently much cooler; his face was crimson, and streaming with perspiration, and something seemed to have irritated him.

A large portion of the cylinder had been uncovered, though its lower end was still imbedded. As soon as Ogilvy saw me among the staring crowd on the edge of the pit, he called to me to come down, and asked me if I would mind going over to see Lord Hilton, the lord of Horsell Manor. The growing crowd, he said, was becoming a serious impediment to their excavations, especially the boys. They wanted a light railing put up, and help to keep the people back. He told me that a faint stirring was occasionally still audible within the case, but that the workmen had failed to unscrew the top, as it afforded no grip to them. The case appeared to be enormously thick, and it was possible that the faint sounds we heard represented a noisy tumult in the interior.

I was very glad to do as he asked, and so become one of the privileged spectators within the contemplated inclosure. I failed to find Lord Hilton at his house, but I was told he was expected from London by the six o'clock train from Waterloo, and as it was then about a quarter past five I went home and had some tea, and walked up to the station to waylay him.

IV.—THE CYLINDER UNSCREWS.

WHEN I returned to the common the sun was setting. Scattered groups were hurrying from the direction of Woking, and one or two persons were returning. The crowd about the pit had increased, and stood out black against the lemon yellow of the sky—a couple of hundred people perhaps. There were a number of voices raised, and some sort of struggle appeared to be going on about the pit. Strange imaginings passed through my mind. As I drew nearer I heard Stent's voice : " Keep back—keep back ! " A boy came running towards me. " It's a-movin'," he said to me as he passed.

I ran slantingly and stumbling.

" A-screwin' and a-screwin' out. I don't like it. I'm a-goin' 'ome, I am." I went on to the crowd.

There were really, I should think, two or three hundred people, elbowing and jostling one another, the one or two ladies there being by no means the least active.

" He's fallen in the pit ! " cried some one. " Keep back ! " said several. The crowd swayed a little, and I elbowed my way through.

Everyone seemed greatly excited. I heard a peculiar humming sound from the pit. " I say ! " said Ogilvy ; " help keep these idiots back. We don't know what's in the confounded thing, you know ! " I saw a young man, a shop assistant in Woking, I believe he was, standing on the cylinder and trying to scramble out of the hole again. The crowd had pushed him in.

The end of the cylinder was being screwed out from within. Nearly two feet of shining screw projected. Somebody blundered against me and I narrowly missed being pitched on to the top of the screw. I turned, and as I did so the screw must have come out, and the lid of the cylinder fell upon the gravel with a ringing concussion. I struck my elbow into the person behind and turned my head towards the Thing again. For a moment that circular cavity seemed perfectly black. I had the sunset in my eyes.

I think everyone expected to see a man emerge—possibly something a little unlike us terrestrial men, but in all essentials a man. I know I did. But looking, I presently saw something stirring within the shadow, greyish billowy movements, one above another, and then two luminous discs like eyes. Then something resembling a little grey snake, about the thickness of a walking stick, coiled up out of the writhing middle, and wriggled in the air towards me. And then another.

A sudden chill came upon me. There was a loud shriek from a woman behind. I half turned, keeping my eyes fixed upon the cylinder still, from which other tentacles were now projecting, and began pushing my way back from the edge of the pit. I saw astonishment giving place to horror on the faces of the people about me. I heard inarticulate exclamations on all sides. There was a general movement backward. I saw the shopman struggling still on the edge of the pit. I found myself alone, and saw the people on the other side of the pit running off, Stent among them. I looked again at the cylinder, and ungovernable terror gripped me. I stood petrified and staring.

A big greyish rounded bulk, the size perhaps of a bear, was rising slowly and painfully out of the cylinder. As it bulged up and caught the light, it glistened like wet leather. Two large dark-coloured eyes were regarding me steadfastly. It was rounded and had—one might say—a face. There was a mouth under the eyes, the lipless brim of which quivered and panted, and dropped saliva. The body heaved and pulsated convulsively. A lank tentacular appendage gripped the edge of the cylinder, another swayed in the air.

You who have only seen the dead monsters in spirit in the Natural History Museum, shrivelled brown bulks, can scarcely imagine the strange horror of their appearance. The peculiar V-shaped mouth, with its pointed upper lip, the absence of brow ridges, the absence of a chin beneath the wedge-like lower lip, the incessant quivering of this mouth, the Gorgon circlet of tentacles, the tumultuous breathing of the lungs in a strange atmosphere, the evident heaviness and painfulness of movement, due to the greater gravitational energy of the earth—above all, the extraordinary intensity of the immense eyes, culminated in an effect akin to nausea. There was something fungoid in the oily brown skin, something in the clumsy deliberation of their tedious movements unspeakably terrible. Even at this first encounter, this first glimpse, I was overcome with disgust and dread.

Suddenly the monster vanished. It had toppled over the brim of the cylinder, and fallen into the pit, with a thud like the fall of a great mass of leather. I heard it give a peculiar, thick cry, and forthwith another of these creatures appeared darkly in the deep shadow of the aperture.

At that my rigour of terror passed away. I turned, and, running madly, made for the first group of trees perhaps a hundred yards away. But I ran slantingly and stumbling, for I could not avert my face from these things.

There, among some young pine trees and furze bushes, I stopped, panting, and waited for further developments. The common round the sand-pits was dotted with people, standing like myself in a half fascinated terror, staring at these creatures, or rather at the heaped gravel at the edge of the pit in which they lay. And then, with a renewed horror, I saw a round black object bobbing up and down on the edge of the pit. It was the head of the shopman who had fallen in, but showing as a little black object against the hot western sky. Now he got his shoulder and knee up, and again he seemed to slip back until only his head was visible. Suddenly he vanished, and I could have fancied a faint shriek had reached me. I had a momentary impulse to go back and help him, that my fears overruled.

Everything was then quite invisible, hidden by the deep pit and the heap of sand that the fall of the cylinder had made. Anyone coming along the road from Chobham or Woking would have been amazed at the sight—a dwindling multitude of perhaps a hundred people or more standing in a great irregular circle, in ditches, behind bushes, behind gates and hedges, saying little to one another, and that in short excited shouts, and staring, staring hard, at a few heaps of sand. The barrow of ginger beer stood, a queer derelict, black against the burning sky, and in the sand-pits was a row of deserted vehicles, with their horses feeding out of nosebags or pawing the ground.

Suddenly he vanished.

The mounted policeman came galloping through the confusion with his hands clasped over his head.

By H. G. Wells.

SUMMARY.

THE first indication of the invasion of the earth by the inhabitants of Mars is the falling of a cylinder on the common between Horsell, Ottershaw, and Woking. Many persons, including the narrator of the story, go to inspect the cylinder. They notice that it is being very slowly unscrewed from the inside. At length the top comes off and a fearful-looking monster emerges, and then another. Everyone beats a hasty retreat.

V.—THE HEAT RAY.

AFTER the glimpse I had had of the Martians emerging from the cylinder in which they had come to the earth from their planet, a kind of fascination paralysed my actions. I remained standing knee-deep in the heather staring at the mound that hid them. I was a battle ground of fear and curiosity.

I did not dare to go back towards the pit, but I felt a passionate longing to peer into it. I began walking, therefore, in a big curve, seeking some point of vantage, and continually looking at the sand heaps that hid these new comers to our earth. Once a leash of thin black whips like the arms of an octopus flashed across the sunset and was immediately withdrawn, and afterwards a thin rod rose up, joint by joint, bearing at its apex a circular disc that spun with a wobbling motion. What could be going on there?

Most of the spectators had gathered in one or two groups, one a little crowd towards Woking, the other a knot of people in the direction of Chobham. Evidently they shared my mental conflict. There were few near me. One man I approached —he was, I perceived, a neighbour of mine, though I did not know his name—and accosted. But it was scarcely a time for articulate conversation. "What ugly *brutes!*" he said. "Good God! What Ugly Brutes!" He repeated this over and over again.

"Did you see a man in the pit?" I said; but he made me no answer to that. We became silent, and stood watching for a time side by side, deriving, I fancy, a certain comfort in one another's company. Then I shifted my position to a little knoll that gave me the advantage of a yard or more of elevation, and when I looked for him presently he was walking towards Woking.

The sunset faded to twilight before anything further happened. The crowd far away on the left towards Woking seemed to grow, and I heard now a faint murmur from it. The little knot of people towards Chobham dispersed. There was scarcely an intimation of movement from the pit.

It was this, as much as anything, that gave people courage, and I suppose the new arrivals from Woking also helped to raise confidence again. At any rate, as the dusk came on, a slow, intermittent movement upon the sand pits began, that seemed to gather force as the stillness of the evening about the cylinder remained unbroken. Vertical black figures in twos and threes would advance, stop, watch, and advance again, spreading out as they did so in a thin, irregular crescent that promised to inclose the pit in its attenuated horns. I, too, on my side began to move towards the pit.

Then I saw some cabmen and others had walked boldly into the sand pits, and heard the clatter of hoofs and the grind of wheels. A man ran forward and began wheeling off the barrow of apples. And then, within thirty yards of the pit, advancing from the direction of Horsell, I saw a little black knot of men, the foremost of whom was waving a white flag.

This was the Deputation. There had been a hasty consultation, and, since the Martians were evidently, in spite of their repulsive forms, intelligent creatures, it had been resolved to show them that we too were intelligent by approaching them with signals.

Flutter, flutter, went the flag, first to the right, then to the left. It was impossible to recognise anyone there, but afterwards I learnt that Ogilvy, Stent, and Henderson were with others in this attempt at communication. This little group had in its advance dragged inward, so to speak, the circumference of

Slowly a humped shape rose out of the pit.

the now almost complete circle of people, and a number of dim, black figures followed it at more or less discreet distances.

Suddenly there was a flash of light, and a quantity of luminous, greenish smoke came out of the pit in three distinct puffs, which drove up, one after the other, straight into the still air. This smoke (or flame, perhaps, would be the better word for it) was so bright that the deep blue sky overhead, and the hazy stretches of brown common towards Chertsey, set with black pine trees, seemed to darken abruptly as these puffs arose, and to remain the darker after their dispersal. At the same time a faint hissing sound became audible.

Beyond the pit stood the little wedge of people with the white flag at its apex, arrested by the phenomenon, a little knot of small vertical black shapes upon the black ground. As the green smoke rose their faces flashed out pallid green and faded again as it vanished. And then something happened, so swift, so incredible, that for a time it left me dumfounded, not understanding at all the thing that I had seen. The hissing passed into a humming, into a long, loud droning noise.

Slowly a humped shape rose out of the pit, and the ghost of a beam of light seemed to flicker out from it. Forthwith flashes of actual flame, a bright glare leaping from one to another, sprung from the scattered group of men. It was as if some invisible jet impinged upon them and splashed into white flame. It was as if each man were suddenly and momentarily turned to fire.

Then by the light of their destruction I saw them staggering and falling, and their supporters half-turning to run. It was the occurrence of a second, this swift, unanticipated, inexplicable death.

I cannot describe the swiftness of the thing I saw. The death seemed leaping from man to man in the distant flying crowd. An almost noiseless and blinding flash of light and a man fell headlong and lay still, and as the unseen shaft of heat passed over them, pine trees burst into fire, and every dry furze bush with one dull thud became a mass of flames. And far away towards Knap Hill we saw the flashes of trees and hedges and wooden buildings suddenly set alight.

It was sweeping round swiftly and steadily, this flaming death, this invisible, inevitable sword of heat. I heard the crackle of fire in the sand pits and the sudden squeal of a horse that was as suddenly stilled. I perceived it coming towards me by the flashing bushes it touched, and was too terror-stricken and astounded to stir. Then it was as if an invisible yet intensely heated finger was drawn through the heather, and all along a curving line beyond the sand pits the dark ground smoked and crackled. Something fell with a crash, far away to the left where the road from Woking Station opens out on the common. Forthwith the hissing and humming ceased, and the black, dome-like object sank slowly out of sight into the pit.

All this had happened with such bewildering swiftness that I had stood motionless, dumfounded and dazzled by the flashes of light. Had that death swept through a full circle it must inevitably have slain me in my surprise. But it passed and spared me, and left the night about me suddenly dark and full of terror.

The undulating common seemed now dark almost to blackness except where its roadways lay grey and pale, under the deep blue sky of the early night. Overhead the stars were mustering, and in the west, the sky was still a pale, bright, almost greenish, blue. The tops of the pine trees and the

The death seemed leaping from man to man.

I perceived it coming
towards me.

roofs of Horsell came out sharp and black against the western after-glow. The Martians were altogether invisible, save for one thin mast, upon which their restless mirror wobbled. The dead lay hidden, for the most part, among the dark heather. Nothing seemed unusual, save the patches of bush and the isolated trees here and there, that smoked and glowed still, and the trees towards Woking Station that were sending up spires of flame into the stillness of the evening air. Thence, too, came a murmur of excited voices. Nothing was unusual save that and a terrible astonishment. The little group of black specks with the flag of white, had been swept out of existence, and the peace of the evening, so it seemed to us, had scarcely been broken.

It came to me that I was upon the common, visible to these death dealing monsters, helpless, unprotected and alone. At any moment they might discover that a man was still near them. At any moment that black dome might creep over the verge of the pit again, and inexorable death smite me down! My momentary paralysis passed into active fear. I turned, and began a stumbling run through the heather, bowing myself almost double.

This new death seemed hovering over me, pursuing me, waiting to pounce upon me. Such an extraordinary effect in unmanning me had this thing, that I ran along weeping, much as a child might do. Once I had turned I did not dare to look back. I had an extraordinary persuasion that I was being played with, that presently, when I was upon the very verge of safety, that strange death, as swift as the passage of light, would leap after me from the pit about the cylinder, and strike me down.

VI.—THE HEAT RAY IN THE CHOBHAM ROAD.

It is still a matter of wonder how the Martians are able to slay men so swiftly and so silently. Many think that in some way they are able to generate an intense heat in a chamber of practically absolute non-conductivity. This intense heat they project by means of a polished parabolic mirror of unknown composition, in a parallel beam against any object they choose, much as the parabolic mirror of a lighthouse projects a beam of light. But no one has absolutely proved these details. However it is done, it is certain that a beam of heat is the essence of the matter. Heat, and invisible, instead of visible light. Whatever is combustible flashes into flame at its touch, lead runs like water, it softens iron, cracks and melts glass, and when it falls upon water incontinently that explodes into steam. That night nearly forty people lay under the starlight about the pit, charred and distorted beyond recognition, and all night long the common from Horsell to Maybury was deserted, and brightly ablaze.

The news of the massacre probably reached Chobham, Woking, and Ottershaw about the same time. In Woking the shops had closed when the tragedy happened, and a number of people, shop-people and

I began a stumbling run through the heather.

so forth, attracted by the stories they had heard, were walking over Horsell Bridge and along the road between the hedges that runs out at last upon the common. You may imagine the young people brushed up after the labours of the day, and making this novelty, as they would make any novelty, the excuse for walking together and enjoying a little innocent flirtation, you may figure to yourself the hum of voices along the road in the gloaming.

As yet, of course, few people in Woking even knew that the cylinder had opened, though poor Henderson had sent a messenger on a bicycle to the post office with a special wire to an evening paper. As these folks came out upon the open by twos and threes, however, they found little knots of people standing talking excitedly, and peering at the spinning mirror over the sand-pits, and the newcomers were soon infected by the strange excitement of the occasion.

By half-past eight, when the Deputation was destroyed, there may have been a crowd there of three hundred or more, besides those who had left the road to approach the Martians nearer. There were three policemen, too, one of whom was mounted, doing their best, under instructions from Stent, to keep the people back and deter them from approaching the cylinder. There was some booing from those more thoughtless and excitable souls to whom a crowd is always an occasion for noise and horseplay.

Stent and Ogilvy, anticipating some possibilities of a collision, had telegraphed from Horsell to the barracks as soon as the Martians emerged, for the help of a company of soldiers to protect these strange creatures from violence. After that it was they returned to lead that ill-fated advance. The description of their death as it was seen by the crowd tallies very closely with my own impressions : the three puffs of green smoke, the deep humming note, and the splashes of flame.

But that crowd of people had a far nearer escape than mine. Only the fact that a hummock of heathery sand intercepted the lower part of the Heat Ray saved them Had the elevation of the parabolic mirror been a few yards higher none could have lived to tell the tale. They saw the flashes, and the men falling, and an invisible hand, as it were, lit the bushes as it hurried towards them through the twilight. Then with a whistling note mingling with the droning of the pit, the beam swung close over their heads, lighting the tops of the beech trees that line the road, and splitting the bricks, smashing the windows, firing the window-frames, and bringing down in crumbling ruin a portion of the gable of a house nearest the corner.

In the sudden thud and hiss and glare of the ignited trees, the panic-stricken crowd seems to have swayed hesitatingly for some moments. The unexpected burst of flame overhead, and the black shadows jumping about them must have been intensely disconcerting in themselves. There were shrieks and shouts, and the mounted policeman came galloping through the confusion with his hands clasped over his head and screaming.

Sparks and burning twigs began to fall into the road, and single leaves like puffs of flame, that never reached the ground. A girl's dress caught fire. Then came a crying from the common : " They're coming ! " A woman shrieked, and incontinently everyone was turning and pushing at those behind, in order to clear their way to Woking again. Where the road grows narrow between the high banks the crowd jammed ; a hideous struggle occurred, and two women and a little boy were crushed and left dying there amidst the terror and the darkness.

VII.—HOW I CAME HOME.

For my own part, I remember nothing of my flight except the stress of frantic exertion, and my agony of blundering against trees and tumbling through the heather. I ran into the road between the cross-roads and Horsell, and along this to the cross-roads. To think of it brings back very vividly the whooping of my panting breath as I ran. All about me gathered the invisible terrors of the Martians, that pitiless sword of heat seemed whirling to and fro, flourishing overhead before it descended and smote me out of life.

At last I could go no further ; I was exhausted with the violence of my emotion and of my flight, my knees smote together and I staggered and fell by the wayside. That was near the bridge that crosses the canal by the gasworks. I fell and lay panting. I must have remained there some time.

I sat up, strangely perplexed. For a moment, perhaps, I could not clearly understand how I came there. My terror had fallen from me like a garment. My hat had gone, and my collar had burst away from its stud. A few minutes before, there had only been three real things before me—the immensity of the night and space and nature, my own feebleness and anguish, and the near approach of death. Now it was as if something turned over, and the point of view altered abruptly. There was no sensible transition from one state of mind to the other. I was immediately the self of every day again, a decent ordinary citizen. The silent common, the impulse of my flight, the starting flames, were as if it were a dream. I asked myself had these latter things indeed happened? I could not credit it.

I rose and walked unsteadily up the steep incline of the bridge. My mind was blank wonder. My knees, I found, were stiff; my muscles and nerves seemed drained of their strength. I daresay I staggered drunkenly. A head rose over the arch, and the figure of a workman carrying a basket appeared. Beside him ran a little boy. He passed me, wishing me good-night. I was minded to speak to him, and did not. I answered his greeting with a mumble, and went on over the bridge.

Over the Maybury arch a train, a billowing tumult of white, firelit smoke, and a long caterpillar of lighted windows, went flying south, clatter, clatter, clap, rap, and it had gone. A dim group of people talked at the gate of one of the houses in the pretty little row of gables that was called Oriental Terrace. It was all so real and so familiar. And that behind me! It was frantic, fantastic! Such things, I told myself, could not be.

Perhaps I am a man of exceptional moods. I do not know how far my experience is common. At times I suffer from the strangest sense of utter detachment from myself and the world about me; I seem to watch it all from the outside, from somewhere inconceivably remote, out of time, out of space, out of the stress and tragedy of it all. This feeling was very strong upon me that night. Here was another side to my dream.

But the trouble was the blank incongruity of this security and quiet, and the swift death flying yonder, not two miles away. There was a noise of business from the gasworks, and the electric lamps were all alight. I stopped at the group of people. "What news from the common?" said I.

There were two men and a woman at the gate. "Eigh?" said one of the men, turning.

"What news from the common?" I said.

"Ain't yer just *been* there?" asked the men.

"People seem fair silly about the Common," said the woman over the gate. "What's it all about?"

It seemed impossible to make these people grasp a terror upon which my mind even could not retain its grip of realisation.

"Haven't you heard of the Men from Mars?" said I.

"Quite enough," said the woman over the

I startled my wife at the doorway, so haggard and dishevelled was I.

gate. "Thenks," and all three of them laughed.

I felt foolish and angry. I could not tell them what I had seen. "You'll hear more yet," I gasped, and went on to my home. I startled my wife at the doorway, so haggard and dishevelled was I. I went into the dining-room, sat down and told her all that I had seen. The dinner, which was a cold one, had already been served and remained neglected on the table while I told my story.

"There is one thing," I said, to allay the fears I had aroused, "they are the most sluggish things I ever saw crawl. They may keep the pit and kill people who come near them, but they cannot get out of it. . . . . . But the horror of them!"

"Don't, dear!" said my wife, knitting her brows and putting her hand on mine.

"Poor Ogilvy!" I said. "To think he may be lying dead there!"

My wife at least did not find my experience incredible. She ate scarcely a mouthful of dinner, and ever and again she shuddered at my too vivid story of the death of the flag-bearers. When I saw how deadly white her face was, I ceased describing. "They may come here," she said again and again. I pressed her to take wine, and tried to reassure her. "They can scarcely move," I said. I repeated all that Ogilvy had told me, of the impossibility of the Martians establishing themselves on the earth, at first for her comfort, and then I found for my own.

In particular I laid stress on the gravitation difficulty. On the surface of the earth, the force of gravity is three times what it is on the surface of Mars. A Martian, therefore, would weigh three times more than on Mars, albeit his muscular strength would be the same. His own body would be a cope of lead to him therefore. Both the *Times* and the *Daily Telegraph* repeated this consideration the next morning, and both overlooked two modifying influences. The atmosphere of the earth, we now know, contains far more oxygen or far less argon (whichever way one likes to put it), than does Mars. The invigorating influence of this excess of oxygen upon the Martians indisputably did much to counterbalance the increased weight of their bodies. And, in the second place, we all overlooked the fact that such mechanical intelligence as the Martian possessed, was quite able to dispense with muscular exertion at a pinch. But I did not consider these points at the time. With wine and food, the confidence of my own table, and the necessity of reassuring my wife, I grew, by insensible degrees, courageous.

"They have done a foolish thing," said I, fingering my wine-glass. "They are dangerous because no doubt they are mad with terror. Perhaps they expected to find no living things—certainly no intelligent living things.

"A shell in the pit," said I, "if the worst comes to the worst, will kill them all."

The intense excitement of the events had no doubt left my perceptive powers in a state of erethism. I remember that dinner table with extraordinary vividness even now. My dear wife's sweet anxious face peering at me from under the pink lamp shade, the white cloth, with its silver and glass table furniture—for in those days even philosophical writers had many little luxuries—the crimson purple wine in my glass, are photographically distinct. At the end of it I sat, tempering nuts with a cigarette, regretting Ogilvy's rashness, and denouncing the short-sighted timidity of the Martians.

So some respectable dodo in the Mauritius might have lorded it in his nest, and discussed the arrival of that shipful of pitiless sailors in want of animal food. "We will peck them to death to-morrow, my dear."

I did not know it, but that was the last civilised dinner I was to eat for very many strange and terrible days.

VIII.—FRIDAY NIGHT.

THE most extraordinary thing to my mind, of all the strange and wonderful things that happened upon that Friday, was the dove-tailing of the commonplace habits of our social order with the first beginnings of the series of events that was to topple that social order headlong. If, on Friday night, you had taken a pair of compasses and drawn a circle with a radius of five miles round the Woking sand-pits, I doubt if you would have had one human being outside it, unless it was some relation of Stent, or the three or four cyclists or London people who lay dead on the Common, whose emotions or habits were at all affected by the newcomers. Many people had heard of the cylinder, of course, and talked about it in their leisure, but it certainly did not make the sensation an ultimatum to Germany would have done.

In London, that night, poor Henderson's telegram, describing the gradual unscrewing of the shot, was judged to be a *canard*, and his evening paper, after wiring for authentication from him and receiving no reply—the man was killed—decided not to print a special edition.

Within the five-mile circle, even, the great majority of people were inert. I have already described the behaviour of the man and woman I spoke to. All over the district people were dining and supping; working men were gardening after the labours of the day, children were being put to bed, young people were wandering through the lanes love-making, students sat over their books.

Maybe there was a murmur in the village streets, a novel and dominant topic in the public-houses, and here and there a messenger, or even an eye-witness of the later occurrences caused a whirl of excitement, a shouting and a running to and fro; but, for the most part, the daily routine of working, eating, drinking, sleeping, went on as it had done for countless years—as though no planet Mars existed in the sky. Even at Woking Station and Horsell and Chobham that was the case.

In Woking Junction, until a late hour, trains were stopping and going on, others were shunting on the sidings, passengers were alighting and waiting, and everything was proceeding in the most ordinary way. A boy from the town, trenching on Smith's monopoly, was selling papers with the afternoon's news. The ringing and impact of trucks, the sharp whistle of the engines from the junction, mingled with their shouts of "Men from Mars." Excited men came into the station with incredible tidings about nine o'clock, and caused no more disturbance than drunkards might have done. People rattling Londonwards peered into

One or two adventurous souls never returned.

the darkness outside the carriage windows and saw only a rare, flickering, vanishing spark dance up from the direction of Horsell, a red glow and a thin veil of smoke driving across the stars, and thought that nothing more serious than a heath fire was happening.

It was only round the edge of the common that any disturbance was perceptible. There were half-a-dozen villas burning on the Woking border; there were lights in all the houses on the common side of the three villages, and the people there kept awake till dawn.

A curious crowd lingered restlessly, people coming and going, but the crowd remaining, both on the Chobham and Horsell bridges. One or two adventurous souls, it was afterwards found, went into the darkness and crawled quite near the Martians, but they never returned, for now and again a light-ray, like the beam of a warship's search-light, swept the Common, and the Heat Ray was ready to follow. Save for such that big area of Common was silent and desolate, and the charred bodies lay about on it all night, under the stars, and all the next day.

A noise of hammering from the pit was heard by many people.

So you have the state of things on Friday night. In the centre, sticking into the skin of our old planet Earth, like a poisoned dart, was this cylinder. But the poison was scarcely working yet. Around it was a patch of silent Common, smouldering in places and with a few dark, dimly seen objects lying in contorted attitudes here and there. Here and there was a burning bush or tree. Beyond was a fringe of excitement, and further than that fringe the inflammation had not crept as yet. In the rest of the world the stream of life still flowed as it has flowed for immemorial years. The fever of war that would presently clog vein and artery, deaden nerve and destroy brain, had still to develop.

All night long the Martians were hammer-ing and stirring, sleepless, indefatigable, at work upon the machines they were making ready, and ever and again a puff of greenish white smoke whirled up to the starlit sky.

About eleven a company of soldiers came through Horsell and deployed along the edge of the common to form a cordon. Later a second company marched through Chobham to deploy on the north side of the Common. Several officers from the Inkerman barracks had been on the Common earlier in the day, and one, Major Eden, was reported to be missing. The colonel of the regiment came on with them and was busy questioning the crowd at midnight. The military authorities were certainly early alive to the seriousness of the business. About eleven, the next morning's papers were able to say, a squadron of Hussars, two Maxims, and about four hundred men of the Cardigan regiment started from Aldershot.

A few seconds after midnight the crowd in the Chertsey road, Woking, saw a star fall from Heaven into the pine woods to the north-west. It fell with a greenish light, causing a flash of light like summer lightning. Soon after these pine woods and others about the Byfleet Golf Links were seen to be on fire.

"Wiped out!"

THE WAR OF THE WORLDS

By H. G. Wells.

SUMMARY.

There fall near Woking certain flaming stars, which prove to be huge cylinders from Mars containing Martians. The cylinders open and the Martians come forth. Friendly advances are made to them, but they display a hostile disposition. At first they appear to be heavy, sluggish, soft-bodied creatures with tentacles. The story is told by an inhabitant of Woking.

IX.—THE FIGHTING BEGINS.

Saturday lives in my memory as a day of suspense. It was a day of lassitude, too, hot and close, with, I am told, a rapidly fluctuating barometer. I had slept but little, though my wife had succeeded in sleeping, and I rose early. I went into my garden before breakfast and stood listening, but towards the Common there was nothing stirring but a lark.

The milkman came as usual. I heard the rattle of his chariot, and I went round to the side gate to ask the latest news. He told me that during the night the Martians had been surrounded by troops, and that guns were expected. Then—a reassuring note—I heard a train running towards Woking. "They aren't to be killed," said the milkman, "if that can possibly be avoided."

I saw my neighbour gardening, chatted with him for a time, and then strolled in to breakfast. It was a most unexceptional morning. My neighbour was of opinion that the troops would be able to capture or to destroy the Martians during the day. "It's a pity they make themselves so unapproachable," he said. "It would be curious to learn how they live on another planet. We might learn a thing or two."

He came up to the fence and extended a handful of strawberries—for his gardening was as generous as it was enthusiastic. At the same time, he told me of the burning of the pine woods about the Byfleet Golf Links. "They say," said he, "that there's another of these blessed things fallen there—number two. But one's enough—surely. This lot 'll cost the insurance people a pretty penny, before everything's settled." He laughed with an air of the greatest good humour, as he said this. The woods, he said, were still burning, and pointed out a haze of smoke to me. "They will be hot underfoot on account of the thick soil of pine needles and turf, for days," he said, and then grew serious over "Poor Ogilvy."

After breakfast, instead of working, I decided to walk down towards the Common. Under the railway bridge I found a group of soldiers, sappers I think, men in small round caps, dirty red jackets unbuttoned and showing their blue shirts, dark trousers and boots coming to the calf. They told me no one was allowed over the canal, and, looking along the road towards the bridge, I saw one of the Cardigan men standing sentinel there. I talked with these soldiers for a time ; I told them of my sight of the Martians on the previous evening. None of them had seen the Martians, and they had but the vaguest ideas of them, so that they plied me with questions. They said that they did not know who had authorised the movements of the troops ; their idea was that a dispute had arisen at the Horse Guards. The ordinary sapper is a great deal better educated than the common soldier, and they discussed the peculiar conditions of the possible fight with some acuteness. I described the heat-ray to them, and they began to argue among themselves.

" Crawl up under cover and rush 'em, say I," said one.

" Get aht ! " said another. " Wot's cover against this 'ere 'eat ? Sticks to cook yer ! What we got to do is to go as near as the ground'll let us and then drive a trench."

" Blow yer trenches ! You always want trenches. You ought to ha' been born a rabbit, Snippy."

" Ain't they got any necks, then ? " said a third, abruptly—a little, contemplative, dark man, smoking a pipe.

I repeated my description.

" Octupuses," said he ; " that's what I calls 'em. Talk about fishers of men !— fighters of fish it is this time."

" It ain't no murder killin' beasts like that," said the first speaker.

" Why not shell the darned things strite off and finish 'em ? " said the little dark man. " You carn tell what they might do."

" Where's your shells ? " said the first speaker. " There ain't no time. Do it in a rush—that's my tip. And do it at once."

So they discussed it. After a while I left them and went on to the railway station to get as many morning papers as I could. But I will not weary the reader with a discussion of that long morning, and of the longer afternoon. I did not succeed in getting a glimpse of the Common, for even Horsell and Chobham church towers were in the hands of the military authorities. The soldiers I addressed didn't know anything ; the officers were mysterious as well as busy. I found people in the town quite secure again in the presence of the military, and I heard for the first time

from Marshall, the tobacconist, that his son was among the dead on the Common. The soldiers had made the people on the outskirts of Horsell lock up and leave their houses.

I got back to lunch about two, very tired, for as I have said, the day was extremely hot and dull, and, in order to refresh myself, I took a cold bath in the afternoon. About half past four I went up to the railway station to get an evening paper, for the morning papers had contained only a very inaccurate description of the killing of Stent, Henderson, Ogilvy and the others. But there was little I didn't know. The Martians did not show an inch of themselves. They seemed busy in their pit, and there was a sound now of digging, as well as hammering, and an almost continuous streamer of smoke. Apparently they were busy getting ready for a struggle. " Fresh attempts have been made to signal, but without success," was the stereotyped formula of the papers. A sapper told me it was done by a man in a ditch, with a flag on a long pole. The Martians took as much notice of such advances as we should of a lowing cow.

I must confess the sight of all this armament, all this preparation, greatly excited me. My imagination became belligerent, and defeated the invaders in a dozen striking ways ; something of my schoolboy dreams of battle and heroism came back to me. They seemed so helpless in this pit of theirs.

About three o'clock there began the thud of a gun at measured intervals from Chertsey or Addlestone. I learnt that the smouldering pine wood into which the second cylinder had fallen was being shelled, in the hope of destroying that object before it opened. It was only about five, however, that a field gun reached Chobham for use against the first body of Martians.

About six in the evening, as I sat at tea with my wife in the summer house, talking vigorously about the battle that was lowering upon us, I heard a muffled detonation from the common, and immediately after a gust of firing. Close on the heels of that came a violent, rattling crash, quite close to us, that shook the ground ; and, starting out upon the lawn, I saw the tops of the trees about the Oriental College burst into smoky red flame, and the tower of the little church beside it slide down into ruin. The pinnacle of the mosque had vanished, and the roof line of the college itself looked as if a hundred-ton gun had been at work upon it. One of our chimneys cracked as though a shot had hit it, flew, and the piece of it came clattering down the tiles, and made a heap of broken red fragments upon the flower-bed by my study window.

I and my wife stood amazed. A moment before, peace, and then this earth-quake and fire smiting out of the invisible, and black smoke streaming up all about us. Then I realised that the crest of Maybury Hill must be with-in range of the Martians' heat-ray, now that the college was cleared out of the way.

As soon as my astonish-ment would let me I gripped my wife's arm and ran her out into the road. Then I fetched out the servant, telling her I would go up-stairs myself for the box she was clamouring for. "We can't possibly stay here," I said, and as I spoke, the firing re-opened for a moment upon the common.

"But where are we to go?" said my wife in terror.

I thought perplexed. Then I remembered her cousins at Leatherhead.

"Leatherhead!" I shouted above the sudden noise. She looked away from me downhill. The people were coming out of their houses astonished.

"How am I to get to Leatherhead?" she said.

Down the hill I saw a bevy of hussars ride under the railway bridge. Three galloped through the open gates of the Oriental College; two others dismounted, and began running from house to house. The sun, shining through the smoke that drove up from the tops of the trees, seemed blood red, and threw an un-familiar lurid light upon everything.

"Stop here," said I. "You are safe here," and I started off at once for the "Spotted Dog," for I knew the landlord had a horse and dog-cart. I ran, for I perceived that in a moment everyone upon this side of the hill would be moving. I found him in his bar, quite unaware of what was going on behind his house. A man stood with his back to me, talking to him.

"I must have a pound," said the landlord, "and I've no one to drive it."

"I'll give you two," said I, over the stranger's shoulder.

"What for?"

"And I'll bring it back by midnight," I said.

"Lord!" said the landlord, "what's the hurry? I'm selling my bit of a pig. Two pounds and you bring it back! What's going on now?"

I explained hastily that I had to leave my

Signalling with a flag on a long pole.

home, and so secured the dog-cart. At the time it did not seem to me nearly so urgent that the landlord should leave his. I took care to have it there and then, drove it off down the road, and, leaving it in charge of my wife and servant, rushed into my house and packed a few valuables, such plate as we had, and so forth. The beech trees below the house were burning while I did this, and the palings up the hill glowed red. While I was occupied in this way, one of the dismounted hussars came running up. He was going from house to house, warning people to leave. He was going on as I came out of my front door, lugging my treasures done up in a table-cloth. I shouted after him: "What news ?"

He turned, stared, bawled something about "crawling out in a thing like a dish cover," and ran on to the gate of the house at the crest. A sudden whirl of black smoke driving across the road, hid him for a moment. I ran to my neighbour's door, and rapped, to satisfy myself, what I already knew, that his wife had gone to London with him, and had locked up their house. I went in again for my servant's box, according to my promise, lugged it out, clapped it beside her on the tail of the dog-cart, and then caught the reins and jumped up into the driver's seat beside my wife. In another moment we were clear of the smoke and noise, and spanking down the opposite slope of Maybury Hill towards Old Woking.

In front was a quiet sunny landscape, a wheat field ahead on either side of the road, and the "Maybury Inn," with its swinging sign. At the bottom of the hill I turned my head to look at the hillside I was leaving. Thick streamers of black smoke shot with threads of red fire were driving up into the still air, and throwing dark shadows upon the green tree tops eastward. The smoke already extended far away to the east and west, to the Byfleet pine woods eastward, and to Woking on the west. And very faint now, but very distinct through the hot quiet air, one heard the whirr of a machine gun, that was presently stilled, and an intermittent cracking of rifles.

Apparently the Martians were setting fire to everything within range of their heat ray.

I am an inexpert driver, and I had immediately to turn my head to the horse again. But that strange sight of the swift confusion and destruction of war, the first real glimpse of warfare that had ever come into my life, was photographed in an instant upon my memory. When I looked back again the second hill had hidden the black smoke. I slashed the horse with the whip, and gave him a loose rein until Woking and Send lay between us and that quivering tumult.

X.—IN THE STORM.

LEATHERHEAD is about twelve miles from Maybury Hill. We got there without misadventure about nine o'clock, and the horse had an hour's rest while I took supper with my cousins, and commended my wife to their care. The evening had been a pleasant one, a little hot and close perhaps at first, but the rapid drive had made an artificial breeze for us. The scent of hay was in the air through the lush meadows beyond Pyrford, and the hedges on either side were sweet and gay with multitudes of dog roses. The heavy firing that had broken out while we were driving down Maybury Hill ceased as abruptly as it began, leaving the evening very peaceful and still.

My wife was curiously silent throughout the drive, and seemed oppressed with forebodings of evil. I talked to her reassuringly, pointing out that the Martians were tied to the pit by sheer heaviness, and, at the utmost, could but crawl a little out of it, but she answered only in monosyllables. Had it not been for my promise to the innkeeper she would, I think, have urged me to stay in Leatherhead. Her face, I remember, was very white as we parted. For my own part I had been feverishly excited all day. Something very like the war-fever, that occasionally runs through a civilised community, had got into my blood, and in my heart I was not so very sorry that I had to return to Maybury that night. I was even afraid that last fusillade I had heard might mean the extermination of our invaders from Mars. I wanted to be in at the death.

It was nearly eleven when I started to return. The night was unexpectedly dark; to me, walking out of the lighted passage of my cousin's house, it seemed indeed black, and it was as hot and close as the day. Overhead the clouds were driving fast, albeit not a breath stirred the shrubs about us. My cousin's man lit both lamps. Happily I knew the road intimately. My wife stood in the light of the doorway and watched me until I jumped up into the dog-cart. Then abruptly she turned and went in, leaving my cousins side by side wishing me good hap.

I was a little depressed at first with the contagion of my wife's fears, but very soon my thoughts reverted to the Martians. At that time I was absolutely in the dark as to the course of the evening's fighting. I did not know even the circumstances that had precipitated the conflict. As I came through Ockham (for that was the way I returned, and not through Send and Old Woking), I saw along the western horizon a blood-red glow, which, as I drew nearer, crept slowly up the sky. The driving clouds of the gathering thunderstorm mingled there with masses of black and red smoke.

Ripley Street was deserted, and except for a lighted window or so the village showed not a sign of life, but I narrowly escaped an accident at the corner of the road to Pyrford, where a knot of people stood with their backs to me.

They said nothing to me as I passed. I do not know what they knew of the things happening beyond the hill, nor do I know if the silent houses I passed on my way were sleeping securely, or deserted and empty, or harrassed and watching against the terror of the night. Until I came through Pyrford, I was in the valley of the Wey, and the red glare was hidden from me. As I ascended the little hill beyond Pyrford church, the glare came into view again, and the trees about me shivered with the first intimation of the storm that was upon me. Then I heard midnight pealing out from Pyrford church behind me, and then came the clear sight of Maybury Hill with its treetops and roofs black and sharp against the red.

Even as I beheld this a lurid green glare lit the road about me, and showed the distant woods towards Addlestone. I felt a tug at the reins. I saw, only with half an eye, that the driving clouds had been pierced as it were by a thread of green fire, suddenly lighting their confusion, and falling into the fields to my left. It was the Third Falling Star. Close on its apparition, and blindingly violet by contrast, danced out the first lightning of the gathering storm, and the thunder burst like a rocket overhead.

The horse took the bit between his teeth and bolted. I gripped the reins, and we went whirling along between the hedges, and emerged in a minute or so upon the open common. A moderate incline runs down towards the foot of Maybury Hill, and down this we clattered. Once the lightning had begun it went on in as rapid a succession of flashes as I have ever seen. The thunder claps, treading one on the heels of another, and with a strange crackling accompaniment, sounded more like the working of a gigantic electric machine than the usual detonating reverberations. The flickering light was blinding and confusing, and a thin hail smote in gusts at my face as I drove down the slope.

At first I regarded little but the road before me, and then abruptly my attention was arrested by something that was moving rapidly down the opposite slope of Maybury Hill. At first I took it for the wet roof of a house, but one flash following another showed it to be in swift rolling movement. It was an elusive vision; a moment bewildering darkness, and then a flash like daylight, the red masses of the Orphanage, near the crest of the hill, and the green tops of the pine trees coming out clear and sharp and bright.

And this Thing! How can I describe it? A monstrous tripod, higher than many houses, striding over the young pine trees, and smashing them aside in its wallowing career: a walking engine of glittering metal, reeling now across the heather; articulate ropes of steel dangling from it, and the clattering tumult of its passage mingling with the riot of the thunder. A flash, and it came out vividly, heeling over one way with two feet in the air, to vanish and reappear almost instantly as it seemed, with the next flash, a hundred yards nearer. Can you imagine a milking stool tilted and bowled violently along the ground? But instead of a milking stool, imagine it a great thing of metal, like the body of a colossal steam engine on a tripod stand.

Then suddenly the trees in the pine wood ahead of me were parted, as brittle reeds are parted by a man thrusting through them; they were snapped off and driven headlong, and a second huge tripod appeared, rushing as it seemed headlong towards me. And I was galloping hard to meet it! At the sight of the second monster my nerve went altogether. Not stopping to look again I wrenched the horse's head hard round to the right, and in another moment the

Suddenly the trees in the pinewood were parted.

dog-cart had heeled over upon the horse; the shafts smashed noisily, and I was flung sideways and fell heavily into a shallow pool of water.

I crawled out almost immediately and crouched, my feet still in the water, under a clump of furze. The horse lay motionless (his neck was broken, poor brute!) and by the lightning flashes I saw the black bulk of

the over-turned dog-cart, and the silhouette of the wheel still spinning slowly. In another moment the colossal mechanism went striding by me, and passed uphill towards Pyrford.

Seen nearer, the Thing was incredibly strange. For it was no mere insensate machine driving on its way. Machine it was, with a ringing metallic pace, and long flexible glittering tentacles (one of which gripped a young pine tree) swinging and rattling about its strange body. It picked its road as it went striding along, and the brazen hood that surmounted it moved to and fro with the inevitable suggestion of a head looking about it.

In this was the Martian. Behind the body was a huge thing of white metal, like a gigantic fisherman's basket, and puffs of green smoke squirted out from the joints of the limbs as the monster swept by me. So much I saw then, all vaguely for the flickering of the lightning, in blinding high lights and dense black shadow.

As it passed, it set up an exultant deafening howl, that drowned the thunder, "aloo, aloo," and in another minute it was with the other, half a mile away, stooping over something in the fields. I made no doubt this thing in the field, was the third of the ten cylinders they had fired at us from Mars.

For some minutes I lay there simply stupefied, watching, by the intermittent light, these monstrous beings of metal moving about in the distance over the hedge tops. A thin hail was now beginning, and as it came and went, their figures grew misty and then flashed into clearness again. Now and then came a gap in the lightning, and the night swallowed them up. I was soaked with hail above and puddle water below. It was some time before my blank astonishment would let me struggle up the bank to a drier position, or think at all of my imminent peril.

Not far from me, was a little one-roomed squatter's hut of wood, surrounded by a patch of potato garden. I struggled to my feet at last, and, crouching and making use of every chance of cover, I made a run for this. I hammered at the door, but I could not make the people hear (if there were any people inside), and after a time I desisted, and, availing myself of a ditch for the greater part of the way, succeeded in crawling, unobserved by these monstrous machines, into the pine wood towards Maybury.

Under cover of this I pushed on, wet and shivering now, towards my own house. I walked among the trees trying to find the footpath. It was very dark indeed in the wood, for the lightning was now becoming infrequent, and the hail, which was pouring down in a torrent, fell in columns through the gaps in the heavy foliage. The steaming air was full of a hot resinous smell.

If I had fully realised the meaning of all the things I had seen I should have immediately worked my way round through Byfleet to Street Chobham and so gone back to rejoin my wife at Leatherhead. But that night the strangeness of things about me and my physical wretchedness prevented me, for I was bruised, weary, and wet to the skin, deafened and blinded by the storm. I had a vague idea of going on to my own house, and that was as much motive as I had. I staggered through the trees, fell into a ditch and bruised my knees against a plank, and finally splashed out into the lane that ran down from the "College Arms." I say splashed, for the storm water was sweeping the sand down the hill in a muddy torrent. There in the darkness, a man blundered into me and sent me reeling back.

He gave a cry of terror, sprung sideways, and rushed on before I could gather my wits together sufficiently to speak to him. So heavy was the stress of the storm just at this place, that I had the hardest task to win my way up the hill. I went close up to the fence on the left, and worked my way along its palings.

Near the top, I stumbled upon something soft, and, by a flash of lightning, saw between my feet a heap of black broadcloth and a pair of boots. Before I could distinguish clearly how the man lay, the flicker of light had passed. I stood over him waiting for the next flash. When it came, I saw that he was a sturdy man, cheaply but not shabbily dressed; his head was bent under his body, and he lay crumpled up close to the fence, as though he had been flung violently against it.

Overcoming the repugnance natural to one who had never before touched a dead body, I stooped and turned him over to feel for his heart. He was quite dead. Apparently his neck had been broken. The lightning flashed for a third time, and his face leapt upon me. I sprang to my feet. It was the landlord of the "Spotted Dog," whose conveyance I had taken.

I stepped over him gingerly and pushed on up the hill. I made my way by the police station and the "College Arms" towards my own house. Nothing was burning on the hillside, though from the common there still came a red glare and a rolling tumult of ruddy smoke beating up against the drenching hail. So far as I could see by the two or three distant flashes, the houses about me were mostly uninjured. By the "College Arms" a dark heap lay in the road, but I did not care to examine it.

Down the road towards Maybury Bridge there were voices and the sound of feet, but I had not the courage to shout or to go to them. I saw nothing unusual in my garden that night, though the gate was off its hinges, and the shrubs seemed trampled. I let myself in with my latchkey, closed, locked, and bolted the door, staggered to the foot of the staircase, and sat down. My strength and courage seemed absolutely exhausted. A great horror of this darkness and desolation about me came upon me. My imagination was full of those striding metallic monsters, and of the dead body smashed against the fence. I felt like a rat in a corner. I crouched at the foot of the staircase, with my back to the wall, shivering violently.

XI.—AT THE WINDOW.

I HAVE said already that my storms of emotion have a trick of exhausting themselves. I seem to remember noting that I was cold and wet, and with little pools of water about me on the stair carpet. I got up almost mechanically, went into the dining room and drank some whisky, and then I was moved to change my clothes. After I had done that I went upstairs to my study, but why I did so I do not know. The window of my study looks over the trees and the railway towards Horsell Common. In the hurry

of our departure this window had been left open. The passage was dark, and by contrast with the picture the window frame inclosed, that side of the room seemed impenetrably dark. I stopped in the doorway, staring.

The thunderstorm had passed. The towers of the Oriental College and the pine trees about it had gone, and very far away, lit by a vivid red glare, the common about the sand pits was visible. Across the light, huge black shapes, grotesque and strange, moved busily to and fro. The light itself came from Chobham.

It seemed, indeed, as if the whole country in that direction was on fire, a broad hillside set with minute tongues of flame, swaying and writhing with the gusts of the dying storm, and throwing a red reflection upon the cloud scud above. Every now and then a haze of smoke from some nearer conflagration drove across the window and hid the Martian shapes. I could not see what they were doing

Huge, black shapes moved busily to and fro.

nor the clear form of them, nor recognise the black objects they were busied upon. Neither could I see the nearer fire, though the reflections of it danced on the wall and ceiling of the study. A sharp resinous twang of burning was in the air.

I closed the door noiselessly and crept towards the window. As I did so the view opened out until on the one hand it reached to the houses about Woking station, and on the other to the charred and blackened pine woods of Byfleet. There was a light down below the hill, on the railway near the arch, and several of the houses along the Maybury road, and the streets near the station were glowing ruins. The light upon the railway puzzled me at first; there was a black heap and a vivid glare, and to the right of that a row of yellow oblongs. Then I perceived this was a wrecked train, the forepart smashed and on fire, the hinder carriages still upon the rails.

Between these three main centres of light, the houses, the train, and the burning country towards Chobham, stretched irregular patches of dark country, broken here and there by intervals of dimly glowing and smoking ground. It was the strangest spectacle, that black expanse set with fire. It reminded me, more than anything else, of the potteries seen at night. People, at first I could distinguish none, though I peered intently for them. Later I saw, against the light of Woking station, a number of black figures hurrying one after the other across the line.

And this was the little world in which I had been living securely for years, this fiery chaos! What had happened in the last seven hours, I still did not know, nor did I know, though I was beginning to guess, the relation between these mechanical Colossi and the sluggish lumps I had seen disgorged from the cylinder. With a queer feeling of impersonal interest, I turned my desk chair to the window, sat down, and stared at the blackened country, and particularly at the three gigantic black things that were going to and fro in the glare about the sand pits. They seemed amazingly busy. I began to ask myself what they could be. Were they intelligent mechanisms? Was such a thing

possible? Or did a Martian sit within each, ruling, directing, using, much as a man's brain sits and rules in his body?

Later I was to learn that this was the case. That with incredible rapidity these bodiless brains, these limbless intelligences, had built up these monstrous structures since their arrival, and, no longer sluggish and inert, were now able to go to and fro, destroying and irresistible.

The storm had left the sky clear, and over the smoke of the burning land the little fading pin point of Mars was dropping into the west, when the soldier came into my garden. I heard a slight scraping at the fence, and rousing myself from the lethargy that had fallen upon me, and looking down, I saw him dimly, clambering over the palings. I was so delighted at the sight of another human being, that my torpor passed, and I leant out of the window eagerly.

"Hist!" said I in a whisper.

He stopped, astride of the fence, in doubt. Then he came over and across the lawn to the corner of the house. He bent down and stepped softly.

"Who's there?" he said (also whispering), standing under the window and peering up.

"Where are you going?" I asked.

"God knows."

"Are you trying to hide?"

"That's it."

"Come into the house," I said.

I went down, unfastened the door, and let him in, and locked the door again. I could not see his face. He was hatless, and his coat was unbuttoned.

"My God!" he said as I drew him in.

"What has happened?" I asked.

"What hasn't?" In the obscurity I could see he made a gesture of despair. "They wiped us out: simply wiped us out," he repeated again and again. He followed me almost mechanically into the dining room.

"Take some whisky," I said, pouring out a stiff dose. He drank it. Then abruptly he sat down before the table, put his head on his arms, and began to sob and weep like a little boy, in a perfect passion of emotion, while I, with a curious forgetfulness of my own recent despair, stood beside him wondering.

It was a long time before he could steady

his
nerves
to answer
my questions,
and then he answered
perplexingly and bro-
kenly. He
was a dri-
ver in the
Artil-
lery, and
had onl
come into
action
about
seven. At
that time
firing was going
on across the
common, and
it was said the
Martians were crawling towards
their second cylinder under
cover of a metal shield.

Later this shield staggered up
on tripod legs, and became the
first of the fighting machines I
had seen. The gun he drove
had been unlimbered near Horsell in order to command the
sand pits, and it was this had
precipitated the action. As the
limber gunners went to the rear,
his horse trod in a rabbit hole
and came down, throwing him
into a depression of the ground.
At the same moment the gun
exploded behind him, the ammunition blew up, there was
fire all about him, and
he found himself ly-
ing under a heap
of charred dead
men and dead
horses. "I lay
still," he said,
" scared out of
my wits, with
the fore-
quarter of
a horse

atop of me. We've been wiped out. And
the smell! Good God! Like burnt
meat! I was hurt across the back by the
fall of the horse, and there I had to lie
for a time until I felt better. Just like
parade it had been a minute before, then
stumble, bang! swish!" He threw out
his hands. "Wiped out!" he said.

I asked him a hundred questions. He
had hid under the dead horse for a long
time, peeping out furtively across the
common. The Cardigan men had tried
a rush, in skirmishing order, at the pit,
simply to be swept out of existence.
Then the monster had risen to its feet,
and had begun to walk leisurely to and fro
across the common among the few fugitives, with its head-like hood turning

A second glittering Titan built itself up out of the pit.

about exactly like the head of a cowled human being. A kind of arm carried a thing like a huge photographic camera, and out of the eye of this there smote the Heat Ray.

In a few minutes there was, so far as the soldier could see, not a living thing left upon the common, and every bush and tree upon it that was not already a blackened skeleton was burning. The Hussars had been on the road beyond the curvature of the ground and he saw nothing of them. He heard the Maxims rattle for a time and then become still. The giant saved Woking Station and its cluster of houses until last. Then in a moment the Heat Ray was brought to bear and the town became a heap of fiery ruins. Then the thing shut off the Heat Ray and, turning its back upon the artilleryman, began to waddle away towards the smouldering pinewoods that sheltered the second cylinder. As it did so a second glittering Titan built itself up out of the pit.

The second monster followed the first, and at that the artilleryman began to crawl very cautiously across the hot heather ash towards Horsell. He managed to get alive into the ditch along by the side of the road, and so escaped to Woking. There his story became ejaculatory. The place was impassable. It seems there were a few people alive there, frantic for the most part. He was turned aside by the fire, and hid among some almost scorching heaps of broken wall, as one of the Martian giants returned. He saw this one pursue a man, catch him up in one of its steely tentacles and knock his head against the trunk of a pine tree. At last, after night-

He saw this one pursue a man and catch him up in one of its steely tentacles.

fall, the artilleryman made a rush for it, and got over the railway embankment.

Since then he had been skulking along towards Maybury, in the hope of getting out of danger Londonward. People were hiding in trenches and cellars, and many of the survivors had made off towards Woking village and Send. He had been consumed with thirst until he found one of the water mains near the railway arch smashed, and the water bubbling out like a spring upon the road.

That was the story I won from him bit by bit. He grew calmer telling me, and trying to make me see the things he had seen. He had eaten no food since midday he told me early in his narrative, and I found some mutton and bread in the pantry and brought it into the room. We lit no lamp for fear of attracting the Martians, and ever and again our hands would touch upon bread or meat. As he talked, things about us came darkly out of the darkness, and the trampled bushes and broken rose-trees outside the window grew distinct. It would seem that a number of men or animals

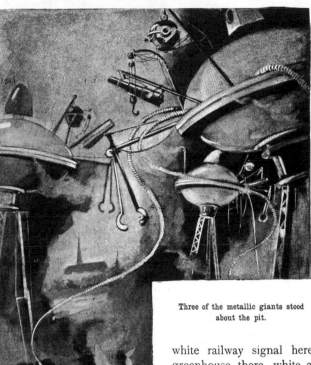

Three of the metallic giants stood about the pit.

had rushed across the lawn. I began to see his face, blackened and haggard, as no doubt mine was also.

When we had finished eating we went softly upstairs to my study, and I looked again out of the open window.

In one night the valley had become a valley of ashes. The fires had dwindled now. Where flames had been there were now streamers of smoke, but the countless ruins of shattered and gutted houses and blasted and blackened trees that the night had hidden stood out now, gaunt and terrible, in the pitiless light of dawn. Yet here and there some object had had the luck to escape—a white railway signal here, the end of a greenhouse there, white and fresh amidst the wreckage. Never before in the history of warfare had destruction been so indiscriminate and so universal. And, shining with the growing light of the east, three of the metallic giants stood about the pit, their cowls rotating as though they were surveying the desolation they had made.

It seemed to me that the pit had been enlarged, and ever and again puffs of vivid green vapour streamed up out of it towards the brightening dawn—streamed up, coiled, whirled, broke, and vanished. Beyond them were the pillars of fire about Chobham. They became pillars of bloodshot smoke at the first touch of day.

By H. G. WELLS.

SUMMARY.

THE inhabitants of Mars invade the earth, descending at Woking. They are sluggish creatures with tentacles, but they possess huge fighting machines, by means of which they destroy the troops sent to encircle them. The story is told by an inhabitant of Woking. At the outbreak of hostilities he takes his wife to Leatherhead for safety, and returns to find his house deserted and partly destroyed. The only human being he meets is an artilleryman hiding in his garden.

XII.—WHAT I SAW OF THE DE-STRUCTION OF WEYBRIDGE AND SHEPPERTON.

As the dawn grew brighter we withdrew ourselves from the window, from which we had watched the Martians, and went very quietly downstairs.

The artilleryman agreed with me that the house was no place to stay in. He proposed, he said, to make his way Londonward, and thence rejoin his battery—No. 12, of the Horse Artillery. My plan was to return at once to Leatherhead, and, so greatly had the strength of the Martians impressed me, that I had determined to take my wife to Newhaven and out of the country forthwith.

I perceived clearly that the country about London must inevitably be the scene of an unparalleled struggle before such creatures as these, constantly reinforced as it seemed they were by fresh falling meteors, could be destroyed. Between us and Leatherhead, however, lay the Third Cylinder with its guarding giants, and so I resolved to go with the artilleryman, under cover of the woods, northward as far as Street Chobham before I parted with him. Thence I would make a big detour by Epsom to reach Leatherhead.

I should have started at once, but my companion had been in active service, and he knew better than that. He made me ransack the house for a flask, which he filled with whisky; and we lined every available pocket with packets of biscuits and slices of meat. Then we crept out of the house, and ran as quickly as we could down the ill-made road by which I had come overnight. The houses seemed deserted. In the road lay a group of three charred bodies close together, struck dead by the Heat Ray, and here and there were things that the people had dropped, a clock, a slipper, in one place a worn silver spoon, and so forth. At the corner turning up towards the post office, a little cart, filled with boxes and furniture, and horseless, heeled over on a broken wheel. A cash box had been hastily smashed open, and thrown under the *débris*.

Except the lodge of the Orphanage, which was still on fire, none of the houses had suffered very greatly here. The Heat Ray had shaved the chimney tops and passed. Yet, save ourselves, there did not seem to be a living soul on Maybury Hill. The majority of the inhabitants had escaped, I suppose, by way of the Old Woking road—the road I had taken when I drove to Leatherhead; or they had hidden.

We went down the lane by the body of the man in black, sodden now from the overnight hail, and broke into the woods at the foot of the hill. We pushed through these towards the railway, without meeting a soul. The woods across the line were but the scarred and blackened ruins of woods; for the most part the trees had fallen, but a certain proportion still stood, dismal grey stems with dark brown foliage instead of green.

On our side, the fire had done no more than scorch the nearer trees; it had failed to secure its footing. In one place, the woodmen had been at work on Saturday; trees, felled and freshly trimmed. lay in a clearing, with heaps of sawdust, by the sawing machine and its engine. Hard by was a temporary hut, deserted. There was not a breath of wind this morning, and everything was strangely still. Even the birds were hushed, and as we hurried along, I and the artilleryman talked in whispers, and looked now and again over our shoulders. Once or twice we stopped to listen.

After a time, we drew near the road, and as we did so, we heard the clatter of hoofs, and saw through the tree stems, three cavalry soldiers riding slowly towards Woking. We hailed them, and they halted while we hurried towards them. It was a lieutenant and a couple of privates of the Eighth Hussars, with a stand like a theodolite, which the artilleryman told me was a heliograph. "You are the first men I've seen coming this way this morning," said the lieutenant. "What's brewing?" His voice and face were eager. The men behind him stared curiously. The artilleryman jumped down the bank into the road and saluted. "Gun destroyed last night, Sir. Have been hiding. Trying to rejoin battery, Sir. You'll come in sight of the Martians I expect about half a mile along this road."

"What the dickens are they like?" asked the lieutenant.

"Giants in armour, Sir. Hundred feet high. Three legs and a body like 'luminium, with a mighty great head in a hood, Sir."

"Get out!" said the lieutenant. "What confounded nonsense!"

"You'll see, Sir. They carry a kind of box, Sir, that shoots fire and strikes you dead."

"What d'ye mean—a gun?"

"No, Sir," and the artilleryman began a vivid account of the Heat Ray. Halfway through the lieutenant interrupted him and looked up at me. I was still standing on the bank by the side of the road. "Did you see it?" said the lieutenant.

"It's perfectly true," I said.

"Well," said the lieutenant, "I suppose it's my business to see it too. Look here,"—to the artilleryman, "we're detailed here clearing people out of their houses. You'd better go along and report yourself to Brigadier-General Marvin, and tell him all you know. He's at Weybridge. Know the way?"

"I do," I said; and he turned his horse southward again. "Half a mile, you say?" said he. "At most," I answered, and pointed over the tree tops southward. He thanked me and rode on, and we saw them no more.

Farther along we came upon a group of three women and two children in the road, busy clearing out a labourer's cottage. They had got hold of a kind of hand-truck, and were piling it up with unclean-looking bundles and shabby furniture. They were all too assiduously engaged to talk to us as we passed.

By Byfleet station we emerged from the pine trees, and found the country calm and peaceful under the morning sunlight. We were far beyond the range of the Heat Ray there, and had ,it not been for the silent desertion of some of the houses, the stirring movement of packing in others, and the knot of soldiers standing on the bridge over the railway and staring down the line towards Woking, the day would have seemed very like any other Sunday.

Several farm waggons and carts were moving creakily along the road to Addlestone, and suddenly through the gate of a field we saw, across a stretch of flat meadow, six twelve-pounders, standing neatly at equal distances and pointing towards Woking. The gunners stood by the guns waiting, and the ammunition waggons were at a business-like distance. The men stood almost as if under inspection.

"That's good!" said I. "They will get one fair shot at any rate." The artilleryman hesitated at the gate. "I shall go on," he said. Farther on towards Weybridge, just over the bridge, there were a number of men in white fatigue jackets throwing up a long rampart, and more guns behind. "It's bows and arrows against the lightning, anyhow," said the artilleryman. "They 'aven't seen that fire beam yet." The officers who were not actively engaged stood and stared over the tree-tops south-westward, and the men digging would stop every now and again to stare in the same direction.

Byfleet was in a tumult, people packing, and a score of hussars perhaps hunting them about, some of them dismounted, some on horseback. Three or four black Government waggons, with crosses in white circles, and an old omnibus, among other vehicles, were being loaded in the village street. There were scores of people, most of them sufficiently Sabbatical to have assumed their best clothes. The soldiers were having the greatest difficulty in making them realise the gravity of their position. We saw one shrivelled old fellow with a huge box and a score or more of flower-pots containing orchids, angrily expostulating with the corporal who would leave them behind. I stopped, and gripped his arm. "Do you know what's over there?" I said, pointing at the pine-tops that hid the Martians.

"Eh?" said he, turning. "I was explainin' these is vallyble."

"Death!" I shouted. "Death is coming! Death!" and, leaving him to digest that if he could, I hurried on after the artilleryman. At the corner I looked back. The soldier had left him, and he was still standing by his box with the pots of orchids on the lid of it and staring vaguely over the trees.

No one in Weybridge could tell us where the headquarters were established, the whole place was in such confusion as I had never seen in any town before. Carts, carriages everywhere, the most astonishing miscellany of conveyances and horseflesh. The respectable inhabitants of the place, men in golf and boating costumes, wives prettily dressed, were packing, riverside loafers energetically helping, children excited, and, for the most part, highly delighted at this astonishing variation of their Sunday experiences. In the midst of it all the worthy vicar was very pluckily holding an early celebration, and his bell was jangling out above the excitement.

I and the artilleryman, seated on the step of the drinking fountain, made a very passable meal upon what we had brought with us. Patrols of soldiers— here no longer hussars but grenadiers in white—were warning people to move now or to take refuge in their cellars as soon as the firing began. We saw as we crossed the railway bridge that a growing crowd of people had assembled in and about the railway station, and the swarming platform was piled with boxes and packages. The ordinary traffic had been stopped, I believe, in order to allow of the passage of troops and guns to Chertsey, and I have heard since that a savage struggle occurred for places in the special trains that were put on at a later hour.

We remained in Weybridge until midday, and at that hour we found ourselves at the place near Shepperton Lock, where the Wey and Thames join. Part of the time we spent helping two old women to pack a little cart. The Wey has a treble mouth, and at this point boats are to be hired, and there was a ferry across the river. On the Shepperton side was an inn, with a lawn, and beyond that the tower of Shepperton church —it has been replaced by a spire—rose above the trees.

Here we found an excited and noisy crowd of fugitives. As yet the flight had not grown to a panic, but there were already far more people than all the boats going to and fro could enable to cross. Quite respectable people came panting along under heavy burdens; one decent husband and wife were even carrying a small outhouse door between them, with some of their household goods piled thereon. One man told us he meant to try to get away from Shepperton station.

There was a lot of shouting, and one man even was jesting. The idea people seemed to have here was that the Martians were simply formidable human beings, who might attack and sack the town, to be certainly destroyed in the end. Every now and then people would glance nervously across the Wey, at the meadows towards Chertsey, but everything over there was still. Across the Thames, except just where the boats landed, everything was quiet, in vivid contrast with the Surrey side. The people who landed there from the boats went tramping off down the lane. The big ferry boat had just made a journey. Three or four soldiers stood on the lawn of the inn, staring and jesting at the fugitives without offering to help. The inn was closed, as it was now within the prohibited hours.

"What's that?" cried a boatman, and "Shut up, you fool," said a man near me to a yelping dog. Then the sound came again, this time from the direction of Chertsey, a muffled thud—the sound of a gun.

The fighting was beginning. Almost immediately unseen batteries across the river to our right, unseen because of the trees, took up the chorus, firing heavily one after the other. A woman screamed. Everyone stood arrested by the sudden stir of battle, near us and yet invisible to us. Nothing was to be seen save flat meadows, cows for the most part feeding unconcernedly, and silvery pollard willows motionless in the

"Hit!" shouted I.

warm sunlight. "The sojers 'll stop 'em," said a woman beside me doubtfully. A haziness rose over the tree tops.

Then suddenly we saw a rush of smoke far away up the river, a puff of smoke that jerked up into the air, and hung, and forthwith the ground heaved under foot and a heavy explosion shook the air, smashing two or three windows in the houses near, and leaving us astonished.

"Here they are!" shouted a man in a blue jersey. "Yonder. D' yer see them? Yonder."

Quickly, one after the other, one, two, three, four of the armed Martians appeared, far away over the little trees, across the flat meadows that stretch towards Chertsey, and striding hurriedly towards the river. Little cowled figures they seemed at first, going with a rolling motion, and as fast as flying birds.

Then, advancing obliquely towards us, came a fifth. Their armoured bodies glittered in the sun, as they swept swiftly forward upon the guns, growing rapidly larger as they drew nearer. One on the extreme left, the remotest that is, flourished a huge box high in the air, and the ghostly terrible Heat Ray I had already seen on Friday night smote towards Chertsey, and struck the town.

At sight of these strange, swift, and terrible creatures, the crowd along by the water's edge seemed to me to be for a moment horrorstruck. There was no screaming or shouting, but a silence.

Then a hoarse murmur and a movement of feet. A splashing from the water. A man, too frightened to drop the portmanteau he carried on his shoulder, swung round and sent me staggering with a blow from the corner of his burden. A woman thrust at me with her hand, and rushed past me. I turned too, with the rush of people all about me. But I was not too terrified for thought. The terrible Heat Ray was in my mind. To get under water! That was it! "Get under water," I shouted. I faced about again, and rushed towards the approaching Martian, rushed right down the gravelly beach, and headlong into the water. Others did the same. A boatload of people, putting back, came leaping out as I rushed past. The stones under my feet were muddy and

slippery, and the river was so low that I ran perhaps twenty feet scarcely waist-deep. Then, as the Martian towered overhead scarcely a couple of hundred yards away, I flung myself forward under the surface. The splashes of the people in the boats leaping into the river sounded like thunderclaps in my ears.

In my convulsive excitement I took no heed of the artilleryman behind me, and to this day I do not know what became of him. I never set eyes on him again. People were landing hastily on both sides of the river.

But the Martian machine took no more notice for the moment of the people running this way and that, than a man would of the confusion of ants in a nest against which his foot has kicked. When, half suffocated, I raised my head above water—there were dripping faces all about me—the Martian's hood pointed at the batteries that were still firing far away across the river, and as it advanced it swung loose what must have been the generator of the Heat Ray.

In another moment it was on the bank, and in a stride wading halfway across. The knees of its foremost legs bent at the further bank, and in another moment it had raised itself to its full height again, close to the village of Shepperton. Forthwith the six guns which, unknown to all of us on the right bank, had been hidden behind the outskirts of that village, fired simultaneously. The sudden concussions, the last close upon the first, made my heart jump. The monster was already raising the case generating the Heat Ray, as the shell burst six yards above the hood.

I gave a cry of astonishment. I saw and thought nothing of the other four Martian monsters; my attention was riveted upon this nearer incident. Simultaneously two other shells burst in the air near the body as the hood twisted round in time to receive, but not in time to dodge, the fourth shell.

The shell burst clean in the face of the thing. The hood bulged, flashed, was whirled off in a dozen tattered fragments of red flesh and glittering metal. "Hit!" shouted I, with something between a scream and a cheer. I heard answering shouts from the people in the water about me. I could have leaped out of the water with that momentary exultation.

The decapitated colossus reeled like a drunken giant. But it did not go over. It recovered its balance by a miracle, and, no longer heeding its steps, and with the camera that fired the Heat Ray now rigidly upheld, it marched swiftly towards Shepperton. The living intelligence, the Martian within the hood, was slain and splashed to the four winds of heaven; and the thing was now but a mere intricate device of metal driving mechanically to destruction. It reeled along in a straight line, incapable of guidance. It struck the tower of Shepperton church, smashing it down as the impact of a battering ram might have done, staggered pitifully like a wounded man, swerved aside, blundered on, and collapsed into the river, out of my sight.

As the camera of the Heat Ray hit the water.

A violent explosion shook the air, and a spout of water, steam, mud, and shattered metal shot far up into the sky. As the camera of the Heat Ray hit the water, the latter had incontinently flashed into steam. In another moment a huge wave like a muddy tidal bore, but almost scaldingly hot, came sweeping round the bend up stream. I heard people struggling shorewards, and screaming and shouting.

I was so excited by this tremendous disaster, that for the moment I heeded nothing of the heat, forgot the patent need of self-preservation. I splashed through the tumultuous water, pushing aside a man in black to do so, until I could see round the bend. Half-a-dozen deserted boats pitched aimlessly upon the confusion of waves. The fallen Martian came into sight, lying across the water, and for the most part submerged.

Thick clouds of steam were pouring off the boiling water, and through the tumultuously whirling whisps of it I could see, intermittently and vaguely, the gigantic limbs churning the water and flinging a black spray of mud and water into the air. The tentacles swayed like living arms. and, save for the helpless purposelessness of these movements, it was exactly like some sensitive wounded thing struggling for its life amidst the waves. To add to the resemblance, enormous quantities of a ruddy brown fluid were spirting up out of the machine.

My attention was diverted from their struggles by the sudden outbreak of a furious yelling, like that of the thing called a siren in our manufacturing towns. A man knee-deep near the towing path shouted to me and pointed. Looking back I saw the other Martians advancing with gigantic strides down the river bank from the direction of Chertsey. The Shepperton guns spoke again unavailingly. At that I ducked at once under water, and, holding my breath until movement was an agony, blundered painfully along under the surface as long as I could. The water was in a tumult about me, and rapidly growing hotter.

When for a moment I raised my head to take breath, and throw the hair and water from my eyes, the steam was rising all round me in a whirling white fog that at first hid the Martians altogether. Then I saw them dimly, colossal figures of grey, magnified by the mist. They had passed by me, and two were stooping over the frothing tumultuous ruins of their comrade. The third and fourth stood beside him in the water, one perhaps two hundred yards from me, the other

The tentacles swayed like living arms.

towards Laleham. The generators of the Heat Rays waved high, and the hissing beam smote down this way and that.

The air was full of sound, a deafening and confusing conflict of noises, the clangorous din of the Martians, the crash of falling houses, the thud of trees, fences, sheds, flashing into flame, and the crackling and roaring of fire. Dense, black smoke was leaping up to mingle with the steam from the river, and as the Heat Ray went to and fro over Weybridge, its impact was marked by flashes of incandescent white, that gave place at once to a smoky dance of lurid flame. The nearer houses still stood intact, awaiting their fate, shadowy, faint and pallid in the mist, with the fire behind them going to and fro.

For a moment, perhaps, I stood there, breast high in the almost boiling water, dumfounded at my position, hopeless of escape. Through the reek I could see the people who had been with me in the river scrambling out of the water through the reeds like little frogs hurrying through grass from the advance of a man, or running to

The four carrying the *débris* of their comrade between them.

and fro in utter dismay on the towing path.

Then suddenly the white flashes of the Heat Ray came leaping towards me. The houses caved in as they dissolved at its touch, and darted out flames ; the trees changed to fire with a roar. It flickered up and down the towing path, licking off the people who ran this way and that, and came down to the water's edge not fifty yards from where I stood. It swept across the river to Shepperton, and the water in its track rose in a boiling wheal crested with steam. I lost sight of everything in a whirling torrent of steam.

In another moment the huge wave, wellnigh at the boiling point, had rushed upon me. I screamed aloud, turned to run as it leapt at my face, and, scalded, half blinded, agonised, I staggered through the hissing, leaping water towards the shore. Had my foot stumbled it would have been the end. I fell helplessly in full sight of the Martians, upon the broad, bare gravelly spit that runs down to mark the angle of the Wey and Thames. I expected nothing but death.

I have a dim memory of the foot of a Martian coming down within a yard of my head, driving straight into the loose gravel, whirling it this way and that, and lifting again ; of a long suspense, and then of the four carrying the *débris* of their comrade between them, now clear, and then presently faint through a veil of smoke, receding interminably, as it seemed to me, across a vast space of river and meadow. And then very slowly I realised that by a miracle of chance I had escaped.

XIII.—HOW I FELL IN WITH THE CURATE.

AFTER this sudden lesson in the power of terrestrial weapons, the Martians retreated to their original position upon Horsell Common, and in their haste and incumbered with the *débris* of their smashed companion, they no doubt overlooked many such a stray and unnecessary victim as myself. Had they left their comrade and pushed on forthwith, there was nothing at that time between them and London but batteries of twelve-pounder guns, and they would certainly have reached the capital in advance of the tidings of their approach,—as sudden, dreadful and destructive their advent would have been as the earthquake that destroyed Lisbon a century ago.

I contrived to paddle, as much as my
parboiled hands would allow.

and desolated area — perhaps twenty square miles altogether — that encircled the Martian encampment on Horsell Common, through charred and ruined villages among the green trees, through the blackened and smoking arcades that had been but a day ago pine spinneys, crawled the devoted scouts with the heliographs that were presently to warn the gunners of the Martian approach. But the Martians now understood our command of artillery and the danger of human proximity, and not a man ventured within a mile of either cylinder save at the price of his life.

But they were in no hurry. Cylinder followed cylinder in its interplanetary flight; every twenty-four hours brought them reinforcement. And meanwhile the military and naval authorities now fully alive to the tremendous power of their antagonists, worked with furious energy. Every minute a fresh gun came into position, until, before twilight, every copse, every row of suburban villas on the hilly slopes about Kingston and Richmond, masked an expectant black muzzle. And through the charred

It would seem these giants spent the earlier part of the afternoon in going to and fro, transferring everything from the second and third cylinders—the second in Addlestone Golf Links and the third at Pyrford—to their original pit on Horsell Common. Over that, one stood sentinel above the blackened heather and ruined buildings that stretched far and wide, while the rest abandoned their vast fighting machines and descended into the pit. They were hard at work there far into the night, and the towering pillar of dense green smoke that rose thencefrom, could be seen from the hills about Merrow, and even, it is said, from Banstead and Epsom Downs.

And while the Martians behind me were thus preparing for their next sally, and in front of me Humanity gathered for the battle, I made my way with infinite pains and labour from the fire and smoke of burning Weybridge towards London. When I realised that the Martians had passed I struggled to my feet, giddy and smarting from the scalding I received, and for a space I stood sick and helpless between the drifting steam and the suffocating, burning, and smouldering behind.

Presently, through a gap in the thinning steam, I saw an abandoned boat, very small and remote, drifting down stream, and throwing off the most of my sodden and blackened clothes, I went after it, gained it, and so escaped out of that destruction. There were no oars in the boat, but I contrived to paddle, as much as my parboiled hands would allow, down the river towards Halliford and Walton, going very tediously, and continually looking behind me, as you may well understand.

The hot water from the Martian's overthrow drifted down stream with me, so that for the best part of a mile I could see little of either bank. Once, however, I made out a string of black figures hurrying across the meadows from the direction of Weybridge. Halliford, it seemed, was quite deserted, and several of the houses facing the river were afire. It was strange to see the place quite tranquil, quite desolate, under the hot blue sky, with the smoke and little threads of flame going straight up into the heat of the afternoon. Never before had I seen houses burning without the accompaniment of an inconvenient crowd. A little further on the dry reeds up the bank were smoking and glowing, and a line of fire inland was marching steadily across a late field of hay.

For a long time I drifted, so painful and weary was I after the violence I had been through, and so intense the heat upon the water. Then my fears got the better of me again, and I resumed my paddling. The sun scorched my bare back. At last, as the bridge at Walton was coming into sight round the bend, my fever and faintness overcame my fears, and I landed on the Middlesex bank, and lay down, deadly sick, amidst the long grass. I suppose the time was then about four or five o'clock. I got up presently, walked perhaps half a mile without meeting a soul, and then lay down again in the shadow of a hedge. I seem to remember talking wanderingly to myself during that last spurt. I was also very thirsty, and bitterly regretful I had drunk no more water.

I do not clearly remember the arrival of the curate, so that I probably dozed. I became aware of him as a seated figure in soot-smudged shirt sleeves, and with his upturned clean-shaven face, staring at a faint flickering that danced over the sky. The sky was what is called a mackerel sky, rows and rows of faint down-plumes of cloud, just tinted with the midsummer sunset.

I sat up, and, at the rustle of my motion, he looked at me quickly. " Have you any water?" I asked abruptly.

He shook his head. " You have been asking for water for the last hour," he said unsympathetically.

For a moment we were silent, taking stock of one another. I daresay he found me a strange enough figure, naked save for my water-soaked trousers and socks, scalded, and my face and shoulders blackened from the smoke. His face was a dead white, his eyes were pale grey, and blankly staring. He spoke abruptly, looking vacantly away from me.

" What does it mean?" he said. " What do these things mean?"

I stared at him and made him no answer.

He extended a thin, white hand and spoke in almost a complaining tone. " Why are these things permitted? What sins have we done? The morning service was over, I was walking through the roads to clear my brain for the afternoon's catechism, and then comes fire, earthquake, Death! As if it were Sodom and Gomorrah! All our work undone, all the work and the lives of hundreds of men. . . . . . Does God care? What are these Martians?"

"What are we?" I answered, clearing my throat.

He gripped his knees and turned to look at me again. For half a minute, perhaps, he stared silently. "Aye!" he said; "what are we?" He relapsed into silence, with his chin now sunken almost to his knees.

"Poor worms," he began, waving his hand rhetorically, "creatures of a day. We have lived in peace and security for a couple of hundred years, neither war, nor pestilence, nor famine, nor earthquake, nor flood, has touched the land — neither war, nor pestilence, nor famine, nor earthquake, nor flood — and we have come to think ourselves kings, lords of it all. Religion! Minister of religion! I have been nothing but human self-complacency in a cassock and gown. Social work! Bazaars! —Folly! The fear of the Lord is the beginning of wisdom—the *fear* of the Lord is the beginning of wisdom."

Another pause, and he broke out again like one demented. "The smoke of her burning goeth up for ever and ever," he shouted, and pointed in the direction of Weybridge.

By this time I was beginning to take his measure. The tremendous tragedy in which he had been involved—it was evident he was a fugitive from Weybridge—had driven him to the very verge of religious mania. "Are we far from Sunbury?" I said, in a matter-of-fact tone.

"What are we to do?" he asked. "Are these creatures everywhere? Has the earth been given over to them?"

"Are we far from Sunbury?"

"Only this morning I officiated at early celebration. . ."

"Things have changed," I said quietly. "You must keep your head. These monsters are not everywhere. There is still hope. They are only in this part of the world, unless I am much mistaken."

"But how are you to know that?"

I told him of the shots I had seen fired from Mars. He listened at first, but as I spoke briefly and drily of what I had seen, the interest in his eyes faded slowly to dejection, and he stared before him again.

"Don't you think," he said, interrupting me, "that this may be the beginning of the end? The end! The great and terrible Day of the Lord. When men shall call upon the

"The smoke of her burning goeth up for ever and ever."

mountains and the rocks to fall upon them and hide them—hide them from the face of Him that sitteth upon the Throne?"

I stared blankly by way of answer, then rose painfully to my feet and, standing over him, laid my hand on his shoulder. "Drop that Book of Revelations," said I, "and be a man. You are scared out of your wits. After all, this is the way of Nature. What good is religion if it collapses at calamity? Think of what earthquakes and floods, wars and volcanoes, have done before to men. Did you think God had exempted Weybridge on your account? One would think, to hear you, that He had made you a special promise —and broken it. . . . . . God is not an insurance agent, man."

"But how can we escape?" he asked more quietly. "They are invulnerable, they are pitiless."

"Neither the one nor perhaps the other," I answered. "And the mightier they are the more sane and wary should we be. One of them was killed yonder not three hours ago.

"I saw it happen," I said, and told him.

"We have chanced to come in for the thick of it, and that is all."

"What is that flicker in the sky?" he said abruptly.

I told him it was simply the heliograph signalling. A cockchafer came droning over the hedge and past us. High in the west the crescent moon hung faint and pale, above the smoke of Weybridge and Shepperton and the hot splendour of the sunset.

"We are in the midst of it," I said, "quiet as it is. That flicker in the sky tells of the gathering storm. Yonder, I take it, are the Martians, and Londonward where those hills rise about Richmond and Kingston, and the trees give cover, earthworks are being thrown up and guns are being laid. Presently the Martians will be coming this way again. . ."

And even as I spoke, he sprang to his feet and stopped me by a gesture. "Listen!" he said. And from far away from beyond the low hills across the water, came the dull resonance of guns and a remote, weird crying.

"We had better follow this path," I said, "northward."

By H. G. WELLS.

SUMMARY.

THE Martians, the inhabitants of Mars, invade the earth by means of huge cylinders shot across the intervening space. The first cylinder descends at Woking. The narrator of the story describes its arrival, the emergence of the Martians, and their hostility to men. Fighting begins on Friday. He narrowly escapes from a great battle at Weybridge, and falls in with a curate near Sunbury.

XIV.—IN LONDON.

My younger brother was in London when the Martians fell at Woking. He was a medical student working for an imminent examination, and he heard nothing of the arrival until Saturday morning. The morning papers on Saturday contained, in addition to lengthy special articles on the planet Mars, on life in the planets, and so forth, a brief and vaguely worded telegram, all the more striking for its brevity.

The Martians, alarmed by the approach of a crowd, had killed a number of people with a quick-firing gun, so the story ran. The telegram concluded with the words : " Formi- " dable as they seem to be, the Martians " have not moved from the pit into which " they have fallen, and indeed seem in- " capable of doing so. Probably this is due " to the relative strength of the Earth's gravi- " tational energy." On that last text, their leader-writer expanded very comfortingly.

Of course, all the students in the crammer's biology class, to which my brother went that day, were intensely interested, but there were no signs of any unusual excitement in the streets. The afternoon papers puffed scraps of news under big headlines. They had nothing to tell beyond the movements of troops about the common, and the burning of the pine woods between Woking and Weybridge, until eight. Then the *St. James' Gazette*, in an extra special edition, announced the bare fact of the interruption of telegraphic communication. This was thought to be due to the falling of burning pine trees across the line. Nothing more of the fighting was known that night, the night of my drive to Leatherhead and back again.

My brother felt no anxiety about us, as he knew from the description of the papers that the shot was a good two miles from my house. He made up his mind to run down that night to me in order, as he says, to see the things before they were killed. He dispatched a telegram (which never reached me) about four o'clock and spent the evening at a music-hall.

In London also on Saturday night there was a thunderstorm, and my brother reached Waterloo in a cab. On the platform from which the midnight train usually starts he

He was a medical student.

a matter of fact there was nothing to justify that very extravagant phrase. Plenty of people in London did not hear of the Martians until the panic of Monday morning. Those who did took some time to realise all that the hastily worded telegrams in the Sunday papers conveyed. The majority of people in London do not read Sunday papers.

The habit of personal security, moreover, is so deeply fixed in the Londoner's mind, and startling intelligence so much a matter of course in the papers, that they could read without any personal tremors :— "About seven o'clock last night the Martians came out of the cylinder, and, moving about under an armour of metallic shields, have completely wrecked Woking station with the adjacent houses, and massacred an entire battalion of the Cardigan Regiment. No details are known. Maxims have been absolutely useless against their armour. The field guns have been disabled by them. Flying Hussars have been galloping into Chertsey. The Martians appear to be moving slowly towards Chertsey or Windsor. Great anxiety prevails in West Surrey, and earthworks are being thrown up to check the advance Londonward." That was how the *Sunday Sun* put it, and a clever, and remarkably prompt " hand-book " article in the *Referee*, compared the affair to a menagerie suddenly let loose in a village.

No one in London knew positively of the nature of the armoured Martians, and there was also a fixed idea that these monsters must be sluggish—"crawling," "creeping painfully," such expressions occurred in almost all the earlier reports. None of the telegrams could have been written by an eyewitness of their advance. The Sunday papers printed separate editions as further news came to hand, some even in default of it. But there was practically nothing more to tell people until late in the afternoon, when the authorities gave the press agents the news in their possession. It was stated that the people of Walton and Weybridge, and all that district, were pouring along the roads Londonward, and that was all.

learnt, after some waiting, that an accident prevented trains from reaching Woking that night. The nature of the accident he could not ascertain. Indeed the railway authorities did not clearly know at that time. There was very little excitement in the station, as the officials, failing to realise that anything further than a breakdown between Byfleet and Woking Junction had occurred, were running the theatre trains which usually passed through Woking round by Virginia Water or Guildford. They were busy making the necessary arrangements to alter the route of the Southampton and Portsmouth Sunday League Excursions. A nocturnal newspaper reporter, mistaking my brother for the traffic manager, whom he does to a slight extent resemble, waylaid-and-tried to interview him. Few people, excepting the railway officials, connected the breakdown with the Martians.

I have read in another account of these events that on Sunday morning " all London was electrified by the news from Woking." As

My brother went to church at the Foundling Hospital in the morning, still in ignorance of what had happened on the previous night. There he heard allusions made to the invasion, and a special prayer for peace. Coming out he bought a *Referee.* He became alarmed at the news in this, and went again to Waterloo station, to find out if communication were restored. The omnibuses, carriages, cyclists, and innumerable people walking in their best clothes, seemed scarcely affected by the strange intelligence that the newsvendors were disseminating. People were interested, or if alarmed, alarmed only on account of the local residents. At the station he heard for the first time that the Windsor and Chertsey lines were now interrupted. The porters told him that several remarkable telegrams had been received in the morning from Byfleet and Chertsey stations, but that these had abruptly ceased. My brother could get very little precise detail out of them. " There's fighting going on about Weybridge," was the extent of their information.

The train service was now very much disorganised. Quite a number of people who had been expecting friends from places on the South-Western network were standing about the station. One grey-headed old gentleman came and abused the South-Western Company bitterly to my brother. " It wants showing up," he said.

One or two trains came in from Richmond, Putney, and Kingston, containing people who had gone out for a day's boating and found the locks closed and a feeling of panic in the air. A man in a blue and white blazer addressed my brother, full of strange tidings. " There's hosts of people driving into Kingston in traps and carts and things, with boxes of valuables and all that," he said. " They come from Molesey and Weybridge and Walton, and they say there's been guns heard at Chertsey, heavy firing, and that mounted soldiers have told them to get off at once because the Martians are coming. *We* heard guns firing at Hampton Court station, but we thought it was thunder. What the dickins does it all mean? The Martians can't get out of their pit, can they ? " My brother could not tell him.

Afterwards he found that the vague feeling of alarm had spread to the clients of the underground railway, and that the Sunday excursionists began to return from all the South-Western " lungs," Barnes, Wimbledon, Richmond Park, Kew, and so forth, at unnaturally early hours. But not a soul had

"The Martians appear to be moving slowly towards Chertsey or Windsor."

anything but vague hearsay to tell of. Every one connected with the terminus seemed ill-tempered.

About five o'clock the gathering crowd in the station was immensely excited by the opening of the line of communication (which is almost invariably closed) between the South-Eastern and South-Western stations, and the passage of carriage-trucks bearing huge guns and carriages crammed with soldiers. These were the guns that were brought up from Woolwich and Chatham to cover Kingston. There was an exchange of pleasantries: "You'll get eaten!" "We're the beast tamers!" and so forth. A little while after that a squad of police came into the station and began to clear the public off the platforms, and my brother went out into the street again.

The church bells were ringing for even-song, and a squad of the Salvation Army lasses came singing down Waterloo Road. On the bridge a number of idle loafers were watching a curious brown scum that came drifting down the stream in patches. The sun was just setting, and the Clock Tower and the Houses of Parliament rose against one of the most peaceful skies it is possible to imagine, a sky of gold barred with long transverse stripes of reddish purple cloud. There was talk of a floating body. One of the men there, a reservist he said he was, told my brother he had seen the heliograph flickering in the west.

In Wellington Street my brother met a couple of sturdy roughs who had just rushed out of Fleet Street with still wet newspapers and staring placards. "Dreadful Catastrophe," they bawled one to the other down Wellington Street. "Fighting at Weybridge. Full description. Repulse of the Martians. London said to be in danger!" He had to give threepence for a copy of that paper.

Then it was and then only that he realised something of the full power and terror of these monsters. He learnt that they were not merely a handful of small sluggish creatures, but that they were minds swaying vast mechanical bodies, and that they could move swiftly and smite with such power that even the mightiest guns could not stand against them.

They were described as "vast spider-like machines, nearly a hundred feet high, capable of the speed of an express train and able to shoot out a beam of intense heat." Masked batteries, chiefly of field guns, had been planted in the country about Horsell Common, and especially between the Woking district and London. Five of the machines had been seen moving towards the Thames, and one, by a freak of chance, had been destroyed. In the other cases the shells had

On the bridge were a number of idle loafers.

missed, and the batteries had been at once annihilated by the Heat Rays. Heavy losses of soldiers were mentioned, but the tone of the dispatch was optimistic.

The Martians had been repulsed; they were not invulnerable. They had retreated to their triangle of cylinders again, in the circle about Woking. Signallers with heliographs were pushing forward upon them from all sides. Guns were in rapid transit from Windsor, Portsmouth, Aldershot, Woolwich, even from the north. Among others, long wire guns of 95 tons from Woolwich. Altogether one hundred and sixteen were in position or being hastily laid, chiefly covering London. Never before in England had there been such a vast or rapid concentration of military material.

Any further cylinders that fell, it was hoped, could be destroyed at once by high explosives, which were being rapidly manufactured and distributed. No doubt, ran the report, the situation was of the strangest and gravest description, but the public was exhorted to avoid and discourage panic. No doubt the Martians were strange and powerful, and their warfare terrible in the extreme, but at the outside, there could not be more than twenty of them against our millions.

The authorities had reason to suppose, from the size of the cylinders, that at the outside there could not be more than five in each cylinder—fifteen altogether. And one, at least, was disposed of, perhaps more. The public would be fairly warned of the approach of danger, and elaborate measures were being taken for the protection of the people in the

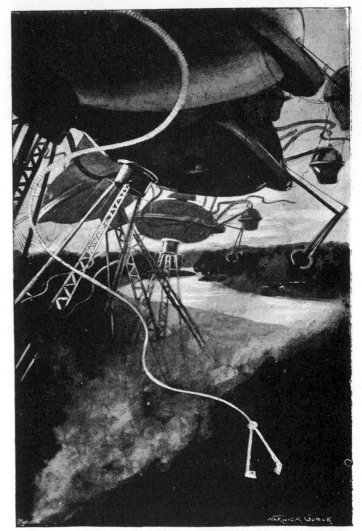

Five of the machines had been seen moving towards the Thames.

threatened south-western suburbs. And so, with reiterated assurances of the safety of London, and the confidence of the authorities to cope with the difficulty, this *quasi* proclamation closed.

This was printed in enormous type, so fresh that the paper was wet still, and there had been no time to add a word of comment. It was curious, my brother said, to see how ruthlessly the other contents of the paper had been hacked and taken out, to give this place.

All down Wellington Street, people could be seen fluttering out the pink sheets, and reading, and the Strand was suddenly noisy with the voices of an army of hawkers following these pioneers. Men came scrambling off 'buses to secure copies. Certainly this news excited people intensely, whatever their previous apathy. The shutters of a map shop in the Strand were being taken down, my brother said, and a man in his Sunday raiment, lemon yellow gloves even, was visible inside the window, hastily fastening maps of Surrey to the glass.

Going on along the Strand to Trafalgar Square, the paper in his hand, my brother saw some of the fugitives from West Surrey. There was a man driving a cart such as greengrocers use, and his wife and two boys and some articles of furniture. He was driving from the direction of Westminster Bridge, and close behind him came a hay waggon with five or six respectable-looking people in it, and some boxes and bundles. The faces of these people were haggard, and their entire appearance contrasted conspicuously with the Sabbath-best appearance of the people on the omnibuses. People in fashionable clothing peeped at them out of cabs. They stopped at the Square as if undecided which way to take, and finally turned eastward along the Strand. Some way after these came a man in work-day clothes, riding one of those old-fashioned tricycles with a small front wheel. He was dirty and white in the face.

My brother turned down towards Victoria and met a number of such people. He had a vague idea that he might see something of me. He noticed an unusual number of police regulating the traffic. Some of the refugees were exchanging news with the people on the omnibuses. One was professing to have seen the Martians. "Boilers on stilts, I tell you, striding along like men." Most of them were excited and animated by this strange experience.

Beyond Victoria the public houses were doing a lively trade with these arrivals. At all the street corners groups of people were reading papers, talking excitedly, or staring at these unusual Sunday visitors. They seemed to increase as night drew on, until at last the roads, my brother says, were like the Sutton High Street on a Derby Day. My

brother addressed several of these fugitives, and got unsatisfactory answers from most.

None of them could tell him any news of Woking, except one man, who assured him that Woking had been entirely destroyed on the previous night. "I come from Byfleet," he said; "a man on a bicycle came through the place in the early morning, and ran from door to door warning us to come away. Then came soldiers. We went out to look and there were clouds of smoke to the south— nothing but smoke, and not a soul coming that way. Then we heard the guns at Chertsey and folks coming from Weybridge. So I've locked up my house and come on." At that time there was a strong feeling in the streets that the authorities were to blame for their incapacity to dispose of the invaders without all this inconvenience.

About eight o'clock, a noise of heavy firing was distinctly audible all over the south of London. My brother could not hear it for the traffic in the main streets, but by striking through the quiet back streets to the river, he was able to distinguish it quite plainly.

He walked back from Westminster to his apartments near Regent's Park about two. He was now very anxious on my account, and disturbed at the evident magnitude of the trouble. His mind was inclined to run, even as mine had run on Saturday, in military details. He thought of all those silent, expectant guns, of the suddenly nomadic country side; he tried to imagine "boilers on stilts," a hundred feet high.

There were one or two cartloads of refugees passing along Oxford Street, and several in the Marylebone Road, but so slowly was the news spreading, that Regent Street and Portland Road were full of their usual Sunday night promenaders, albeit they talked in groups, and, along the edge of Regent's Park, there were as many silent couples "walking out" together under the scattered yellow gas-lamps, as ever there had been. The night was warm and still, and a little oppressive, the sound of guns continued intermittently, and after midnight, there seemed to be sheet lightning in the south.

He read and re-read the paper, fearing

the worst had happened to me. He was restless, and after supper prowled out again aimlessly. He returned and tried to divert his attention by his examination notes in vain. He went to bed a little after midnight and he was awakened out of some lurid dreams, in the small hours of Monday, by the sound of door knockers, feet running in the street, distant drumming and a clamour of bells. Red reflections danced on the ceiling. For a moment, he lay astonished, wondering whether day had come or the world had gone mad. Then he jumped out of bed, and ran to the window.

His room was an attic, and as he thrust his head out, up and down the street there were a dozen echoes to the noise of his window sash, and heads, in every kind of night disarray, appeared. Inquiries were being shouted. "They are coming," bawled a policeman, hammering at the door; "the Martians are coming!" and hurried to the next door.

The noise of drumming and trumpeting came from the Albany Street barracks, and every church within earshot was hard at work killing sleep with a vehement disorderly tocsin. There was a noise of doors opening, and window after window in the houses opposite flashed from darkness into yellow illumination.

Up the street came galloping a closed carriage, bursting abruptly into noise at the corner, rising to a clattering climax under the window, and dying away slowly in the distance. Close on the rear of this came a couple of cabs, the forerunners of a long procession of flying vehicles, going for the most part to Chalk Farm station, where the North-Western special trains were loading up, instead of coming down the gradient into Euston.

For a long time my brother stared out of the window in blank astonishment, watching the policemen hammering at door after door and delivering their incomprehensible message. Then the door behind him opened, and the man who lodged across the landing came in, dressed only in shirt, trousers and slippers, his braces loose about his waist, his hair disordered from his pillow. "What the devil is it?" he asked. "A fire? What a devil of a row!"

They both craned their heads out of the window, straining to hear what the policemen were shouting. People were coming out of side streets and standing in groups at the corners, talking.

"What the devil's it all about?" said my brother's fellow lodger.

My brother answered him vaguely and began to dress, running with each garment to the window, in order to miss nothing of the growing excitement of the streets. And presently men selling unnaturally early newspapers came bawling into the street:

"London in danger of suffocation! The Kingston and Richmond defences forced! Fearful massacres in the Thames Valley!"

And all about him—in the rooms below, in the houses on either side, and across the road, and behind in the Park terraces and in the hundred other streets of that

Then he jumped out of bed, and ran to the window.

"The Martians are able to discharge enormous clouds of a black and poisonous vapour."

part of Marylebone, and in the Westbourne Park district and Saint Pancras, and westward and northward in Kilburn and St. John's Wood and Hampstead, and eastward in Shoreditch and Highbury and Haggerston and Hoxton, and indeed through all the vastness of London from Ealing to East Ham—people were rubbing their eyes, and opening windows to stare out and ask aimless questions, and dressing hastily as the first breath of the coming storm of Fear blew through the streets. It was the dawn of the great panic. London, which had gone to bed on Sunday night stupid and inert, was awakened in the small hours of Monday morning to a vivid sense of danger.

Unable, from his window, to learn what was happening, my brother went down and out into the street, just as the sky between the parapets of the houses grew pink with the early dawn. The flying people, on foot and in vehicles, grew more numerous every moment. "Black Smoke!" he heard people crying, and again, "Black Smoke!" The contagion of such a unanimous fear was inevitable. As my brother hesitated on the doorstep he saw another newsvendor approaching him, and got a copy forthwith. The man was running away with the rest, and selling his papers as he ran for a shilling each—a grotesque mingling of profit and panic.

And from this paper my brother read that catastrophic dispatch of the Commander-in-Chief: "The Martians are able to discharge enormous

clouds of a black and poisonous
vapour by means of rockets. They
have smothered our batteries, destroyed
Richmond, Kingston, and Wimbledon,
and are advancing slowly towards London,
destroying everything on the way. It is
impossible to stop them. There is no safety
from the Black Smoke but in instant flight."
That was all, but it was enough. The whole
population of the great five-million city was stirring,
slipping, running; presently it would be pouring, *en
masse*, northward.

"Black Smoke!" the voices cried. "Fire!" The
bells of the neighbouring church made a jangling
tumult, a cart carelessly driven smashed, amid shrieks
and curses, against the water trough up the street.
Sickly yellow light went to and fro in the houses,
and some of the passing cabs flaunted unextin-
guished lamps. And overhead the dawn was
growing brighter, clear and steady and
calm.

He heard footsteps running to and
fro in the rooms and up and down
stairs behind him. His landlady
came to the door, loosely
wrapped in dressing-gown and
shawl; her husband followed,
ejaculating.

As my brother began to
realise the import of all these
things, he turned hastily to
his own room, put all his
available money—some ten
pounds altogether—into
his pockets, and went
out again into the
streets.

A leg of the tripod had been smashed.

XV.—WHAT HAD HAPPENED IN
SURREY.

It was while I and the curate had sat and talked under the hedge in the flat meadows near Halliford, and while my brother was watching the fugitives stream over Westminster Bridge, that the Martians resumed the offensive. So far as one can ascertain from the conflicting accounts that have been put forth, the majority of them remained busied with preparations in the Horsell pit until nine that night, hurrying on some operation that disengaged huge volumes of green smoke. But three certainly came out about eight o'clock, and, advancing slowly and cautiously, made their way through Byfleet and Pyrford towards Ripley and Weybridge, and so came in sight of the expectant batteries against the setting sun. These Martians did not advance in a body but in a line, each perhaps a mile and a half from his nearest fellow. They communicated with each other by means of siren-like howls, running up and down the scale from one note to another.

It was this howling and the firing of the guns at Ripley and Saint George's Hill that we had heard at Upper Halliford. The Ripley gunners, unseasoned Artillery volunteers who ought never to have been placed in such a position, fired one wild, premature, ineffectual volley, and bolted on horse and foot through the deserted village, and the Martian walked over their guns serenely without using his Heat Ray, stepped gingerly among them, passed in front of them, and so came unexpectedly upon the guns in Painshill Park, which he destroyed. The St. George's Hill men, however, were better led or of a better mettle. Hidden by a pine wood as they were, they seem to have been quite unexpected by the Martian nearest to them. They laid their guns as deliberately as if they had been on parade, and fired at about a thousand yards range.

The shells flashed all round the Martian, and they saw him advance a few paces, stagger, and go down. Everybody yelled together, and the guns were reloaded in frantic haste. The overthrown Martian set up a prolonged ululation, and immediately a second glittering giant, answering him, appeared over the trees to the south. It would seem that a leg of the tripod had been smashed by one of the shells. The whole of the second volley flew wide of the Martian on the ground, and simultaneously both his companions brought their Heat Rays to bear on the battery. The ammunition blew up, the pine trees all about the guns flashed into fire, and only one or two of the men who were already running over the crest of the hill escaped.

After this it would seem that the three took counsel together and halted, and the scouts who were watching them report that they remained absolutely stationary for the next half hour. The Martian who had been overthrown crawled tediously out of his hood, a small brown figure oddly suggestive from that distance of a speck of blight, and apparently engaged in the repair of his support. About nine he had finished, for his cowl was then seen above the trees again.

It was a few minutes past nine that night when these three sentinels were joined by other Martians carrying thick black tubes in their tentacles. A similar tube was handed to each of the three, and the seven proceeded to distribute themselves at equal distances along a curved line between Saint George's Hill, Weybridge, and the village of Send, south-west of Ripley.

A dozen rockets sprang out of the hills before them so soon as they began to move, and warned the waiting batteries about Ditton and Esher. At the same time four of their fighting machines, similarly armed with tubes, crossed the river, and two of them, black against the western sky, came into sight of myself and the curate, as we hurried wearily and painfully along the road that runs northward out of Halliford, looking back every moment expecting this thing.

They moved, as it seemed to us, upon a cloud, for a milky mist covered the fields and rose to a third of their height. At the sight the curate shouted and began running, but I knew it was no good running from a Martian, and I turned aside and crawled through dewy nettles and brambles into the broad ditch by the side of the road.

He looked
back, saw
what I was do-
ing and turned to
join me.

The two Martians halted,
the nearer to us standing and
facing Sunbury, the remoter being
a grey indistinctness beneath the evening star far away towards Staines.

The occasional howling of the Martians had
ceased; they took up
their positions in the
huge crescent about
their cylinders in
absolute
silence.

They moved,
as it seemed to
us, upon a cloud.

It was a crescent
with twelve miles
between its horns.
Never since the devising
of gunpowder was the be-
ginning of a battle so still.
To us and to an observer
about Ripley it would have
had precisely the same effect
—the Martians seemed in
solitary possession of the darkling night, lit only as it was by
the slender moon, the stars, the
after-glow of the daylight, and
the ruddy glare from Saint George's
Hill and the woods of Painshill.

But facing that crescent everywhere, at Staines, Hounslow, Ditton,
Esher, Ockham, behind hills and
woods south of the river, and across
the flat grass meadows to the north of
it, wherever a cluster of trees or village
houses gave sufficient cover, the guns were
waiting. The signal rockets burst and
rained their sparks through the night and
vanished, and the spirit of all those watching

batteries rose to a tense expectation. The Martians had but to advance into the line of fire, and instantly those motionless black forms of men, those tubes glittering so darkly in the early night, would explode into a thunderous fury of battle.

No doubt the thought that was uppermost in a thousand of those vigilant minds, even as it was uppermost in mine, was the riddle, how much they understood of us? Did they grasp that we in our millions were organised, disciplined, working together? Or did they interpret our spurts of fire, the sudden stinging of our shells, our steady investment of their encampment, as we should the furious unanimity of onslaught in a disturbed hive of bees? Did they dream they might exterminate us? (At that time no one knew what food they needed.) A hundred such questions struggled together in my mind as I watched that vast sentinel shape. And in the back of my mind was the sense of all the huge unknown and hidden forces Londonward. Had they prepared pitfalls? Were the powder mills at Hounslow ready as a snare? Would the Londoners have the heart and courage to make a greater Moscow of their mighty province of houses?

Then, after an interminable time as it seemed to us, crouching there and peering through the hedge, came the sound like the distant concussion of a gun. Another, nearer, and then another. And then the Martian beside us raised his tube on high and discharged it gunwise, with a heavy report that made the ground heave. The Martian towards Staines answered him. There was no flash, no smoke, simply that loaded detonation.

I was so excited by these heavy minute guns following one another, that I so far forgot my personal safety and my scalded hands as to clamber up into the hedge and stare towards Sunbury. As I did so a second report followed, and a big projectile hurtled overhead towards Hounslow. I expected at least to see smoke or fire or some such evidence of its work. But all I saw was the deep blue sky above, with one solitary star, and the white mist spreading wide and low beneath. And there had been no crash, no answering explosion. The silence was restored, the minute lengthened to three. "What has happened?" said the curate, standing up beside me. "Heaven knows!" said I.

A bat flickered by and vanished. A distant tumult of shouting began and ceased. I looked again at the Martian, and saw he was now moving eastward, along the river bank, with a swift rolling motion.

Every moment I expected the fire of some hidden battery to spring upon him. But the evening calm was unbroken. The figure of the Martian grew smaller as he receded, and presently the mist and the gathering night had swallowed him up. By a common impulse we clambered higher. Towards Sunbury was a dark appearance, as though a conical hill had suddenly come into being there, hiding our view of the further country. And then, remoter across the river, over Walton, we saw another such summit. These hill-like forms grew lower and broader even as we stared.

Moved by a sudden thought, I looked northward, and there I perceived a third of these cloudy black kopjes had arisen.

Everything had suddenly become very still. Far away to the south-east, marking the quiet, we heard the Martians hooting to one another, and then the air quivered again with the distant thud of their guns. But the earthly artillery made no reply.

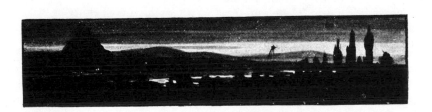

SUMMARY.

THE Martians, the inhabitants of Mars, invade the earth by means of huge cylinders, shot across the intervening space. The first cylinder descends at Woking. The narrator of the story describes its arrival, the emergence of the Martians, and their hostility to men. Fighting begins on Friday. He narrowly escapes from a great battle at Weybridge, and falls in with a curate near Sunbury.

XV.—WHAT HAD HAPPENED IN
SURREY *(continued)*.

AND here I come upon the most obscure of all the problems that centre about the Martians, the riddle of the Black Gas. Each of the Martians standing in the great crescent I have described, seems, at some unknown signal, to have discharged by means of the gun-like tube he carried a huge canister over whatever hill, copse, cluster of houses, or other possible cover for guns chanced to be in front of him.

Some fired only one of them, some two, as in the case of the one we had seen; the one at Ripley is said to have discharged no fewer than five at that time. These canisters seemed to have smashed or exploded on striking the ground, and incontinently to have disengaged an enormous volume of a heavy inky vapour, coiling and pouring upwards in a huge and ebony cumulus cloud, a gaseous hill that sank and spread itself slowly over the surrounding country. And the touch of that vapour, the inhaling of its pungent wisps, was death to all that breathe.

It was heavy, this vapour, heavier than the densest smoke, so that after the first tumultuous uprush and outflow of its impact, it sank down through the air and poured over the ground in a manner rather liquid than gaseous, abandoning the hills and streaming into the valleys and ditches and water-courses, even as I have heard the carbonic acid gas that pours from volcanic clefts is wont to do. And where it came upon water some chemical action occurred, and the surface would be instantly covered with a powdery scum that sank slowly and made way for more. That scum was absolutely insoluble, and it is a strange thing, seeing the instant effect of the gas, that one could drink the water from which it had been strained without hurt.

The vapour did not diffuse as a true gas would do. It hung together in banks, flowing sluggishly down the slope of the land and driving reluctantly before the wind, and very slowly it combined with the mist and moisture of the air and sank to the earth in the form of dust.

Once the tumultuous upheaval of its dispersion was over, it clung so closely to the ground, even before this precipitation, that fifty feet up in the air, on the roofs and upper storeys of high houses and on great trees, there was a chance of escaping its poison altogether, as was proved even that night at Street Chobham and Ditton. The man who escaped at the former place tells a wonderful story of the strangeness of its coiling flow, and how he looked down from the church spire and saw the houses of the village rising like ghosts out of its inky nothingness. For a day and a half he remained there, weary, starving and sun-scorched—the earth under the blue sky and against the prospect of the distant blue hills a velvet black expanse, with red roofs, green trees, and, later, black-veiled shrubs and gates, barns, outhouses and walls rising here and there into the sunlight.

But that was at Street Chobham, where the black vapour was allowed to remain until it sank of its own accord to the ground. As a rule, the Martians, when it had served its purpose, cleared the air of it again by wading into it and directing a jet of steam upon it.

That they did with the vapour banks near us, as we saw in the starlight from the window of a deserted house at Upper Halliford, whither we had returned. From there we could see the search lights on Richmond Hill and Kingston Hill going to and fro, and about eleven the window rattled, and we heard the sound of the huge siege guns that had been put in position there. These continued intermittently for the space of a quarter of an hour, sending chance shots at the invisible Martians at Hampton and Ditton, and then the pale beams of the electric light vanished, and were replaced by a bright red glow.

Then the fourth cylinder fell—a brilliant green meteor—as I learnt afterwards, in Bushey Park. Before the guns on the Richmond and Kingston line of hills began, there was a fitful cannonade far away in the south-west, due, I believe, to guns being fired haphazard before the black vapour could overwhelm the gunners.

So, setting about it as methodically as men might smoke out a wasp's nest, the Martians spread this strange stifling vapour over the London-ward country. The horns of the crescent slowly spread apart, until at last they formed a line from Hanwell to Coombe and Malden. All night through, their destructive tubes advanced. Never once, after the Martian at St. George's Hill was brought down, did they give the artillery the ghost of a chance against them. Wherever there was a possibility of guns being laid for them unseen, a fresh canister of the black vapour was discharged, and where the guns were openly displayed, the Heat Ray was brought to bear.

By midnight, the blazing trees along the slopes of Richmond Park, and the glare of Kingston Hill, threw their light upon a network of black smoke, blotting out the whole valley of the Thames and extending as far as the eye could reach. And through this two Martians slowly waded and turned their hissing steam jets this way and that.

The Martians were sparing of the Heat Ray that night, either because they had but a limited supply of material for its production, or because they did not wish to destroy the country, but only to crush and overawe the opposition they had aroused. In the latter aim they certainly succeeded. Sunday night was the end of the organised opposition to their movements. After that no body of men could stand against them, so hopeless was the enterprise. Even the crews of the torpedo boats and destroyers that had brought their quick-firers up the Thames, refused to stop, mutinied, and went down again. The only offensive operation men ventured upon after that night was the preparation of mines and pitfalls, and even in those, men's energies were frantic and spasmodic.

One has to imagine the fate of those batteries towards Esher waiting so tensely in the twilight, as well as one may. Survivors there were none. One may picture the orderly expectation, the officers alert and watchful, the gunners ready, the ammunition piled to hand, the limber gunners with their horses and waggons, the groups of civilian spectators standing as near as they were permitted, the evening stillness; the ambulances and hospital tents with the burnt and wounded from Weybridge; then the dull resonance of the shots the Martians fired, and the clumsy projectile whirling over the trees and houses, and smashing amidst the neighbouring fields.

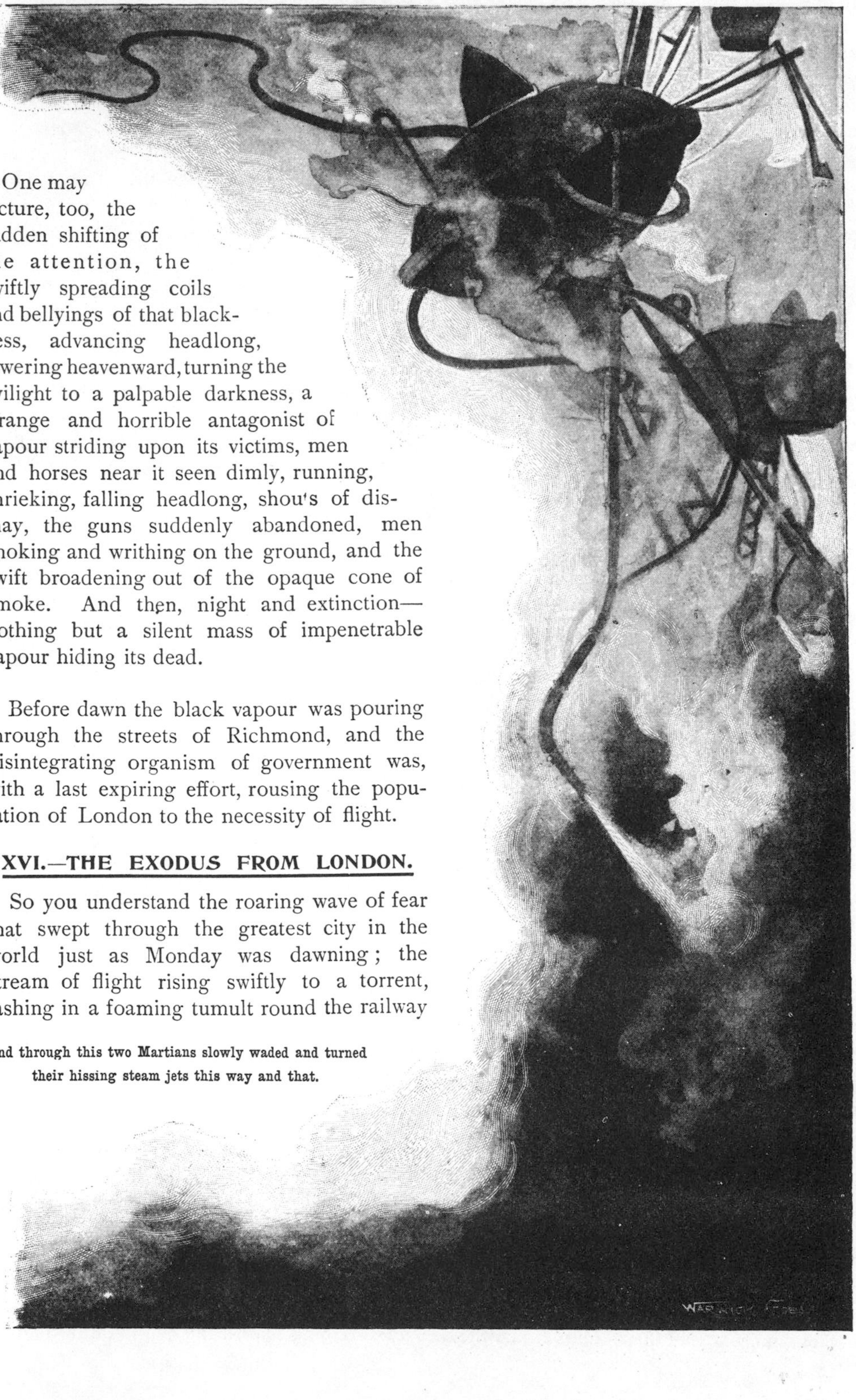

One may
picture, too, the
sudden shifting of
the attention, the
swiftly spreading coils
and bellyings of that blackness, advancing headlong,
towering heavenward, turning the
twilight to a palpable darkness, a
strange and horrible antagonist of
vapour striding upon its victims, men
and horses near it seen dimly, running,
shrieking, falling headlong, shou's of dismay, the guns suddenly abandoned, men
choking and writhing on the ground, and the
swift broadening out of the opaque cone of
smoke. And then, night and extinction—
nothing but a silent mass of impenetrable
vapour hiding its dead.

Before dawn the black vapour was pouring
through the streets of Richmond, and the
disintegrating organism of government was,
with a last expiring effort, rousing the population of London to the necessity of flight.

XVI.—THE EXODUS FROM LONDON.

So you understand the roaring wave of fear
that swept through the greatest city in the
world just as Monday was dawning; the
stream of flight rising swiftly to a torrent,
lashing in a foaming tumult round the railway

And through this two Martians slowly waded and turned
their hissing steam jets this way and that.

A strange and horrible antagonist of vapour striding upon its victims.

stations, banked up into a horrible struggle about the shipping in the Thames, and hurrying by every available channel northward and eastward. By ten o'clock the police organisation, the telegraphic organisation, and by midday even the railway organisations, were losing coherency, losing shape and efficiency, guttering, softening, running at last in that swift liquefaction of the social body.

All the railway lines north of the Thames and the South-Eastern people at Cannon Street had been warned by midnight of Sunday, and trains were being filled, people were fighting savagely for standing room in the carriages, even at two o'clock. By three, people were being trampled and crushed even in Bishopsgate Street; a couple of hundred yards or more from Liverpool Street station, revolvers were fired, people stabbed, and the policemen who had been sent to direct the traffic exhausted and infuriated, were breaking the heads of the people they were called out to protect.

And as the day advanced and the engine-drivers and stokers refused to return into London, the pressure of the flight drove the people in an ever thickening multitude away from the stations and along the northward running roads. By midday a Martian had been seen at Barnes, and a cloud of slowly sinking black vapour drove along the Thames and across the flats of Lambeth, cutting off all escape over the bridges in its sluggish advance. Another bank drove over Ealing and surrounded a little island of survivors on Castle Hill, alive but unable to escape.

My brother has described the flight of the people through Chipping Barnet very vividly. And the account of his Monday morning may serve to give an idea how it was with the individuals in that pouring multitude. He himself was no longer alone when he came to Chipping Barnet. After a fruitless struggle to get aboard a North-Western train at Chalk Farm—the engines of the trains that had loaded in the goods yard there, *ploughed* through shrieking people, and a dozen stalwart men fought to keep the crowd from crushing the driver against his furnace—my brother emerged upon the Chalk Farm road, dodged across through a hurrying swarm of vehicles, and had the luck to be foremost in the sack of a cycle shop. The front tyre of the machine he got was punctured in dragging it through the window, but he got up and off notwithstanding, with no further injury than a cut wrist. The steep foot of Haverstock Hill was impassable owing to several overturned horses, and my brother struck into Belsize Road.

So he got out of the fury of the panic, and, skirting the Edgware Road, reached Edgware about seven, fasting and wearied but well ahead of the crowd. A mile from Edgware the rim of the bicycle broke, and the machine became unrideable. He trudged into the village. Here, as yet, the panic had scarcely arrived, and he succeeded in getting some food at an inn. There were shops half opened in the main street of the place, and people in the doorways and windows staring astonished at this extraordinary procession of fugitives that was beginning.

At Edgware the roads were crowded, but as yet far from congested. Most of the fugitives at that hour were mounted on cycles, but there were also motor cars, hansom cabs, and carriages hurrying along, and the dust hung in heavy clouds along the road to Saint Albans. It was perhaps a vague idea of making his way to Chelmsford, where some friends of his lived, that made my brother strike into a quiet lane running eastward. The torrent of people flowed on past him. For a few minutes he thought he had the lane to himself. And then he came upon two ladies, just in time to save them.

He heard their screams, and hurrying round the corner saw a couple of men struggling to drag them out of the little pony chaise in which they had been driving, while a third with difficulty held the frightened pony's head. One of the ladies, a short woman dressed in white, was simply screaming, the other, a dark slender figure, slashed at the man who gripped her arm with a whip she held in her disengaged hand. My brother immediately grasped the situation, shouted and hurried towards the struggle. One of the men desisted and turned towards him, and my brother, realising from his antagonist's face that a fight was unavoidable, and being an expert boxer, went into him forthwith and sent him down against the wheel of the chaise.

It was no time for pugilistic chivalry, and my brother laid him quiet with a kick, and gripped the collar of the man who pulled at the slender lady's arm. He heard the clatter of hoofs, the whip stung across his face, a third antagonist struck him between the eyes, and the man he held wrenched himself free and made off down the lane in the direction from which he had come.

Partly stunned, he found himself facing the man who had held the horse's head, and became aware of the chaise receding from him down the lane, swaying from side to side and with the women in it looking back. The man before him, a burly rough, tried to close, and he stopped him with a blow in the face. Then realising that he was deserted, he dodged round and made off down the lane after the chaise, with the sturdy man close behind him, and the fugitive who had turned now, following remotely.

Suddenly he stumbled and fell, his immediate pursuer went headlong, and he rose to his feet to find himself with a couple of antagonists again. He would have had little chance against them had not the slender lady very pluckily pulled up and returned to his help. It seems she had had a revolver all this time, but it had been under the seat when she and her companions were attacked. She fired at six yards distance, narrowly missing my brother. The less courageous of the robbers made off, and his companion followed him cursing his cowardice. They both stopped in sight down the lane where the third man lay insensible.

"Take this!" said the slender lady, and gave my brother her revolver.

"Go back to the chaise," said my brother, wiping the blood from his split lip.

She turned without a word—they were both panting—and they went back to where the lady in white struggled to hold back the frightened pony. The robbers had evidently had enough of it. "I'll sit here," said my brother, "if I may," and he got upon the empty front seat. The lady looked over her shoulder. "Give me the reins," she said, and laid the whip along the pony's side. In another moment a bend in the road hid the three men from my brother's eyes.

So, quite unexpectedly, my brother found himself, panting, with a cut mouth, a bruised jaw, and bloodstained knuckles, driving along an unknown lane with these two women. Such extraordinary introductions were by no means uncommon in those strange and wonderful days. These women had no idea where to go. They were wife and younger sister of a surgeon living at Stanmore, who had come in the small hours from a dangerous case at Pinner, and heard at some railway-station on his way of the Martian advance. He had hurried home, roused the women —their servant had left them two days before— packed some provisions, put his revolver under the seat—luckily for my brother—and told them to drive on to Edgware, with the idea of

She fired at six yards distance.

their getting a train there. He stopped behind to tell the neighbours. He would overtake them, he said, at about half past four in the morning, and now it was nearly nine and they had seen nothing of him since. They could not stop in Edgware because of the growing traffic through the place, and so they had come into this side lane.

That was the story they told my brother in fragments when presently they stopped again, nearer to New Barnet. He promised to stay with them at least until they could determine what to do or until the missing man arrived, and professed to be an expert shot with the revolver—a weapon strange to him—in order to give them confidence. He told them of his own escape out of London, and all that he knew of these Martians and their ways. The sun crept higher in the sky, and after a time their talk died out and gave place to an uneasy state of anticipations.

"What is that murmur?" asked the stouter woman suddenly. They all listened and heard a sound like the droning of wheels in a distant factory, a murmurous sound, rising and falling. "If one did not know this was Middlesex," said my brother, "we might take that for the sound of the sea."

"Do you think George can possibly find us here?" asked the slender woman abruptly.

The man's wife was for returning to their house, but my brother urged a hundred cogent reasons against that suicide. "We have money," said the slender woman, and hesitated. Her eyes met my brother's, and her hesitation ended. "So have I," said my brother. She explained that they had as much as thirty pounds in gold besides a five pound note, and suggested that with that, they might get upon a train at Saint Albans or New Barnet. My brother thought that was hopeless, seeing the fury of the Londoners to crowd upon the trains, and broached his own idea of striking across Essex towards Harwich. Mrs. Elphinstone—that was the name of the woman in white—would listen to no reasoning, and kept calling upon "George," but her sister-in-law was astonishingly quiet and deliberate; and at last agreed to my brother's suggestion. So they went on towards Barnet, my brother leading the pony to save it as much as possible.

As the sun crept up the sky, the day became excessively hot, and under foot a thick whitish sand grew burning and blinding, so that they travelled only very slowly. The hedges were grey with dust. And slowly as they advanced towards Barnet, the tumultuous murmuring grew stronger.

"That sound," said Miss Elphinstone presently, "is growing. It sounds now like the noise of a waterfall in the distance."

"Or that deep note one hears from a fire," said my brother. "It is the voice of a multitude of people. And very soon now we shall come upon the great North Road."

As they went up a little hill towards the cross roads they saw a woman approaching the road across some fields on their left, carrying a child, and with two other children, and then a man in dirty black, with a thick stick in one hand and a small portmanteau in the other passed them. Mrs. Elphinstone suddenly cried out at a number of tongues of smoky red flame leaping up above the houses against the hot blue sky. Then round the corner of the lane, from between the villas that guarded it at its confluence with the high road, came a little cart drawn by a sweating black pony and driven by a sallow youth in a bowler hat, grey with dust. There were three girls like East End factory girls, and a couple of little children, crowded in the cart.

"This'll tike us rahnd Edgware?" asked the driver, and when my brother told him it would if he turned to the left, he looked over his shoulder and remarked, "told yer so," to his following.

My brother noticed a pale grey smoke or haze rising among the houses in front of them, and veiling the white façade of a terrace beyond the road that appeared between the backs of the villas. Then, as the noise of the cartwheels died away behind the man, the tumultous noise before them asserted itself again, but stronger now and clearer, the disorderly mingling of many voices, the gride of many wheels, the creaking of waggons, and in another minute the cross roads were visible. The lane came round abruptly not fifty yards from the turning. "Good heavens!" cried Mrs. Elphinstone. "What is this you are driving us into?" My brother stopped. Then, fascinated by what he saw, led the pony into the very throat of the lane, and stood amazed.

For the main road was a boiling stream of people, a torrent of human beings rushing northward, one pressing on another. A great bank of dust, white and luminous in the blaze of the sun, made everything within twenty feet of the ground grey and indistinct, and was perpetually renewed by the hurrying feet of a dense crowd of horses and men and women on foot, and by the wheels of vehicles of every description. "Way!" my brother heard voices crying. "Make way." It was like riding into the smoke of a fire to approach the meeting point of the lane and road: the crowd roared like a fire, and the dust was hot and pungent. And, indeed, a little way up the road a villa was burning, and sending rolling masses of black smoke across the road to add to the confusion.

So much as they could see of the road Londonward between the houses to the right, was a tumultuous stream of dirty, hurrying people pent in between the villas on either side; the black heads, the crowded forms, grew into distinctness as they rushed towards the corner, hurried past and merged their individuality again in a receding multitude that was swallowed up at last in a cloud of dust. "Go on! Go on!" cried the voices. "Way! Way!" One man's hands pressed on the back of another.

Edgware had been a scene of confusion, Chalk Farm a riotous tumult, but this was a whole population in movement. It is hard to imagine that host. It had no character of its own. The figures poured out past the corner and receded with their backs to the group in the lane. Along the margin came those who were on foot, threatened by the wheels, stumbling in the ditches, blundering into one another. There were sad, haggard women rushing by, well dressed, with children that cried and stumbled, their dainty clothes smothered in dust, their weary faces smeared with tears. With many of these came men, sometimes helpful, sometimes lowering and savage.

Fighting side by side with them pushed some weary street outcast in faded black rags, wide-eyed, loud-voiced, and foul-mouthed. There were sturdy workmen thrusting their way along, wretched un-kempt men clothed like clerks or shopmen, struggling spasmodically, a wounded soldier my brother noticed, men dressed in the clothes of railway porters, one wretched creature in a night-shirt with a coat thrown over it. The carts and carriages crowded close upon one another, making little way for those swifter and more impatient vehicles that darted forward every now and then when an oppor-tunity showed itself of do-ing so, sending the people scattering against the fences and gates of the villas. "Push on!" was the cry. "Push on! they are com-ing."

In one cart stood a blind man in the uniform of the Salvation Army, gesticulating with his crooked fingers and bawling "Eternity! Eternity!" His voice was hoarse and very loud, so that my brother could hear him long after he was lost to sight in the southward dust. Some of the people who crowded in the carts, whipped stupidly at their horses and quarrelled with other drivers; some sat motionless, staring at nothing with

miserable eyes, some gnawed their hands with thirst, or lay prostrate in the bottoms of their conveyances. The horses' bits were covered with foam, their eyes bloodshot.

There were cabs, carriages, shop carts, waggons, beyond counting; once my brother saw a mail cart, and once a road cleaner's cart marked "Vestry

The shaft of a cab struck his shoulder.

of Saint Pan-cras"; there was even a huge timber waggon, crowded with roughs. A brewer's dray rumbled by with its two near wheels splashed with recent blood. "Clear the way!" cried the voices. "Clear the way!" "Eter—nity! Eter—nity!" came echoing up the road.

But varied as its composition was, certain things all that host had in common. There was fear and pain on their faces, and fear behind them, a tumult up the road—a quarrel for a place in a waggon, sent the whole host of them quickening their pace, even as a man so scared and broken that his knees bent under him was galvanised for a moment into renewed activity. The heat and dust had already been at work on this multitude. Their skins were dry, their lips black and cracked. They were all thirsty, weary and footsore. And amid the various cries one heard disputes, reproaches, groans of weariness and fatigue—the voices of most of them were hoarse and weak—through it all ran a refrain: "Way! Way! The Martians are coming."

Few stopped and came aside from that flow of men. The lane opened slantingly into the main road with a narrow opening, and had a delusive appearance of coming from the direction of London. Yet a kind of eddy of people drove into its mouth; weaklings elbowed out of the stream, who for the most part rested but a moment before plunging into it again. A little way down the lane with two friends bending over him lay a man with a bare leg, wrapped about with bloody rags. He was a lucky man to have friends.

A little old man with a grey military moustache, and a filthy black frock coat, limped out and sat down beside the trap, removed his boot—his sock was bloodstained—shook out a pebble and hobbled on again; and then a little girl of eight or nine, all alone, threw herself under the hedge close by my brother—weeping. "I can't go on. I can't go on."

My brother woke from his torpor of astonishment and lifted her up, speaking gently to her, and carried her to Miss Elphinstone. So soon as my brother touched her she became quite still as if frightened. "What does it all mean?" whispered Miss Elphinstone. "I don't know," said my brother. "But this poor child is dropping with fear and fatigue." "Ellen, Ellen!" shrieked a woman in the crowd, with tears in her voice, and the child suddenly dashed away from my brother, crying: "Mother!"

"They are coming," said a man on horseback riding past along the lane.

"Out of the way there!" bawled a coachman towering high, and my brother saw he was turning his carriage, a closed carriage such as doctors use, into the lane. The people crushed back on one another to avoid his horse. My brother pushed the pony and chaise back into the hedge, and he drove by and stopped at the turn of the way. It was a carriage for a pair of horses, but only one was in the shafts. From the chaise they saw dimly through the dust that two men were lifting out a man on a white stretcher, and putting him gently on the grass beneath the privet hedge. One of the men came running to my brother. "Where is there water?" he said. "He is dying fast and very thirsty. It is Lord Garrick."—"Lord Garrick!" said my brother, "the Chief Justice?"—"The water?" he said.—"There may be a tap," said my brother, "in some of the houses. We have no water. I dare not leave my people." The man pushed his way against the crowd towards the gate of the corner house. "Go on!" said the people thrusting at him. "They are coming. Go on!"

Then my brother's attention was distracted by a bearded eagle-faced man lugging a small handbag which split even as my brother's eyes rested on it and disgorged a mass of sovereigns that seemed to break up into separate coins as it struck the ground.

They rolled hither and thither among the struggling feet of men and horses. The Jew stopped and looked stupidly at the heap, and the shaft of a cab struck his shoulder and sent him reeling. He gave a shriek and dodged back, and a cartwheel shaved him narrowly. "Way!" cried the men all about him. "Make way!" So soon as the cab had passed, he flung himself, with both hands open, upon the heap of coins, and began clutching handfuls in his pocket; a horse rose close upon him, and in another moment he had half risen and had been borne down under the horse's hoofs. "Stop!" screamed my brother, and, pushing a woman out of his way, tried to clutch the bit of the horse.

Before he could get to it, he heard a scream under the wheels and saw through the dust, the tire passing over the poor wretch's back. The driver of the cart slashed his whip at my brother, who ran round behind the cart. That multitudinous shouting dimmed and confused his ears. The man was writhing in the dust among his scattered money, unable to rise, for the wheel had broken his back and his limbs lay limp and dead. My brother stood up and yelled at the next driver, and a man on a black horse came to his assistance.

"Get him out of the road," said he, and, clutching the Jew's collar with his free hand, my brother lugged him sideways. But he still clung to his money, and regarded my brother fiercely, hammering at his arm with a handful of gold. He thought they were robbing him, and he did not know as yet, what had happened to him. "Go on! Go on!" shouted angry voices behind. "Way! Way!"

My brother heard a smash, the pole of a carriage crashing into the cart that the man on horseback stopped. My brother looked up, and the man with the gold twisted his head round and bit the wrist that held his collar. There was a concussion and the black horse came staggering sideways, his hind hoof missing my brother's foot by

They wrecked the railways.

a hair's breadth, and the cart horse pushed beside it. He released his grip on the fallen man and jumped back. He saw anger change to terror on the face of the poor wretch on the ground, and in a moment my brother was borne backward and carried past the entrance of the lane, and had to fight hard in the torrent to recover it.

He saw Miss Elphinstone covering her eyes, and a little child with all a child's want of sympathetic imagination, staring with dilated eyes at a dusty something that lay black and still, ground and crushed under the rolling wheels. "Let us go back!" shouted my brother and began turning the pony round. "We cannot cross this—hell," he said; and they went back a hundred yards the way they had come, until the fighting crowd was hidden. The two women sat silent, crouching in their seats and shivering. As they passed the bend in the lane my brother saw the face of the dying man in the ditch under the privet, deadly white and drawn, and shining with perspiration. . . .

So my brother describes one striking phase of the great flight out of London on the morning of Monday. So vividly did that scene at the corner of the lane impress him, so vividly did he describe it, that I can now see the details of it almost as distinctly as if I had been present at the time. I wish I had the skill to give the reader the effect of his description. And that was just *one drop* of the flow of the panic taken and magnified.

Not only along the road through Barnet, but also through Edgware and Waltham Abbey, and along the roads eastward to Southend and Shoeburyness, and south of the Thames to Deal and Broadstairs, poured the same frantic rout. If one could have hung that June morning in a balloon in the blazing blue above London, every northward and eastward road running out of the infinite tangle of streets would have seemed stippled black with the streaming fugitives, each dot a human agony of terror and physical distress.

Never before in the history of the world had such a mass of human beings moved and suffered together. The legendary hosts of Goths and Huns, the hugest armies Asia has ever seen, would have been but a drop in that current. And this was no disciplined march, it was a stampede—a stampede gigantic and terrible, without order and without a goal, six million people unarmed and unprovisioned, driving headlong. It was the beginning of the route of civilisation, of the massacre of mankind.

Directly below him the balloonist would have seen the network of streets far and wide, houses, churches, squares, crescents, gardens —already empty and derelict—spread out like a huge map; and in the southward *blotted*. Over Ealing, Richmond, Wimbledon, it would have seemed as if some monstrous pen had flung ink upon the chart, and each black splash grew and spread, shooting out ramifications this way and that, now banking itself against rising ground, now pouring swiftly over a crest into a new found valley, very much as a gout of ink spreads itself upon blotting-paper.

And beyond, over the blue hills that rise southward of the river, the glittering Martians went to and fro, calmly and methodically, spreading their poison cloud over this patch of country, and then over that, laying it again with the steam jets when it had served its purpose, and then serenely taking possession of the conquered country. They do not seem to have aimed at extermination, so much as at complete demoralisation and the destruction of any opposition. They exploded any stores of powder they came upon, cut every telegraph, and wrecked the railways here and there. They seemed in no hurry to extend the field of their operations, and did not come beyond the central parts of London all that day.

Just after midnight the fifth cylinder fell, green and livid, crushing a house, as I shall presently tell in fuller detail, beside the road between Richmond and Barnes. The fifth cylinder—and there were five more yet to come !

XVII.—THE THUNDER-CHILD.

HAD the Martians aimed only at destruction they might on Monday have annihilated the entire population of London, as it spread itself slowly through the home counties. To a balloonist, I say, that exodus would have seemed a matter of little black dots running northward over green Essex as blight might move over a leaf. I have set forth at length in the last chapter my brother's account of the road through Chipping Barnet, in order that my reader may realise how that swarming of black dots appeared to one of those concerned, but I do not, of course, propose to give at equal length his subsequent experiences, to tell of the hot day, passed in attempts to strike the road higher up and struggle across it, of the gradual slackening of the haste in the crowded roads as the day wore on and no Martians appeared, of the leaking of the people out of the dusty ways into the dusty fields where they flung themselves down, exhausted and hungry and parched with thirst, of the multitudes of people drinking water from the New River, some kneeling, some face down to the water, others fighting to come at it, of the feeble endeavours of the local authorities to restore their demoralised police, and of the renewal of terror with the oncoming night. There was no properly organised news distribution, of course, but with the twilight came the report that the whole of London was under the black smoke.

It is possible that a very considerable number of people in London stuck to their houses through Monday morning. Certain it is that many died at home, suffocated by the Black Smoke.

Until about midday the Pool of London was an astonishing scene, steamboats and shipping of all sorts lay there, tempted by the enormous sums of money offered by fugitives, and it is said that many who swam out to these vessels were thrust off with boat-hooks and drowned.

About one o'clock in the afternoon, the thinning remnant of a cloud of the Black Vapour appeared between the arches of Blackfriars Bridge. At that the Pool became a scene of mad confusion, fighting and collision, and for some time a multitude of boats and barges jammed in the northern arch of the Tower Bridge, and the sailors and lightermen had to fight savagely against the people who swarmed upon them from the river front. People were actually clambering down the piers of the bridge from above. . . .

When, an hour later, a Martian appeared beyond the Clock Tower and waded down the river, nothing but wreckage floated above Limehouse.

On Monday night came the sixth star, and it fell at Wimbledon. My brother, keeping watch beside the women sleeping in the chaise in a meadow, saw the green flash of its fall beyond the hills. On Tuesday the little party, still set upon getting across the

73

sea, made its way through the swarming country towards Colchester. The news that the Martians were now in possession of the whole of London was confirmed. They had been seen at Highgate and even it was said at Neasden. But they did not come into my brother's view that day. That day the scattered multitudes began to realise the urgent need of provisions. As they grew hungry the rights of property ceased to be regarded.

Farmers were out to defend the cattle sheds, granaries, and ripening root crops, with arms in their hands. A number of people now, like my brother, had their faces eastward, and there were some desperate souls even going back towards London to get food. These were chiefly people from the northern suburbs, whose knowledge of the Black Smoke came by hearsay. He heard that about half the members of the Government had gathered at Birmingham, and that enormous quantities of high explosives were being prepared to be used in automatic mines across the Midland counties.

He was also told that the Midland Railway Company had replaced the desertions of the first day's panic, had resumed traffic, and were running northward trains from St. Albans to relieve the congestion of the home counties. There was also a placard in Chipping Ongar announcing that large stores of flour were available in the northern towns and that within twenty-four hours bread would be distributed among the starving people in the neighbourhood. But this intelligence did not deter him from the plan of escape he had formed, and the three pressed eastward all day, and saw no more of the bread distribution than this promise. Nor, as a matter of fact, did anyone else see more of it. That night fell the seventh star, falling upon Primrose Hill. It fell while Miss Elphinstone was watching, for she took that duty alternately with my brother. She saw it.

On Wednesday the three fugitives—they had passed the night in a field of unripe wheat—reached Chelmsford, and a body of the inhabitants calling itself the Committee of Public Supply, promptly seized the pony as provisions, and would give nothing in exchange for it but the promise of a share in it the next day. Here there were rumours of

Martians at Epping, and news of the destruction of Waltham Abbey Powder Mills in a vain attempt to blow up one of the invaders.

People were watching for Martians here from the church towers. My brother, very luckily for him as it chanced, preferred to push on at once to the coast, rather than wait for food, although all three of them were very hungry. By midday they passed through Tillingham, which was, strangely enough, absolutely silent and deserted, save for a few plundering fugitives, who were hunting food : and so they came in sight of the sea, and the most amazing crowd of shipping of all sorts that it is possible to imagine.

For after the sailors could no longer come up the Thames, they came on to the Essex coast, to Harwich, and Walton, and Clacton, and afterwards to Foulness and Shoebury, to bring off the people. They lay in a huge sickle-shaped curve that vanished into mist at last towards the Naze. Close in shore was a multitude of fishing-smacks, English, Scotch, French, Dutch, and even Swedish ; steam launches from the Thames, yachts, electric boats ; and beyond were ships of larger burthen, a multitude of filthy colliers, trim merchantmen, cattle ships, passenger boats, petroleum tanks, ocean tramps, an old white transport even, neat white and grey liners from Southampton and Hamburg ; and along the blue coast across the Blackwater my brother could make out dimly a dense swarm of boats chaffering with the people on the beach, a swarm which also extended up the Blackwater almost to Maldon.

About a couple of miles out lay an ironclad very low in the water, almost, to my brother's perception, like a water-logged ship. This was the ram *Thunder Child*. It was the only warship in sight, but far away to the right over the smooth surface of the sea—for that day there was a dead calm—lay a serpent of black smoke to mark the next ironclads of the Channel Fleet, which hovered in an extended line, steam up and ready for action, across the Thames estuary during the course of the Martian conquest, vigilant and yet powerless to prevent it.

At the sight of the sea Mrs. Elphinstone, in spite of the assurances of her sister-in-law, gave way to panic. She had never been out of England before, she would rather die than trust herself friendless in a foreign country, and so forth. She seemed, poor woman, to imagine that the French and the Martians might prove very similar. She had been growing increasingly hysterical, fearful and depressed, during the two days' journeyings.

Her great idea was to return to Stanmore. Things had always been well and safe at Stanmore. They would find George at Stanmore. . . . It was with the greatest difficulty they could get her down to the beach, where presently my brother succeeded in attracting the attention of the men on a paddle-steamer out of the Thames. They sent a boat and drove a bargain for thirty-six pounds for the three. The steamer was going, these men said, to Ostend.

It was about two o'clock when my brother, having paid their fares at the gangway, found himself safely aboard the steamboat with his charges. There was food aboard, albeit at exorbitant prices, and the three of them contrived to eat a meal on one of the seats forward.

They were all stalking seaward.

There were already a couple of score of passengers aboard, some of whom had expended their last money in securing a passage, but the captain lay off the Blackwater until five in the afternoon, picking up passengers the whole time until the seated decks were even dangerously crowded. He would probably have remained longer, had it not been for the sound of guns that began about that hour in the south. As if in answer, the ironclad seaward fired a small gun and hoisted a string of flags. A jet of smoke sprang out of her funnels.

Some of the passengers were of opinion that this firing came from Shoeburyness, until it was noticed that it was growing louder. At the same time, far away in the south-east, the masts and upperworks of three ironclads rose one after the other out of the sea, beneath clouds of black smoke. But my brother's attention speedily reverted to the distant firing in the south. He fancied he saw a column of smoke rising out of the distant grey haze.

The little steamer was already flapping her way eastward of the big crescent of shipping, and the low Essex coast was growing blue and hazy, when a Martian appeared, small and faint in the remote distance, advancing along the muddy coast from the direction of Foulness. At that the captain on the bridge swore at the top of his voice with fear and anger at his own delay, and the paddles seemed infected with his terror. Every soul aboard stood at the bulwarks or on the seats of the steamer and stared at that distant shape, higher than the trees or church towers inland, and advancing with a leisurely parody of a human stride.

It was the first Martian my brother had seen, and he stood, more amazed than terrified, watching this Titan advancing deliberately towards the shipping, wading farther and farther into the water as the coast fell away. Then, far away beyond the Crouch, came another striding over some stunted trees, and then yet another, still farther off, wading deeply through a shiny mudflat that seemed to hang halfway up between sea and sky. They were all stalking seaward, as if to intercept the escape of the multitudinous vessels that were crowded between Foulness and the Naze. In spite of the throbbing exertions of the engines of the little paddle boat, and the pouring foam that her wheels flung behind her, she receded with terrifying slowness from this ominous advance.

Glancing north-westward, my brother saw the large crescent of shipping already

It hit her larboard side.

writhing with the approaching terror ; one ship passing behind another, another coming round from broadside to end on, steamships whistling and giving off volumes of steam, sails being let out, launches rushing hither and thither. He was so fascinated by this and by the creeping danger away to the left that he had no eyes for anything seaward. And then a swift movement of the steamboat (she had suddenly come about to escape being run down) flung him headlong from the seat upon which he was standing. There was a shouting all about him, a trampling of feet, and a cheer that seemed to be answered faintly. The steamboat lurched, and rolled him over upon his hands.

He sprang to his feet and saw to starboard, and not a hundred yards from their heeling, pitching boat, a vast iron bulk like the blade of a plough tearing through the water, tossing it on either side in huge waves of foam that leapt towards the steamer, flinging her paddles helplessly in the air and then sucking her deck down almost to the water line.

A douche of spray blinded my brother for a moment. When his eyes were clear of that he saw the monster had passed and was rushing landward. Big iron upperworks rose out of this headlong structure, and from that twin funnels projected, and spat a smoking blast shot with fire into the air. It was the torpedo ram, *Thunder Child*, steaming headlong, coming to the rescue of the threatened shipping.

Keeping his footing on the heaving deck by clutching the bulwarks, my brother looked past this charging leviathan at the Martians again, and he saw the three of them now close together, and standing so far out to sea that their tripod supports were

In another moment he was cut down.

almost entirely submerged. Thus sunken, and seen in remote perspective, they appeared far less formidable than the huge iron bulk, in whose wake the steamer was pitching so helplessly. It would seem they were regarding this new antagonist with astonishment. To their intelligence, it may be, the giant was even such another as themselves. The *Thun-*

der Child fired no gun, but simply drove full speed towards them. It was probably her not firing that enabled her to get so near the enemy as she did. They did not know what to make of her. One shell, and they would have sent her to the bottom forthwith with the Heat Ray.

She was steaming at such a pace that in a minute she seemed half way between the steamboat and the Martians, a diminishing black bulk against the receding horizontal expanse of the Essex coast.

Suddenly the foremost Martian lowered his tube, and discharged a canister of the black gas at the ironclad. It hit her larboard side and glanced off in an inky jet, that rolled away to seaward an unfolding torrent of black smoke, from which the ironclad drove clear. To the watchers from the steamer, low in the water and with the sun in their eyes, it seemed as though she was already among the Martians.

They saw the gaunt figures separating and rising out of the water as they retreated shoreward, and one of them raised the camera-like generator of the Heat Ray. He held it pointing obliquely downward, and a bank of steam sprang from the water at its touch. It must have driven through the iron of the ship's side like a white-hot iron rod through paper.

A flicker of flame went up through the rising steam, and then the Martian reeled and staggered. In another moment he was cut down, and a great body of water and steam shot high in the air. The guns of the *Thunder Child* sounded through the reek going off one after the other, and one shot splashed the water high close by the steamer, ricocheted towards the other flying ships to the north and smashed a smack to matchwood.

But no one heeded that very much. At the sight of the Martian's collapse the captain on the bridge yelled inarticulately and all the crowding passengers on the steamer's stern shouted together. And then they yelled again. For surging out beyond the white tumult, drove something long and black, the flames streaming from its middle parts, its ventilators and funnels spouting fire.

She was alive still—the steering gear, it seems, was intact and her engines working. She headed straight for a second Martian, and was within a hundred yards of him when the Heat Ray came to bear. Then with a violent thud, a blinding flash, her decks, her funnels, leapt upward. The Martian staggered with the violence of her explosion, and in another moment the flaming wreckage, still driving forward with the impetus of its pace, had struck him and crumpled him up like a thing of cardboard. My brother shouted involuntarily. A boiling tumult of steam hid everything again.

" Two ! " yelled the captain. Everyone was shouting—the whole steamer from end to end rang with frantic cheering that was taken up first by one and then by all in the crowding multitude of ships and boats that was driving out to sea.

The steam hung upon the water for many minutes, hiding the third Martian and the coast altogether. And all this time the boat was paddling steadily out to sea and away from the fight ; and when at last the confusion cleared, the drifting bank of black vapour intervened, and nothing of the *Thunder Child* could be made out, nor could the third Martian be seen. But the iron-

clads to seaward were now quite close and standing in towards shore past the steamboat.

The little vessel continued to beat its way seaward, and the ironclads receded slowly towards the coast, which was hidden still by a marbled bank of vapour, part steam, part black gas eddying and combining in the strangest ways. The fleet of refugees was scattering to the north-east, several smacks were sailing between the ironclads and the steamboat. After a time, and before they reached the sinking cloud bank, the warships turned northward, and then abruptly went about and passed into the thickening haze of evening southward. The coast grew faint, and at last indistinguishable amidst the low banks of clouds that were gathering about the sinking sun.

Then suddenly out of the golden haze of the sunset came the vibration of guns, and a form of black shadows moving. Everyone struggled to the rail of the steamer and peered into the blinding furnace of the west, but nothing was to be distinguished clearly. A mass of smoke rose slantingly and barred the face of the sun.

The steamboat throbbed on its way through an interminable suspense. The sun sank into grey clouds, the sky flushed and darkened, the evening star trembled into sight.

It was deep twilight when the captain cried out and pointed. My brother strained his eyes. Something rushed up into the sky out of the greyness, rushed slantingly upward and very swiftly into the luminous clearness above the clouds in the western sky, something flat and broad and very large, that swept round in a vast curve, grew smaller, sank slowly, and vanished again into the grey mystery of the night. As it flew it rained down darkness upon the land.

XVIII.—LONDON UNDER THE MARTIANS.

My inexpertness as a story writer insists on appearing. I have wandered away from my own adventures to tell of the experiences of my brother, and for all these last chapters I and the curate have still been lurking in the empty house at Halliford. Even in writing fiction I expect—since it is the commonest failure—it is hard to make each circumstance flow from its predecessors in a natural fashion, and to do so with the huge history I am sketching is certainly quite beyond my ability. I can fancy how some of our new romance writers would have pictured my brother escaping out of the destruction of England with the two women he had so strangely encountered, and what a fine figure they could have made of my sister-in-law—Miss Elphinstone that was, with her courage and resolution. But the Martians, their hissing Heat Ray, their strange machines, their torrents of Black Smoke, and the far reaching desolation and panic they created, trample across everything in my memory, and insist on being heroes, characters, plot, to the exclusion of every human interest, even as they trampled over the beaten world during that terrible June.

I know it would have been more picturesque if I could have told of the two standing side by side on the steamer, hand in hand, she with shining eyes and parted lips, watching that wonderful fight. I could imagine her grip tightening, I could imagine her enthusiasm rising, for she is not the type to be cowed by danger. And my brother's attention divided between her beauty and the war.

But the truth is the truth, and when the time came for us to meet again, and I asked my

As it flew it rained down darkness upon the land.

brother how she faced that last strange spectacle, hoping to find a touch of the true romantic colour, he answered prosaically : " I don't know. I didn't notice her. She was forward, I think, in the empty part of the boat, attending to Mrs. Elphinstone, who was hysterical. I'd offered to help but I didn't see anything that I could do, so I went aft to watch the fight." So poor Romance, with its craving for situations, goes down under the pitiless heels of fact.

The curate and I stopped in our house at Upper Halliford all that Sunday night, and all the next day, the day of the panic, judging ourselves safest in that deserted spot. The Black Smoke drifted slowly riverward, all

We hurried across the exposed bridge.

through Monday morning, creeping nearer and nearer to us, driving at last along the roadway outside the house that hid us.

A Martian came across the fields about midday, laying the stuff with a jet of superheated steam that hissed against the walls, frightened us dreadfully, smashed all the windows it touched, and scalded the curate's hand. When we looked out again, the country northward was as though a black snowstorm had passed over it. Looking towards the river we were astonished to see an unaccount-

able redness mingling with the black of the scorched meadows.

I was for staying in the village indefinitely, for there we had provisions for weeks, if necessary, and only the remotest chance of capture, but the curate was insistent, and I could not find it in me to stop alone. So, all being quiet throughout the afternoon, we started along the blackened road to Sunbury about five. I had availed myself of a hat and a flannel shirt that I found in one of the Halliford rooms. In Sunbury, and at intervals along the road, were dead bodies lying in contorted attitudes, and covered thickly with black dust. It made me think of what I had read of Pompeii. We got to Hampton Court about six, and there our eyes were relieved to find a patch of green that had escaped the suffocating drift. We went through Bushey Park, with its deer going to and fro under the chestnuts, and came to Twickenham.

Away across the road the woods beyond Ham and Petersham were still afire. Twickenham was intact, and there were no signs of the Black Smoke, but it seemed quite deserted save for a prowling muzzled dog or so, and we crossed Richmond bridge about half-past eight. We hurried across the exposed bridge, of course, but I noticed floating down the stream a number of red masses, some many feet across. Here again on the Surrey side was black dust that had once been smoke, and dead bodies—a heap near the approach to the station—and never a sight of the Martians until we were some way towards Barnes. Up the hill Richmond town was burning briskly; outside the town of Richmond there was no trace of the Black Smoke.

Then suddenly, as we were going towards Kew, a Martian came in sight over the housetops, not a hundred yards away from us. We stood aghast at our danger, and had he looked down we must immediately have perished.

We were so terrified that we dared not go on, but turned aside and hid in a tool-shed in a garden. From Halliford to this place we must have tramped a dozen miles or more, and never a living man had we seen all that time except once at Richmond—a group of three people, with their backs to us, running down a side street towards the river.

In the twilight we ventured out again, and going through a shrubbery and along a passage beside a big house standing in its own grounds, we emerged upon the road towards Kew. But scarcely had we got to the road, before we saw a Martian far away across the meadows in the direction of Kew Lodge. We saw four or five little black figures hurrying across the green-grey of the field, and it was evident this Martian pursued them. In a stride or two he was among them, and they ran radiating from his feet in all directions. He used no Heat Ray to destroy them, but picked them up one by one. Apparently he tossed them into the great metallic carrier which projected behind him, much as a workman's basket hangs over his shoulder.

In a stride or two he was among them.

It was the first time that I realised that the Martians might have any other purpose with humanity than destruction. This sight so appalled us, however, that we hastily clambered over a fence and got into a garden, and lay in a ditch there, scarcely daring to whisper to one another until the stars were out.

I suppose it was nearly eleven at night before we gathered courage to start again,

no longer venturing into the road, but sneaking along hedgerows and through plantations, and watching keenly through the darkness, he on the right hand and I on the left, for the Martians, who seemed to be all about us. In one place we blundered upon a scorched and blackened area, now cooling and grey, and a number of scattered dead bodies of men, burnt horribly about the heads and bodies, but with their legs and boots mostly intact; and of dead horses, fifty feet, perhaps, behind a line of four ripped guns and smashed gun carriages. Sheen, it seemed, had escaped destruction, but the place was silent and deserted. But here we happened on no dead, though the night was too dark for us to see into the side roads of the place.

In Sheen my companion suddenly complained of faintness and thirst, and we decided to try one of the houses. The first house we entered, after a little difficulty with the window, was a small semi-detached villa, and I found nothing eatable left in the place but some mouldy cheese. There was, however, water to drink, and I took a hatchet which promised to be useful in our next housebreaking. We crossed the road to a place near the cross roads towards Mortlake, a white house within a walled garden, and in the pantry of this we found a store of food, two loaves of bread in a pan, an uncooked steak, and the half of a ham. I give this catalogue so precisely because, as it happened, we were destined to subsist upon this store for the next fortnight. Bottled beer stood under a shelf, and there were two bags of haricot beans and some limp lettuces. This pantry opened into a kind of wash-up kitchen, and in this was firewood, and a cupboard in which we found nearly a dozen of Burgundy, tinned soups and salmon, and two tins of biscuits.

We sat in the adjacent kitchen—in the dark, for we dared not strike a light—and ate bread and ham and drank beer out of one bottle. The curate, who was still timorous and restless, was for pushing on, and I was urging him to keep up his strength by eating, when the thing that was to imprison us happened.

"It can't be midnight yet," I said, and then came a blinding glare of vivid green light. Everything in the kitchen leapt out clearly visible in green and black, and then vanished again. And then followed such a concussion as I have never heard before or since. So close on the heels of this as to seem instantaneous, came a thud behind me, a clash of glass, a crash and rattle of falling masonry all about us, and incontinently the plaster of the ceiling came down on us, smashing into a multitude of fragments upon our heads.

I was knocked headlong across the floor against the oven handle, and stunned. I was insensible for a long time, the curate told me, and when I came to we were in darkness again, and he, with a face wet, as I found afterwards, with blood from a cut forehead, was pouring water over me.

For some time I could not recollect what had happened. Then things came to me slowly. A bruise on my temple asserted itself. "Are you better?" asked the curate in a whisper again and again. At last I answered him. I sat up.

"Don't move," he said. "The floor is covered with smashed crockery from the dresser. You can't possibly move without making a noise, and I fancy *they* are outside."

We both sat quite silent, so that we could scarcely hear one another breathing. Everything seemed deadly still, though once something near us, some plaster or broken brickwork, slid down with a rumbling sound. Outside and very near was an intermittent, metallic rattle. "That!" said the curate when presently it happened again.

"Yes," I said, and then, with a flash of comprehension, "I have it!"

"What is it?"

"The fifth cylinder, the fifth shot from Mars, has struck this house!"

"God help us!" said the Curate.

Our situation was so strange and dangerous that for three or four hours, until the dawn came, we scarcely moved. And then the light filtered in, not through the window, which remained black, but through a triangular aperture in the wall behind us. The interior of the kitchen, which we now saw greyly for the first time, presented a strange appearance. The window had been burst in by a mass of garden mould, which flowed over the table upon which we had been sitting and lay about our feet. Outside the soil was banked high against the house. At the top of the window frame we could see an uprooted drainpipe. The floor was littered with smashed hardware. The end of the kitchen towards the house was broken into, and since the daylight shone in there it was evident the greater part of the house had collapsed. Contrasting vividly with this ruin was the neat dresser, stained a pleasant light green and with a number of burnished copper and tin vessels below it, the bright wall paper imitating blue and white tiles, and a couple of gay coloured supplements fluttering from the walls above the kitchen range.

We afterwards found the Fifth Cylinder had fallen just in front of the house, pulverising the garden wall and burying itself partly in the garden and partly in the road. The mass of the house and the displaced earth had—"splashed" is really the only possible word—over us, had behaved just like mud under the blow of a hammer. By a miracle the kitchen and scullery had stood the impact, and we were now imprisoned under an unknown quantity of soil and ruins. The scullery door was shut by tons of earth; we were shut in, in fact, in every direction except towards the cylinder. And there was a rough triangular aperture, between a beam and a heap of broken bricks, through which a dim light came, and through which we saw the body of a Martian standing sentinel, I suppose, over the still glowing cylinder.

At the sight of that we crawled as circumspectly as possible out of the twilight of the kitchen into the darkness of the scullery.

THE WAR OF THE WORLDS

WARWICK GOBLE

By H.G.WELLS

XIX.—WHAT WE SAW FROM THE RUINED HOUSE.

So it came about that I and the curate were imprisoned out of the sight of, and yet within sound of, the Martians, and by creeping up to the triangular hole in the broken wall, we could even lie (and to that our courage attained on the second day) peeping through a narrow crack between two masses of plaster at them. The dreadful thing that happened at last between myself and the curate, and how in the end I escaped from that house, I will defer telling in this chapter.

Here I will simply set down an account of what we could make out of the Martians by our observations, together with certain things that have since been learned concerning them. The period until our provisions ran short, and the trouble between myself and the curate arose, was, in all, ten days.

During that period we peeped often by night and day, notwithstanding that once a Martian came and peered into the kitchen through our hole. We had this in our favour, that the kitchen was very dark, and when any body stood across the triangular patch not a gleam of light could enter, while outside was the brightest sunlight. During the first few days the din of hammering, the thunderous roar and penetrating seething of their machinery left us free to talk and walk about without restraint, and afterwards, when a stillness came on the pit, and the number of Martians dwindled to one or two, we went to and fro so quietly, that until the tenth day they never suspected our existence.

At first the pit in which the cylinder lay was, like the pit on Horsell Common, simply the hole the thing had made in its fall. But very speedily, before the unscrewing in fact, this was rounded and enlarged, and a huge cavernous extension of perhaps a hundred yards radius on its floor, was made a little way under the house we were in, and more so in the opposite direction. Of the cylinder we could see nothing but the top, nor could we see anything of the cage in which they put the men and women they had caught. This was placed overhead on the top of the mound of rubble in which we were entombed, so that we saw nothing of these wretched creatures, until they were killed, nor did we hear their voices very distinctly. We were quite unable to communicate with them. In fact, for some time we did not suspect their neighbourhood. We saw, however, all the upper works of the peculiar and still problematical machine from which the green vapour was disengaged. The vapour came hissing out of the stem of the pear-shaped part at the end, and invariably before it was given off, the pear-shaped part oscillated rapidly to and fro with a low, roaring note. We saw, too, very distinctly the corner in which the Martians took nourishment.

It did not take me long to confirm my idea, that the metallic giants I had seen were mere machines, in which the real Martian sat, for the very first time I dared look out of the hole in the wall, I saw one swing out of his apparatus into the pit. The actual Martians were the most extraordinary creatures it is possible to conceive. They had huge round bodies — or rather heads —about four feet in diameter, with a peculiar face in the front of these.

The face had no nostrils, indeed, the Martians do not seem to possess any sense of smell, but it had a pair of very large dark-coloured eyes, and just beneath this a kind of fleshy beak. In the back of the body was the ear, a single tight tympanic surface. In a crescent round the mouth were sixteen slender, almost whip-like, tentacles. The internal anatomy, dissection has shewn, is almost equally simple. The greater part of the structure is the brain, sending enormous nerves to the eyes, ear and tactile tentacles. Besides this are the complex lungs, into

The actual Martians were the most extraordinary creatures it is possible to conceive.

which the mouth opens, and the heart and its vessels. Strange as it may seem to a human being, all the complex apparatus of digestion which makes up the bulk of our bodies, does not exist in the Martians. They do not eat, much less digest. Instead, they take the fresh living blood of other creatures and *inject* it into their own veins. I have myself seen this being done, but, squeamish as I may seem, I cannot bring myself to describe what I could not endure even to continue watching. Let it suffice, blood obtained from a still living animal — in most cases from a human being, was run directly by means of a little pipette into the recipient vessel.

The bare idea of this is no doubt horribly repulsive to us, but at the same time I think that we should remember how repulsive our carnivorous habits would seem to an intelligent rabbit. I know it is the fashion to write of these Martians as being incredibly cruel, but for my own part I cannot see that we are justified in calling ourselves, as certain recent flatterers of humanity have called men, their Moral Superiors. The fact that in the pit at

Wimbledon (the pit made by the tenth Cylinder) the still living body of an eminent physician was found fixed so that he could not move, and horribly mutilated, does not seem to me to carry the point.

Let us clear our minds of cant. We are not justified in supposing that the Martians had been amusing themselves by torturing him. All the circumstances point to the view that they were satisfying their curiosity upon some structural point, and that afterwards, through interruption or inadvertency, they omitted to put him out of his misery. Man who vivisects the lower animals certainly has no claim to exemption when in his turn he becomes a lower animal. Certainly nothing else that we know of the Martians points to their being needlessly cruel. They did not, for the gratification of their personal vanity, tear out the hair of the living women they captured, in order to deck themselves with the spoils; nor did they, in my judgment, carry the sporting instinct quite so far as men.

In the Heat Ray matches they certainly held, every one of the men was killed outright, none escaped, charred and mutilated, to die in a slow agony after they had served their turn. Compared with the lot of the birds used in pigeon shooting, theirs was indisputably a fortunate one. And the aimless collecting spirit which encourages the systematic impalement of insects by children, is apparently absent altogether from the Martian mind.

Indisputably they inflicted enormous agonies; indisputably Martians and men cannot exist permanently upon the same planet; but that is no reason why we should tell lies upon ethical points. They fought for their kind and we for ours. But, as for right, I do not believe that there is any right in the world, save the sense of justice between man and man. All the rest, I hold, is physical law.

But I wander from my subject. The physiological advantage at any rate of this practice of injection is undeniable, if one thinks of the tremendous waste of human time and energy occasioned by eating and the digestive process. Our bodies are half made up of glands and tubes and organs, occupied in turning heterogeneous food into blood. The digestive processes and their reaction upon the nervous system, sap our strength, colour our minds. Men go miserable or happy as they have healthy or unhealthy livers, or sound gastric glands. But the Martians are lifted above all these organic fluctuations of mood and emotion.

Their undeniable preference for men as their source of nourishment, is partly explained by the nature of the remains of the victims they had brought with them as provisions from Mars. These creatures, to judge from the shrivelled remains that have fallen into human hands, were bipeds, with flimsy siliceous skeletons (almost like those of the siliceous sponges) and feeble musculature, standing about six feet high, and having round erect heads, and large eyes in flinty sockets. Two or three of these seem to have been brought in each cylinder, and all were killed before earth was reached. It was just as well for them, for the mere attempt to stand upright upon our planet would have crushed them.

In three other points the Martian physiology differs from ours. Their organisms do not sleep, any more than the heart of man sleeps. Since they have no extensive muscular mechanism to recuperate, that periodical extinction is unknown to them. In twenty-four hours they do twenty-four hours of work —as, even on earth is, perhaps, the case with the ants.

In the next place, wonderful as it seems in a sexual world, the Martians are absolutely without sex, and, therefore, free from the tumultuous emotions that arise from that difference among men. A young Martian was born upon earth during the war, and it was *budded* off just as young lily bulbs bud off, or the young animals in the fresh water polyp.

In man, in all the higher terrestrial animals, such a method of increase has disappeared, but even on this earth it was certainly the primitive method. Among the lower animals, up even to those first cousins of the vertebrated animals, the Tunicates, the two processes occur side by side, but finally the sexual method superseded its competitor altogether. On Mars, however, just the reverse has apparently been the case.

The Handling Machine.

The last point in which their systems differ from ours is in what one might have thought a very trivial particular. Micro-organisms, which cause so much disease and pain on earth, have either never appeared upon Mars, or Martian sanitary science eliminated them ages ago. But of that I will write more at length later.

But, speaking of the differences between the life on Mars and terrestrial life, I may allude here to the curious suggestions of the Red Weed. Apparently, the vegetable kingdom in Mars, instead of having green for a dominant colour, is of a vivid blood-red tint. At any rate, the seeds which the Martians (intentionally or accidentally) brought with them, in all cases, gave rise to red coloured growths. Only that now known popularly as the Red Weed, however, gained any footing in competition with terrestrial forms. For a time, the Red Weed grew with astonishing vigour and luxuriance. It spread up the sides of the pit, by the third or fourth day of our imprisonment, and its cactus-like branches formed a carmine fringe to the edges of our triangular window. And afterwards I found it broadcast throughout the county, and especially wherever there was a stream of water.

The Martians wore no clothing, their conceptions of ornament and decorum are necessarily different from ours, and not only were they evidently much less sensible of changes of temperature than we are, but changes of pressure do not seem to have affected their health at all seriously. But if they wore no clothing, yet it was in the other artificial additions to their bodily resources, certainly, that their great superiority over man lay.

We men, with our bicycles and road

skates, our Lilienthal soaring machines, our guns and sticks, and so forth, are just in the beginning of the evolution that the Martians have worked out. They have become mere brains, wearing different bodies according to their need, just as men wear suits of clothes and take a bicycle in a hurry or an umbrella in the wet. There was the gigantic marching, fighting body of metal, carrying the generator of the Heat Ray, which I have already described. At the pit, however, the Martian descended from this huge thing, leaving it to straddle motionless against his need, and assumed, as a rule, a machine body, which might perhaps be called the Handling Machine.

In this he sat unprotected amidst a two-score rayed star of many jointed arms and tentacles bearing a miscellany of gripping, hooking, hammering, and stabbing ends. These he played through the agency of a sort of key, and he certainly used them as swiftly, subtly and dexterously as a man his fingers.

It was hard when one saw a Handling Machine (as I have done) go clambering up a vertical bank of sand, and hold itself by one arm to the brow of the pit, while it caught bars of rock crystal flung up to it by two others, not to regard it as a living organism. But I suppose, after all, it was no more wonderful to me than a steam engine would be to a thoughtful ape.

We were able to see from our peephole the upper works of the green-vapour machine, the precipitous side of the pit to the north, and part of the westward slope down which the Martians came into the pit. And in the north-west corner of the pit were the shambles, where it was their custom to kill their prey. Only once did I see that done, and then only indistinctly, for I lay almost stunned with fear and repulsion. I heard suddenly a dismal crying and saw one of the many armed Handling Machines clambering crab-like down the slope, with a lad gripped in one of its flexible tentacles. It emitted a cheerful hooting as it did so, and immediately three of the round brown-bodied unarmed Martians gathered about it. . . . . I must admit it seemed a painless death.

XX.—THE DEATH OF THE CURATE.

OUR life, pent up in the kitchen and scullery of the ruined house, was a strange one. During the earlier days we spent the greater part of our time sitting motionless in the scullery, scarcely exchanging a word with one another. The curate talked to himself in an undertone, seeming to be reasoning out some perplexing theological problem. He ate more than I did, and it was in vain that I pointed out that a time might presently come when we should need food. He ate and drank impulsively, in heavy meals at long intervals. He slept but little. As the days passed the peephole began to exercise a horrible fascination upon him. He would lie watching for hours together, eating nothing.

I was quite unused to seeing mental trouble, or I suppose I should have understood that from the first the swift tragedy that had burst upon the world had deranged his mind.

After the eighth day he began to talk aloud instead of whisper, and nothing I could do would moderate his speech. " It is just, O God! " he would say over and over again. " It is just. On me and mine be the punishment laid. We have sinned, we have fallen short. There was poverty, sorrow ; the poor were trodden in the dust, and I held my peace. I preached acceptable folly — my God, what folly ! — to fat stockbrokers, to landlords who drew their rent as though it came from God, to idle, foolish women, to cheating, over-reaching tradesmen, to braggart half-pay gentility, when I should have stood up, though I died for it, and called upon them to Repent, Repent. The brotherhood of man ! To make the best of every child that comes into the world ! . . How we have wasted our brothers ! . . . . . Oppressors of the poor and needy. . . . The Wine Press of God ! "

So he would talk with his voice rising slowly, through the greater part of the eighth and ninth days, a torrent of half sane and always frothy repentance for his vacant sham of God's service, such as made me pity him. Then he slept awhile, and began again with renewed strength, so loudly that I must needs make him desist. " Be still," I implored.

He rose to his knees—for he had been sitting in the darkness near the copper. "I have been still too long," he said, in a tone that must have reached the pit, "and now I must bear my witness! Woe unto this unfaithful city. Woe, woe! Woe, woe, woe, to the inhabitants of the earth by reason of the other voices of the trumpet. . . ."

"Shut up," I said, rising to my feet, and in a terror lest the Martians should hear us, I looked round for something wherewith I might stun him.

"Nay," shouted the curate at the top of his voice, standing likewise and extending his arms. "Speak! The word of the Lord is upon me!"

In three strides he was at the door into the kitchen. "I must bear my witness. I go. It has already been too long delayed!"

I put out my hand and felt the meat chopper hanging to the wall. In a flash I was after him. I was fierce with fear. Before he was half way across the kitchen I had overtaken him. I turned the blade back and struck him with the butt. He went headlong forward, and lay stretched on the ground. Just at that moment the triangular aperture was darkened by a Martian. I stumbled over the curate, staggered, and stood petrified for a moment.

Then I rushed to the door into the scullery. As I did so a long snake of metallic tentacle came feeling slowly through the hole. I went into the scullery and turned. I did not know how long their tentacles were, whether one could reach across the kitchen. Suppose

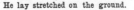

He lay stretched on the ground.

It was like a black worm swaying its blind head to and fro.

it could! Had the Martian seen me? What was it doing now? I could imagine that snaky thing, twisting and turning this way and that. I opened the door of the coal cellar, and stood there in the darkness staring at the faintly lit doorway into the kitchen, and listening.

Something was moving to and fro there very quietly; every now and then it tapped against the wall with a faint metallic ringing like the movement of keys on a split ring. Then the curate's insensible body was dragged across the floor of the kitchen towards the opening.

I crept to the door and peeped into the kitchen. In the triangle of bright outer sunlight I saw the Martian in its Briareus of a Handling Machine, scrutinising the curate's head. I thought at once that it would tell of my presence from the mark of the blow I had given him. I rushed back to the coal cellar, shut the door, and began to cover myself up as much as I could and as noiselessly as possible, in the darkness among the firewood and coal therein. Every now and then I paused rigid, to hear if the Martian had thrust its tentacle through the opening again.

Then the faint metallic jingle returned. I traced it slowly feeling over the kitchen. Presently I heard it nearer—in the scullery as I judged. It passed, scraping faintly, across the cellar door. An age of almost intolerable suspense intervened. Then I heard it fumbling at the latch. It had found the door! The Martian understood doors. It worried at the catch for a minute perhaps, and then the door opened.

In the darkness I could just see the thing—like an elephant's trunk more than anything else—waving towards me and touching and examining the wall, coals, wood and ceiling.

It was like a black worm swaying its blind head to and fro. Once even it touched my boot. At any moment the blind filament might discover me. I was on the verge of screaming—I bit my hand. For a time it was silent. I could have fancied it had been withdrawn. Presently with an abrupt click it gripped something—I thought it had me!—and seemed to go out of the cellar again. For a minute I was not sure. Apparently it had taken a lump of coal to examine.

I seized the opportunity of slightly shifting my position, which had become cramped, and listened. I whispered passionate prayers for

A multitude of crows hopped and fought over the skeletons of the dead.

safety. Then I heard the slow deliberate sound creeping towards me again. Slowly, slowly it drew near, scratching against walls and tapping furniture. While I was still doubtful it rapped suddenly against the cellar door. I heard it go into the pantry, and the biscuit tins rattled and a bottle smashed, and then came a heavy bump against the cellar door. Then silence, that passed into an infinity of suspense. Had it gone? At last I decided that it had.

It came into the scullery no more. But I lay all the tenth day, in the close darkness, buried among coals and firewood, not daring even to crawl out for the drink for which I craved. It was the eleventh day before I ventured so far from my security. My first act, before I went into the pantry, was to fasten the door between kitchen and scullery. But the pantry was empty; every scrap of food had gone. Apparently the Martian had taken it all on the previous day. At that discovery I despaired for the first time.

I took no food and no drink either on the eleventh or the twelfth day. At first my mouth and throat were parched and my strength ebbed sensibly. I sat about in the darkness of the scullery, in a state of despondent wretchedness. My mind ran on eating. I thought I had become deaf, for the noises of movement I had been accustomed to hear from the pit ceased absolutely. I did not feel strong enough to crawl noiselessly to the peephole, or I would have gone there. On the twelfth day, my throat was so painful that, taking the chance of alarming the Martians, I attacked the creaking rain water pump that stood by the sink, and got a couple of glassfuls of blackened and tainted rain water. I was greatly refreshed by this, and emboldened by the fact that no inquiring tentacle followed the noise of my pumping.

On the thirteenth day I drank some more water, and dozed and thought disjointedly of eating and of vague impossible plans of escape. Whenever I dozed I dreamt of sumptucus dinners, but, sleeping or awake, I felt a keen pain that urged me to drink again and again. On the fourteenth day I went into the kitchen, and I was surprised to find that the fronds of the Red Weed had grown right across the hole in the wall, turning the half-light of the place into a crimson coloured obscurity. It was early on the fifteenth day that I heard a curious familiar sequence of sounds in the kitchen, and listening, identified it as the snuffing and scratching of a dog. Going into the kitchen I saw a dog's nose peering in through a break among the ruddy fronds. This greatly surprised me. At the scent of me he barked shortly.

I thought if I could induce him to come into the place quietly I should be able perhaps to kill and eat him, and in any case it would be advisable to kill him, lest his actions attracted the attention of the Martians. I crept forward, saying " Good dog! " very softly. But he suddenly withdrew his head and disappeared. I listened—I was not deaf—but certainly the pit was still. I heard a sound like the flutter of a bird's wings, and a hoarse croaking, and that was all.

For a long while I lay close to our peephole, but not daring to move aside the red plants that obscured it. Once or twice I heard a faint pitter-patter like the feet of a dog going hither and thither on the sand far below me, and there were more bird-like sounds, but that was all. At length, encouraged by the silence, I looked out. Except in the corner, where a multitude of crows hopped and fought over the skeletons of the dead the Martians had consumed, there was not a living thing in the pit.

I stared about me, scarcely believing my eyes. All the machinery had gone. Save for a big mound of greyish blue powder in one place, certain broken bars of metal in another, the black birds and the skeletons of the killed, the place was merely an empty pit in the sand. I hesitated for some time, and then, with considerable exertion, I scrambled out of the hole and on to the top of the mound in which I had been buried so long. There I found empty and silent the big cage of white metal in which the victims had been confined.

XXI.—AFTER THE FIFTEEN DAYS.

I looked about me. When I had last seen this part of Sheen in the daylight, it had been a straggling street of comfortable white and red houses, interspersed with abundant shady trees. Now I stood by this cage on a mound of clay and gravel, over which spread a multitude of red cactus shaped plants, knee high, without a solitary terrestrial growth to dispute their footing. The trees near me were dead and brown, but further, a network of red threads scaled the still living stems.

The neighbouring houses had all been wrecked, but none had been burned; their walls stood sometimes to the second storey, with smashed windows and shattered doors. The red weed grew tumultuously in their roofless rooms. Below me was the great pit, with the crows struggling for its refuse. A number of other birds hopped about among the ruins. Far away I saw a gaunt cat slink crouchingly along a wall, but traces of men there were none.

The day seemed, by contrast with my recent confinement, dazzlingly bright, the sky a glowing blue, and a gentle breeze kept the red weeds that had covered every scrap of unoccupied ground, gently swaying.

For a time I stood marvelling at the change that had come over the world. Then the fact of my insecurity came to mind, and, clambering past the empty cage, I crossed the summit of the mound and descended on the other side, away from the pit. I was of course alert for food, and here was a patch of garden unburied. I found some young onions, a couple of gladiolus bulbs, and a quantity of immature carrots, all of which I secured, and, scrambling over a ruined wall, went on my way through the trees towards Kew, possessed with two ideas—to get more food, and to limp, as soon and as far as my strength permitted, out of the region of the pit. For I did not know when the Martians might return.

Some way further in a grassy place was a group of mushrooms which I also devoured, and then I came upon a brown sheet of flowing shallow water, where meadows used to be. At first I was sur-

At Putney, the bridge was almost lost in a tangle of this weed.

prised at this flood in a hot, dry summer, but afterwards I discovered that this was caused by the tropical exuberance of the Red Weed. Directly this extraordinary growth encountered water, it straightway became gigantic and of unparalleled fecundity. Its seeds were simply poured down into the water of the Wey and Thames, and its swiftly growing and Titanic waterfronds speedily choked both these rivers.

At Putney, as I afterwards saw, the bridge was almost lost in a tangle of this weed; and at Richmond, too, the Thames water poured in a broad and shallow stream across the meadows of Hampton and Twickenham. As the waters spread, the weed followed them, until the ruined villas of the Thames valley were for a time lost in a red swamp, and much of the

desolation the Martians had caused was concealed.

In the end the Red Weed succumbed almost as quickly as it spread. A cankering disease, due it is believed to the action of certain bacteria, presently seized upon it. The fronds became bleached, and then shrivelled and brittle. They broke off at the least touch, and the waters that had stimulated their early growth carried their last vestiges out to sea. . . . . But this is an anticipation.

My first act on coming to this water was, of course, to slake my thirst. I found the water was sufficiently shallow for me to wade securely, although the Red Weed impeded my feet a little, but it evidently got deeper towards the river, and I turned back to Mortlake.

I managed to make out the road by means of its villas and fences and lamps, and so presently got out of this spate, and made my way to the hill going up towards Roehampton, and came out on Putney Common. Here I hunted for food among the trees, finding nothing, and I also raided a couple of silent houses, but they had already been broken into and ransacked. I rested for the remainder of the daylight in a shrubbery, being, in my enfeebled condition, too fatigued to push on.

All this time I saw no human beings and

no signs of the Martians. I encountered a couple of hungry-looking dogs, but both hurried away from the advances I made them. Near Roehampton, I had seen two human skeletons—not bodies, but skeletons, picked clean, and in the wood by me, I found the crushed and scattered bones of several cats and rabbits, and the skull of a sheep. But though I gnawed parts of these in my mouth, there was nothing to be got from them.

After sunset, I struggled on along the road towards Putney, where I think the Heat Ray must have been used for some reason. The aspect of the place in the dusk was singularly desolate, blackened trees, stark and blackened ruins, and down the hill, the sheets of the flooded river, red-tinged with the weed; and over it all—silence. It filled me with terror to look at it all, and think how swiftly that desolating change had come. For a time I believed that all mankind had been swept out of existence, and that I stood there alone, the last man left alive.

I went down Putney High Street, and at the corner of the Upper Richmond Road came upon another skeleton, with the arms dislocated and removed several yards from the rest of the body.

I crossed the bridge, and found a man at last, lying at the corner of the lane to Putney Bridge. He was as black as a sweep with the black dust, and helplessly and speechlessly drunk. There was black dust along the roadway from the bridge onwards, and it grew thicker in Fulham. The streets were horribly quiet. I got food, sour and mouldy, but still quite eatable, in a baker's shop here. Some way towards Walham Green, the streets became clear of powder, and I passed a white terrace of houses on fire—the noise of the burning was an absolute relief. Going on towards Brompton the streets were quiet again.

Here I came once more upon the black powder in the streets, and dead bodies. I saw altogether about a dozen in the length of the Fulham Road. They had been dead some days, so that I hurried quickly past them. The black powder covered them over and softened their outlines. One or two had been disturbed by dogs. Where there was no black powder, it was curiously like a Sunday in the City, with the closed shops, the houses locked up and the blinds drawn, the desertion and the stillness. In some places plunderers had been at work, but rarely at other than the provision and wine shops. A little jeweller's window had been broken open in one place, but apparently the thief had been disturbed, and a number of gold chains and a watch were scattered on the pavement. I did not trouble to touch them. Further on was a tattered woman in a heap on a doorstep; the hand that hung over her knee was gashed and had bled down her rusty brown dress, and a smashed magnum of champagne formed a pool across the pavement.

I became more and more convinced that the extermination of mankind was, save for such stragglers as myself, already accomplished in this part of the world. The Martians, I thought, had gone on, and left the country desolated, seeking food elsewhere. Perhaps even now they were destroying Berlin or Paris, or it might be they had gone northward. . . . . .

XXI.—AFTER THE FIFTEEN

DAYS (*continued*).

THE further I penetrated into London, the profounder grew the silence. But it was not so much the stillness of death, it was the stillness of suspense, of expectation. Somehow I felt that this was not the end. I had a sense of things still impending. Suppose the Martians were, after all, at hand. At any time the destruction that already singed the north-western borders of the Metropolis, and had annihilated Ealing and Kilburn, might strike among these houses and leave them smoking ruins. It was a city condemned and derelict. . . . That, at any rate, would be completion.

In South Kensington the streets were clear of dead and of black powder. It was near South Kensington that I first heard the howling. It crept almost imperceptibly upon my senses. It was a sobbing alternation of two notes, "*Ulla, ulla, ulla, ulla,*" keeping on perpetually. When I passed streets that ran northward it grew in volume, and houses and buildings seemed to deaden and cut it off again. It came in a full tide down Exhibition Road. I stopped staring towards Kensington Gardens, wondering at this strange remote wailing. It was as if that mighty desert of houses had found a voice for its fear and solitude.

"Ulla, ulla, ulla, ulla," wailed that super-human note; great waves of sound sweeping down the broad, sunlit roadway, between the tall buildings on either side. I turned northward, marvelling, towards the iron gates of Hyde Park. I had half a mind to break into the Natural History Museum and find my way up to the summits of the towers, in order to see across the Park. But I decided to keep to the ground, where quick hiding was possible, and so went on up the Exhibition Road. All the large mansions on either side of the road were empty and still, and my footsteps echoed against the sides of the houses. At the top, near the park gate, I came upon a strange sight—a 'bus over-turned, and the skeleton of a horse picked clean. I puzzled over this for a time, and then went on to the bridge over the Serpentine. The Voice grew stronger and stronger, though I could see nothing above the house-tops on the north side of the park, save a haze of smoke to the north-west.

"Ulla, ulla, ulla, ulla," cried the voice, coming, as it seemed to me, from somewhere beyond Baker Street. The desolating cry worked upon my mind. The mood that had sustained me passed. The wailing took pos-session of me. I found I was intensely weary, footsore, and now again hungry and thirsty.

It was already past noon. Why was I wandering alone in this city of the dead? Why was I alone when all London was lying in state, and in its black shroud? I was intolerably lonely. My mind ran on old friends that I had forgotten for years. I thought of the poisons in the chemists' shops, of the liquors the wine merchants stored, I recalled the two sodden creatures of despair who, so far as I knew, shared the city with myself . . . . We were the last of men.

I came into Oxford Street by the Marble Arch, and here again was black powder and several bodies, and an evil, ominous smell from the gratings of the cellars of some of the houses. I grew very thirsty after the heat of my long walk. With infinite trouble I managed to break into a public-house and get food and drink. I was weary after eating, and went into the parlour behind the bar and slept on a black horsehair sofa I found there.

I awoke to find that dismal howling still in my ears : " Ulla, ulla, ulla, ulla." It was now dusk, and after I had routed out some biscuits and a cheese in the bar—there was cold beef there also in a safe, but it was too bad to eat —I wandered on through the silent residential squares to Baker Street—Portman Square is the only one I can name—and so came out at last upon Regent's Park. And as I emerged from the top of Baker Street, I saw far away over the trees in the clearness of the sunset, the hood of the Martian giant from which this howling proceeded. I was not terrified. I came upon him as if it were a matter of course. I watched him for some time, but he did not move. He appeared to be standing and yelling, for no reason that I could discover.

I tried to formulate a plan of action. That perpetual sound of " Ulla, ulla, ulla, ulla," confused my mind. Perhaps I was too tired to be very fearful. Certainly I was rather curious than afraid to know the reason of this monotonous crying. I turned back away from the park and struck into Park Road, intending to skirt the park, and went along under shelter of the terraces and got a view of this stationary howling Martian from the direction of St. John's Wood. A couple of hundred yards out of Baker Street I heard a yelping chorus, and saw, first, a dog with a piece of putrescent red meat in his jaws coming headlong towards me, and then a pack of starving mongrels in pursuit of him. He made a wide curve to avoid me, as though he feared I might prove a fresh competitor. As the yelping died away down the silent road, the wailing sound of " Ulla, ulla, ulla," reasserted itself.

I came upon the wrecked Handling Machine half way to St. John's Wood station. At first I thought that a house had fallen across the road. It was only as I clambered among the ruins that I saw, with a start, this mechanical Samson lying, with its tentacles bent and smashed and twisted, among the ruins it had made. The forepart was shattered. It seemed as if it had driven blindly straight at the house and had been overwhelmed in its overthrow. It seemed to me then that this might have happened by a Handling Machine escaping from the guidance of its Martian. I could not clamber among the ruins to see it, and the twilight was now so far advanced that the blood with which its seat was smeared and the gnawed gristle of the Martian that the dogs had left, was invisible to me.

Wondering still more at all that I had seen, I pushed on towards Primrose Hill. Far away, through a gap in the trees, I saw a second Martian, motionless as the first, standing in the park towards the Zoological Gardens, and silent. A little beyond the ruins about the smashed Handling Machine I came upon the Red Weed again, and found the Regent's Canal a spongy mass of dark red vegetation.

Abruptly, as I crossed the bridge, the sound of " Ulla, ulla, ulla," ceased. It was, as it were, cut off. The silence came like a thunderclap.

The dusky houses about me stood faint, and tall and dim, the trees towards the park were growing black. Night, the Mother of Fear and Mystery, was coming upon me. But while that voice sounded the solitude, the desolation had been endurable ; by virtue of it London had still seemed alive, and the sense of life about me had upheld me. Then suddenly, a change, the passing of something —I knew not what—and then a stillness that could be felt. Nothing but this gaunt quiet of death !

London about me gazed at me spectrally. The windows in the white houses were like the eye-sockets of skulls. About me my imagination found a thousand noiseless enemies moving. Terror seized me, a horror of my temerity. In front of me the road became pitchy black as though it was tarred, and I saw a contorted shape lying across the pathway. I could not bring myself to go on. I turned down St. John's Wood Road, and ran headlong from this unendurable stillness towards Kilburn. I hid from the night and the silence, until long after midnight, in a cabmen's shelter in the Harrow Road. But before the dawn my courage returned, and while the stars were still in the sky, I turned once more towards the Regent's Park. I missed my way among the streets, and presently saw, down a long avenue, in the half light of early dawn, the curve of Primrose Hill. On the summit, towering up to the fading stars, was a

third Martian, erect and motionless like the others.

A strange insanity seized upon me. I would die and end it. And I would save myself even the trouble of killing myself. I marched on recklessly towards this Titan, and then, as I drew nearer and the light grew, I saw that a multitude of black birds was circling and clustering about the hood. At that my heart gave a bound, and I began running along the road. I hurried through the red weed that choked St. Edmund's Terrace (a torrent of water was rushing down from the waterworks towards the Albert Road) and emerged upon the grass before the rising of the sun. Great mounds had been heaped about the crest of the hill, making a huge redoubt of it, and from behind them rose a thin smoke against the sky. Against the skyline an eager dog ran and disappeared. The thought that had flashed into my mind, grew real, grew credible. I felt no fear, only a wild exultation, as I ran up the hill, towards the motionless monster. Out of the hood hung lank shreds of brown at which the hungry birds pecked and tore.

In another moment I had scrambled up the earthen rampart and stood upon its crest, and the interior of the redoubt was below me. A mighty space it was, with gigantic machines here and there within it, huge mounds of material, and rough hewn shelter places. And scattered about it, some in their overturned war machines, some in the now rigid Handling Machines, and a dozen of them, stark and silent and laid in a row, were the Martians—*dead!*—Slain by the putrefactive and disease bacteria, against which their systems were unprepared; slain, after all man's devices had failed, by the humblest things that God has put upon this earth.

Here and there they were scattered, nearly fifty altogether in that great gulf they had made, overtaken by a death that must have

I hurried through the red weed.

Nearly fifty together in that great gulf.

seemed to em as incomprehensible as any death could be. But how they had died I did not know at this time. All I knew was, that these things that had been alive and so terrible to men, were dead. For a moment I believed that the destruction of Sennacherib had been repeated—that God had repented, that the Angel of Death had slain them in the night.

I stood staring into the pit, and my heart lightened gloriously, even as the rising sun struck the world to fire about me with his rays. The pit was still sunk in darkness, the mighty engines, so great and wonderful in their power and complexity, so unearthly in their tortuous forms, rose weird and strange out of the shadows. The dogs, I could hear, fought over the bodies that lay darkly in the depth of the pit, far below me. Then at the sound of a cawing overhead, I looked up at the huge Fighting Machine, that would fight no more for ever, at the tattered red shreds of flesh that dripped down upon the overturned seats on the summit of Primrose Hill.

I turned and looked down the slope of the hill, to where, enhaloed now in birds, stood those other two Martians that I had seen overnight, just as death had overtaken them. The one had died, even as it had been crying to its companions; perhaps it was the last to die, and its voice had gone on perpetually until the force of its machinery was exhausted. They glittered now, harmless tripod towers of shining metal, in the brightness of the rising sun. . . . . .

All about the pit, and saved as by a miracle from everlasting destruction, stretched the great Mother of Cities. Those who have only seen London veiled in her robes of smoke, can scarcely imagine the naked clearness and beauty of the silent wilderness of houses.

Eastward, over the blackened ruins of the Albert Terrace and the splintered spire of the church, the sun blazed dazzling in a clear sky, and here and there some facet in the great wilderness of roofs caught the light and glared with a white intensity. There is a round store place for wines by the Chalk Farm Station, and vast railway yards, marked once with a graining of black rails, but red lined now with the quick rusting of a fortnight's disuse. Northward, Kilburn and Hampstead rose blue and crowded with houses; westward, the great city was haze-

I extended my hands
towards the sky.

Surrey hills rose up, and the towers of the Crystal Palace glittered like two silver rods. The dome of St. Paul's was dark against the sunrise, and injured, I saw for the first time, by a huge gaping cavity on its westward side.

And, as I looked at this wide expanse of houses, and factories, and churches, silent and abandoned, as I thought of the multitudinous hopes and efforts, the innumerable hosts of lives that had gone to build this human reef, and of the swift and ruthless destruction that had hung over it all, when I realised that the shadow had been rolled back, and that men might still live in its streets, and this dear vast dead city of mine be once more alive and powerful, I felt a wave of emotion, that was near akin to tears.

The torment was over. Even that day, the healing would begin. The survivors of the people scattered over the country, leaderless, lawless, foodless, like sheep without a shepherd, the thousands who had fled by sea would begin to return; the pulse of life, growing stronger and stronger, would beat again in the empty streets, and pour across the vacant squares. Whatever destruction was done, the hand of the destroyer was stayed. All the gaunt wrecks, the blackened skeletons of houses that stared so dismally at the sunlit grass of the hill, would presently be echoing under the hammers of the restorers, and ringing with the tintinnabulations of the trowels. At the thought, I extended my hands towards the sky, and began thanking God. In a year, thought I,—in a year. . . . and then, with overwhelming force, came the thought of myself, of my wife, and the old life, that I had to imagine done with for ever.

dimmed; and southward, beyond the Martians, the green waves of Regent's Park, the Langham Hotel, the dome of the Albert Hall, the Imperial Institute, and the giant mansions of the Brompton Road came out clear and little in the sunrise with the jagged ruins of Westminster beyond. Far away the

XXII.—THE EPILOGUE.

But here the story that will interest the general reader, the story of the Martians, ends. The rest, the return, the Thanksgiving, has been written by a thousand pens. This is indeed no history, it is a mere clumsy narrative of my own personal adventures during this strange time, eked out by my brother's experience where the gaps were too great. Such narratives we must have first in abundance, and afterwards the history may be written. In the fact that I was among the first to see the Martians at their arrival, and the second man—indeed, I had fancied myself first—to discover them dead, I have presumed to think my impressions might be of value. And by an odd coincidence, of the four Martians killed by Man, I saw the death of one and my brother the overthrow of two others. But to tell of the torrent of people that presently flowed back into London, chiefly from the north—for the Martians had never gone further than forty miles in that direction—of the riots and plundering, and murders, of the restoration of government, of the terrific explosion of the Heat Ray powder that wrecked the north of London, hundreds are better qualified than I.

Nor have I any qualification to speak of the distresses in the home counties, the famine, the violence, even it is said, the cannibalism, the disappearance of all law and order during the fortnight of the war, and afterwards the struggle with the pestilence. It speaks eloquently for the lesson that humanity had learned that no attack was made on our stricken Empire during the months of reconstruction.

I plundered a grocer's shop in Camden Town for food, on the morning of my discovery, and afterwards tramped down to the docks with the idea of spreading the good news there. In Shoreditch I met people again, and told them what I had seen; and it was from the General Post Office, by a Jewess who had learned the trade of a telegraph operator, that the news was first flashed out of London, to Paris first, and then to certain English towns.

I remember that I laughed hysterically until I cried, when, after infinite trouble and muddling, we managed the telephone, and heard the French operator say, over and over again as though they were his only words: "Dead! *Nom de Dieu!* A Tousand Congratulation. You have kill dem? *Vive l'Angleterre!* Hooray!" Its kindly insipidity offered such an infinite contrast to the half dozen haggard yellow faced dirty and hungry people who crowded into the room. That night, I have heard since, Paris, by no set contrivance, but of its own impulsive emotion, was a fairy-land of blazing illuminations from end to end, and ten thousand thronged cities in Europe and Asia and America shouted aloud and held festival at the news of the world's release.

I lingered in London ten days, serving as a special constable. I dreaded to go back to my house, desolate among the ashes of Maybury Hill, the house in which I had hoped to live the best part of my days. I believed my wife was dead. I feared to find a solitude that should confirm my fears. But at last, I induced myself to resign my white badge and staff and return by one of the Government trains, by which people were taken back free of charge to their proper dwelling places. The Surrey country was pitifully scarred and blackened on either side, and every watercourse was scarlet with the red weed.

I descended at Byfleet Station, and took the road to Maybury, past the place where I and the artilleryman had talked to the hussars, and on by the spot where the Martian had appeared to me in the thunderstorm. Here I turned aside to find, among a tangle of red fronds, the warped and broken dog-cart with the whitened bones of the horse, scattered and gnawed. Then I returned through the pine wood, neck high with weed here and there, to find that the landlord of the 'Spotted Dog' had already found burial, and so home, past the College Arms. A man standing at an open cottage door greeted me by name as I passed.

I looked at my house with a quick flash of hope that faded immediately. The door had been forced; it was unfastened and was opening slowly as I approached. Then it slammed again. The curtains of my study fluttered out of the open window from which

I and the artilleryman had watched the dawn. No one had closed it since. The smashed bushes were just as I had left them nearly four weeks ago. I stumbled into the hall, and the house felt empty. The stair carpet was ruffled and discoloured where I had crouched, soaked to the skin from the thunderstorm, on the night of the catastrophe. Our muddy footsteps I saw still went up the stairs.

I went into the dining-room, and there was the mutton and the bread, both far gone now in decay, and a beer bottle overturned just as I and the artilleryman had left them. My home was desolate. I perceived the folly of the faint hope I had cherished so long. And then a strange thing occurred. "It is no use," said a voice. "The house is deserted. No one has been here these ten days. Do not stay here to torment yourself. No one escaped but you."

I was startled. Had I spoken my thought aloud? I turned, and the French window was open behind me. I made a step to it, and stood looking out. And there, amazed and afraid, even as I stood amazed and afraid, were my cousin and my wife. My wife, white and tearless. She gave a faint cry. "I came," she said. "I knew. Knew . . ."

She put her hand to her throat—swayed. I dashed out and caught her in my arms.

I turned aside to find the warped and broken dog-cart with the whitened bones of the horse.

I cannot but regret now that I am concluding my story how little I am able to contribute to the discussion of the many debatable questions which are still unsettled. In one respect I shall certainly provoke criticism. My particular province is speculative philosophy; my knowledge of comparative physiology is confined to a book or two, but it seems to me that Carver's suggestions as to the reason of the rapid death of the Martians is so probable as to be regarded almost as a proven conclusion. I have assumed that in the body of my narrative.

At the very base of the vegetable kingdom in this world are those exceedingly minute and abundant things, the Bacteria. They will be better known, perhaps, to the unscientific reader as "Germs." Various species of them cause putrefaction and such diseases as Cholera, Anthrax, and Typhoid. Others are less mischievous, and some even beneficial. Multitudes of them occurring about the roots of trees are said to be absolutely necessary to the feeding of these trees, and it has even been supposed that those always present in the stomach and intestines of men and animals are conducive to digestion and even essential.

They are everywhere, in the air we breathe, in the water we drink, in the dust, in our food, in our veins even. To guard us against the perpetual attacks of those that generate disease, there are in our blood a multitude of microscopic particles, the *leucocytes*, which have the property of consuming them. Our bodies, in fact, carry on a perpetual defensive warfare against these unseen activities; we have been drilled and disciplined and to a large extent inured against them. But on Mars, the development of life has been so far dissimilar from the development of life on Earth, that there do not seem to be any bacteria there at all. The Martians arrived here

And there, amazed and afraid, were my cousin and my wife.

without any such resisting power as we possess, Carver supposes, and they must have begun to rot almost as soon as they arrived.

At any rate, in all the bodies of the Martians that were examined after the war, no bacteria except those already known as terrestrial species, were found. That they did not bury any of their dead, and the reckless slaughter they perpetrated, point also to an entire ignorance of the putrefactive process. But

probable as this seems, it is by no means a proven conclusion.

Neither is the composition of the Black Smoke known, which the Martians used with such deadly effect, and the generator of the Heat Ray remains a puzzle. The terrible disasters at the Ealing and South Kensington laboratories have disinclined analysts for further investigations upon the latter. Spectrum analysis of the black powder points unmistakably to the presence of an unknown element with a brilliant group of three lines in the green and it is possible that it combines with argon to form a compound which acts at once with deadly effect upon some constituent in the blood. But such unproven speculations will scarcely be of interest to the general reader to whom this story is addressed. None of the brown scum that drifted down the Thames after the destruction of Shepperton was examined at the time, and none now is forthcoming.

The results of an anatomical examination of the Martians, so far as the prowling dogs had left such an examination possible, I have already given. But everyone is familiar with the magnificent and almost complete specimen in spirits at the Natural History Museum, and the countless drawings that have been made from it ; and beyond that the interest of the physiology and structure is purely scientific.

It has often been asked why the Martians did not fly immediately after their arrival. They certainly did use a flying apparatus for several days, but only for brief flights of a score or so of miles, in order to reconnoitre and spread their black powder. The framework found at Kilburn was certainly this flying machine. I never saw this thing flying myself, but my brother, as I have already told in its proper place, had just a glimpse of it. It is hard to believe, seeing their other power, that this was their limit in this direction.

Two things must have prevented the immediate resort to aeronautics. In the first place it must have been impossible to pack the necessary wings into the cylinder by which the Martians came, and in the next the problem of flying in our atmosphere was one they could scarcely calculate in detail upon Mars, since it would be almost impossible for them to estimate the density of our lower air, until they reached it. But these are of course merely suggestions. The fact remains, that they did not fly fifty miles from London all through the war. Had they done so, then the destruction they would have caused must have been infinitely greater than it was, though it could not have averted the end, of course, even by a day.

A question of graver and universal interest is the possibility of another attack from the Martians. I do not think that nearly enough attention has been given to this aspect of the matter. At present the planet Mars is in conjunction, but with every return to opposition I, for one, anticipate a renewal of their adventure. In any case we should be prepared. It seems to me that it should be possible to define the position of the gun from which the shots are discharged, to keep a sustained watch upon this part of the planet, and to anticipate the arrival of the next attack.

In that case the cylinder might be destroyed with dynamite or artillery before it was sufficiently cool for the Martians to emerge, or they might be butchered by means of guns so soon as the screw opened. It

seems to me that they have lost a vast advantage in the failure of their first surprise. Possibly they see it in the same light.

Lessing had advanced excellent reasons for supposing that the Martians have actually succeeded in effecting a landing on the planet Venus. Seven months ago now Venus and Mars were in alignment with the sun, that is to say, Mars was in opposition from the point of view of an observer on Venus. Subsequently a peculiar luminous and sinuous marking appeared on the unillumined half of the inner planet, and almost simultaneously a faint dark mark of a similar sinuous character was detected upon a photograph of the Martian disc. One needs to see the drawings of these appearances in order to appreciate fully their remarkable resemblance in character. The photographs were reproduced in *Knowledge* in July of last year; Lessing's sketch of the luminous marks on Venus appeared in the corresponding column of *Nature* in the previous April.

At any rate, whether we expect another invasion or not, our views of the human future must be greatly modified by these events. We have learned now that we cannot regard this planet as being fenced in and a secure abiding place for Man ; we can never anticipate the unseen good or evil that may come upon us suddenly out of space. It may be that in the larger design of the universe this invasion from Mars is not without its ultimate benefit for men ; it has robbed us of that serene confidence in the future which is the most fruitful source of decadence, and it has done much to promote the conception of the commonweal of mankind. It may be that across the immensity of space the Martians have watched the fate of these pioneers of theirs and learned their lesson, and that on the planet Venus they have found a securer settlement. Be that as it may, for many years yet there will certainly be no relaxation of the eager scrutiny of the Martian disc, and those fiery darts of the sky, the shooting stars, will bring with them as they fall an unavoidable apprehension to all the sons of men.

The broadening of men's views that has resulted can scarcely be exaggerated. Before the cylinder fell there was a general persuasion that through all the deep of space no life existed beyond the petty surface of our minute sphere. Now we see further. If the Martians can reach Venus, there is no reason to suppose that the thing is impossible for men, and when the slow cooling of the sun makes, as it must do at last, this earth uninhabitable, it may be that the thread of life that has begun here will have streamed out and caught our sister planet within its toils. Should we conquer? Dim and wonderful is the vision I have conjured up in my mind of life spreading slowly from this little seed bed of the solar system throughout the inanimate vastness of sidereal space. But that is a remote dream. It may be, on the other hand, that the destruction of the Martians is only a reprieve. To them and not to us perhaps is the future ordained.

For my own part, the stress and danger of this time have left an abiding sense of doubt and insecurity in my mind. I sit in my study writing by lamplight, and suddenly I see again the healing valley below set with writhing flames, and feel the house behind and about me empty and desolate. I go out into the Byfleet Road and vehicles pass me, a butcher boy in a cart, a cabful of visitors, a workman on a bicycle, children going to school, and suddenly they become vague and unreal, and I hurry again with the artilleryman through the hot brooding silence. Of a night I see the black powder darkening the silent streets, and the contorted bodies shrouded in that layer; they rise upon me tattered and dogbitten. They gibber and grow fiercer, paler, uglier, mad distortions of humanity at last, and I wake cold and wretched in the darkness of the night.

I go to London and see the busy multitudes in Fleet Street and the Strand, and it comes across my mind that they are but the ghosts of the past haunting the streets that I have seen silent and wretched, going to and fro, phantasms in a dead city, the mockery of life in a galvanised body. And strange, too, it is to stand on Primrose Hill, as I did but a day before writing this last chapter, to see the great province of houses, dim and blue through the haze of the smoke and mist, vanishing at last into the vague lower sky, to see the people walking to and fro among the flower beds on the hill, to see the sightseers about the Martian machine that

They gibber and grow fiercer.

stands there still, to hear the tumult of playing children, and to recall the time when I saw it all bright and clear cut, hard and silent, under the dawn of that last great day. . .

And strangest of all is it to hold my wife's hand again, and to think that I have counted her and that she has counted me, among the dead.

THE END.

—2—

THE COUNTRY OF THE BLIND

Originally published in *The Strand Magazine*
April 1904

The Country of the Blind.

By H. G. Wells.

THREE HUNDRED miles and more from Chimborazo, one hundred from the snows of Cotopaxi, in the wildest wastes of Ecuador's Andes, there lies that mysterious mountain valley, cut off from all the world of men, the Country of the Blind. Long years ago that valley lay so far open to the world that men might come at last through frightful gorges and over an icy pass into its equable meadows, and thither indeed men came, a family or so of Peruvian half-breeds fleeing from the lust and tyranny of an evil Spanish ruler. Then came the stupendous outbreak of Mindobamba, when it was night in Quito for seventeen days, and the water was boiling at Yaguachi and all the fish floating dying even as far as Guayaquil ; everywhere along the Pacific slopes there were landslips and swift thawings and sudden floods, and one whole side of the old Arauca crest slipped and came down in thunder, and cut off the Country of the Blind for·ever from the exploring feet of men. But one of these early settlers had chanced to be on the hither side of the gorges when the world had so terribly shaken itself, and he perforce had to forget his wife and his child and all the friends and possessions he had left up there, and start life over again in the lower world. He started it again but ill, blindness overtook him, and he died of punishment in the mines ; but the story he told begot a legend that lingers along the length of the Cordilleras of the Andes to this day.

He told of his reason for venturing back from that fastness, into which he had first been carried lashed to a llama, beside a vast bale of gear, when he was a child. The valley, he said, had in it all that the heart of man could desire—sweet water, pasture, an even climate, slopes of rich brown soil with tangles of a shrub that bore an excellent fruit, and on one side great hanging forests of pine that held the avalanches high. Far overhead, on three sides, vast cliffs of grey-green rock were capped by cliffs of ice ; but the glacier stream came not to them, but flowed away by the farther slopes, and only now and then huge ice masses fell on the valley side. In this valley it neither rained nor snowed, but the abundant springs gave a rich green pasture, that irrigation would spread over all the valley space. The settlers did well indeed there. Their beasts did well and multiplied, and but one thing marred their happiness. Yet it was enough to mar it greatly. A strange disease had come upon them and had made all the children born to them there—and, indeed, several older children also—blind. It was to seek some charm or antidote against this plague of blindness that he had with fatigue and danger and difficulty returned down the gorge. In those days, in such cases, men did not think of germs and infections, but of sins, and it seemed to him that the reason of this affliction must lie in the negligence of these priestless immigrants to set up a shrine so soon as they entered the valley. He wanted a shrine—a handsome, cheap, effectual shrine—to be erected in the valley ; he wanted relics and such-like potent things of faith, blessed objects and mysterious medals and prayers. In his wallet he had a bar of native silver for which he would not account ; he insisted there was none in the valley with something of the insistence of an inexpert liar. They had all clubbed their money and ornaments together, having little need for such treasure up there, he said, to buy them holy help against their ill. I figure this dim-eyed young mountaineer, sunburnt, gaunt, and anxious, hat brim clutched feverishly, a man all unused to the ways of the lower world, telling this story to some keen-eyed, attentive priest before the great convulsion ; I can picture him presently seeking to return with pious and infallible remedies against that trouble, and the infinite dismay with which he must have faced the tumbled vastness where the gorge had once come out. But the rest of his story of mischances is lost to me, save that I know of his evil death after several years. Poor stray from that remoteness ! The stream that had once made the gorge now bursts from the mouth of a rocky cave, and the legend his poor, ill-told story set going developed into the legend of a race of blind men somewhere " over there " one may still hear to-day.

And amidst the little population of that

now isolated and forgotten valley the disease ran its course. The old became groping and purblind, the young saw but dimly, and the children that were born to them saw never at all. But life was very easy in that snow-rimmed basin, lost to all the world, with neither thorns nor briers, with no evil insects nor any beasts save the gentle breed of llamas they had lugged and thrust and followed up the beds of the shrunken rivers in the gorges up which they had come. The seeing had become purblind so gradually that they scarcely noted their loss. They guided the sightless youngsters hither and thither until they knew the whole valley marvellously, and when at last sight died out among them the race lived on. They had even time to adapt themselves to the blind control of fire, which they made carefully in stoves of stone. They were a simple strain of people at the first, unlettered, only slightly touched with the Spanish civilization, but with something of a tradition of the arts of old Peru and of its lost philosophy. Generation followed generation. They forgot many things; they devised many things. Their tradition of the greater world they came from became mythical in colour and uncertain. In all things save sight they were strong and able, and presently chance sent one who had an original mind and who could talk and persuade among them, and then afterwards another. These two passed, leaving their effects, and the little community grew in numbers and in understanding, and met and settled social

"THEY FOUND NUÑEZ HAD GONE FROM THEM."

and economic problems that arose. Generation followed generation. Generation followed generation. There came a time when a child was born who was fifteen generations from that ancestor who went out of the valley with a bar of silver to seek God's aid, and who never returned. Thereabout it chanced that a man came into this community from the outer world. And this is the story of that man.

He was a mountaineer from the country near Quito, a man who had been down to the sea and had seen the world, a reader of books in an original way, an acute and enterprising man, and he was taken on by a party of Englishmen who had come out to Ecuador to climb mountains, to replace one of their three Swiss guides who had fallen ill. He climbed here and he climbed there, and then came the attempt on Parascotopetl, the Matterhorn of the Andes, in which he was lost to the outer world. The story of that accident has been written a dozen times. Pointer's narrative is the best. He tells how the little party worked their difficult and almost vertical way up to the very foot of the last and greatest precipice, and how they built a night shelter amidst the snow upon a little shelf of rock, and, with a touch of real dramatic power, how presently they found Nuñez had gone from them. They shouted, and there was no reply; shouted and whistled, and for the rest of that night they slept no more.

As the morning broke they saw the traces

of his fall. It seems impossible he could have uttered a sound. He had slipped eastward towards the unknown side of the mountain; far below he had struck a steep slope of snow, and ploughed his way down it in the midst of a snow avalanche. His track went straight to the edge of a frightful precipice, and beyond that everything was hidden. Far, far below, and hazy with distance, they could see trees rising out of a narrow, shut-in valley—the lost Country of the Blind. But they did not know it was the lost Country of the Blind, nor distinguish it in any way from any other narrow streak of upland valley. Unnerved by this disaster, they abandoned their attempt in the afternoon, and Pointer was called away to the war before he could make another attack. To this day Parascotopetl lifts an unconquered crest, and Pointer's shelter crumbles unvisited amidst the snows.

And the man who fell survived.

At the end of the slope he fell a thousand feet, and came down in the midst of a cloud of snow upon a snow-slope even steeper than the one above. Down this he was whirled, stunned and insensible, but without a bone broken in his body; and then at last came to gentler slopes, and at last rolled out and lay still, buried amidst a softening heap of the white masses that had accompanied and saved him. He came to himself with a dim fancy that he was ill in bed; then realized his position with a mountaineer's intelligence and worked himself loose and, after a rest or so, out until he saw the stars. He rested flat upon his chest for a space, wondering where he was and what had happened to him. He explored his limbs, and discovered that several of his buttons were gone and his coat turned over his head. His knife had gone from his pocket and his hat was lost, though he had tied it under his chin. He recalled that he had been looking for loose stones to raise his piece of the shelter wall. His ice-axe had disappeared.

He decided he must have fallen, and looked up to see, exaggerated by the ghastly light of the rising moon, the tremendous flight he had taken. For a while he lay, gazing blankly at that vast, pale cliff towering above, rising moment by moment out of a subsiding tide of darkness. Its phantasmal, mysterious beauty held him for a space, and then he was seized with a paroxysm of sobbing laughter. . . .

After a great interval of time he became aware that he was near the lower edge of the snow. Below, down what was now a moon-lit and practicable slope, he saw the dark and broken appearance of rock-strewn turf. He struggled to his feet, aching in every joint and limb, got down painfully from the heaped loose snow about him, went downward until he was on the turf, and there dropped rather than lay beside a boulder, drank deep from the flask in his inner pocket, and instantly fell asleep. . . .

He was awakened by the singing of birds in the trees far below.

He sat up and perceived he was on a little alp at the foot of a vast precipice that sloped only a little in the gully down which he and his snow had come. Over against him another wall of rock reared itself against the sky. The gorge between these precipices ran east and west and was full of the morning sunlight, which lit to the westward the mass of fallen mountain that closed the descending gorge. Below him it seemed there was a precipice equally steep, but behind the snow in the gully he found a sort of chimney-cleft dripping with snow-water, down which a desperate man might venture. He found it easier than it seemed, and came at last to another desolate alp, and then after a rock climb of no particular difficulty to a steep slope of trees. He took his bearings and turned his face up the gorge, for he saw it opened out above upon green meadows, among which he now glimpsed quite distinctly a cluster of stone huts of unfamiliar fashion. At times his progress was like clambering along the face of a wall, and after a time the rising sun ceased to strike along the gorge, the voices of the singing birds died away, and the air grew cold and dark about him. But the distant valley with its houses was all the brighter for that. He came presently to talus, and among the rocks he noted—for he was an observant man—an unfamiliar fern that seemed to clutch out of the crevices with intense green hands. He picked a frond or so and gnawed its stalk, and found it helpful.

About midday he came at last out of the throat of the gorge into the plain and the sunlight. He was stiff and weary; he sat down in the shadow of a rock, filled up his flask with water from a spring and drank it down, and remained for a time, resting before he went on to the houses.

They were very strange to his eyes, and indeed the whole aspect of that valley became, as he regarded it, queerer and more unfamiliar. The greater part of its surface was lush green meadow, starred with many beautiful flowers, irrigated with extraordinary care, and bearing evidence of systematic cropping piece by piece. High up and ringing the valley about was a wall, and what appeared to be a circumferential water channel, from which the little trickles of water that fed the meadow plants came, and on the higher slopes above this flocks of llamas cropped the scanty herbage. Sheds, apparently shelters or feeding-places for the llamas, stood against the boundary wall here and there. The irrigation streams ran together into a main channel down the centre of the valley, and this was enclosed on either side by a wall breast high. This gave a singularly urban quality to this secluded place, a quality that was greatly enhanced by the fact that a number of paths paved with black and white stones, and each with a curious little kerb at the side, ran hither and thither in an orderly manner. The houses of the central village were quite unlike the casual and higgledy-piggledy agglomeration of the mountain villages he knew; they stood in a continuous row on either side of a central street of astonishing cleanness, here and there their parti-coloured

sometimes slate-coloured or dark brown; and it was the sight of this wild plastering first brought the word "blind" into the thoughts of the explorer. "The good man who did that," he thought, "must have been as blind as a bat."

He descended a steep place, and so came to the wall and channel that ran about the valley, near where the latter spouted out its surplus contents into the deeps of the gorge in a thin and wavering thread of cascade. He could now see a number of men and women resting on piled heaps of grass, as if taking a siesta, in the remoter part of the meadow, and nearer the village a number of recumbent children, and then nearer at hand three men carrying pails on yokes along a little path that ran from the encircling wall towards the houses. These latter were clad in garments of llama cloth and boots and belts of leather, and they wore caps of cloth with back and ear flaps. They followed one another in single file, walking slowly and yawning as they walked, like men who have been up all night. There was something so

"NUÑEZ STOOD FORWARD AS CONSPICUOUSLY AS POSSIBLE UPON HIS ROCK."

façade was pierced by a door, and not a solitary window broke their even frontage. They were parti-coloured with extraordinary irregularity, smeared with a sort of plaster that was sometimes grey, sometimes drab,

reassuringly prosperous and respectable in their bearing that after a moment's hesitation Nuñez stood forward as conspicuously as possible upon his rock, and gave vent to a mighty shout that echoed round the valley.

The three men stopped, and moved their heads as though they were looking about them. They turned their faces this way and that, and Nuñez gesticulated with freedom. But they did not appear to see him for all his gestures, and after a time, directing themselves towards the mountains far away to the right, they shouted as if in answer. Nuñez bawled again, and then once more, and as he gestured ineffectually the word " blind " came up to the top of his thoughts. "The fools must be blind," he said.

When at last, after much shouting and wrath, Nuñez crossed the stream by a little bridge, came through a gate in the wall, and approached them, he was sure that they were blind. He was sure that this was the Country of the Blind of which the legends told. Conviction had sprung upon him, and a sense of great and rather enviable adventure. The three stood side by side, not looking at him, but with their ears directed towards him, judging him by his unfamiliar steps. They stood close together like men a little afraid, and he could see their eyelids closed and sunken, as though the very balls beneath had shrunk away. There was an expression near awe on their faces.

" A man," one said, in hardly recognisable Spanish. " A man it is—a man or a spirit—coming down from the rocks."

But Nuñez advanced with the confident steps of a youth who enters upon life. All the old stories of the lost valley and the Country of the Blind had come back to his mind, and through his thoughts ran this old proverb, as if it were a refrain :—

" In the Country of the Blind the One-Eyed Man is King."

" In the Country of the Blind the One-Eyed Man is King."

And very civilly he gave them greeting. He talked to them and used his eyes.

"Where does he come from, brother Pedro ?" asked one.

" Down out of the rocks."

" Over the mountains I come," said Nuñez, " out of the country beyond there—where men can see. From near Bogota—where there are a hundred thousands of people, and where the city passes out of sight."

"Sight ?" muttered Pedro. " Sight ?"

" He comes," said the second blind man, " out of the rocks."

The cloth of their coats Nuñez saw was curiously fashioned, each with a different sort of stitching.

They startled him by a simultaneous movement towards him, each with a hand outstretched. He stepped back from the advance of these spread fingers.

" Come hither," said the third blind man, following his motion and clutching him neatly.

And they held Nuñez and felt him over, saying no word further until they had done so.

"Carefully," he cried, with a finger in his eye, and found they thought that organ, with its fluttering lids, a queer thing in him. They went over it again.

" A strange creature, Correa," said the one called Pedro. "Feel the coarseness of his hair. Like a llama's hair."

" Rough he is as the rocks that begot him," said Correa, investigating Nuñez's unshaven chin with a soft and slightly moist hand. " Perhaps he will grow finer."

Nuñez struggled a little under their examination, but they gripped him firm.

" Carefully," he said again.

" He speaks," said the third man. " Certainly he is a man."

" Ugh !" said Pedro, at the roughness of his coat.

"And you have come into the world ?" asked Pedro.

"*Out* of the world. Over mountains and glaciers ; right over above there, half-way to the sun. Out of the great, big world that goes down, twelve days' journey to the sea."

They scarcely seemed to heed him. " Our fathers have told us men may be made by the forces of Nature," said Correa. " It is the warmth of things, and moisture, and rotten-ness—rottenness."

" Let us lead him to the elders," said Pedro.

" Shout first," said Correa, " lest the children be afraid. This is a marvellous occasion."

So they shouted, and Pedro went first and took Nuñez by the hand to lead him to the houses.

He drew his hand away. "I can see," he said.

" See ?" said Correa.

" Yes ; see," said Nuñez, turning towards him, and stumbled against Pedro's pail.

" His senses are still imperfect," said the third blind man. " He stumbles, and talks unmeaning words. Lead him by the hand."

" As you will," said Nuñez, and was led along, laughing.

It seemed they knew nothing of sight.

Well, all in good time he would teach them.

He heard people shouting, and saw a

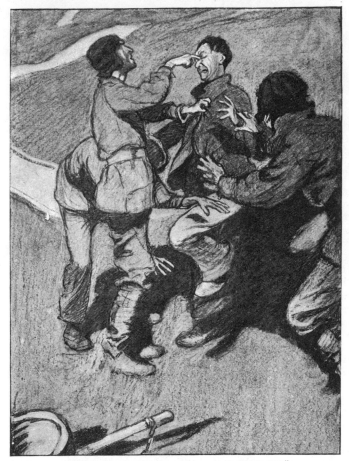

"'CAREFULLY,' HE CRIED, WITH A FINGER IN HIS EYE."

"Bogota," he said. "Bogota. Over the mountain crests."

"A wild man—using wild words," said Pedro. "Did you hear that — *Bogota?* His mind has hardly formed yet. He has only the beginnings of speech."

A little boy nipped his hand. "Bogota!" he said, mockingly.

"Aye! A city to your village. I come from the great world — where men have eyes and see."

"His name's Bogota," they said.

"He stumbled," said Correa — "stumbled twice as we came hither."

"Bring him in to the elders."

And they thrust him suddenly through a doorway into a room as black as pitch, save at the end there faintly glowed a fire. The crowd closed in behind him and shut out all but the faintest glimmer of day, and before he could arrest himself he had fallen headlong over the feet of a seated man. His arm, outflung, struck the face of someone else as he went down; he felt the soft impact of features and heard a cry of anger, and for a moment he struggled against a number of hands that clutched him. It was a one-sided fight. An inkling of the situation came to him and he lay quiet.

"I fell down," he said; "I couldn't see in this pitchy darkness."

There was a pause as if the unseen persons about him tried to understand his words. Then the voice of Correa said: "He is but newly formed. He stumbles as he walks and mingles words that mean nothing with his speech."

Others also said things about him that he heard or understood imperfectly.

"May I sit up?" he asked, in a pause. "I will not struggle against you again."

They consulted and let him rise.

The voice of an older man began to question him, and Nuñez found himself trying to explain the great world out of which he had

number of figures gathering together in the middle roadway of the village.

He found it tax his nerve and patience more than he had anticipated, that first encounter with the population of the Country of the Blind. The place seemed larger as he drew near to it, and the smeared plasterings queerer, and a crowd of children and men and women (the women and girls he was pleased to note had, some of them, quite sweet faces, for all that their eyes were shut and sunken) came about him, holding on to him, touching him with soft, sensitive hands, smelling at him, and listening at every word he spoke. Some of the maidens and children, however, kept aloof as if afraid, and indeed his voice seemed coarse and rude beside their softer notes. They mobbed him. His three guides kept close to him with an effect of proprietorship, and said again and again, "A wild man out of the rocks."

fallen, and the sky and mountains and sight and such-like marvels, to these elders who sat in darkness in the Country of the Blind. And they would believe and understand nothing whatever that he told them, a thing quite outside his expectation. They would not even understand many of his words. For fourteen generations these people had been blind and cut off from all the seeing world ; the names for all the things of sight had faded and changed ; the story of the outer world was faded and changed to a child's story ; and they had ceased to concern themselves with anything beyond the rocky slopes above their circling wall. Blind men of genius had arisen among them and questioned the shreds of belief and tradition they had brought with them from their seeing days, and had dismissed all these things as idle fancies and replaced them with new and saner explanations. Much of their imagination had shrivelled with their eyes, and they had made for themselves new imaginations with their ever more sensitive ears and finger-tips. Slowly Nuñez realized this : that his expectation of wonder and reverence at his origin and his gifts was not to be borne out ; and after his poor attempt to explain sight to them had been set aside as the confused version of a new-made being describing the marvels of his incoherent sensations, he subsided, a little dashed, into listening to their instruction. And the eldest of the blind men explained to him life and philosophy and religion, how that the world (meaning their valley) had been first an empty hollow in the rocks, and then had come first inanimate things without the gift of touch, and llamas and a few other creatures that had little sense, and then men, and at last angels, whom one could hear singing and making fluttering sounds, but whom no one could touch at all, which puzzled Nuñez greatly until he thought of the birds.

He went on to tell Nuñez how this time had been divided into the warm and the cold, which are the blind equivalents of day and night, and how it was good to sleep in the warm and work during the cold, so that now, but for his advent, the whole town of the blind would have been asleep. He said Nuñez must have been specially created to learn and serve the wisdom they had acquired, and that for all his mental incoherency and stumbling behaviour he must have courage and do his best to learn, and at that all the people in the doorway murmured encouragingly. He said the night—for the blind call their day night—was now far gone, and

it behoved everyone to go back to sleep. He asked Nuñez if he knew how to sleep, and Nuñez said he did, but that before sleep he wanted food. They brought him food, llama's milk in a bowl and rough salted bread, and led him into a lonely place to eat out of their hearing, and afterwards to slumber until the chill of the mountain evening roused them to begin their day again. But Nuñez slumbered not at all.

Instead, he sat up in the place where they had left him, resting his limbs and turning the unanticipated circumstances of his arrival over and over in his mind.

Every now and then he laughed, sometimes with amusement and sometimes with indignation.

"Unformed mind !" he said. "Got no senses yet ! They little know they've been insulting their Heaven - sent King and master. . . .

"I see I must bring them to reason.

"Let me think.

"Let me think."

He was still thinking when the sun set.

Nuñez had an eye for all beautiful things, and it seemed to him that the glow upon the snow-fields and glaciers that rose about the valley on every side was the most beautiful thing he had ever seen. His eyes went from that inaccessible glory to the village and irrigated fields, fast sinking into the twilight, and suddenly a wave of emotion took him, and he thanked God from the bottom of his heart that the power of sight had been given him.

He heard a voice calling to him from out of the village.

"Yaho there, Bogota ! Come hither !"

At that he stood up, smiling. He would show these people once and for all what sight would do for a man. They would seek him, but not find him.

"You move not, Bogota," said the voice.

He laughed noiselessly and made two stealthy steps aside from the path.

"Trample not on the grass, Bogota ; that is not allowed."

Nuñez had scarcely heard the sound he made himself. He stopped, amazed.

The owner of the voice came running up the piebald path towards him.

He stepped back into the pathway. "Here I am," he said.

"Why did you not come when I called you ?" said the blind man. "Must you be led like a child ? Cannot you hear the path as you walk ?"

Nuñez laughed. "I can see it," he said.

"There is no such word as *see*," said the blind man, after a pause. "Cease this folly and follow the sound of my feet."

Nuñez followed, a little annoyed.

"My time will come," he said.

"You'll learn," the blind man answered. "There is much to learn in the world."

"Has no one told you, 'In the Country of the Blind the One-Eyed Man is King'?"

"What is blind?" asked the blind man, carelessly, over his shoulder.

Four days passed and the fifth found the King of the Blind still incognito, as a clumsy and useless stranger among his subjects.

It was, he found, much more difficult to proclaim himself than he had supposed, and in the meantime, while he meditated his *coup d'état,* he did what he was told and learnt the manners and customs of the Country of the Blind. He found working and going about at night a particularly irksome thing, and he decided that that should be the first thing he would change.

They led a simple, laborious life, these people, with all the elements of virtue and happiness as these things can be understood by men. They toiled, but not oppressively; they had food and clothing sufficient for their needs; they had days and seasons of rest; they made much of music and singing, and there was love among them and little children. It was marvellous with what confidence and precision they went about their ordered world. Everything, you see, had

"THE GLOW UPON THE SNOW-FIELDS AND GLACIERS WAS THE MOST BEAUTIFUL THING HE HAD EVER SEEN."

been made to fit their needs; each of the radiating paths of the valley area had a constant angle to the others, and was distinguished by a special notch upon its kerbing; all obstacles and irregularities of path or meadow had long since been cleared away; all their methods and procedure arose naturally from their special needs. Their senses had become marvellously acute; they could hear and judge the slightest gesture of a man a dozen paces away—could hear the very beating of his heart. Intonation had long replaced expression with them, and touches gesture, and their work with hoe and spade and fork was as free and confident as garden work can be. Their sense of smell was extraordinarily fine; they could distinguish individual differences as readily as a dog can, and they went about the tending of llamas, who lived among the rocks above and came to the wall for food and shelter, with ease and confidence. It was only when at last Nuñez sought to assert himself that he found how easy and confident their movements could be.

He rebelled only after he had tried persuasion.

He tried at first on several occasions to tell them of sight. "Look you here, you people," he said. "There are things you do not understand in me."

Once or twice one or two of them attended to him; they sat with faces downcast and ears turned intelligently towards him, and he did his best to tell them what it was to see. Among his hearers was a girl, with eyelids less red and sunken than the others, so that one could almost fancy she was hiding eyes, whom especially he hoped to persuade. He spoke of the beauties of sight, of watching the mountains, of the sky and the sunrise, and they heard him with amused incredulity that presently became condemnatory. They told him there were indeed no mountains at all, but that the end of the rocks where the llamas grazed was indeed the end of the world ; thence sprang a cavernous roof of the universe, from which the dew and the avalanches fell ; and when he maintained stoutly the world had neither end nor roof such as they supposed, they said his thoughts were wicked. So far as he could describe sky and clouds and stars to them it seemed to them a hideous void, a terrible blankness in the place of the smooth roof to things in which they believed—it was an article of faith with them that the cavern roof was exquisitely smooth to the touch. He saw that in some manner he shocked them, and gave up that aspect of the matter altogether, and tried to show them the practical value of sight. One morning he saw Pedro in the path called Seventeen and coming towards the central houses, but still too far off for hearing or scent, and he told them as much. "In a little while," he prophesied, "Pedro will be here." An old man remarked that Pedro had no business on path Seventeen, and then, as if in confirmation, that individual as he drew near turned and went transversely into path Ten, and so back with nimble paces towards the outer wall. They mocked Nuñez when Pedro did not arrive, and afterwards, when he asked Pedro questions to clear his character, Pedro denied and outfaced him, and was afterwards hostile to him.

Then he induced them to let him go a long way up the sloping meadows towards the wall with one complaisant individual, and to him he promised to describe all that happened among the houses. He noted certain goings and comings, but the things that really seemed to signify to these people happened inside of or behind the windowless houses—the only things they took note of to test him by—and of those he could see or tell nothing ; and it was after the failure of this attempt, and the ridicule they could not repress, that he resorted to force. He thought of seizing a spade and suddenly smiting one or two of them to earth, and so in fair combat showing the advantage of eyes. He went so far with that resolution as to seize his spade, and then

he discovered a new thing about himself, and that was that it was impossible for him to hit a blind man in cold blood.

He hesitated, and found them all aware that he had snatched up the spade. They stood all alert, with their heads on one side, and bent ears towards him for what he would do next.

"Put that spade down," said one, and he felt a sort of helpless horror. He came near obedience.

Then he had thrust one backwards against a house wall, and fled past him and out of the village.

He went athwart one of their meadows, leaving a track of trampled grass behind his feet, and presently sat down by the side of one of their ways. He felt something of the buoyancy that comes to all men in the beginning of a fight, but more perplexity. He began to realize that you cannot even fight happily with creatures who stand upon a different mental basis to yourself. Far away he saw a number of men carrying spades and sticks come out of the street of houses and advance in a spreading line along the several paths towards him. They advanced slowly, speaking frequently to one another, and ever and again the whole cordon would halt and sniff the air and listen.

The first time they did this Nuñez laughed. But afterwards he did not laugh.

One struck his trail in the meadow grass and came stooping and feeling his way along it.

For five minutes he watched the slow extension of the cordon, and then his vague disposition to do something forthwith became frantic. He stood up, went a pace or so towards the circumferential wall, turned, and went back a little way. There they all stood in a crescent, still and listening.

He also stood still, gripping his spade very tightly in both hands. Should he charge them ?

The pulse in his ears ran into the rhythm of "In the Country of the ·Blind the One-Eyed Man is King !"

Should he charge them ?

He looked back at the high and unclimbable wall behind—unclimbable because of its smooth plastering, but withal pierced with many little doors, and at the approaching line of seekers. Behind these others were now coming out of the street of houses.

Should he charge them ?

"Bogota !" called one. "Bogota ! where are you ?"

He gripped his spade still tighter and

advanced down the meadows towards the place of habitations, and directly he moved they converged upon him. "I'll hit them if they touch me," he swore; "by Heaven, I will. I'll hit." He called aloud, "Look here, I'm going to do what I like in this valley! Do you hear? I'm going to do what I like and go where I like."

They were moving in upon him quickly, groping, yet moving rapidly. It was like

where to run. He ran from the nearest blind man, because it was a horror to hit him. He stopped, and then made a dash to escape from their closing ranks. He made for where a gap was wide, and the men on either side, with a quick perception of the approach of his paces, rushed in on one another. He sprang forward, and then saw he must be caught, and *swish!* the spade had struck. He felt the soft thud of hand

"THEY WERE MOVING IN UPON HIM QUICKLY."

playing blind man's buff with everyone blind-folded except one. "Get hold of him!" cried one. He found himself in the arc of a loose curve of pursuers. He felt suddenly he must be active and resolute.

"You don't understand," he cried, in a voice that was meant to be great and resolute, and which broke. "You are blind and I can see. Leave me alone!"

"Bogota! Put down that spade and come off the grass!"

The last order, grotesque in its urban familiarity, produced a gust of anger. "I'll hurt you," he said, sobbing with emotion. "By Heaven, I'll hurt you! Leave me alone!"

He began to run—not knowing clearly

and arm, and the man was down with a yell of pain, and he was through.

Through! And then he was close to the street of houses again, and blind men, whirling spades and stakes, were running with a sort of reasoned swiftness hither and thither.

He heard steps behind him just in time, and found a tall man rushing forward and swiping at the sound of him. He lost his nerve, hurled his spade a yard wide at this antagonist, and whirled about and fled, fairly yelling as he dodged another.

He was panic-stricken. He ran furiously to and fro, dodging when there was no need to dodge, and, in his anxiety to see on every side of him at once, stumbling. For a moment he was down and they heard his fall. Far away in the circumferential wall a little doorway looked like Heaven, and he set off in a wild rush for it. He did not even look round at his pursuers until it was gained, and he had stumbled across the bridge, clambered a little way among the rocks, to the surprise and dismay of a young llama, who went leaping out of sight, and lay down sobbing for breath.

And so his *coup d'état* came to an end.

He stayed outside the wall of the valley of the blind for two nights and days without food or shelter, and meditated upon the Unexpected. During these meditations he repeated very frequently and always with a profounder note of derision the exploded proverb : " In the Country of the Blind the One-Eyed Man is King." He thought chiefly of ways of fighting and conquering these people, and it grew clear that for him no practicable way was possible. He had no weapons, and now it would be hard to get one.

The canker of civilization had got to him even in Bogota, and he could not find it in himself to go down and assassinate a blind man. Of course, if he did that, he might then dictate terms on the threat of assassinating them all. But——— Sooner or later he must sleep ! . . .

He tried also to find food among the pine trees, to be comfortable under pine boughs while the frost fell at night, and—with less confidence—to catch a llama by artifice in order to try to kill it—perhaps by hammering it with a stone—and so finally, perhaps, to eat some of it. But the llamas had a doubt of him and regarded him with distrustful brown eyes and spat when he drew near. Fear came on him the second day and fits of shivering. Finally he crawled down to the wall of the Country of the Blind and tried to make his terms. He crawled along by the stream, shouting, until two blind men came out to the gate and talked to him.

" I was mad," he said. " But I was only newly made."

They said that was better.

He told them he was wiser now, and repented of all he had done.

Then he wept without intention, for he was very weak and ill now, and they took that as a favourable sign.

They asked him if he still thought he could " *see*."

" No," he said. " That was folly. The word means nothing. Less than nothing ! "

They asked him what was overhead.

" About ten times ten the height of a man

there is a roof above the world—of rock—and very, very smooth. So smooth—so beautifully smooth. . . ." He burst again into hysterical tears. " Before you ask me any more, give me some food or I shall die ! "

He expected dire punishments, but these blind people were capable of toleration. They regarded his rebellion as but one more proof of his general idiocy and inferiority, and after they had whipped him they appointed him to do the simplest and heaviest work they had for anyone to do, and he, seeing no other way of living, did submissively what he was told.

He was ill for some days and they nursed him kindly. That refined his submission. But they insisted on his lying in the dark, and that was a great misery. And blind philosophers came and talked to him of the wicked levity of his mind, and reproved him so impressively for his doubts about the lid of rock that covered their cosmic *casserole* that he almost doubted whether indeed he was not the victim of hallucination in not seeing it overhead.

So Nuñez became a citizen of the Country of the Blind, and these people ceased to be a generalized people and became individualities to him, and familiar to him, while the world beyond the mountains became more and more remote and unreal. There was Yacob, his master, a kindly man when not annoyed ; there was Pedro, Yacob's nephew ; and there was Medina-saroté, who was the youngest daughter of Yacob. She was little esteemed in the world of the blind, because she had a clear-cut face and lacked that satisfying, glossy smoothness that is the blind man's ideal of feminine beauty, but Nuñez thought her beautiful at first, and presently the most beautiful thing in the whole creation. Her closed eyelids were not sunken and red after the common way of the valley, but lay as though they might open again at any moment ; and she had long eyelashes, which were considered a grave disfigurement. And her voice was weak and did not satisfy the acute hearing of the valley swains. So that she had no lover.

There came a time when Nuñez thought that, could he win her, he would be resigned to live in the valley for all the rest of his days.

He watched her ; he sought opportunities of doing her little services, and presently he found that she observed him. Once at a rest-day gathering they sat side by side in the dim starlight, and the music was sweet. His hand came upon hers and he dared to clasp it. Then very tenderly she returned his pressure. And one day, as they were at their meal in the darkness, he felt her hand very softly seeking him, and as it chanced the fire leapt then, and he saw the tenderness of her face.

He sought to speak to her.

He went to her one day when she was sitting in the summer moonlight spinning. The light made her a thing of silver and mystery. He sat down at her feet and told her he loved her, and told her how beautiful she seemed to him. He had a lover's voice,

"HE SAT DOWN AT HER FEET."

he spoke with a tender reverence that came near to awe, and she had never before been touched by adoration. She made him no definite answer, but it was clear his words pleased her.

After that he talked to her whenever he could take an opportunity. The valley became the world for him, and the world beyond the mountains where men lived by day seemed no more than a fairy tale he would some day pour into her ears. Very tentatively and timidly he spoke to her of sight.

Sight seemed to her the most poetical of fancies, and she listened to his description of the stars and the mountains and her own

sweet white-lit beauty as though it was a guilty indulgence. She did not believe, she could only half understand, but she was mysteriously delighted, and it seemed to him that she completely understood.

His love lost its awe and took courage. Presently he was for demanding her of Yacob and the elders in marriage, but she became fearful and delayed. And it was one of her elder sisters who first told Yacob that Medina-saroté and Nuñez were in love.

There was from the first very great opposition to the marriage of Nuñez and Medina-saroté ; not so much because they valued her as because they held him as a being apart, an idiot, incompetent thing below the permissible level of a man. Her sisters opposed it bitterly as bringing discredit on them all ; and old Yacob, though he had formed a sort of liking for his clumsy, obedient serf, shook his head and said the thing could not be. The young men were all angry at the idea of corrupting the race, and one went so far as to revile and strike Nuñez. He struck back. Then for the first time he found an advantage in seeing, even by twilight, and after that fight was over no one was disposed to raise a hand against him. But they still found his marriage impossible.

Old Yacob had a tenderness for his last little daughter, and was grieved to have her weep upon his shoulder.

"You see, my dear, he's an idiot. He has delusions ; he can't do anything right."

"I know," wept Medina-saroté. "But he's better than he was. He's getting better. And he's strong, dear father, and kind—stronger and kinder than any other man in the world. And he loves me—and, father, I love him."

Old Yacob was greatly distressed to find her inconsolable, and, besides—what made it more distressing—he liked Nuñez for many things. So he went and sat in the windowless council-chamber with the other elders and watched the trend of the talk, and said, at the proper time, "He's better than he was. Very likely, some day, we shall find him as sane as ourselves."

Then afterwards one of the elders, who thought deeply, had an idea. He was the great doctor among these people, their medicine-man, and he had a very philosophical and inventive mind, and the idea of curing Nuñez of his peculiarities appealed to him. One day when Yacob was present he returned to the topic of Nuñez. "I have examined Nuñez," he said, "and the case is clearer to me. I think very probably he might be cured."

"That is what I have always hoped," said old Yacob.

"His brain is affected," said the blind doctor.

The elders murmured assent.

"And then he will be sane?"

"Then he will be perfectly sane, and a quite admirable citizen."

"Thank Heaven for science!" said old Yacob, and went forth at once to tell Nuñez of his happy hopes.

But Nuñez's manner of receiving the good news struck him as being cold and disappointing.

"One might think," he said, "from the tone you take that you did not care for my daughter."

It was Medina - saroté who persuaded Nuñez to face the blind surgeons.

" *You* do not want me," he said, "to lose my gift of sight?"

"'HIS BRAIN IS AFFECTED,' SAID THE BLIND DOCTOR."

"Now, *what* affects it?"

"Ah!" said old Yacob.

" *This,*" said the doctor, answering his own question. "Those queer things that are called the eyes, and which exist to make an agreeable depression in the face, are diseased, in the case of Nuñez, in such a way as to affect his brain. They are greatly distended, he has eyelashes, and his eyelids move, and consequently his brain is in a state of constant irritation and distraction."

"Yes?" said old Yacob. "Yes?"

"And I think I may say with reasonable certainty that, in order to cure him completely, all that we need to do is a simple and easy surgical operation—namely, to remove these irritant bodies."

She shook her head.

"My world is sight."

Her head drooped lower.

"There are the beautiful things, the beautiful little things — the flowers, the lichens amidst the rocks, the light and softness on a piece of fur, the far sky with its drifting down of clouds, the sunsets and the stars. And there is *you.* For you alone it is good to have sight, to see your sweet, serene face, your kindly lips, your dear, beautiful hands folded together. . . . It is these eyes of mine you won, these eyes that hold me to you, that these idiots seek. Instead, I must touch you, hear you, and never see you again. I must come under that roof of rock and stone and darkness, that horrible roof under which your imaginations stoop. . . . *No; you* would not have me do that ?"

A disagreeable doubt had arisen in him. He stopped and left the thing a question.

"I wish," she said, "sometimes——" She paused.

"Yes?" said he, a little apprehensively.

"I wish sometimes—you would not talk like that."

"Like what ?"

"I know it's pretty—it's your imagination. I love it, but *now*——"

He felt cold. "*Now ?*" he said, faintly.

She sat quite still.

"You mean —you think— I should be better, better perhaps——"

He was realizing things very swiftly. He felt anger perhaps, anger at the dull course of fate, but also sympathy for her lack of understanding —a sympathy near akin to pity. "*Dear*," he said, and he could see by her whiteness how tensely her spirit pressed against the things she could not say. He put his arms about her, he kissed her ear, and they sat for a time in silence.

"If I were to consent to this?" he said at last, in a voice that was very gentle.

She flung her arms about him, weeping wildly. "Oh, if you would," she sobbed, "if only you would !"

For a week before the operation that was to raise him from his servitude and inferiority to the level of a blind citizen Nuñez knew nothing of sleep, and all through the warm, sunlit hours, while the others slumbered happily, he sat brooding or wandered aim-

"HE HAD A FEW MINUTES WITH MEDINA-SAROTÉ BEFORE SHE WENT APART TO SLEEP."

lessly, trying to bring his mind to bear on his dilemma. He had given his answer, he had given his consent, and still he was not sure. And at last work-time was over, the sun rose in splendour over the golden crests, and his last day of vision began for him. He had a few minutes with Medina-saroté before she went apart to sleep.

"To-morrow," he said, "I shall see no more."

"Dear heart !" she answered, and pressed his hands with all her strength.

"They will hurt you but little," she said ; "and you are going through this pain, you are going through it, dear lover, for *me*. . . . Dear, if a woman's heart and life can do it, I will repay you. My dearest one, my dearest with the tender voice, I will repay."

He was drenched in pity for himself and her.

He held her in his arms, and pressed his lips to hers and looked on her sweet face for the last time. "Good-bye !" he whispered to that dear sight, "good-bye !"

And then in silence he turned away from her.

She could hear his slow retreating footsteps, and something in the rhythm of them threw her into a passion of weeping.

He walked away.

He had fully meant to go to a lonely place where the meadows were beautiful with white narcissus, and there remain until the hour of his sacrifice should come, but as he walked he lifted up his eyes and saw the morning, the morning like an angel in golden armour, marching down the steeps. . .

It seemed to him that before this splendour he and this blind world in the valley, and his love and all, were no more than a pit of sin.

He did not turn aside as he had meant to do, but went on and passed through the wall of the circumference and out upon the rocks, and his eyes were always upon the sunlit ice and snow.

He saw their infinite beauty, and his imagination soared over them to the things beyond he was now to resign for ever !

He thought of that great free world that he was parted from, the world that was his own, and he had a vision of those further slopes, distance beyond distance, with Bogota, a place of multitudinous stirring beauty, a glory by day, a luminous mystery by night, a place of palaces and fountains and statues and white houses, lying beautifully in the middle distance. He thought how for a day or so one might come down through passes drawing ever nearer and nearer to its busy streets and ways. He thought of the river journey, day by day, from great Bogota to the still vaster world beyond, through towns and villages, forest and desert places, the rushing river day by day, until its banks receded and the big steamers came splashing by and one had reached the sea—the limitless sea, with its thousand islands, its thousands of islands, and its ships seen dimly far away in their incessant journeyings round and about that greater world. And there, unpent by mountains, one saw the sky—the sky, not such a disc as one saw it here, but an arch of immeasurable blue, a deep of deeps in which the circling stars were floating. . . .

His eyes began to scrutinize the great curtain of the mountains with a keener inquiry.

For example : if one went so, up that gully and to that chimney there, then one might come out high among those stunted pines that ran round in a sort of shelf and rose still higher and higher as it passed above the gorge. And then ? That talus might be managed. Thence perhaps a climb might be found to take him up to the precipice that came below the snow ; and if that chimney failed, then another farther to the east might serve his purpose better. And then ? Then one would be out upon the amber-lit snow there, and half-way up to the crest of those beautiful desolations. And suppose one had good fortune !

He glanced back at the village, then turned right round and regarded it with folded arms.

He thought of Medina-saroté, and she had become small and remote.

He turned again towards the mountain wall down which the day had come to him.

Then very circumspectly he began his climb.

When sunset came he was no longer climbing, but he was far and high. His clothes were torn, his limbs were blood-stained, he was bruised in many places, but he lay as if he were at his ease, and there was a smile on his face.

From where he rested the valley seemed as if it were in a pit and nearly a mile below. Already it was dim with haze and shadow, though the mountain summits around him were things of light and fire. The mountain summits around him were things of light and fire, and the little things in the rocks near at hand were drenched with light and beauty, a vein of green mineral piercing the grey, a flash of small crystal here and there, a minute, minutely-beautiful orange lichen close beside his face. There were deep, mysterious shadows in the gorge, blue deepening into purple, and purple into a luminous darkness, and overhead was the illimitable vastness of the sky. But he heeded these things no longer, but lay quite still there, smiling as if he were content now merely to have escaped from the valley of the Blind, in which he had thought to be King. And the glow of the sunset passed, and the night came, and still he lay there, under the cold, clear stars.

THE FLOWERING OF THE STRANGE ORCHID

Originally published in *Pearson's Magazine*
April 1905

The Flowering of the Strange Orchid

OF THE

A Tale of an Orchid Enthusiast.

By H. G. Wells.

The buying of orchids always has in it a certain speculative flavour. You have before you the brown shrivelled lump of tissue, and for the rest you must trust your judgment, or the auctioneer, or your good-luck, as your taste may incline. The plant may be moribund or dead, or it may be just a respectable purchase, fair value for your money, or perhaps—for the thing has happened again and again—there slowly unfolds before the delighted eyes of the happy purchaser, day after day, some new variety, some novel richness, a strange twist of the labellum, or some subtler coloration or unexpected mimicry.

Pride, beauty, and profit blossom together on one delicate green spike, and it may be, even immortality. For the new miracle of Nature may stand in need of a new specific name, and what so convenient as that of its discoverer? "Johnsmithia!" There have been worse names.

It was perhaps the hope of some such happy discovery that made Winter-Wedderburn such a frequent attendant at these sales —that hope, and also, maybe, the fact that he had nothing else of the slightest interest to do in the world. He was a shy, lonely, rather ineffectual man, provided with just enough income to keep off the spur of necessity, and not enough nervous energy to make him seek any exacting employments. He might have collected stamps or coins, or translated Horace, or bound books, or invented new species of diatoms. But, as it happened, he grew orchids, and had one ambitious little hothouse.

"I have a fancy," he said over his coffee, "that something is going to happen to me to-day."

He spoke—as he moved and thought—slowly.

"Oh, don't say *that!*" said his house-keeper—who was also his remote cousin. For "something happening" was a euphemism that meant only one thing to her.

"You misunderstand me. I mean nothing unpleasant . . . though what I do mean I scarcely know.

"To-day," he continued, after a pause, "Peters' are going to sell a batch of plants from the Andamans and the Indies. I shall go up and see what they have. It may be I shall buy something good, unawares. That may be it."

He passed his cup for his second cupful of coffee.

"Are these the things collected by that poor young fellow you told me of the other day?" asked his cousin as she filled his cup.

"Yes," he said, and became meditative over a piece of toast.

"Nothing ever does happen to me," he remarked presently, beginning to think aloud.

"I wonder why? Things enough happen to other people. There is Harvey. Only the other week; on Monday he picked up six-pence, on Wednesday his chicks all had the staggers, on Friday his cousin came home from Australia, and on Saturday he broke his ankle. What a whirl of excitement—compared to me."

"I think I would rather be without so much excitement," said his housekeeper. "It can't be good for you."

"I suppose it's troublesome. Still . . . you see, nothing ever happens to me. When I was a little boy I never had accidents. I never fell in love as I grew up. Never married . . . I wonder how it feels to have something happen to you, something really remarkable.

"That orchid-collector was only thirty-six—twenty years younger than myself—when he died. And he had been married twice, and divorced once; he had had malarial fever four times, and once he broke his thigh. He killed a Malay once, and once he was wounded by a poisoned dart. And in the end he was killed by jungle-leeches. It must have all been very troublesome, but then it must have been very interesting, you know—except, perhaps, the leeches."

"I am sure it was not good for him," said the lady, with conviction.

"Perhaps not." And then Wedderburn looked at his watch. "Twenty-three minutes past eight. I am going up by the quarter to twelve train, so that there is plenty of time. I think I shall wear my alpaca jacket—it is quite warm enough—and my grey felt hat and brown shoes. I suppose——"

He glanced out of the window at the serene sky and sunlit garden, and then nervously at his cousin's face.

"I think you had better take an umbrella if you are going to London," she said, in a voice that admitted of no denial. "There's all between here and the station coming back."

When he returned he was in a state of mild excitement. He had made a purchase. It was rarely that he could make up his mind quickly enough to buy, but this time he had done so.

"There are Vandas," he said, "and a Dendrobe and some Palæonophis." He surveyed his purchases lovingly as he consumed his soup. They were laid out on the spotless tablecloth before him, and he was telling his cousin all about them as he slowly meandered through his dinner. It was his custom to live all his visits to London over again in the evening for her and his own entertainment.

"I knew something would happen to-day. And I have bought all these. Some of them—some of them—I feel sure, do you know, that some of them will be remarkable. I don't know how it is, but I feel just as sure as if someone had told me that some of these will turn out remarkable.

"That one"—he pointed to a shrivelled rhizome—"was not identified. It may be a Palæonophis—or it may not. It may be a new species, or even a new genus. And it was the last that poor Batten ever collected."

"I don't like the look of it," said his housekeeper. "It's such an ugly shape."

"To me it scarcely seems to have a shape."

"I don't like those things that stick out," said his housekeeper.

"It shall be put away in a pot to-morrow."

"It looks," said the housekeeper, "like a spider shamming dead."

Wedderburn smiled and surveyed the root with his head on one side. "It is certainly not a pretty lump of stuff. But you can never judge of these things from their dry appearance. It may turn out to be a very beautiful orchid indeed. How busy I shall be to-morrow! I must see to-night just exactly what to do with these things, and to-morrow I shall set to work.

"They found poor Batten lying dead, or dying, in a mangrove swamp—I forget which," he began again presently, "with one of these very orchids crushed up under his body. He had been unwell for some days with some kind of native fever, and I suppose he fainted. These mangrove swamps are very unwholesome. Every drop of blood, they say, was taken out of him by the jungle-leeches. It may be that very plant that cost him his life to obtain."

"I think none the better of it for that."

"Men must work though women may weep," said Wedderburn, with profound gravity.

" Fancy dying away from every comfort in a nasty swamp ! Fancy being ill of fever with nothing to take but chlorodyne and quinine—if men were left to themselves they would live on chlorodyne and quinine—and no one round you but horrible natives ! They say the Andaman islanders are most disgusting wretches—and, anyhow, they can scarcely make good nurses, not having the necessary training. And just for people in England to have orchids ! "

" I don't suppose it was comfortable, but some men seem to enjoy that kind of thing," said Wedderburn. " Anyhow, the natives of his party were sufficiently civilised to take care of all his collection until his colleague, who was an ornithologist, came back again from the interior ; though they could not tell the species of the orchid and had let it wither. And it makes these things more interesting."

" It makes them disgusting. I should be afraid of some of the malaria clinging to them. And just think, there has been a dead body lying across that ugly thing ! I never thought of that before. There ! I declare I cannot eat another mouthful of dinner ! "

" I will take them off the table if you like, and put them in the window-seat. I can see them just as well there."

The next few days he was indeed singularly busy in his steamy little hot-house, fussing about with charcoal, lumps of teak, moss, and all the other mysteries of the orchid cultivator. He considered he was having a wonderfully eventful time. In the evening he would talk about these new orchids to his friends, and over and over again he reverted to his expectation of something strange.

Several of the Vandas and the Dendrobium died under his care, but presently the strange orchid began to show signs of life. He was delighted and took his housekeeper right away from jam-making to see it at once, directly he made the discovery.

" That is a bud," he said, " and presently there will be a lot of leaves there, and those little things coming out here are aërial rootlets."

" They look to me like little white fingers poking out of the brown," said his housekeeper. " I don't like them."

" Why not ? "

" I don't know. They look like fingers trying to get at you. I can't help my likes and dislikes."

" I don't know for certain, but I don't *think* there are any orchids I know that have aërial rootlets quite like that. It may be my fancy, of course. You see they are a little flattened at the ends."

" I don't like 'em," said his housekeeper, suddenly shivering and turning away. " I know it's very silly of me—and I'm very sorry, particularly as you like the thing so much. But I can't help thinking of that corpse."

" But it may not be that particular plant. That was merely a guess of mine."

His housekeeper shrugged her shoulders. " Anyhow I don't like it," she said.

Wedderburn felt a little hurt at her dislike to the plant. But that did not prevent his talking to her about orchids generally, and this orchid in particular, whenever he felt inclined.

" There are such queer things about orchids," he said one day ; " such possibilities of surprises. You know, Darwin studied their fertilisation, and showed that the whole structure of an ordinary orchid flower was contrived in order that moths might carry the pollen from plant to plant. Well, it seems that there are lots of orchids known the flower of which cannot possibly be used for fertilisation in that way. Some of the Cypripediums, for instance ; there are no insects known that can possibly fertilise them, and some of them have never been found with seed."

" But how do they form new plants ? "

" By runners and tubers, and that kind of outgrowth. That is easily explained. The puzzle is, what are the flowers for ?

" Very likely," he added, " *my* orchid may be something extraordinary in that way. If so, I shall study it. I have often thought of making researches as Darwin did. But hitherto I have not found the time, or something else has happened to prevent it. The leaves are beginning to unfold now. I do wish you would come and see them ! "

But she said that the orchid-house was so hot it gave her the headache. She had seen the plant once again, and the aërial rootlets, which were now some of them more than a foot long, had unfortunately reminded her of tentacles reaching out after something ; and they got into her dreams, growing after her with incredible rapidity. So that she had settled to her entire satisfaction that she would not see that plant again, and Wedderburn had to admire its leaves alone. They were of the ordinary broad form, and a deep, glossy green, with splashes and dots of deep red towards the base. He knew of no other leaves quite like them.

The plant was placed on a low bench near the thermometer, and close by was a simple arrangement by which a tap dripped on the hot-water pipes and kept the air steamy. And he spent his afternoons now with some regularity meditating on the approaching flowering of this strange plant.

And at last the great thing happened. Directly he entered the little glass house he knew that the spike had burst out, although his great *Palæonophis Lowii* hid the corner where his new darling stood. There was a new odour in the air—a rich, intensely sweet scent, that overpowered every other in that crowded, steaming little greenhouse.

Directly he noticed this he hurried down to the strange orchid. And, behold ! the trailing green spikes bore now three great splashes of blossom, from which this overpowering sweetness proceeded. He stopped before them in an ecstasy of admiration.

The flowers were white, with streaks of golden orange upon the petals ; the heavy labellum was coiled into an intricate projection, and a wonderful bluish purple mingled there with the gold. He could see at once that the genus was altogether a new one. And the insufferable scent ! How hot the place was ! The blossoms swam before his eyes.

He would see if the temperature was right. He made a step towards the thermometer. Suddenly everything appeared unsteady. The bricks on the floor were dancing up and down. Then the white blossoms, the green leaves behind them, the whole greenhouse, seemed to sweep sideways, and then in a curve upward.

* * * * *

At half-past four his cousin made the tea, according to their invariable custom. But Wedderburn did not come in for his tea.

"He is worshipping that horrid orchid," she told herself, and waited ten minutes. "His watch must have stopped. I will go and call him."

She went straight to the hothouse, and, opening the door, called his name. There was no reply. She noticed that the air was very close, and loaded with an intense perfume. Then she saw something lying on the bricks between the hot-water pipes.

For a minute, perhaps, she stood motionless.

He was lying, face upward, at the foot of the strange orchid. The tentacle-like aërial rootlets no longer swayed freely in the air, but were crowded together, a tangle of grey ropes, and stretched tight, with their ends closely applied to his chin and neck and hands.

She did not understand. Then she saw from one of the exultant tentacles upon his cheek there trickled a little thread of blood.

With an inarticulate cry she ran towards him, and tried to pull him away from the leech-like suckers. She snapped two of these tentacles, and their sap dripped red.

Then the overpowering scent of the blossom began to make her head reel. How they clung to him ! She tore at the tough ropes, and he and the white inflorescence swam about her. She felt she was fainting, knew she must not. She left him and hastily opened the nearest door, and, after she had panted for a moment in the fresh air, she had a brilliant inspiration. She caught up a flower-pot and smashed in the windows at the end of the greenhouse. Then she re-entered. She tugged now with renewed strength at Wedderburn's motionless body, and brought the strange orchid crashing to the floor. It still clung with the grimmest tenacity to its victim. In a frenzy, she lugged it and him into the open air.

Then she thought of tearing through the sucker rootlets one by one, and in another minute she had released him and was dragging him away from the horror.

He was white and bleeding from a dozen circular patches.

The odd-job man was coming up the garden, amazed at the smashing of glass, and saw her emerge, hauling the inanimate body with red-stained hands. For a moment he thought impossible things.

"Bring some water!" she cried, and her voice dispelled his fancies. When, with unnatural alacrity, he returned with the water, he found her weeping with excitement, and with Wedderburn's head upon her knee, wiping the blood from his face.

"What's the matter?" said Wedderburn, opening his eyes feebly, and closing them again at once.

"Go and tell Annie to come out here to me, and then go for Dr. Haddon at once," she said to the odd-job man so soon as he had brought the water; and added, seeing he hesitated: "I will tell you all about it when you come back."

Presently Wedderburn opened his eyes again, and, seeing that he was troubled by the puzzle of his position, she explained to him: "You fainted in the hothouse."

"And the orchid?"

"I will see to that," she said.

She tugged with renewed strength at Wedderburn's motionless body, and brought the strange orchid crashing to the floor.

Wedderburn had lost a good deal of blood, but beyond that he had suffered no very great injury. They gave him brandy mixed with some pink extract of meat, and carried him upstairs to bed. His housekeeper told her incredible story in fragments to Dr. Haddon. "Come to the orchid-house and see," she said.

The cold outer air was blowing in through the open door, and the sickly perfume was almost dispelled. Most of the torn aërial rootlets lay already withered amidst a number of dark stains upon the bricks. The stem of the inflorescence was broken by the fall of the plant, and the flowers were growing limp and brown at the edges of the petals. The doctor stooped towards it, then saw that one of the aërial rootlets still stirred feebly, and hesitated.

The next morning the strange orchid still lay there, black now and putrescent. The door banged intermittently in the morning breeze, and all the array of Wedderburn's orchids was shrivelled and prostrate. But Wedderburn himself was bright and garrulous upstairs in the glory of his strange adventure.

AEPYORNIS ISLAND

Originally published in *Pearson's Magazine*
February 1905

ÆPYORNIS ISLAND

An Unvarnished Narrative.

By H. G. Wells.

The man with the scarred face leant over the table and looked at my bundle.

" Orchids ? " he asked.

" A few," I said.

"Cypripediums," he said.

"Chiefly," said I.

"Anything new ? I thought not. *I* did these islands twenty-five—twenty-seven years ago. If you find anything new here—well, it's brand new. I didn't leave much."

" I'm not a collector," said I.

" I was young then," he went on. " Lord ! how I used to fly round." He seemed to take my measure. " I was in the East Indies two years, and in Brazil seven. Then I went to Madagascar."

" I know a few explorers by name," I said, anticipating a yarn. " Whom did you collect for ? "

" Dawsons'. I wonder if you've heard the name of Butcher ever ? "

" Butcher—Butcher ? " The name seemed vaguely present in my memory ; then I recalled *Butcher* v. *Dawson*. " Why ! " said I, " you are the man who sued them for four years' salary—got cast away on a desert island. . . . "

" Your servant," said the man with the scar, bowing. " Funny case, wasn't it ? Here was me, making a little fortune on that island, doing nothing for it neither, and them quite unable to give me notice. It often used to amuse me thinking over it while I was there. I did calculations of it—big—all over the blessed atoll in ornamental figuring."

" How did it happen ? " said I. " I don't rightly remember the case."

" Well. . . . You've heard of the Æpyornis ? "

" Rather. Andrews was telling me of a new species he was working on only a month or so ago. Just before I sailed. They've got a thigh bone, it seems, nearly a yard long. Monster the thing must have been ! "

" I believe you," said the man with the scar. " It *was* a monster. Sinbad's roc was just a legend of 'em. But when did they find these bones ? "

" Several years ago—'91, I fancy. Why ? "

" Why ? Because *I* found 'em—Lord !— it's nearly twenty years ago. If Dawsons hadn't been silly about that salary they might have made a perfect ring in 'em. . . . *I* couldn't help the infernal boat going adrift."

He paused. " I suppose it's the same place. A kind of swamp about ninety miles north of Antananarivo. Do you happen to know ? You have to go to it along the coast by boats. You don't happen to remember, perhaps ? "

"I don't. I fancy Andrews said something about a swamp."

"It must be the same. It's on the east coast. And somehow there's something in the water that keeps things from decaying. Like creosote it smells. It reminded me of Trinidad. Did they get any more eggs? Some of the eggs I found were a foot and a half long. The swamp goes circling round, you know, and cuts off this bit. It's mostly salt, too. Well. . . . What a time I had of it! I found the things quite by accident. We went for eggs, me and two native chaps in one of those rum canoes all tied together, and found the bones at the same time. We had a tent and provisions for four days, and we pitched on one of the firmer places. To think of it brings that odd tarry smell back even now. It's funny work. You go probing into the mud with iron rods, you know. Usually the egg gets smashed.

"I wonder how long it is since these Æpyornises really lived. The missionaries say the natives have legends about when they were alive, but I never heard any such stories myself.* But certainly those eggs we got were as fresh as if they had been new laid. Fresh! Carrying them down to the boat, one of my nigger chaps dropped one on a rock and it smashed. How I lammed into the beggar! But sweet it was, as if it was new laid, not even smelly, and its mother dead these four hundred years, perhaps. Said a centipede had bit him.

"However, I'm getting off the straight with the story. It had taken us all day to dig into the slush and get these eggs out unbroken, and we were all covered with beastly black mud, and naturally I was cross. So far as I know they were the only eggs that have ever been got out not even cracked. I went afterwards to see the ones they have at the Natural History Museum in London; all of them were cracked and just stuck together like a mosaic, and bits missing. Mine were perfect, and I meant to blow them when I got back. Naturally I was annoyed at the silly duffer dropping three hours' work just on account of a centipede. I hit him about rather."

* No European is known to have seen a live Æpyornis, with the doubtful exception of Mac-Andrew, who visited Madagascar in 1745.—H. G. W.

The man with the scar took out a clay pipe. I placed my pouch before him. He filled up absent-mindedly.

"How about the others? Did you get those home? I don't remember——"

"That's the queer part of the story. I had three others. Perfectly fresh eggs. Well, we put 'em in the boat, and then I went up to the tent to make some coffee, leaving my two heathens down by the beach—the one fooling about with his sting and the other helping him. It never occurred to me that the beggars would take advantage of the peculiar position I was in to pick a quarrel. But I suppose the centipede poison and the kicking I had given him had upset the one—he was always a cantankerous sort—and he persuaded the other.

"I remember I was sitting and smoking and boiling up the water over a spirit-lamp business I used to take on these expeditions. Incidentally I was admiring the swamp under the sunset. All black and blood-red it was, in streaks—a beautiful sight. And up beyond the land rose grey and hazy to the hills, and the sky behind them red, like a furnace mouth. And fifty yards behind the back of me were these blessed heathen—regardless of the tranquil air of things—plotting to cut off with the boat and leave me all alone with three days' provisions and a canvas tent, and nothing to drink whatsoever, beyond a little keg of water.

"I heard a kind of yelp behind me, and there they were in this canoe affair—it wasn't properly a boat—and, perhaps, twenty yards from land. I realised what was up in a moment. My gun was in the tent, and, besides, I had no bullets—only duck shot. They knew that. But I had a little revolver in my pocket, and I pulled that out as I ran down to the beach.

"'Come back!' says I, flourishing it.

"They jabbered something at me, and the man that broke the egg jeered. I aimed at the other—because he was unwounded and had the paddle, and I missed. They laughed. However, I wasn't beat. I knew I had to keep cool, and I tried him again and made him jump with the whang of it. He didn't laugh that time. The third time I got his head, and over he went, and the paddle with him. It was a precious lucky shot for a revolver. I reckon it was fifty yards. He went right under. I don't know if he was shot, or simply stunned and drowned. Then I began to shout to the other chap to come back, but he huddled up in the canoe and refused to answer. So I fired out my revolver at him and never got near him.

"I felt a precious fool, I can tell you. There I was on this rotten, black beach, flat swamp all behind me, and the flat sea, cold after the sunset, and just this black canoe drifting steadily out to sea. I tell you I cursed Dawsons' and Jamrachs' and Museums and all the rest of it just to rights. I bawled to this nigger to come back, until my voice went up into a scream.

"There was nothing for it but to swim after him and take my luck with the sharks. So I opened my clasp-knife and put it in my mouth, and took off my clothes and waded in. As soon as I was in the water I lost sight of the canoe, but I aimed, as I judged, to head it off. I hoped the man in it was too bad to navigate it, and that it would keep on drifting in the same direction. Presently it came up over the horizon again to the south-westward about. The after glow of sunset was well over now and the dim of night creeping up. The stars were coming through the blue. I swam like a champion, though my legs and arms were soon aching.

'However, I came up to him by the time the stars were fairly out. As it got darker I began to see all manner of glowing things in the water—phosphorescence, you know. At times it made me giddy. I hardly knew which was stars and which was phosphorescence, and whether I was swimming on my head or my heels. The canoe was as black as sin, and the ripple under the bows like liquid fire.

"I was naturally chary of clambering up into it. I was anxious to see what he was up to first. He seemed to be lying cuddled up in a lump in the bows, and the stern was all out of water. The thing kept turning round slowly as it drifted—kind of waltzing, don't you know. I went to the stern and pulled it down, expecting him to wake up. Then I began to clamber in with my knife in my hand, ready for a rush. But he never

stirred. So there I sat in the stern of the little canoe, drifting away over the calm phosphorescent sea, and with all the host of the stars above me, waiting for something to happen.

"After a long time I called him by name, but he never answered. I was too tired to take any risks by going along to him. So we sat there. I fancy I dozed once or twice. When the dawn came I saw he was as dead as a doornail and all puffed up and purple. My three eggs and the bones were lying in the middle of the canoe, and the keg of water and some coffee and biscuits wrapped in a Cape *Argus* by his feet, and a tin of methylated spirit underneath him. There was no paddle, nor, in fact, anything except the spirit-tin that one could use as one, so I settled to drift until I was picked up. I held an inquest on him, brought in a verdict against some snake, scorpion, or centipede unknown, and sent him overboard.

"After that I had a drink of water and a few biscuits, and took a look round. I suppose a man low down as I was don't see very far; leastways, Madagascar was clean out of sight, and any trace of land at all. I saw a sail going south-westward—looked like a schooner, but her hull never came up. Presently the sun got high in the sky and began to beat down upon me. Lord! It pretty near made my brains boil. I tried dipping my head in the sea, but after a while my eye fell on the Cape *Argus*, and I lay down flat in the canoe and spread this over me. Wonderful things, these newspapers! I never read one through thoroughly before, but it's odd what you get up to when you're alone, as I was. I suppose I read that blessed old Cape *Argus* twenty times. The pitch in the canoe simply reeked with the heat, and rose up into big blisters.

"I drifted ten days," said the man with the scar. "It's a little thing in the telling, isn't it? Every day was like the last. Except in the morning and the evening I never kept a look-out even—the blaze was so infernal. I didn't see a sail after the first three days, and those I saw took no notice of me. About the sixth night a ship went by scarcely half-a-mile away from me, with all its lights ablaze and its ports open, looking like a big firefly.

There was music aboard. I stood up and shouted and screamed at it.

"The second day I broached one of the Æpyornis eggs, scraped the shell away at the end bit by bit, and tried it, and I was glad to find it was good enough to eat. A bit flavoury—not bad, I mean—but with something of the taste of a duck's egg. There was a kind of circular patch, about six inches across, on one side of the yolk, and with streaks of blood and a white mark like a ladder in it that I thought queer, but I did not understand what this meant at the time, and I wasn't inclined to be particular. The egg lasted me three days, with biscuits and a drink of water. I chewed coffee berries too—invigorating stuff. The second egg I opened about the eighth day, and it scared me."

The man with the scar paused. "Yes," he said, "developing.

"I dare say you find it hard to believe. *I* did, with the thing before me. There the egg had been, sunk in that cold black mud, perhaps three hundred years. But there was no mistaking it. There was the—what is it? —embryo, with its big head and curved back, and its heart beating under its throat, and the yolk shrivelled up and the great membranes spreading inside of the shell and all over the yolk. Here was I hatching out the eggs of one of the biggest of all extinct birds, in a little canoe in the midst of the Indian Ocean. If old Dawson had known that! It was worth four years' salary. What do *you* think?

"However, I had to eat that precious thing up, every bit of it, before I sighted the reef, and some of the mouthfuls were beastly unpleasant. I left the third one alone. I held it up to the light, but the shell was too thick for me to get any notion of what might be happening inside; and though I fancied I heard blood pulsing, it might have been the rustle in my own ears, like what you listen to in a sea-shell.

"Then came the atoll. Came out of the sunrise, as it were, suddenly, close up to me. I drifted straight towards it until I was about half-a-mile from the shore, not more, and then the current took a turn, and I had to paddle as hard as I could with my hands and bits of the Æpyornis shell to make the place. However, I got there. It was just a common

atoll about four miles round, with a few trees growing and a spring in one place, and the lagoon full of parrot-fish. I took the egg ashore and put it in a good place well above the tide lines and in the sun, to give it all the chance I could, and pulled the canoe up safe, and loafed about prospecting.

"It's rum how dull an atoll is. As soon as I had found a spring all the interest seemed to vanish. When I was a kid I thought nothing could be finer or more adventurous than the Robinson Crusoe business, but that place was as monotonous as a book of sermons. I went round finding eatable things and generally thinking; but I tell you I was bored to death before the first day was out. It shows my luck—the very day I landed the weather changed. A thunderstorm went by to the north and flicked its wing over the island, and in the night there came a drencher and a howling wind slap over us. It wouldn't have taken much, you know, to upset that canoe.

"I was sleeping under the canoe, and the egg was luckily among the sand higher up the beach, and the first thing I remember was a sound like a hundred pebbles hitting the boat at once, and a rush of water over my body. I'd been dreaming of Antananarivo, and I sat up and halloaed to Intoshi to ask what the blazes was up, and clawed out at the chair where the matches used to be.

"Then I remembered where I was. There were phosphorescent waves rolling up as if they meant to eat me, and all the rest of the night as black as pitch. The air was simply yelling. The clouds seemed down on your head almost, and the rain fell as if heaven were sinking and they were baling out the waters above the firmament. One great roller came writhing at me like a fiery serpent, and I bolted. Then I thought of the canoe, and ran down to it as the water went hissing back again; but the thing had gone. I wondered about the egg then, and felt my way to it. It was all right and well out of reach of the maddest waves, so I sat down beside it and cuddled it for company. Lord! what a night that was!

"The storm was over before the morning. There wasn't a rag of cloud left in the sky when the dawn came, and all along the beach there were bits of plank scattered—which was the disarticulated skeleton, so to speak, of my canoe. However, that gave me something to do, for taking advantage of two of the trees being together, I rigged up a kind of storm-shelter with these vestiges. And that day the egg hatched.

"Hatched, sir, when my head was pillowed on it and I was asleep. I heard a whack and felt a jar and sat up, and there was the end of the egg pecked out and a rum little brown head looking out at me. 'Lord!' I said, ' you're welcome ;' and with a little difficulty he came out.

"He was a nice friendly little chap, at first, about the size of a small hen—very much like most other young birds, only bigger. His plumage was a dirty brown to begin with, with a sort of grey scab that fell off it very soon, and scarcely feathers—a kind of downy hair. I can hardly express how pleased I was to see him. I tell you Robinson Crusoe don't make near enough of his loneliness. But here was interesting company. He looked at me and winked his eye from the front backwards, like a hen, and gave a chirp and began to peck about at once, as though being hatched three hundred years too late was just nothing.

"' Glad to see you, Man Friday !' says I, for I had naturally settled that he was to be called Man Friday if ever he was hatched, as soon as I found the egg in the canoe had developed. I was a bit anxious about his feed, so I gave him a lump of raw parrot-fish at once. He took it, and opened his beak for more. I was glad of that, for, under the circumstances, if he'd been at all fanciful, I should have had to eat him after all.

"You'd be surprised what an interesting bird that Æpyornis chick was. He followed me about from the very beginning. He used to stand by me and watch while I fished in the lagoon, and go shares in anything I caught. And he was sensible, too. There were nasty green warty things, like pickled gherkins, used to lie about on the beach, and he tried one of these and it upset him. He never even looked at any of them again.

"And he grew. You could almost see

"Though I fancied I heard blood pulsing, it might have been the rustle in my own ears."

him grow. And as I was never much of a society man, his quiet, friendly ways suited me to a T. For nearly two years we were as happy as we could be on that island. I had no business worries, for I knew my salary was mounting up at Dawsons'. We could see a sail now and then, but nothing ever came near us. I amused myself, too, by decorating the island with designs worked in sea-urchins and fancy shells of various kinds.

" I put Æpyornis Island all round the place very nearly, in big letters, like what you see done with coloured stones at railway stations in the old country, and mathematical calculations and drawings of various sorts. And I used to lie watching the blessed bird stalking round and growing, growing ; and think how I could make a living out of him by showing him about if I ever got taken off.

" After his first moult he began to get handsome, with a crest and a blue wattle, and a lot of green feathers in his tail. And then I used to puzzle whether Dawsons' had any right to claim him or not. In stormy weather and in the rainy season we lay snug under the shelter I had made out of the old canoe, and I used to tell him lies about my friends at home. And after a storm we would go round the island together to see if there was any drift. It was a kind of idyll, you might say. If only I had had some tobacco it would have been simply just like Heaven.

" It was about the end of the second year our little paradise went wrong. Friday was then about fourteen feet high to the bill of him, with a big, broad head like the end of a pickaxe, and two huge brown eyes with yellow rims, set together like a man's—not out of sight of each other like a hen's. His plumage was fine—none of the half-mourning style of your ostrich—more like a cassowary as far as colour and texture go. And then it was he began to cock his comb at me and give himself airs, and show signs of a nasty temper. . . . .

" At last came a time when my fishing had been rather unlucky, and he began to hang about me in a queer, meditative way. I thought he might have been eating sea-cucumbers or something, but it was really just discontent on his part. I was hungry, too, and when at last I landed a fish I wanted it for myself. Tempers were short that morning on both sides. He pecked at it and grabbed it, and I gave him a whack on the head to make him leave go. And at that he went for me. Lord ! . . .

" He gave me this in the face." The man indicated his scar. " Then he kicked me. It was like a cart-horse. I got up, and seeing he hadn't finished, I started off full tilt with my arms doubled up over my face. But he ran on those gawky legs of his faster than a racehorse, and kept landing out at me with sledge-hammer kicks, and bringing his pick-axe down on the back of my head. I made for the lagoon, and went in up to my neck. He stopped at the water, for he hated getting his feet wet, and began to make a shindy, something like a peacock's, only hoarser. He started strutting up and down the beach. I'll admit I felt small to see this blessed fossil lording it there. And my head and face were all bleeding, and—well, my body just one jelly of bruises.

" I decided to swim across the lagoon and leave him alone for a bit, until the affair blew over. I shinned up the tallest palm-tree, and sat there thinking of it all. I don't suppose I ever felt so hurt by anything before or since. It was the brutal ingratitude of the creature. I'd been more than a brother to him. I'd hatched him, educated him. A great gawky, out-of-date bird ! And me a human being—heir of the ages and all that.

" I thought after a time he'd begin to see things in that light himself, and feel a little sorry for his behaviour. I thought if I were to catch some nice little bits of fish, perhaps, and go to him presently in a casual kind of way, and offer them to him, he might do the sensible thing. It took me some time to learn how unforgiving and cantankerous an extinct bird can be. Malice !

" I won't tell you all the little devices I tried to get that bird round again. I simply can't. It makes my cheek burn with shame even now to think of the snubs and buffets I had from this infernal curiosity. I tried violence. I chucked lumps of coral at him

"He ran on those gawky legs of his faster than a racehorse, and kept landing out at me with sledge-hammer kicks."

from a safe distance, but he only swallowed them. I shied my open knife at him and almost lost it, though it was too big for him to swallow. I tried starving him out and struck fishing, but he took to picking along the beach at low water after worms, and rubbed along on that.

"Half my time I spent up to my neck in the lagoon, and the rest up the palm-trees. One of them was scarcely high enough, and when he caught me up it he had a regular Bank Holiday with the calves of my legs. It got unbearable. I don't know if you have ever tried sleeping up a palm-tree. It gave me the most horrible nightmares. Think of the shame of it, too! Here was this extinct animal mooning about my island like a sulky duke, and me not allowed to rest the sole of my foot on the place. I used to cry with weariness and vexation. I told him straight that I didn't mean to be chased about a desert island by any infernal anachronisms. I told him to go and peck a navigator of his own age. But he only snapped his beak at me. Great ugly bird—all legs and neck!

"I shouldn't like to say how long that went on altogether. I'd have killed him sooner if I'd known how. However, I hit on a way of settling him at last. It is a South American dodge. I joined all my fishing-lines together with stems of seaweed and things, and made a stoutish string, perhaps twelve yards in length or more, and I fastened two lumps of coral rock to the ends of this. It took me some time to do, because every now and then I had to go into the lagoon or up a tree as the fancy took me. This I whirled rapidly round my head, and then let it go at him. The first time I missed, but the next time the string caught his legs beautifully, and wrapped round them again and again. Over he went. I threw it standing waist-deep in the lagoon, and as soon as he went down I was out of the water and sawing at his neck with my knife. . . .

"I don't like to think of that even now. I felt like a murderer while I did it, though my anger was hot against him. When I stood over him and saw him bleeding on the white sand, and his beautiful great legs and neck writhing in his last agony . . . Pah!

"With that tragedy loneliness came upon me like a curse. Good lord! you can't imagine how I missed that bird. I sat by his corpse and sorrowed over him, and shivered as I looked round the desolate reef. I thought of what a jolly little bird he had been when he was hatched, and of a thousand pleasant tricks he had played before he went wrong. I thought if I'd only wounded him I might have nursed him round into a better understanding. If I'd had any means of digging into the coral rock I'd have buried him. I felt exactly as if he was human. As it was, I couldn't think of eating him, so I put him in the lagoon, and the little fishes picked him clean. I didn't even save the feathers. Then one day a chap cruising about in a yacht had a fancy to see if my atoll still existed.

"He didn't come a moment too soon, for I was about sick enough of the desolation of it, and only hesitating whether I should walk out into the sea and finish up the business that way, or fall back on the green things. . . .

"I sold the bones to a man named Winslow—a dealer near the British Museum, and he says that he sold them to old Havers. It seems Havers didn't understand they were extra large, and it was only after his death they attracted attention. They called 'em Æpyornis—what was it?"

"*Æpyornis vastus*," said I. "It's funny, the very thing was mentioned to me by a friend of mine. When they found an Æpyornis, with a thigh a yard long, they thought they had reached the top of the scale, and called him *Æpyornis maximus*. Then someone turned up another thigh-bone four feet six or more, and that they called *Æpyornis Titan*. Then your *vastus* was found after old Havers died, in his collection, and then a *vastissimus* turned up."

"Winslow was telling me as much," said the man with the scar. "If they get any more Æpyornises, he reckons some scientific swell will go and burst a blood-vessel. But it was a queer thing to happen to a man; wasn't it—altogether?"

THE FIRST MEN IN THE MOON

Originally published in *The Strand Magazine*
December 1900–August 1901

The First Men in the Moon.

By H. G. Wells.

MENIPPUS: "Three thousand stadia from the earth to the moon. . . . Marvel not, my comrade, if I appear talking to you on superterrestrial and aerial topics. The long and the short of the matter is that I am running over the order of a Journey I have lately made."—LUCIAN'S ICAROMENIPPUS.

CHAPTER I.

MR. BEDFORD MEETS MR. CAVOR AT LYMPNE.

 AS I sit down to write here, amidst the shadows of vine leaves under the blue sky of Southern Italy, it comes to me with a certain quality of astonishment that my participation in these amazing adventures of Mr. Cavor was, after all, the outcome of the purest accident. It might have been anyone. I fell into these things at a time when I thought myself removed from the slightest possibility of disturbing experiences. I had gone to Lympne because I had imagined it the most uneventful place in the world. "Here, at any rate," said I, "I shall find peace and a chance to work!"

And this book is the sequel. So utterly at variance is Destiny with all the little plans of men.

I may perhaps mention here that very recently I had come an ugly cropper in certain business enterprises. Sitting now surrounded by all the circumstances of wealth, there is a luxury in admitting my extremity. I can admit even that to a certain extent my disasters were conceivably of my own making. It may be there are directions in which I have some capacity, but the conduct of business operations is not among these. In those days I was young. I am young still in years, but the things that have happened to me have rubbed something of the youth from my mind. Whether they have brought any wisdom to light below it is a more doubtful matter.

It is scarcely necessary to go into the details of the speculations that landed me at Lympne, in Kent. Nowadays even about business transactions there is a strong spice of adventure. I took risks. In these things there is invariably a certain amount of give and take, and it fell to me finally to do the giving—reluctantly enough. Even when I had got out of everything one cantankerous creditor saw fit to be malignant. It seemed to me at last that there was nothing for it but to write a play, unless I wanted to drudge for my living as a clerk. I know there is nothing a man can do outside legitimate business transactions that has such opulent possibilities. I had, indeed, got into the habit of regarding this unwritten drama as a convenient little reserve put by for a rainy day. That rainy day had come.

I soon discovered that writing a play was a longer business than I had supposed—at first I had reckoned ten days for it—and it was to have a *pied-à-terre* while it was in hand that I came to Lympne. I reckoned

"I CAME TO LYMPNE."

myself lucky in getting that little bungalow. I got it on a three years' agreement. I put in a few sticks of furniture, and while the play was in hand I did my own cooking. My cooking would have shocked Mrs. Bond. I had a coffee-pot, a saucepan for eggs and one for potatoes, and a frying-pan for sausages and bacon. Such was the simple apparatus of my comfort. For the rest I laid in an eighteen-gallon cask of beer on credit, and a trustful baker came each day. It was not, perhaps, in the style of Sybaris, but I have had worse times.

Certainly if anyone wants solitude the place is Lympne. It is in the clay part of Kent, and my bungalow stood on the edge of an old sea cliff and stared across the flats of Romney Marsh at the sea. In very wet weather the place is almost inaccessible, and I have heard that at times the postman used to traverse the more succulent portions of his route with boards upon his feet. I never saw him doing so, but I can quite imagine it. Outside the doors of the few cottages and houses that make up the present village big birch besoms are stuck to wipe off the worst of the clay, which will give some idea of the texture of the district. I doubt if the place would be there at all if it were not a fading memory of things gone for ever. It was the big port of England in Roman times, Portus Lemanus, and now the sea is four miles away. All down the steep hill are boulders and masses of Roman brickwork, and from it old Watling Street, still paved in places, starts like an arrow to the north. I used to stand on the hill and think of it all—the galleys and legions, the captives and officials, the women and traders, the speculators like myself, all the swarm and tumult that came clanking in and out of the harbour. And now just a few lumps of rubble on a grassy slope and a sheep or two—and me! And where the port had been were the levels of the marsh, sweeping round in a broad curve to distant Dungeness, and dotted here and there with tree clumps and the church towers of old mediæval towns that are following Lemanus now towards extinction.

That outlook on the marsh was, indeed, one of the finest views I have ever seen. I

suppose Dungeness was fifteen miles away; it lay like a raft on the sea, and farther westward were the hills by Hastings under the setting sun. Sometimes they hung close and clear, sometimes they were faded and low, and often the drift of the weather took them clean out of sight. And all the nearer parts of the marsh were laced and lit by ditches and canals.

The window at which I worked looked over the skyline of this crest, and it was from this window that I first set eyes on Cavor. It was just as I was struggling with my scenario, holding down my mind to the sheer hard work of it, and, naturally enough, he arrested my attention.

The sun had set, the sky was a vivid tranquillity of green and yellow, and against that he came out black, the oddest little figure.

He was a short, round-bodied, thin-legged little man with a jerky quality in his motions; he had seen fit to clothe his extraordinary mind in a cricket cap, an overcoat, and cycling knickerbockers and stockings. Why he did so I do not know, for he never cycled and he never played cricket. It was a fortuitous concurrence of garments arising I know not how. He gesticulated with his hands and arms, and jerked his head about

" HE GESTICULATED WITH HIS HANDS AND ARMS."

and *buzzed.* He buzzed like something electric. You never heard such buzzing. And ever and again he cleared his throat with a most extraordinary noise.

There had been rain, and that spasmodic walk of his was enhanced by the extreme slipperiness of the footpath. Exactly as he came against the sun he stopped, pulled out a watch, hesitated. Then, with a sort of convulsive gesture, he turned and retreated with every manifestation of haste, no longer gesticulating, but going with ample strides that showed the relatively large size of his feet—they were, I remember, grotesquely exaggerated in size by adhesive clay—to the best possible advantage.

This occurred on the first day of my sojourn, when my play-writing energy was at its height, and I regarded the incident simply as an annoying distraction—the waste of five minutes. I returned to my scenario. But when next evening the apparition was repeated with remarkable precision, and again the next evening, and, indeed, every evening when rain was not falling, concentration upon the scenario became a considerable effort. "Confound the man," said I. "One would think he was learning to be a marionette," and for several evenings I cursed him pretty heartily.

Then my annoyance gave way to amazement and curiosity. Why on earth should a man do this thing? On the fourteenth evening I could stand it no longer, and so soon as he appeared I opened the French window, crossed the veranda, and directed myself to the point where he invariably stopped.

He had his watch out as I came up to him. He had a chubby, rubicund face, with reddish-brown eyes—previously I had seen him only against the light. "One moment, sir," said I, as he turned.

He stared. "One moment," he said, "certainly. Or if you wish to speak to me for longer, and it is not asking too much—your moment is up—would it trouble you to accompany me?"

"Not in the least," said I, placing myself beside him.

"My habits are regular. My time for intercourse—limited."

"This, I presume, is your time for exercise?"

"It is. I come here to enjoy the sunset."

"You don't."

"Sir?"

"You never look at it."

"Never look at it?"

"No. I've watched you thirteen nights, and not once have you looked at the sunset —not once."

He knitted his brows like one who encounters a problem.

"Well, I enjoy the sunlight—the atmosphere—I go along this path, through that gate"—he jerked his head over his shoulder —"and round."

"You don't. You never have been. It's all nonsense. There isn't a way. To-night, for instance——"

"Oh, to-night! Let me see. Ah! I just glanced at my watch, saw that I had already been out just three minutes over the precise half-hour, decided there was not time to go round, turned——"

"You always do."

He looked at me, reflected. "Perhaps I do—now I come to think of it . . . . . But what was it you wanted to speak to me about?"

"Why—this!"

"This?"

"Yes. Why do you do it? Every night you come making a noise——"

"Making a noise?"

"Like this." I imitated his buzzing noise.

He looked at me, and it was evident the buzzing awakened distaste. "Do I do *that?*" he asked.

"Every blessed evening."

"I had no idea."

He stopped dead. He regarded me gravely. "Can it be," he said, "that I have formed a Habit?"

"Well, it looks like it. Doesn't it?"

He pulled down his lower lip between finger and thumb. He regarded a puddle at his feet.

"My mind is much occupied," he said. "And you want to know *why?* Well, sir, I can assure you that not only do I not know why I do these things, but I did not even know I did them. Come to think, it is just as you say: I never *have* been beyond that field. . . . . And these things annoy you?"

For some reason I was beginning to relent towards him. "Not *annoy,*" I said. "But —imagine yourself writing a play!"

"I couldn't."

"Well, anything that needs concentration."

"Ah!" he said, "of course," and meditated. His expression became so eloquent of distress that I relented still more. After all, there *is* a touch of aggression in demanding of a man you don't know why he hums on a public footpath.

"You see," he said, weakly, "it's a habit."

"Oh! I recognise that."

"I must stop it."

"But not if it puts you out. After all, I had no business -- it's something of a liberty."

"Not at all, sir," he said. "Not at all. I am greatly indebted to you. I should guard myself against these things. In future I will. Could I trouble you—once again? That noise?"

"Something like this," I said. "Zuzzoo, zuzzoo. But really, you know——"

"I am greatly obliged to you. In fact— I know—I am getting absurdly absent-minded. You are quite justified, sir— perfectly justified. Indeed, I am indebted to you. The thing shall end. And now, sir, I have already brought you farther than I should have done."

"I do hope my impertinence——"

"Not at all, sir, not at all."

We regarded each other for a moment. I raised my hat and wished him a good-evening. He responded convulsively, and so we went our ways.

At the stile I looked back at his receding figure. His bearing had changed remarkably; he seemed limp, shrunken. The contrast with his former gesticulating, zuzzooing self took me in some absurd way as pathetic. I watched him out of sight. Then, wishing very heartily I had kept to my own business, I returned to my bungalow and my play.

The next evening I saw nothing of him, nor the next. But he was very much in my mind, and it had occurred to me that as a sentimental comic character he might serve a useful purpose in the development of my plot. The third day he called upon me.

For a time I was puzzled to think what had brought him—he made indifferent conversation in the most formal way—then abruptly

"I LOOKED BACK AT HIS RECEDING FIGURE."

he came to business. He wanted to buy me out of my bungalow.

"You see," he said, "I don't blame you in the least, but you've destroyed a habit, and it disorganizes my day. I've walked past here for years—years. No doubt I've hummed . . . . . You've made all that impossible!"

I suggested he might try some other direction.

"No. There is no other direction. This is the only one. I've inquired. And now every afternoon at four—I come to a dead wall."

"But, my dear sir, if the thing is so important to you——"

"It's vital. You see I'm—I'm an investigator. I am engaged in a scientific research. I live"—he paused, and seemed to think—"just over there," he said, and pointed suddenly dangerously near my eye. "The house with white chimneys that you see just over the trees. And my circumstances are abnormal — abnormal. I am on the point of completing one of the most important demonstrations—I can assure you one of *the most important* demonstrations—that have ever been made. It requires constant thought, constant mental ease, and activity. And the afternoon was my brightest time!—effervescing with new ideas — new points of view."

"But why not come by still?"

"It would be all different. I should be self-conscious. I should think of you at your play—watching me, irritated! Instead of thinking of my work. . . . No! I must have the bungalow."

I meditated. Naturally I wanted to think the matter over thoroughly before anything decisive was said. I was generally ready enough for business in those days, and selling always attracted me; but in the first place it was not my bungalow, and even if I sold it to him at a good price I might get inconvenienced in the delivery of goods if the current owner got wind of the transaction; and in the second I was—well, undischarged. It was clearly a business that required delicate handling. Moreover, the possibility of his being in pursuit of some valuable invention also interested me. It occurred to me that I would like to know more of this research, not with any dishonest intention, but simply with an idea that to know what it was would be a relief from play-writing. I threw out feelers.

He was quite willing to supply information. Indeed, once he was fairly under way the conversation became a monologue. He talked like a man long pent up, who has had

" HE TALKED LIKE A MAN LONG PENT UP."

it over with himself again and again. He talked for nearly an hour, and I must confess I found it a pretty stiff bit of listening. But through it all there was the under-tone of satisfaction one feels when one is neglecting work one has set oneself. During that first interview I gathered very little of the drift of his work. Half his words were technicalities entirely strange to me, and he illustrated one or two points with what he was pleased to call elementary

mathematics, computing on an envelope with a copying-ink pencil, in a manner that made it hard even to seem to understand. " Yes," I said. " Yes. Go on ! " Nevertheless I made out enough to convince me that he was no mere crank playing at discoveries. In spite of his crank-like appearance there was a force about him that made that impossible. Whatever it was, it was a thing with mechanical possibilities. He told me of a work-shed he had, and of three assistants, originally jobbing carpenters, whom he had trained. Now, from the work-shed to the patent office is clearly only one step. He invited me to see these things. I accepted readily, and took care, by a remark or so, to underline that. The proposed transfer of the bungalow remained very conveniently in suspense.

At last he rose to depart with an apology for the length of his call. Talking over his work was, he said, a pleasure enjoyed only too rarely. It was not often he found such an intelligent listener as myself; he mingled very little with professional scientific men.

" So much pettiness," he explained ; " so much intrigue ! And really, when one has an idea—a novel, fertilizing idea——. I don't wish to be unchari-table, but——."

I am a man who believes in im-pulses. I made what was perhaps a rash proposition. But you must re-member that I had been alone, play-writing in Lympne, for fourteen days, and my compunction for his ruined walk still hung about me. " Why not," said I, " make this your new habit ? In the place of the one I spoilt. At least—until we can settle about the bun-galow. What you want is to turn over your work in your mind. That you have always done during your afternoon walk. Unfortunately that's over — you can't get things back as they were. But why not come and talk about your work to me, use me as a sort of wall against which you may throw your thoughts and catch them again ? It's certain I don't know enough to steal your idea myself—and I know no scientific men."

I stopped. He was considering. Evidently the thing attracted him. " But I'm afraid I should bore you," he said.

" You think I'm too dull ? "

" Oh, no, but technicalities—— "

" Anyhow, you have interested me im-mensely this afternoon."

" Of course it *would* be a great help to me.

Nothing clears up one's ideas so much as explaining them. Hitherto——"

" My dear sir, say no more."

" But really, can you spare the time ? "

" There is no rest like change of occupation," I said, with profound conviction.

The affair was over. On my veranda steps he turned. " I am greatly indebted to you," he said.

I made an interrogative noise.

" You have completely cured me of that ridiculous habit of humming," he explained.

I think I said I was glad to be of any service to him, and he turned away.

Immediately the train of thought that our conversation had suggested must have resumed its sway. His arms began to wave in their former fashion. The faint echo of " zuzzoo " came back to me on the breeze . . . . .

Well, after all, that was not my affair. . . . .

He came the next day, and again the next day after that, and delivered two lectures on physics to our mutual satisfaction. He talked with an air of being extremely lucid about the " ether," and " tubes of force," and " gravitational potential," and things like that, and I sat in my other folding-chair and said " Yes," " Go on," " I follow you," to keep him going.

It was tremendously difficult stuff, but I do not think he ever suspected how much I did not understand him. There were moments when I doubted whether I was well employed, but at any rate I was resting from that confounded play. Now and then things gleamed on me clearly for a space, only to vanish just when I thought I had hold of them. Sometimes my attention failed altogether, and I would give it up, and sit and stare at him, wondering whether, after all, it would not be better to use him as a central figure in a good farce, and let all this other stuff slide. And then perchance I would catch on again for a bit.

At the earliest opportunity I went to see his house. It was large and carelessly furnished ; there were no servants other than his three assistants, and his dietary and private life were characterized by a philosophical simplicity. He was a water-drinker, a vegetarian, and all those logical disciplinary things. But the sight of his equipment settled many doubts. It looked like business from cellar to attic—an amazing little place to find in an out-of-the-way village. The ground-floor rooms contained benches and apparatus, the bakehouse and scullery boiler had developed into respectable furnaces,

dynamos occupied the cellar, and there was a gasometer in the garden. He showed it to me with all the confiding zest of a man who has been living too much alone. His seclusion was overflowing now in an excess of confidence, and I had the good luck to be the recipient.

The three assistants were creditable specimens of the class of " handy men " from which they came. Conscientious if unintelligent, strong, civil, and willing. One, Spargus, who did the cooking and all the metal work, had been a sailor ; a second, Gibbs, was a joiner, and the third was an ex - jobbing gardener and now general assistant. They were the merest labourers. All the intelligent work was done by Cavor. Theirs was the darkest ignorance compared even with my muddled impression.

And now, as to the nature of these inquiries. Here, unhappily, comes a grave difficulty. I am no scientific expert, and if I were to attempt to set forth in the highly scientific language of Mr. Cavor the aim to which his experiments tended I am afraid I should confuse not only the reader but myself, and almost certainly I should make some blunder that would bring upon me the mockery of every up-to-date student of mathematical physics in the country. The best thing I can do, therefore, is, I think, to give my impressions in my own inexact language, without any attempt to wear a garment of knowledge to which I have no claim.

The object of Mr. Cavor's search was a substance that should be " opaque "—he used some other word I have forgotten, but " opaque " conveys the idea—to " all forms of radiant energy." " Radiant energy," he made me understand, was anything like light or heat, or those Röntgen rays there was so much talk about a year or so ago, or the electric waves of Marconi, or gravitation. All these things, he said, *radiate* out from centres and act on bodies at a distance, whence comes the term " radiant energy." Now, almost all substances are opaque to some form or other of radiant energy. Glass, for example, is transparent to light, but much less so to heat, so that it is useful as a fire screen ; and alum is transparent to light, but blocks heat completely. A solution of iodine in carbon bisulphide, on the other hand, completely blocks light, but is quite transparent to heat. It will hide a fire from you, but permit all its warmth to reach you. Metals are not only opaque to light and heat, but also to electrical energy, which passes through both iodine solution and glass almost as though they were not interposed. And so on.

Now, all known substances are "transparent" to gravitation. You can use screens of various sorts to cut off the light or heat or electrical influence of the sun, or the warmth of the earth from anything ; you can screen things by sheets of metal from Marconi's rays, but nothing will cut off the gravitational attraction of the sun or the gravitational attraction of the earth. Yet why there should be nothing is hard to say. Cavor did not see why such a substance did not exist, and certainly I could not tell him. I had never thought of such a possibility before. He showed me by calculations on paper, which Lord Kelvin, no doubt, or Professor Lodge or Professor Karl Pearson, or any of those great scientific people might have understood, but which simply reduced me to a hopeless muddle, that not only was such a substance possible, but that it must satisfy certain conditions. It was an amazing piece of reasoning. Much as it amazed and exercised me at the time, it would be impossible to reproduce it here. "Yes," I said to it all, "yes, go on !" Suffice it for this story that he believed he might be able to manufacture this possible substance opaque to gravitation out of a complicated alloy of metals and something new—a new element, I fancy—called, I believe, *helium*, which was sent to him from London in sealed stone jars. Doubt has been thrown upon this detail, but I am almost certain it was *helium* he had sent him in sealed stone jars. It was certainly something very gaseous and thin.

If only I had taken notes . . . .

But, then, how was I to foresee the necessity of taking notes ?

Anyone with the merest germ of an imagination will understand the extraordinary possibilities of such a substance, and will sympathize a little with the emotion I felt as this understanding emerged from the haze of abstruse phrases in which Cavor expressed himself. Comic relief in a play indeed ! It was some time before I would believe that I had interpreted him aright, and I was very careful not to ask questions that would have enabled him to gauge the profundity of misunderstanding into which he dropped his daily exposition. But

no one reading the story of it here will sympathize fully, because, from my barren narrative, it will be impossible to gather the strength of my conviction that this astonishing substance was positively going to be made.

I do not recall that I gave my play an hour's consecutive work at any time after my visit to his house. My imagination had other things to do. There seemed no limit to the possibilities of the stuff; which ever way I tried, I came on miracles and revolutions. For example, if one wanted to lift a weight, however enormous, one had only to get a sheet of this substance beneath it, and one might lift it with a straw. My first natural impulse was to apply this principle to guns and ironclads, and all the material and methods of war, and from that to shipping, locomotion, building, every conceivable form of human industry. The chance that had brought me into the very birth-chamber of this new time—it was an epoch, no less— was one of those chances that come once in a thousand years. The thing unrolled, it expanded and expanded. Among other things I saw in it my redemption as a business man. I saw a parent company and daughter companies, applications to right of us, applications to left, rings and

"THE THING UNROLLED, IT EXPANDED."

trusts, privileges and concessions, spreading and spreading, until one vast, stupendous Cavorite company ran and ruled the world.

And I was in it !

I took my line straight away. I knew I was staking everything, but I jumped there and then.

" We're on absolutely the biggest thing that has ever been invented," I said, and put the accent on " we." " If you want to keep me out of this, you'll have to do it with a gun. I'm coming down to be your fourth labourer to-morrow."

He seemed surprised at my enthusiasm, but not a bit suspicious or hostile. Rather he was self-depreciatory.

He looked at me doubtfully. " But do you really think——?" he said. " And your play ! How about that play ? "

" It's vanished !" I cried. " My dear sir, don't you see what you've got ? Don't you see what you're going to do ? "

That was merely a rhetorical turn, but positively he didn't ! At first I could not believe it. He had not had the beginning of the inkling of an idea ! This astonishing little man had been working on purely theoretical grounds the whole time ! When he said it was " the most important " research the world had ever seen, he simply meant it squared up so many theories, settled so much that was in doubt ; he had troubled no more about the application of the stuff he was going to turn out than if he had been a machine that makes guns. This was a possible substance, and he was going to make it ! *V'la tout*, as the Frenchman says.

Beyond that—he was childish ! If he made it, it would go down to posterity as Cavorite or Cavorine, and he would be made an F.R.S., and his portrait given away as a scientific worthy with *Nature*, and things like that. And that was all he saw ! He would have dropped this bomb-shell into the world as though he had discovered a new species of gnat if it had not happened that I had come along. And there it would have lain and fizzled, like one or two other little things that scientific people have lit and dropped about us.

When I realized this it was I did the talking and Cavor who said " Go on ! " I jumped up. I paced the room, gesticulating like a boy of twenty. I tried to make him understand his duties and responsibilities in the matter—*our* duties and responsibilities in the matter. I assured him we might make wealth enough to work any sort of social revolution we fancied ; we might own and

order the whole world. I told him of companies and patents, and the case for secret processes. All these things seemed to take him much as his mathematics had taken me. A look of perplexity came into his ruddy little face. He stammered something about indifference to wealth, but I brushed all that aside. He had got to be rich, and it was no good his stammering. I gave him to understand the sort of man I was, and that I had had very considerable business experience. I did not tell him I was an undischarged bankrupt at the time, because that was temporary ; but I think I reconciled my evident poverty with my financial claims. And quite insensibly, in the way such projects grow, the understanding of a Cavorite monopoly grew up between us. He was to make the stuff and I was to make the boom.

I stuck like a leech to the " we "—" you " and " I " didn't exist for me.

His idea was that the profits I spoke of might go to endow research, but that, of course, was a matter we had to settle later. " That's all right," I shouted, " that's all right." The great point, as I insisted, was to get the thing done.

" Here is a substance," I cried, " no home, no factory, no fortress, no ship can dare to be without—more universally applicable even than a Patent Medicine ! There isn't a solitary aspect of it, not one of its ten thousand possible uses that will not make us rich, Cavor, beyond the dreams of avarice ! "

" No !" he said. " I begin to see. It's extraordinary how one gets new points of view by talking over things ! "

" And as it happens you have just talked to the right man ! "

" I suppose no one," he said, " is absolutely *averse* to enormous wealth. Of course, there is one thing——"

He paused. I stood still.

" It is just possible, you know, that we may not be able to make it after all ! It may be one of those things that are a theoretical possibility but a practical absurdity. Or when we make it there may be some little hitch——! "

" We'll tackle the hitch when it comes," said I.

CHAPTER II.

THE FIRST MAKING OF CAVORITE.

BUT Cavor's fears were groundless so far as the actual making was concerned. On the 14th of October, 1899, this incredible substance was made !

Oddly enough, it was made at last by accident when Cavor least expected it. He had fused together a number of metals and certain other things—I wish I knew the particulars now—and he intended to leave the mixture a week, and then allow it to cool slowly. Unless he had miscalculated, the last stage in the combination would occur when the stuff sank to a temperature of 60deg. Fahr. But it chanced that, unknown to Cavor, dissension had arisen among the men about the furnace tending. Gibbs, who had previously seen to this, had suddenly attempted to shift it to the man who had been a gardener, on the score that coal was soil, being dug, and therefore could not possibly fall within the province of a joiner; the man who had been a jobbing gardener alleged however that coal was a metallic or ore-like substance, let alone that he was cook. But Spargus insisted on Gibbs doing the coaling, seeing that he was a joiner and that coal is notoriously fossil wood. Consequently Gibbs ceased to replenish the furnace, and no one else did so, and Cavor was too much immersed in certain interesting problems concerning a Cavorite flying machine (neglecting the resistance of the air and one or two other points) to perceive that anything was wrong. And the premature birth of his invention took place just as he was coming across the field to my bungalow for our afternoon talk and tea.

I remember the occasion with extreme vividness. The water was boiling and everything was prepared, and the sound of his "zuzzoo" had brought me out upon the veranda. His active little figure was black against the autumnal sunset, and to the right the chimneys of his house just rose above a gloriously-tinted group of trees. Remoter rose the Wealden Hills, faint and blue, while to the left the hazy marsh spread out spacious and serene. And then——!

The chimneys jerked heavenward, smashing into a string of bricks as they rose, and the roof and a miscellany of furniture followed. Then, overtaking them, came a huge, white flame. The trees about the building swayed and whirled and tore themselves to pieces that sprang towards the flare. My ears were smitten with a clap of thunder that left me deaf on one side for life, and all about me windows smashed unheeded.

I took three steps from the veranda towards Cavor's house, and even as I did so came the wind.

Instantly my coat-tails were over my head and I was progressing in great leaps and bounds and quite against my will towards him. In the same moment the discoverer was seized, whirled about, and flew through the screaming air. I saw one of my chimney-pots hit the ground within six yards of me, leap a score of feet, and so hurry in great strides towards the focus of the disturbance. Cavor, kicking and flapping, came down again, rolled over and over on the ground for a space, struggled up and was lifted and borne forward at an enormous velocity, vanishing at last among the labouring, lashing trees that writhed about his house.

A mass of smoke and ashes and a square of

"I WAS PROGRESSING IN GREAT LEAPS AND BOUNDS."

bluish, shining substance rushed up towards the zenith. A large fragment of fencing came sailing past me, dropped edgeways, hit the ground and fell flat, and then the worst was over. The aerial commotion fell swiftly until it was a mere strong gale, and I became once more aware that I had breath and feet. By leaning back against the wind I managed to stop and could collect such wits as still remained to me.

In that instant the whole face of the world had changed. The tranquil sunset had vanished, the sky was dark with scurrying clouds, everything was flattened and swaying with the gale. I glanced back to see if my bungalow was still, in a general way, standing, then staggered forward towards the trees amongst which Cavor had vanished, and through whose tall and leaf-denuded branches shone the flames of his burning house. I entered the copse, dashing from one tree to another and clinging to them, and for a space I sought him in vain. Then, amidst a heap of smashed branches and fencing that had banked itself against a portion of his garden-wall I perceived something stir. I made a run for this, but before I reached it a brown object separated itself, rose on two muddy legs, and protruded two drooping, bleeding hands. Some tattered ends of garment fluttered out from its middle portion and streamed before the wind.

For a moment I did not recognise this earthy lump, and then I saw that it was Cavor, caked in the mud in which he had rolled. He leant forward against the wind, rubbing the dirt from his eyes and mouth.

He extended a muddy lump of hand, and staggered a pace towards me. His face worked with emotion, little lumps of mud kept falling from it. He looked as damaged and pitiful as any living creature I have ever seen, and his remark, therefore, amazed me exceedingly.

" 'Gratulate me," he gasped, " 'gratulate me !"

" Congratulate you ? " I said. " Good heavens ! what for ? "

" I've done it."

" You *have*. What on earth caused that explosion ? "

A gust of wind blew his words away. I understood him to say that it wasn't an explosion at all. The wind hurled me into collision with him, and we stood clinging to one another.

" Try and get back to my bungalow," I bawled in his ear. He did not hear me, and shouted something about " three martyrs —science," and also something about " not much good." At the time he laboured under the impression that his three attendants had perished in this whirlwind. Happily this was incorrect. Directly he had left for my bungalow they had gone off to the public-house in Lympne to discuss the question of the furnaces over some trivial refreshment.

I repeated my suggestion of getting back to my bungalow, and this time he understood.

"WE CLUNG ARM-IN-ARM, AND STARTED."

We clung arm-in-arm and started, and managed at last to reach the shelter of as much roof as was left to me. For a space we sat in arm-chairs and panted. All the windows were broken, and the lighter articles of furniture were in great disorder, but no irrevocable damage was done. Happily the kitchen door had stood the pressure upon it, so that all my crockery and cooking materials had survived. The oil-stove was still burning, and I put on the water to boil again for tea. And that prepared, I could turn on Cavor for his explanation.

" Quite correct," he insisted ; " quite correct. I've done it, and it's all right."

" But——" I protested. " All right ! Why, there can't be a rick standing, or a fence or a thatched roof undamaged, for twenty miles round."

" It's all right, *really*. I didn't, of course, foresee this little upset. My mind was preoccupied with another problem, and I'm apt to disregard these practical side issues. But it's all right."

" My dear sir," I cried, " don't you see you've done thousands of pounds' worth of damage ? "

" There, I throw myself on your discretion. I'm not a practical man, of course, but don't you think they will regard it as a cyclone ? "

" But the explosion——"

" It was *not* an explosion. It's perfectly simple. Only, as I say, I'm apt to overlook these little things. It's that zuzzoo business on a larger scale. Inadvertently I made this substance of mine—this Cavorite—in a thin, wide sheet——"

He paused. " You are quite clear that the stuff is opaque to gravitation ; that it cuts off things from gravitating towards each other ? "

" Yes," said I. " Yes ? "

" Well, so soon as it reached a temperature of 6odeg. Fahr., and the process of its manufacture was complete, the air above it, the portions of roof and ceiling and floor above it, ceased to have weight. I suppose you know—everybody knows nowadays—that, as a usual thing, the air *has* weight ; that it presses on everything at the surface of the earth ; presses, in all directions, with a pressure of 14½lb. to the square inch ? "

" I know that," said I. " Go on."

" I know that too," he remarked. " Only this shows you how useless knowledge is unless you apply it. You see, over our Cavorite, this ceased to be the case ; the air there ceased to exert any pressure, and the air round it and not over the Cavorite was exerting a pressure of 14½lb. to the square inch upon this suddenly weightless air. Ah! you begin to see! The air all about the Cavorite crushed in upon the air above it with irresistible force. The air above the Cavorite was forced upward violently, the air that rushed in to replace it immediately lost weight, ceased to exert any pressure, followed suit, blew the ceiling through and the roof off. . . . .

" You perceive," he said, " it formed a sort of atmospheric fountain, a kind of chimney in the atmosphere. And if the Cavorite itself hadn't been loose and so got sucked up the chimney, does it occur to you what would have happened ? "

I thought. " I suppose," I said, " the air would be rushing up and up over that infernal piece of stuff now."

" Precisely," he said ; " a huge fountain !"

" Spouting into space ! Good heavens ! Why, it would have squirted all the atmosphere of the earth away ! It would have robbed the world of air. It would have been the death of all mankind ! That little lump of stuff !"

" Not exactly into space," said Cavor, " but as bad—practically. It would have whipped the air off the world as one peels a banana, and flung it thousands of miles. It would have dropped back again, of course, but on an asphyxiated world ! From our point of view, very little better than if it never came back !"

I stared. As yet I was too amazed to realize how all my expectations had been upset. " What do you mean to do now ? " I asked.

" In the first place, if I may borrow a garden trowel, I will remove some of this earth with which I am encased, and then, if I may avail myself of your domestic conveniences, I will have a bath. This done, we will converse more at leisure. It will be wise, I think "—he laid a muddy hand on my arm—" if nothing were said of this affair beyond ourselves. I know I have caused great damage — probably even dwelling-houses may be ruined here and there upon the country-side. But on the other hand I cannot possibly pay for the damage I have done, and if the real cause of this is published it will lead only to heartburning and the obstruction of my work. One cannot foresee *everything*, you know, and I cannot consent for one moment to add the burden of practical considerations to my theorizing. Later on, when you have come in with your practical mind and Cavorite is floated—floated *is* the word, isn't it ?—and it has realized all you anticipate for it, we may set matters right with these people. But not now—not now. If no other explanation is offered people, in the present unsatisfactory state of meteorological science, will ascribe all this to a cyclone; there might be a public subscription, and, as my house has collapsed and been burnt, I should in that case receive a considerable share in the compensation, which would be extremely helpful to the prosecution of our researches. But if it is known that *I* caused this there will be no public subscription, and everybody will be put out. Practically, I shall never get a chance of working in peace again. My three assistants may or may not have perished. That is a detail. If they have it is no great loss; they were more zealous than able, and this premature event must be largely due to their joint neglect of the furnace. If they have not perished I doubt if they have the intelligence to explain the affair. They will accept the cyclone story. And if during the temporary unfitness of my house for occupation I may lodge in one of the untenanted rooms of this bungalow of yours——"

He paused and regarded me.

A man of such possibilities, I reflected, is no ordinary guest to entertain.

"Perhaps," said I, rising to my feet, "we had better begin by looking for a trowel," and I led the way to the scattered vestiges of the greenhouse.

And while he was having his bath I considered the entire question alone. It was clear there were drawbacks to Mr. Cavor's society I had not foreseen. The absent-mindedness that had just escaped depopulating the terrestrial globe might at any moment result in other grave inconvenience. On the other hand, I was young, my affairs were in a mess, and I was in just the mood for reckless adventure—with a chance of something good at the end of it. I had quite settled in my mind that I was to have half at least in that aspect of the affair. Fortunately I held my bungalow, as I have already explained, on a three years' agreement without being responsible for repairs, and my furniture, such as there was of it, had been hastily purchased, was unpaid for, insured,

"I CONSIDERED THE ENTIRE QUESTION ALONE."

and altogether devoid of associations. In the end I decided to keep on with him and see the business through.

Certainly the aspect of things had changed very greatly. I no longer doubted at all the enormous possibilities of the substance, but I began to have doubts about the gun-carriage and the patent boots.

We set to work at once to reconstruct his laboratory and proceed with our experiments. Cavor talked more on my level than he had ever done before when it came to the question of how we should make the stuff next.

"Of course we must make it again," he said, with a sort of glee I had not expected in him; "of course we must make it again. We have caught a tartar, perhaps, but we have left the theoretical behind us for good and all. If we can possibly avoid wrecking this little planet of ours we will. But — there *must* be risks! There must be. In experimental work there always are. And here, as a practical man, *you* must come in. For my own part it seems to me we might make it edgeways perhaps, and very thin. Yet I don't know. I have a certain dim perception of another method. I can hardly explain it yet. But, curiously enough, it came into my mind while I was rolling over and over in the mud before the wind, and very doubtful how the whole adventure was to end, as being absolutely the thing I ought to have done."

Even with my aid we found some little difficulty, and meanwhile we kept at work restoring the laboratory. There was plenty to do before it was absolutely necessary to decide upon the precise form and method of our second attempt. Our only hitch was the strike of the three labourers, who objected to my activity as a foreman. But that matter we compromised after two days' delay.

The First Men in the Moon.

By H. G. Wells.

CHAPTER III.

THE BUILDING OF THE SPHERE.

 REMEMBER the occasion very distinctly when Cavor told me of his idea of the sphere. He had had intimations of it before, but at the time it seemed to come to him in a rush. We were returning to the bungalow for tea, and on the way he fell humming. Suddenly he shouted, " That's it. That finishes it ! A sort of roller blind ! "

" Finishes what ? " I asked.

" Space—anywhere ! The moon ! "

" What do you mean ? "

" Mean ? Why—it must be a sphere ! That's what I mean ! "

I saw I was out of it, and for a time I let him talk in his own fashion. I hadn't the ghost of an idea then of his drift. But after he had taken tea he made it clear to me.

" It's like this," he said. " Last time I ran this stuff that cuts things off from gravitation into a flat tank with an overlap that held it down. And directly it had cooled and the manufacture was completed all that uproar happened; nothing above it weighed anything; the air went squirting up, the house squirted up, and if the stuff itself hadn't squirted up too, I don't know what would have happened. But suppose the substance is loose and quite free to go up ? "

" It will go up at once ! "

" Exactly. With no more disturbance than firing a big gun."

" But what good will that do ? "

" I'm going up with it ! "

I put down my teacup and stared at him.

" Imagine a sphere," he explained, " large enough to hold two people and their luggage. It will be made of steel lined with thick glass ; it will contain a proper store of solidified air, concentrated food, water, distilling apparatus, and so forth, and enamelled, as it were, on the outer steel——"

" Cavorite ? "

" Yes."

" But how will you get inside ? "

" There was a similar problem about a dumpling."

" Yes, I know. But how ? "

" That's perfectly easy. An air-tight manhole is all that is needed. That, of course, will have to be a little complicated ; there will have to be a valve so that things may be thrown out if necessary, without much loss of air."

" Like Jules Verne's thing in 'A Trip to the Moon' ? "

But Cavor was not a reader of fiction.

" I begin to see," I said slowly. " And you could get in and screw yourself up while the Cavorite was warm, and as soon as it cooled it would become impervious to gravitation, and off you would fly——"

" At a tangent."

" You would go off in a straight line "—I stopped abruptly. " What is to prevent the thing travelling in a straight line into space for ever ? " I asked. " You're not safe to get anywhere, and if you do, how will you get back ? "

" I've just thought of that," said Cavor. " That's what I meant when I said the thing was finished. The inner glass sphere can be air-tight, and, except for the man-hole, continuous, and the steel sphere can be made in sections, each section capable of rolling up after the fashion of a roller blind. These can easily be worked by springs, and released and checked by electricity conveyed by platinum wires fused through the glass. All that is merely a question of detail. So you see that, except for the thickness of the blind rollers, the Cavorite exterior of the sphere will consist of windows or blinds, which ever you like to call them. Well, when all these windows or blinds are shut, no light, no heat, no gravitation, no radiant energy of any sort will get at the inside of the sphere ; it will fly on through space in a straight line as you say. But open a window, imagine one of the windows open ! Then at once any heavy body that chances to be in that direction will attract us."

I sat taking it in.

" You see ? " he said.

" Oh, I *see*."

" Practically, we shall be able to tack about in space just as we wish. Get attracted by this and that."

" Oh, yes. *That's* clear enough. Only——"

" Well ? "

" I don't quite see what we shall do it for ! It's really only jumping off the world and back again."

" Surely ! For example, one might go to the moon."

" And when one got there ! What would you find ? "

" We should see——! Oh ! Consider the new knowledge."

" Is there air there ? "

" There may be."

"It's a fine idea," I said, "but it strikes me as a large order all the same. The moon! I'd much rather try some smaller things first."

"They're out of the question. Because of the air difficulty."

"Why not apply that idea of spring blinds—Cavorite blinds in strong steel cases—to lifting weights?"

"It wouldn't work," he insisted. "After all, to go into outer space is not so much worse, if at all, than a Polar expedition. Men go on Polar expeditions."

"Not business men. And besides they get paid for Polar expeditions. And if anything goes wrong there are relief parties. But this—it's just firing ourselves off the world for nothing."

"Call it prospecting."

"You'll have to call it that. One might make a book of it, perhaps," I said.

"I have no doubt there will be minerals," said Cavor.

"For example?"

"Oh, sulphur, ores, gold perhaps, possibly new elements."

"Cost of carriage," I said. "You know you're *not* a practical man. The moon is a quarter of a million miles away."

"It seems to me it wouldn't cost much to cart any weight anywhere if you packed it in a Cavorite case."

I · had not thought of that. "Delivered free on head of purchaser, eh?"

"It isn't as though we were confined to the moon."

"You mean——?"

"There's Mars—clear atmosphere, novel surroundings, exhilarating sense of lightness. It might be pleasant to go there."

"Is there air on Mars?"

"Oh, yes!"

"Seems as though you might run it as a sanatorium. By the way, how far is Mars?"

"Two hundred million miles at present," said Cavor, airily; "and you go close by the sun."

My imagination was picking itself up again. "After all," I said, "there's something in these things. There's travel——"

An extraordinary possibility came rushing into my mind. Suddenly I saw as in a vision the whole solar system threaded with Cavorite liners and spheres *de luxe.* "Rights of pre-emption" came floating into my head—planetary rights of pre-emption. I recalled the old Spanish monopoly in American gold. It wasn't as though it was just this planet or that, it was all of them. I stared at Cavor's rubicund face, and suddenly my imagination was leaping and dancing. I stood up, I walked up and down; my tongue was unloosened.

"I'm beginning to take it in," I said. "I'm beginning to take it in." The transition from doubt to enthusiasm seemed to take scarcely any time at all. "But this is tremendous!" I cried. "This is Imperial! I haven't been dreaming of this sort of thing."

Once the chill of my opposition was removed his own pent-up excitement had play. He too got up and paced; he too gesticulated and shouted. We behaved like men inspired. We *were* men inspired.

"We'll settle all that!" he said, in answer to some incidental difficulty that had pulled me up. "We'll soon settle all that! We'll start the drawings for mouldings this very night."

"We'll start them now," I responded, and we hurried off to the laboratory to begin upon this work forthwith.

I was like a child in wonderland all that night. The dawn found us both still at work—we kept our electric light going heedless of the day. I remember now exactly how those drawings looked—I shaded and tinted while Cavor drew—smudged and haste-marked they were in every line, but wonderfully correct. We got out the orders for the steel blinds and frames we needed from that night's work, and the glass sphere was designed within a week. We gave up our afternoon conversations and our old routine altogether. We worked, and we slept and

"AN EXTRAORDINARY POSSIBILITY CAME RUSHING INTO MY MIND."

ate when we could work no longer for hunger and fatigue. Our enthusiasm infected our three men, though they had no idea what the sphere was for. Through those days the man Gibbs gave up walking and went everywhere, even across the room, at a sort of fussy run.

And it grew, the sphere. December passed, January. — I spent a day with a broom, sweeping a path through the snow from bungalow to laboratory. — February, March. By the end of March the completion was in sight. In January had come a team of horses, a huge packing-case ; we had our thick glass sphere now ready and in position under the crane we had rigged to sling it into the steel shell. All the bars and blinds of the steel shell—it was not really a spherical shell, but polyhedral with a roller blind to each facet—had arrived by February, and the lower half was bolted together. The Cavorite was half made by March, the metallic paste had gone through two of the stages in its manufacture, and we had plastered quite half of it on to the steel bars and blinds. It was astonishing how closely we kept to the lines of Cavor's first inspiration in working out the scheme. When the bolting together of the sphere was finished he proposed to remove the rough roof of the temporary laboratory in which the work was done and build a furnace about it. So the last stage of Cavorite making, in which the paste is heated to a dull red glow in a stream of helium, would be accomplished when it was already on the sphere.

And then we had to discuss and decide what provisions we were to take—compressed foods, concentrated essences, steel cylinders containing reserve oxygen, an arrangement for removing carbonic acid and waste from the air and restoring oxygen by means of sodium peroxide, water condensers, and so forth. I remember the little heap they made in the corner, tins and rolls and boxes— convincingly matter-of-fact.

It was a strenuous time, with little chance of thinking. But one day, when we were drawing near the end, an odd mood came over me. I had been bricking up the furnace all the morning, and I sat down by these possessions, dead beat. Everything seemed dull and incredible.

" But look here, Cavor," I said, " after all, what's it all for ? "

He smiled. " The thing now is to go."

" The moon," I reflected. " But what do you expect ? I thought the moon was a dead world."

He shrugged his shoulders.

" What do you expect ? "

" We're going to see."

" *Are* we ? " I said, and stared before me.

" You are tired," he remarked. " You'd better take a walk this afternoon."

" No," I said, obstinately ; " I'm going to finish this brickwork."

And I did, and insured myself a night of insomnia.

I don't think I have ever had such a night. I had some bad times before my business collapse, but the very worst of those was sweet slumber compared to this infinity of aching wakefulness. I was suddenly in the most enormous funk at the thing we were going to do.

I do not remember thinking at all of the risks we were running before that night. Now they came like that array of spectres that once beleaguered Prague and camped around me. The strangeness of what we were about to do, the unearthliness of it, overwhelmed me. I was like a man awakened out of pleasant dreams to the most horrible surroundings. I lay, eyes wide open, and the sphere seemed to get more flimsy and feeble, and Cavor more unreal and fantastic, and the whole enterprise madder and madder, every moment.

I got out of bed and wandered about. I sat at the window and stared at the immensity of space. Between the stars was the void, the unfathomable darkness. I tried to recall the fragmentary knowledge of astronomy I had gained in my irregular reading, but it was all too vague to furnish any idea of the things we might expect. At last I got back to bed and snatched some moments of sleep, moments of nightmare rather, in which I fell and fell and fell for evermore into the abyss of the sky.

I astonished Cavor at breakfast. I told him shortly : " I'm not coming with you in the sphere."

I met all his protests with a sullen persistence. " The thing's too mad," I said ; " and I won't come. The thing's too mad."

I would not go with him to the laboratory. I fretted about my bungalow for a time, and then took hat and stick and set off alone, I knew not whither. It chanced to be a deep glorious morning ; a warm wind and deep blue sky, the first green of spring abroad and multitudes of birds singing. I lunched on beef and beer in a little public-house near Flham, and startled the landlord by remarking, *apropos* of the weather, " A man who leaves the world when days of this sort are about is a fool !"

"That's what I says when I heerd on it !" said the landlord ; and I found that for one poor soul at least this world had proved excessive, and there had been a throat-cutting. I went on with a new twist to my thoughts.

In the afternoon I had a pleasant sleep in a sunny place, and went on my way refreshed.

I came to a comfortable-looking inn near Canterbury. It was bright with creepers, and the landlady was a clean old woman, and took my eye. I found I had just enough money to pay for my lodging with her. I decided to stop the night there. She was a talkative body, and among many other

"I FELL AND FELL FOR EVERMORE INTO THE ABYSS OF THE SKY."

particulars I learnt she had never been to London. "Canterbury's as far as ever I been," she said. "I'm not one of your gad-about sort."

"How would you like a trip to the moon?" I cried.

"I never did hold with them ballooneys," she said, evidently under the impression that this was a common excursion enough. "I wouldn't go up in one—not for ever so."

This struck me as being funny. After I had supped I sat on a bench by the door of the inn and gossiped with two labourers about brickmaking and motor-cars and the cricket of last year. And in the sky a faint new crescent, blue and vague as a distant Alp, sank westward over the sun.

The next day I returned to Cavor. "I am coming," I said. "I've been a little out of order—that's all."

That was the only time I felt any serious doubt of our enterprise. Nerves purely ! After that I worked a little more carefully

and took a trudge for an hour every day. And at last, save for the heating in the furnace, our labours were at an end.

CHAPTER IV.
INSIDE THE SPHERE.

"Go on," said Cavor, as I sat across the edge of the man-hole and looked down into the black interior of the sphere. We two were alone. It was evening, the sun had set, and the stillness of the twilight was upon everything.

I drew my other leg inside and slid down the smooth glass to the bottom of the sphere ; then turned to take the cans of food and other impedimenta from Cavor. The interior was warm — the thermometer stood at 80deg. — and as we should lose little or none of this by radiation, we were dressed in slippers and thin flannels. We had, however, a bundle of thick woollen clothing and several thick blankets to guard against mischance. By Cavor's direction I placed the packages, the cylinders of oxygen, and so forth loosely about my feet, and soon we had everything in. He walked about the roofless shed for a time, seeking anything we had overlooked, and then crawled in after me. I noted something in his hand.

"What have you there ?" I asked.

"Haven't you brought anything to read ?"

"Good Lord ! *No !*"

"I forgot to tell you. There are uncertainties—— The voyage may last—— We may be weeks !"

"But——"

"We shall be floating in this sphere with absolutely no occupation."

"I wish I'd known."

"I SAT ACROSS THE EDGE OF THE MAN-HOLE AND LOOKED DOWN INTO THE BLACK INTERIOR."

He peered out of the man-hole. "Look!" he said; "there's something there!"

"Is there time?"

"We shall be an hour."

I looked out. It was an old number of *Tit-Bits* that one of the men must have brought. Farther away in the corner I saw a torn *Lloyd's News*. I scrambled back into the sphere with these things. "What have you got?" I said.

I took the book from his hand and read, "The Works of William Shakespeare."

He coloured slightly. "My education has been so purely scientific," he said, apologetically.

"Never read him?"

"Never."

"You're in for a treat," I said. It's the sort of thing one must say, though as a matter of fact I had never read Shakespeare myself much. I doubt if many people do.

I assisted him to screw in the glass cover of the man-hole, and then he pressed a stud to close the corresponding blind in the outer case. The little oblong of twilight vanished. We were in darkness.

For a time neither of us spoke. Although our case would not be impervious to sound, everything was very still. I perceived there was nothing to grip when the shock of our start should come, and I realized that I should be uncomfortable for want of a chair.

"Why have we no chairs?" I asked.

"I've settled all that," said Cavor. "We sha'n't need them."

"Why not?"

"You will see," he said, in the tone of a man who refuses to talk.

I became silent. Suddenly it had come to me clear and vivid that I was a fool to be inside that sphere. "Even now," I asked myself, "is it too late to withdraw?" The world outside the sphere, I knew, would be cold and inhospitable enough to me—for weeks I had been living on subsidies from Cavor—but, after all, would it be as cold as the infinite zero, as inhospitable as empty space? If it had not been for the appearance of cowardice I believe that even then I should have made him let me out. But I hesitated on that score and hesitated, and grew fretful and angry, and the time passed.

There came a little jerk, a noise like champagne being uncorked in another room, and a faint, whistling sound. For just one instant I had a sense of enormous tension, a transient conviction that my feet were pressing downward with a force of countless tons. It lasted for an infinitesimal time.

But it stirred me to action. "Cavor!" I said into the darkness, "my nerve's in rags. . . . . . I don't think——"

I stopped. He made no answer.

"Confound it!" I cried; "I'm a fool! What business have I here? I'm not coming, Cavor; the thing's too risky; I'm getting out!"

"You can't," he said.

" Can't ! We'll soon see about that."

He made no answer for ten seconds. "It's too late for us to quarrel now, Bedford," he said. "That little jerk was the start. Already we are flying as swiftly as a bullet up into the gulf of space."

" I——," I said, and then it didn't seem to matter what happened. For a time I was, as it were, stunned. I had nothing to say. It was just as if I had never heard of this idea of leaving the world before. Then I perceived an unaccountable change in my bodily sensations. It was a feeling of lightness, of unreality. Coupled with that was a queer sensation in the head, an apoplectic effect almost, and a thumping of blood-vessels at the ears. Neither of these feelings diminished as time went on, but at last I got so used to them that I experienced no inconvenience.

I heard a click, and a little glow-lamp came into being.

I saw Cavor's face, as white as I felt my own to be. We regarded one another in silence. The transparent blackness of the glass behind him made him seem as though he floated in a void.

"Well, we're committed," I said, at last.

"Yes," he said, " we're committed."

" Don't move," he exclaimed, at some suggestion of a gesture. " Let your muscles keep quite lax—as if you were in bed. We are in a little universe of our own. Look at those things ! "

He pointed to the loose cases and bundles that had been lying on the blankets in the bottom of the sphere. I was astonished to see that they were floating now nearly a foot from the spherical wall. Then I saw from his shadow that Cavor was no longer leaning against the glass. I thrust out my hand behind me, and found that I too was suspended in space, clear of the glass.

I did not cry out or gesticulate, but fear came upon me. It was like being held and lifted by something—you know not what. The mere touch of my hand against the glass moved me rapidly. I understood what had happened, but that did not prevent my being afraid. We were cut off from all exterior gravitation, only the attraction of objects within our sphere had effect. Consequently everything that was not fixed to the glass was falling—slowly because of the slightness of our masses—towards the centre of gravity of our little world, to the centre of our sphere.

" We must turn round," said Cavor, " and float back to back, with the things between us."

It was the strangest sensation conceivable, floating thus loosely in space ; at first indeed horribly strange, and, when the horror passed, not disagreeable at all, exceeding restful ; indeed, the nearest thing in earthly experience to it that I know is lying on a very thick, soft feather bed. But the quality of utter detachment and independence ! I had not reckoned on things like this. I had expected a violent jerk at starting, a giddy sense of speed. Instead I felt—as if I were disembodied. It was not like the beginning of a journey ; it was like the beginning of a dream.

CHAPTER V.
THE JOURNEY TO THE MOON.

PRESENTLY Cavor extinguished the light. He said we had not overmuch energy stored, and that which we had we must economize for reading. For a time, whether it was long or short I do not know, there was nothing but blank darkness.

A question floated up out of the void. " How are we pointing ? " I said. " What is our direction ? "

" We are flying away from the earth at a tangent, and as the moon is near her third quarter we are going somewhere towards her. I will open a blind——"

Came a click, and then a window in the outer case yawned open. The sky outside was as black as the darkness within the sphere, but the shape of the open window was marked by an infinite number of stars.

Those who have only seen the starry sky from the earth cannot imagine its appearance when the vague, half-luminous veil of our air has been withdrawn. The stars we see on earth are the mere scattered survivors that penetrate our misty atmosphere. But now at last I could realize the meaning of the hosts of heaven !

Stranger things we were presently to see, but that airless, star-dusted sky ! Of all things I think that will be one of the last I shall forget.

The little window vanished with a click ; another beside it snapped open and instantly closed, and then a third, and for a moment I had to close my eyes because of the blinding splendour of the waning moon.

For a space I had to stare at Cavor and the white-lit things about me to season my eyes to light again, before I could turn them towards that pallid glare.

Four windows were open in order that the gravitation of the moon might act upon all the substances in our sphere. I found I was

"THE LITTLE WINDOW VANISHED WITH A CLICK."

no longer floating freely in space, but that my feet were resting on the glass in the direction of the moon. The blankets and cases of provisions were also creeping slowly down the glass, and presently came to rest so as to block out a portion of the view. It seemed to me, of course, that I looked "down" when I looked at the moon. On earth "down" means earthward, the way things fall, and "up" the reverse direction. Now, the pull of gravitation was towards the moon, and, for all I knew to the contrary, our earth was overhead. And, of course, when all the Cavorite blinds were closed, "down" was towards the centre of our sphere, and "up" towards its outer wall.

It was curiously unlike earthly experience, too, to have the light coming *up* to one. On earth light falls from above, or comes slanting down sideways; but here it came from beneath our feet, and to see our shadows we had to look up.

At first it gave me a sort of vertigo to stand only on thick glass, and look down upon the

moon through hundreds of thousands of miles of vacant space. But this sickness passed very speedily. And then—the splendour of the sight!

The reader may imagine it best if he will lie on the ground some warm summer's night and look between his upraised feet at the moon; but for some reason, probably because the absence of air made it so much more luminous, the moon seemed already considerably larger than it does from earth. The minutest details of its surface were acutely clear. And since we did not see it through air, its outline was bright and sharp, there was no glow or halo about it, and the star dust that covered the sky came right to its very margin and marked the outline of its unilluminated part. And as I stood and stared at the moon between my feet, that perception of the impossible that had been with me off and on ever since our start returned again with tenfold conviction.

"Cavor," I said, "this takes me queerly. Those companies we were going to run and all that about minerals——"

"Well?"

"I don't see 'em here."

"No," said Cavor, "but you'll get over all that."

"I suppose I'm made to turn right side up again. Still, *this*——. For a moment I could half believe there never was a world."

"That copy of *Lloyd's News* might help you."

I stared at the paper for a moment, then held it above the level of my face and found I could read it quite easily. I struck a column of mean little advertisements. "A gentleman of private means is willing to lend money," I read. I knew that gentleman. Then somebody eccentric wanted to sell a Cutaway bicycle, "quite new and cost fifteen pounds," for five pounds; and a lady in distress wished to dispose of some fish knives and forks, "a wedding present," at a great sacrifice. No doubt some simple soul was sagely examining those knives and forks, and another triumphantly riding off on that bicycle, and a third trustfully consulting that benevolent gentleman of means even as I

"I STOOD AND STARED AT THE MOON BETWEEN MY FEET."

read. I laughed, and let the paper drift from my hand.

"Are we visible from the earth?" I asked.

"Why?"

"I knew someone — who was rather interested in astronomy. It occurred to me that it would be rather odd if—my friend—chanced to be looking through some telescope."

"It would need the most powerful telescope on earth even now to see us as the minutest speck."

For a time I stared in silence at the moon.

"It's a world," I said; "one feels that infinitely more than one ever did on earth. People, perhaps——"

"People!" he exclaimed. "*No!* Banish all that! Think yourself a sort of ultra-Arctic voyager exploring the desolate places of space. Look at it!"

He waved his hand at the shining whiteness below. "It's dead—dead! Vast extinct volcanoes, lava wildernesses, tumbled wastes of snow or frozen carbonic acid or frozen air, and everywhere landslips, seams and cracks and gulfs. Nothing happens. Men have watched this planet systematically with telescopes for over two hundred years.

How much change do you think they have seen?"

"None."

"They have traced two indisputable landslips, a doubtful crack, and one slight periodic change of colour. And that's all."

"I didn't know they'd traced even that."

"Oh, yes. But as for people——"

"By the way," I asked, "how small a thing will the biggest telescopes show upon the moon?"

"One could see a fair-sized church. One could certainly see any towns or buildings or anything like the handiwork of men. There might, perhaps, be insects, something in the way of ants, for example, so that they could hide in deep burrows from the lunar night. Or some new sort of creatures having no earthly parallel. That is the most probable thing if we are to find life there at all. Think of the difference in conditions! Life must fit itself to a day as long as fourteen earthly days, a cloudless sun blaze of fourteen days, and then a night of equal length, growing ever colder and colder under these cold, sharp stars. In that night there must be cold, the ultimate cold, absolute zero, 273deg. C. below the earthly freezing-point. Whatever life there is must hibernate through *that*. And rise again each day."

He mused. "One can imagine something wormlike," he said, "taking its air solid, as an earthworm swallows earth or thick-skinned monsters——"

"By-the-bye," I said, "why didn't we bring a gun?"

He did not answer that question. "No," he concluded, "we just have to go. We shall see when we get there."

I remembered something. "Of course, there's my minerals, anyhow," I said; "whatever the conditions may be."

Presently he told me he wished to alter our course a little by letting the earth tug at us for a moment. He was going to open one earthward blind for thirty seconds. He warned me that it would make my head swim, and advised me to extend my hands against the glass to break my fall. I did as he directed, and thrust my feet against the bales of food cases and air cylinders to prevent their falling upon me. Then with a click the window flew open; I fell clumsily upon hands and face, and saw for a moment weight make all we had to do, that the necessity for taking refreshment did not occur to us for nearly six hours (by Cavor's chronometer) after our start. I was amazed at that lapse of time. Even then I was satisfied with very little. Cavor examined the

"I FELL CLUMSILY UPON HANDS AND FACE."

between my black, extended fingers our mother earth—a planet in a downward sky.

We were still very near—Cavor told me the distance was perhaps eight hundred miles —and the huge terrestrial disc filled all heaven. But already it was plain to see that the world was a globe. The land below us was in twilight and vague; but westward the vast grey stretches of the Atlantic shone like molten silver under the receding day. I think I recognised the cloud-dimmed coast lines of France and Spain and the south of England, and then with a click the shutter closed again, and I found myself in a state of extraordinary confusion sliding slowly over the smooth glass.

When at last things settled themselves in my mind again it seemed quite beyond question that the moon was "down" and under my feet, and that the earth was somewhere away on the level of the horizon, the earth that had been "down" to me and my kindred since the beginning of things.

So slight were the exertions required of us, so easy did the practical annihilation of our apparatus for absorbing carbonic acid and water, and pronounced it to be in satisfactory order, our consumption of oxygen having been extraordinarily slight; and our talk being exhausted for the time, and there being nothing further for us to do, we gave way to a curious drowsiness that had come upon us, and, spreading our blankets on the bottom of the sphere in such a manner as to shut out most of the moonlight, wished each other "Good-night!" and almost immediately fell asleep.

And so—sleeping and sometimes talking and reading a little, and at times eating, though without any keenness of appetite,[*] but for the most part in a sort of quiescence that was neither waking nor slumber—we fell through a space of time that had neither night nor day in it, silently, softly, and swiftly down towards the moon.

---

[*] It is a curious thing that while we were in the sphere we felt not the slightest desire for food nor did we feel the want of it when we abstained. At first we forced our appetites, but afterwards we fasted completely. Altogether we did not consume one-twentieth part of the compressed provision we had brought with us. The amount of carbonic acid we breathed was also unnaturally low, but why this was so I am quite unable to explain.

The First Men in the Moon.

By H. G. Wells.

CHAPTER VI.

THE LANDING ON THE MOON.

 REMEMBER how one day Cavor suddenly opened six of our shutters and blinded me so that I cried aloud at him. The whole area was moon, a stupendous scimitar of white dawn with its edge hacked out by notches of darkness, the crescent shore of an ebbing tide of darkness, out of which peaks and pinnacles came climbing into the blaze of the sun. I take it the reader has seen pictures or photographs of the moon, so that I need not describe the broader features of that landscape, those spacious, ring-like ranges vaster than any terrestrial mountains, their summits shining in the day, their shadows harsh and deep ; the grey, disordered plains, the ridges, hills, and craterlets all passing at last from a blazing illumination into a common mystery of black. Athwart this world we were flying scarcely a hundred miles above its crests and pinnacles. And now we could see what no eye on earth will ever see, that under the blaze of the day the harsh outlines of the rocks and ravines of the plains and crater floor grew grey and indistinct under a thickening haze, that the white of their lit surfaces broke into lumps and patches and broke again and shrank and vanished, and that here and there strange tints of brown and olive grew and spread.

But little time we had for watching then. For now we had come to the real danger of our journey. We had to drop ever closer to the moon as we spun about it, to slacken our pace and watch our chance until at last we could dare to drop upon its surface.

For Cavor that was a time of intense exertion ; for me it was an anxious inactivity. I seemed perpetually to be getting out of his way. He leapt about the sphere from point to point with an agility that would have been impossible on earth. He was perpetually opening and closing the Cavorite windows, making calculations, consulting his chronometer by means of the glow-lamp during those last eventful hours. For a long time we had all our windows closed, and hung silently in darkness, hurtling through space.

Then he was feeling for the shutter studs, and suddenly four windows were open. I staggered and covered my eyes, drenched and scorched and blinded by the unaccustomed splendour of the sun beneath my feet. Then again the shutters snapped, leaving my brain spinning in a darkness that pressed against the eyes. And after that I floated in another vast black silence.

Then Cavor switched on the electric light, and told me he proposed to bind all our luggage together with the blankets about it, against the concussion of our descent. We did this with our windows closed, because in that way our goods arranged themselves naturally at the centre of the sphere. That, too, was a strange business : we two men floating loose in that spherical space and packing and pulling ropes. Imagine it if you can ! No up or down, and every effort resulting in unexpected movements. Now I would be pressed against the glass with the full force of Cavor's thrust ; now I would be kicking helplessly in a void. Now the star of the electric light would be overhead, now under foot. Now Cavor's feet would float up before my eyes, and now we would be crossways to each other. But at last our goods were safely bound together in a big soft bale, all except two blankets with head holes that we were to wrap about ourselves.

Then for a flash Cavor opened a window moonward, and we saw that we were dropping towards a huge central crater, with a number of minor craters grouped in a sort of cross about it. And then again Cavor flung our little sphere open to the scorching, blinding sun. I think he was using the sun's attraction as a brake. "Cover yourself with a blanket," he cried, thrusting himself from me, and for a moment I did not understand.

Then I hauled the blanket from beneath my feet and got it about me and over my head and eyes. Abruptly he closed the shutters again, snapped one open again, and closed it ; then suddenly began snapping them all open, each safely into its steel roller. There came a jar, and then we were rolling over and over, bumping against the glass and against the big bale of our luggage, and clutching at each other ; and outside some white substance splashed as if we were rolling down a slope of snow. . . . . .

Over, clutch, bump, clutch, bump, over. . .

Came a thud, and I was half buried under the bale of our possessions, and for a space everything was still. Then I could hear Cavor puffing and grunting and the snapping of a shutter in its sash. I made an effort,

"FLOATING LOOSE IN THAT SPHERICAL SPACE."

We might have been in a sphere of steel for all that we could see. My rubbing with the blanket simply smeared the glass, and as fast as I wiped it it became opaque again with freshly - condensed moisture mixed with an increasing quantity of blanket hairs. Of course I ought not to have used the blanket. In my efforts to clear the glass I slipped upon the damp surface and hurt my shin against one of the oxygen cylinders that protruded from our bale.

The thing was exasperating — it was absurd. Here we were just arrived upon the moon, amidst we knew not what wonders, and all we could see was the grey and streaming wall of the bubble in which we had come.

thrust back our blanket - wrapped luggage, and emerged from beneath it. Our open windows were just visible as a deeper black set with stars.

We were still alive, and we were lying in the darkness of the shadow of the wall of the great crater into which we had fallen.

We sat getting our breath again and feeling the bruises on our limbs. I don't think either of us had had a very clear expectation of such rough handling as we had received. I struggled painfully to my feet. "And now," said I, "to look at the landscape of the moon! But——! It's tremendously dark, Cavor!"

The glass was dewy, and as I spoke I wiped at it with my blanket. "We're half an hour or so beyond the day," he said. "We must wait."

It was impossible to distinguish anything.

"Confound it," I said, "but at this rate we might have stopped at home!" and I squatted on the bale and shivered and drew my blanket closer about me.

Abruptly the moisture turned to spangles and fronds of frost. "Can you reach the electric heater?" said Cavor. "Yes—that black knob. Or we shall freeze."

I did not wait to be told twice. "And now," said I, "what are we to do?"

"Wait," he said.

"Wait?"

"Of course. We shall have to wait until our air gets warm again, and then this glass will clear. We can't do anything till then. It's night here yet—we must wait for the day to overtake us. Meanwhile, don't you feel hungry?"

For a space I did not answer him, but sat fretting. I turned reluctantly from the

"WE WERE LYING IN THE DARKNESS OF THE SHADOW OF THE WALL OF THE GREAT CRATER."

smeared puzzle of the glass and stared at his face. " Yes," I said, " I am hungry. I feel somehow enormously disappointed. I had expected——. I don't know what I had expected, but not this."

I summoned my philosophy, and, rearranging my blanket about me, sat down on the bale again and began my first meal on the moon. I don't think I finished it—I forget. Presently, first in patches, then running rapidly together into wider spaces, came the clearing of the glass, came the drawing of the misty veil that hid the moon-world from our eyes.

We peered out upon the landscape of the moon.

CHAPTER VII.
SUNRISE ON THE MOON.

As we saw it first it was the wildest and most desolate of scenes. We were in an enormous amphitheatre, a vast circular plain, the floor of the giant crater. Its cliff-like walls closed us in on every side. From the westward the light of the unseen sun fell upon them, reaching to the very foot of the cliff, and showed a disordered escarpment of drab and greyish rock, lined here and there with banks and crevices of snow. This was, perhaps, a dozen miles away, but at first no intervening atmosphere diminished in the slightest the minutely-detailed brilliancy with which these things glared at us. They stood out clear and dazzling against a background of starry blackness that seemed to our earthly eyes rather a gloriously-spangled velvet curtain than the spaciousness of the sky.

The eastward cliff was at first merely a starless selvedge to the starry dome. No rosy flush, no creeping pallor, announced the commencing day. Only the Corona, the Zodiacal light, a huge, cone-shaped, luminous haze, pointing up towards the splendour of the morning star, warned us of the imminent nearness of the sun.

Whatever light was about us was reflected by the westward cliffs. It showed a huge, undulating plain, cold and grey—a grey that deepened eastward into the absolute raven darkness of the cliff shadow, innumerable rounded grey summits, ghostly hummocks, billows of snowy substance, stretching crest beyond crest into the remote obscurity, gave us our first inkling of the distance of the crater wall. These hummocks looked like snow. At the time I thought they were snow. But they were not—they were mounds and masses of frozen air !

So it was at first, and then, sudden, swift, and amazing, came the lunar day.

The sunlight had crept down the cliff, it touched the drifted masses at its base, and incontinently came striding with seven-leagued boots towards us. The distant cliff seemed to shift and quiver, and at the touch of the dawn a reek of grey vapour poured upward from the crater floor, whirls and puffs and drifting wraiths of grey, thicker and broader and denser, until at last the whole westward plain was steaming like a wet handkerchief held before the fire, and the westward cliffs were no more than a refracted glare beyond.

"It is air," said Cavor. "It must be air —or it would not rise like this—at the mere touch of a sunbeam. And at this pace . . ."

He peered upwards. "Look !" he said.

"What ?" I asked.

"In the sky. Already. On the blackness —a little touch of blue. See ! The stars seem larger. And the little ones and all those dim nebulosities we saw in empty space—they are hidden !"

Swiftly, steadily the day approached us. Grey summit after grey summit was overtaken by the blaze, and turned to a smoking white intensity. At last there was nothing to the west of us but a bank of surging fog, the tumultuous advance and ascent of cloudy haze. The distant cliff had receded farther and farther, had loomed and changed through the whirl, had foundered and vanished at last in its confusion.

Nearer came that steaming advance, nearer and nearer, coming as fast as the shadow of a cloud before the south-west wind. About us rose a thin, anticipatory haze.

Cavor gripped my arm.

"What ?" I said.

"Look ! The sunrise ! The sun !"

He turned me about and pointed to the brow of the eastward cliff, looming above the haze about us, scarce lighter than the darkness of the sky. But now its line was marked by strange reddish shapes—tongues of vermilion flame that writhed and danced. I fancied it must be spirals of vapour that had caught the light and made this crest of fiery tongues against the sky, but, indeed, it was the solar prominences I saw, a crown of fire about the sun that is for ever hidden from earthly eyes by our atmospheric veil.

And then—the sun !

Steadily, inevitably, came a brilliant line— came a thin edge of intolerable effulgence that took a circular shape, became a bow, became a blazing sceptre, and hurled a shaft of heat at us as though it were a spear.

It seemed verily to stab my eyes ! I cried aloud and turned about blinded, groping for my blanket beneath the bale.

And with that incandescence came a sound, the first sound that had reached us from without since we left the earth, a hissing and rustling, the stormy trailing of the aerial garment of the advancing day. And with the coming of the sound and the light the sphere lurched, and, blinded and dazzled, we staggered helplessly against each other. It lurched again, and the hissing grew louder. I had shut my eyes perforce ; I was making clumsy efforts to cover my head with my blanket, and this second lurch sent me helplessly off my feet. I fell against the bale, and, opening my eyes, had a momentary glimpse of the air just outside our glass. It was running — it was boiling—like snow into which a white-hot rod is thrust. What had been solid air had suddenly, at the touch of the sun, become a paste, a mud, a slushy liquefaction, that hissed and bubbled into gas.

There came a still more violent whirl of the sphere, and we had clutched one another. In another moment we were spun about again. Round we went and over, and then I was on all fours. The lunar dawn had hold of us. It meant to show us little men what the moon could do with us.

I caught a second glimpse of things without, puffs of vapour, half-liquid slush, excavated, sliding, falling, sliding. We dropped into darkness. I went down with Cavor's knees in my chest. Then he seemed to fly away from me, and for a moment I lay, with all the breath out of my body, staring upward. A huge landslip, as it were, of the melting stuff had splashed over us, buried us, and now it thinned and boiled off us. I saw the bubbles dancing on the glass above. I heard Cavor exclaiming feebly.

Then some huge landslip in the thawing air had caught us and, spluttering expostulation, we began to roll down a slope, rolling faster and faster, leaping crevasses and rebounding from banks, faster and faster, westward into the white-hot boiling tumult of the lunar day.

Clutching at one another we spun about, pitched this way and that, our bale of packages leaping at us, pounding at us. We collided, we gripped, we were torn asunder—

"WE BEGAN TO ROLL DOWN A SLOPE."

upside down, his eyes also protected by tinted goggles. His breath came irregularly, and his lip was bleeding from a bruise. "Better?" he said, wiping the blood with the back of his hand.

Everything seemed swaying for a space, but that was simply my giddiness. I perceived that he had closed some of the shutters in the outer sphere to save me from the direct blaze of the sun. I was aware that everything about us was very brilliant.

"Lord!" I gasped.   "But this——"

I craned my neck to see. I perceived there was a blinding glare outside, an utter change from the gloomy darkness of our first impressions. "Have I been insensible long?" I asked.

"I don't know — the chronometer is broken. Some little time . . . . My dear chap! I have been afraid . . . ."

I lay for a space taking this in. I saw his face still bore evidences of emotion. For a while I said nothing. I passed an inquisitive hand over my contusions, and surveyed his face for similar damages. The back of my right hand had suffered most, and was skinless and raw. My forehead was bruised and had bled. He handed me a little measure with some of the restorative—I forget the name of it—he had brought with us. After a time I felt a little better. I began to stretch my limbs carefully. Soon I could talk.

"It wouldn't have done," I said, as though there had been no interval.

"No, it *wouldn't.*"

He thought, his hands hanging over his knees. He peered through the glass and then stared at me. "Good Lord!" he said. "*No!*"

"What has happened?" I asked, after a pause; "have we jumped to the tropics?"

"It was as I expected. This air has evaporated. If it is air. At any rate it has evaporated, and the surface of the moon is showing. We are lying on a bank of earthy rock. Here and there bare soil is exposed; a queer sort of soil."

It occurred to him that it was unnecessary

our heads met, and the whole universe burst into fiery darts and stars! On the earth we should have smashed one another a dozen times, but on the moon luckily for us our weight was only one-sixth of what it is terrestrially, and we fell very mercifully. I recall a sensation of utter sickness, a feeling as if my brain were upside down within my skull, and then——

Something was at work upon my face; some thin feelers worried my ears. Then I discovered the brilliance of the landscape around was mitigated by blue spectacles. Cavor bent over me, and I saw his face to explain. He assisted me into a sitting position, and I could see with my own eyes.

CHAPTER VIII.
A LUNAR MORNING.

THE harsh emphasis, the pitiless black and white of the scenery, had altogether disappeared. The glare of the sun had taken upon itself a faint tinge of amber; the shadows upon the cliff of the crater wall were deeply purple. To the eastward a dark bank of fog still crouched and sheltered from the sunrise, but to the westward the sky was blue and clear. I began to realize the length of my insensibility.

We were no longer in a void. An atmosphere had arisen about us. The outline of things had gained in character, had grown acute and varied; save for a shadowed space of white substance here and there, white substance that was no longer air but snow, the Arctic appearance had gone altogether. Everywhere broad, rusty-brown spaces of bare and tumbled earth spread to the blaze of the sun. Here and there at the edge of the snow-drifts were transient little pools and eddies of water, the only things stirring in that expanse of barrenness. The sunlight inundated the upper two-thirds of our sphere and turned our climate to high summer, but our feet were still in shadow and the sphere was lying upon a drift of snow.

And scattered here and there upon the slope, and emphasized by little white threads of unthawed snow upon their shady sides, were shapes like sticks—dry, twisted sticks of the same rusty hue as the rock upon which they lay. That caught one's thoughts sharply. Sticks! On a lifeless world? Then as my eye grew more accustomed to the texture of their substance I perceived that almost all this surface had a fibrous texture, like the carpet of brown needles one finds beneath the shade of pine trees.

"Cavor!" I said.

"Yes?"

"It may be a dead world now—but once——"

Something arrested my attention. I had discovered among these needles a number of little round objects. And it seemed to me that one of these had moved.

"Cavor," I whispered.

"What?"

But I did not answer at once. I stared incredulous. For an instant I could not believe my eyes. I gave an inarticulate cry. I gripped his arm. I pointed. "Look!" I cried, finding my tongue. "There! Yes! And there!"

His eyes followed my pointing finger. "Eh?" he said.

How can I describe the thing I saw? It is so petty a thing to state, and yet it seemed so wonderful, so pregnant with emotion. I have said that amidst the stick-like litter were these rounded bodies, these little oval bodies that might have passed as very small pebbles. And now first one and then another had stirred, had rolled over and cracked, and down the crack of each of them showed a minute line of yellowish green, thrusting outward to meet the hot encouragement of the newly-risen sun. For a moment that was all, and then there stirred and burst a third!

"It is a seed," said Cavor. And then I heard him whisper, very softly, "*Life!*"

"Life!" and immediately it poured upon us that our vast journey had not been made in vain, that we had come to no arid waste of minerals, but to a world that lived and moved! We watched intensely. I remember I kept rubbing the glass before me with my sleeve, jealous of the faintest suspicion of mist.

The picture was clear and vivid only in the middle of the field. All about that centre the dead fibres and seeds were magnified and distorted by the curvature of the glass. But we could see enough! One after another all down the sunlit slope these miraculous little brown bodies burst and gaped apart, like seed-pods, like the husks of fruits; opened eager mouths that drank in the heat and light pouring in a cascade from the newly-risen sun.

Every moment more of these seed-coats ruptured, and even as they did so the swelling pioneers overflowed their rent-distended seed-cases and passed into the second stage of growth. With a steady assurance, a swift deliberation, these amazing seeds thrust a rootlet downward to the earth and a queer little bundle-like bud into the air. In a little while the whole slope was dotted with minute plantlets standing at attention in the blaze of the sun.

They did not stand for long. The bundle-like buds swelled and strained and opened with a jerk, thrusting out a coronet of little sharp tips, spreading a whorl of tiny, spiky, brownish leaves, that lengthened rapidly, lengthened visibly, even as we watched. The movement was slower than any animal's, swifter than any plant's I have ever seen before. How can I suggest it to you—the way that growth went on? The leaf tips

"WE WATCHED INTENSELY."

blinding glare of the sun. And beyond this fringe was the silhouette of a plant mass, branching clumsily like a cactus and swelling visibly, swelling like a bladder that fills with air.

Then to the westward also I discovered tha᷈ another such distendec form was rising over the scrub. But here the light fell upon its sleek sides, and I could see that its colour was a vivid orange hue. It rose as one watched it; if one looked away from it for a minute and then back, its outline had changed: it thrust out blunt, congested branches, until in a little time it rose a coral-line shape of many feet in height. Compared with such a growth the terrestrial puff-ball, which will sometimes swell a foot in diameter in a single night, would be a hopeless laggard. But then the puff-ball grows against a gravitational pull six times that of the moon. Beyond, out of gullies and flats that had been hidden from us, but not from the quickening sun, over reefs and banks of shining rock, a bristling beard of spiky and fleshy vegetation was straining into view, hurrying tumultuously to take advantage of the brief day in which it must flower, and fruit, and seed again, and die. It was like a miracle, that growth. So, one must imagine, the trees and plants arose at the Creation, and covered the desolation of the new-made earth.

Imagine it! Imagine that dawn! The resurrection of the frozen air, the stirring and quickening of the soil, and then this silent uprising of vegetation, this unearthly ascent of fleshliness and spikes. Conceive it all lit by a blaze that would make the intensest sunlight of earth seem watery and weak. And still amidst this stirring jungle wherever there was shadow lingered banks of bluish snow. And to have the picture of our impression complete you must bear in mind that we saw it all through a thick bent glass,

grew so that they moved onward even while we looked at them. The brown seed-case shrivelled and was absorbed with an equal rapidity. Have you ever on a cold day taken a thermometer into your warm hand and watched the little thread of mercury creep up the tube? These moon-plants grew like that.

In a few minutes, as it seemed, the buds of the more forward of these plants had lengthened into a stem, and were even putting forth a second whorl of leaves, and all the slope that had seemed so recently a lifeless stretch of litter was now dark with the stunted, olive-green herbage of bristling spikes that swayed with the vigour of their growing.

I turned about, and behold! along the upper edge of a rock to the eastward a similar fringe, in a scarcely less forward condition, swayed and bent, dark against the distorting it as things are distorted by a lens, acute only in the centre of the picture and very bright there, and towards the edge magnified and unreal.

CHAPTER IX.

PROSPECTING BEGINS.

WE ceased to gaze. We turned to each other, the same thought, the same question, in our eyes. For these plants to grow there must be some air, however attenuated — air that we also should be able to breathe.

"The man-hole?" I said.

"Yes," said Cavor; "if it is air we see!"

"In a little while," I said, "these plants will be as high as we are. Suppose— suppose, after all—— Is it certain? How do you know that stuff *is* air? It may be nitrogen; it may be carbonic acid even!"

"That is easy," he said, and set about proving it. He produced a big piece of crumpled paper from the bale, lit it, and thrust it hastily through the man-hole valve. I bent forward and peered down through the thick glass for its appearance outside, that little flame on whose evidence depended so much!

I saw the paper drop out and lie lightly upon the snow. The pink flame of its burning vanished. For an instant it seemed to be extinguished . . . And then I saw a little blue tongue upon the edge of it that trembled and crept and spread!

Quietly the whole sheet, save where it lay in immediate contact with the snow, charred and shrivelled and sent up a quivering thread of smoke. There was no doubt left to me: the atmosphere of the moon was either pure oxygen or air, and capable therefore, unless its tenuity were excessive, of supporting our alien life. We might emerge—and live!

I sat down with my legs on either side of the man-hole and prepared to unscrew it, but Cavor stopped me. "There is first a little precaution," he said. He pointed out that, although it was certainly an oxygenated atmosphere outside, it might still be so rarefied as to cause us grave injury. He reminded me of mountain sickness and of the bleeding that often afflicts aeronauts who have ascended too swiftly, and he spent some time in the preparation of a sickly-tasting drink which he insisted on my sharing. It made me feel a little numb, but otherwise had no effect on me. Then he permitted me to begin unscrewing.

Presently the glass stopper of the man-hole was so far undone that the denser air within

our sphere began to escape along the thread of the screw, singing as a kettle sings before it boils. Thereupon he made me desist. It speedily became evident that the pressure outside was very much less than it was within. How much less it was we had no means of telling.

I sat grasping the stopper with both hands, ready to close it again if, in spite of our intense hope, the lunar atmosphere should after all prove too rarefied for us, and Cavor sat with a cylinder of compressed oxygen at hand to restore our pressure. We looked at one another in silence, and then at the fantastic vegetation that swayed and grew visibly and noiselessly without. And ever that shrill piping continued.

The blood-vessels began to throb in my ears, and the sound of Cavor's movements diminished. I noted how still everything had become because of the thinning of the air.

As our air sizzled out from the screw the moisture of it condensed in little puffs.

Presently I experienced a peculiar short-ness of breath—that lasted, indeed, during the whole of the time of our exposure to the moon's exterior atmosphere, and a rather unpleasant sensation about the ears and finger-nails and the back of the throat grew upon my attention, and presently passed off again.

But then came vertigo and nausea that abruptly changed the quality of my courage. I gave the lid of the man-hole half a turn and made a hasty explanation to Cavor, but now he was the more sanguine. He answered me in a voice that seemed extraordinarily small and remote, because of the thinness of the air that carried the sound. He recommended a nip of brandy, and set me the example, and presently I felt better. I turned the man-hole stopper back again. The throbbing in my ears grew louder, and then I remarked that the piping note of the outrush had ceased. For a time I could not be sure that it had ceased.

"Well?" said Cavor, in the ghost of a voice.

"Well?" said I.

"Shall we go on?"

I thought. "Is this all?"

"If you can stand it."

By way of answer I went on unscrewing. I lifted the circular operculum from its place and laid it carefully on the bale. A flake or so of snow whirled and vanished as that thin and unfamiliar air took possession of our sphere. I knelt and then seated myself at the edge of the man-hole, peering over it.

Beneath, within a yard of my face, lay the untrodden snow of the moon.

There came a little pause. Our eyes met.

"It doesn't distress your lungs too much?" said Cavor.

"No," I said. "I can stand this."

He stretched out his hand for his blanket, thrust his head through its central hole, and wrapped it about him. He sat down on the edge of the man-hole; he let his feet drop until they were within six inches of the lunar snow. He hesitated for a moment, then thrust himself forward, dropped these intervening inches, and stood upon the untrodden soil of the moon.

As he stepped forward he was refracted grotesquely by the edge of the glass. He stood for a moment looking this way and that. Then he drew himself together and leapt.

The glass distorted everything, but it seemed to me even then to be an extremely big leap. He had at one bound become remote. He seemed twenty or thirty feet off. He was standing high upon a rocky mass and gesticulating back to me. Perhaps he was shouting — but the sound did not reach me. But how the deuce had he done this? I felt like a man who has just seen a new conjuring trick.

Still in a puzzled state of mind, I too dropped through the man-hole. I stood up. Just in front of me the snowdrift had fallen away and made a sort of ditch. I made a step and jumped.

I found myself flying through the air, saw the rock on which he stood coming to meet me, clutched it, and clung in a state of infinite amazement. I gasped a painful

laugh. I was tremendously confused. Cavor bent down and shouted in piping tones for me to be careful. I had forgotten that on the moon, with only an eighth part of the earth's mass and a quarter of its diameter, my weight was barely a sixth what it was on earth. But now that fact insisted on being remembered.

"We are out of Mother Earth's leading-strings now," he said.

With a guarded effort I raised myself to the top and, moving as cautiously as a rheumatic patient, stood up beside him under the blaze of the sun. The sphere lay behind us on its dwindling snowdrift thirty feet away.

As far as the eye could see over the enormous disorder of rocks that formed the

" HE WAS STANDING HIGH UPON A ROCKY MASS."

crater floor the same bristling scrub that surrounded us was starting into life, diversified here and there by bulging masses of a cactus form, and scarlet and purple lichens that grew so fast they seemed to crawl over the rocks. The whole area of the crater seemed to me then to be one similar wilderness up to the very foot of the surrounding cliff.

This cliff was apparently bare of vegetation save at its base, and with buttresses and terraces and platforms that did not very greatly attract our attention at the time. It was many miles away from us in every direction; we seemed to be almost at the centre of the crater, and we saw it through a certain haziness that drove before the wind. For there was even a wind now in the thin air—a swift yet weak wind that chilled exceedingly, but exerted little pressure. It was blowing round the crater, as it seemed, to the hot, illuminated side from the foggy darkness under the sunward wall. It was difficult to look into this eastward fog; we had to peer with half-closed eyes beneath the shade of our hands, because of the fierce intensity of the motionless sun.

"It seems to be deserted," said Cavor, "absolutely desolate."

I looked about me again. I retained even then a clinging hope of some quasi-human evidence, some pinnacle of building, some house or engine; but everywhere one looked spread the tumbled rocks in peaks and crests, and the darting scrub and those bulging cacti that swelled and swelled, a flat negation as it seemed of all such hope.

"It looks as though these plants had it to themselves," I said. "I see no trace of any other creature."

"No insects—no birds—no! Not a trace, not a scrap or particle of animal life. If there was—what would they do in the night? .... No; there's just these plants alone."

I shaded my eyes with my hand. "It's like the landscape of a dream. These things are less like earthly land plants than the things one imagines among the rocks at the bottom of the sea. Look at that, yonder! One might imagine it a lizard changed into a plant. And the glare!"

"This is only the fresh morning," said Cavor.

He sighed and looked about him. "This is no world for men," he said. "And yet in a way . . . . . it appeals."

He became silent for a time, then commenced his meditative humming. I started at a gentle touch, and found a thin sheet of livid lichen lapping over my shoe. I kicked at it and it fell to powder, and each speck began to grow. I heard Cavor exclaim sharply, and perceived that one of the fixed bayonets of the scrub had pricked him.

He hesitated, his eyes sought among the rocks about us. A sudden blaze of pink had crept up a ragged pillar of crag. It was a most extraordinary pink, a livid magenta.

"Look!" said I, turning, and behold Cavor had vanished!

For an instant I stood transfixed. Then I made a hasty step to look over the verge of the rock. But, in my surprise at his disappearance, I forgot once more that we were on the moon. The thrust of my foot that I made in striding would have carried me a yard on earth; on the moon it carried me six—a good five yards over the edge. For the moment the thing had something of the effect of those nightmares when one falls and falls. For while one falls sixteen feet in the first second of a fall on earth, on the moon one falls two, and with only a sixth of one's weight. I fell, or rather I jumped down, about ten yards I suppose. It seemed to take quite a long time—five or six seconds, I should think. I floated through the air and fell like a feather, knee-deep in a snowdrift in the bottom of a gully of blue-grey, white-veined rock.

I looked about me. "Cavor!" I cried, but no Cavor was visible.

"Cavor!" I cried louder, and the rocks echoed me.

I turned fiercely to the rocks and clambered to the summit of them. "Cavor," I cried. My voice sounded like the voice of a lost lamb.

The sphere too was not in sight, and for a moment a horrible feeling of desolation pinched my heart.

Then I saw him. He was laughing and gesticulating to attract my attention. He was on a bare patch of rock twenty or thirty yards away. I could not hear his voice, but "Jump!" said his gestures. I hesitated, the distance seemed enormous. Yet I reflected that surely I must be able to clear a greater distance than Cavor.

I made a step back, gathered myself together, and leapt with all my might. I seemed to shoot right up in the air as though I should never come down. . .

It was horrible and delightful, and as wild as a nightmare to go flying off in this fashion. I realized my leap had been altogether too violent. I flew clean over Cavor's head, and beheld a spiky confusion in a gully spreading

"I REALIZED MY LEAP HAD BEEN TOO VIOLENT."

He helped me to my feet. "You exerted yourself too much," he said, dabbing at the yellow stuff with his hand to remove it from my garments.

I stood passive and panting, allowing him to beat off the jelly from my knees and elbows and lecture me upon my misfortunes. "We don't quite allow for the gravitation. Our muscles are scarcely educated yet. We must practise a little. When you have got your breath."

I pulled two or three little thorns out of my hand, and sat for a time on a boulder of rock. My muscles were quivering, and I had that feeling of personal disillusionment that comes at the first fall to the learner of cycling on earth.

It suddenly occurred to Cavor that the cold air in the gully after the brightness of the sun might give me a fever. So we clambered back into the sunlight. We found that beyond a few abrasions I had received no serious injuries from my tumble, and at Cavor's suggestion we were presently looking round for some safe and easy landing-place for my next leap. We chose a rocky slab some ten yards off, separated from us by a little thicket of olive-green spikes.

"Imagine it there !" said Cavor, who was assuming the airs of a trainer, and he pointed to a spot about four feet from my toes. This leap I managed without difficulty, and I must confess I found a certain satisfaction in Cavor's falling short by a foot or so and tasting the spikes of the scrub. "One has to be careful, you see," he said, pulling out his thorns, and with that he ceased to be my Mentor and became my fellow-learner in the art of lunar locomotion.

We chose a still easier jump and did it without difficulty, and then leapt back again and to and fro several times, accustoming our muscles to the new standard. I could never have believed, had I not experienced it, how rapid that adaptation would be. In a very little time indeed, certainly after fewer than thirty leaps, we could judge the effort

to meet my fall. I gave a yelp of alarm. I put out my hands and straightened my legs.

I hit a huge fungoid bulk that burst all about me, scattering a mass of orange spores in every direction, and covering me with orange powder. I rolled over spluttering, and came to rest convulsed with breathless laughter.

I became aware of Cavor's little round face peering over a bristling hedge. He shouted some faded inquiry. "Eh?" I tried to shout, but could not do so for want of breath. He made his way towards me, coming gingerly among the bushes.

"We've got to be careful !" he said. "This moon has no discipline. She'll let us smash ourselves."

necessary for a distance with almost terrestrial assurance.

And all this time the lunar plants were growing around us, higher and denser and more entangled, every moment thicker and taller, spiked plants, green cactus masses, fungi, fleshy and lichenous things, strangest radiate and sinuous shapes. But we were so intent upon our leaping that for a time we gave no heed to their unfaltering expansion.

"I STOOD FOR A MOMENT STRUCK BY THE GROTESQUE EFFECT OF HIS SOARING FIGURE."

experimental as a Cockney would do placed for the first time among mountains; and I do not think it occurred to either of us, face to face though we were with the Unknown, to be very greatly afraid.

We were bitten by a spirit of enterprise. We selected a lichenous kopje, perhaps fifteen yards away, and landed neatly on its summit one after the other. "Good!" we cried to each other, "good"; and Cavor made three steps and went off to a tempting slope of snow a good twenty yards and more beyond. I stood for a moment struck by the grotesque effect of his soaring figure, his dirty cricket cap and spiky hair, his little round body, his arms and his knicker-bockered legs tucked up tightly against the weird spaciousness of the lunar scene. A gust of laughter seized me, and then I stepped off to follow. Plump! I dropped beside him.

We made a few Gargantuan strides, leapt three or four times more, and sat down at last in a lichenous hollow. Our lungs were painful. We sat holding our sides and recovering our breath, looking appreciation at one another. Cavor panted something about "Amazing sensations." And then came a thought into my head. For the moment it did not seem a particularly appalling thought, simply a natural question arising out of the situation.

"By the way," I said, "where exactly is the sphere?"

Cavor looked at me. "Eh?"

The full meaning of what we were saying struck me sharply.

"Cavor!" I cried, laying a hand on his arm; "where is the sphere?"

An extraordinary elation had taken possession of us. Partly I think it was our sense of release from the confinement of the sphere. Mainly, however, the thin sweetness of the air which I am certain contained a much larger proportion of oxygen than our terrestrial atmosphere. In spite of the strange quality of all about us, I felt as adventurous and

The First Men in the Moon.

By H. G. Wells.

CHAPTER X.

LOST MEN IN THE MOON.

AVOR'S face caught something of my dismay. He stood up and stared about him at the scrub that fenced us in and rose about us, straining upward in a passion of growth. He put a dubious hand to his lips. He spoke with a sudden lack of assurance. "I think," he said, slowly, "we left it . . . . somewhere . . . . about *there*."

He pointed a hesitating finger that wavered in an arc.

"I'm not sure." His look of consternation deepened. "Anyhow," he said, with his eyes on me, "it can't be far."

We had both stood up. We made unmeaning ejaculations ; our eyes sought in the twining, thickening jungle round about us.

All about us on the sunlit slopes frothed and swayed the darting shrubs, the swelling cactus, the creeping lichens, and wherever the shade remained the snowdrifts lingered. North, south, east, and west spread an identical monotony of unfamiliar forms. And somewhere, buried already among this tangled confusion, was our sphere, our home, our only provision, our only hope of escape from this fantastic wilderness of ephemeral growths into which we had come.

"I think, after all," he said, pointing suddenly, "it might be over there."

"No," I said. "We have turned in a curve. See ! here is the mark of my heels. It's clear the thing must be more to the eastward, much more. No ! the sphere must be over there."

"I *think*," said Cavor, "I kept the sun upon my right all the time."

"Every leap, it seems to *me*," I said, "my shadow flew before me."

We stared into one another's eyes. The area of the crater had become enormously vast to our imaginations, the growing thickets already impenetrably dense.

"Good heavens ! What fools we have been !"

"It's evident that we must find it again," said Cavor, "and that soon. The sun grows stronger. We should be fainting with the heat already if it wasn't so dry. And . . . . I'm hungry."

I stared at him. I had not suspected this aspect of the matter before. But it came to me at once—a positive craving. "Yes," I said with emphasis, "I am hungry too."

He stood up with a look of active resolution. "Certainly we must find the sphere."

As calmly as possible we surveyed the interminable reefs and thickets that formed the floor of the crater, each of us weighing in silence the chances of our finding the sphere before we were overtaken by heat and hunger.

"It can't be fifty yards from here," said Cavor, with indecisive gestures. "The only thing is to beat round about until we come upon it."

"That is all we can do," I said, without any alacrity to begin our hunt. "I wish this confounded spike bush did not grow so fast !"

"That's just it," said Cavor. "But it *was* lying on a bank of snow."

I stared about me in the vain hope of recognising some knoll or shrub that had been near the sphere. But everywhere was a confusing sameness, everywhere the aspiring bushes, the distending fungi, the dwindling snow-banks, steadily and inevitably changed. The sun scorched and stung ; the faintness of an unaccountable hunger mingled with our infinite perplexity. And even as we stood there, confused and lost amidst unprecedented things, we became aware for the first time of a sound upon the moon other than the stir of the growing plants, the faint sighing of the wind, or those that we ourselves had made.

Boom . . . Boom . . . Boom . . .

It came from beneath our feet, a sound in the earth. We seemed to hear it with our feet as much as with our ears. Its dull resonance was muffled by distance, thick with the quality of intervening substance. No sound that I can imagine could have astonished us more, or have changed more completely the quality of things about us. For this sound, rich, slow, and deliberate, seemed to us as though it could be nothing but the striking of some gigantic buried clock.

Boom . . . Boom . . . Boom . . .

Sound suggestive of still cloisters, of sleepless nights in crowded cities, of vigils and the awaited hour, of all that is orderly and methodical in life, booming out pregnant and mysterious in this fantastic desert ! To the eye everything was unchanged ; the desolation of bushes and cacti waving silently in the wind stretched unbroken to the distant cliffs ; the still, dark sky was empty overhead, and the hot sun hung and burned. And through it all, a warning, a threat, throbbed this enigma of sound.

Boom . . . Boom . . . Boom . . .

We questioned one another in faint and faded voices. "A clock?"

"Like a clock!"

"What is it?"

"What can it be?"

"Count," was Cavor's belated suggestion, and at that word the striking ceased.

The silence, the rhythmic disappointment of the silence, came as a fresh shock. For a moment one could doubt whether one had ever heard a sound. Or whether it might not still be going on! Had I indeed heard a sound?

I felt the pressure of Cavor's hand upon my arm. He spoke in an undertone as though he feared to wake some sleeping thing. "Let us keep together," he whispered, "and look for the sphere. We must get back to the sphere. This is beyond our understanding."

"Which way shall we go?"

He hesitated. An intense persuasion of presences, of unseen things about us and near us, dominated our minds. What could they be? Where could they be? Was this arid desolation, alternately frozen and scorched, only the outer rind and mask of some subterranean world? And if so, what sort of world? What sort of inhabitants might it not presently disgorge upon us?

And then stabbing the aching stillness, as vivid and sudden as an unexpected thunderclap, came a clang and rattle as though great gates of metal had suddenly been flung apart.

It arrested our steps. We stood gaping helplessly. Then Cavor stole towards me.

"BOOM . . . BOOM . . . BOOM."

"I do not understand!" he whispered, close to my face. He waved his hand vaguely skyward, the vague suggestion of still vaguer thoughts.

"A hiding-place! If anything came——"

I looked about us. I nodded my head in assent to him.

We started off, moving stealthily, with the most exaggerated precautions against noise. We went towards a thicket of scrub. A clangour like hammers flung about a boiler hastened our steps. "We must crawl," whispered Cavor.

The lower leaves of the bayonet plants, already overshadowed by the newer ones above, were beginning to wilt and shrivel so that we could thrust our way in among the thickening stems without any serious injury. A stab in the face or arm we did not heed. At the heart of the thicket I stopped and stared panting into Cavor's face.

"Subterranean," he whispered. "Below."

"They may come out."

"We must find the sphere!"

"Yes," I said, "but how?"

"Crawl till we come to it."

"But if we don't?"

"Keep hidden. See what they are like."

"We will keep together," said I.

He thought. "Which way shall we go?"

"We must take our chance."

We peered this way and that. Then very circumspectly we began to crawl through the lower jungle, making so far as we could judge a circuit, halting now at every waving fungus, at every sound, intent only on the sphere from which we had so foolishly emerged. Ever and again from out of the. earth beneath us came concussions, beatings, strange, inexplicable, mechanical sounds, and once and then again we thought we heard something, a faint rattle and tumult, borne to us through the air. But fearful as we were we dared essay no vantage-point to survey the crater. For long we saw nothing of the beings whose sounds were so abundant and insistent. But for the faintness of our hunger and the drying of our throats that crawling would have had the quality of a very vivid dream. It was so absolutely unreal. The only element with any touch of reality was these sounds.

Figure it to yourself! About us the dreamlike jungle, with the silent bayonet leaves darting overhead, and the silent, vivid, sun-splashed lichens under our hands and knees, waving with the vigour of their growth as a carpet waves when the wind gets beneath it. Ever and again one of the bladder fungi, bulging and distending under the sun, loomed upon us. Ever and again some novel shape in vivid colour obtruded. The very cells that built up these plants were as large as my thumb, like beads of coloured glass. And all these things were saturated in the unmitigated glare of the sun, were seen against a sky that was bluish-black and spangled still, in spite of the sunlight, with a few surviving stars. Strange! the very forms and texture of the stones were strange. It was all strange: the feeling of one's body was unprecedented, every other movement ended in a surprise. The breath sucked thin in one's throat, the blood flowed through one's ears in a throbbing tide, thud, thud, thud, thud . . .

And ever and again came gusts of turmoil, hammering, the clanging and throb of machinery, and presently — the bellowing of great beasts!

CHAPTER XI.

THE MOONCALF PASTURES.

So we two poor terrestrial castaways, lost in that wild-growing moon jungle, crawled in terror before the sounds that had come upon us. We crawled as it seemed a long time before we saw either Selenite or mooncalf, though we heard the bellowing and gruntulous noises of these latter continually drawing nearer to us. We crawled through stony ravines, over snow slopes, amidst fungi that ripped like thin bladders at our thrust, emitting a watery humour; over a perfect pavement of things like puff balls and beneath interminable thickets of scrub. And ever more hopelessly our eyes sought for our abandoned sphere. The noise of the mooncalves would at times be a vast, flat, calf-like sound, at times it rose to an amazed and wrathy bellowing, and again it would become a clogged, bestial sound as though these unseen creatures had sought to eat and bellow at the same time.

Our first view was but an inadequate, transitory glimpse, yet none the less disturbing because it was incomplete. Cavor was crawling in front at the time, and he first was aware of their proximity. He stopped dead, arresting me with a single gesture.

A crackling and smashing of the scrub appeared to be advancing directly upon us, and then, as we squatted close and endeavoured to judge of the nearness and direction of this noise, there came a terrific bellow behind us,

" THERE CAME A TERRIFIC BELLOW BEHIND US."

so close and vehement that the tops of the bayonet scrub bent before it, and one felt the breath of it hot and moist. And turning about we saw indistinctly through a crowd of swaying stems the mooncalf's shining sides and the long line of its back looming out against the sky.

Of course it is hard for me now to say how much I saw at that time, because my impressions were corrected by subsequent observation. First of all impressions was its enormous size : the girth of its body was some fourscore feet, its length perhaps two hundred. Its sides rose and fell with its laboured breathing. I perceived that its gigantic flabby body lay along the ground and that its skin was of a corrugated white, dappling into blackness along the backbone. But of its feet we saw nothing. I think also that we saw then the profile at least of the almost brainless head, with its fat-encumbered neck, its slobbering, omnivorous mouth, its little nostrils, and tight shut eyes. (For the mooncalf invariably shut its eyes in the presence of the sun.) We had a glimpse of a vast red pit as it opened its mouth to bleat and bellow again, we had a breath from the pit, and then the monster heeled over like a ship, dragged forward along the ground, creasing all his leathery skin, rolled again, and so wallowed past us, smashing a path amidst the scrub, and was speedily hidden from our eyes by the dense interlacings beyond. Another appeared more distantly, and then another, and then, as though he was guiding these animated lumps of provender to their pasture, a Selenite came momentarily into ken. My grip upon Cavor's foot became convulsive at the sight of him, and we remained motionless and peering long after he had passed out of our range.

By contrast with the mooncalves he seemed a trivial being, a mere ant, scarcely 5ft. high. He was wearing garments of some leathery substance so that no portion of his actual body appeared—but of this of course we were entirely ignorant. He presented himself therefore as a compact bristling creature, having much of the quality of a complicated insect, with whip-like tentacles, and a clanging arm projecting from his shining cylindrical body-case. The form of his head was hidden by his enormous, many-spiked helmet—we discovered afterwards that he used the spikes for prodding refractory mooncalves—and a pair of goggles of darkened glass set very much at the side gave a bud-like quality to the metallic apparatus that covered his face. His arms did not project beyond his body-case, and he carried himself upon short legs that, wrapped though they were in warm coverings, seemed to our terrestrial eyes inordinately flimsy. They had very short thighs, very long shanks, and little feet.

In spite of his heavy-looking clothing he was progressing with what would be from the terrestrial point of view very considerable strides, and his clanging arm was busy. The quality of his motion during the instant of his passing suggested haste and a certain anger, and soon after we had lost sight of him we heard the bellow of a mooncalf change abruptly into a short sharp squeal, followed by the scuffle of its acceleration. And gradually that bellowing receded, and then came to an end, as if the pastures sought had been attained.

We listened. For a space the moon world was still. But it was some time before we resumed our crawling search for the vanished sphere.

When next we saw mooncalves they were some little distance away from us, in a place of tumbled rocks. The less vertical surfaces of the rocks were thick with a speckled green plant, growing in dense, mossy clumps, upon which these creatures were browsing. We stopped at the edge of the reeds, amidst which we were crawling, at the sight of them, peering out at them, and looking round for a second glimpse of a Selenite. They lay against their food like stupendous slugs, huge, greasy hulls, eating greedily and noisily, with a sort of sobbing avidity. They seemed monsters of mere fatness, clumsy and overwhelmed to a degree that would make a Smithfield ox seem a model of agility. Their busy, writhing, chewing mouths, and eyes closed, together with the appetizing sound of their munching, made up an effect of animal enjoyment that was singularly stimulating to our empty frames.

"Hogs!" said Cavor, with unusual passion. "Disgusting hogs!" and after one glare of angry envy crawled off through the bushes to our right. I stayed long enough to see that the speckled plant was quite hopeless for human nourishment, then crawled after him, nibbling a quill of it between my teeth.

Presently we were arrested again by the proximity of a Selenite, and this time we were able to observe him more exactly. Now we could see that the Selenite covering was indeed clothing, and not a sort of crustacean integument. He was quite similar in his costume to the former one we had glimpsed, except that ends of something like wadding were protruding from his neck, and he stood on a promontory of rock and moved his head this way and that as though he was surveying the crater. We lay quite still, fearing to attract his attention if we moved, and after a time he turned about and disappeared.

We came upon another drove of moon-calves bellowing up a ravine, and then we passed over a place of sounds, sounds of beating machinery, as if some huge hall of industry came near the surface there. And while these sounds were still about us we came to the edge of a great open space, perhaps two hundred yards in diameter, and perfectly level. Save for a few lichens that advanced from its margin, this space was bare, and presented a powdery surface of a dusty yellow colour. We were afraid to strike out across this space, but as it presented less obstruction to our crawling than the scrub, we went down upon it and began very circum-spectly to skirt its edge.

For a little while the noises from below ceased, and everything, save for the faint stir of the growing vegetation, was very still. Then abruptly there began an uproar, louder, more vehement, and nearer than any we had so far heard. Of a certainty it came from below. Instinctively we crouched as flat as we could, ready for a prompt plunge into the thicket beside us. Each knock and throb seemed to vibrate through our bodies. Louder grew this throbbing and beating, and that irregular vibration increased until the whole moon world seemed to be jerking and pulsing.

"Cover," whispered Cavor, and I turned towards the bushes.

At that instant came a thud like the thud of a gun, and then a thing happened—it still haunts me in my dreams. I had turned my head to look at Cavor's face, and thrust out my hand in front of me as I did so. And my hand met nothing! Plunged suddenly into a bottomless hole!

My chest hit something hard, and I found myself with my chin on the edge of an un-fathomable abyss that had suddenly opened beneath me, my hand extended stiffly into the void. The whole of that flat circular area was no more than a gigantic lid, that was now sliding sideways from off the pit it had covered into a slot prepared for it.

Had it not been for Cavor I think I should have remained rigid, hanging over this margin and staring into the enormous gulf below until at last the edges of the slot scraped me off and hurled me into its depths. But Cavor had not received the shock that had paralyzed me. He had been a little distance from the edge when the lid had first opened, and, perceiving the peril that held me helpless, gripped my legs and pulled me backward. I came into a sitting position, crawled away from the edge for a space on all fours, then staggered up and ran after him across the thundering, quivering sheet of metal. It seemed to be swinging open with a steadily-accelerated velocity, and the bushes in front of me shifted sideways as I ran.

"CAVOR GRIPPED MY LEGS AND PULLED ME BACKWARD."

I was none too soon. Cavor's back vanished amidst the bristling thicket, and as I scrambled up after him the monstrous valve came into its position with a clang. For a long time we lay panting, not daring to approach the pit.

But at last, very cautiously, and bit by bit, we crept into a position from which we could peer down. The bushes about us creaked and waved with the force of a breeze that was blowing down the shaft. We could see nothing at first except smooth, vertical walls descending at last into an impenetrable black. And then very gradually we became aware of a number of very faint and little lights going to and fro.

For a time that stupendous gulf of mystery held us so that we forgot even our sphere. In time as we grew more accustomed to the darkness we could make out very small, dim, illusive shapes moving about among those needle - point illuminations. We peered, amazed and incredulous, understanding so little that we could find no words to say. We could distinguish nothing that would give us a clue to the meaning of the faint shapes we saw.

"What can it be?" I asked; "what can it be?"

"The engineering! . . . . They must live in these caverns during the night and come out during the day."

"Cavor!" I said. "Can they be—*that*—it was something like—men?"

"*That* was not a man."

"We dare risk nothing!"

"We dare do nothing until we find the sphere."

He assented with a groan and stirred himself to move. He stared about him for a space, sighed, and indicated a direction. We struck out through the jungle. For a time we crawled resolutely, then with diminishing vigour. Presently among great shapes of flabby purple there came a noise of trampling and cries about us. We lay close, and for a long time the sounds went to and fro and very near. But this time we saw nothing. I tried to whisper to Cavor that I could hardly go without food much longer, but my mouth had become too dry for whispering.

"Cavor," I said, "I must have food."

He turned a face full of dismay towards me. "It's a case for holding out," he said.

"But I *must*," I said; "and look at my lips!"

"I've been thirsty some time."

"If only some of that snow had remained!"

"It's clean gone! We're driving from Arctic to tropical at the rate of a degree a minute. . . ."

I gnawed my hand.

"The sphere!" he said. "There is nothing for it but the sphere." We roused ourselves to another spurt of crawling. My mind ran entirely on edible things, on the hissing profundity of summer drinks; more particularly I craved for beer. I was haunted by the memory of an eighteen-gallon cask that had swaggered in my Lympne cellar. I thought of the adjacent larder, and especially of steak and kidney pie—tender steak and plenty of kidney, and rich, thick gravy between. Ever and again I was seized with fits of hungry yawning. We came to flat places overgrown with fleshy red things, monstrous coralline growths; as we pushed against them they snapped and broke. I noted the quality of the broken surfaces. The confounded stuff certainly looked of a biteable texture. Then it seemed to me that it smelt rather well.

I picked up a fragment and sniffed at it.

"Cavor," I said, in a hoarse undertone.

He glanced at me with his face screwed up. "Don't," he said. I put down the fragment, and we crawled on through this tempting fleshiness for a space.

"Cavor," I asked, "why *not*?"

"Poison," I heard him say, but he did not look round.

We crawled some way before I decided.

"I'll chance it," said I.

He made a belated gesture to prevent me. I stuffed my mouth full. He crouched, watching my face, his own twisted into the oddest expression. "It's good," I said.

"Oh, Lord!" he cried.

He watched me munch, his face wrinkled between desire and disapproval, then suddenly succumbed to appetite, and began to tear off huge mouthfuls. For a time we did nothing but eat.

The stuff was not unlike a terrestrial mushroom, only it was much laxer in texture, and as one swallowed it it warmed the throat. At first we experienced a mere mechanical satisfaction in eating. Then our blood began to run warmer, and we tingled at the lips and fingers, and then new and slightly irrelevant ideas came bubbling up in our minds.

"It's good," said I. "Infernally good! What a home for our surplus population! Our poor surplus population," and I broke off another large portion.

It filled me with a curiously benevolent satisfaction that there was such good food in the moon. The depression of my hunger gave way to an irrational exhilaration. The dread and discomfort in which I had been living vanished entirely. I perceived the moon no longer as a planet from which I most earnestly desired the means of escape, but as a possible refuge for human destitution. I think I forgot the Selenites, the mooncalves, the lid, and the noises completely so soon as I had eaten that fungus.

Cavor replied to my third repetition of my "surplus population" remark with similar words of approval. I felt that my head swam, but I put this down to the stimulating effect of food after a long fast. "Ess'lent discov'ry, yours, Cavor," said I. "Se'nd on'y to the 'tato."

"Whajer mean?" asked Cavor. "'Scovery of the moon—se'nd on'y to the 'tato?"

I looked at him, shocked at his suddenly hoarse voice and by the badness of his articulation. It occurred to me in a flash that he was intoxicated, possibly by the fungus It also occurred to me that he erred in imagining that he had discovered the moon —he had not discovered it, he had only reached it. I tried to lay my hand on his arm and explain this to him, but the issue was too subtle for his brain. It was also unexpectedly difficult to express. After a momentary attempt to understand me—I remember wondering if the fungus had made my eyes as fishy as his—he set off upon some observations on his own account.

"We are," he announced, with a solemn hiccup, "the creashurs o' what we eat and drink."

He repeated this, and as I was now in one of my subtle moods I determined to dispute it. Possibly I wandered a little from the point. But Cavor certainly did not attend at all properly. He stood up as well as he could, putting a hand on my head to steady himself, which was disrespectful, and stood staring about him, quite devoid now of any fear of the moon beings.

I tried to point out that this was dangerous, for some reason that was not perfectly clear to me ; but the word "dangerous" had somehow got mixed with "indiscreet," and came out rather more like "injurious" than either, and after an attempt to disentangle them I resumed my argument, addressing myself principally to the unfamiliar but attentive coralline growths on either side. I felt that it was necessary to clear up this confusion between the moon and a potato at once—I wandered into a long parenthesis on the importance of precision of definition in argument. I did my best to ignore the fact that my bodily sensations were no longer agreeable.

In some way that I have now forgotten my

"HE STOOD UP AS WELL AS HE COULD."

mind was led back to projects of colonization. "We must annex this moon," I said. "There must be no shilly-shally. This is part of the White Man's Burthen. Cavor— we are—*hic*—Satap—mean Satraps ! Nempire Cæsar never dreamt. B'in all the newspapers. Cavorecia. Bedfordecia. Bedfordecia. Hic — Limited. Mean — unlimited ! Practically."

Certainly I was intoxicated. I embarked upon an argument to show the infinite benefits our arrival would confer upon the moon. I involved myself in a rather difficult proof that the arrival of Columbus was, after all, beneficial to America. I found I had forgotten the line of argument I had intended to pursue, and continued to repeat "simlar to Clumbus" to fill up time.

From that point my memory of the action of that abominable fungus becomes confused. I remember vaguely that we declared our intention of standing no nonsense from any confounded insects, that we decided it ill became men to hide shamefully upon a mere satellite, that we equipped ourselves with huge armfuls of the fungus—whether for missile purposes or not I do not know —and, heedless of the stabs of the bayonet shrub, we started forth into the sunshine.

Almost immediately we must have come upon the Selenites. There were six of them, and they were marching in single file over a rocky place, making the most remarkable piping and whining sounds. They all seemed to become aware of us at once, all instantly became silent and motionless like animals, with their faces turned towards us.

For a moment I was sobered.

"Insects," murmured Cavor, "insects !— and they think I'm going to crawl about on my stomach—on my vertebrated stomach!

"Stomach" he repeated, slowly, as though he chewed the indignity.

Then suddenly, with a shout of fury, he made three vast strides and leapt towards them. He leapt badly, he made a series of somersaults in the air, whirled right over them, and vanished with an enormous splash amidst the cactus bladders. What the Selenites made of this amazing, and to my mind undignified, irruption from another planet, I have no means of guessing. I seem to remember the sight of their backs as they ran in all directions—but I am not sure. All these last incidents before oblivion came are vague and faint in my mind. I know I made a step to follow Cavor, and tripped and fell headlong among the rocks. I was, I am certain, suddenly and vehemently ill. I seem to remember a violent struggle, and being gripped by metallic clasps. . . . .

My next clear recollection is that we were prisoners at we knew not what depth beneath the moon's surface; we were in darkness amidst strange, distracting noises; our bodies were covered with scratches and bruises, and our heads racked with pain.

" 'INSECTS,' MURMURED CAVOR, 'INSECTS !' "

CHAPTER XII.

THE SELENITE'S FACE.

I FOUND myself sitting crouched together in a tumultuous darkness. For a long time I could not understand where I was nor how I had come to this perplexity. I thought of the cupboard into which I had been thrust at times when I was a child, and then of a very dark and noisy bedroom in which I had slept during an illness. But these sounds about me were not the noises I had known, and there was a thin flavour in the air like the wind of a stable. Then I supposed we must still be at work upon the sphere, and that somehow I had got into the cellar of Cavor's house. I remembered we had finished the sphere, and fancied I must still be in it and travelling through space.

"Cavor," I said, "cannot we have some light?"

There came no answer.

"Cavor!" I insisted.

I was answered by a groan. "My head!" I heard him say, "my head!"

I attempted to press my hands to my brow, which ached, and discovered they were tied together. This startled me very much. I brought them up to my mouth and felt the cold smoothness of metal. They were chained together. I tried to separate my legs and made out they were similarly fastened, and also that I was fastened to the ground by a much thicker chain about the middle of my body.

I was more frightened than I had yet been by anything in all our strange experiences. For a time I tugged silently at my bonds. "Cavor!" I cried out, sharply, "why am I tied? Why have you tied me hand and foot?"

" I haven't tied you," he answered. " It's the Selenites."

The Selenites ! My mind hung on that for a space. Then my memories came back to me : the snowy desolation, the thawing of the air, the growth of the plants, our strange hopping and crawling among the rocks and vegetation of the crater. All the distress of our frantic search for the sphere returned to me. . . . Finally the opening of the great lid that covered the pit !

Then as I strained to trace our later movements down to our present plight the pain in my head became intolerable. I came to an insurmountable barrier, an obstinate blank.

" Cavor ! "

" Yes."

" Where are we ? "

" How should I know ? "

" Are we dead ? "

" What nonsense ! "

" They've got us, then ! "

He made no answer but a grunt. The lingering traces of the poison seemed to make him oddly irritable.

" What do you mean to do ? "

" How should I know what to do ? "

" Oh, very well," said I, and became silent. Presently I was roused from a stupor. " Oh, *Lord !* " I cried, " I wish you'd stop that buzzing."

We lapsed into silence again, listening to the dull confusion of noises like the muffled sounds of a street or factory that filled our ears. I could make nothing of it ; my mind pursued first one rhythm and then another, and questioned it in vain. But after a long time I became aware of a new and sharper element, not mingling with the rest, but standing out, as it were, against that cloudy background of sound. It was a series of relatively very little definite sounds, tappings and rubbings like a loose spray of ivy against a window or a bird moving about upon a box. We listened and peered about us, but the darkness was a velvet pall. There followed a noise like the subtle movement of the wards of a well-oiled lock. And then there appeared before me, hanging as it seemed in an immensity of black, a thin bright line.

" Look ! " whispered Cavor, very softly.

" What is it ? "

" I don't know."

We stared.

The thin bright line became a band and broader and paler. It took upon itself the quality of a bluish light falling upon a white-washed wall. It ceased to be parallel sided ;

it developed a deep indentation on one side. I turned to remark this to Cavor, and was amazed to see his ear in a brilliant illumination — all the rest of him in shadow. I twisted my head round as well as my bonds would permit. "Cavor ! " I said, "it's behind !"

His ear vanished—gave place to an eye !

Suddenly the crack that had been admitting the light broadened out and revealed itself as the space of an opening door. Beyond was a sapphire vista, and in the doorway stood a grotesque outline silhouetted against the glare.

We both made convulsive efforts to turn, and, failing, sat staring over our shoulders at this. My first impression was of some clumsy quadruped with lowered head. Then I perceived it was the slender, pinched body and short and extremely attenuated bandy legs of a Selenite, with his head depressed between his shoulders. He was without the helmet and body-covering they wear upon the exterior.

He was a blank black figure to us, but instinctively our imaginations supplied features to his very human outline. I at least took it instantly that he was somewhat hunchbacked, with a high forehead and long features.

He came forward three steps and paused for a time. His movements seemed absolutely noiseless. Then he came forward again. He walked like a bird—his feet fell one in front of the other. He stepped out of the ray of light that came through the doorway, and it seemed as though he vanished altogether in the shadow.

For a moment my eyes sought him in the wrong place, and then I perceived him standing facing us both in the full light. Only the human features I had attributed to him were not there at all ! The front of his face was a gap.

Of course I ought to have expected that, only I didn't. It came to me as an absolute, for a moment an overwhelming, shock. It seemed as though it wasn't a face ; as though it must needs be a mark, a horror, a deformity that would presently be disavowed or explained.

It was rather like a visored helmet . . . But I can't explain the thing. Have you ever seen the face of some insect greatly magnified ? There was no nose, no expression, it was all shiny and hard and invariable, with bulging eyes—in the silhouette I had supposed they were ears . . . I have tried to draw one of these heads, but I cannot. The point one cannot get is the horrible want of expression, or rather the horrible want of change of expression. Every head and face a man meets with on earth in the usual way resorts to expression. This was like being stared at suddenly by an engine. There the thing was, looking at us!

But when I say there was a want of change of expression I do not mean that there was not a sort of set expression on the face—just as there is a sort of set expression about a coal-scuttle, or a chimney-cowl, or the ventilator of a steamship. There was a mouth, downwardly curved, like a human mouth in a face that stares ferociously. . . .

The neck on which the head was poised was jointed in three places, almost like the short joints in the leg of a crab. The joints of the limbs I could not see because of the puttee-like straps in which they were swathed, and which formed the only clothing this being wore.

At the time my mind was taken up by the mad impossibility of the creature. I suppose he also was amazed—and with more reason, perhaps, for amazement than we. Only, confound him, he did not show it. We did at least know what had brought about this meeting of incompatible creatures. But conceive how it would seem to decent Londoners, for example, to come upon a couple of living things, as big as men and absolutely unlike any other earthly animals, careering about among the sheep in Hyde Park!

It must have taken him like that.

Figure us! We were bound hand and foot, fagged and filthy, our beards two inches long, our faces scratched and bloody. Cavor you must imagine in his knickerbockers (torn in several places by the bayonet scrub), his Jaeger shirt and old cricket cap, his wiry hair wildly disordered, a tail to every quarter of the heavens. In that blue light his face

"THERE THE THING WAS, LOOKING AT US."

did not look red, but very dark; his lips and the drying blood upon his hands seemed black. If possible, I was in a worse plight than he, on account of the yellow fungus into which I had jumped. Our jackets were unbuttoned, and our shoes had been taken off and lay at our feet. And we were sitting with our backs to the queer, bluish light peering at such a monster as Dürer might have invented.

Cavor broke the silence, started to speak, went hoarse, and cleared his throat. Outside began a terrific bellowing, as if a mooncalf were in trouble. It ended in a shriek, and everything was still again.

Presently the Selenite turned about, flickered into the shadow, stood for a moment retrospective at the door, and then closed it on us, and once more we were in that murmurous mystery of darkness into which we had awakened.

The First Men in the Moon.

By H. G. Wells.

CHAPTER XIII.

MR. CAVOR MAKES SOME SUGGESTIONS.

OR a time neither of us spoke. To focus together all the things we had brought upon ourselves seemed beyond my mental powers.

"They've got us," I said at last.

"It was that fungus."

"Well, if I hadn't taken it we should have fainted and starved."

"We might have found the sphere."

I lost my temper at his persistence and swore to myself. For a time we hated one another in silence. I drummed with my fingers on the floor between my knees and gritted the links of my fetters together. Presently I was forced to talk again.

"What do you make of it, anyhow?" I asked humbly.

"They are reasonable creatures—they can make things and do things. Those lights we saw . . . ."

He stopped. It was clear he could make nothing of it.

When he spoke again it was to confess. "After all, they are more human than we had a right to expect. I suppose——"

He stopped, irritatingly.

"Yes?"

"I suppose, anyhow—on any planet, where there is an intelligent animal, it will carry its brain case upward, and have hands and walk erect. . . ."

Presently he broke away in another direction.

"We are some way in," he said. "I mean—perhaps a couple of thousand feet or more."

"Why?"

"It's cooler. And our voices are so much louder. That faded quality—it has altogether gone. And the feeling in one's ears and throat."

I had not noted that, but I did now.

"The air is denser. We must be some depth—a mile even we may be—inside the moon."

"We never thought of a world inside the moon."

"No."

"How could we?"

"We might have done. Only——one gets into habits of mind."

He thought for a time.

"*Now*," he said, "it seems such an obvious thing. Of course! The moon must be enormously cavernous with an atmosphere within, and at the centre of its caverns a sea. One knew that the moon had a lower specific gravity than the earth; one knew that it had little air or water outside; one knew, too, that it was sister planet to the earth and that it was unaccountable that it should be different in composition. The inference that it was hollowed out was as clear as day. And yet one never saw it as a fact. Kepler, of course——" His voice had the interest now of a man who has discovered a pretty sequence of reasoning.

"Yes," he said, "Kepler, with his *sub-volvani*, was right after all."

"I wish you had taken the trouble to find that out before we came," I said.

He answered nothing, buzzing to himself softly as he pursued his thoughts. My temper was going. "What do you think has become of the sphere, anyhow?" I asked.

"Lost," he said, like a man who answers an uninteresting question.

"Among those plants?"

"Unless they find it."

"And then?"

"How can I tell?"

"Cavor," I said, with a sort of hysterical bitterness, "things look bright for my Company . . . ."

He made no answer.

"Good Lord!" I exclaimed. "Just think of all the trouble we took to get into this pickle! What did we come for? What are we after? What was the moon to us, or we to the moon? We wanted too much, we tried too much. We ought to have started the little things first. It was you proposed the moon! Those Cavorite spring blinds! I am certain we could have worked them for terrestrial purposes. Certain! Did you really understand what I proposed? A steel cylinder——"

"Rubbish!" said Cavor.

We ceased to converse.

For a time Cavor kept up a broken monologue without much help from me.

"If they find it," he began; "if they find it. . . . what will they do with it? Well, that's a question! It may be that's *the* question. They won't understand it, anyhow. If they understood that sort of thing they would have come long since to the earth. Would they? Why shouldn't they? But they would have sent something—— They couldn't keep their hands off such a possibility. No! But they will examine it. Clearly they are intelligent and inquisitive. They will examine it—get inside it—trifle with the studs. Off! . . . That would mean the moon for us for all the rest of our lives. Strange creatures, strange knowledge . . . ."

"As for strange knowledge—— !" said I, and language failed me.

"Look here, Bedford," said Cavor. "You came on this expedition of your own free will."

"You said to me — 'call it prospecting.'"

"There's always risks in prospecting."

"Especially when you do it unarmed and without thinking out every possibility."

"I was so taken up with the sphere. The thing rushed on us and carried us away."

"Rushed on *me*, you mean."

"Rushed on me just as much. How was *I* to know when I set to work on molecular physics that the business would bring me here—of all places?"

"It's this accursed Science," I cried.

"It's the very Devil. The mediæval priests and persecutors were right, and the Moderns are all wrong. You tamper with it and it offers you gifts. And directly you take them

it knocks you to pieces in some unexpected way. Old passions and new weapons— now it upsets your religion, now it upsets your social ideas, now it whirls you off to desolation and misery!

"Anyhow, it's no use your quarrelling with me now. These creatures — these Selenites—or whatever we choose to call them, have got us tied hand and foot. Whatever temper you choose to go through with it in, you will have to go through with it . . . . We have experiences before us that will need all our coolness."

He paused as if he required my assent. But I sat sulking.

"Confound your Science!" I said.

"The problem is communication. Gestures, I fear, will be different. Pointing, for example. No creatures but men and monkeys point."

That was too obviously wrong for me. "Pretty nearly every animal," I cried, "points with its eyes or nose."

Cavor meditated over that. "Yes," he said at last, "and we don't. There's such differences! Such differences!

"One might . . . . But how can I tell? There is speech. The sounds they make,

"I SAT SULKING."

a sort of fluting and piping. I don't see how we are to imitate that. Is it their speech, that sort of thing? They may have different senses, different means of communication. Of course they are minds and we are minds—there must be something in common. Who knows how far we may not get to an understanding?"

"The things are outside us," I said. "They're more different from us than the strangest animals on earth. They are a different clay. What is the good of talking like this?"

Cavor thought. "I don't see that. Where there are minds, they will have something *similar*—even though they have been evolved on different planets. Of course, if it was a question of instinct—if we or they were no more than animals——"

" Well, *are* they? They're much more like ants on their hind legs than human beings, and who ever got to any sort of understanding with ants?"

" But these machines and clothing! No, I don't hold with you, Bedford. The difference is wide——"

" It's insurmountable."

" The resemblance must bridge it. I remember reading once a paper by the late Professor Galton on the possibility of communication between the planets. Unhappily at that time it did not seem probable that that would be of any material benefit to me, and I fear I did not give it the attention I should have done—in view of this state of affairs. Yet . . . Now, let me see!

" His idea was to begin with those broad truths that must underlie all conceivable mental existences and establish a basis on those. The great principles of geometry, to begin with. He proposed to take some leading proposition of Euclid's, and show by construction that its truth was known to us; to demonstrate, for example, that the angles at the base of an isosceles triangle are equal, and that if the equal sides be produced the angles on the other side of the base are equal also; or that the square on the hypotenuse of a right-angled triangle is equal to the sum of the squares on the two other sides. By demonstrating our knowledge of these things we should demonstrate our possession of a reasonable intelligence. . . . Now, suppose I . . . I might draw the geometrical figure with a wet finger or even trace it in the air . . ."

He fell silent. I sat meditating his words. For a time his wild hope of communication, of interpretation with these weird beings, held me. Then that angry despair that was a part of my exhaustion and physical misery resumed its sway. I perceived with a sudden novel vividness the extraordinary folly of everything I had ever done. " Ass!" I said, " Oh, ass, unutterable ass . . . I seem to exist only to go about doing preposterous things. . . . Why did we ever leave the thing? . . . Hopping about looking for patents and concessions in the craters of the moon! . . . If only we had had the sense to fasten a handkerchief to a stick to show where we had left the sphere!"

I subsided, fuming.

" It is clear," meditated Cavor, " they are intelligent. One can hypotheticate certain things. As they have not killed us at once they must have ideas of mercy. Mercy! At any rate of restraint. Possibly of intercourse. They may meet us. And this apartment and the glimpses we had of its guardian. These fetters! A high degree of intelligence. . . ."

" I wish to Heaven," cried I, " I'd thought even twice! Plunge after plunge. First one fluky start and then another. It was my confidence in you. *Why* didn't I stick to my play? That was what I was equal to. That was my world and the life I was made for. I could have finished that play. I'm certain . . . . it was a good play. I had the scenario as good as done. Then . . . . Conceive it! Leaping to the moon! Practically—I've thrown my life away! That old woman in the inn near Canterbury had better sense."

I looked up, and stopped in mid-sentence. The darkness had given place to that bluish light again. The door was opening, and several noiseless Selenites were coming into the chamber. I became quite still, staring at the chitinous impassiveness of their faces.

Then suddenly my sense of disagreeable strangeness changed to interest. I perceived that the foremost and second carried bowls. One elemental need at least our minds could understand in common. They were bowls of some metal that, like our fetters, looked dark in that bluish light; and each contained a number of whitish fragments. All the cloudy pain and misery that oppressed me rushed together and took the shape of hunger. I eyed these bowls wolfishly, and, though it returned to me i. ɹeams, at that time it seemed a small matter that at the end of the arms that lowered one towards me were not hands, but a sort of flap and thumb, like the end of an elephant's trunk.

The stuff in the bowl was loose in texture and whitish-brown in colour—rather like lumps of some cold soufflé, and it smelt faintly like mushrooms. From a partially-divided carcass of a mooncalf that we presently saw I am inclined to believe it must have been mooncalf flesh.

My hands were so tightly chained that I could barely contrive to reach the bowl, but when they saw the effort I made two of them dexterously released one of the turns about my wrist. Their tentacle hands were soft and cold to my skin. I immediately seized a mouthful of the food. It had the same laxness in texture that all organic structures seem to have upon the moon; it tasted rather like a *gauffre*, or a damp meringue, but in no way was it disagreeable. I took two other mouthfuls. "I *wanted*—foo'!" said I, tearing off a still larger piece. . . . .

For a time we ate with an utter absence of self-consciousness. We ate and presently drank like tramps in a soup kitchen. Never before, nor since, have I been hungry to the ravenous pitch, and save that I have had this very experience I could never have believed that a quarter of a million of miles out of our proper world, in utter perplexity of soul, surrounded, watched, touched by beings more grotesque and inhuman than the worst creatures of a nightmare, it would be possible for me to eat in utter forgetfulness of all these things. They stood about us, watching us, and ever and again making a slight elusive twittering that stood them, I suppose, in the stead of speech. I did not even shiver at their touch. And when the first zeal of my feeding was over I could note that Cavor too had been eating with the same shameless abandon.

"I EYED THESE BOWLS WOLFISHLY."

eating the Selenites linked our hands closely together again, and then untwisted the chains about our feet and rebound them, so as to give us a limited freedom of movement. Then they unfastened the chains about our waists. To do all this they had to handle us freely, and ever and again one of their queer heads came down close to my face, or a soft tentacle-hand touched my head or neck. I don't remember that I was afraid then or repelled by their proximity. I think that our incurable anthropomorphism made us imagine there were human heads inside these crustacean masks. The skin, like everything else, looked bluish, but that was on account of the light, and it was hard and shiny, quite in the beetle-wing fashion, not soft or moist or hairy as a vertebrated animal's would be. Along the crest of the head was a low ridge of whitish spines running from back to front, and a much larger ridge curved on either side over the eyes. The Selenite who untied me used his mouth to help his hands.

"They seem to be releasing us," said Cavor. "Remember, we are on the moon! Make no sudden movements!"

"Are you going to try that geometry?"

"If I get a chance. But, of course, they may make an advance first."

CHAPTER XIV.

EXPERIMENTS IN INTERCOURSE.

WHEN at last we had made an end of

"THE SELENITES STOOD BACK FROM US, AND SEEMED TO BE LOOKING AT US."

We remained passive, and the Selenites having finished their arrangements stood back from us, and seemed to be looking at us. I say seemed to be, because as their eyes were at the side and not in front one had the same difficulty in determining the direction in which they were looking as one has in the case of a hen or a fish. They conversed with one another in their reedy tones that seemed to me impossible to imitate or define. The door behind us opened wider, and glancing over my shoulder I saw a vague large space beyond in which quite a little crowd of Selenites were standing.

"Do they want us to imitate those sounds?" I asked Cavor.

"I don't think so," he said.

"It seems to me that they are trying to make us understand something."

"I can't make anything of their gestures. Do you notice this one, who is worrying with his head like a man with an uncomfortable collar?"

"Let us shake our heads at him."

We did that, and finding it ineffectual, attempted an imitation of the Selenite's movements. That seemed to interest them. At any rate, they all set up the same movement. But as that seemed to lead to nothing we desisted at last, and so did they, and fell into a piping argument among themselves. Then one of them, a little shorter and thicker than the other, and with a particularly wide mouth, squatted down suddenly beside Cavor, and put his hands and feet in the same posture as Cavor's were bound, and then by a dexterous movement stood up.

"Cavor," I shouted, "they want us to get up!"

He stared open-mouthed. "That's it!" he said.

And with much heaving and grunting, because our hands were tied together, we contrived to struggle to our feet. The Selenites made way for our elephantine heavings, and seemed to twitter more volubly. As soon as we were on our feet the thick-set Selenite came and patted each of our faces with his tentacles, and walked towards the open doorway. That also was plain enough, and we followed him. We saw that four of the Selenites standing in the doorway were taller than the others, and clothed in the same manner as those we had seen in the crater, namely, with spiked, round helmets and cylindrical body-cases, and that each of the four carried a goad, with spike and guard made of that same dull-looking metal as the bowls. These four closed about us, one on either side of each of us, as we emerged from our chamber into the cavern from which the light had come.

We did not get our impression of that cavern all at once. Our attention was taken up by the movements and attitudes of the Selenites immediately about us, and by the necessity of controlling our motion, lest we should startle and alarm them and ourselves by some excessive stride. In front of us was the short, thick-set being who had solved the problem of asking us to get up, moving with gestures that seemed, almost all of them, intelligible to us, inviting us to follow him. His spout-like face turned from one of us to the other with a quickness that was clearly interrogative. For a time, I say, we were taken up with these things.

But at last the great place that formed a background to our movements asserted itself. It became apparent that the source of much at least of the tumult of sounds which had filled our ears ever since we had recovered from the stupefaction of the fungus was a vast mass of machinery in active movement, whose flying and whirling parts were visible indistinctly over the heads and between the bodies of the Selenites who walked about us. And not only did the web of sounds that filled the air proceed from this mechanism, but also the peculiar blue light that irradiated the whole place. We had taken it as a natural thing that a subterranean cavern should be artificially lit, and even now, though the fact was patent to my eyes, I did not really grasp its import until presently the darkness came. The meaning and structure of this huge apparatus we saw I cannot explain, because we neither of us learnt what it was for or how it worked. One after another, big shafts of metal flung out and up from its centre, their heads travelling in what seemed to me to be a parabolic path; each dropped a sort of dangling arm as it rose towards the apex of its flight and plunged down into a vertical cylinder, forcing this down before it. And as each of these arms plunged down there was a clank and then a roaring, and out of the top of the vertical cylinder came pouring this incandescent substance, that lit the place and ran over as milk runs over a boiling pot and dripped luminously into a tank of light below. It was a cold blue light, a sort of phosphorescent glow, but infinitely brighter, and from the tanks into which it fell it ran in conduits athwart the cavern.

Thud, thud, thud, thud, came the sweeping arms of this unintelligible apparatus, and the light substance hissed and poured. At first the thing seemed only reasonably large and

near to us; and then I saw how exceedingly little the Selenites upon it seemed, and I realized the full immensity of cavern and machine. I looked from this tremendous affair to the faces of the Selenites with a new respect. I stopped, and Cavor stopped, and stared at this thunderous engine.

" But this is stupendous ! " I said. " What can it be for ? "

Cavor's blue-lit face was full of an intelligent respect. " I can't dream ! Surely these beings——. Men could not make a thing like that ! Look at those arms : are they on connecting rods ? "

The thick-set Selenite had gone some paces unheeded. He came back and stood between us and the great machine. I avoided seeing him, because I guessed somehow that his idea was to beckon us onward. He walked away in the direction he wished us to go, and turned and came back, and flicked our faces to attract our attention.

Cavor and I looked at one another.

" Cannot we show him we are interested in the machine ? " I said.

" Yes," said Cavor. " We'll try that." He turned to our guide, and smiled, and pointed to the machine, and pointed again, and then to his head, and then to the machine. By some defect of reasoning he seemed to imagine that broken English might help these gestures. " Me look 'im," he said ; " me think 'im very much. Yes."

His behaviour seemed to check the Selenites in their desire for our progress for a moment. They faced one another, their queer heads moved, the twittering voices came quick and liquid. Then one of them, a lean, tall creature, with a sort of mantle added to the puttee in which the others were dressed, twisted his elephant trunk of a hand about Cavor's waist, and pulled him gently to follow our guide, who again went on ahead.

Cavor resisted. " We may just as well begin explaining ourselves now ! They may think we are new animals, a new sort of mooncalf, perhaps ! It is most important that we should show an intelligent interest from the outset."

He began to shake his head violently. " No, no," he said ; " me not come on one minute. Me look at 'im."

" Isn't there some geometrical point you might bring in *àpropos* of that affair ? " I suggested, as the Selenites conferred again.

" Possibly a parabolic——" he began. He yelled loudly and leaped six feet or more !

One of the four armed moon-men had pricked him with a goad !

I turned on the goad-bearer behind me with a swift, threatening gesture and he started back. This and Cavor's sudden shout and leap clearly astonished all the Selenites. They receded hastily, facing us with their stupid, unchanging stare. For one of those moments that seem to last for ever

CHAPTER XV.

THE GIDDY BRIDGE.

JUST for a moment that hostile pause endured. I suppose that both we and the Selenites did some very rapid thinking. My clearest impression was that there was nothing to put my back against and that we were bound to be surrounded and killed. The overwhelming folly of our presence there

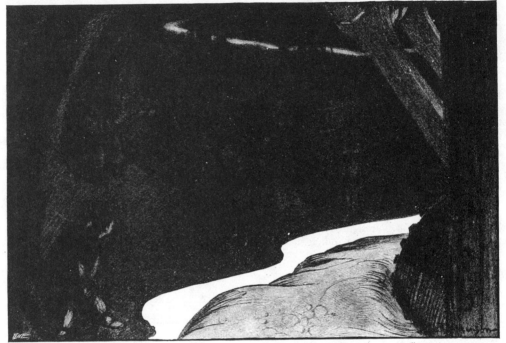

"THEY RECEDED HASTILY, FACING US WITH THEIR STUPID, UNCHANGING STARE."

we stood in angry protest, with a scattered semi-circle of these inhuman beings about us.

"He pricked me !" said Cavor, with a catching of the voice.

"I saw him," I answered.

"Confound it !" I said to the Selenites ; "we're not going to stand that ! What on earth do you take us for ?"

I glanced quickly right and left. Far away across the blue wilderness of cavern I saw a number of other Selenites running towards us. The cavern spread wide and low, and receded in every direction into darkness. Its roof, I remember, seemed to bulge down as if with the weight of the vast thickness of rocks that prisoned us. There was no way out of it—no way out of it. Above, below, in every direction, was the unknown, and these inhuman creatures with goads and gestures confronting us, and we two unsupported men !

loomed over me in black, enormous reproach. Why had I ever launched myself on this mad, inhuman expedition ?

Cavor came to my side and laid his hand on my arm. His pale and terrified face was ghastly in the blue light.

"We can't do anything," he said. "It's a mistake. They don't understand. We must go—as they want us to go."

I looked down at him, and then at the fresh Selenites who were coming to help their fellows. "If I had my hands free——"

"It's no use," he panted.

"No."

"We'll go."

And he turned about and led the way in the direction that had been indicated for us.

I followed, trying to look as subdued as possible, and feeling at the chains about my wrists. My blood was boiling. I noted nothing more of that cavern, though it seemed to take a long time before we had marched across it, or if I noted anything I forgot it as I saw it. My thoughts were concentrated, I think, upon my chains and the Selenites, and particularly upon the helmeted ones with the goads. At first they marched parallel with us, and at a respectful distance, but presently they were overtaken by three others, and then they drew nearer until they were within arms' length again. I winced like a spurred horse as they came near to us. The shorter, thicker Selenite marched at first on our right flank, but presently came in front of us again.

How well the picture of that grouping has bitten into my brain: the back of Cavor's downcast head just in front of me, and the dejected droop of his shoulders, and our guide's gaping visage, perpetually jerking

Clang, clang, clang, we passed right under the thumping levers of another vast machine, and so came at last to a wide tunnel, in which we could even hear the pad, pad of our shoeless feet, and which, save for the trickling thread of blue to the right of us, was quite unlit. The shadows made gigantic travesties of our shapes and those of the Selenites on the irregular wall and roof of the tunnel. Ever and again crystals in the walls of the tunnel scintillated like gems, ever and again the tunnel expanded into a stalactitic cavern, or gave off branches that vanished into darkness.

We seemed to be marching down that tunnel for a long time. "Trickle, trickle," went the flowing light very softly, and our footfalls and their echoes made an irregular paddle, paddle. My mind settled down to

"'TRICKLE, TRICKLE,' WENT THE FLOWING LIGHT VERY SOFTLY."

about him, and the goad-bearers on either side, watchful yet open-mouthed—a blue monochrome. And after all, I do remember one other thing besides the purely personal affair, which is that a sort of gutter came presently across the floor of the cavern and then ran along by the side of the path of rock we followed. And it was full of that same bright blue luminous stuff that flowed out of the great machine. I walked close beside it, and I can testify it radiated not a particle of heat. It was brightly shining, and yet it was neither warmer nor colder than anything else in the cavern.

the question of my chains. If I were to slip off one turn *so*, and then to twist it *so*. . . .

If I tried to do it very gradually, would they see I was slipping my wrist out of the looser turn? If they did, what would they do?

"Bedford," said Cavor, "it goes down. It keeps on going down."

His remark roused me from my sullen preoccupation.

"If they wanted to kill us," he said, dropping back to come level with me, "there is no reason why they should not have done it."

"No," I admitted; "that's true."

"They don't understand us," he said;

"they think we are merely strange animals, some wild sort of mooncalf birth, perhaps. It will be only when they have observed us better that they will begin to think we have minds——"

"When you trace those geometrical problems?" said I.

"It may be that."

We tramped on for a space.

"You see," said Cavor, "these may be Selenites of a lower class."

"The infernal fools," said I, viciously, glancing at their exasperating faces.

"If we endure what they do to us——"

"We've got to endure it," said I.

"There may be others less stupid. This is the mere outer fringe of their world. It must go down and down, cavern, passage, tunnel, down at last to the sea—hundreds of miles below."

His words made me think of the mile or so of rock and tunnel that might be over our heads already. It was like a weight dropping on my shoulders. "Away from the sun and air," I said. "Even a mine half a mile deep is stuffy."

"This is not—anyhow. It's probable—— Ventilation! The air would blow from the dark side of the moon to the sunlit, and all the carbonic acid would well out there and feed those plants. Up this tunnel, for example—there is quite a breeze. And what a world it must be! The earnest we have in that shaft, and those machines——"

"And the goad," I said. "Don't forget the goad!"

He walked a little in front of me for a time.

"Even that goad——" he said.

"Well?"

"I was angry at the time. But—— it was perhaps necessary we should get on. They have different skins and probably different nerves. They may not understand our objection—just as a being from Mars might not like our earthly habit of nudging."

"They'd better be careful how they nudge *me*."

"And about that geometry. After all, their way is a way of understanding too. They begin with the elements of life and not of thought. Food. Compulsion. Pain. They strike at fundamentals."

"There's no doubt about *that*," I said.

He went on to talk of the enormous and wonderful world into which we were being taken. I realized slowly from his tone that even now he was not absolutely in despair at the prospect of going ever deeper into this inhuman planet burrow. His mind ran on machines and invention to the exclusion of a thousand dark things that beset me. It wasn't that he intended to make any use of these things: he simply wanted to know them.

"After all," he said, "this is a tremendous occasion. It is the meeting of two worlds. What are we going to see? Think of what is below us here."

"We sha'n't see much if the light isn't better," I remarked.

"This is only the outer crust. Down below——. On this scale——. There will be everything. The story we shall take back!"

"Some rare sort of animal," I said, "might comfort himself in that way while they were bringing him to the Zoo. . . . It doesn't follow that we are going to be shown all these things."

"When they find we have reasonable minds," said Cavor, "they will want to learn about the earth. Even if they have no generous emotions they will teach in order to learn. . . . And the things they must know! The unanticipated things!"

He went on to speculate on the possibility of their knowing things he had never hoped to learn on earth, speculating in that way, with a raw wound from that goad already in his skin! Much that he said I forget, for my attention was drawn to the fact that the tunnel along which we had been marching was opening out wider and wider. We seemed from the feeling of the air to be going out into a huge space. But how big the space might really be we could not tell, because it was unlit. Our little stream of light ran in a dwindling thread and vanished far ahead. Presently the rocky walls had vanished altogether on either hand. There was nothing to be seen but the path in front of us and the trickling, hurrying rivulet of blue phosphorescence. The figures of Cavor and the guiding Selenite marched before me; the sides of their legs and heads that were towards the rivulet were clear and bright blue; their darkened sides, now that the reflection of the tunnel wall no longer lit them, merged indistinguishably in the darkness beyond.

And soon I perceived that we were approaching a declivity of some sort, because the little blue stream dipped suddenly out of sight.

In another moment, as it seemed, we had reached the edge. The shining stream gave one meander of hesitation and then rushed over. It fell to a depth at which the sound of its descent was absolutely lost to us. And the darkness it dropped out of became utterly void and black, save that a thing like a plank projected from the edge of the cliff and stretched out and faded and vanished altogether.

For a moment I and Cavor stood as near the edge as we dared peering into an inky profundity. And then our guide was pulling at my arm.

Then he left me and walked to the end of that plank and stepped upon it, looking back. Then when he perceived we watched him he turned about and went on along it, walking as surely as though he was on firm earth. For a moment his form was distinct, then he became a blue blur, and then vanished into the obscurity.

There was a pause. " Surely —— ! " said Cavor.

One of the other Selenites walked a few paces out upon the plank and turned and looked back at us unconcernedly. The others stood ready to follow after us. Our guide's expectant gape reappeared. He was returning to see why we had not advanced.

" We can't cross that at any price," said I.

" I could not go three steps on it," said Cavor, " even with my hands free."

We looked at each other's drawn faces in blank consternation.

"'They can't know what it is to be giddy," said Cavor.

" It's quite impossible for us to walk that plank."

" I don't believe they see as we do. I've been watching them. I wonder if they know this is simply blackness for us. How can we make them understand ? "

" Anyhow, we must make them understand."

I think we said these things with a vague, half hope the Selenites might somehow understand. I knew quite clearly that all that was needed was an explanation. Then, as I saw their blank faces, I realized that an explanation was impossible. Just here it was that our resemblances were not going to bridge our differences. Well, I wasn't going to walk the plank anyhow. I slipped my wrist very quickly out of the coil of chain that was loose, and then began to twist my wrists in opposite directions. I was standing nearest to the bridge, and as I did this two of the Selenites laid hold of me and pulled me gently towards it.

I shook my head violently. " No go," I said, " no use. You don't understand."

Another Selenite added his compulsion. I was forced to step forward.

" Look here ! " I exclaimed. " Steady on ! It's all very well for you —— "

I sprang round upon my heel : I burst out into curses. For one of the armed Selenites had stabbed me behind with his goad.

I wrenched my wrists free from the little tentacles that held them. I turned on the goad-bearer. " Confound you ! " I cried. " I've warned you of that. What on earth do you think I'm made of, to stick that into me ? If you touch me again —— ! "

By way of answer he pricked me forthwith.

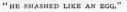

" HE SMASHED LIKE AN EGG."

I heard Cavor's voice in alarm and entreaty. Even then I think he wanted to compromise with these creatures. But the sting of that second stab seemed to set free some pent-up reserve of energy in my being. Instantly a link of the wrist chain snapped, and with it snapped all considerations that had held us unresisting in the hands of these moon-creatures. For that second, at least, I was mad with fear and anger. I took no thought of consequences. I hit straight out, at the face of the thing with the goad. The chain was twisted round my fist. . . . .

There came another of those beastly surprises of which the moon world is full. My mailed hand seemed to go clean through him. He smashed like an egg. It was like hitting one of those hard sweets that have liquid inside. It broke right in, and the flimsy body went spinning a dozen yards and fell with a flabby impact. I was astonished. I was incredulous that any living thing could be so flimsy. For an instant I could have believed the whole thing a dream.

Then it had become real and imminent again. Neither Cavor nor the other Selenites seemed to have done anything from the time when I had turned about to the time when the dead Selenite hit the ground. Everyone stood back from us two, everyone alert. That arrest seemed to last at least a second after the Selenite was down. Everyone must have been taking the thing in. I seem to remember myself standing with my arm half retracted, trying also to take it in. "What next?" clamoured my brain; "what next?" Then in a moment everyone was moving!

I perceived we must get our chains loose, and that before we could do this these Selenites had to be beaten off. I faced towards the group of the three goad-bearers. Instantly one threw his goad at me. It swished over my head, and I suppose went flying into the abyss behind.

I leaped right at him with all my might as the goad flew over me. He turned to run as I jumped, and I bore him to the ground, came down right upon him, and slipped upon his smashed body and fell.

I came into a sitting position, and on every hand the blue backs of the Selenites were receding into the darkness. I bent a link by main force and untwisted the chain that had hampered me about the ankles, and sprang to my feet, with the chain in my hand. Another goad, flung javelin-wise, whistled by me, and I made a rush towards the darkness out of which it had come. Then I turned back towards Cavor, who was still standing in the light of the rivulet near the gulf, convulsively busy with his wrists.

"Come on!" I cried.

"My hands!" he answered.

Then, realizing that I dared not run back to him because my ill-calculated steps might carry me over the edge, he came shuffling towards me, with his hands held out before him.

I gripped his chains at once to unfasten them.

"Where are they?" he panted.

"Run away. They'll come back. They're throwing things! Which way shall we go?"

"By the light. To that tunnel. Eh?"

"Yes," said I, and his hands were free.

I dropped on my knees and fell to work on his ankle bonds. Whack came something—I know not what—and splashed the livid streamlet into drops about us. Far away on our right a piping and whistling began.

I whipped the chain off his feet, and put it in his hand. "Hit with that!" I said, and without waiting for an answer set off in big bounds along the path by which we had come. I heard the impact of his leaps come following after me.

We ran in vast strides. But that running, you must understand, was an altogether different thing from any running on earth. On earth one leaps and almost instantly hits the ground again; but on the moon, because of its weaker pull, one shot through the air for several seconds before one came to earth. In spite of our violent hurry this gave an effect of long pauses, pauses in which one might have counted seven or eight. Step, and one soared off. All sorts of questions ran through my mind: "Where are the Selenites? What will they do? Shall we ever get to that tunnel? Is Cavor far behind? Are they likely to cut him off?" Then whack, stride, and off again for another step.

I saw a Selenite running in front of me, his legs going exactly as a man's would go on earth, saw him glance over his shoulder, and heard him shriek as he ran aside out of my way into the darkness. He was, I think, our guide, but I am not sure. Then in another vast stride the walls of rock had come into view on either hand, and in two more strides I was in the tunnel, and tempering my pace to its low roof. I went on to a bend, then stopped and turned back, and plug, plug, plug, Cavor came into view, splashing into the stream of blue light at every stride, and grew larger and blundered into me. We stood clutching each other. For a moment, at least, we had shaken off our captors and were alone.

We were both very much out of breath. We spoke in panting, broken sentences.

" What are we to do ? "

" Hide."

" Where ? "

" Up one of these side caverns."

" And then ? "

" Think."

"Right—come on."

We strode on, and presently came to a radiating, dark cavern. Cavor was in front. He hesitated, and chose a black mouth that seemed to promise good hiding. He went towards it and turned.

" It's dark," he said.

"Your legs and feet will light us. You are all wet with that luminous stuff."

" But——"

A tumult of sounds, and in particular a sound like a clanging gong advancing up the main tunnel, became audible. It was horribly suggestive of a tumultuous pursuit. We made a bolt for the unlit side cavern forthwith. As we ran along it our way was lit by the irradiation of Cavor's legs. " It's lucky," I panted, " they

" ' BEDFORD,' HE WHISPERED ; ' THERE'S A SORT OF LIGHT IN FRONT OF US.' "

took off our boots, or we should fill this place with clatter." On we rushed, taking as small steps as we could to avoid striking the roof of the cavern. After a time we seemed to be gaining on the uproar. It became muffled, it dwindled, it died away.

I stopped and looked back, and I heard the pad, pad of Cavor's feet receding. Then he stopped also. "Bedford," he whispered; "there's a sort of light in front of us."

I looked, and at first could see nothing. Then I perceived his head and shoulders dimly outlined against a fainter darkness. I saw also that this mitigation of the darkness was not blue, as all the other light within the moon had been, but a pallid grey, a very vague faint white, the daylight colour. Cavor noted this difference as soon as, or sooner than, I did, and I think, too, that it filled him with much the same wild hope.

" Bedford," he whispered, and his voice trembled, "that light—it is possible——"

He did not dare to say the thing he hoped. There came a pause. Suddenly I knew by the sound of his feet that he was striding towards that pallor. I followed him, with a beating heart.

CHAPTER XVI.

POINTS OF VIEW.

THE light grew stronger as we advanced. In a little time it was nearly as strong as the phosphorescence on Cavor's legs. Our tunnel was expanding into a cavern and this new light was at the farther end of it. I perceived something that set my hopes leaping and bounding.

"Cavor," I said, "it comes from above! I am certain it comes from above!"

He made no answer, but hurried on.

Indisputably it was a grey light, a silvery light.

In another moment we were beneath it. It filtered down through a chink in the walls of the cavern, and as I stared up, drip, came a huge drop of water upon my face. I started, and stood aside ; drip, fell another drop quite audibly on the rocky floor.

"Cavor," I said, "if one of us lifts the other, he can reach that crack!"

"I'll lift you," he said, and incontinently hoisted me as though I was a baby.

I thrust an arm into the crack, and just at my finger-tips found a little ledge by which I could hold. I could see the white light was very much brighter now. I pulled myself up by two fingers with scarcely an effort, though on earth I weigh twelve stone, reached to a still higher corner of rock, and so got my feet on the narrow ledge. I stood up and searched up the rocks with my fingers ; the cleft broadened out upwardly. "It's climbable," I said to Cavor. "Can you jump up to my hand if I hold it down to you?"

I wedged myself between the sides of the cleft, rested knee and foot on the ledge, and extended a hand. I could not see Cavor, but I could hear the rustle of his movements as he crouched to spring. Then whack, and he was

hanging to my arm—and no heavier than a kitten! I lugged him up until he had a hand on my ledge and could release me.

"Confound it!" I said, "anyone could be a mountaineer on the moon," and so set myself in earnest to the climbing. For a few minutes I clambered steadily, and then I looked up again. The cleft opened out gradually, and the light was brighter. Only——

It was not daylight after all! In another moment I could see what it was, and at the sight I could have beaten my head against the rocks with disappointment. For I beheld simply an irregularly sloping open space, and all over its slanting floor stood a forest of little club-shaped fungi, each shining gloriously with that pinkish, silvery light. For a moment I stared at their soft radiance, then sprang forward and upward among them. I plucked up half-a-dozen and flung them against the rocks, and then sat down, laughing bitterly, as Cavor's ruddy face came into view.

"It's phosphorescence again," I said. "No need to hurry. Sit down and make

"CAVOR'S RUDDY FACE CAME INTO VIEW."

yourself at home." And as he spluttered over our disappointment I began to lob more of these growths into the cleft.

" I thought it was daylight," he said.

" Daylight!" cried I. " Daybreak, sunset, clouds, and windy skies! Shall we ever see such things again?"

As I spoke a little picture of our world seemed to rise before me, bright and little and clear, like the background of some Italian picture. " The sky that changes, and the sea that changes, and the hills and the green trees, and the towns and cities shining in the sun. Think of a wet roof at sunset, Cavor! Think of the windows of a westward house!"

He made no answer.

" Here we are burrowing in this beastly world that isn't a world, with its inky ocean hidden in some abominable blackness below, and outside that torrid day and that death stillness of night. And all those things that are chasing us now, beastly men of leather— insect men, that come out of a nightmare! After all, they're right! What business have we here, smashing them and disturbing their world? For all we know the whole planet is up and after us already. In a minute we may hear them whimpering and their gongs going. What are we to do? Where are we to go? Here we are as comfortable as snakes from Jamrach's loose in a Surbiton villa!"

I resumed my destruction of the fungi. Then suddenly I saw something and shouted.

" Cavor," I said, " these chains are of gold!"

He was sitting, thinking intently, with his hands gripping his cheeks. He turned his head slowly and stared at me and, when I had repeated my words, at the twisted chain about his right hand. " So they are," he said, " so they are." His face lost its transitory interest even as he looked. He hesitated for a moment, then went on with his interrupted meditation. I sat for a space puzzling over the fact that I had only just observed this, until I considered the blue light in which we had been and which had taken all the colour out of the metal. And from that discovery I also started upon a train of thought that carried me wide and far. I forgot that I had just been asking what business we had in the moon. I was dreaming of gold. . . .

It was Cavor who spoke first. " It seems to me that there are two courses open to us."

" Well?"

" Either we can attempt to make our way —fight our way if necessary—out to the

exterior again and then hunt for our sphere until either we find it or the cold of the night comes to kill us, or else——"

He paused. " Yes," I said, though I knew what was coming.

" We might attempt once more to establish some sort of understanding with the minds of the people in the moon."

" So far as I'm concerned—it's the first."

" I doubt."

" I don't."

" You see," said Cavor, " I do not think we can judge the Selenites by what we have seen of them. Their central world, their civilized world, will be far below in the profounder caverns about their sea. This region of the crust in which we are is an outlying district, a pastoral region. At any rate, that is my interpretation. These Selenites we have seen may be only the equivalent of cow-boys and engine-tenders. Their use of goads—in all probability mooncalf goads—the lack of imagination they show in expecting us to be able to do just what they can do, their indisputable brutality, all seem to point to something of that sort. But if we endured——"

" Neither of us could endure a six-inch plank across the bottomless pit for very long."

" No," said Cavor, " that's true."

He discovered a new line of possibilities. " Suppose we got ourselves into some corner, where we could defend ourselves against these hinds and labourers. If, for example, we could hold out for a week or so, it is probable that the news of our appearance would filter down to the more intelligent and populous parts——"

" If they exist."

" They must exist, or whence come those tremendous machines?"

" That's possible, but it's the worst of the two chances."

" We might write up inscriptions on walls——"

" How do we know their eyes would see the sort of marks we made?"

" If we cut them——"

" That's possible, of course."

I took up a new thread of thought. " After all," I said, " I suppose you don't think these Selenites so infinitely wiser than men?"

" They must know a lot more—or at least a lot of different things."

" Yes, but——" I hesitated. " I think you'll quite admit, Cavor, that you're rather an exceptional man."

" How?"

" Well, you—you're a rather lonely man ; have been, that is. You haven't married."

" Never wanted to. But why ? "

" And you never grew richer than you happened to be ? "

" Never wanted that either."

" You've just rooted after knowledge."

" Well, a certain curiosity is natural——"

" You think so. That's just it. You think every other mind wants to *know*. I remember once, when I asked you why you conducted all these researches, you said you wanted your F.R.S., and to have the stuff called Cavorite, and things like that. You know perfectly well you didn't do it for that ; but at the time my question took you by surprise, and you felt you ought to have something to look like a motive. Really, you conducted researches because you *had* to. It's your twist."

" Perhaps it is——"

" It isn't one man in a million has that twist. Most men want—well, various things, but very few want knowledge for its own sake. I don't, I know perfectly well. Now these Selenites seem to be a driving, busy sort of being, but how do you know that even the most intelligent will take an interest in us or our world ? I don't believe they'll even know we have a world. They never come out at night—they'd freeze if they did. They've probably never seen any heavenly body at all except blazing sun. How are they to know there *is* another world ? What does it matter to them if they do ? Well, even if they *have* had a glimpse of a few stars or even of the earth crescent, what of that ? Why should people living *inside* a planet trouble to observe that sort of thing ? Men wouldn't have done it except for the seasons and sailing ; why should the moon people ? . . . .

"Well, suppose there are a few philosophers like yourself. They are just the very Selenites who'll never hear of our existence. Suppose a Selenite had dropped on the earth when you were at Lympne ; you'd have been the last man in the world to hear he had come. You never read a newspaper. You see the chances against you. Well, it's for these chances we're sitting here doing nothing while precious time is flying. I tell you we've got into a fix. We've come unarmed, we've lost our sphere, we've got no food, we've shown ourselves to the Selenites and made them think we're strange, strong, dangerous animals, and unless these Selenites are perfect fools they'll set about now and hunt us till they find us, and when they find us they'll try and take us if they can and kill us if they can't,

and that's the end of the matter. After they take us they'll probably kill us, through some misunderstanding. After we're done for they may discuss us, perhaps, but we sha'n't get much fun out of that."

" Go on."

" On the other hand, here's gold knocking about like cast-iron at home. If only we can get some of it back, if only we can find our sphere again before they do and get back, then——"

" Yes ? "

" We might put the thing on a sounder footing. Come back in a bigger sphere with guns."

" Good Lord ! " cried Cavor, as though that was horrible.

I shied another luminous fungus down the cleft.

" Look here, Cavor," I said, " I've half the voting power anyhow in this affair, and this is a case for a practical man. I'm a practical man, and you are not. I'm not going to trust to Selenites and geometrical diagrams again if I can help it. . . . That's all. Get back. Drop all this secrecy—or most of it. And come again."

He reflected. " When I came to the moon," he said, " I ought to have come alone."

" The question before the meeting," I said, " is how to get back to the sphere."

For a time we nursed our knees in silence. Then he seemed to decide to accept my reasons.

" I think," he said, " one can get data. It is clear that, while the sun is on this side of the moon, the air will be blowing through this planet sponge from the dark side hither. On this side, at any rate, the air will be expanding and flowing out of the moon caverns into the crater. . . . Very well, there's a draught here."

" So there is."

" And that means that this is not a dead end ; somewhere behind us this cleft goes on and up. The draught is blowing up, and that is the way we have to go. If we try and get up any sort of chimney or gully there is, we shall not only get out of these passages where they are hunting for us——"

" But suppose the gully is too narrow."

" We'll come down again."

" 'Ssh ! " I said, suddenly ; " what's that ? "

We listened. At first it was an indistinct murmur, and then one picked out the clang of a gong. " They must think we are mooncalves," said I, " to be frightened at that."

"They're coming along that passage," said Cavor.

"They must be."

"They'll not think of the cleft. They'll go past."

I listened again for a space. "This time," I whispered, "they're likely to have some sort of weapon."

Then suddenly I sprang to my feet. "Good heavens, Cavor!" I cried. "But they *will!* They'll see the fungi I have been pitching down. They'll——"

I didn't finish my sentence. I turned about and made a leap over the fungus-tops towards the upper end of the cavity. I saw that the space turned upward and became a draughty cleft again, ascending to impenetrable darkness. I was about to clamber up into this, and then with a happy inspiration turned back.

"What are you doing?" asked Cavor.

"Go on!" said I, and went back and got two of the shining fungi, and putting one into the breast pocket of my flannel jacket so that it stuck out to light our climbing, went back with the other for Cavor. The noise of the Selenites was now so loud that it seemed they must be already beneath the cleft. But it might be they would have difficulty in clambering into it, or might hesitate to ascend it against our possible resistance. At any rate we had now the comforting knowledge of the enormous muscular superiority our birth on another planet gave us. In another minute I was clambering with gigantic vigour after Cavor's blue-lit heels.

"CLAMBERING WITH GIGANTIC VIGOUR AFTER CAVOR'S BLUE-LIT HEELS."

CHAPTER XVII.

THE FIGHT IN THE CAVE OF THE MOON BUTCHERS.

I DO not know how far we clambered before we came to the grating. It may be we ascended only a few hundred feet, but at the time it seemed to me we might have hauled and jammed and hopped and wedged ourselves through a mile or more of vertical ascent. Whenever I recall that time there comes into my head the heavy clank of our golden chains that followed every movement. Very soon my knuckles and knees were raw, and I had a bruise on one cheek. After a time the first violence of our efforts diminished, and our movements became more deliberate and less painful. The noise of the pursuing Selenites had died away altogether. It seemed almost as though they had not traced us up the crack after all, in spite of the tell-tale heap of broken fungi that must have lain beneath, it. At times the cleft narrowed so much that we could scarce squeeze up it, at others it expanded into great drusy cavities studded with prickly crystals, or thickly beset with dull, shining fungoid pimples. Sometimes it twisted spirally and at other times slanted down nearly to the horizontal direction. Ever and again there was the intermittent drip and trickle of water by us. Once or twice it seemed to us that small living things had rustled out of our reach, but what they were we never saw. They may have been venomous beasts for all I know, but they did us no harm, and we were now tuned to a pitch when a weird creeping thing more or less mattered little. And, at last, far above came the familiar bluish light again, and then we saw that it filtered through a grating that barred our way.

We whispered as we pointed this out to one another and became more and more cautious in our ascent. Presently we were close under the grating, and by pressing my face against its bars I could see a limited portion of the cavern beyond. It was clearly a large space, and lit no doubt by some rivulet of the same blue light that we had seen flow from the beating machinery. An intermittent trickle of water dropped ever and again between the bars near my face.

My first endeavour was naturally to see what might be upon the floor of the cavern, but our grating lay in a depression whose rim hid all this from our eyes. Our foiled attention then fell back upon the suggestion of the various sounds we heard, and presently my eye caught a number of faint shadows that played across the dim roof, far overhead.

Indisputably there were several Selenites, perhaps a considerable number in this space, for we could hear the noises of their intercourse and faint sounds that I identified as their footfalls. There was also a succession of regularly repeated sounds, chid, chid, chid, which began and ceased, suggestive of a knife or spade hacking at some soft substance. Then came a clank as if of chains, a whistle and a rumble as of a truck running over a hollowed place, and then again that chid, chid, chid, resumed. The shadows told of shapes that moved quickly and rhythmically in agreement with that regular sound, and rested when it ceased.

We put our heads close together and began to discuss these things in noiseless whispers.

"They are occupied," I said; "they are occupied in some way."

"Yes."

"They're not seeking us or thinking of us."

"Perhaps they have not heard of us."

"Those others are hunting about below. If suddenly we appeared here——"

We looked at one another.

"There might be a chance to parley," said Cavor.

"No," I said, "not as we are."

For a space we remained, each occupied with his own thoughts.

Chid, chid, chid went the chipping, and the shadows moved to and fro.

I looked at the grating. "It's flimsy," I said. "We might bend two of the bars and crawl through."

We wasted a little time in vague discussion. Then I took one of the bars in both hands, and got my feet up against the rock until they were almost on a level with my head, and so thrust against the bar. It bent so suddenly that I almost slipped. I clambered about and bent the adjacent bar in the opposite direction, and then took the luminous fungus from my pocket and dropped it down the fissure.

"Don't do anything hastily," whispered Cavor, as I twisted myself up through the opening I had enlarged. I had a glimpse of busy figures as I came through the grating, and immediately bent down, so that the rim of the depression in which the grating lay hid me from their eyes, and so lay flat, signalling advice to Cavor as he also prepared to come through. Presently we were side by side in the depression, peering over the edge at the cavern and its occupants.

It was a much larger cavern than we had supposed from our first glimpse of it, and we looked up from the lowest portion of its sloping floor. It widened out as it receded from us, and its roof came down and hid the remoter portion altogether. And lying in a line along its length, vanishing at last far away in that tremendous perspective, were a number of huge shapes, huge pallid hulls, upon which the Selenites were busy. At first they seemed big white cylinders of vague import. Then I noted the heads upon them lying towards us, eyeless and skinless like the heads of sheep at a butcher's, and perceived they were the carcasses of mooncalves being cut up, much as the crew of a whaler might cut up a moored whale. They were cutting off the flesh in strips, and on some of the farther trunks the white ribs were showing. It was the sound of their hatchets that made that chid, chid. Some way away a thing like a trolley, cable-drawn and loaded with chunks of lax meat, was running up the slope of the cavern floor. That enormous busy avenue of hulls that were destined to be food gave us a sense of the vast populousness of the moon world second only to the effect of our first glimpse down the shaft.

It seemed to me at first that the Selenites must be standing on trestle-supported planks,[*] and then I saw that the planks and supports and their hatchets were really of the same leaden hue as my fetters had seemed before white light came to bear on them. A number of very thick-looking crowbars lay about the floor and had apparently assisted to turn the dead mooncalf over on its side. They were perhaps 6ft. long, with shaped handles; very tempting looking weapons.

---

[*] I do not remember seeing any wooden things on the moon; doors, tables, everything corresponding to our terrestrial joinery was made of metal, and I believe for the most part of gold, which as a metal would, of course, naturally recommend itself—other things being equal—on account of the ease in working it and its toughness and durability.

"HUGE PALLID HULLS, UPON WHICH THE SELENITES WERE BUSY."

The whole place was lit by three transverse streams of the blue fluid.

We lay for a long time noting all these things in silence. "Well?" said Cavor at last.

I crouched lower and turned to him. I had come upon a brilliant idea. "Unless they lowered those bodies by a crane," I said, "we must be nearer the surface than I thought."

"Why?"

"The mooncalf doesn't hop and it hasn't got wings."

He peered over the edge of the hollow again. "I wonder, now——" he began. "After all we have never gone far from the surface."

I stopped him by a grip on his arm. I had heard a noise from the cleft below us !

We twisted ourselves about and lay as still as death, with every sense alert. In a little while I did not doubt that something was quietly ascending the cleft. Very slowly and quite noiselessly I assured myself of a good grip on my chain, and waited for that something to appear.

"Just look at those chaps with the hatchets again," I said.

"They're all right," said Cavor.

I took a sort of provisional aim at the gap in the grating. I could hear now quite distinctly the soft twittering of the ascending Selenites, the dab of their hands against the rock, and the falling of dust from their grips, as they clambered.

Then I could see that there was something moving dimly in the blackness below the grating, but what it might be I could not distinguish. The whole thing seemed to hang fire just for a moment; then, smash ! I had sprung to my feet, struck savagely at something that had flashed out at me. It was the keen point of a spear. I have thought since that its length in the narrowness of the cleft must have prevented its being sloped to reach me. Anyhow, it shot out from the grating like the tongue of a snake and missed, and flew back and flashed again. But the second time I snatched and caught it, and wrenched it away, but not before another had darted ineffectually at me.

I shouted with triumph as I felt the hold of the Selenite resist my pull for a moment and give, and then I was jabbing down through the bars, amidst squeals from the darkness, and Cavor had snapped off the other spear, and was leaping and flourishing it beside me and making inefficient jabs. "Clang, clang," came up through the grating, and then an axe hurtled through the air and whacked against the rocks beyond to remind me of the fletchers at the carcasses up the cavern.

I turned, and they were all coming towards

us in open order, waving their axes. If they had not heard of us before they must have realized the situation with incredible swiftness. I stared at them for a moment, spear in hand. "Guard that grating, Cavor," I cried, and howled to intimidate them, and rushed to meet them. Two of them missed with their hatchets, and the rest fled incontinently. Then the two also were sprinting away up the cavern, with hands clenched and heads down. I never saw men run like them!

I knew the spear I had was no good for me. It was thin and flimsy, only effectual for a thrust, and too long for a quick recover. So I only chased the Selenites as far as the first carcass, and stopped there and picked up one of the crowbars that were lying about. It felt comfortingly heavy and equal to smashing any number of Selenites. I threw away my spear, and picked up a second crowbar for the other hand. I felt five times better than I had with the spear. I shook the two threateningly at the Selenites, who had come to a halt in a little crowd far away up the cavern, and then turned about to look at Cavor.

He was leaping from side to side of the grating making threatening jabs with his broken spear. That was all right. It would keep the Selenites down—for a time at any rate. I looked up the cavern again. What on earth were we going to do now?

We were cornered in a sort of way already. But these butchers and fletchers up the cavern had been surprised; they were probably scared, and they had no special weapons, only those little hatchets of theirs. And that way lay escape. Their sturdy little forms—for most of them were shorter and thicker than the mooncalf herds — were scattered up the slope in a way that was eloquent of indecision. But for all that there was a tremendous crowd of them. Those Selenites down the cleft had certainly some infernally long spears. It might be they had other surprises for us. . . . But, confound it! if we charged up the cave we should let them up behind us; and if we didn't, those little brutes up the cave

would probably get reinforced. Heaven alone knew what tremendous engines of warfare— guns, bombs, terrestrial torpedoes—this unknown world below our feet, this vaster world of which we had only pricked the outer cuticle, might not presently send up to our destruction. It became clear the only thing to do was to charge! It became clearer as the legs of a number of fresh Selenites appeared running down the cavern towards us.

"Bedford!" cried Cavor, and behold! he was half-way between me and the grating.

"Go back!" I cried. "What are you doing——"

"They've got—it's like a gun!"

And struggling in the grating between those defensive spears appeared the head and shoulders of a Selenite bearing some complicated apparatus.

I realized Cavor's utter incapacity for the fight we had in hand. For a moment I hesitated. Then I rushed past him whirling my crowbars, and shouting to confound the aim of the Selenite. He was aiming in the queerest way with the thing against his stomach. "*Chuzz!*" The thing wasn't a gun; it went off like a cross-bow more, and dropped me in the middle of a leap.

"I RUSHED PAST HIM WHIRLING MY CROWBARS."

I didn't fall down—I simply came down a little shorter than I should have done if I hadn't been hit, and from the feel of my shoulder the thing might have tapped me and glanced off. Then my left hand hit against the shaft, and I perceived there was a sort of spear sticking half through my shoulder. The moment after I got home with the crowbar in my right hand, and hit the Selenite fair and square. Hitting those Selenites was like hitting dry sunflower canes with a rod of iron. He collapsed—he broke into pieces.

I dropped a crowbar, pulled the spear out of my shoulder, and began to jab it down the grating into the darkness. At each jab came a shriek and twitter. Finally I hurled the spear down upon them with all my strength, leapt up, picked up the crowbar again, and started for the multitude up the cavern.

"Bedford!" cried Cavor, "Bedford!" as I flew past him.

I seem to remember his footsteps coming on behind me.

Step, leap . . . . whack, step, leap . . . . Each leap seemed to last ages. • With each, the cave opened out and the number of Selenites visible increased. At first they seemed all running about like ants in a disturbed ant-hill, one or two waving hatchets and coming to meet me, more running away, some bolting sideways into the avenue of carcasses; then presently others came in sight carrying spears, and then others. The cavern grew darker farther up. Flick! something flew over my head. Flick! As I soared in mid-stride I saw a spear hit and quiver in one of the carcasses to my left. Then as I came down one hit the ground before me and I heard the remote chuzz! with which their things were fired. Flick! Flick! for a moment it was a shower. They were volleying!

I stopped dead.

I don't think I thought clearly then. I seem to remember a kind of stereotyped phrase running through my mind: "Zone of fire, seek cover!" I know I made a dash for the space between two of the carcasses, and stood there, panting and feeling very wicked.

I looked round for Cavor, and for a moment it seemed as if he had vanished from the world. Then he came out of the darkness between the row of the carcasses and the rocky wall of the cavern. I saw his little face, dark and blue, and shining with perspiration and emotion.

He was saying something, but what it was

I did not heed. I had realized that we might work from mooncalf to mooncalf up the cave until we were near enough to charge home. "Come on!" I said, and led the way.

"Bedford!" he cried, unavailingly.

My mind was busy as we went up that narrow alley between the dead bodies and the wall of the cavern. The rocks curved about—they could not enfilade us. Though in that narrow space we could not leap, yet with our earth-born strength we were still able to go very much faster than the Selenites. I reckoned we should presently come right among them. Once we were on them they would be hardly as formidable as black-beetles. Only, there would first of all be a volley. I whipped off my flannel jacket as I ran.

"Bedford!" panted Cavor, behind me.

I glanced back. "What?" said I.

He was pointing upward over the carcasses. "White light!" he said. "White light again!"

I looked, and it was even so: a faint white ghost of twilight in the remoter cavern roof. That seemed to give me double strength.

"Keep close," I said. A Selenite dashed out of the darkness and squealed and fled. I halted and stopped Cavor with my hand. I hung my jacket over my crowbar, ducked round the next carcass, dropped jacket and crowbar, showed myself, and darted back.

"Chuzz—flick," just one arrow came. We were close on the Selenites, and they were standing in a crowd, with a little battery of their shooting implements pointing down the cave. Three or four other arrows followed the first, and then their fire ceased.

I stuck out my head, and escaped by a hair's breadth. This time I drew a dozen shots or more, and heard the Selenites shouting and twittering as if with excitement as they shot. I picked up jacket and crowbar again.

"*Now!*" said I, and thrust out the jacket.

"Chuzz-zz-zz-zz! Chuzz!" In an instant my jacket had grown a thick beard of arrows, and they were quivering all over the carcass behind us. Instantly I slipped the crowbar out of the jacket, dropped the jacket—for all I know to the contrary it is lying up there in the moon now—and rushed out upon them.

For a minute perhaps it was massacre. I was too fierce to discriminate, and the Selenites were probably too scared to fight. At any rate they made no sort of fight against me. I saw scarlet, as the saying is. I remember I seemed to be wading among those insect helmets as a man wades through tall grass, mowing and hitting, first right then left—smash, smash ! Little drops of moisture flew about. I trod on things that crushed and piped and went slippery. The crowd seemed to open and close and flow like water. There were spears flew about me ; I was grazed over the ear by one. I was

"MOWING AND HITTING, FIRST RIGHT THEN LEFT—SMASH, SMASH !"

stabbed once in the arm and once in the cheek, but I only found that out afterwards when the blood had had time to run and cool and feel wet.

What Cavor did I do not know. For a space it seemed that this fighting had lasted for an age and must needs go on for ever. Then suddenly it was all over, and there was nothing to be seen but the backs of heads bobbing up and down as their owners ran in

all directions. . . . I seemed altogether unhurt. I ran forward some paces, shouting, then turned about. I was amazed.

I ran right through them, taking vast flying strides. They were all behind me, and running hither and thither to hide.

I felt an enormous astonishment at the evaporation of the great fight into which I had hurled myself, and not a little of exultation.

It did not seem to me that I had discovered the Selenites were unexpectedly flimsy, but that I was unexpectedly strong. I laughed stupidly. This fantastic moon !

I leapt the smashed and writhing bodies that were scattered over the cavern floor, and hurried on after Cavor.

CHAPTER XVIII.
IN THE SUNLIGHT.

PRESENTLY we saw that the cavern before us opened on a hazy void. In another moment we had emerged upon a sort of slanting gallery that projected into a vast circular space, a huge cylindrical pit running vertically up and down. Round this pit the slanting gallery ran without any parapet or protection for a turn and a half, and then plunged high above into the rock again. Somehow it reminded me then of one of those spiral turns of the railway through the Saint Gothard. It was all tremendously huge. I can scarcely hope to convey to you the Titanic proportion of all that place —the Titanic effect of it. Our eyes followed up the vast declivity of the pit wall, and overhead and far above we beheld a round opening set with faint stars, and half of the lip about it well-nigh blinding with the white light of the sun. At that we cried aloud simultaneously.

"Come on !" I said, leading the way.

"But there?" said Cavor, and very carefully stepped nearer the edge of the gallery. I followed his example and craned forward and looked down, but I was dazzled by that gleam of light above, and I could see only a bottomless darkness with spectral patches of crimson and purple floating therein. Yet if I could not see I could hear. Out of this darkness came a sound—a sound like the angry hum one can hear if one puts one's ear outside a hive of bees, a sound out of that enormous hollow, it may be, four miles beneath our feet. . . .

For a moment I listened, then tightened my grip on my crowbar and led the way up the gallery.

"This must be the shaft we looked down upon," said Cavor. "Under that lid."

"And below there is where we saw the lights."

"The lights!" said he. "Yes—the lights of the world that now we shall never see."

"We'll come back," I said, for now we had escaped so much I was rashly sanguine that we should recover the sphere.

His answer I did not catch.

"Eh?" I asked.

"It doesn't matter," he answered, and we hurried on in silence.

I suppose that slanting lateral way was four or five miles long, allowing for its curvature, and it ascended at a slope that would have made it almost impossibly steep on earth, but which one strode up easily under lunar conditions. We saw only two Selenites during all that portion of our flight, and directly they became aware of us they ran headlong. It was clear that the knowledge of our strength and violence had reached them. Our way to the exterior was unexpectedly plain. The spiral gallery straightened into a steeply ascendent tunnel, its floor bearing abundant traces of the mooncalves, and so straight and short in proportion to its vast arch that no part of it was absolutely dark. Almost immediately it began to lighten, and then far off and high up, and quite blindingly brilliant, appeared its opening on the exterior, a slope of Alpine steepness surmounted by a crest of bayonet shrub tall and broken down now and dry and dead, in spiky silhouette against the sun.

And it is strange that we men, to whom this very vegetation had seemed so weird and horrible a little time ago, should now behold it with the emotion a home-coming exile might feel at sight of his native land. We welcomed even the rareness of the air that made us pant as we ran and which rendered speaking no longer the easy thing it had been, but an effort to make oneself heard. Larger grew the sunlit circle above us and larger, and all the nearer tunnel sank into a rim of indistinguishable black. We saw the dead bayonet shrub no longer with any touch of green in it, but brown and dry and thick, and the shadow of its upper branches high out cf sight made a densely interlaced pattern upon the tumbled rocks. And at the immediate mouth of the tunnel was a wide trampled space where the mooncalves had come and gone.

We came out upon this space at last into a light and heat that hit and pressed upon us. We traversed the exposed area painfully, and clambered up a slope among the scrub-stems, and sat down at last panting in a high place beneath the shadow of a mass of twisted lava. Even in the shade the rock felt hot.

The air was intensely hot, and we were in great physical discomfort, but for all that we were no longer in a nightmare. We seemed to have come to our own province again, beneath the stars. All the fear and stress of our flight through the dim passages and fissures below had fallen from us. That last fight had filled us with an enormous confidence in ourselves so far as the Selenites were concerned. We looked back almost incredulously at the black opening from which we had just emerged. Down there it was, in a blue glow that now in our memories seemed the next thing to absolute darkness, we had met with things like mad mockeries of men, helmet-headed creatures, and had walked in fear before them, and had submitted to them until we could submit no longer. And behold, they had smashed like wax and scattered like chaff, and fled and vanished like the creatures of a dream!

I rubbed my eyes, doubting whether we had not slept and dreamt these things by reason of the fungus we had eaten, and suddenly discovered the blood upon my face, and then that my shirt was sticking painfully to my shoulder and arm.

"Confound it!" I said, gauging my injuries with an investigatory hand, and suddenly that distant tunnel-mouth became, as it were, a watching eye.

"Cavor!" I said, "what are they going to do now? And what are we going to do?"

He shook his head, with his eyes fixed upon the tunnel. "How can one tell what they will do?"

"It depends on what they think of us, and I don't see how we can begin to guess that. And it depends upon what they have in reserve. It's as you say, Cavor: we have touched the merest outside of this world. They may have all sorts of things inside here. Even with those shooting things they might make it bad for us. . . . . ."

"Yet, after all," I said, "even if we *don't* find the sphere at once, there is a chance for us. We might hold out. Even through the night. We might go down there again and make a fight for it."

The First Men in the Moon.

By H. G. Wells.

CHAPTER XVIII.—(Continued.)

STARED about me with speculative eyes. The character of the scenery had altered altogether by reason of the enormous growth and subsequent drying of the scrub. The crest on which we sat was high and commanded a wide prospect of the crater landscape, and we saw it now all sere and dry in the late autumn of the lunar afternoon. Rising one behind the other were long slopes and fields of trampled brown where the mooncalves had pastured, and far away in the full blaze of the sun a drove of them basked slumberously, scattered shapes, each with a blot of shadow against it like sheep on the side of a down. But never a sign of Selenite was to be seen. Whether they had fled on our emergence from the interior passages, or whether they were accustomed to retire after driving out the mooncalves, I cannot guess. At the time I believed the former was the case.

"If we were to set fire to all this stuff," I said, "we might find the sphere among the ashes."

Cavor did not seem to hear me. He was peering under his hand at the stars, that still, in spite of the intense sunlight, were abundantly visible in the sky. "How long do you think we have been here?" he asked, at last.

"Been where?"

"On the moon."

"Two days, perhaps."

"WE MUST GET A FIXED POINT WE CAN RECOGNISE."

"More nearly ten. Do you know, the sun is past its zenith, and sinking in the west! In four days' time or less it will be night."

"But—we've only eaten once!"

"I know that. And—— But there are the stars!"

"But why should time seem different because we are on a smaller planet?"

"I don't know. There it is!"

"How does one tell time?"

"Hunger—fatigue—all those things are different. Everything is different —everything. To me it seems that since first we came out of the sphere has been only a question of hours— long hours—at most."

"Ten days," I said; "that leaves ——" I looked up at the sun for a moment, and then saw that it was halfway from the zenith to the western edge of things. "Four days! . . . . Cavor, we mustn't sit here and dream. How do you think we may begin?"

I stood up.

"We must get a fixed point we can recognise; we might hoist a flag, or a handkerchief, or something, and quarter the ground and work round that."

He stood up beside me.

"Yes," he said, "there is nothing for it but to hunt for the sphere. Nothing. We may find it—certainly we may find it. And if not——"

"We must keep on looking."

He looked this way and that, glanced up at the sky and down at the tunnel, and astonished me by a sudden gesture of impatience. " Oh ! but we have done foolishly ! To have come to this pass ! Think how it might have been, and the things we might have done ! "

" We may do something yet."

" Never the thing we might have done. Here below our feet is a world. Think of what that world must be ! Think of that machine we saw, and the lid and the shaft ! They were just remote, outlying things ; and those creatures we have seen and fought with, no more than ignorant peasants, dwellers in the outskirts, yokels and labourers half akin to brutes. Down below ! Caverns beneath caverns, tunnels, structures, ways. . . . . It must open out and be greater and wider, and more populous as one descends. Assuredly. Right down at last to the central sea that washes round the core of the moon. Think of its inky waters under the spare lights ! If, indeed, their eyes *need* lights. Think of the cascading tributaries pouring down their channels to feed it. Think of the tides upon its surface and the rush and swirl of its ebb and flow. Perhaps they have ships that go upon it ; perhaps down there are mighty cities and swarming ways and wisdom and order passing the wit of man. And we may die here upon it and never see the masters who *must* be—ruling over these things. We may freeze and die here, and the air will freeze and thaw upon us, and then——! Then they will come upon us ; come on our stiff and silent bodies and find the sphere we cannot find, and they will understand at last too late all the thought and effort that ended here in vain ! " His voice for all that speech sounded like the voice of someone heard in a telephone, weak and far away.

" But the darkness ? " I said.

" One might get over that."

" How ? "

" I don't know. How am I to know ? One might carry a torch, one might have a lamp——! The others — might understand."

He stood for a moment with his hands held down and a rueful face, staring out over the waste that defied him. Then with a gesture of renunciation he turned towards me with proposals for the systematic hunting of the sphere.

" We can return," I said.

He looked about him. " First of all we shall have to get to earth."

" We could bring back lamps to carry and climbing irons and a hundred necessary things."

" Yes," he said.

" We can take back an earnest of success in this gold."

He looked at my golden crowbars and said nothing for a space. He stood with his hands clasped behind his back staring across the crater. At last he sighed and spoke : " It was *I* found the way here, but to find a way isn't always to be master of a way. If I take my secret back to earth, what will happen ? I do not see how I can keep my secret for a year—for even a part of a year. Sooner or later it must come out, even if other men rediscover it. And then . . . . Governments and Powers will struggle to get hither ; they will fight against one another and against these moon people ; it will only spread warfare and multiply the occasions of war. In a little while, in a very little while, if I tell my secret, this planet to its deepest galleries will be strewn with human dead. Other things are doubtful, but that is certain. . . . It is not as though man had any use for the moon. What good would the moon be to men ? Even of their own planet what have they made but a battle-ground and theatre of infinite folly ? Small as his world is, and short as his time, he has still in his little life down there far more than he can do. No ! Science has toiled too long forging weapons for fools to use. It is time she held her hand. Let him find it out for himself again—in a thousand years' time."

" There are methods of secrecy," I said.

He looked up at me and smiled. " After all," he said, " why should one worry ? There is little chance of our finding the sphere, and down below things are brewing. It's simply the human habit of hoping till we die that makes us think of return. Our troubles are only beginning. We have shown these moon-folk violence, we have given them a taste of our quality, and our chances are about as good as a tiger's that has got loose and killed a man in Hyde Park. The news of us must be running down from gallery to gallery, down towards the central parts. . . . No sane beings will ever let us take that sphere back to earth after so much as they have seen of us."

" We aren't improving our chances," said I, " by sitting here."

We stood up side by side.

" After all," he said, " we must separate. We must stick up a handkerchief on these tall spikes here and fasten it firmly, and from this as a centre we must work over the crater. You must go westward, moving out in semi-circles to and fro towards the setting sun. You must move first with your shadow on your right until it is at right angles with the direction of your handkerchief, and then with your shadow on your left. And I will do the same to the east. We will look into every gully, examine every skerry of rocks ; we will do all we can to find my sphere. If we see Selenites we will hide from them as well as we can. For drink we must take snow, and if we feel the need of food we must kill a mooncalf if we can, and eat such flesh as it has—raw ; and so each will go his own way."

" And if one of us comes upon the sphere ? "

" He must come back to the white handkerchief and stand by and signal to the other."

" And if neither ——? "

Cavor glanced up at the sun. " We go on seeking until the night and cold overtake us."

" Suppose the Selenites have found the sphere and hidden it ? "

He shrugged his shoulders.

" Or if presently they come hunting us ? "

He made no answer.

" You had better take a club," I said.

He shook his head and stared away from me across the waste. " Let us start," he said.

But for a moment he did not start. He looked at me shyly, hesitated. " Au revoir," he said.

I felt an odd stab of emotion. I was on the point of asking him to shake hands—for that somehow was how I felt just then—— when he put his feet together and leapt away from me towards the north. He seemed to drift through the air as a dead leaf would do, fell lightly, and leapt again. I stood for a moment watching him, then faced westward reluctantly, pulled myself together and, with something of the feeling of a man who leaps into icy water, selected a leaping-point, and plunged forward to explore my solitary half of the moon world. I dropped rather

clumsily among rocks, stood up and looked about me, clambered on to a rocky slab, and leapt again. When presently I looked for Cavor he was hidden from my eyes, but the handkerchief showed out bravely on its headland, white in the blaze of the sun. I determined not to lose sight of that handkerchief whatever might betide.

CHAPTER XIX.
MR. BEDFORD ALONE.

IN a little while it seemed to me as though I had always been alone on the moon. I hunted for a time with a certain intentness, but the heat was still very great and the thinness of the air felt like a hoop about one's chest. I came presently into a hollow basin bristling with tall, brown, dry fronds about its edge, and I sat down under these to rest and cool. I intended to rest for only

" HE SEEMED TO DRIFT THROUGH THE AIR AS A DEAD LEAF WOULD DO."

a little while. I put down my clubs beside me and sat resting my chin on my hands. I saw with a sort of colourless interest that the rocks of the basin, where here and there the crackling dry lichens had shrunk away to show them, were all veined and splattered with gold, that here and there bosses of rounded and wrinkled gold projected from among the litter. What did that matter now? A sort of languor had possession of my limbs and mind. I did not believe for a moment that we should ever find the sphere in that vast desiccated wilderness. I seemed to lack a motive for effort until the Selenites should come. Then I supposed I should exert myself, obeying that unreasonable imperative that urges a man before all things to preserve and defend his life, albeit he may preserve it only to die more painfully in a little while.

Why had we come to the moon?

The thing presented itself to me as a perplexing problem. What is this spirit in man that urges him for ever to depart from happiness and security, to toil, to place himself in danger, to risk even a reasonable certainty of death? It dawned upon me up there in the moon, as a thing I ought always to have known, that man is not made simply to go about being safe and comfortable and well fed and amused; but

"THE HANDKERCHIEF SHOWED OUT BRAVELY ON ITS HEADLAND."

that man himself, if you put the thing to him — not in words, but in the shape of opportunities — will show that he knows that this is so. Sitting there in the midst of that useless moon-gold, amidst the things of another world, I took count of all my life. Assuming I was to die a castaway upon the moon, I failed altogether to see what purpose I had served. I got no light on that point, but at any rate it was clearer to me than it had ever been in my life before that I was not serving my own purpose, that all my life I

had in truth never served the purposes of my private life. I ceased to speculate on why we had come to the moon and took a wider sweep. Why had I come to the earth? Why had I a private life at all? . . . . I lost myself at last in bottomless speculations. . . . .

My thoughts became vague and cloudy, no longer leading in definite directions. I had not felt heavy or weary — I cannot imagine one doing so upon the moon—but I suppose I was greatly fatigued. At any rate, I slept.

Slumbering there rested me greatly, I think, and the sun was setting and the violence of the heat abating through all the time I slumbered. When at last I was roused from my slumbers by a remote clamour I felt active and capable again. I rubbed my eyes and stretched my arms. I rose to my feet—I was a little stiff—and at once prepared to resume my search. I shouldered my golden clubs one on each shoulder and went on out of the ravine of the golden-veined rocks.

The sun was certainly lower, much lower than it had been; the air was very much cooler. I perceived I must have slept some time. It seemed to me that a faint touch of misty blueness hung about the western cliff. I leaped to a little boss of rock and surveyed the crater. I could see no signs of mooncalves or Selenites, nor could I see Cavor, but I could see my handkerchief afar off spread out on its thicket of thorns. I looked about me, and then leapt forward to the next convenient view-point.

I beat my way round in a semi-circle and back again in a still remoter crescent. It was very fatiguing and hopeless. The air was really very much cooler, and it seemed to me that the shadow under the westward cliff was growing broad. Ever and again I stopped and reconnoitred, but there was no sign of Cavor, no sign of Selenites, and it seemed to me the mooncalves must have been driven into the interior again. I could see none of them. I became more and more desirous of seeing Cavor. The winged outline of the sun had sunk now until it was scarcely the distance of its diameter from the rim of the sky. I was oppressed by the idea that the Selenites would presently close their lids and valves and shut us out under the inexorable onrush of the lunar night. It seemed to me high time that he abandoned his search and that we took counsel together. We must decide soon. Once these valves were closed we were lost men. We must get into the moon again, though we were slain in doing it. I had a vision of our freezing to death, and hammering with our last strength on the valve of the great pit.

Indeed, I took no thought any more of the sphere. I thought only of finding Cavor again. I was weighing the advisability of a prompt return to our handkerchief, when suddenly——

I saw the sphere!

I did not find it so much as it found me. It was lying much farther to the westward than I had come, and the sloping rays of the sinking sun reflected from its glass had suddenly proclaimed its presence in a dazzling beam. For an instant I thought this was some new device of the Selenites against us, and then I understood and

"I WAS IN A STATE OF HYSTERICAL AGITATION."

shouted a ghostly shout, and set off in vast leaps towards it. I missed one of my leaps and dropped into a deep ravine and turned over my ankle, and after that I stumbled at almost every leap. I was in a state of hysterical agitation, trembling violently and quite breathless long before I got to it. Three times at least I had to stop with my hands resting on my side, and spite of the thin dryness of the air the perspiration was wet upon my face.

I thought of nothing but the sphere until I reached it; I forgot even my trouble of Cavor's whereabouts. My last leap flung me with my hands hard against its glass, then I lay against it panting and trying vainly to shout "Cavor! Here is the sphere!" I peered through the thick glass and the things inside seemed tumbled. When at last I could move I hoisted it over a little and thrust my head through the man-hole. The screw stopper was inside, and I could see now that nothing had been touched, nothing had suffered. It lay there as we had left it when we had dropped out amidst the snow. For a time I was wholly occupied in making and re-making this inventory. I was trembling violently I found when I came to handle one of the blankets. But it was good to see that familiar dark interior again. Presently I crept inside and sat down among the things. I packed up my gold clubs in the bale and took a little food, not so much because I wanted it, but because it was there. Then it occurred to me that it was time to go out and signal for Cavor.

After all, everything was coming right!

There would be still time for us to get more of the magic stone that gives one mastery over men. Away there close handy was gold for the picking up, and the sphere would travel as well half full of gold as though it were empty. We could go back now masters of ourselves and our world, and then——!

I had an enormous vision of vast and dazzling possibilities that held me dreaming for a space. What monopolist, what emperor, that could compare for a moment with the men who owned the moon?

I roused myself, and it was time to fetch Cavor. No doubt he was toiling despairfully away there to the east.

I clambered out of the sphere again at last and looked about me. The growth and decay of the vegetation had gone on apace and the whole aspect of the rocks had changed, but still it was possible to make out the slope on which the seeds had germinated and the rocky mass from which we had taken our first view of the crater. But the spiky scrub on the slope stood brown and sere now and 30ft. high, and cast long shadows that stretched out of sight, and the little seeds that clustered in its upper branches were black and ripe. Its work was done, and it was brittle and ready to fall and crumple under the freezing air so soon as the nightfall came. And the huge cacti that had swollen as we watched them had long since burst and scattered their spores to the four quarters of the moon. Amazing little corner in the universe this—the landing-place of men! Some day I would have an inscription standing there, right in the midst of the hollow. It came to me if only this teeming world within knew of the full import of the moment how furious its tumult would become! But as yet it could scarcely be dreaming of the significance of our coming. For if it did, then the crater would surely be an uproar of pursuit instead of as still as death! I looked about for some place from which I might signal to Cavor, and saw that same patch of rock to which he had first leapt still bare and barren in the sun. For a moment I hesitated at going so far from the sphere. Then, with a pang of shame at that hesitation, I leapt. . . .

From this vantage-point I surveyed the crater again. Far away at the top of the enormous shadow I cast was the little white handkerchief fluttering on the bushes. It seemed to me that by this time Cavor ought to be looking for me. But he was nowhere to be seen.

I stood waiting and watching, hands shading my eyes, expecting every moment to distinguish him. Very probably I stood there for quite a long time. I tried to shout, and was reminded of the thinness of the air. I made an undecided step back towards the sphere. But a lurking dread of the Selenites made me hesitate to signal my whereabouts by hoisting one of our blankets on to the adjacent scrub. I searched the crater again.

It had an effect of complete emptiness that chilled me. And it was still. Any sound of the Selenites in the world beneath even had died away. It was as still as death. Save for the faint stir of the scrub about me in the little breeze that was rising, there was no sound—no shadow of a sound. And it was not warm now; the breeze was even a little fresh.

Confound Cavor!

I took a deep breath. I put my hands to the sides of my mouth. "Cavor!" I bawled, and the sound was like some manikin shouting far away.

I looked at the handkerchief; I looked behind me at the broadening shadow of the westward cliff; I looked under my hand at the sun. It seemed to me that almost visibly it was creeping down the sky.

I felt I must act instantly if I was to save Cavor, and set off in a straight line towards the handkerchief. Perhaps it was a couple of miles away—a matter of a few hundred leaps and strides. I have already told how one seemed to hang through those lunar leaps. In each suspense I sought Cavor, and marvelled why he should be hidden. I tried to think of it only in that way, as if that were the only possibility.

A last leap, and I was in the depression below our handkerchief; a stride, and I stood on our former vantage-point within arm's reach of it. I stood up straight and scanned the world about me, between its lengthening bars of shadow. Far away, down a long declivity, was the opening of the tunnel up which we had fled, and my shadow reached towards it, stretched towards it and touched it like a finger of the night.

Not a sign of Cavor, not a sound in all the stillness, only that the stir and waving of the scrub and of the shadows increased. And suddenly and violently I shivered. "Cav——" I began, and realized once more the uselessness of the human voice in that thin air.

Silence. The silence of death.

Then it was my eye caught something—a little thing, lying perhaps fifty yards away down the slope, amidst a litter of bent and broken branches. What was it? I knew, and yet for some reason I would not know.

I went nearer to it. It was the little cricket cap Cavor had worn.

I saw then that the scattered branches about it had been forcibly smashed and trampled. I hesitated, stepped forward, and picked it up.

I stood with Cavor's cap in my hand, staring at the trampled ground about me. On some of them were little smears of some dark stuff, stuff that I dared not touch. A dozen yards away, perhaps, the rising breeze dragged something into view, something small and vividly white.

It was a little piece of paper crumpled tightly as though it had been clutched tightly. I picked it up, and on it were smears of red. My eye caught faint pencil marks. I smoothed it out and saw uneven and broken writing, ending at last in a crooked streak upon the paper.

I set myself to decipher this.

"I have been injured about the knee — I think my knee-cap is smashed, and I cannot run or crawl," it began — pretty distinctly written.

Then, less legibly: "They have been chasing me for some time and it is only a question of——" the word "time" seemed to have been written here and erased in favour of something illegible — "before they get me. They are beating all about me."

Then the writing became convulsive. "I can hear them," I guessed the tracing meant, and then it was quite unreadable for a space. Then came a little string of words that was quite distinct: "a different sort of Selenite altogether who appears to be directing the

"I SET MYSELF TO DECIPHER THIS."

——" The writing became a mere hazy confusion again.

"They have larger brain-cases, and are clothed, as I take it, in thin plates of gold. They make gentle noises and move with organized deliberation. . . . .

"And though I am wounded and helpless here, their appearance still gives me hope." (That was like Cavor.) "They have not shot at me or attempted . . . injury. I intend——"

Then came the sudden streak of the pencil across the paper, and brown on the back and edges was—blood!

And as I stood there, stupid and perplexed with this dumfounding relic in my hand, something very, very soft and light and chill touched my hand for a moment and ceased to be, and then a thing, a little white speck, drifted athwart a shadow. They were tiny snowflakes, the first snowflakes, the heralds of the night.

I looked up with a start, and the sky had darkened almost to blackness, and was thick with a gathering multitude of coldly watchful stars. I looked eastward, and the light of that shrivelled world was touched with a sombre bronze, westward, and the sun, robbed now by a thickening white mist of half its heat and splendour, was touching the crater rim, was sinking out of sight, and all the shrubs and jagged and tumbled rocks stood out against it in a bristling disorder of black shapes. Into the great lake of darkness westward a vast wreath of mist was sinking. A cold wind set all the crater shivering. Suddenly, for a moment, I was in a puff of falling snow, and all the world about me grey and dim.

And then it was I heard, not loud and penetrating as at first, but faint and dim like a dying voice, that tolling—that same tolling that had welcomed the coming of the day:

"Boom . . . . Boom . . . . Boom . . . ."
And suddenly the open mouth of the tunnel down below there shut like an eye and vanished out of sight.

Then, indeed, I was alone.

Over me, among me, closing in on me, embracing me ever nearer, was the Eternal, that which was before the beginning and that which triumphs over the end ; that enormous void in which all light and life and being is but the thin and vanishing splendour of a falling star, the cold, the stillness, the silence, the infinite and final Night of space.

"No !" I cried. "*No !* Not yet ! not yet ! Wait ! Wait ! Oh, wait !" And frantic and convulsive, shivering with cold and terror, I flung the crumpled paper from me, scrambled back to the crest to take my bearings, and then, with all the will that was in me, leapt out towards the mark I had left, dim and distant now in the very margin of the shadow.

Leap, leap, leap, and each leap was seven ages. Before me the pale, serpent-girdled sector of the sun sank and sank, and the advancing shadow swept to seize the sphere before I could reach it. Once, and then again my foot slipped on the gathering snow as I leapt and shortened my leap ; once I fell short into bushes that crashed and smashed into dusty chips and nothingness, and once I stumbled as I dropped and rolled head over heels into a gully and rose bruised and bleeding and confused as to my direction.. But such incidents were as nothing to the intervals, those awful pauses when one drifted through the air towards that pouring tide of night. "Shall I reach it ? Oh, Heaven ! shall I reach it ? "—a thousand times repeated, until it passed into a prayer, into a sort of litany. And with the barest margin of time I reached the sphere.

Already it had passed into the chill

"ALREADY THE SNOW WAS THICK UPON IT."

penumbra of the cold. Already the snow was thick upon it, and the cold reaching my marrow. But I reached it — the snow was already banking against it—and crept into its refuge, with the snowflakes dancing in about me, as I turned with chilling hands to thrust the valve in and spun it tight and hard. And then with fingers that were already thick and clumsy I turned to the shutter-studs.

As I fumbled with the switches—for I had never controlled them before—I could see dimly through the steaming glass the blazing red streamers of the sinking sun dancing and flickering through the snowstorm, and the black forms of the scrub thickening and bending and breaking beneath the accumulating snow. Thicker whirled the snow and thicker, black against the light. What if even now the switches failed to obey me ?

Then something clicked under my hands,

and in an instant that last vision of the moon-world was hidden from my eyes. I was in the silence and darkness of the interplanetary sphere.

CHAPTER XX.
MR. BEDFORD IN INFINITE SPACE.

IT was almost as though I had been killed. Indeed, I could imagine a man suddenly and violently killed would feel very much as I did. One moment, a passion of agonizing existence and fear ; the next, darkness and stillness, neither light nor life nor sun, moon, nor stars—the blank Infinite. Although the thing was done by my own act, although I had already tasted this very effect in Cavor's company, I felt astonished, dumfounded, and overwhelmed. I seemed to be borne upward into an enormous darkness. My fingers floated off the studs, I hung as if I were annihilated, and at last very softly and gently I came against the bale and the golden chain and the crowbars that had drifted to meet me at our common centre of gravity.

I do not know how long that drifting took. In the sphere, of course, even more than on the moon, one's earthly time-sense was ineffectual. At the touch of the bale it was as if I had awakened from a dreamless sleep. I immediately perceived that if I wanted to keep awake and alive I must get a light or open a window, so as to get a grip of something with my eyes. And, besides, I was cold. I kicked off from the bale, therefore, clawed on to the thin cords within the glass, crawled along until I got to the man-hole rim, and so got my bearings for the light and blind studs ; took a shove-off, and, flying once round the bale and getting a scare from something big and flimsy that was drifting loose, I got my hand on the cord quite close to the studs and reached them. I lit the little lamp first of all to see what it was I had collided with, and discovered that old copy of *Lloyd's News* had slipped its moorings and was adrift in the void. That brought me out of the infinite to my own proper dimensions again. It made me laugh and pant for a time, and suggested the idea of a little oxygen from one of the cylinders. After that I lit the heater until I felt warm, and then I took food. Then I set to work in a very gingerly fashion on the Cavorite blinds to see if I could guess by any means how the sphere was travelling.

The first blind I opened I shut at once, and hung for a time flattened and blinded by the sunlight that had hit me. After thinking a little I started upon the windows at right angles to this one, and got the huge crescent moon and the little crescent earth behind it, the second time. I was amazed to find how far I was from the moon. I had reckoned that not only should I have little or none of the " kick-off " that the earth's atmosphere had given us at our start, but that the tangential " fly-off " of the moon's spin would be at least twenty-eight times less than the earth's. I had expected to discover myself hanging over our crater and on the edge of the night, but all that was now only a part of the outline of the white crescent that filled the sky. And Cavor——?

He was already infinitesimal.

Under the inspiring touch of the drifting newspaper I became very practical again for awhile. It was quite clear to me that what I had to do was to get back to earth, but as far as I could see I was drifting away from it. Whatever had happened to Cavor, I was powerless to help him. There he was, living or dead, behind the mantle of that rayless night, and there he must remain until I could summon our fellow-men to his assistance. That briefly was the plan I had in my mind : to come back to earth and then, as maturer consideration might determine, either to show and explain the sphere to a few discreet persons and act with them, or else to keep my secret, sell my gold, obtain weapons, provisions, and an assistant, and return with these advantages to deal on equal terms with the flimsy people of the moon, and either to rescue Cavor or to procure a sufficient supply of gold to place my subsequent proceedings on a firmer basis. All this was pretty clear and obvious, and I set myself to decide just exactly how the return to earth should be contrived.

I puzzled out at last that I must drop back towards the moon as near as I dared to gather velocity, then shut my windows and fly behind it, and when I was past open my earthward windows, and so get off at a good pace homeward. But whether I should ever reach the earth by that device or whether I might not simply find myself spinning about it in some hyperbolic or parabolic curve or other, I could not tell. Later I had a happy inspiration, and, by opening certain windows to the moon which had appeared in the sky in front of the earth, I turned my course aside so as to head off the earth, which it had become evident to me I must pass behind without some such expedient. I did a very great deal of complicated thinking over these problems— for I am no mathematician—and in the end I am certain it was much more my good luck than my reasoning that enabled me to hit the earth. Had I known then, as I know now, the mathematical chances there were against me, I doubt if I should have troubled even to touch the studs to make any attempt. And having puzzled out what I considered to be the thing to do, I opened all my moonward windows and squatted down—the effort lifted me for a time some foot or so into the air, and I hung there in the oddest way—and waited for the crescent to get bigger and bigger until I felt I was near enough for safety. Then I would shut the windows, fly past the moon with the velocity I had got from it—if I did not smash upon it —and so go on towards the earth.

A time came when this was done, and I shut out the sight of the moon from my eyes, and in a state of mind singularly free from anxiety or any distressful quality, I sat down to begin my vigil in that little speck of matter in infinite space that would last until I should strike the earth. The heater had made the sphere tolerably warm, the air had

"I WAS IN DARKNESS SAVE FOR THE EARTH SHINE AND THE GLITTER OF THE STARS BELOW ME."

been refreshed by the oxygen, and, except for that faint congestion of the head that was always with me while I was away from earth, I felt entire physical comfort. I had extinguished the light again lest it should fail me in the end ; I was in darkness save for the earth shine and the glitter of the stars below me. Everything was so absolutely silent and still that I might indeed have been the only being in the universe, and yet, strangely enough, I had no more feeling of loneliness or fear than if I had been lying in bed on earth. Now, this seems all the stranger to me since during my last hours in the crater of the moon the sense of my utter loneliness had been an agony. . . .

Incredible as it will seem, this interval of time that I spent in space has no sort of proportion to any other interval of time in my life. Sometimes it seemed that I sat through

immeasurable eternities like some god upon a lotus leaf, and again as though there was a momentary pause as I leapt from moon to earth. In truth, it was altogether some weeks of earthly time. But I had done with care and anxiety, hunger or fear, for that space. I sat thinking with a strange breadth and freedom of all that we had undergone, and of all my life and motives and the secret issues of my being. I seemed to myself to have grown greater and greater ; to have lost all sense of movement ; to be floating amidst the stars, and always the sense of earth's littleness and the infinite littleness of my life upon it was implicit in my thoughts.

I can't profess to explain the things that happened in my mind. No doubt they could all be traced directly or indirectly to the curious physical conditions under which I was living. I set them down here just for what they are worth, and without any comment. The most prominent quality of it was a pervading doubt of my own identity. I became, if I may so express it, dissociate from Bedford ; I looked down on Bedford as a trivial, incidental thing with which I chanced to be connected. I saw Bedford in many relations—as an ass or as a poor beast where I had hitherto been inclined to regard him with a quiet pride as a very spirited or rather forcible person. I saw him, not only as an ass, but as the son of many generations of asses. I reviewed his schooldays and his early manhood and his first encounter with love very much as one might review the proceedings of an ant in the sand. . . . Something of that period of lucidity, I regret, still hangs about me, and I doubt if I shall ever recover the full-bodied self-satisfaction of my early days. But, at the time, the thing was not in the least painful, because I had that extraordinary persuasion that, as a matter of fact, I was no more Bedford than I was anyone else, but only a mind floating in the still serenity of space. Why should I be disturbed about this Bedford's shortcomings? I was not responsible for him or them.

For a time I struggled against this really very grotesque delusion. I tried to summon the memory of vivid moments, of tender or intense emotions, to my assistance; I felt that if I could recall one genuine twinge of feeling the growing severance would be stopped. But I could not do it. I saw Bedford rushing down Chancery Lane, hat on the back of his head, coat-tails flying out, *en route* for his public examination. I saw him dodging and bumping against and even saluting other similar little creatures in that swarming gutter of people. *Me?* I saw Bedford that same evening in the sitting-room of a certain lady, and his hat was on the table beside him, and it wanted brushing badly, and he was in tears. *Me?* I saw him with that lady in various attitudes and emotions—I never felt so detached before. . . . I saw him hurrying off to Lympne to write a play, and accosting Cavor, and in his shirt-sleeves working at the sphere, and walking out to Canterbury because he was afraid to come! *Me?* I did not believe it.

I still reasoned that all this was hallucination due to my solitude and the fact that I had lost all weight and sense of resistance. I endeavoured to recover that sense by banging myself about the sphere, by pinching my hands and clasping them together. Among other things I lit the light, captured that torn copy of *Lloyd's*, and read those convincingly realistic advertisements again about the Cutaway bicycle, and the gentleman of private means, and the lady in distress who was selling those "forks and spoons." There was no doubt *they* existed surely enough, and, said I, "This is your world, and you are Bedford, and you are going back to live among things like that for all the rest of your life." But the doubts within me could still argue: "It is not you that is reading — it is Bedford; but *you are not Bedford*, you know. That's just where the mistake comes in."

"Confound it!" I cried, "and if I am not Bedford, what *am* I?"

But in that direction no light was forthcoming, though the strangest fancies came drifting into my brain, queer, remote suspicions like shadows seen from far away . . . Do you know I had a sort of idea that really I was something quite outside not only the world, but all worlds, and out of space and time, and that this poor Bedford was just a peephole through which I looked at life? . . . .

Bedford! However I disavowed him, there I was most certainly bound up with him, and I knew that wherever and whatever I might be I must needs feel the stress of his desires and sympathize with all his joys and sorrows until his life should end. And with the dying of Bedford —what then? . . . .

Enough of this remarkable phase of my experiences! I tell it here simply to show how one's isolation and departure from this planet touched not only the functions and feeling of every organ of the body, but indeed also the very fabric of the mind with strange and unanticipated disturbances. All through the major portion of that vast space journey I hung thinking of such immaterial things as these, hung dissociated and apathetic, a cloudy megalo-maniac as it were, amidst the stars and planets in the void of space, and not only the world to which I was returning, but the blue-lit caverns of the Selenites, their helmet faces, their gigantic and wonderful machines, and the fate of Cavor, dropped helpless into that world, seemed infinitely minute and altogether trivial things to me.

Until at last I began to feel the pull of the earth upon my being, drawing me back again to the life that is real for men. And then, indeed, it grew clearer and clearer to me that I was quite certainly Bedford after all, and returning after amazing adventures to this world of ours, and with a life that I was very likely to lose in this return. I set myself to puzzle out the conditions under which I must fall to earth.

The First Men in the Moon.

By H. G. Wells.

CHAPTER XXI.

MR. BEDFORD AT LITTLESTONE.

Y line of flight was about parallel with the surface as I came into the upper air. The temperature of the sphere began to rise forthwith. I knew it behoved me to drop at once. Far below me in a darkening twilight stretched a great expanse of sea. I opened every window I could and fell—out of sunshine into evening and out of evening into night. Vaster grew the earth and vaster, swallowing up the stars, and the silvery, translucent, starlit veil of cloud it wore spread out to catch me. At last the world seemed no longer a sphere but flat, and then concave. It was no longer a planet in the sky, but the World — the world of man. I shut all but an inch or so of earthward window and dropped with a slackening velocity. The broadening water, now so near that I could see the dark glitter of the waves, rushed up to meet me. I snapped the last strip of window and sat scowling and biting my knuckles waiting for the impact. . . .

The sphere hit the water with a huge splash; it must have sent it fathoms high. At the splash I flung the Cavorite shutters open. Down I went, but slower and

slower, and then I felt the sphere pressing against my feet and so drove up again as a bubble drives. And at the last I was floating and rocking upon the surface of the sea, and my journey in space was at an end.

The night was dark and overcast. Two yellow pin-points far away showed the passing of a ship, and nearer was a red glare that

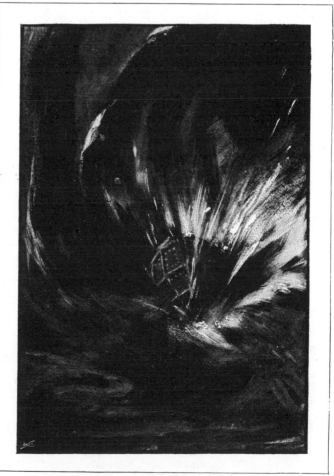

"THE SPHERE HIT THE WATER WITH A HUGE SPLASH."

219

came and went. Had not the electricity of my glow-lamp exhausted itself I could have got picked up that night. In spite of the inordinate fatigue I was beginning to feel I was excited now, and for a time hopeful in a feverish, impatient way that so my travelling might end.

But at last I ceased to move about, and sat, wrists on knees, staring at that distant red light. It swayed up and down, rocking, rocking. My excitement passed. I realized I had yet to spend another night, at least, in the sphere. I perceived myself infinitely heavy and fatigued. And so I fell asleep.

A change in my rhythmic motion awakened me. I peered through the refracting glass and saw that I had come aground upon a huge shallow of sand. Far away I seemed to see houses and trees, and seaward a curved, vague distortion of a ship hung between sea and sky.

I stood up and staggered. My one desire was to emerge. The man-hole was upward and I wrestled with the screw. Slowly I opened the man-hole. At last the air was singing in again as once it had sung out. But this time I did not wait until the pressure was adjusted. In another moment I had the weight of the window on my hands and I was open, wide open, to the old familiar sky of earth.

The air hit me on the chest so that I gasped. I dropped the glass screw. I cried out, put my hands to my chest, and sat down. For a time I was in pain. Then I took deep breaths. At last I could rise and move about again.

I tried to thrust my head through the man-hole, and the sphere rolled over. It was as though something had lugged my head down directly it emerged. I ducked back sharply or I should have been pinned face under water. After some wriggling and shoving I managed to crawl out upon sand, over which the retreating waves still came and went.

I did not attempt to stand up. It seemed to me that my body must be suddenly changed to lead. Mother Earth had her grip on me now—no Cavorite intervening. I sat down, heedless of the water that came over my feet.

It was dawn—a grey dawn—rather overcast, but showing here and there a long patch of greenish grey. Some way out a ship was lying at anchor—a pale silhouette of a ship, with one yellow light. The water came rippling in in long, shallow waves. Away to the right curved the land, a shingle bank with little hovels, and at last a light-house, a sailing mark, and a point. Inland stretched a space of level sand, broken here and there by pools of water, and ending a mile away, perhaps, in a low shore of scrub. To the north-east some isolated watering-place was visible, a row of gaunt lodging-houses, the tallest things that I could see on earth, dull dabs against the brightening sky. What strange men can have reared these vertical piles in such an amplitude of space I do not know. There they are, like pieces of Brighton lost in the waste.

For a long time I sat there, yawning and rubbing my face. At last I struggled to rise. It made me feel that I was lifting a weight. I stood up.

I stared at the distant houses. For the first time since our starvation in the crater I thought of earthly food. "Bacon," I whispered, "eggs. Good toast and good coffee. . . . And how the dickens am I going to get all this stuff to Lympne?" I wondered where I was. It was an east shore anyhow, and I had seen Europe before I dropped.

I heard footsteps scrunching in the sand, and a little, round-faced, friendly-looking man in flannels, with a bathing towel wrapped about his shoulders and his bathing dress over his arm, appeared up the beach. I knew instantly that I must be in England. He was staring almost intently at the sphere and me. He advanced staring. I daresay I looked a ferocious savage enough—dirty, unkempt, ragged to an indescribable degree, but it did not occur to me at the time. He stopped at a distance of twenty yards. "Hal-loa, my man!" he said, doubtfully.

"Halloa yourself!" said I.

He advanced, reassured by that. "What on earth is that thing?" he asked.

"Can you tell me where I am?" I asked.

"That's Littlestone," he said, pointing to the houses; "and that's Dungeness! Have you just landed? What's that thing you've got? Some sort of machine?"

"Yes."

"Have you floated ashore? Have you been wrecked or something? What is it?"

I meditated swiftly. I made an estimate of the little man's appearance as he drew nearer. "By Jove!" he said, "you've had a time of it! I thought you—— Well—where were you cast away? Is that thing a sort of floating thing for saving life?"

I decided to take that line for the present. I made a few vague affirmatives. "I want help," I said, hoarsely. "I want to get some stuff up the beach—stuff I can't very well leave about." I became aware of three other pleasant-looking young men with towels, blazers, and straw hats coming down the sands towards me. Evidently the early bathing section of this Littlestone!

"Help!" said the young man; "rather!" He became vaguely active. "What particularly do you want done?" He turned round and gesticulated. The three young men accelerated their pace. In a minute they were about me, plying me with questions I was indisposed to answer. "I'll tell all that later," I said. "I'm dead-beat. I'm a rag."

"Come up to the hotel," said the foremost little man. "We'll look after that thing there."

I hesitated. "I can't," I said. "In that sphere there's two big bars of gold."

They looked incredulously at one another, then at me with a new inquiry. I went to the sphere, stooped, crept in, and presently they had the Selenite's crowbars and the broken chain before them. If I had not been so horribly fagged I could have laughed at them. It was like kittens round a beetle. They didn't know what to do with the stuff. The fat little man stooped and lifted the end of one of the bars and then dropped it with a grunt. Then they all did.

"It's lead or gold!" said one.

"Oh, it's *gold!*" said another.

"Gold, right enough," said the third.

Then they all stared at me, and then they all stared at the ship lying at anchor.

"I say!" cried the little man. "But where did you get that?"

I was too tired to keep up a lie. "I got it in the moon!"

I saw them stare at one another.

"Look here!" said I; "I'm not going to argue now. Help me carry these lumps of gold up to the hotel—I guess with rests two of you can manage one, and I ll trail this

" 'I WANT HELP,' I SAID, HOARSELY."

chain thing—and I'll tell you more when I've had some food."

"And how about that thing?"

"It won't hurt there," I said. "Anyhow—confound it!—it must stop there now. If the tide comes up it will float all right."

And, in a state of enormous wonderment, these young men most obediently hoisted my treasures on their shoulders, and with limbs that felt like lead I headed a sort of procession towards that distant fragment of "seafront." Half-way there we were reinforced by two awe-stricken little girls with spades, and later a lean little boy with a penetrating sniff appeared. He was, I remember, wheeling a bicycle, and he accompanied us at a distance of about a hundred yards on our right flank, and then I suppose gave us up as uninteresting, mounted his bicycle, and rode off over the level sands in the direction of the sphere.

I glanced back after him.

"*He* won't touch it," said the stout young man, reassuringly, and I was only too willing to be reassured.

At first something of the grey of the morning was in my mind, but presently the sun disengaged itself from the level clouds of the horizon and lit the world and turned the leaden sea to glittering waters. My spirits rose. A sense of the vast importance of the things I had done and had yet to do came with the sunlight into my mind. I laughed aloud as the foremost man staggered under my gold. When indeed I took my place in the world, how amazed the world would be!

If it had not been for my inordinate fatigue the landlord of the Littlestone hotel would have been amusing, as he hesitated between my gold and my respectable company on one hand and my filthy appearance on the other. But at last I found myself in a terrestrial bath-room once more, with warm water to wash myself with and a change of raiment, preposterously small indeed, but anyhow clean, that the genial little man had lent me. He lent me a razor too, but I could not screw up my resolution to attack even the outposts of the bristling beard that covered my face.

I sat down to an English breakfast and ate with a sort of languid appetite, an appetite many weeks old and very decrepit, and stirred myself to answer the questions of the four young men. And I told them the truth.

"Well," said I, "as you press me—I got it in the moon."

"The moon?"

"Yes; the moon in the sky."

"But how do you mean?"

"What I say, confound it!"

"That you have just come from the moon?"

"Exactly!—through space—in that ball." And I took a delicious mouthful of egg. I made a private note that when I went back to find Cavor I would take a box of eggs.

I could see clearly that they did not believe one word of what I told them, but evidently they considered me the most respectable liar they had ever met. They glanced at one another, and then concentrated the fire of their eyes on me. I fancy they expected a clue to me in the way I helped myself to salt. They seemed to find something significant in my peppering my egg. Those strangely-shaped masses of gold they had staggered under held their minds. There the lumps lay in front of me, each worth thousands of pounds, and as impossible for anyone to steal as a house or a piece of land. As I looked at their curious faces over my coffee-cup I realized something of the enormous wilderness of explanations into which I should have to wander to render myself comprehensible again.

"You don't *really* mean——" began the youngest young man in the tone of one who speaks to an obstinate child.

"Just pass me that toast-rack," I said, and shut him up completely.

"But look here, I say," began one of the others, "we're not going to believe that, you know."

"Ah, well," said I, and shrugged my shoulders.

"He doesn't want to tell us," said the youngest young man in a stage aside, and then, with an appearance of great *sang-froid*, "You don't mind if I take a cigarette?"

I waved him a cordial assent, and proceeded with my breakfast. Two of the others went and looked out of the farther window and talked inaudibly. I was struck by a thought. "The tide," I said, "is running out."

There was a pause as to who should answer me.

"It's near the ebb," said the fat little man.

"Well, anyhow," I said, "it won't float far."

I decapitated my third egg and began a little speech. "Look here," I said, "please don't imagine I'm surly or telling you uncivil lies or anything of that sort. I'm forced almost to be a little short and mysterious. I can quite understand this is as queer as it can be and that your imaginations must be going it. I can assure you you're in at a memorable time. But I can't make it clear to you now—it's impossible. I give you my word of honour I've come from the moon, and that's all I can tell you . . . . . All the same, I'm tremendously obliged to you, you know, tremendously. I hope that my manner hasn't in any way given you offence."

"Oh, not in the least!" said the youngest young man, affably. "We can quite understand," and staring hard at me all the time he heeled his chair back until it very nearly upset, and recovered with some exertion. "Not a bit of it," said my fat young man. "Don't you imagine *that!*" and they all got up and dispersed and walked about and lit cigarettes and generally tried to show they were perfectly amiable and disengaged and entirely free from the slightest curiosity about me and the sphere. "I'm going to keep an eye on that ship out there all the same," I heard one of them remarking in an undertone. If only they could have forced themselves to it they would, I believe, even have gone out and left me. I went on with my third egg.

"The weather," the fat little man remarked, presently, "has been immense, has it not? I don't know *when* we have had such a summer——"

"Phoo-whizz!" Like a tremendous rocket! And somewhere a window was broken. . . .

"What's that?" cried I.

"It isn't——?" cried the little man and rushed to the corner window.

All the others rushed to the window likewise. I sat staring at them.

Suddenly I leapt up, knocked over my third egg, and rushed for the window also. I had just thought of something. "Nothing to be seen there," cried the little man, rushing for the door.

"It's that boy!" I cried, bawling in hoarse fury; "it's that accursed boy!" and turning about I pushed the waiter aside—he was just bringing me some more toast—and rushed violently out of the room and down and out upon the queer little esplanade in front of the hotel.

The sea which had been smooth was rough now with hurrying catspaws, and all about where the sphere had been was tumbled water like the wake of a ship. Above, a little puff of cloud whirled like dispersing smoke, and the three or four people on the beach were staring up with interrogative faces towards the point of that unexpected report. And that was all! Boots and waiter and the four young men in blazers came rushing out behind me. Shouts came from windows and doors, and all sorts of worrying people came into sight —agape.

For a time I stood there too overwhelmed by this new development to think of the people about me.

"There's Cavor," I said. "Up there! And no one knows anything of how to make the stuff. Good Lord!"

I felt as though somebody was pouring funk out of a can down the back of my neck. My legs became feeble. Then there was that confounded-boy — sky-high! I was utterly "left." There was the gold in the coffee-room — my only possession on earth. There were my creditors. Good heavens! How would it all work out? The general effect was of a gigantic, unmanageable confusion.

"I say," said the voice of the little man behind; "I say, you know!"

I wheeled about, and there were twenty or

"ABOVE, A LITTLE PUFF OF CLOUD WHIRLED LIKE DISPERSING SMOKE."

thirty people, a sort of irregular investment of people, all bombarding me with dumb interrogation, with infinite doubt and suspicion. I felt the compulsion of their eyes intolerably. I groaned aloud.

"I *can't*," I shouted. "I tell you I can't. I'm not equal to it. You must puzzle and—and be d——d to you!"

I gesticulated convulsively. He receded a step as though I had threatened him. I made a bolt through them into the hotel. I charged back into the coffee-room, rang the bell furiously. I gripped the waiter as he entered. "D'ye hear?" I shouted. "Get help and carry these bars up to my room right away."

He failed to understand me, and I shouted and raved at him. A scared-looking little old man in a green apron appeared, and further, two of the young men in flannels. I made a dash at them and commandeered their services. As soon as the gold was in my room I felt free to quarrel. "Now get out!" I shouted; "all of you get out if you don't want to see a man go mad before your eyes!" And I helped the waiter by the shoulder as he hesitated in the doorway. Then as soon as I had the door locked on them all I tore off the little man's clothes again, shied them right and left, and got into bed forthwith. And there I lay swearing and panting and cooling for a very long time.

At last I was calm enough to get out of bed and ring up the round-eyed waiter for a flannel nightshirt, a soda and whisky, and some good cigars. And these things being procured me, I locked the door again and proceeded very deliberately to look the entire situation in the face.

The net result of the great experiment presented itself as an absolute failure. It was a rout, and I was the sole survivor. It was an absolute collapse, and this was the final disaster. There was nothing for it but to save myself and as much as I could in the way of prospects from our debâcle. At one fatal crowning blow all my vague resolutions of return and recovery had vanished. My intention of going back to the moon, of rescuing Cavor, or at any rate of getting a

speedily convinced myself on that point. And as for any responsibility I might have in the matter, the more I reflected upon that, the clearer it became that, if only I kept quiet about things, I need not trouble myself on the point. If I were faced by sorrowing parents demanding their lost boy, I had merely to demand my lost sphere—or ask them what they meant. At first I had had a

"I GESTICULATED CONVULSIVELY."

sphereful of gold, and afterwards of having a fragment of Cavorite analyzed and so recovering his great secret—all these ideas vanished altogether.

I was the sole survivor, and that was all!

I think that going to bed was one of the luckiest ideas I have ever had in an emergency. I really believe I should either have got loose-headed or done some fatal, indiscreet thing. But there, locked in and secure from all interruption, I could think out the position in all its bearings, and make my arrangements at leisure.

Of course it was quite clear to me what had happened to the boy. He had crawled into the sphere, meddled with the studs, shut the Cavorite windows, and gone up. It was highly improbable he had screwed in the man-hole stopper, and, even if he had, the chances were a thousand to one against his getting back. It was fairly evident that he would gravitate to the middle of the sphere and remain there, and so cease to be of legitimate terrestrial interest, however remarkable he might seem to the inhabitants of some remote quarter of space. I very

vision of weeping parents and guardians and all sorts of complications, but now I saw that I simply had to keep my mouth shut and nothing in that way could arise. And, indeed, the more I lay and smoked and thought the more evident became the wisdom of impenetrability. It is within the right of every British citizen, provided he does not commit damage or indecorum, to appear suddenly wherever he pleases, and as ragged and filthy as he pleases, and with whatever amount of virgin gold he sees fit to encumber himself with, and no one has any right at all to hinder and detain him in this procedure. I formulated that at last to myself, and repeated it over as a sort of private Magna Charta of my liberty.

Once I had put that issue on one side I could take up and consider in an equable manner certain considerations I had scarcely dared to think of before, namely, those arising out of the circumstances of my bankruptcy. But now, looking at this matter calmly and at leisure, I could see that if only I suppressed my identity by a temporary assumption of some less well-known name, and if I retained the two months' beard that had grown upon me, the risks of any annoyance from the spiteful creditor to whom I have already alluded became very small indeed. From that to a definite course of rational worldly action was plain sailing.

I ordered up writing materials and addressed a letter to the New Romney Bank—the nearest, the waiter informed me—telling the manager I wished to open an account with him and requesting him to send two trustworthy persons properly authenticated in a cab with a good horse to fetch some hundredweight of gold with which I happened to be encumbered. I signed the letter "H. G. Wells," which seemed to me to be a thoroughly respectable sort of name. This done, I got a Folkestone directory, picked out an outfitter, and asked him to send a cutter to measure me for a tweed suit, ordering at the same time a valise, dressing-bag, shirts, hats (to fit), and so forth, and from a watchmaker I also ordered a watch. And these letters being dispatched I had up as good a lunch as the hotel could give, and then lay smoking a cigar until, in accordance with my instructions, two duly authenticated clerks came from the bank and weighed and took away my gold. After which I pulled the clothes over my ears in order to drown any knocking and went very comfortably to sleep.

I went to sleep. No doubt it was a prosaic thing for the first man back from the moon to do, and I can imagine that the young and imaginative reader will find my behaviour disappointing. But I was horribly fatigued and bothered, and, confound it, what else was there to do? There certainly was not the remotest chance of my being believed, if I had told my story, and it would certainly have subjected me to intolerable annoyances.

I went to sleep. When at last I woke up again I was ready to face the world as I have always been accustomed to face it since I came to years of discretion. And so I got away to Italy, and there it is I am writing this story. If the world will not have it as fact, then the world may take it as fiction. It is no concern of mine.

And now that the account is finished I am amazed to think how completely this adventure is gone and done with. Everybody believes that Cavor was merely a not very brilliant scientific experimenter, who blew up his house and himself at Lympne, and they explain the bang that followed my arrival at Littlestone by a reference to the experiments with explosives that are going on continually at the Government establishment of Lydd, two miles away. I must confess that hitherto I have not acknowledged my share in the disappearance of Master Tommy Simmons, which was that little boy's name. That, perhaps, may prove a difficult item of corroboration to explain away. They account for my appearance in rags with two bars of indisputable gold upon the Littlestone beach in various ingenious ways—it doesn't worry me what they think of me. They say I have strung all these things together to avoid being questioned too closely as to the source of my wealth. I would like to see the man who could invent a story that would hold together like this one. Well, they must take it as fiction—there it is!

I have told my story—and now I suppose I have to take up the worries of this terrestrial life again. Even if one has been to the moon, one has still to earn a living. So I am working here at Amalfi on the scenario of that play I sketched before Cavor came walking into my world, and I am trying to piece my life together as it was before ever I saw him. I must confess that I find it hard to keep my mind on the play when the moonshine comes into my room. It is full moon here, and last night I was out on the pergola for hours staring away at that shining blankness that hides so much. Imagine it! Tables and chairs, and trestles, and bars of gold! Confound it!—if only one could hit on that Cavorite again! But a thing like that doesn't come twice in a life. Here I am, a little better off than I was at Lympne, and that is all. And Cavor has committed suicide in a more elaborate way than any human being ever did before. So the story closes as finally and completely as a dream. It fits in so little with all the other things of life—so much of it was so utterly remote from all human experience, the leaping, the eating, the breathing of these weightless times—that indeed there are moments when, in spite of my moon gold, I do more than half believe myself that the whole thing was a dream.

[Here the story, as we originally received it, ends. But we have just received a most extraordinary communication which certainly gives a curious and unexpected air of conviction to the narrative. If our correspondent is to be believed, Mr. Cavor is alive in the moon, and he is sending messages to the earth]

The First Men in the Moon.

By H. G. Wells.

CHAPTER XXII.

THE ASTONISHING COMMUNICATION OF MR. JULIUS WENDIGEE.

WHEN I had finished my account of my return to the earth at Littlestone I wrote "The End," made a flourish, and threw my pen aside, fully believing that the whole story of the First Men in the Moon was done. Not only had I done this, but I had placed my manuscript in the hands of a literary agent, had permitted it to be sold, had seen the greater portion of it appear in THE STRAND MAGAZINE, and was setting to work again upon the scenario of the play I had commenced at Lympne before I realized that the end was not yet. And then, following me from Amalfi to Algiers, there reached me (it is now about six weeks ago) one of the most astounding communications I have ever been fated to receive. Briefly, it informed me that Mr. Julius Wendigee, a Dutch electrician, who has been experimenting with certain apparatus akin to the apparatus used by Mr. Tesla in America, in the hope of discovering some method of communication with Mars, was receiving day by day a curiously fragmentary message in English, which was indisputably emanating from Mr. Cavor in the moon.

At first I thought the thing was an elaborate practical joke by someone who had seen the manuscript of my narrative. I answered Mr. Wendigee jestingly, but he replied in a manner that put such suspicion altogether aside, and in a state of inconceivable excitement I hurried from Algiers to the little observatory upon the St. Gothard in which he was working. In the presence of his record and his appliances—and above all of the messages from Mr. Cavor that were

"ONE OF THE MOST ASTOUNDING COMMUNICATIONS."

coming to hand — my lingering doubts vanished. I decided at once to accept a proposal he made me to remain with him, assisting him to take down the record from day to day, and endeavouring with him to send a message back to the moon. Cavor, we learnt, was not only alive but free, in the midst of an almost inconceivable community of these ant-like beings, these ant-men, in the blue darkness of the lunar caves. He was lamed, it seemed, but otherwise in quite good health—in better health, he distinctly said, than he usually enjoyed on earth. He had had a fever, but it had left no bad effects. But curiously enough he seemed to be labouring under a conviction that I was either dead in the moon crater or lost in the deep of space.

His message began to be received by Mr. Wendigee when that gentleman was engaged in quite a different investigation. The reader will no doubt recall the little excitement that began the century, arising out of an announcement by Mr. Nikola Tesla, the American electrical celebrity, that he had received a message from Mars. His announcement renewed attention to a fact that had long been familiar to scientific people, namely: that from some unknown source in space, waves of electro-magnetic disturbance, entirely similar to those used by Signor Marconi for his wireless telegraphy, are constantly reaching the earth. Besides Mr. Tesla quite a number of other observers have been engaged in perfecting apparatus for receiving and recording these vibrations, though few would go so far as to consider them actual messages from some extra-terrestrial sender. Among that few, however, we must certainly count Mr. Wendigee. Ever since 1898 he had devoted himself almost entirely to this subject, and being a man of ample means he had erected an observatory on the flanks of Monte Rosa, in a position singularly adapted in every way for such observations.

My scientific attainments, I must admit, are not great, but so far as they enable me to judge, Mr. Wendigee's contrivances for detecting and recording any disturbances in the electro-magnetic conditions of space are singularly original and ingenious. And by a happy combination of circumstances they were set up and in operation about two months before Cavor made his first attempt to call up the earth. Consequently we have fragments of his communication even from the beginning. Unhappily, they are only fragments, and the most momentous of all the things that he had to tell humanity —the instructions, that is, for the making of Cavorite, if, indeed, he ever transmitted them—have throbbed themselves away unrecorded into space. We never succeeded in getting a response back to Cavor. He was unable to tell, therefore, what we had received or what we had missed ; nor, indeed, did he certainly know that anyone on earth was really aware of his efforts to reach us. And the persistence he displayed in sending eighteen long descriptions of lunar affairs—as they would be if we had them complete—shows how much his mind must have turned back towards his native planet since he left it two years ago.

You can imagine how amazed Mr. Wendigee must have been when he discovered his record of electro-magnetic disturbances interlaced by Cavor's straightforward English. Mr. Wendigee knew nothing of our wild journey moonward, and suddenly—this English out of the void !

It is well the reader should understand the conditions under which it would seem these messages were sent. Somewhere within the moon Cavor certainly had access for a time to a considerable amount of electrical apparatus, and it would seem he rigged up— perhaps furtively—a transmitting arrangement of the Marconi type. This he was able to operate at irregular intervals : sometimes for only half an hour or so, sometimes for three or four hours at a stretch. At these times he transmitted his earthward message, regardless of the fact that the relative position of the moon and points upon the earth's surface is constantly altering. As a consequence of this and of the necessary imperfections of our recording instruments his communication comes and goes in our records in an extremely fitful manner ; it becomes blurred; it "fades out" in a

mysterious and altogether exasperating way. And added to this is the fact that he was not an expert operator ; he had partly forgotten, or never completely mastered, the code in general use, and as he became fatigued he dropped words and misspelt in a curious manner.

Altogether we have probably lost quite half of the communications he made, and much we have is damaged, broken, and partly effaced. In the abstract that follows the reader must be prepared therefore for a considerable amount of break, hiatus, and change of topic. Mr. Wendigee and I are collaborating in a complete and annotated edition of the Cavor record, which we hope to publish, together with a detailed account of the instruments employed, beginning with the first volume in January next. That will be the full and scientific report, of which this is only the popular first transcript. But here we give at least sufficient to complete the story I have told, and to give the broad outlines of the state of that other world so near, so kin, and yet so dissimilar to our own.

CHAPTER XXIII.

AN ABSTRACT OF THE SIX MESSAGES FIRST RECEIVED FROM MR. CAVOR.

THE two earlier messages of Mr. Cavor may very well be reserved for that larger volume. They simply tell with greater brevity and with a difference in several details that is interesting, but not of any vital importance, the bare facts of the making of the sphere and our departure from the world. Throughout, Cavor speaks of me as a man who is dead, but with a curious change of temper as he approaches our landing on the moon. " Poor Bedford," he says of me, and " this poor young man," and he blames himself for inducing a young man, " by no means well equipped for such adventures," to leave a planet " on which he was indisputably fitted to succeed " on so precarious a mission. I think he underrates the part my energy and practical capacity played in bringing about the realization of his theoretical sphere. " We arrived," he says, with no more account of our passage through space than if we had made a journey of common occurrence in a railway train.

And then he becomes increasingly unfair to me. Unfair, indeed, to an extent I should not have expected in a man trained in the search for truth. Looking back over my previously written account of these things I must insist that I have been altogether juster to Cavor than he has been to me. I have extenuated little and suppressed nothing. But his account is :—

" It speedily became apparent that the entire strangeness of our circumstances and surroundings—great loss of weight, attenuated but highly oxygenated air, consequent exaggeration of the results of muscular effort, rapid development of weird plants from obscure spores, lurid sky—was exciting my companion unduly. On the moon his character seemed to deteriorate. He became impulsive, rash, and quarrelsome. In a little while his folly in devouring some gigantic vesicles and his consequent intoxication led to our capture by the Selenites—before we had had the slightest opportunity of properly observing their ways. . . . "

(He says, you observe, nothing of his own concession to these same " vesicles.")

And he goes on from that point to say that " We came to a difficult passage with them, and Bedford mistaking certain gestures of theirs "—pretty gestures they were !— " gave way to a panic violence. He ran amuck, killed three, and perforce I had to flee with him after the outrage. Subsequently we fought with a number who endeavoured to bar our way, and slew seven or eight more. It says much for the tolerance of these beings that on my recapture I was not instantly slain. We made our way to the exterior and separated in the crater of our arrival, to increase our chances of recovering our sphere. But presently I came upon a body of Selenites, led by two who were curiously different, even in form, from any of those we had seen hitherto, with larger heads and smaller bodies and much more elaborately wrapped about. And after evading them for some time I fell into a crevasse, cut my head rather badly and displaced my patella, and, finding crawling very painful, decided to surrender—if they would still permit me to do so. This they did, and, perceiving my helpless condition, carried me with them again into the moon. And of Bedford I have heard or seen nothing more, nor, so far as I can gather, has any Selenite. Either the night overtook him in the crater, or else, which is more probable, he found the sphere, and, desiring to steal a march upon me, made off with it—only, I fear, to find it uncontrollable, and to meet a more lingering fate in outer space."

And with that Cavor dismisses me and goes on to more interesting topics. I dislike the idea of seeming to use my position as his editor to deflect his story in my own interest, but I am obliged to protest here

against the turn he gives these occurrences. He says nothing about that gasping message on the blood-stained paper in which he told, or attempted to tell, a very different story. The dignified self-surrender is an altogether new view of the affair that has come to him, I must insist, since he began to feel secure among the lunar people ; and as for the " stealing a march " conception, I am quite willing to let the reader decide between us on what he has before him. I know I am not a model man—I have made no pretence to be. But am I *that*?

However, that is the sum of my wrongs. From this point I can edit Cavor with an untroubled mind, for he mentions me no more.

It would seem the Selenites who had come upon him carried him to some point in the interior down " a great shaft " by means of what he describes as " a sort of balloon." We gather from the rather confused passage in which he describes this, and from a number of chance allusions and hints in other and subsequent messages, that this " great shaft " is one of an enormous system of artificial shafts that run, each from what is called a lunar "crater," downwards for very nearly a hundred miles towards the central portion of our satellite. These shafts communicate by transverse tunnels, they throw out abyssmal caverns and expand into great globular places ; the whole of the moon's substance for a hundred miles inward, indeed, is a mere sponge of rock. " Partly," says Cavor, "this sponginess is natural, but very largely it is due to the enormous industry of the Selenites in the past. The enormous circular mounds of the excavated rock and earth it is that form these great circles about the tunnels known to earthly astronomers (misled by a false analogy) as volcanoes."

It was down this shaft they took him, in this " sort of balloon " he speaks of, at first into an inky blackness and then into a region of continually increasing phosphorescence. Cavor's despatches show him to be curiously regardless of detail for a scientific man, but we gather that this light was due to the streams and cascades of water—"no doubt containing some phosphorescent organism " —that flowed ever more abundantly downward towards the Central Sea. And as he descended, he says, "The Selenites also became luminous." And at last far below him he saw as it were a lake of heatless fire, the waters of the Central Sea, glowing and eddying in strange perturbation, "like luminous blue milk that is just on the boil."

"This Lunar Sea," says Cavor, in a later passage, "is not a stagnant ocean; a solar tide sends it in a perpetual flow around the lunar axis, and strange storms and boilings and rushings of its waters occur, and at times cold winds and thunderings that ascend out of it into the busy ways of the great ant-hill above. It is only when the water is in motion that it gives out light; in its rare seasons of calm it is black. Commonly, when one sees it, its waters rise and fall in an oily swell, and flakes and big rafts of shining, bubbly foam drift with the sluggish, faintly-glowing current. The Selenites navigate its cavernous straits and lagoons in little shallow boats of a canoe-like shape; and even before my journey to the galleries about the Grand Lunar, who is Master of the Moon, I was permitted to make a brief excursion on its waters.

"The caverns and passages are naturally very tortuous. A large proportion of these ways are known only to expert pilots among the fishermen, and not infrequently Selenites are lost for ever in their labyrinths. In their remoter recesses, I am told, strange creatures lurk, some of them terrible and dangerous creatures that all the science of the moon has been unable to exterminate. There is particularly the Rapha, an inextricable mass of clutching tentacles that one hacks to pieces only to multiply; and the Tzee, a darting creature that is never seen, so subtly and suddenly does it slay. . . ."

He gives us a gleam of description.

"I was reminded on this excursion of what I have read of the Mammoth Caves; if only I had had a yellow flambeau instead of the pervading blue light, and a solid-looking boatman with an oar instead of a scuttle-faced Selenite working an engine at the back of the canoe, I could have imagined I had suddenly got back to earth. The rocks about us were very various, sometimes black, sometimes pale blue and veined, and once they flashed and glittered as though we had come into a mine of sapphires. And below one saw the ghostly phosphorescent fishes flash and vanish in the hardly less phosphorescent deep. Then, presently, a long ultra-marine vista down the turgid stream of one of the channels of traffic, and a landing-stage, and then, perhaps, a glimpse up the enormous crowded shaft of one of the vertical ways.

"In one great place heavy with glistening stalactites a number of boats were fishing. We went alongside one of these and watched the long-armed fishing Selenites winding in a net. They were little, hunchbacked insects with very strong arms, short, bandy legs, and crinkled face-masks. As they pulled at it that net seemed the heaviest thing I had come upon in the moon; it was loaded with weights—no doubt of gold—and it took a

"A LAKE OF HEATLESS FIRE."

"THE FISH IN THE NET CAME UP LIKE A BLUE MOONRISE."

long time to draw, for in those waters the larger and more edible fish lurk deep. The fish in the net came up like a blue moonrise—a blaze of darting, tossing blue.

"Among their catch was a many-tentaculate, evil-eyed black thing, ferociously active, whose appearance they greeted with shrieks and twitters, and which with quick, nervous movements they hacked to pieces by means of little hatchets. All its dissevered limbs continued to lash and writhe in a vicious manner. Afterwards when fever had hold of me I dreamt again and again of that bitter, furious creature rising so vigorous and active out of the unknown sea. It was the most active and malignant thing of all the living creatures I have yet seen in this world inside the moon . . . . .

"The surface of this sea must be very nearly two hundred miles (if not more) below the level of the moon's exterior; all the cities of the moon lie, I learnt, immediately above this Central Sea, in such cavernous spaces and artificial galleries as I have described, and they communicate with the exterior by enormous vertical shafts which open invariably in what are called by earthly astronomers the 'craters' of the moon. The lid covering

one such aperture I had already seen during the wanderings that had preceded my capture.

"Upon the condition of the less central portion of the moon I have not yet arrived at very precise knowledge. There is an enormous system of caverns in which the mooncalves shelter during the night; and there are abattoirs and the like—in one of these it was that I and Bedford fought with the Selenite butchers—and I have since seen balloons laden with meat descending out of the upper dark. I have as yet scarcely learnt as much of these things as a Zulu in London would learn about the British corn supplies in the same time. It is clear, however, that these vertical shafts and the vegetation of the surface must play an essential *rôle* in ventilating and keeping fresh the atmosphere of the moon. At one time, and particularly on my first emergence from my prison, there was certainly a cold wind blowing *down* the shaft, and later there was a kind of sirocco upward that corresponded with my fever. For at the end of about three weeks I fell ill of an indefinable sort of fever, and in spite of sleep and the quinine tabloids that very fortunately I had brought in my pocket, I remained ill and fretting miserably, almost to the time when I was taken into the palace of the Grand Lunar, who is Master of the Moon.

" I will not dilate on the wretchedness of my condition," he remarks, "during those days of ill-health." And he goes on with great amplitude with details I omit here. " My temperature," he concludes, "kept abnormally high for a long time, and I lost all desire for food. I had stagnant waking intervals, and sleep tormented by dreams, and at one phase I was, I remember, so weak as to be earth-sick and almost hysterical. I longed almost intolerably for colour to break the everlasting blue. . . ."

He reverts again presently to the topic of this sponge caught lunar atmosphere. I am told by astronomers and physicists that all he tells is in absolute accordance with what was already known of the moon's condition. Had earthly astronomers had the courage and imagination to push home a bold induction, says Mr. Wendigee, they might have foretold almost everything that Cavor has to say of the general structure of the moon. They know now pretty certainly that moon and earth are not so much satellite and primary as smaller and greater sisters, made out of one mass, and consequently made of the same material. And since the density of the moon is only three-fifths that of the earth, there can be nothing for it but that she is hollowed out by a great system of caverns. There was no necessity, said Sir Jabez Flap, F.R.S., that most entertaining exponent of the facetious side of the stars, that we should ever have gone to the moon to find out such easy inferences, and points the pun with an allusion to Gruyère, but he certainly might have announced his knowledge of the hollowness of the moon before. And if the moon is hollow, then the apparent absence of air and water is, of course, quite easily explained. The sea lies within at the bottom of the caverns, and the air travels through the great sponge of galleries, in accordance with simple physical laws. The caverns of the moon, on the whole, are very windy places. As the sunlight comes round the moon the air in the outer galleries on that side is heated, its pressure increases, some flows out on the exterior and mingles with the evaporating air of the craters (where the plants remove its carbonic acid), while the greater portion flows round through the galleries to replace the shrinking air of the cooling side that the sunlight has left. There is, therefore, a constant eastward breeze in the air of the outer galleries, and an up-flow during the lunar day up the shafts, compli-

cated, of course, very greatly by the varying shape of the galleries and the ingenious contrivances of the Selenite mind. . . .

CHAPTER XXIV.

THE NATURAL HISTORY OF THE SELENITES.

THE messages of Cavor from the sixth up to the sixteenth are for the most part so much broken, and they abound so in repetitions, that they scarcely form a consecutive narrative. They will be given in full, of course, in the scientific report, but here it will be far more convenient to continue simply to abstract and quote as in the former chapter. We have subjected every word to a keen critical scrutiny, and my own brief memories and impressions of lunar things have been of inestimable help in interpreting what would otherwise have been impenetrably dark. And, naturally, as living beings our interest centres far more upon the strange community of lunar insects in which he is living, it would seem, as an honoured guest than upon the mere physical condition of their world.

I have already made it clear, I think, that the Selenites I saw resembled man in maintaining the erect attitude and in having four limbs, and I have compared the general appearance of their heads and the jointing of their limbs to that of insects. I have mentioned, too, the peculiar consequence of the smaller gravitation of the moon on their fragile slightness. Cavor confirms me upon all these points. He calls them "animals," though of course they fall under no division of the classification of earthly creatures, and he points out "the insect type of anatomy had, fortunately for men, never exceeded a relatively very small size on earth." The largest terrestrial insects, living or extinct, do not, as a matter of fact, measure 6in. in length; " but here, against the lesser gravitation of the moon, a creature certainly as much an insect as vertebrate seems to have been able to attain to human and ultra-human dimensions."

He does not mention the ant, but throughout his allusions the ant is continually being brought before my mind, in its sleepless activity, in its intelligence and social organization, in its structure, and more particularly in the fact that it displays, in addition to the two forms, the male and the female form, that almost all other animals possess, a number of other sexless creatures, workers, soldiers, and the like, differing from one another in structure, character, power, and use, and yet all members of the same species,

For these Selenites have a great variety of forms. Of course these Selenites are not only colossally greater in size than ants, but also, in Cavor's opinion, in respect to intelligence, morality, and social wisdom are they colossally greater than men. And instead of the four or five different forms of ant that are found there are almost innumerably different forms of Selenite. I have endeavoured to indicate the very considerable difference observable in such Selenites of the outer crust as I happened to encounter; the differences in size, hue, and shape were certainly as wide as the differences between the most widely-separated races of men. But such differences as I saw fade absolutely to nothing in comparison with the huge distinctions of which Cavor tells. It would seem the exterior Selenites I saw were, indeed, mostly of one colour and occupation — mooncalf herds, butchers, fleshers, and the like. But within the moon, practically unsuspected by me, there are, it seems, a number of other sorts of Selenite, differing in size, differing in form, differing in power and appearance, and yet not different species of creatures, but only different forms of one species. The moon is, indeed, a sort of vast ant-hill, only, instead of there being only four or five sorts of ant, worker, soldier, winged male, queen, and slave, there are many hundred different sorts of Selenite, and almost every gradation between one sort and another.

It would seem the discovery came upon Cavor very speedily. I infer rather than learn from his narrative that he was captured by the mooncalf herds under the direction of those other Selenites who "have larger brain-cases (heads?) and very much shorter legs." Finding he would not walk even under the goad, they carried him into darkness, crossed a narrow, plank-like bridge that may have been the identical bridge I had refused, and put him down in something that must have seemed at first to be some sort of lift. This was the balloon — it had certainly been absolutely invisible to us in the darkness — and what had seemed to me a mere plank-walking into the void was really, no doubt, the passage of the gangway. In this he descended towards constantly more luminous strata of the moon. At first they descended in silence—save for the twitterings of the Selenites — and then into a stir of windy movement. In a little while the profound blackness had made his eyes so sensitive that he began to see more and more of the things about him, and at last the vague took shape.

"THEY CARRIED HIM INTO DARKNESS."

"Conceive an enormous cylindrical space," says Cavor in his seventh message, "a quarter of a mile across, perhaps; very dimly lit at first and then bright, with big platforms twisting down its sides in a spiral that vanishes at last below in a blue profundity; and lit even more brightly—one could not tell how or why. Think of the well of the very largest spiral staircase or lift-shaft that you have ever looked down, and magnify that by a hundred.

Imagine it at twilight seen through blue glass. Imagine yourself looking down that; only imagine also that you feel extraordinarily light and have got rid of any giddy feeling you might have on earth, and you will have the first conditions of my impression. Round this enormous shaft imagine a broad gallery running in a much steeper spiral than would be credible on earth, and forming a steep road protected from the gulf only by a little parapet that vanishes at last in perspective a couple of miles below.

"Looking up, I saw the very fellow of the downward vision; it had, of course, the effect of looking into a very steep cone. A wind was blowing down the shaft, and far above I

"IT WAS AN INCREDIBLE CROWD."

fancy I heard, growing fainter and fainter, the bellowing of the mooncalves that were being driven down again from their evening pasturage on the exterior. And up and down the spiral galleries were scattered numerous moon people, pallid, faintly self-luminous insects, regarding our appearance or busied on unknown errands.

"Either I fancied it or a flake of snow came drifting swiftly down on the icy breeze. And then, falling like a snowflake, a little figure, a little man-insect clinging to a parachute, drove down very swiftly towards the central places of the moon.

"The big-headed Selenite sitting beside me, seeing me move my head with the gesture of one who saw, pointed with his trunk-like 'hand' and indicated a sort of jetty coming into sight very far below: a little landing-stage, as it were, hanging into the void. As it swept up towards us our pace diminished very rapidly, and in a few moments as it seemed we were abreast of it and at rest. A mooring-rope was flung and grasped, and I found myself pulled down to a level with a great crowd of Selenites, who jostled to see me.

"It was an incredible crowd. Suddenly and violently there was forced upon my attention the vast amount of difference there is amongst these beings of the moon.

"Indeed, there seemed not two alike in all that jostling multitude. They differed in shape, they differed in size! Some bulged and overhung, some ran about among the feet of their fellows, some twined and interlaced like snakes. All of them had a grotesque and disquieting suggestion of an insect that has somehow contrived to mock humanity; all seemed to present an incredible exaggeration of some particular feature: one had a vast right fore-limb, an enormous antennal arm, as it were; one seemed all leg, poised, as it were, on stilts; another protruded an enormous nose-like organ beside a sharply speculative eye that made him startlingly human until one saw his expressionless mouth. One has seen punchinellos made of lobster claws—he was like that. The strange and (except for the want of mandibles and palps) most insect-like head of the mooncalf-minders underwent astounding transformations : here it was broad and low, here high and narrow; here its vacuous brow was drawn out into horns and strange features ; here it was whiskered and divided, and there with a grotesquely human profile. There were several brain-cases distended like bladders to a huge size. The eyes, too, were strangely varied, some quite elephantine in their small alertness, some huge pits of darkness. There were amazing forms with heads reduced to microscopic proportions and blobby bodies ; and fantastic, flimsy things that existed it would seem only as a basis for vast, white-rimmed, glaring eyes. And oddest of all, as it seemed to me for the moment, two or three of these weird inhabitants of a subterranean world, a world sheltered by innumerable miles of rock from sun or rain, *carried umbrellas* in their tentaculate hands ! — real terrestrial-looking umbrellas ! And then I thought of the parachutist I had watched descend.

" These moon people behaved exactly as a human crowd might have done in similar circumstances : they jostled and thrust one another, they shoved one another aside, they even clambered upon one another to get a glimpse of me. Every moment they increased in numbers, and pressed more urgently upon the discs of my ushers "— Cavor does not explain what he means by this—" every moment fresh shapes forced themselves upon my astounded attention. And presently I was signed and helped into a sort of litter, and lifted up on the shoulders of strong-armed bearers and so borne over this seething nightmare towards the apartments that were provided for me in the moon. All about me were eyes, faces, masks, tentacles, a leathery noise like the rustling of beetle wings, and a great bleating and twittering of Selenite voices . . . . . "

We gather he was taken to a " hexagonal apartment," and there for a space he was confined. Afterwards he was given a much more considerable liberty ; indeed, almost as much freedom as one has in a civilized town on earth. And it would appear that the mysterious being who is the ruler and master of the moon appointed two Selenites " with large heads " to guard and study him, and to establish whatever mental communications were possible with him. And, amazing and incredible as it may seem, these two creatures, these fantastic men-insects, these beings of another world, were presently communicating with Cavor by means of terrestrial speech.

Cavor speaks of them as Phi-oo and Tsi-puff. Phi-oo, he says, was about 5ft. high ; he had small, slender legs about 18in. long, and slight feet of the common lunar pattern. On these balanced a little body, throbbing with the pulsations of his heart. He had long, soft, many-jointed arms ending in a tentacled grip, and his neck was many-jointed in the usual way, but exceptionally short and thick. His head, says Cavor—apparently alluding to some previous description that has gone astray in space—" is of the common lunar type, but strangely modified. The mouth has the usual expressionless gape, but it is unusually small and pointing downward, and the mask is reduced to the size of a large flat nose-flap. On either side are the little hen-like eyes.

The rest of the head is distended into a huge globe, and the chitinous leathery cuticle of the mooncalf herds thins out to a mere membrane, through which the pulsating brain movements are distinctly visible. He is a creature, indeed, with a tremendously hypertrophied brain, and with the rest of his organism both relatively and absolutely dwarfed."

In another passage Cavor compares the back view of him to Atlas supporting the world. Tsi-puff, it seems, was a very similar insect, but his " face " was drawn out to a considerable length, and, the brain hypertrophy being in different regions, his head was not round but pear-shaped, with the stalk downward. There were also litter-carriers, lop-sided beings with enormous shoulders, very spidery ushers, and a squat foot attendant in Cavor's retinue.

The manner in which Phi-oo and Tsi-puff attacked the problem of speech was fairly obvious. They came into this " hexagonal cell " in which Cavor was confined, and began imitating every sound he made, beginning with a cough. He seems to have grasped their intention with great quickness, and to have begun repeating words to them and pointing to indicate the application. The procedure was probably always the same. Phi-oo would attend to Cavor for a space, then point also and say the word he had heard.

The first word he mastered was " man," and the second " Mooney "—which Cavor on the spur of the moment seems to have used instead of " Selenite " for the moon race. As soon as Phi-oo was assured of the meaning of a word he repeated it to

"REPEATING WORDS TO THEM AND POINTING TO INDICATE THE APPLICATION."

came a fourth assistant, a being with a huge, football‑shaped head, whose *forte* was clearly the pursuit of intricate analogy. He entered in a preoccupied manner, stumbling against a stool, and the difficulties that arose had to be presented to him with a certain amount of clamour and hitting and pricking before they reached his apprehension. But once he was involved his penetration was amazing. Whenever there came a need of thinking beyond Phi‑oo's by no means limited scope, this prolate‑headed person was in request, but he invariably told the conclusion to Tsi‑puff, in order that it might be remembered ; Tsi‑puff was ever the arsenal for facts. And so we advanced again.

"It seemed long and yet brief — a matter of days before I was positively talking with these insects of the moon. Of course, at first it was an intercourse infinitely tedious and exasperating, but imperceptibly it has grown to comprehension. And my patience has grown to meet its limitations. Phi‑oo it is who does all the talking. He does it with a vast amount of meditative provisional 'M'm—M'm,' and he has caught up one or two phrases, 'If I may say,' 'If you understand,' and beads all his speech with them.

"Thus he would discourse. Imagine him explaining his artist.

"'M'm—M'm—he—if I may say—draw. Eat little—drink little—draw. Love draw. No other thing. Hate all who not draw like him. Angry. Hate all who draw like him better. Hate most people. Hate all who not think all world for to draw. Angry. M'm. All things mean nothing to him— only draw. He like you. . . . . if you understand . . . . New thing to draw. Ugly—striking. Eh ?

"'He '—turning to Tsi‑puff—'love remember words. Remember wonderful more than any. Think no, draw no—remember. Say '—here he referred to his gifted assistant for a word—'histories—all things. He hear once—say ever.'

Tsi‑puff, who remembered it infallibly. They mastered over one hundred English nouns at their first session.

Subsequently it seems they brought an artist with them to assist the work of explanation with sketches and diagrams—Cavor's drawings being rather crude. He was, says Cavor, "a being with an active arm and an arresting eye," and he seemed to draw with incredible swiftness.

The eleventh message is undoubtedly only a fragment of a longer communication. After some broken sentences, the record of which is unintelligible, it goes on :—

"But it will interest only linguists, and delay me too long, to give the details of the series of intent parleys of which these were the beginning, and, indeed, I very much doubt if I could give in anything like the proper order all the twistings and turnings that we made in our pursuit of mutual comprehension. Verbs were soon plain sailing— at least, such active verbs as I could express by drawings ; some adjectives were easy, but when it came to abstract nouns, to prepositions, and the sort of hackneyed figures of speech by means of which so much is expressed on earth, it was like diving in cork jackets. Indeed, these difficulties were insurmountable until to the sixth lesson

"It is more wonderful to me than I ever dreamt that anything ever could be again to hear these extraordinary creatures—for even familiarity fails to weaken the inhuman effect of their appearance—continually piping a nearer approach to coherent earthly speech, asking questions, giving answers. I feel that I am casting back to the fable-hearing period of childhood again when the ant and the grasshopper talked together and the bee judged between them. . . ."

And while these linguistic exercises were going on Cavor seems to have experienced a considerable relaxation of his confinement. The first dread and distrust our unfortunate conflict aroused was being, he says, "continually effaced by the deliberate rationality of all I do." . . . . "I am now able to come and go as I please, or I am restricted only for my own good. So it is I have been able to get at this apparatus, and, assisted by a happy find among the material that is littered in this enormous store-cave, I have contrived to dispatch these messages. So far not the slightest attempt has been made to interfere with me in this, though I have made it quite clear to Phi-oo that I am signalling to the earth.

" ' You talk to other ? ' he asked, watching me.

" ' Others,' said I.

" ' Others,' he said. ' Oh, yes. Men ? '

" And I went on transmitting."

Cavor was continually making corrections in his previous accounts of the Selenites as fresh facts flowed in upon him to modify his conclusions, and accordingly one gives the quotations that follow with a certain amount of reservation. They are quoted from the ninth, thirteenth, and sixteenth messages, and, altogether vague and fragmentary as they are, they probably give as complete a picture of the social life of this strange community as mankind can now hope to have for many generations.

"In the moon," says Cavor, "every citizen knows his place. He is born to that place, and the elaborate discipline of training and education and surgery he undergoes fits him at last so completely to it that he has neither ideas nor organs for any purpose beyond it. 'Why should he ?' Phi-oo would ask. If, for example, a Selenite is destined to be a mathematician, his teachers and trainers set out at once to that end. They check any incipient disposition to other pursuits, they encourage his mathematical bias with a perfect psychological skill. His brain grows, or at least the mathematical faculties of his brain grow, and the rest of him only so much

as is necessary to sustain this essential part of him. At last, save for rest and food, his one delight lies in the exercise and display of his faculty, his one interest in its application, his sole society with other specialists in his own line. His brain grows continually larger, at least so far as the portions engaging in mathematics are concerned ; they bulge ever larger and seem to suck all life and vigour from the rest of his frame. His limbs shrivel, his heart and digestive organs diminish, his insect face is hidden under its bulging contours. His voice becomes a mere squeak for the stating of formulæ ; he seems deaf to all but properly enunciated problems. The faculty of laughter, save for the sudden discovery of some paradox, is lost to him ; his deepest emotion is the evolution of a novel computation. And so he attains his end.

"Or, again, a Selenite appointed to be a minder of mooncalves is from his earliest years induced to think and live mooncalf, to find his pleasure in mooncalf lore, his exercise in their tending and pursuit. He is trained to become wiry and active, his eye is indurated to the tight wrappings, the angular contours that constitute a 'smart mooncalfishness.' He takes at last no interest in the deeper part of the moon ; he regards all Selenites not equally versed in mooncalves with indifference, derision, or hostility. His thoughts are of mooncalf pastures, and his dialect an accomplished mooncalf technique. So also he loves his work, and discharges in perfect happiness the duty that justifies his being. And so it is with all sorts and conditions of Selenites— each is a perfect unit in a world machine . . .

"These beings with big heads, to whom the intellectual labours fall, form a sort of aristocracy in this strange society, and at the head of them, quintessential of the moon, is that marvellous gigantic ganglion the Grand Lunar, into whose presence I am finally to come. The unlimited development of the minds of the intellectual class is rendered possible by the absence of any bony skull in the lunar anatomy, that strange box of bone that clamps about the developing brain of man, imperiously insisting 'thus far and no farther' to all his possibilities. They fall into three main classes differing greatly in influence and respect. There are the administrators of whom Phi-oo was one, Selenites of considerable initiative and versatility, responsible each for a certain cubic content of the moon's bulk ; the experts like the football-headed thinker who are trained to perform certain special operations; and the erudite who are the repositories of all knowledge. To this latter class belongs Tsi-puff, the first lunar professor of terrestrial languages. With regard to these latter it is a curious little thing to note that the unlimited growth of the lunar brain has rendered unnecessary the invention of all those mechanical aids to brain work which have distinguished the career of man. There are no books, no records of any sort, no libraries or inscriptions. All knowledge is stored in distended brains much as the honey-ants of Texas store honey in their distended abdomens. The lunar Somerset House and the lunar British Museum Library are collections of living brains. . . .

"The less specialized administrators, I note, do for the most part take a very lively interest in me whenever they encounter me. They will come out of the way and stare at me and ask questions to which Phi-oo will reply. I see them going hither and thither with a retinue of bearers, attendants, shouters, parachute-carriers, and so forth—queer groups to see. The experts for the most part ignore me completely, even as they ignore each other, or notice me only to begin a clamorous exhibition of their distinctive skill. The erudite for the most part are rapt in an impervious and apoplectic complacency from which only a denial of their erudition can rouse them. Usually they are led about by little watchers and attendants, and often there are small and active-looking creatures, small females usually, that I am inclined to think are a sort of wife to them; but some of the profounder scholars are altogether too great for locomotion, and are carried from place to place in a sort of sedan tub, wabbling jellies of knowledge that enlist my respectful astonishment. I have just passed one in coming to this place where I am permitted to amuse myself with these electrical toys, a vast, shaven, shaky head, bald and thin-skinned, carried on his grotesque stretcher. In front and behind came his bearers, and curious, almost trumpet-faced, news disseminators shrieked his fame.

"I have already mentioned the retinues that accompanied most of the intellectuals: ushers, bearers, valets, extraneous tentacles and muscles as it were, to replace the abortive physical powers of these hypertrophied minds. Porters almost invariably accompany them. There are also extremely swift messengers with spider-like legs, and 'hands' for grasping parachutes, and attendants with vocal organs that could well-nigh wake the dead. Apart

" WABBLING JELLIES OF KNOWLEDGE."

from their controlling intelligence these subordinates are as inert and helpless as umbrellas in a stand. They exist only in relation to the orders they have to obey, the duties they have to perform.

"The bulk of these insects, however, who go to and fro upon the spiral ways, who fill the ascending balloons and drop past me clinging to flimsy parachutes, are, I gather, of the operative class. 'Machine hands,' indeed, some of these are in actual nature— it is no figure of speech, the single tentacle of the mooncalf herd is replaced by huge single or paired bunches of three, or five, or seven digits for clawing, lifting, guiding, the rest of them no more than necessary subordinate appendages to these important parts. Some, who I suppose deal with bell-striking mechanisms, have enormous, rabbit-like ears just behind the eyes ; some whose work lies in delicate chemical operations project a vast olfactory organ ; others again have flat feet for treadles with anchylozed joints ; and others—who I have been told are glass-blowers—seem mere lung-bellows. But every one of these common Selenites I have seen at work is exquisitely adapted to the social need it meets. Fine work is done by fined-down workers amazingly dwarfed and neat. Some I could hold on the palm of my hand. There is even a sort of turnspit Selenite, very common, whose duty and only delight it is to supply the motive power for various small appliances. And to rule over these things and order any erring tendency there might be in some aberrant nature are the finest muscular beings I have seen in the moon, a sort of lunar police, who must have been trained from their earliest years to give a perfect respect and obedience to the swollen heads.

"The making of these various sorts of operative must be a very curious and interesting process. I am still very much in the dark about it, but quite recently I came upon a number of young Selenites confined in jars from which only the fore-limbs protruded, who were being compressed to become machine-minders of a special sort. The extended 'hand' in this highly developed system of technical education is stimulated by irritants and nourished by injection while the rest of the body is starved. Phi-oo, unless I misunderstood him, explained that in the earlier stages these queer little creatures are apt to display signs of suffering in their various cramped situations, but they easily become indurated to their lot ; and he took me on to where a number of flexible-limbed messengers were being drawn out and broken in. It is quite unreasonable, I know, but these glimpses of the educational methods of these beings has affected me disagreeably. I hope, however, that may pass off and I may be able to see more of this aspect of this wonderful social order. That wretched-looking-hand sticking out of its jar seemed to have a sort of limp appeal for lost possibilities ; it haunts me still, although, of course, it is really in the end a far more humane proceeding than our earthly method of leaving children to grow into human beings, and then making machines of them.

"Quite recently, too—I think it was on the eleventh or twelfth visit I made to this apparatus—I had a curious light upon the lives of these operatives. I was being guided through a short cut hither instead of going down the spiral and by the quays of the Central Sea. From the devious windings of a long, dark gallery we emerged into a vast, low cavern, pervaded by an earthy smell, and rather brightly lit. The light came from a tumultuous growth of livid fungoid shapes—some indeed singularly like our terrestrial mushrooms, but standing as high or higher than a man.

" ' Mooneys eat these ? ' said I to Phi-oo.

" ' Yes, food.'

" ' Goodness me ! ' I cried, ' what's that ? '

" My eye had just caught the figure of an exceptionally big and ungainly Selenite lying motionless among the stems, face downward. We stopped.

" ' Dead ? ' I asked. (For as yet I have seen no dead in the moon, and I have grown curious.)

" ' *No !* ' exclaimed Phi-oo. ' Him—worker—no work to do. Get little drink then—make sleep—till we him want. What good him wake, eh ? No want him walking about.'

" ' There's another ! ' cried I.

" And indeed all that huge extent of mushroom ground was, I found, peppered with these prostrate figures sleeping under an opiate until the moon had need of them. There were scores of them of all sorts, and we were able to turn over some of them, and examine them more precisely than I had been able to do previously. They breathed noisily at my doing so, but did not wake. One I remember very distinctly : he left a strong impression, I think, because some trick of the light and of his attitude was strongly suggestive of a drawn-up human figure. His fore-limbs were long, delicate tentacles—he was some kind of refined manipulator—and the pose of his slumber suggested a submissive suffering. No doubt it was quite a mistake for me to interpret his expression in that way, but I did. And as Phi-oo rolled him over into the darkness among the livid fleshiness again I felt a distinctly unpleasant sensation, although as he rolled the insect in him was confessed.

" It simply illustrates the unthinking way in which one acquires habits of thought and feeling. To drug the worker one does not want and toss him aside is surely far better than to expel him from his factory to wander starving in the streets. In every complicated social community there is necessarily a certain intermittency in the occupation of all specialized labour, and in this way the trouble of an unemployed problem is altogether anticipated. And yet, so unreasonable are even scientifically trained minds, I still do not like the memory of those prostrate forms amidst those quiet, luminous arcades of fleshy growth, and I avoid that short cut in spite of the inconveniences of its longer, more noisy, and more crowded alternative.

" My alternative route takes me round by a huge, shadowy cavern, very crowded and clamorous, and here it is I see peering out of the hexagonal openings of a sort of honeycomb wall, or parading a large open space behind, or selecting the toys and amulets made to please them by the acephalic dainty - fingered jewellers who work in kennels below, the mothers of the moon-world —the queen bees, as it were, of the hive. They are noble-looking beings, fantastically and sometimes quite beautifully adorned, with a proud carriage and, save for their mouths, almost microscopic heads.

" HIS ATTITUDE WAS STRONGLY SUGGESTIVE OF A DRAWN-UP HUMAN FIGURE."

" Of the condition of the moon sexes, marrying and giving in marriage, and of birth and so forth among the Selenites, I have as yet been able to learn very little. With the steady progress of Phi-oo in English, however, my ignorance will no doubt as steadily disappear. I am of opinion that as with the ants and bees there is a large majority of the members in this community of the neuter sex. Of course on earth in our cities there are now many who never live that life of parentage which is the natural life of man. Here, as with the ants, this thing has become a normal condition of the race, and the

whole of such replacement as is necessary falls upon this special and by no means numerous class of matrons, the mothers of the moon - world, large and stately beings beautifully fitted to bear the larval Selenite. Unless I misunderstand an explanation of Phi-oo's, they are absolutely incapable of cherishing the young they bring into the moon ; periods of foolish indulgence alternate with moods of aggressive violence, and as soon as possible the little creatures, who are quite soft and flabby and pale coloured, are transferred to the charge of a variety of celibate females, women " workers " as it were, who in some cases possess brains of almost masculine dimensions."

Just at this point, unhappily, this message broke off. Fragmentary and tantalizing as the matter constituting this chapter is, it does nevertheless give a vague, broad impression of an altogether strange and wonderful world — a world with which our own must now prepare to reckon very speedily. This intermittent trickle of messages, this whispering of a record needle in the darkness of the mountain slopes, is the first warning of such a change in human conditions as mankind has scarcely imagined heretofore. In that planet there are new elements, new appliances, new traditions, an overwhelming avalanche of new ideas, a strange race with whom we must inevitably struggle for mastery — gold as common as iron or wood. . . . .

The First Men in the Moon.

By H. G. Wells.

CHAPTER XXV.
THE GRAND LUNAR.

 HE penultimate message describes, with occasionally even elaborate detail, the encounter between Cavor and the Grand Lunar, who is the ruler or master of the moon. Cavor seems to have sent most of it without interference, but to have been interrupted in the concluding portion. The second came after an interval of a week.

The first message begins : " At last I am able to resume this ———" ; it then becomes illegible for a space, and after a time resumes in mid-sentence.

The missing words of the following sentence are probably "the crowd." There follows quite clearly : " grew ever denser as we drew near the palace of the Grand Lunar — if I may call a series of excavations a palace. Everywhere faces stared at me — blank, chitinous gapes and masks, big eyes peering over tremendous nose tentacles, and little eyes beneath monstrous forehead plates ; below an undergrowth of smaller creatures dodged and yelped, and grotesque heads poised on sinuous, swanlike, long-jointed necks appeared craning over shoulders and beneath armpits. Keeping a welcome space about me marched a cordon of stolid, scuttle-headed guards, who had joined us on our leaving the boat in which we had come along the channels of the Central Sea. The flea-like artist with the little brain joined us also, and a thick bunch of lean porter-ants swayed and struggled under the multitude of conveniences that were considered essential to my state. I was carried in a litter during the final stage of our journey. It was made of some very ductile metal that looked dark to me, meshed and woven and with bars of paler metal, and about me as I advanced there grouped itself a long and complicated procession.

" In front, after the manner of heralds, marched four trumpet-faced creatures making a devastating bray ; and then came squat, almost beetle-like, ushers before and behind, and on either hand a galaxy of learned heads, a sort of animated encyclopædia, who were,

Phi-oo explained, to stand about the Grand Lunar for purposes of reference. (Not a thing in lunar science, not a point of view or method of thinking, that these wonderful beings did not carry in their heads.) Followed guards and porters, and then Phi-oo's shivering brain borne also on a litter. Then came Tsi-puff in a slightly less important litter ; then myself on a litter of greater elegance than any other and surrounded by my food and drink attendants. More trumpeters came next, splitting the ear with vehement outcries, and then several big brains, special correspondents one might well call them or historiographers, charged with the task of observing and remembering every detail of this epoch-making interview. A company of attendants, bearing and dragging banners and masses of scented fungus and curious symbols, completed the procession. The way was lined by ushers and officers in caparisons that gleamed like steel, and beyond their line the heads and tentacles of that enormous crowd surged on either hand.

" I will own that I am still by no means indurated to the peculiar effect of the Selenite appearance, and to find myself as it were adrift on this broad sea of excited entomology was by no means agreeable. Just for a space I had something like I should imagine people mean when they speak of the ' horrors.' It had come to me before in these lunar caverns, when on occasion I have found myself weaponless and with an undefended back, amidst a crowd of these Selenites, but never quite so vividly. It is, of course, as absolutely irrational a feeling as one could well have, and I hope gradually to subdue it. But just for a moment, as I swept forward into the welter of the vast crowd, it was only by gripping my litter tightly and summoning all my will-power that I succeeded in avoiding an outcry or some such manifestation. It lasted perhaps three minutes ; then I had myself in hand again.

" We ascended the spiral of a vertical way for some time and then passed through a series of huge halls, dome-roofed and gloriously decorated. The approach to the Grand Lunar was certainly contrived to give one a vivid impression of his greatness. The halls—all happily sufficiently luminous for my terrestrial eye—were a cunning and elaborate crescendo of space and decoration. The effect of their progressive size was enhanced by the steady diminution in the lighting, and by a thin haze of incense that thickened as one advanced. In the earlier ones the vivid, clear light made everything finite and concrete to me. I seemed to advance continually to something larger, dimmer, and less material.

" I must confess that all this splendour made me feel extremely shabby and unworthy. I was unshaven and unkempt ; I had brought no razor ; I had a coarse beard over my mouth. On earth I have always been inclined to despise any attention to my person beyond a proper care for cleanliness ; but under the exceptional circumstances in which I found myself, representing, as I did, my planet and my kind, and depending very largely upon the attractiveness of my appearance for a proper reception, I could have given much for something a little more artistic and dignified than the husks I wore. I had been so serene in the belief that the moon was uninhabited as to overlook such precautions altogether. As it was I was dressed in a flannel jacket, knickerbockers, and golfing stockings, stained with every sort of dirt the moon offered ; slippers (of which the left heel was wanting), and a blanket, through a hole in which I thrust my head. (These clothes, indeed, I still wear.) Sharp bristles are anything but an improvement to my cast of features, and there was an unmended tear at the knee of my knickerbockers that showed conspicuously as I squatted in my litter ; my right stocking, too, persisted in getting about my ankle. I am fully alive to the injustice my appearance did humanity, and if by any expedient I could have improvised something a little out of the way and imposing I would have done so. But I could hit upon nothing. I did what I could with my blanket—folding it somewhat after the fashion of a toga, and for the rest I sat as upright as the swaying of my litter permitted.

" Imagine the largest hall you have ever been in, elaborately decorated with blue and whitish-blue Majolica, lit by blue light, you know not how, and surging with metallic or livid-white creatures of such a mad diversity as I have hinted. Imagine this hall to end in an open archway beyond which is a still larger hall, and beyond this yet another and still larger one, and so on. At the end of the vista a flight of steps, like the steps of Ara Cœli at Rome, ascend out of sight. Higher and higher these steps appear to go as one draws nearer their base. But at last I came under a huge archway and beheld the summit of these steps, and upon it the Grand Lunar exalted on his throne.

" He was seated in a blaze of incandescent blue. A hazy atmosphere filled the place so that its walls seemed invisibly remote. This gave him an effect of floating in a blue-black void. He seemed a small, self-luminous cloud at first, brooding on his glaucous throne ; his brain-case must have measured many yards in diameter. For some reason that I cannot fathom a number of blue search-lights radiated from behind the throne on which he sat, as though he were a star, and immediately encircling him was a halo. About him, and little and indistinct in this glow, a number of body-servants sustained and supported him, and overshadowed and standing in a huge semicircle beneath him were his intellectual subordinates, his remembrancers and computators and searchers, his flatterers and servants, and all the distinguished insects of the court of the moon. Still lower stood ushers and messengers, and then all down the countless steps of the throne were guards, and at the base, enormous, various, indistinct, a vast swaying multitude of the minor dignitaries of the moon. Their feet made a perpetual scraping whisper on the rocky floor, their limbs moved with a rustling murmur.

"As I entered the penultimate hall the music rose and expanded into an imperial magnificence of sound, and the shrieks of the newsbearers died away. . . .

"I entered the last and greatest hall. . . .

"My procession opened out like a fan. My ushers and guards went right and left, and the three litters bearing myself and Phi-oo and Tsi-puff marched across a shiny waste of floor to the foot of the giant stairs. Then began a vast throbbing hum, that mingled with the music. The two Selenites dismounted, but I was bidden remain seated—I imagine as a special honour. The music ceased, but not that humming, and by a simultaneous movement of ten thousand respectful eyes my attention was directed to the enhaloed supreme intelligence that hovered above us.

"At first as I peered into the radiating blaze this quintessential brain looked very much like an opaque, featureless bladder with dim, undulating ghosts of convolutions writhing visibly within. Then beneath its enormity and just above the edge of the throne one saw with a start minute elfin eyes peering out of the blaze. No face, but eyes, as if they peered through holes. At first I could see no more than these two staring little eyes, and then below I distinguished the little dwarfed body and its insect-jointed limbs shrivelled and white. The eyes stared down at me with a strange intensity, and the lower part of the swollen globe was wrinkled. Ineffectual-looking little hand-tentacles steadied this shape on the throne. . . .

"It was great. It was pitiful. One forgot the hall and the crowd.

"I ascended the staircase by jerks. It seemed to me that the purple glowing brain-case above us spread over me, and took more and more of the whole effect into itself as I drew nearer. The tiers of attendants and helpers grouped about their master seemed to dwindle and fade into the glare. I saw that the shadowy attendants were busy spraying that great brain with a cooling spray, and patting and sustaining it. For my own part I sat gripping my swaying litter and staring at the Grand Lunar, unable to turn my gaze aside. And at last, as I reached a little landing that was separated only by ten steps or so from the supreme seat, the woven splendour of the music reached a climax and

"THE GRAND LUNAR."

ceased, and I was left naked, as it were, in that vastness, beneath the still scrutiny of the Grand Lunar's eyes.

"He was scrutinizing the first man he had ever seen. . . . .

"My eyes dropped at last from his greatness to the faint figures in the blue mist about him, and then down the steps to the massed Selenites, still and expectant in their thousands, packed on the floor below. Once again an unreasonable horror reached out towards me. . . . . And passed.

"After the pause came the salutation. I was assisted from my litter, and stood awkwardly while a number of curious and no doubt deeply symbolical gestures were vicariously performed for me by two slender officials. The encyclopædic galaxy of the learned that had accompanied me to the entrance of the last hall appeared two steps above me and left and right of me, in readiness for the Grand Lunar's need, and Phi-oo's white brain placed itself about half-way up to the throne in such a position as to com-

"I BECAME AWARE OF A FAINT WHEEZY NOISE."

municate easily between us without turning his back on either the Grand Lunar or myself. Tsi-puff took up a position behind him. Dexterous ushers sidled sideways towards me, keeping a full face to the Presence. I seated myself Turkish fashion, and Phi-oo and Tsi-puff also knelt down above me. There came a pause. The eyes of the nearer court went from me to the Grand Lunar and came back to me, and a

hissing and piping of expectation passed across the hidden multitudes below and ceased.

"That humming ceased.

"For the first and last time in my experience the moon was silent.

"I became aware of a faint wheezy noise. The Grand Lunar was addressing me. It was like the rubbing of a finger upon a pane of glass.

"I watched him attentively for a time and then glanced at the alert Phi-oo. I felt amidst these filmy beings ridiculously thick and fleshy and solid; my head all jaw and black hair. My eyes went back to the Grand Lunar. He had ceased; his attendants were busy, and his shining superfices was glistening and running with cooling spray.

"Phi-oo meditated through an interval. He consulted Tsi-puff. Then he began piping his recognisable English —at first a little nervously, so that he was not very clear.

"'M'm — the Grand Lunar—wishes to say—wishes to say —he gathers you are—m'm—men —that you are a man from the planet earth. He wishes to say that he welcomes you—welcomes you—and wishes to learn——learn, if I may use the word—the state of your world, and the reason why you came to this.'

"He paused. I was about to reply when he resumed. He proceeded to remarks of which the drift was not very clear, though I am inclined to think they were intended to be complimentary. He told me that the earth was to the moon what the sun is to the earth, and that the Selenites desired very greatly to learn about the earth and men. He then told me, no doubt in compliment also, the relative magnitude and diameter of earth and moon, and the perpetual wonder and speculation with which the Selenites had regarded our planet. I meditated with downcast eyes and decided to reply that men too had wondered what might lie in the moon, and had judged it dead, little recking of such magnificence as I had seen that day. The Grand Lunar, in token of recognition, caused his blue search-light to rotate in a very confusing manner, and all about the great hall ran the pipings and whisperings and rustlings of the report of what I had said. He then proceeded to put to Phi-oo a number of inquiries which were easier to answer.

"I WAS DAZZLED AND BLINDED FOR SOME LITTLE TIME."

"He understood, he explained, that we lived on the surface of the earth, that our air and sea were outside the globe; the latter part, indeed, he already knew from his astronomical specialists. He was very anxious to have more detailed information of what he called this extraordinary state of affairs, for from the solidity of the earth there had always been a disposition to regard it as uninhabitable. He endeavoured first to ascertain the extremes of temperature to which we earth beings were exposed, and he was deeply interested by my descriptive treatment of clouds and rain. His imagination was assisted by the fact that the lunar atmosphere in the outer galleries of the night side is not infrequently very foggy. He seemed inclined to marvel that we did not find the sunlight too intense for our eyes, and was interested in my attempt to explain that the sky was tempered to a bluish colour through the refraction of the air, though I doubt if he clearly understood that. I explained how the iris of the human eyes can contract the pupil and save the delicate internal structure

from the excess of sunlight, and was allowed to approach within a few feet of the Presence in order that this structure might be seen. This led to a comparison of the lunar and terrestrial eyes. The former is not only excessively sensitive to such light as men can see, but it can also *see* heat, and every difference in temperature within the moon renders objects visible to it.

"The iris was quite a new organ to the Grand Lunar. For a time he amused himself by flashing his rays into my face and watching my pupils contract. As a consequence, I was dazzled and blinded for some little time. . . . .

"But in spite of that discomfort I found something reassuring by insensible degrees in the rationality of this business of question and answer. I could shut my eyes, think of my answer, and almost forget that the Grand Lunar has no face. . . . .

"When I had descended again to my proper place the Grand Lunar asked how we sheltered ourselves from heat and storms, and I expounded to him the arts of building and furnishing. Here we wandered into misunderstandings and cross-purposes, due largely, I must admit, to the looseness of my expressions. For a long time I had great difficulty in making him understand the nature of a house. To him and his attendant Selenites it seemed no doubt the most whimsical thing in the world that men should build houses when they might descend into excavations, and an additional complication was introduced by the attempt I made to explain that men had originally begun their homes in caves, and that they were now taking their railways and many establishments beneath the surface. Here I think a desire for intellectual completeness betrayed me. There was also a considerable tangle due to an equally unwise attempt on my part to explain about mines. Dismissing this topic at last in an incomplete state, the

Grand Lunar inquired what we did with the interior of our globe.

" A tide of twittering and piping swept into the remotest corners of that great assembly when it was at last made clear that we men know absolutely nothing of the contents of the world upon which the immemorial generations of our ancestors had been evolved. Three times had I to repeat that of all the 4,000 miles of substance between the earth and its centre men knew only to the depth of a mile, and that very vaguely. I understood the Grand Lunar to ask why had I come to the moon seeing we had scarcely touched our own planet yet, but he did not trouble me at that time to proceed to an explanation, being too anxious to pursue the details of this mad inversion of all his ideas.

" He reverted to the question of weather, and I tried to describe the perpetually changing sky, and snow, and frost and hurricanes. ' But when the night comes,' he asked, ' is it not cold ? '

" I told him it was colder than by day.

" ' And does not your atmosphere freeze ? '

" I told him not; that it was never cold enough for that, because our nights were so short.

" ' Not even liquefy ? '

" I was about to say ' No,' but then it occurred to me that one part at least of our atmosphere, the water vapour of it, does sometimes liquefy and form dew and sometimes freeze and form frost—a process perfectly analogous to the freezing of all the external atmosphere of the moon during its longer night. I made myself clear on this point, and from that the Grand Lunar went on to speak with me of sleep. For the need of sleep that comes so regularly every twenty-four hours to all things is part also of our

" HE ORDERED COOLING SPRAYS UPON HIS BROW."

earthly inheritance. On the moon they rest only at rare intervals and after exceptional exertions. Then I tried to describe to him the soft splendours of a summer night, and from that I passed to a description of those animals that prowl by night and sleep by day. I told him of lions and tigers, and here it seemed as though we had come to a deadlock. For, save in their waters, there are no creatures in the moon not absolutely domestic and subject to his will, and so it has been for immemorial years. They have monstrous water creatures, but no evil beasts, and the idea of anything strong and large existing ' outside ' in the night is very difficult for them. . . .

[The record is here too broken to transcribe for the space of perhaps twenty words or more.]

" He talked with his attendants, as I suppose, upon the strange superficiality and unreasonableness of (man), who lives on the mere surface of a world, a creature of waves and winds and all the chances of space, who cannot even unite to overcome the beasts that prey upon his kind, and yet who dares to invade another planet. During this aside I sat thinking, and then at his desire I told him of the different sorts of men. He searched me with questions. ' And for all sorts of work you have the same sort of men. But who thinks ? Who governs ? '

" I gave him an outline of the democratic method.

" When I had done he ordered cooling sprays upon his brow, and then requested me to repeat my explanation, conceiving something had miscarried.

" ' Do they not do different things, then ? ' said Phi-oo.

" Some I admitted were thinkers and some

officials ; some hunted, some were mechanics, some artists, some toilers. 'But *all* rule,' I said.

" 'And have they not different shapes to fit them to their different duties ? '

" 'None that you can see,' I said, 'except perhaps for clothes. Their minds perhaps differ a little,' I reflected.

" 'Their minds must differ a great deal,' said the Grand Lunar, 'or they would all want to do the same things.'

" In order to bring myself into a closer harmony with his preconceptions I said that his surmise was right. 'It was all hidden in the brain,' I said ; 'but the difference was there. Perhaps if one could see the minds and souls of men they would be as varied and unequal as the Selenites. There were great men and small men, men who could reach out far and wide, and men who could go swiftly ; noisy, trumpet-minded men, and men who could remember without thinking. . . . . [The record is indistinct for three words.]

" He interrupted me to recall me to my previous statement. 'But you said all men rule ? ' he pressed.

" 'To a certain extent,' I said, and made, I fear, a denser fog with my explanation.

" He reached out to a salient fact. 'Do you mean,' he asked, 'that there is no Grand Earthly ? '

" I thought of several people, but assured him finally there was none. I explained that such autocrats and emperors as we had tried upon earth had usually ended in drink, or vice, or violence, and that the large and influential section of the people of the earth to which I belonged, the Anglo-Saxons, did not mean to try that sort of thing again. At which the Grand Lunar was even more amazed.

" 'But how do you keep even such wisdom as you have ? ' he asked ; and I explained to him the way we helped our limited [a word omitted here, probably " brains."] with libraries of books. I explained to him how our science was growing by the united labours of innumerable little men, and on that he made no comment save that it was evident we had mastered much in spite of our social savagery, or we could not have come to the moon. Yet the contrast was very marked. With knowledge the Selenites grew and changed ; mankind stored their knowledge about them and remained brutes—equipped. He said this . . . [Here there is a short piece of the record indistinct.]

" He then caused me to describe how we went about this earth of ours, and I described to him our railways and ships. For a time he could not understand that we had had the use of steam only one hundred years, but when he did he was clearly amazed. (I may mention as a singular thing that the Selenites use years to count by, just as we do on earth, though I can make nothing of their numeral system. That however does not matter, because Phi-oo understands ours.) From that I went on to tell him that mankind had dwelt in cities only for nine or ten thousand years, and that we were still not united in one brotherhood, but under many different forms of government. This astonished the Grand Lunar very much, when it was made clear to him. At first he thought we referred merely to administrative areas.

" 'Our States and Empires are still the rawest sketches of what order will some day be,' I said, and so I came to tell him. . . . [At this point a length of record that probably represents thirty or forty words is totally illegible.]

" The Grand Lunar was greatly impressed by the folly of men in clinging to the inconvenience of diverse tongues. 'They want to communicate, and yet not to communicate,' he said, and then for a long time he questioned me closely concerning war.

" He was at first perplexed and incredulous. 'You mean to say,' he asked, seeking confirmation, 'that you run about over the surface of your world—this world, whose riches you have scarcely begun to scrape—killing one another for beasts to eat ? '

" I told him that was perfectly correct.

" He asked for particulars to assist his imagination. 'But do not your ships and your poor little cities get injured ? ' he asked, and I found the waste of property and conveniences seemed to impress him almost as much as the killing. 'Tell me more,' said the Grand Lunar ; 'make me see pictures. I cannot conceive these things.'

" And so, for a space, though something loth, I told him the story of earthly War.

" I told him of the first orders and ceremonies of war, of warnings and ultimatums, and the marshalling and marching of troops. I gave him an idea of manœuvres and positions and battle joined. I told him of sieges and assaults, of starvation and hardship in trenches, and of sentinels freezing in the snow. I told him of routs and surprises, and desperate last stands and faint hopes, and the pitiless pursuit of fugitives and the dead upon the field. I told, too, of the past, of invasions and massacres, of the Huns and Tartars, and the wars of Mahomet and the Caliphs and of the Crusades. And as I went on, and Phi-oo translated, the Selen-

"THE SELENITES COOED AND MURMURED IN A STEADILY INTENSIFIED EMOTION."

ites cooed and murmured in a steadily intensified emotion.

"I told them an ironclad could fire a shot of a ton twelve miles, and go through 20ft. of iron—and how we could steer torpedoes under water. I went on to describe a Maxim gun in action and what I could imagine of the Battle of Colenso. The Grand Lunar was so incredulous that he interrupted the translation of what I had said in order to have my verification of my account. They particularly doubted my description of the men cheering and rejoicing as they went into (? battle).

"'But surely they do not like it!' translated Phi-oo.

"I assured them men of my race considered battle the most glorious experience of life, at which the whole assembly was stricken with amazement.

"'But what good is this war?' asked the Grand Lunar, sticking to his theme.

"'Oh! as for *good!*' said I; 'it thins the population!'

"'But why should there be a need——?' . . . .

"There came a pause, the cooling sprays impinged upon his brow, and then he spoke again."

At this point there suddenly becomes predominant in the record a series of undulations that have been apparent as a perplexing complication as far back as Cavor's description of the silence that fell before the first speaking of the Grand Lunar. These undulations are evidently the result of radiations proceeding from a lunar source, and their persistent approximation to the alternating signals of Cavor is curiously suggestive of some operator deliberately seeking to mix them in with his message and render it illegible. At first they are small and regular, so that with a little care and the loss of very few words we have been able to disentangle Cavor's message; then they become broad and larger, then suddenly they are irregular, with an irregularity that gives the effect at last of someone scribbling through a line of writing. For a long time nothing can be made of this madly zigzagging trace; then quite abruptly the interruption ceases, leaves a few words clear, and then resumes and continues for all the rest of the message, completely obliterating whatever Cavor was attempting to transmit. Why, if this is indeed a deliberate intervention, the Selenites should have preferred to let Cavor go on transmitting his message in happy ignorance of their obliteration of its record, when it was clearly quite in their power and much more easy and convenient for them to stop his proceedings at any time, is a problem to which I can contribute nothing. The thing seems to have happened so, and that is all I can say. This last rag of his description of the Grand Lunar begins, in mid-sentence :—

"interrogated me very closely upon my secret. I was able in a little while to get to an understanding with them, and at last to elucidate what has been a puzzle to me ever since I realized the vastness of their science, namely, how it is they themselves have never discovered 'Cavorite.' I find they know of it as a theoretical substance, but they have always regarded it as a practical impossibility, because for some reason there is no helium in the moon, and helium——"

Across the last letters of helium slashes the resumption of that obliterating trace. Note that word "secret," for on that, and that alone, I base my interpretation of the last message, as both Mr. Wendigee and myself now believe it to be, that he is ever likely to send us.

CHAPTER XXVI.

THE LAST MESSAGE CAVOR SENT TO THE EARTH.

IN this unsatisfactory manner the pen-ultimate message of Cavor dies out. One seems to see him away there amidst his blue-lit apparatus intently signalling us to the last, all unaware of the curtain of confusion that drops between us; all unaware, too, of the final dangers that even then must have been creeping upon him. His disastrous want of vulgar common-sense had utterly betrayed him. He had talked of war, he had talked of all the strength and irrational violence of men, of their insatiable aggressions, their tireless futility of conflict. He had filled the whole moon-world with this impression of our race, and then I think it is plain that he admitted upon himself alone hung the possibility— at least for a long time — of any further men reaching the moon. The line the cold, inhuman reason of the moon would take seems plain enough to me, and a suspicion of it, and then perhaps some sudden sharp realization of it, must have come to him. One imagines him going about the moon with the remorse of this fatal indiscretion growing in his mind. During a certain time most assuredly the Grand Lunar was deliberating the new situation, and for all that time Cavor went as free as ever he had gone. We imagine obstacles of some sort prevented Cavor getting to his electro-magnetic apparatus again after that last message I have given. For some days we received nothing. Perhaps he was having fresh audiences, and trying to evade his previous admissions. Who can hope to guess?

And then suddenly, like a cry in the night, like a cry that is followed by a stillness, came the last message. It is the briefest fragment, the broken beginnings of two sentences.

The first was: "I was mad to let the Grand Lunar know——"

There was an interval of perhaps a minute. One imagines some interruption from without. A departure from the instrument—a dreadful hesitation among the looming masses of apparatus in that dim, blue-lit cavern—a sudden rush back to it, full of a resolve that came too late. Then, as if it were hastily transmitted, came: "Cavorite made as follows: take——"

There followed one word, a quite unmeaning word as it stands: "uless."

And that is all.

It may be he made a hasty attempt to spell "useless" when his fate was close upon him. Whatever it was that was happening about that apparatus, we cannot tell. Whatever it was we shall never, I know, receive another message from the moon. For my own part a vivid dream has come to my help, and I see, almost as plainly as though I had seen it in actual fact, a blue-lit dishevelled Cavor struggling in the grip of a great multitude of those insect Selenites, struggling ever more desperately and hopelessly as they swarm upon him, shouting, expostulating, perhaps even at last fighting, and being forced backward step by step out of all speech or sign of his fellows, for evermore into the Unknown — into the dark, into that silence that has no end . . . .

"STRUGGLING EVER MORE DESPERATELY AND HOPELESSLY."

THE END.

—6—

THE DIAMOND MAKER

Originally published in *Pearson's Magazine*
March 1905

The Diamond Maker.

The Story of an Unappreciated Genius.

By H. G. Wells.

Some business had detained me in Chancery Lane until nine in the evening, and thereafter, having some inkling of a headache, I was disinclined either for entertainment or further work. So much of the sky as the high cliffs of that narrow cañon of traffic left visible spoke of a serene night, and I determined to make my way down to the Embankment, and rest my eyes and cool my head by watching the variegated lights upon the river.

Beyond comparison the night is the best time for this place; a merciful darkness hides the dirt of the waters, and the lights of this transition age, red, glaring orange, gas-yellow, and electric white, are set in shadowy outlines of every possible shade between grey and deep purple. Through the arches of Waterloo Bridge a hundred points of light mark the sweep of the Embankment, and above its parapet rise the towers of Westminster, warm grey against the starlight. The black river goes by with only a rare ripple breaking its silence, and disturbing the reflections of the lights that swim upon its surface.

"A warm night," said a voice at my side.

I turned my head, and saw the profile of a man who was leaning over the parapet beside me. It was a refined face, not unhandsome, though pinched and pale enough, and the coat collar turned up and pinned round the throat marked his status in life as sharply as a uniform. I felt I was committed to the price of a bed and breakfast if I answered him.

I looked at him curiously. Would he have anything to tell me worth the money, or was he the common incapable — incapable even of telling his own story? There was a quality of intelligence in his forehead and eyes, and a certain tremulousness in his nether lip that decided me.

"Very warm," said I; "but not too warm for us here."

"No," he said, still looking across the water, "it is pleasant enough here . . . just now."

"It is good," he continued after a pause, "to find anything so restful as this in London. After one has been fretting about business all day, about getting on, meeting obligations, and parrying dangers, I do not know what one would do if it were not for such pacific corners." He spoke with long pauses between the sentences. "You must know a little of the irksome labour of the world, or you would not be here. But I doubt if you can be so brain-weary and footsore as I am . . . Bah! Sometimes I doubt if the

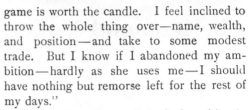

He pulled out a little canvas bag that was hanging by a cord round his neck. From this he produced a brown pebble. "I wonder if you know enough to know what that is?"

game is worth the candle. I feel inclined to throw the whole thing over—name, wealth, and position—and take to some modest trade. But I know if I abandoned my ambition—hardly as she uses me—I should have nothing but remorse left for the rest of my days."

He became silent. I looked at him in astonishment. If ever I saw a man hopelessly hard-up it was the man in front of me. He was ragged and he was dirty, unshaven and unkempt; he looked as though he had been left in a dust-bin for a week. And he was talking to *me* of the irksome worries of a large business. I almost laughed outright. Either he was mad or playing a sorry jest on his own poverty.

" If high aims and high positions," said I, " have their drawbacks of hard work and anxiety, they have their compensations. Influence, the power of doing good, of assisting those weaker and poorer than ourselves; and there is even a certain gratification in display . . . ."

My banter under the circumstances was in very vile taste. I spoke on the spur of the contrast of his appearance and speech. I was sorry even while I was speaking.

He turned a haggard but very composed face upon me. Said he: " I forget myself. Of course you would not understand."

He measured me for a moment. " No doubt it is very absurd. You will not believe me even when I tell you, so that it is fairly safe to tell you. And it will be a comfort to tell someone. I really have a big business in hand, a very big business. But there are troubles just now. The fact is . . . I make diamonds."

" I suppose," said I, " you are out of work just at present ?"

" I am sick of being disbelieved," he said

impatiently, and suddenly unbuttoning his wretched coat he pulled out a little canvas bag that was hanging by a cord round his neck. From this he produced a brown pebble. "I wonder if you know enough to know what that is?" He handed it to me.

Now, a year or so ago, I had occupied my leisure in taking a London science degree, so that I have a smattering of physics and mineralogy. The thing was not unlike an uncut diamond of the darker sort, though far too large, being almost as big as the top of my thumb. I took it, and saw it had the form of a regular octahedron, with the curved faces peculiar to the most precious of minerals. I took out my penknife and tried to scratch it— vainly. Leaning forward towards the gas-lamp, I tried the thing on my watch-glass, and scored a white line across that with the greatest ease.

I looked at my interlocutor with rising curiosity. "It certainly is rather like a diamond. But, if so, it is a Behemoth of diamonds. Where did you get it?"

"I tell you I made it," he said. "Give it back to me."

He replaced it hastily and buttoned his jacket. "I will sell it you for one hundred pounds," he suddenly whispered eagerly. With that my suspicions returned. The thing might, after all, be merely a lump of that almost equally hard substance, corundum, with an accidental resemblance in shape to the diamond. Or if it was a diamond, how came he by it, and why should he offer it at a hundred pounds?

We looked into one another's eyes. He seemed eager, but honestly eager. At that moment I believed it was a diamond he was trying to sell. Yet I am a poor man, a hundred pounds would leave a visible gap in my fortunes, and no sane man would buy a diamond by gaslight from a ragged tramp on his personal warranty only. Still, a diamond that size conjured up a vision of many thousands of pounds. Then, thought I, such a stone could scarcely exist without being mentioned in every book on gems, and again I called to mind the stories of contraband and light-fingered Kaffirs at the Cape. I put the question of purchase on one side.

"How did you get it?" said I.

"I made it."

I had heard something of Moissan, but I knew his artificial diamonds are very small. I shook my head.

"You seem to know something of this kind of thing. I will tell you a little about myself. Perhaps then you may think better of the purchase." He turned round with his back to the river, and put his hands in his pockets. He sighed. "I know you will not believe me."

"Diamonds," he began—and as he spoke his voice lost its faint flavour of the tramp and assumed something of the easy tone of an educated man—"are to be made by throwing carbon out of combination in a suitable flux and under a suitable pressure; the carbon crystallises out, not as black-lead or charcoal powder, but as small diamonds. So much has been known to chemists for years, but no one yet has hit upon exactly the right flux in which to melt up the carbon, or exactly the right pressure for the best results. Consequently the diamonds made by chemists are small and dark, and worthless as jewels. Now I, you know, have given up my life to this problem—given my life to it.

"I began to work at the conditions of diamond making when I was seventeen, and now I am thirty-two. It seemed to me that it might take all the thought and energies of a man for ten years, or twenty years, but, even if it did, the game was still worth the candle. Suppose one to have at last just hit the right trick, before the secret got out and diamonds became as common as coal, one might realise millions. Millions!"

He paused and looked for my sympathy. His eyes shone hungrily. "To think," said he, "that I am on the verge of it all, and here!

"I had," he proceeded, "about a thousand pounds when I was twenty-one, and this, I thought, eked out by a little teaching, would keep my researches going. A year or two was spent in study, at Berlin chiefly, and then I continued on my own account. The trouble was the secrecy. You see, if once I had let out what I was doing, other men might have been spurred on by my belief in the practicability of the idea; and I do not pretend to be such a genius as to have been sure of coming in first, in the case of a race for the discovery.

And you see it was important that if I really meant to make a pile, people should not know it was an artificial process and capable of turning out diamonds by the ton. So I had to work all alone.

"At first I had a little laboratory, but as my resources began to run out I had to conduct my experiments in a wretched unfurnished room in Kentish Town, where I slept at last on a straw mattress on the floor among all my apparatus. The money simply flowed away. I grudged myself everything except scientific appliances. I tried to keep things going by a little teaching, but I am not a very good teacher, and I have no university degree, nor very much education except in chemistry, and I found I had to give a lot of time and labour for precious little money. But I got nearer and nearer the thing. Three years ago I settled the problem of the composition of the flux, and got near the pressure by putting this flux of mine and a certain carbon composition into a closed-up gun-barrel, filling up with water, sealing tightly, and heating."

He paused.

"Rather risky," said I.

"Yes. It burst, and smashed all my windows and a lot of my apparatus; but I got a kind of diamond powder nevertheless. Following out the problem of getting a big pressure upon the molten mixture from which the things were to crystallise, I hit upon some researches of Daubrée's at the Paris *Laboratorie des Poudres et Salpêtres*. He exploded dynamite in a tightly screwed steel cylinder, too strong to burst, and I found he could crush rocks into a muck not unlike the South African bed in which diamonds are found.

"It was a tremendous strain on my resources, but I got a steel cylinder made for my purpose after his pattern. I put in all my stuff and my explosives, built up a fire in my furnace, put the whole concern in, and—went out for a walk."

I could not help laughing at his matter-of-fact manner. "Did you not think it would blow up the house? Were there other people in the place?"

"It was in the interests of science," he said ultimately. "There was a costermonger family on the floor below, a begging-letter writer in the room behind mine, and two flower-women were upstairs. Perhaps it was a bit thoughtless. But possibly some of them were out.

"When I came back the thing was just where I left it, among the white hot coals. The explosive hadn't burst the case. And then I had a problem to face. You know time is an important element in crystallisation. If you hurry the process the crystals are small—it is only by prolonged standing that they grow to any size. I resolved to let this apparatus cool for two years, letting the temperature go down slowly during that time. And I was now quite out of money; and with a big fire and the rent of my room, as well as my hunger to satisfy, I had scarcely a penny in the world.

"I can hardly tell you all the shifts I was put to while I was making the diamonds. I have sold newspapers, held horses, opened cab-doors. For many weeks I addressed envelopes. I had a place as assistant to a man who owned a barrow, and used to call down one side of the road while he called down the other. Once, for a week, I had absolutely nothing to do, and I begged. What a week that was! One day the fire was going out and I had eaten nothing all day, and a little chap, taking his girl out, gave me sixpence—to show off. Thank heaven for vanity! How the fish-shops smelt! But I went and spent it all on coals, and had the furnace bright red again, and then—Well, hunger makes a fool of a man.

"At last, three weeks ago, I let the fire out. I took my cylinder and unscrewed it while it was still so hot that it punished my hands, and I scraped out the crumbling lava-like mass with a chisel, and hammered it into a powder upon an iron plate. And I found three big diamonds and five small ones. As I sat on the floor hammering, my door opened, and my neighbour, the begging-letter writer, came in. He was drunk—as he usually is. ''Nechist,' said he. 'You're drunk,' said I. ''Structive scoundrel,' said he, 'Go to your father,' said I, meaning the Father of Lies. 'Never you mind,' said he, and gave me a cunning wink, and hiccuped, and leaning up against the door, with his other eye against the door-post, began to babble of how he had been prying in my room, and how he had gone to the police that morning, and how they had taken down everything he had to say —' 'siffiwas a ge'm,' said he.

"Then I suddenly realised I was in a hole. Either I should have to tell these police my little secret, and get the whole thing blown upon, or be lagged as an Anarchist. So I went up to my neighbour and took him by the collar, and rolled him about a bit, and then I gathered up my diamonds and cleared out. The evening newspapers called my den the Kentish Town Bomb Factory. And now I cannot part with the things for love or money.

"If I go to a respectable jeweller's they ask me to wait, and go and whisper to a clerk to fetch a policeman, and then I say I cannot wait. And I found out a receiver of stolen goods, and he simply stuck to the one I gave him and told me to prosecute if I wanted it back. I am going about now with several hundred thousand pounds' worth of diamonds round my neck, and without either food or shelter. You are the first person I have taken into my confidence. But I like your face and I am hard driven."

He looked into my eyes.

"It would be madness," said I, "for me to buy a diamond under the circumstances.

"I took him by the collar, and rolled him about a bit."

Besides, I do not carry hundreds of pounds about in my pocket. Yet I more than half believe your story. I will, if you like, do this: come to my office to-morrow. . . ."

"You think I am a thief!" said he keenly. "You will tell the police. I am not coming into a trap."

"Somehow I am assured you are no thief. Here is my card. Take that, anyhow. You need not come to any appointment. Come when you will."

He took the card, and an earnest of my good-will.

"Think better of it and come," said I.

He shook his head doubtfully. " I will pay back your half-crown with interest some day—such interest as will amaze you," said he. " Anyhow, you will keep the secret? . . . Don't follow me."

He crossed the road and went into the darkness towards the little steps under the archway leading into Essex Street, and I let him go. And that was the last I ever saw of him.

Afterwards I had two letters from him asking me to send banknotes—not cheques— to certain addresses. I weighed the matter over, and took what I conceived to be the wisest course. Once he called upon me when I was out. My urchin described him as a very thin, dirty, and ragged man, with a dreadful cough. He left no message. That was the finish of him so far as my story goes.

I wonder sometimes what has become of him. Was he an ingenious monomaniac, or a fraudulent dealer in pebbles, or has he really made diamonds as he asserted? The latter is just sufficiently credible to make me think at times that I have missed the most brilliant opportunity of my life. He may, of course, be dead, and his diamonds carelessly thrown aside—one, I repeat, was almost as big as my thumb. Or he may be still wandering about trying to sell the things. It is just possible he may yet emerge upon society, and, passing athwart my heavens in the serene altitude sacred to the wealthy and the well advertised, reproach me silently for my want of enterprise. I sometimes think I might at least have risked five pounds.

THE STORY OF
THE INEXPERIENCED GHOST

Originally published in *The Strand Magazine*
March 1902

THE STORY OF THE INEXPERIENCED GHOST

By H. G. Wells.

THE scene amidst which Clayton told his last story comes back very vividly to my mind. There he sat, for the most part of the time, in the corner of the authentic settle by the spacious open fire, and Sanderson sat beside him smoking the Broseley clay that bore his name. There was Evans, and that marvel among actors, Wish, who is also a modest man. We had all come down to the Mermaid Club that Saturday morning, except Clayton, who had slept there overnight—which indeed gave him the opening of his story. We had golfed until golfing was invisible; we had dined, and we were in that mood of tranquil kindliness when men will suffer a story. When Clayton began to tell one, we naturally supposed he was lying. It may be that indeed he was lying—of that the reader will speedily be able to judge as well as I. He began, it is true, with an air of matter-of-fact anecdote, but that we thought was only the incurable artifice of the man.

"I say!" he remarked, after a long con-sideration of the upward rain of sparks from the log that Sanderson had thumped, "you know I was alone here last night?"

"Except for the domestics," said Wish.

"Who sleep in the other wing," said Clayton. "Yes. Well——" He pulled at his cigar for some little time as though he still hesitated about his confidence. Then he said, quite quietly, "I caught a ghost!"

"Caught a ghost, did you?" said Sanderson. "Where is it?"

And Evans, who admires Clayton immensely and has been four weeks in America, shouted, "*Caught* a ghost, did you, Clayton? I'm glad of it! Tell us all about it right now."

Clayton said he would in a minute, and asked him to shut the door.

He looked apologetically at me. "There's no eavesdropping of course, but we don't want to upset our very excellent service with any rumours of ghosts in the place. There's too much shadow and oak panelling to trifle with that. And this, you know, wasn't a regular ghost. I don't think it will come again—ever."

259

"You mean to say you didn't keep it?" said Sanderson.

"I hadn't the heart to," said Clayton.

And Sanderson said he was surprised.

We laughed, and Clayton looked aggrieved. "I know," he said, with the flicker of a smile, "but the fact is it really *was* a ghost, and I'm as sure of it as I am that I am talking to you now. I'm not joking. I mean what I say."

Sanderson drew deeply at his pipe, with one reddish eye on Clayton, and then emitted a thin jet of smoke more eloquent than many words.

Clayton ignored the comment. "It is the strangest thing that has ever happened in my life. You know I never believed in ghosts or anything of the sort before, ever; and then, you know, I bag one in a corner; and the whole business is in my hands."

He meditated still more profoundly and produced and began to pierce a second cigar with a curious little stabber he affected.

"You talked to it?" asked Wish.

"For the space, probably, of an hour."

"Chatty?" I said, joining the party of the sceptics.

"The poor devil was in trouble," said Clayton, bowed over his cigar-end and with the very faintest note of reproof.

"Sobbing?" someone asked.

Clayton heaved a realistic sigh at the memory. "Good Lord!" he said; "yes." And then, "Poor fellow! yes."

"Where did you strike it?" asked Evans, in his best American accent.

"I never realized," said Clayton, ignoring him, "the poor sort of thing a ghost might be," and he hung us up again for a time, while he sought for matches in his pocket and lit and warmed to his cigar.

"I took an advantage," he reflected at last.

We were none of us in a hurry. "A character," he said, "remains just the same character for all that it's been disembodied. That's a thing we too often forget. People with a certain strength or fixity of purpose may have ghosts of a certain strength and fixity of purpose—most haunting ghosts, you know, must be as one-idea'd as monomaniacs and as obstinate as mules to come back again and again. This poor creature wasn't." He suddenly looked up rather queerly, and his eye went round the room. "I say it," he said, "in all kindliness, but that is the plain truth of the case. Even at the first glance he struck me as weak."

He punctuated with the help of his cigar.

"I came upon him, you know, in the long passage. His back was to me and I saw him first. Right off I knew him for a ghost. He was transparent and whitish; clean through his chest I could see the glimmer of the little window at the end. And not only his physique but his attitude struck me as being weak. He looked, you know, as though he didn't know in the slightest whatever he meant to do. One hand was on the panelling and the other fluttered to his mouth. Like—*so!*"

"What sort of physique?" said Sanderson.

"Lean. You know that sort of young man's neck that has two great flutings down the back, here and here—so! And a little, meanish head with scrubby hair and rather bad ears. Shoulders bad, narrower than the hips; turndown collar, ready-made short jacket, trousers baggy and a little frayed at the heels. That's how he took me. I came very quietly up the staircase. I did not carry a light, you know—the candles are on the landing table and there is that lamp—and I was in my list slippers, and I saw him as I came up. I stopped dead at that—taking him in. I wasn't a bit afraid. I think that in most of these affairs one is never nearly so afraid or excited as one imagines one would be. I was surprised and interested. I thought, 'Good Lord! Here's a ghost at last! And I haven't believed for a moment in ghosts during the last five-and-twenty years.'"

"Um," said Wish.

"I suppose I wasn't there a moment before he found out I was there. He turned on me sharply and I saw the face of an immature young man, a weak nose, a scrubby little moustache, a feeble chin. So for an instant we stood—he looking over his shoulder at me—and regarded one another. Then he seemed to remember his high calling. He turned round, drew himself up, projected his face, raised his arms, spread his hands in approved ghost fashion—came towards me. As he did so his little jaw dropped, and he emitted a faint, drawn-out 'Boo.' No, it wasn't—not a bit dreadful. I'd dined. I'd had a bottle of champagne and, being all alone, perhaps two or three—perhaps even four or five—whiskies, so I was as solid as rocks and no more frightened than if I'd been assailed by a frog. 'Boo!' I said. 'Nonsense. You don't belong to *this* place. What are you doing here?'

"I could see him wince. 'Boo-oo,' he said.

"'Boo—be hanged! Are you a member?' I said; and just to show I didn't care a pin for him I stepped through a corner of him and made to light my candle. 'Are you a member?' I repeated, looking at him sideways.

"He moved a little so as to stand clear of me, and his bearing became crestfallen. 'No,' he said, in answer to the persistent interrogation of my eye; 'I'm not a member —I'm a ghost.'

"'Well, that doesn't give you the run of the Mermaid Club. Is there anyone you want to see, or anything of that sort?' And doing it as steadily as possible for fear that he should mistake the carelessness of whisky for the distraction of fear, I got my candle alight. I turned on him, holding it. 'What are you doing here?' I said.

business to haunt here. This is a respectable private club; people often stop here with nursemaids and children, and, going about in the careless way you do, some poor little mite might easily come upon you and be scared out of her wits. I suppose you didn't think of that?'

"'No, sir,' he said, 'I didn't.'

"'You should have done. You haven't any claim on the place, have you? Weren't murdered here, or anything of that sort?'

"'None, sir; but I thought as it was old and oak-panelled——'

"'That's *no* excuse.' I regarded him firmly. 'Your coming here is a mistake,' I said, in a tone of friendly superiority. I feigned to see if I had my matches and then looked up at him frankly. 'If I were you

"'WHAT ARE YOU DOING HERE?' I SAID."

"He had dropped his hands and stopped his booing, and there he stood, abashed and awkward, the ghost of a weak, silly, aimless young man. 'I'm haunting,' he said.

"'You haven't any business to,' I said, in a quiet voice.

"'I'm a ghost,' he said, as if in defence.

"'That may be, but you haven't any

I wouldn't wait for cock-crow—I'd vanish right away.'

"He looked embarrassed. 'The fact *is*, sir——' he began.

"'I'd vanish,' I said, driving it home.

"'The fact is, sir, that—somehow—I can't.'

"'You *can't*?'

"'No, sir. There's something I've forgotten. I've been hanging about here since midnight last night, hiding in the cupboards of the empty bedrooms and things like that. I'm flurried. I've never come haunting before, and it seems to put me out.'

"'Put you out?'

"'Yes, sir. I've tried to do it several times, and it doesn't come off. There's some little thing has slipped me, and I can't get back.'

"That, you know, rather bowled me over. He looked at me in such an abject way that for the life of me I couldn't keep up quite the high, hectoring vein I had adopted. 'That's queer,' I said, and as I spoke I fancied I heard someone moving about down below. 'Come into my room and tell me more about it,' I said. 'I didn't, of course, understand this,' and I tried to take him by the arm. But, of course, you might as well have tried to take hold of a puff of smoke! I had forgotten my number, I think; anyhow, I remember going into several bedrooms— it was lucky I was the only soul in that wing

prefer to flit up and down the room if it was all the same to me. And so he did, and in a little while we were deep in a long and serious talk. And presently, you know, something of those whiskies and sodas evaporated out of me, and I began to realize just a little what a thundering rum and weird business it was that I was in. There he was, semi-transparent—the proper conventional phantom, and noiseless except for his ghost of a voice—flitting to and fro in that nice, clean, chintz-hung old bedroom. You could see the gleam of the copper candlesticks through him, and the lights on the brass fender, and the corners of the framed engravings on the wall, and there he was telling me all about this wretched little life of his that had recently ended on earth. He hadn't a particularly honest face, you know, but being transparent, of course, he couldn't avoid telling the truth."

"Eh?" said Wish, suddenly sitting up in his chair.

"What?" said Clayton.

"Being transparent — couldn't avoid

"HE SAID HE WOULDN'T SIT DOWN; HE'D PREFER TO FLIT UP AND DOWN THE ROOM."

—until I saw my traps. 'Here we are,' I said, and sat down in the arm-chair; 'sit down and tell me all about it. It seems to me you have got yourself into a jolly awkward position, old chap.'

"Well, he said he wouldn't sit down; he'd

telling the truth—I don't see it," said Wish.

"*I* don't see it," said Clayton, with inimitable assurance. "But it *is* so, I can assure you nevertheless. I don't believe he got once a nail's breadth off the Bible truth.

He told me how he had been killed—he went down into a London basement with a candle to look for a leakage of gas—and described himself as a senior English master in a London private school when that release occurred."

" Poor wretch ! " said I.

" That's what I thought, and the more he talked the more I thought it. There he was, purposeless in life and purposeless out of it. He talked of his father and mother and his schoolmaster, and all who had ever been anything to him in the world, meanly. He had been too sensitive, too nervous; none of them had ever valued him properly or understood him, he said. He had never had a real friend in the world, I think ; he had never had a success. He had shirked games and failed examinations. ' It's like that with some people,' he said ; ' whenever I get into the examination-room or anywhere everything seems to go.' Engaged to be married of course—to another over-sensitive person, I suppose—when the indiscretion with the gas escape ended his affairs. ' And where are you now ? ' I asked. ' Not in —— ? '

" He wasn't clear on that point at all. The impression he gave me was of a sort of vague, intermediate state, a special reserve for souls too non-existent for anything so positive as either sin or virtue. *I* don't know. He was much too egotistical and unobservant to give me any clear idea of the kind of place, kind of country, there is on the Other Side of Things. Wherever he was, he seems to have fallen in with a set of kindred spirits : ghosts of weak Cockney young men, who were on a footing of Christian names, and among these there was certainly a lot of talk about 'going haunting' and things like that. Yes—going haunting ! They seemed to think 'haunting' a tremendous adventure, and most of them funked it all the time. And so primed, you know, he had come."

" But really ! " said Wish to the fire.

" These are the impressions he gave me, anyhow," said Clayton, modestly. " I may, of course, have been in a rather uncritical state, but that was the sort of background he gave to himself. He kept flitting up and down, with his thin voice going—talking, talking about his wretched self, and never a word of clear, firm statement from first to last. He was thinner and sillier and more pointless than if he had been real and alive. Only then, you know, he would not have been in my bedroom here —— if he *had* been alive. I should have kicked him out."

" Of course," said Evans, " there *are* poor mortals like that."

" And there's just as much chance of their having ghosts as the rest of us," I admitted.

" What gave a sort of point to him, you know, was the fact that he did seem within limits to have found himself out. The mess he had made of haunting had depressed him terribly. He had been told it would be a 'lark'; he had come expecting it to be a 'lark,' and here it was, nothing but another failure added to his record ! He proclaimed himself an utter out-and-out failure. He said, and I can quite believe it, that he had never tried to do anything all his life that he hadn't made a perfect mess of—and through all the wastes of eternity he never would. If he had had sympathy, perhaps—— He paused at that, and stood regarding me. He remarked that, strange as it might seem to me, nobody, not anyone, ever, had given him the amount of sympathy I was doing now. I could see what he wanted straight away, and I determined to head him off at once. I may be a brute, you know, but being the Only Real Friend, the recipient of the confidences of one of these egotistical weaklings, ghost or body, is beyond my physical endurance. I got up briskly. ' Don't you brood on these things too much,' I said. ' The thing you've got to do is to get out of this—get out of this sharp. You pull yourself together and *try*.' ' I can't,' he said. ' You try,' I said, and try he did."

" Try ! " said Sanderson. " *How* ? "

" Passes," said Clayton.

" Passes ? "

" Complicated series of gestures and passes with the hands. That's how he had come in and that's how he had to get out again. Lord ! what a business I had ! "

" But how could *any* series of passes——." I began.

" My dear man," said Clayton, turning on me and putting a great emphasis on certain words, " you want *everything* clear. *I* don't know *how*. All I know is that you *do*—that *he* did, anyhow, at least. After a fearful time, you know, he got his passes right and suddenly disappeared."

" Did you," said Sanderson, slowly, " observe the passes ? "

" Yes," said Clayton, and seemed to think. " It was tremendously queer," he said. " There we were, I and this thin vague ghost, in that silent room, in this silent, empty inn, in this silent little Friday-night town. Not a sound except our voices and a faint panting he made when he swung. There was the bedroom candle, and one candle on the dressing-table alight, that was all—sometimes one or other would flare up into a tall, lean, astonished flame for a space. And queer things happened. 'I can't,' he said; 'I shall never——!' And suddenly he sat down on a little chair at the foot of the bed and began to sob and sob. Lord! what a harrowing, whimpering thing he seemed!

"'You pull yourself together,' I said, and tried to pat him on the back, and, you know, my confounded hand went through him. By that time, you know, I wasn't nearly so —massive as I had been on the landing. I got the queerness of it full. I remember

his finger in his pipe-bowl. "You mean to say this ghost of yours gave away——"

"Did his level best to give away the whole confounded barrier? *Yes.*"

"He didn't," said Wish; "he couldn't. Or you'd have gone there too."

"That's precisely it," I said, finding my elusive idea put into words for me.

"That *is* precisely it," said Clayton, with thoughtful eyes upon the fire.

For just a little while there was silence.

"And at last he did it?" said Sanderson.

"At last he did it. I had to keep him up to it hard, but he did it at last—rather suddenly. He despaired, we had a scene,

"I GOT THE QUEERNESS OF IT FULL."

snatching back my hand out of him, as it were, with a little thrill, and walking over to the dressing-table. 'You pull yourself together,' I said to him, 'and try.' And in order to encourage and help him I began to try as well."

"What!" said Sanderson, "the passes?"

"Yes, the passes."

"But——" I said, moved by an idea that eluded me for a space.

"This is interesting," said Sanderson, with

and then he got up suddenly and asked me to go through the whole performance, slowly, so that he might see. 'I believe,' he said, 'if I could *see* I should spot what was wrong at once.' And he did. '*I* know,' he said. 'What do you know?' said I. '*I* know,' he repeated. Then he said, suddenly, 'I *can't* do it if you look at me—I really *can't;* it's been that, partly, all along. I'm such a nervous fellow that you put me out.' Well, we had a bit of an argument. Naturally I wanted to see ; but he was as obstinate as a mule, and suddenly I had come over as tired as a dog—he tired me out. 'All right,' I said, '*I* won't look at you,' and turned towards the mirror, on the wardrobe, by the bed.

"He started off very fast. I tried to follow him by looking in the looking-glass, to see just what it was had hung. Round went his arms and his hands, so, and so, and so, and then with a rush came to the last gesture of all—you stand erect and open out your arms—and so, don't you know, he stood. And then he didn't ! He didn't ! He wasn't ! I wheeled round from the looking-glass to him. There was nothing ! I was alone, with the flaring candles and a staggering mind. What had happened ? Had

"I WAS ALONE."

anything happened ? Had I been dreaming ? . . . . And then, with an absurd note of finality about it, the clock upon the landing discovered the moment was ripe for striking *one*. So !—Ping ! And I was as grave and sober as a judge, with all my champagne and whisky gone into the vast serene. Feeling queer, you know — confoundedly *queer !* Queer ! Good Lord !' "

He regarded his cigar-ash for a moment. " That's all that happened," he said.

" And then you went to bed ? " asked Evans.

" What else was there to do ? "

I looked Wish in the eye. We wanted to scoff, and there was something, something perhaps in Clayton's voice and manner, that hampered our desire.

" And about these passes ? " said Sanderson.

" I believe I could do them now."

" Oh ! " said Sanderson, and produced a pen-knife and set himself to grub the dottel out of the bowl of his clay.

" Why don't you do them now ? " said Sanderson, shutting his pen-knife with a click.

" That's what I'm going to do," said Clayton.

" They won't work," said Evans.

" If they do——" I suggested.

" You know, I'd rather you didn't," said Wish, stretching out his legs.

" Why ? " asked Evans.

" I'd rather he didn't," said Wish.

" But he hasn't got 'em right," said Sanderson, plugging too much tobacco into his pipe.

" All the same, I'd rather he didn't," said Wish.

We argued with Wish. He said that for Clayton to go through those gestures was like mocking a serious matter. " But you don't believe ——— ? " I said. Wish glanced at Clayton, who was staring into the fire, weighing something in his mind. " I do —more than half, anyhow, I do," said Wish.

" Clayton," said I, " you're too good a liar for us. Most of it was all right. But that disappearance . . . . happened to be convincing. Tell us, it's a tale of cock and bull."

He stood up without heeding me, took the middle of the hearthrug, and faced me. For a moment he regarded his feet thoughtfully, and then for all the rest of the time his eyes were on the opposite wall, with an intent expression. He raised his two hands slowly to the level of his eyes and so began. . . .

Now, Sanderson is a Freemason, a member of the lodge of the Four Kings, which devotes itself so ably to the study and elucidation of all the mysteries of Masonry past and present, and among the students of this lodge Sanderson is by no means the least. He followed Clayton's motions with a singular interest in his reddish eye. "That's not bad," he said, when it was done. "You really do, you know, put things together, Clayton, in a most amazing fashion. But there's one little detail out."

"I know," said Clayton. "I believe I could tell you which."

"Well?"

"This," said Clayton, and did a queer little twist and writhing and thrust of the hands.

"Yes."

"That, you know, was what *he* couldn't get right," said Clayton. "But how do *you*——?"

"Most of this business, and particularly how you invented it, I don't understand at all," said Sanderson, "but just that phase—I do." He reflected. "These happen to be a series of gestures—connected with a certain branch of esoteric Masonry—— Probably you know. Or else—— *How?*" He reflected still further. "I do not see I can do any harm in telling you just the proper twist. After all, if you know, you know; if you don't, you don't."

"I know nothing," said Clayton, "except what the poor devil let out last night."

"Well, anyhow," said Sanderson, and placed his churchwarden very carefully upon the shelf over the fireplace. Then very rapidly he gesticulated with his hands.

"So?" said Clayton, repeating.

"So," said Sanderson, and took his pipe in hand again.

"Ah, *now*," said Clayton, "I can do the whole thing—right."

He stood up before the waning fire and smiled at us all. But I think there was just a little hesitation in his smile. "If I begin——" he said.

"I wouldn't begin," said Wish.

"It's all right!" said Evans. "Matter is indestructible. You don't think any jiggery-pokery of this sort is going to snatch Clayton into the world of shades. Not it! You may try, Clayton, so far as I'm concerned, until your arms drop off at the wrists."

"I don't believe that," said Wish, and stood up and put his arm on Clayton's shoulder. "You've made me half believe in that story somehow, and I don't want to see the thing done."

"Goodness!" said I, "here's Wish frightened!"

"I am," said Wish, with real or admirably feigned intensity. "I believe that if he goes through these motions right he'll *go*."

"He'll not do anything of the sort," I cried. "There's only one way out of this world for men, and Clayton is thirty years from that. Besides . . . And such a ghost! Do you think——?"

Wish interrupted me by moving. He walked out from among our chairs and stopped beside the table and stood there. "Clayton," he said, "you're a fool."

Clayton, with a humorous light in his eyes, smiled back at him. "Wish," he said, "is right and all you others are wrong. I shall go. I shall get to the end of these passes, and as the last swish whistles through the air, Presto!—this hearthrug will be vacant, the room will be blank amazement, and a respectably dressed gentleman of seventeen stone will plump into the world of shades. I'm certain. So will you be. I decline to argue further. Let the thing be tried."

"*No*," said Wish, and made a step and ceased, and Clayton raised his hands once more to repeat the spirit's passing.

By that time, you know, we were all in a state of tension—largely because of the behaviour of Wish. We sat all of us with our eyes on Clayton—I, at least, with a sort of tight, stiff feeling about me as though from the back of my skull to the middle of my thighs my body had been changed to steel. And there, with a gravity that was imperturbably serene, Clayton bowed and swayed and waved his hands and arms before us. As he drew towards the end one piled up, one tingled in one's teeth. The last gesture, I have said, was to swing the arms out wide open, with the face held up. And when at last he swung out to this closing gesture I ceased even to breathe. It was ridiculous, of course, but you know that ghost-story feeling. It was after dinner, in a queer, old shadowy house. Would he, after all——?

There he stood for one stupendous moment, with his arms open and his upturned face, assured and bright, in the glare of the hanging lamp. We hung through that moment as if it were an age, and then came from all of us something that was half a sigh of infinite relief and half a reassuring "*No!*" For visibly—he wasn't going. It was all nonsense. He had told an idle story, and carried it almost to conviction, that was all! . . . . And then in that moment the face of Clayton changed.

It changed. It changed as a lit house

"HE STOOD THERE, VERY GENTLY SWAYING."

changes when its lights are suddenly extinguished. His eyes were suddenly eyes that are fixed, his smile was frozen on his lips, and he stood there still. He stood there, very gently swaying.

That moment, too, was an age. And then, you know, chairs were scraping, things were falling, and we were all moving. His knees seemed to give, and he fell forward, and Evans rose and caught him in his arms. . . . .

It stunned us all. For a minute I suppose no one said a coherent thing. We believed it, yet could not believe it. . . . . I came out of a muddled stupefaction to find myself kneeling beside him, and his vest and shirt were torn open, and Sanderson's hand lay on his heart. . . . .

Well—the simple fact before us could very well wait our convenience ; there was no hurry for us to comprehend. It lay there for an hour ; it lies athwart my memory, black and amazing still, to this day. Clayton had, indeed, passed into the world that lies so near to and so far from our own, and he had gone thither by the only road that mortal man may take. But whether he did indeed pass there by that poor ghost's incantation, or whether he was stricken suddenly by apoplexy in the midst of an idle tale—as the coroner's jury would have us believe—is no matter for my judging ; is just one of those inexplicable riddles that must remain unsolved until the final solution of all things shall come. All I certainly know is that, in the very moment, in the very instant, of concluding these passes he changed, and staggered and fell down before us—dead !

—8—

THE EMPIRE OF THE ANTS

Originally published in *The Strand Magazine*
December 1905

The Empire of the Ants.

By H. G. Wells.

I.

 WHEN Captain Gerilleau received instructions to take his new gunboat, the *Benjamin Constant*, to Badama on the Batemo arm of the Guaramadema and there assist the inhabitants against a plague of ants, he suspected the authorities of mockery. His promotion had been romantic and irregular ; the affections of a prominent Brazilian lady and the captain's liquid eyes had played a part in the process, and the *Diario* and *O Futuro* had been lamentably disrespectful in their comments. He felt he was to give further occasion for disrespect.

He was a Creole, his conceptions of etiquette and discipline were pure-blooded Portuguese, and it was only to Holroyd, the Lancashire engineer who had come over with the boat, and as an exercise in the use of English—his " th " sounds were very uncertain—that he opened his heart.

"It is in effect," he said, "to make me absurd ! What can a man do against ants ? Dey come, dey go."

"They say," said Holroyd, "that these don't go. That chap you said was a Sambo——"

"Zambo ;—it is a sort of mixture of blood."

"Sambo. He said the people are going."

The captain smoked fretfully for a time. " Dese tings 'ave to happen," he said at last. "What is it ? Plagues of ants and suchlike as God wills. Dere was a plague in Trinidad—the little ants that carry leaves. Orl der orange trees, all der mangoes ! What does it matter ? Sometimes ant armies come into your houses—fighting ants ; a different sort. You go and they clean the house. Then you come back again ;—the house is clean, like new ! No fleas, no jiggers in the floor."

"That Sambo chap," said Holroyd, " says these are a different sort of ant."

The captain shrugged his shoulders, fumed, and gave his attention to a cigarette.

Afterwards he reopened the subject. " My dear 'Olroyd, what am I to do about dese infernal ants ? "

"You're asking me ? "

"Yes," said Gerilleau, reluctantly, and broke out. " But it is a confounded shame ! 'Ere I 'ave got dis gun ! Very likely I shall never use it—never ! And an insurrection in Parana—practically—*now*. They will not let me target practise. . . . But about dese ants ! "

"They say corrosive sublimate is rather good for them. You ought to lay in some of that. Then chalk, or lime, or whiting—what you do dancing girls' shoes with."

" Ah, precisely ! " said the captain.

" And carbolic acid. After all—you've got to pull the job *.off*, you know. You've got to make a success of it."

The captain reflected. " It is ridiculous," he said. But in the afternoon he put on his full uniform and went ashore, and jars and boxes came back to the ship and subsequently he did. And Holroyd sat on deck in the evening coolness and smoked profoundly and marvelled at Brazil. They were six days up the Amazon, some hundreds of miles from the ocean, and east and west of him there was an horizon like the sea, and to the south nothing but a sand-bank island with some tufts of scrub. The water was always running like a sluice, thick with dirt, animated with crocodiles and hovering birds, and fed by some inexhaustible source of tree-trunks ; and the waste of it, the headlong waste of it, filled his soul. The town of Alemquer with its meagre church, its thatched sheds for houses, its discoloured ruins of ampler days, seemed a little thing lost in this wilderness of Nature, a sixpence dropped on Sahara. He was a young man, this was his first sight of the tropics, he came straight from England, where Nature is hedged, ditched, and drained into the perfection of submission, and he had suddenly discovered the insignificance of man. For six days they had been steaming up from the sea by unfrequented channels and man had been as rare as a rare butterfly. One saw, one day a canoe, another day a distant station, the next no men at all. He began to perceive that man is indeed a rare animal, having but a precarious hold upon this land.

He perceived it more clearly as the days passed and he made his devious way to the Batemo, in the company of this remarkable commander who ruled over one big gun, and was forbidden to waste his ammunition. Holroyd was learning Spanish industriously, but he was still in the present tense and substantive stage of speech, and the only other person who had any words of English was a negro stoker who had them all wrong. The second in command was a Portuguese " da Cunha " who spoke French, but it was a different sort of French from the French Holroyd had learnt in Southport, and their intercourse was confined to politenesses and simple propositions about the weather. And the weather, like everything else in this amazing new world—the weather had no human aspect, and was hot by night and hot by day, and the air steam, even the wind was hot steam, smelling of vegetation in decay : and the alligators and the strange birds, the flies of many sorts and sizes, the beetles, the ants, the snakes and monkeys, seemed to wonder what man was doing in an atmosphere that had no gladness in its sunshine and no coolness in its night. To wear clothing was intolerable, but to cast it aside was to scorch by day and expose an ampler area to the mosquitoes by night ; to go on deck by day was to be blinded by glare and to stay below was to suffocate. And in the daytime came certain flies, extremely clever and noxious about one's wrist and ankle. Captain Gerilleau, who was Holroyd's sole distraction from these physical distresses, developed into a formidable bore, telling the simple story of his heart's affections day by day, a string of anonymous women, as if he were telling beads. Sometimes he suggested sport, and they shot at alligators, and at rare intervals they came to human aggregations in the waste of trees, and stayed for a day or so, and drank and sat about, and, one night, danced with Creole girls, who found Holroyd's poor elements of Spanish, without either past tense or future, amply sufficient for their purposes. But these were mere luminous chinks in the long grey passage of the steaming river, up which the throbbing engines beat. A certain liberal heathen deity in the shape of a demijohn, held seductive court aft, and, it is probable, forward.

But Gerilleau learnt things about the ants, more things and more, at this stopping place and that, and became interested in his mission.

" Dey are a new sort of ant," he said. " We have got to be—what do you call it ?—entomologie ? Big. Five centimetres ! Some bigger ! It is ridiculous. We are like the monkeys—sent to pick insects. . . . But dey are eating up the country."

He burst out indignantly. " Suppose—suddenly, there are complications with Europe. Here am I—soon we shall be above the Rio Negro—and my gun, useless ! "

He nursed his knee and mused.

" Dose people who were dere at de dancing place, dey 'ave come down. Dey 'ave lost all they got. De ants come to deir 'ouse one afternoon. Everyone run out. You know when de ants come one must—everyone runs out and they go over the house. If you stayed they'd eat you. See ? Well, presently dey go back ; dey say, ' The ants 'ave gone.' . . . De ants 'aven't gone. Dey try to go in—de son, 'e goes in. De ants fight."

" Swarm over him ? "

" Bite 'im. Presently he comes out again —screaming and running. He runs past them to the river. See ? He gets into de water and drowns de ants—yes." Gerilleau paused, brought his liquid eyes close to Holroyd's face, tapped Holroyd's knee with his knuckle. " That night he dies, just as if he was stung by a snake."

" Poisoned—by the ants ? "

" Who knows ? " Gerilleau shrugged his shoulders. " Perhaps they bit him badly. . . . When I joined dis service I joined to fight men. Dese things, dese ants, dey come and go. It is no business for men."

After that he talked frequently of the ants to Holroyd, and whenever they chanced to drift against any speck of humanity in that waste of water and sunshine and distant trees, Holroyd's improving knowledge of the language enabled him to recognise the ascendant word Saüba, more and more completely dominating the whole.

He perceived the ants were becoming interesting, and the nearer he drew to them the more interesting they became. Gerilleau abandoned his old themes, almost suddenly, and the Portuguese lieutenant became a conversational figure ; he knew something about the leaf-cutting ant, and expanded his knowledge. Gerilleau sometimes rendered what he had to tell to Holroyd. He told of the little workers that swarm and fight, and the big workers that command and rule, and how these latter always crawled to the neck and how their bites drew blood. He told how they cut leaves and made fungus beds, and how their nests in Caracas are sometimes a hundred yards across. Two days the three men spent disputing whether ants have eyes. The discussion grew dangerously heated on the second afternoon, and Holroyd saved the situation by going ashore in a boat to catch ants and see. He captured various specimens and returned, and some had eyes and some hadn't. Also, they argued, do ants bite or sting ?

" Dese ants," said Gerilleau after collecting

information at a rancho, "have big eyes. They don't run about blind—not as most ants do. No! Dey get in corners and watch what you do."

"And they sting?" asked Holroyd.

"Yes. Dey sting. Dere is poison in the sting." He meditated. "I do not see what men can do against ants. Dey come and go."

"But these don't go."

"They will," said Gerilleau.

Past Tamandu there is a long low coast of eighty miles without any population, and then one comes to the confluence of the main river and the Batemo arm like a great lake, and then the forest came nearer, came at last intimately near. The character of the channel changes, snags abound, and the *Benjamin Constant* moored by a cable that night, under the very shadow of dark trees. For the first time for many days came a spell of coolness, and Holroyd and Gerilleau sat late, smoking cigars and enjoying this delicious sensation. Gerilleau's mind was full of ants and what they could do. He decided to sleep at last, and lay down on a mattress on deck, a man hopelessly perplexed, his last words, when he already seemed asleep, being to ask with a flourish of despair, "What can one do with ants? . . . De whole thing is absurd."

Holroyd was left to scratch his bitten wrists, and meditate alone. He sat on the bulwark and listened to the little changes in Gerilleau's breathing until he was fast asleep, and then the ripple and lap of the stream took his mind and brought back that sense of immensity that had been growing upon him since first he had left Para and come up the river. The monitor showed but one small light, and there was first a little talking forward and then stillness. His eyes went from the dim black outlines of the middle works of the gunboat towards the bank, to the black, overwhelming mysteries of forest, lit now and then by a firefly, and never still from the murmur of alien and mysterious activities. . . .

It was the inhuman immensity of this land that astonished and oppressed him. He knew the skies were empty of men, the stars were specks in an incredible vastness of space; he knew the ocean was enormous and untamable, but in England he had come to think of the land as man's. In England it is indeed man's; the wild things live by sufferance, grow on lease; everywhere the roads, the fences, and absolute security runs. In an atlas too, the land is man's, and all coloured to show his claim to it—in vivid contrast to the universal independent blueness of the sea. He had taken it for granted that a day

"HOLROYD AND GERILLEAU SAT LATE, SMOKING."

would come when everywhere about the earth, plough and culture, light tramways and good roads, an ordered security, would prevail. But now; he doubted.

This forest was interminable, it had an air of being invincible, and Man seemed at best an infrequent, precarious intruder. One travelled for miles, amidst the still, silent struggle of giant trees, of strangulating creepers, of assertive flowers; everywhere the alligator, the turtle, and endless varieties of birds and insects seemed at home, dwelt irreplaceably; but man, man at most held a footing upon resentful clearings, fought weeds, fought beasts and insects for the barest foothold, fell a prey to snake and beast, insect and fever, and was presently carried away. In many places down the river he had been manifestly driven back, this deserted creek or that preserved the name of a *casa*, and here and there ruinous white walls and a shattered tower enforced the lesson. The puma, the jaguar, were more the masters here. . . .

Who were the real masters?

In a few miles of this forest there must be more ants than there were men in the whole world! This seemed to Holroyd a perfectly new idea. In a few thousand years men had emerged from barbarism to a stage of civilization that made them feel lords of the future and masters of the earth! But what was to prevent the ants evolving also? Such ants as one knew lived in little communities of a few thousand individuals, made no concerted efforts against the greater world. But they had a language, they had an intelligence! Why should things stop at that any more than men had stopped at the barbaric stage? Suppose presently the ants began to store knowledge just as men had done by means of books and records, use weapons, form great empires, sustain a planned and organized war?

Things came back to him that Gerilleau had gathered about these ants they were approaching. They used a poison like the poison of snakes. They obeyed greater leaders even as the leaf-cutting ants do. They were carnivorous, and where they came they stayed. . . .

The forest was very still. The water lapped incessantly against the side. About the lantern overhead there eddied a noiseless whirl of phantom moths.

Gerilleau stirred in the darkness and sighed. "Wha' can one *do?*" he murmured, and turned over and was still again.

Holroyd was roused from meditations that were becoming sinister by the hum of a mosquito.

II.

THE next morning Holroyd learnt they were within forty kilometres of Badama, and his interest in the banks intensified. He came up whenever an opportunity offered to examine his surroundings. He could see no signs of human occupation whatever, save for a weedy ruin of a house and the green-stained façade of the long-deserted monastery at Mojû, with a forest tree growing out of a vacant window space, and great creepers netted across its vacant portals. Several flights of strange yellow butterflies with semi-transparent wings crossed the river that morning, and many alighted on the monitor and were killed by the men. It was towards afternoon that they came upon the derelict *cuberta.*

She did not at first appear to be derelict; both her sails were set and hanging slack in the afternoon calm, and there was the figure of a man sitting on the fore planking beside the shipped sweeps. Another man appeared to be sleeping face downward on the sort of longitudinal bridge these big canoes have in the waist. But it was presently apparent from the sway of her rudder and the way she drifted into the course of the gunboat that something was out of order with her. Gerilleau surveyed her through a field-glass, and became interested in the queer darkness of the face of the sitting man, a red-faced man he seemed, without a nose—crouching he was rather than sitting; and the longer the captain looked the less he liked to look at him, and the less able he was to take his glasses away.

But he did so at last, and went a little way to call up Holroyd. Then he went back to hail the cuberta. He hailed her again, and so she drove past him. *Santa Rosa* stood out clearly as her name.

As she came by and into the wake of the monitor she pitched a little, and suddenly the figure of the crouching man collapsed as though all its joints had given way. His hat fell off, his head was not nice to look at, and his body flopped lax and rolled out of sight behind the bulwarks.

"Caramba!" cried Gerilleau, and resorted to Holroyd forthwith.

Holroyd was half-way up the companion. "Did you see dat?" said the captain.

"Dead!" said Holroyd. "Yes. You'd better send a boat aboard. There's something wrong."

"Did you—by any chance—see his face?"

"What was it like?"

"It was—ugh! I have no words." And the captain suddenly turned his back on Holroyd and became an active and strident commander.

The gunboat came about, steamed parallel to the erratic course of the canoe, and dropped the boat with Lieutenant da Cunha and three sailors to board her. Then the curiosity of the captain made him draw up almost alongside as the lieutenant got aboard the boat, so that the whole of the *Santa Rosa*, deck and hold, was visible to Holroyd.

He saw now clearly that the sole crew of the vessel was these two dead men, and though he could not see their faces, he saw by their outstretched hands, which were all of ragged flesh, that they had been subjected to some strange exceptional process of decay. For a moment his attention concentrated on those two enigmatical bundles of dirty clothes and laxly flung limbs, and then his eyes went forward to discover the open hold piled high with trunks and cases, and aft, to where the little cabin gaped inexplicably empty. Then he became aware that the planks of the middle decking were dotted with moving black specks.

His attention was riveted by these specks. They were all walking in directions radiating from the fallen man in a manner—the image came unsought to his mind—like the crowd dispersing from a bull-fight.

He became aware of Gerilleau beside him. "Capo," he said, "have you your glasses? Can you focus as closely as those planks there?"

Gerilleau made an effort, grunted, and handed him the glasses.

There followed a moment of scrutiny. "It's ants," said the Englishman, and handed the focused field-glass back to Gerilleau.

His impression of them was of a crowd of large black ants, very like ordinary ants except for their size, and for the fact that some of the larger of them bore a sort of clothing of grey. But at the time his inspection was too brief for particulars. The head of Lieutenant da Cunha appeared as he stood erect in the boat and looked over the side of the cuberta, and a brief colloquy ensued between them.

"You must go aboard," said Gerilleau.

"THE TWO MEN DISPUTED WITH A CERTAIN INCREASING VEHEMENCE."

The lieutenant objected that the boat was full of ants.

"You have your boots," said Gerilleau.

The lieutenant changed the subject. "How did these men die?" he asked.

Captain Gerilleau embarked upon speculations that Holroyd could not follow, and the two men disputed with a certain increasing vehemence. Holroyd took up the field-glass and resumed his scrutiny, first of the ants and then of the dead man amidships.

He has described these ants to me very particularly.

He says they were as large as any ants he has ever seen, black, and moving with a steady deliberation very different from the mechanical fussiness of the common ant. About one in twenty was much larger than its fellows and with an exceptionally large head. These reminded him at once of the master workers who are said to rule over the leaf-cutter ants; like them they seemed to be directing and co-ordinating the general movements. They tilted their bodies back in a manner altogether singular as if they made some use of the fore feet. And he had a curious fancy that he was too far off to verify that most of these ants of both kinds were wearing accoutrements, had things strapped about their bodies by bright white bands like white metal threads. . . .

He put down the glasses abruptly, realizing that the question of discipline between the captain and his subordinate had become acute.

"It is your duty," said the captain, "to go aboard. It is my instructions."

The lieutenant seemed on the verge of refusing.

The head of one of the mulatto sailors appeared beside him.

"I believe these men were killed by the ants," said Holroyd abruptly in English.

The captain burst into a rage. He made no answer to Holroyd. "I have commanded you to go aboard," he screamed to his subordinate in Portuguese. "If you do not go aboard forthwith it is mutiny—rank mutiny. Mutiny and cowardice! Where is the courage that should animate us? I will have you in irons, I will have you shot like a dog." He began a torrent of abuse and curses, he danced to and fro. He shook his fists, he behaved as if beside himself with rage, and the lieutenant, white and still, stood looking at him. The crew appeared forward, with amazed faces.

Suddenly in a pause of this outbreak the lieutenant came to some heroic decision, saluted, drew himself together and clambered upon the deck of the cuberta.

"Ah!" said Gerilleau, and his mouth shut like a trap.

Holroyd saw the ants retreating before da Cunha's boots. The Portuguese walked slowly to the fallen man, stooped down, hesitated, clutched his coat and turned him over. A black swarm of ants rushed out of the clothes, and da Cunha stepped back very quickly and trod two or three times on the deck.

Holroyd put up the glasses. He saw the scattered ants about the invader's feet, and doing what he had never seen ants doing before. They had nothing of the blind movements of the common ant; they were looking at him—as a rallying crowd of men might look at some gigantic monster that had dispersed it.

"How did he die?" the captain shouted.

Holroyd understood the Portuguese to say the body was too much eaten to tell.

"What is there forward?" asked Gerilleau.

The lieutenant walked a few paces, and began his answer in Portuguese. He stopped abruptly and beat off something from his leg. He made some peculiar steps as if he was trying to stamp on something invisible and went quickly towards the side. Then he controlled himself, turned about, walked deliberately forward to the hold, clambered up to the fore decking from which the sweeps are worked, stooped for a time over the second man, groaned audibly, and made his way back and aft to the cabin, moving very rigidly. He turned and began a conversation with his captain, cold and respectful in tone on either side, contrasting vividly with the wrath and insult of a few moments before. Holroyd gathered only fragments of its purport. He reverted to the field-glass, and was surprised to find the ants had vanished from all the exposed surfaces of the deck. He turned towards the shadows beneath the decking and it seemed to him they were full of watching eyes.

The cuberta, it was agreed, was derelict, but too full of ants to put men aboard to sit and sleep: it must be towed. The lieutenant went forward to take in and adjust the cable and the men in the boat stood up to be ready to help him. Holroyd's glasses searched the canoe.

He became more and more impressed by the fact that a great, if minute and furtive, activity was going on. He perceived that a number of gigantic ants—they seemed nearly a couple of inches in length—carrying oddly-shaped burthens for which he could imagine no use—were moving in rushes from one point of obscurity to another. They did not move in columns across the exposed places, but in open, spaced out lines, oddly suggestive of the rushes of modern infantry advancing under fire. A number were taking cover under the dead man's clothes, and a perfect swarm was gathering along the side over which da Cunha must presently go.

He did not see them actually rush for the lieutenant as he returned, but he has no doubt they did make a concerted rush. Suddenly the lieutenant was shouting and cursing and beating at his legs. "I'm stung!" he shouted, with a face of hate and accusation towards Gerilleau.

Then he vanished over the side, dropped into his boat, and plunged at once into the water. Holroyd heard the splash.

The three men in the boat pulled him out and brought him aboard, and that night he died.

III.

HOLROYD and the captain came out of the cabin in which the swollen and contorted body of the lieutenant lay, and stood together at the stern of the monitor staring at the sinister vessel they trailed behind them. It was a close dark night that had only phantom flickerings of sheet lightning to illuminate it. The cuberta, a vague black triangle, rocked about in the steamer's wake, her sails bobbing and flapping; and the black smoke from the funnels, spark-lit ever and again, streamed over her swaying masts.

Gerilleau's mind was inclined to run on the unkind things the lieutenant had said in the heat of his last fever.

"HE PLUNGED AT ONCE INTO THE WATER."

"He says I murdered 'im," he protested. "It is simply absurd. Someone 'ad to go aboard. Are we to run away from these confounded ants whenever they show up?"

Holroyd said nothing. He was thinking of a disciplined rush of little black shapes across bare sunlit planking.

"It was his place to go," harped Gerilleau. "He died in the execution of his duty. What has he to complain of? Murdered! . . . But the poor fellow was—what is it?—demented. He was not in his right mind. The poison swelled him. . . . U'm."

They came to a long silence.

"We will sink that canoe—burn it."

"And then?"

The inquiry irritated Gerilleau. His shoulders went up, his hands flew out at right angles from his body. "What is one to *do*?" he said, his voice going up to an angry squeak.

"Anyhow," he broke out vindictively, "every ant in dat cuberta!—I will burn dem alive!"

Holroyd was not moved to conversation. A distant ululation of howling monkeys filled the sultry night with foreboding sounds, and as the gunboat drew near the black, mysterious banks this was reinforced by a depressing clamour of frogs.

"What is one to *do*?" the captain repeated after a vast interval, and suddenly becoming active and savage and blasphemous, decided to burn the *Santa Rosa* without further delay. Everyone aboard was pleased by that idea, everyone helped with zest; they pulled in the cable, cut it, and dropped the boat and fired her with tow and kerosene, and soon the cuberta was crackling and flaring merrily amidst the immensities of the tropical night. Holroyd watched the mounting yellow flare against the blackness, and the livid flashes of sheet lightning that came and went above the forest summits, throwing them into momentary silhouette, and his stoker stood behind him watching also.

The stoker was stirred to the depths of his linguistics. "Saüba go pop, pop," he said, "Wahaw!" and laughed richly.

But Holroyd was thinking that these little creatures on the decked canoe had also eyes and brains.

The whole thing impressed him as incredibly foolish and wrong, but—what was

"THE CUBERTA WAS CRACKLING AND FLARING MERRILY."

one to *do?* This question came back enormously reinforced on the morrow, when at last the gunboat reached Badama.

This place, with its leaf-thatch-covered houses and sheds, its creeper-invaded sugar-mill, its little jetty of timber and canes, was very still in the morning heat, and showed never a sign of living men. Whatever ants there were at that distance were too small to see.

"All the people 'ave gone," said Gerilleau, "but we will do one thing anyhow. We will 'oot and vissel."

So Holroyd hooted and whistled.

Then the captain fell into a doubting fit of the worst kind. "Dere is one thing we can do," he said presently.

"What's that?" said Holroyd.

"'Oot and vissel again."

So they did.

The captain walked his deck and gesticulated to himself. He seemed to have many things on his mind. Fragments of speeches came from his lips. He appeared to be addressing some imaginary public tribunal either in Spanish or Portuguese. Holroyd's improving ear detected something about ammunition. He came out of these preoccupations suddenly into English. "My dear 'Olroyd!" he cried, and broke off with "But what *can* one do?"

They took the boat and the field-glasses, and went close in to examine the place. They made out a number of big ants, whose still postures had a certain effect of watching them, dotted about the edge of the rude embarkation jetty. Gerilleau tried ineffectual pistol shots at these. Holroyd thinks he distinguished curious earthworks running between the nearer houses, that may have been the work of the insect conquerors of those human habitations. The explorers pulled past the jetty, and became aware of a human skeleton wearing a loin cloth, and very bright and clean and shining, lying beyond. They came to a pause regarding this. . . .

"I 'ave all dose lives to consider," said Gerilleau suddenly.

Holroyd turned and stared at the captain, realizing slowly that he referred to the unappetizing mixture of races that constituted his crew.

"To send a landing party—it is impossible —impossible. They will be poisoned, they will swell, they will swell up and abuse me and die. It is totally impossible. . . . If we land, I must land alone, alone, in thick boots and with my life in my hand. Perhaps I should live. Or again—-I might not land. I do not know. I do not know."

Holroyd thought he did, but he said nothing.

"De whole thing," said Gerilleau suddenly, "'as been got up to make me ridiculous. De whole thing!"

They paddled about and regarded the clean white skeleton from various points of view, and then they returned to the gunboat. Then Gerilleau's indecisions became terrible. Steam was got up and in the afternoon the monitor went on up the river with an air of going to ask somebody something, and by sunset came back again and anchored. A thunderstorm gathered and broke furiously, and then the night became beautifully cool and quiet and everyone slept on deck. Except Gerilleau, who tossed about and muttered. In the dawn he roused Holroyd.

"Lord!" said Holroyd, "what now?"

"I have decided," said the captain.

"What — to land?" said Holroyd, sitting up brightly.

"THEY TOOK THE BOAT AND THE FIELD-GLASSES, AND WENT CLOSE IN TO EXAMINE THE PLACE."

"No!" said the captain, and was for a time very reserved. "I have decided," he repeated, and Holroyd manifested symptoms of impatience.

"Well,—yes," said the captain, "*I shall fire de big gun!*"

And he did! Heaven knows what the ants thought of it, but he did. He fired it twice with great sternness and ceremony. All the crew had wadding in their ears, and there was an effect of going into action about the whole affair, and first they hit and wrecked the old sugar-mill and then they smashed the abandoned store behind the jetty. And then Gerilleau experienced the inevitable reaction.

"It is no good," he said to Holroyd; "no good at all. No sort of bally good. We must go back—for instructions. Dere will be de deuce of a row about dis ammunition— oh! de *deuce* of a row! You don't know, 'Olroyd. . . ."

He stood regarding the world in infinite perplexity for a space.

"But what else was there to *do?*" he cried.

In the afternoon the monitor started down stream again, and in the evening a landing party took the body of the lieutenant and buried it on the bank upon which the new ants have so far not appeared. . . .

IV.

I HEARD this story in a fragmentary state from Holroyd not three weeks ago.

These new ants have got into his brain, and he has come back to England with the idea, as he says, of "exciting people" about them "before it is too late." He says they threaten British Guiana, which cannot be much over a trifle of a thousand miles from their present sphere of activity, and that the Colonial Office ought to get to work upon them at once. He declaims with great passion: "These are intelligent ants. Just think what that means!"

There can be no doubt they are a serious pest, and that the Brazilian Government is well advised in offering a prize of five hundred pounds for some effectual method of extirpation. It is certain too that, since they first appeared in the hills beyond Badama about three years ago, they have achieved extraordinary conquests. The whole of the south bank of the Batemo river, for nearly sixty miles, they have in their effectual occupation, they have driven men out completely, occupied plantations and settlements, and boarded and captured at least one ship. It is even said they have in some inexplicable way bridged the very considerable Capuarana arm and pushed many miles towards the Amazon itself. There can be little doubt that they are far more reasonable and with a far better social organization than any previously known ant species; instead of being in dispersed societies they are organized into what is in effect a single nation; but their peculiar and immediate formidableness lies not so much in this as in the intelligent use they make of poison against their larger enemies. It would seem this poison of theirs is closely akin to snake poison, and it is highly probable they actually manufacture it, and that the larger individuals among them carry the needle-like crystals of it in their attacks upon men.

Of course it is extremely difficult to get any detailed information about these new competitors for the sovereignty of the globe. No eye-witnesses of their activity, except for such glimpses as Holroyd's, have survived the encounter. The most extraordinary legends of their prowess and capacity are in circulation in the region of the Upper Amazon, and grow daily as the steady advance of the invader stimulates men's imaginations through their fears. These strange little creatures are credited not only with the use of implements and a knowledge of fire and metals and with organized feats of engineering that stagger our northern minds—unused as we are to such feats as that of the Saübas of Rio de Janeiro, who in 1841 drove a tunnel under the Parahyba where it is as wide as the Thames at London Bridge—but with an organized and detailed method of record and communication analogous to our books. They are increasing rapidly in numbers, and Holroyd at least is firmly convinced that they will finally dispossess man over the whole of tropical South America.

This is a startling outlook, but what is going to check them? And why should they stop at tropical South America?

I confess I felt disposed to echo the inquiry of Captain Gerilleau and ask: "What can one *do?*"

Suppose they go on spreading! Suppose they come down the river to the sea and send off an expedition in the hold of some eastward-travelling ship! What could one do?

There are moments when I am almost disposed to agree with Holroyd and believe that he has seen the beginning of one of the most stupendous dangers that have ever threatened our race.

STORIES OF THE STONE AGE

Originally published in *The Idler*
May-November 1897

STORIES OF THE STONE AGE.

BY H. G. WELLS.

ILLUSTRATED BY COSMO ROWE.

I.—UGH-LOMI AND UYA.

THIS story is of a time beyond the memory of man, before the beginning of history, before the beginning of speech almost, when men still eked out their scarce words by gestures, and talked together as the animals do, by the passing of simple thoughts from mind to mind—being themselves indeed still of the brotherhood of the beasts. Of a time when one might have walked dryshod from France (as we call it now) to England, and when a broad and sluggish Thames flowed through its marshes to meet its father Rhine, flowing through a wide and level country that is under water in these latter days, and which we know by the name of the North Sea. In that remote age the valley which runs along the foot of the Downs did not exist, and the south of Surrey was a range of hills, fir-clad on the middle slopes, and snow-capped for the better part of the year. The cores of its summits still remain as Leith Hill, and Pitch Hill, and Hindhead. On the lower slopes of the range below the grassy spaces where the wild horses grazed were forests of yew and sweet-chestnut and elm, and the thickets and dark places hid the grizzly bear and the hyæna, and the grey apes clambered through the branches. And still lower amidst the woodland and marsh and open grass along the Wey did this little drama play itself out to the end that I have to tell. Fifty thousand years ago it was, fifty thousand years—if the estimates of the geologists are correct.

And in those days the spring-time was as joyful as it is now, and sent the blood coursing in just the same fashion. The afternoon sky was blue with piled white clouds sailing through it, and the south-west wind came like a soft caress. The new-come swallows drove to and fro. The reaches of the river were spangled with white ranunculus, the marshy places were starred with lady's-smock and lit with marsh-mallow wherever the regiments of the sedges lowered their swords, and the northward moving hippopotami, shiny black monsters, sporting clumsily, came floundering and blundering through it all, rejoicing dimly and possessed with one clear idea, to splash the river muddy.

Farther up the river and well in sight of the hippopotami, a number of little buff-coloured animals dabbled in the water. There was no fear, no rivalry, and no enmity between them and the hippopotami. As the great bulks came crashing through the reeds and smashed the mirror of the water into silvery splashes, these little creatures shouted and gesticulated with glee. It was the surest sign of high spring. "Boloo!" they cried. "Baayah. Boloo!" They were the children of the men folk, the smoke of whose encampment rose from the knoll at the river's bend. Wild-eyed youngsters they were, with matted hair and little broad-nosed impish faces, covered (as some children are covered even nowadays) with

He had given her a piece of the liver.

a delicate down of hair. They were narrow in the loins and long in the arms. And their ears had no lobes, and had little pointed tips, a thing that still, in rare instances, survives. Stark-naked vivid little gipsies, as active as monkeys and as full of chatter, though a little wanting in words.

Their elders were hidden from the wallowing hippopotami by the crest of the knoll. The human squatting-place was a trampled area among the dead brown fronds of Royal Fern, through which the crosiers of this year's growth were unrolling to the light and warmth. The fire was a smouldering heap of char, light grey and black, replenished by the old women from time to time with brown leaves. Most of the men were asleep—they slept sitting with their foreheads on their knees. They had killed that morning a good quarry, enough for all, a deer that had been wounded in a rutting fight; so that there had been no quarrelling among them, and some of the women were still gnawing the bones that lay scattered about. Others were making a heap of leaves and sticks to feed Brother Fire when the darkness came again, that he might grow strong and tall therewith, and guard them against the beasts. And two were piling flints that they brought, an armful at a time, from the bend of the river where the children were at play.

None of these buff-skinned savages were clothed, but some wore about their hips rude girdles of adder-skin or crackling undressed hide, from which depended little bags, not made, but torn from the paws of beasts, and carrying the rudely-dressed flints that were men's chief weapons and tools. And one woman, the mate of Uya the Cunning Man, wore a wonderful necklace of perforated fossils—that others had worn before her. Beside some of the sleeping men lay the big antlers of the elk, with the tines chipped to sharp edges, and long sticks, hacked at the ends with flints into sharp points. There was little else save

these things and the smouldering fire to mark these human beings off from the wild animals that ranged the country. But Uya the Cunning did not sleep, but sat with a bone in his hand and scraped busily thereon with a flint, a thing no animal would do. He was the oldest man in the tribe, beetle-browed, prognathous, lank-armed; he had a beard and his cheeks were hairy, and his chest and arms were black with thick hair. And by virtue both of his strength and cunning he was master of the tribe, and his share was always the most and the best.

Eudena had hidden herself among the alders, because she was afraid of Uya. She was still a girl, and her eyes were bright and her smile pleasant to see. He had given her a piece of the liver, a man's piece, and a wonderful treat for a girl to get; but as she took it the other woman with the necklace had looked at her, an evil glance, and Ugh-lomi had made a noise in his throat. At that, Uya had looked at him long and steadfastly, and Ugh-lomi's face had fallen. And then Uya had looked at her. She was frightened and she had stolen away, while the feeding was still going on, and Uya was busy with the marrow of a bone. Afterwards he had wandered about as if looking for her. And now she crouched among the alders, wondering mightily what Uya might be doing with the flint and the bone. And Ugh-lomi was not to be seen.

Presently a squirrel came leaping through the alders, and she lay so quiet the little man was within six feet of her before he saw her. Whereupon he dashed up a stem in a hurry and began to chatter and scold her. "What are you doing here," he asked, "away from the other men beasts?" "Peace," said Eudena, but he only chattered more, and then she began to break off the little black cones to throw at him. He dodged and defied her, and she grew excited and rose up to throw better, and then she saw Uya coming down the knoll. He had seen the movement of her pale arm amidst the thicket —he was very keen-eyed.

At that she forgot the squirrel and set off through the alders and reeds as fast as she could go. She did not care where she went so long as she escaped Uya. She splashed nearly knee-deep through a swampy place, and saw in front of her a slope of ferns—growing more slender and greener as they passed up out of the light into the shade of the young chestnut trees. She was soon amidst the trees—she was very fleet of foot, and she ran on and on, until the forest was old and the trees great, and the vines about their stems where the light came were thick as young trees, and the ropes of ivy stout and tight. On she went, and she doubled and doubled again, and then at last lay down amidst some ferns in a hollow place near a thicket, and listened with her heart beating in her ears.

She heard footsteps presently rustling among the dead leaves, far off, and they died away and everything was still again, except the scandalising of the midges—for the evening was drawing on—and the incessant whisper of the leaves. She laughed silently to think the cunning Uya should go by her. She was not frightened. Sometimes, playing with the other girls and lads, she had fled into the wood, though never so far as this. It was pleasant to be hidden and alone.

She lay a long time there, glad of her escape, and then she sat up listening.

It was a rapid pattering growing louder and coming towards her, and in a little while she could hear grunting noises and the snapping of twigs. It was a drove of the lean grisly wild swine. She turned about her, for a boar is an ill fellow to pass too closely, on account of the sideway slash of his tusks, and she made off slantingly through the trees. But the patter came nearer, they were not feeding as they wandered, but going fast—or else they would not overtake her—and she caught the limb of a tree, swung on to

it, and ran up the stem with something of the agility of a monkey.

Down below the sharp bristling backs of the swine were already passing when she looked down. And she knew the short, sharp grunts they made meant fear. What were they afraid of? A man? They were in a great hurry for just a man.

And then, so suddenly it made her grip on the branch tighten involuntarily, a fawn started in the brake and rushed after the swine. Something else went by, low and grey, with a long body; she did not know what it was, indeed she saw it only momentarily through the interstices of the young leaves; and then there came a pause.

She remained stiff and expectant, as rigid almost as though she was a part of the tree she clung to, peering down.

Then, far away among the trees, clear for a moment, then hidden, then visible knee-deep in ferns, then gone again, ran a man. She knew it was young Ugh-lomi by the fair colour of his hair, and there was red upon his face. Somehow his frantic flight and that scarlet mark made her feel sick. And then nearer, running heavily and breathing hard, came another man also running. At first she could not see, and then she saw, foreshortened and clear to her, Uya, running with great strides and his eyes staring. He was not going after Ugh-lomi. His face was white. It was Uya—*afraid!* He passed, and was still loud hearing, when something else, something large and with grizzled fur, swinging along with soft swift strides, came rushing in pursuit of him.

Eudena suddenly became rigid, ceased to breathe, her clutch convulsive, and her eyes starting.

She had never seen the thing before, she did not even see him clearly now, but she knew at once it was the Terror of the Woodshade. His name was a legend, the children would frighten one another, frighten even themselves with his name, and run screaming to the squatting-place. No man had ever killed any of his kind. Even the mighty mammoth feared his anger. It was the grizzly bear, the lord of the world as the world went then.

As he ran he made a continuous growling grumble. "Men in my very lair! Fighting and blood. At the very mouth of my lair. Men, men, men. Fighting and blood." For he was the lord of the wood and of the caves.

Long after he had passed she remained, a girl of stone, staring down through the branches. All her power of action had gone from her. She gripped by instinct with hands and knees and feet. It was some time before she could think, and then only one thing was clear in her mind, that the Terror was between her and the tribe—that it would be impossible to descend.

Presently when her fear was a little abated she clambered into a more comfortable position, where a great branch forked. The trees rose about her, so that she could see nothing of Brother Fire, who is black by day. Birds began to stir about her, and things that had gone into hiding for fear of her movements crept out. . . .

After a time the blue overhead deepened, and the taller branches flamed out at the touch of the sunset. High overhead the rooks, who were wiser than men, went cawing home to their squatting-places among the elms. Looking down, things were clearer and darker. Eudena thought of going back to the squatting-place; she let herself down some way, and then the fear of the Terror of the Wood-shade came again. While she hesitated a rabbit squealed dismally, and she dared not descend farther.

The shadows gathered, and the deeps of the forest began stirring. Eudena went up the tree again to be nearer the light. Down below the shadows came out of their hiding-places and walked abroad. Overhead the blue deepened. A dreadful stillness came, and then the leaves began whispering. Eudena shivered and thought of Brother Fire.

The shadows now were gathering in the trees, they sat on the branches and watched her. Branches and leaves were turned to ominous, quiet black shapes that would spring on her if she stirred. Then the white owl, flitting silently, came ghostly through the shades. Darker grew the world and darker, until the leaves and twigs against the sky were black, and the ground was hidden.

She remained there all night, an age-long vigil, straining her ears for the things that went on below in the darkness, and keeping motionless lest some stealthy beast should discover her. Man in those days was never alone in the dark, save for such rare accidents as this. Age after age he had learnt the lesson of its terror —a lesson we poor children of his have nowadays painfully to unlearn. Eudena, though in age a woman, was in heart like a little child. She kept as still, poor little animal, as a hare before it is started.

The stars gathered and watched her— her one grain of comfort. In one bright one she fancied there was something like Ugh-lomi. Then she fancied it *was* Ugh-lomi. And near him, red and duller, was Uya, and as the night passed Ugh-lomi fled before him up the sky.

She tried to see Brother Fire, who guarded the squatting-place from beasts, but he was not in sight. And far away she heard the mammoths trumpeting as they went down to the drinking-place, and once some huge bulk with heavy paces hurried along, making a noise like a calf, but what it was she could not see. But she thought from the voice it was Yaaa the rhinoceros, who stabs with his nose, goes always alone, and rages without cause.

At last the little stars began to hide, and then the larger ones. It was like all the animals vanishing before the Terror.

The Sun was coming, lord of the sky, as the grizzly was lord of the forest. Eudena wondered what would happen if one star stayed behind. And then the sky paled to the dawn.

When the daylight came the fear of lurking things passed, and she could descend. She was stiff, but not so stiff as you would have been, dear young lady (by virtue of your upbringing), and as she had not been trained to eat at least once in three hours, but instead had often fasted three days, she did not feel uncomfortably hungry. She crept down the tree very cautiously, and went her way stealthily through the wood, and not a squirrel sprang or deer started but the terror of the grizzly bear froze her marrow.

Her desire was now to find her people again. Her dread of Uya the Cunning was consumed by a greater dread of loneliness. But she had lost her direction. She had run heedlessly overnight, and she could not tell whether the squatting-place was sunward or where it lay. Ever and again she stopped and listened, and at last, very far away, she heard a measured chinking. It was so faint even in the morning stillness that she could tell it must be far away. But she knew the sound was that of a man sharpening a flint.

Presently the trees began to thin out, and then came a regiment of nettles barring the way. She turned aside, and then she came to a fallen tree that she knew, with a noise of bees about it. And so presently she was in sight of the knoll, very far off, and the river under it, and the children and the hippopotami just as they had been yesterday, and the thin spire of smoke swaying in the morning breeze. Far away by the river was the cluster of alders where she had hidden. And at the sight of that the fear of Uya returned, and she crept into a thicket of bracken, out of which a rabbit scuttled, and lay awhile to watch the squatting-place.

The men were mostly out of sight, saving Wau, the flint-chipper ; and at that she felt safer. They were away hunting— food, no doubt. Some of the women, too, were down in the stream, stooping intent, seeking mussels, crayfish, and water-snails, and at the sight of their occupation Eudena felt hungry. She rose, and ran through the fern, designing to join them. As she went she heard a voice among the bracken calling softly. She stopped. Then suddenly she heard a rustle behind her, and turning, saw Ugh-lomi rising out of the fern. There were streaks of brown blood and dirt on his face, and his eyes were fierce, and the white stone of Uya, the white Fire Stone, that none but Uya dared to touch, was in his hand. In a stride he was beside her, and gripped her arm. He swung her about, and thrust her before him towards the woods. "Uya," he said, and waved his arms about. She heard a cry, looked back, and saw all the women standing up, and two wading out of the stream. Then came a nearer howling, and the old woman with the beard, who watched the fire on the knoll, was waving her arms, and Wau, the man who had been chipping the flint, was getting to his feet. The little children too were hurrying and shouting.

"Come !" said Ugh-lomi, and dragged her by the arm.

She still did not understand.

"Uya," said Ugh-lomi, and she glanced back again at the screaming curve of figures, and dimly understood.

Wau and all the women and children were coming towards them, a scattered array of buff shock-headed figures, howling, leaping, and crying. Over the knoll two youths hurried. Down among the ferns to the right came a man, heading them off from the wood. Ugh-lomi left her arm, and the two began running side by side, leaping the bracken and stepping clear and wide. Eudena, knowing her fleetness and the fleetness of Ugh-lomi, laughed aloud at the unequal chase. They were an exceptionally straight-limbed couple for those days.

They soon cleared the open, and drew near the wood of chestnut trees again—neither afraid now because neither was alone. They slackened their pace, already not excessive. And suddenly Eudena cried and swerved aside, pointing, and looking up through the tree-stems. Ugh-lomi saw the feet and legs of men running towards him. Eudena was already running off at a tangent. And as he too turned to follow her they heard the voice of Uya coming through the trees, and roaring out his rage at them.

Then terror came in their hearts, not the terror that numbs, but the terror that makes one silent and swift. They were cut off now on two sides. They were in a sort of corner of pursuit. On the right hand, and near by them, came the men swift and heavy, with bearded Uya, antler in hand, leading them ; and on the left, scattered as one scatters corn, yellow dashes among the fern and grass, ran Wau and the women ; and even the little children from the shallow had joined the chase. The two parties converged upon them. Off they went, with Eudena ahead.

They knew there was no mercy for them. There was no hunting so sweet to these ancient men as the hunting of men. Once the fierce passion of the chase was lit, the feeble beginnings of humanity in them were thrown to the winds. And Uya in the night had marked Ugh-lomi with the death word. Ugh-lomi was the day's quarry.

They ran straight—it was their only chance—taking whatever ground came in the way—a spread of stinging nettles, an open glade, a clump of grass out of which a hyæna fled snarling. Then woods again, long stretches of shady leaf-mould and moss under the green trunks. Then a stiff slope, tree-clad, and long vistas of trees, a glade, a succulent green area of black mud, a wide open space again, and then a clump of lacerating brambles, with beast tracks through it. Behind them

the chase trailed out and scattered, with Uya ever at their heels. Eudena kept the first place, running light and with her breath easy, for Ugh-lomi carried the Fire Stone in his hand.

It told on his pace—not at first, but after a time. His footsteps behind her suddenly grew remote. Glancing over her shoulder as they crossed another open space, Eudena saw that Ugh-lomi was many yards behind her, and Uya close upon him, with antler already raised in the air to strike him down. Wau and the others were but just emerging from the shadow of the woods.

Seeing Ugh-lomi in peril, Eudena ran sideways, looking back, threw up her arms and cried aloud, just as the antler flew. And young Ugh-lomi, expecting this and understanding her cry, ducked his head, so that the missile merely struck his scalp lightly, making but a trivial wound, and flew over him. He turned forthwith, the quartzite Fire Stone in both hands, and hurled it straight at Uya's body as he ran loose from the throw. Uya shouted, but could not dodge it. It took him under the ribs, heavy and flat, and he reeled and went down without a cry. Ugh-lomi caught up the antler—one tine of it was tipped with his own blood—and came running on again with a red trickle just coming out of his hair.

Uya rolled over twice, and lay a moment before he got up, and then he did not run fast. The colour of his face was changed. Wau overtook him, and then others, and he coughed and laboured in his breath. But he kept on.

At last the two fugitives gained the bank of the river, where the stream ran deep and narrow, and they still had fifty yards in hand of Wau, the foremost pursuer, the man who made the smiting stones. He carried one, a large flint, the shape of an oyster and double the size, chipped to a chisel edge, in either hand.

They sprang down the steep bank into the stream, rushed through the water,

It took him under the ribs, heavy and flat.

swam the deep current in two or three strokes, and came out wading again, dripping and refreshed, to clamber up the farther bank. It was undermined, and with willows growing thickly therefrom, so that it needed clambering. And while Eudena was still among the silvery branches and Ugh-lomi still in the water—for the antler had encumbered him—Wau came up against the sky on the opposite bank, and the smiting stone, thrown cunningly, took the side of Eudena's knee. She struggled to the top and fell.

They heard the pursuers shout to one another, and Ugh-lomi, climbing to her and moving jerkily to mar Wau's aim, felt the second smiting stone graze his ear, and heard the water splashing below him.

Then it was Ugh-lomi, the stripling, proved himself to have come to man's estate. For running on, he found Eudena fell behind, limping, and at that he turned, and crying savagely and with a face terrible with sudden wrath and trickling blood, ran swiftly past her back to the bank, whirling the antler round his head. And Eudena kept on, running stoutly still, though she must needs limp at every step, and the pain was already sharp.

So that Wau, rising over the edge and clutching the straight willow branches, saw Ugh-lomi towering over him, gigantic against the blue; saw his whole body swing round, and the grip of his hands upon the antler. The edge of the antler came sweeping through the air, and he saw no more. The water under the osiers whirled and eddied and went crimson six feet down the stream. Uya following, stopped knee-high across the stream, and the man who was swimming turned about.

The other men who trailed after—they were none of them very mighty men (for Uya was more cunning than strong, brooking no sturdy rivals)—slackened momentarily at the sight of Ugh-lomi standing there above the willows, bloody and terrible, between them and the halting

girl, with the huge antler waving in his hand. It seemed as though he had gone into the water a youth, and come out of it a man full grown.

He knew what there was behind him. A broad stretch of grass, and then a thicket, and in that Eudena could hide. That was clear in his mind, though his thinking powers were too feeble to see what should happen thereafter. Uya stood knee-deep, undecided and un-armed. His heavy mouth hung open, showing his canine teeth, and he panted heavily. His side was flushed and bruised under the hair. The other man beside him carried a sharpened stick. The rest of the hunters came up one by one to the top of the bank, hairy, long-armed men clutching flints and sticks. Two ran off along the bank down stream, and then clambered down to the water, where Wau had come to the surface struggling weakly. They gibbered at him without any sane attempt to help, and presently he went under again. Two others threatened Ugh-lomi from the bank.

He answered back, shouts, vague in-sults, gestures. Then Uya, who had been standing hesitating, roared with rage, and whirling his fists came plunging through the water. His followers came splashing after him.

Ugh-lomi glanced over his shoulder and found Eudena already vanished into the thicket. He would perhaps have waited for Uya, but Uya preferred to spar in the water below him until the others were beside him. Human tactics in those days, in all serious fighting, were the tactics of the pack. Prey that turned at bay they gathered around and rushed. Ugh-lomi felt the rush coming, and hurling the antler at Uya, turned about and fled.

When he halted to look back from the shadow of the thicket, he found only three of his pursuers had followed him across the river, and they were going back again. Uya, with a bleeding mouth, was on the farther side of the stream again, but lower down, and he held his hand to his side. The others were in the river dragging something to shore. For a time at least the chase was intermitted.

Ugh-lomi stood watching for a space, and snarled at the sight of Uya. Then he turned and plunged into the thicket.

In a minute, Eudena came hastening to join him, and they went on hand in hand. He dimly perceived the pain she suffered from the cut and bruised knee, and chose the easier ways. But they went on all that day, mile after mile, through wood and thicket, until at last they came to the chalk land, open grass with rare woods of beech, and the birch growing near water, and they saw the Wealden mountains nearer, and groups of horses grazing together. They went circumspectly, keeping always near thicket and cover, for this was a strange region —even its ways were strange. Steadily the ground rose, until the chestnut forests spread wide and blue below them, and the Thames marshes shone silvery, high and far. They saw no men, for in those days men were still only just come into this part of the world, and were moving but slowly along the river-ways. Towards evening they came on the river again, but now it ran in a gorge, between high cliffs of white chalk that sometimes overhung it. Down the cliffs was a scrub of birches and there were many birds there. And high up the cliff was a little shelf by a tree, whereon they clambered to pass the night.

They had had scarcely any food; it was not the time of year for berries, and they had no time to go aside to snare or waylay. They tramped in a hungry weary silence, gnawing at twigs and leaves. But over the surface of the cliffs were a multitude of snails, and in a bush were the freshly laid eggs of a little bird, and then Ugh-lomi threw at and killed a squirrel in a beech tree, so that at last they fed well. Ugh-lomi watched during the

night, his chin on his knees; and he heard young foxes crying hard by, and the noise of mammoths down the gorge, and the hyænas yelling and laughing far away. It was chilly, but they dared not light a fire. Whenever he dozed, his spirit went abroad, and straightway met with the spirit of Uya, and they fought. And always Ugh-lomi was paralysed so that he could not smite nor run, and then he would awake suddenly. Eudena, too, dreamt evil things of Uya, so that they both awoke with the fear of him in their hearts, and by the light of the dawn they saw a woolly rhinoceros go blundering down the valley.

During the day they caressed one another and were glad of the sunshine, and Eudena's leg was so stiff she sat on the ledge all day. Ugh-lomi found great flints sticking out of the cliff face, greater than any he had seen, and he dragged some to the ledge and began chipping, so as to be armed against Uya when he came again. And at one he laughed heartily, and Eudena laughed, and they threw it about in derision. It had a hole in it. They stuck their fingers through it, it was very funny indeed. Then they peeped at one another through it. Afterwards, Ugh-lomi got himself a stick, and thrusting by chance at this foolish flint, the stick went in and stuck there. He had rammed it in too tightly to withdraw it. That was still stranger—scarcely funny, terrible almost, and for a time Ugh-lomi did not greatly care to touch the thing. It was as if the flint had bit and held with its teeth. But then he got familiar with the odd combination. He swung it about, and perceived dimly that the stick with the heavy stone on the end struck a better blow than anything he knew. He went to and fro swinging it, and striking with it; but later he tired of it and threw it aside. In the afternoon he went up over the brow of the white cliff, and lay watching by a rabbit-warren until the rabbits came out to play. There were no men thereabouts, and the rabbits were heedless. He threw a smiting stone he had made and got a kill.

That night they made a fire from flint sparks and bracken fronds, and talked and caressed by it. And in their sleep Uya's spirit came again, and suddenly, while Ugh-lomi was trying to fight vainly, the foolish flint on the stick came into his hand, and he struck Uya with it, and behold ! it killed him. But afterwards came other dreams of Uya—for spirits take a lot of killing, and he had to be killed again. Then after that the stone would not keep on the stick. He awoke tired and rather gloomy, and was sulky all the forenoon, in spite of Eudena's kindliness, and instead of hunting he sat chipping a sharp edge to the singular flint, and looking strangely at her. Then he bound the perforated flint on to the stick with strips of rabbit skin. And afterwards he walked up and down the ledge, striking with it, and muttering to himself, and thinking of Uya. It felt very fine and heavy in the hand.

Several days, more than there was any counting in those days, five days, it may be, or six, did Ugh-lomi and Eudena stay on that shelf in the gorge of the river, and they lost all fear of men, and their fire burnt redly of a night. And they were very merry together ; there was food every day, sweet water, and no enemies. Eudena's knee was well in a couple of days, for those ancient savages had quick-healing flesh. Indeed, they were very happy.

On one of those days, although it has little to do with this story, Ugh-lomi dropped a chunk of flint on the cliff. He saw it fall, and go bounding across the river bank into the river, and after laughing and thinking it over a little he tried another. This smashed a bush of hazel in the most interesting way. They spent all the morning dropping stones from the ledge, and in the afternoon they discovered this new and interesting pastime was also possible from the cliff brow. The next day they had forgotten this delight. Or at least, it seemed they had forgotten.

But Uya came in dreams to spoil the paradise. Three nights he came fighting Ugh-lomi. In the morning after these dreams Ugh-lomi would walk up and down, threatening him and swinging the axe, and at last came the night after Ugh-lomi brained the otter, and they had feasted. Uya went too far. Ugh-lomi awoke, scowling under his heavy brows, and he took his axe, and extending his hand towards Eudena he bade her wait for him upon the ledge. Then he clambered down the white declivity, glanced up once from the foot of it and flourished his axe, and without looking back again went striding along the river bank until the overhanging cliff at the bend hid him.

Two days and nights did Eudena sit alone by the fire on the ledge waiting, and in the night the beasts howled over the cliffs and down the valley, and on the cliff over against her the hunched hyænas prowled black against the sky. But no evil thing came near her save fear. Once, far away, she heard the roaring of a lion, following the horses as they came northward over the grass lands with the spring. All that time she waited—the waiting that is pain.

And the third day Ugh-lomi came back, up the river. The plumes of a raven were in his hair. The axe was red-stained, and had long dark hairs upon it, and he carried the necklace that had marked the favourite of Uya in his hand. He walked in the soft places, giving no heed to his trail. Save a raw cut below his jaw there was not a wound upon him. "Uya!" cried Ugh-lomi exultant, and Eudena saw it was well. He put the necklace on Eudena, and they ate and drank together. And after eating he began to rehearse the whole story from the beginning, when Uya had cast his eyes on Eudena, and Uya and Ugh-lomi, fighting in the forest, had been chased by the bear, eking out his scanty words with abundant pantomime, springing to his feet and whirling the stone axe round when it came to the fighting. The last fight was a mighty one, stamping and shouting, and once a blow at the fire that sent a torrent of sparks up into the night. And Eudena sat red in the light of the fire, gloating on him, her face flushed and her eyes shining, and the necklace Uya had made about her neck. It was a splendid time, and the stars that look down on us looked down on her, our ancestor—who has been dead now these fifty thousand years.

STORIES OF THE STONE AGE.

BY H. G. WELLS.

ILLUSTRATED BY COSMO ROWE.

II.—Ugh-lomi and the Cave Bear.

N the days when Eudena and Ugh-lomi fled from the people of Uya towards the fir-clad mountains of the Weald, across the forests of sweet chestnut and the grass-clad chalkland, and hid themselves at last in the gorge of the river between the chalk cliffs, men were few and their squatting-places far between. The nearest men to them were those of the tribe, a full day's journey down the river, and up the mountains there were none. Man was indeed a newcomer to this part of the world in that ancient time, coming slowly along the rivers, generation after generation, from one squatting-place to another, from the south-westward. And the animals that held the land, the hippopotami and rhinoceri of the river valleys, the horses of the grass plains, the deer and swine of the woods, the grey apes in the branches, the cattle of the uplands, feared him but little—let alone the mammoths in the mountains and the elephants that came through the land in the summer-time out of the south. For why should they fear him, with but the rough, chipped flints that he had not learnt to haft and which he threw but ill, and the poor spear of sharpened wood, as all his weapons against hoof and horn, tooth and claw?

Andoo, the huge cave bear, who lived in the cave up the gorge, had never even seen a man in all his wise and respectable life, until midway through one night, as he was prowling down the gorge along the cliff edge, he saw the glare of Eudena's fire upon the ledge, and Eudena red and shining, and Ugh-lomi, with a gigantic shadow mocking him upon the white cliff, going to and fro, shaking his mane of hair, and waving the axe of stone—the first axe of stone—while he chanted of the killing of Uya. The cave bear was far up the gorge, and he saw the thing slanting-ways and far off. He was so surprised he stood quite still upon the edge, sniffing the novel odour of burning bracken, and wondering whether the dawn was coming up in the wrong place.

He was the lord of the rocks and caves, was the cave bear, as his slighter brother, the grizzly, was lord of the thick woods below, and as the dappled lion—the lion of those days was dappled—was lord of the thorn-thickets, reed-beds, and open plains. He was the greatest of all meat-eaters; he knew no fear, none preyed on him, and none gave him battle; only the rhinoceros was beyond his strength. Even the mammoth shunned his country. This invasion perplexed him. He noticed these new beasts were shaped like monkeys, and sparsely hairy like young pigs. "Monkey and young pig," said the cave bear. "It might not be so bad. But that red thing that jumps, and the black thing jumping with it yonder! Never in my life have I seen such things before."

He came slowly along the brow of the cliff towards them, stopping thrice to sniff and peer, and the reek of the fire grew stronger. A couple of hyænas also were so intent upon the thing below that Andoo, coming soft and easy, was close

Waving the axe of stone, while he chanted of the killing of Uya.

upon them before they knew of him or he of them. They started guiltily and went lurching off. Coming round in a wheel, a hundred yards off, they began yelling and calling him names for the start they had had. " Ya-ha ! " they cried. " Who can't grub his own burrow ? Who eats roots like a pig ? . . . Ya-ha ! " For even in those days the hyæna's manners were just as offensive as they are now.

"Who answers the hyæna ? " growled Andoo, peering through the midnight dimness at them, and then going to look at the cliff edge.

There was Ugh-lomi still telling his story, and the fire getting low, and the scent of the burning hot and strong.

Andoo stood on the edge of the chalk cliff for some time, shifting his vast weight from foot to foot, and swaying his head to and fro, with his mouth open, his ears erect and twitching, and the nostrils of his big, black muzzle sniffing. He was very curious, was the cave bear, more curious than any of the bears that live now, and the flickering fire and the incomprehensible movements of the man, let alone the intrusion into his indisputable province, stirred him with a sense of strange new happenings. He had been after red deer fawn that night, for the cave bear was a miscellaneous hunter, but this quite turned him from that enterprise.

" Ya-ha ! " yelled the hyænas behind. " Ya-ha-ha ! "

Peering through the starlight, Andoo saw there were now three or four going to and fro against the grey hillside. " They will hang about me now all the night . . . until I kill," said Andoo. " Filth of the world ! " And mainly to annoy them, he resolved to watch the red flicker in the gorge until the dawn came to drive the hyæna scum home. And after a time they vanished, and he heard their voices, like a party of Cockney beanfeasters, away in the beech-woods. Then they came slinking near

again. Andoo yawned and went on along the cliff, and they followed. Then he stopped and went back.

It was a splendid night, beset with shining constellations, the same stars, but not the same constellations we know, for since those days all the stars have had time to move into new places. Far away across the open space beyond where the heavy-shouldered, lean-bodied hyænas blundered and howled, was a beech-wood, and the mountain slopes rose beyond, a dim mystery, until their snow-capped summits came out white and cold and clear, touched by the first rays of the yet unseen moon. It was a vast silence, save when the yell of the hyænas flung a vanishing discordance across its peace, or when from down the hills the trumpeting of the new-come elephants came faintly on the faint breeze. And below now, the red flicker had dwindled and was steady, and shone a deeper red, and Ugh-lomi had finished his story and was preparing to sleep, and Eudena sat and listened to the strange voices of unknown beasts, and watched the dark eastern sky growing deeply luminous at the advent of the moon. Down below, the river talked to itself, and things unseen went to and fro.

After a time the bear went away, but in an hour he was back again. Then, as if struck by a thought, he turned, and went up the gorge. . . .

The night passed, and Ugh-lomi slept on. The waning moon rose and lit the gaunt white cliff overhead with a light that was pale and vague. The gorge remained in a deeper shadow, and seemed all the darker. Then by imperceptible degrees the day came stealing in the wake of the moonlight. Eudena's eyes wandered to the cliff brow overhead once, and then again. Each time the line was sharp and clear against the sky, and yet she had a dim perception of something lurking there. The red of the fire grew deeper and deeper, grey scales spread upon it, its vertical column of smoke became more and more visible, and up and down the gorge things that had been unseen grew clear in a colourless illumination. She may have dozed.

Suddenly she started up from her squatting position, erect and alert, scrutinising the cliff up and down.

She made the faintest sound, and Ugh-lomi too, light sleeping like an animal, was instantly awake. He caught up his axe and came noiselessly to her side.

The light was still dim, the world now all in black and dark grey, and one sickly star still lingered overhead. The ledge they were on was a little grassy space, six feet wide, perhaps, and twenty feet long, sloping outwardly, and with a handful of St. John's wort growing near the edge. Below it the soft, white rock fell away in a steep slope of nearly fifty feet to the thick bush of hazel that fringed the river. Down the river this slope increased, until some way off a thin grass held its own right up to the crest of the cliff. Overhead, forty or fifty feet of rock bulged into the great masses characteristic of chalk, but at the end of the ledge a gully, a precipitous groove of discoloured chalk, slashed the face of the cliff, and gave a footing to a scrubby growth, by which Eudena and Ugh-lomi went up and down.

They stood as noiseless as startled deer, with every sense expectant. For a minute they heard nothing, and then came a faint rattling of dust down the gully, and the creaking of twigs.

Ugh-lomi gripped his axe, and went to the edge of the ledge, for the bulge of the chalk overhead had hidden the upper part of the gully. And forthwith, with a sudden contraction of the heart, he saw the cave bear half-way down from the brow, and making a gingerly backward step with his flat hind-foot. His hindquarters were towards Ugh-lomi, and he clawed at the rocks and bushes so that he seemed flattened against the cliff. He

looked none the less for that. From his shining snout to his stumpy tail he was a lion and a half, the length of two tall men. He looked over his shoulder, and his huge mouth was open with the exertion of holding up his great carcase, and his tongue lay out. . . .

He got his footing, and came down slowly, a yard nearer.

"Bear," said Ugh-lomi, looking round with his face white.

But Eudena, with terror in her eyes, was pointing down the cliff.

Ugh-lomi's mouth fell open. For down below, with her big fore-feet against the rock, stood another big brown-grey bulk—the she-bear. She was not so big as Andoo, but she was big enough for all that.

Then suddenly Ugh-lomi gave a cry, and catching up a handful of the litter of ferns that lay scattered on the ledge, he thrust it into the pallid ash of the fire. "Brother Fire!" he cried, "Brother Fire!" And Eudena, starting into activity, did likewise. "Brother Fire! Help, help! Brother Fire!"

Brother Fire was still red in his heart, but he turned to grey as they scattered him. "Brother Fire!" they screamed. But he whispered and passed, and there was nothing but ashes. Then Ugh-lomi danced with anger and struck the ashes with his fist. But Eudena began to hammer the firestone against a flint. And the eyes of each were turning ever and again towards the gully by which Andoo was climbing down. Brother Fire!

Suddenly the huge furry hind-quarters of the bear came into view, beneath the bulge of the chalk that had hidden him. He was still clambering gingerly down the nearly vertical surface. His head was yet out of sight, but they could hear him talking to himself. "Pig and monkey," said the cave bear. "It ought to be good."

Eudena struck a spark and blew at it; it twinkled brighter and then—went out.

At that she cast down flint and firestone and began wringing her hands. Her face was wet with tears. Then she sprang to her feet and scrambled a dozen feet up the cliff above the ledge. How she hung on even for a moment I do not know, for the chalk was vertical and without grip for a monkey. In a couple of seconds she had slid back to the ledge again with bleeding hands.

Ugh-lomi was making frantic rushes about the ledge—now he would go to the edge, now to the gully. He did not know what to do, he could not think. The she-bear looked smaller than her mate—much. If they rushed down on her together, *one* might live. "Eigh?" said the cave bear, and Ugh-lomi turned again and saw his little eyes peering under the bulge of the chalk. "Stand away!" said the bear; "I'm going to jump down."

Eudena, cowering at the end of the ledge, began to scream like a gripped rabbit.

At that a sort of madness came upon Ugh-lomi. With a mighty cry, he caught up his axe and began to clamber up the gully to the bear. He uttered neither word nor cry. The monster gave a grunt of surprise. In a moment Ugh-lomi was clinging to a bush right underneath the bear, and in another he was hanging to its back half buried in fur, with one fist clutched in the hair under its jaw. The bear was too astonished at this fantastic attack to do more than cling passive. And then the axe, the first of all axes, rang in its skull.

The bear's head twisted from side to side, and he began a petulant scolding growl. The axe bit within an inch of the left eye, and the hot blood blinded that side. At that the brute roared with surprise and anger, and his teeth gnashed six inches from Ugh lomi's face. Then the axe, clubbed close, came down heavily on the corner of the jaw.

The next blow blinded the right side

and called forth a roar, this time of pain. Eudena saw the huge, flat feet slipping and sliding, and suddenly the bear gave a clumsy leap sideways, as if for the ledge. Then everything vanished, and the hazels smashed, and a roar of pain and a tumult of shouts and growls came up from far below.

Eudena screamed and ran to the edge and peered over. For a moment, man and bears were a heap together, Ugh-lomi uppermost; and then he had sprung clear and was scaling the gully again, with the bears rolling and striking at one another among the hazels. But he had left his axe below, and three knob-ended streaks of carmine were shooting down his thigh. "Up!" he cried, and in a moment Eudena was preceding him to the top of the cliff.

In half a minute they were at the crest, their hearts pumping noisily, with Andoo and his wife far and safe below them. Andoo was sitting on his haunches, both paws at work, trying with quick exasperated movements to wipe the blindness out of his eyes, and the she-bear stood on all-fours a little way off, ruffled in appearance and growling angrily. Ugh-lomi flung himself flat on the grass, and lay panting and bleeding with his face on his arms.

For a second Eudena regarded the bears, then she came and sat beside him, looking at him. . . .

Presently she put forth her hand timidly and touched him, and made the guttural sound that was his name. He turned over and raised himself on his arm. His face was pale, like the face of one who is afraid. He looked at her steadfastly for a moment, and then suddenly he laughed. "Waugh!" he said exultantly.

"Waugh!" said she—a simple but expressive conversation.

Then Ugh-lomi came and knelt beside her, and on hands and knees peered over the brow and examined the gorge. His

He was hanging to its back half buried in fur.

breath was steady now, and the blood on his leg had ceased to flow, though the scratches the she-bear had made were open and wide. He squatted up and sat staring at the footmarks of the great bear as they came to the gully—they were as wide as his head and twice as long. Then he jumped up and went along the cliff face until the ledge was visible. Here he sat down for some time thinking, while Eudena watched him.

Presently Ugh-lomi rose, as one whose mind is made up. He returned towards the gully, Eudena keeping close by him, and together they clambered to the ledge. They took the firestone and a flint, and then Ugh-lomi went down to the foot of the cliff very cautiously, and found his axe. They returned to the cliff now as quietly as they could, and turning their faces resolutely up-stream set off at a brisk walk. The ledge was a home no longer, with such callers in the neighbourhood. Ugh-lomi carried the axe and Eudena the firestone. So simple was a Palæolithic removal.

They went up-stream, although it might lead to the very lair of the cave bear, because there was no other way to go. Down the stream was the tribe, and had not Ugh-lomi killed Uya and Wau? By the stream they had to keep—because of drinking.

So they marched, through beech trees, with the gorge deepening until the river flowed, a frothing rapid, five hundred feet below them. And of all the changeful things in this world of change, the courses of rivers in deep valleys change least. It was the river Wey, the river we know to-day, and they marched over the very spots where nowadays stand little Guildford and Godalming—the first human beings to come into the land. Once a grey ape chattered and vanished, and all along the cliff edge, vast and even, ran the spoor of the great cave bear.

And then the spoor of the bear fell away from the cliff, showing, Ugh-lomi thought, that he came from some place to the left, and keeping to the cliff's edge, they presently came to an end. They found themselves looking down on a great semi-circular space caused by the collapse of the cliff. It had smashed right across the gorge, banking the up-stream water back in a pool which overflowed in a rapid. The slip had happened long ago. It was grassed over, but the face of the cliffs that stood about the semicircle was still almost fresh-looking and white as on the day when the rock must have broken and slid down. Starkly exposed and black under the foot of these cliffs were the mouths of several caves. And as they stood there, looking at the space, and disinclined to skirt it, because they thought the bears' lair lay somewhere on the left in the direction they must needs take, they saw suddenly first one bear and then two coming up the grass slope to the right and going across the amphitheatre towards the caves. Andoo was first, and he dropped a little on his fore-foot, and his mien was despondent, and the she-bear came shuffling behind.

Eudena and Ugh-lomi stepped quite noiselessly back from the cliff until they could just see the bears over the verge. Then Ugh-lomi stopped. Eudena pulled his arm, but he turned with a forbidding gesture, and her hand dropped. Ugh-lomi stood watching the bears, with his axe in his hand, until they had vanished into the cave. He growled softly, and shook the axe at the she-bear's receding quarters. Then to Eudena's terror, instead of creeping off with her, he lay flat down and crawled forward into such a position that he could just see the cave. It was bears—and he did it as calmly as if it had been rabbits he was watching!

He lay still, like a barked log, sun-dappled, in the shadow of the trees. He was thinking. And Eudena had learnt, even when a little girl, that when Ugh-lomi became still like that, jawbone on fist, novel things presently began to happen.

It was an hour before the thinking was over; it was noon when the two little savages had found their way to the cliff brow that overhung the bears' cave. And all the long afternoon they fought desperately with a great boulder of chalk; trundling it, with nothing but their unaided sturdy muscles, from the gully where it had hung like a loose tooth, towards the cliff top. It was full two yards about, it stood as high as Eudena's waist, it was obtuse-angled and toothed with flints. And when the sun set it was poised, three inches from the edge, above the cave of the great cave bear.

In the cave, conversation languished during the afternoon. The she-bear snoozed sulkily in her corner—for she was fond of pig and monkey—and Andoo was busy licking the side of his paw and smearing his face to cool the smart and inflammation of his wounds. Afterwards he went and sat just within the mouth of the cave, blinking out at the afternoon sun with his uninjured eye, and thinking.

" I never was so startled in my life," he said at last. " They are the most extraordinary beasts. Attacking *me* ! "

" I don't like them," said the she-bear, out of the darkness behind.

" A feebler sort of beast I *never* saw. I can't think what the world is coming to. Scraggy, weedy legs . . . . Wonder how they keep warm in winter ? "

" Very likely they don't," said the she-bear.

" I suppose it's a sort of monkey gone wrong."

" It's a change," said the she-bear.

A pause.

" The advantage he had was merely accidental," said Andoo. " These things *will* happen at times."

" *I* can't understand why you let go," said the she-bear.

That matter had been discussed before, and settled. So Andoo, being a bear of experience, remained silent for a space. Then he resumed upon a different aspect of the matter. " He has a sort of claw—a long claw that he seemed to have first on one paw and then on the other. Just one claw. They're very odd things. The bright thing, too, they seemed to have—like that glare that comes in the sky in daytime—only it jumps about—it's really worth seeing. It's a thing with a root, too—like grass when it is windy."

" Does it bite ? " asked the she-bear.

" If it bites it can't be a plant."

" No——I don't know," said Andoo. " But it's curious, anyhow."

" I wonder if they *are* good eating ? " said the she-bear.

" They look it," said Andoo, with appetite—for the cave bear, like the polar bear, was an incurable carnivore — no roots or honey for *him*.

The two bears fell into a meditation for a space. Then Andoo resumed his simple attentions to his eye. The sunlight up the green slope before the cave mouth grew warmer in tone and warmer, until it was a ruddy amber.

" Curious sort of thing—day," said the cave bear. " Lot too much of it, I think. Quite unsuitable for hunting. Dazzles me always. I can't smell nearly so well by day."

The she-bear did not answer, but there came a measured crunching sound out of the darkness. She had turned up a bone. Andoo yawned. " Well," he said. He strolled to the cave mouth and stood with his head projecting, surveying the amphitheatre. He found he had to turn his head completely round to see objects on his right-hand side. No doubt that eye would be all right to-morrow.

He yawned again. There was a tap overhead, and a big mass of chalk flew out from the cliff face, dropped a yard in front of his nose, and starred into a dozen unequal fragments. It startled him extremely.

When he had recovered a little from his shock, he went and sniffed curiously at the representative pieces of the fallen projectile. They had a distinctive flavour, oddly reminiscent of the two drab animals of the ledge. He sat up and pawed the larger lump, and walked round it several times, trying to find a man about it somewhere. . . .

When night had come he went off down the river gorge to see if he could cut off either of the ledge's occupants. The ledge was empty, there were no signs of the red thing, but as he was rather hungry he did not loiter long that night, but pushed on to pick up a red deer fawn. He forgot about the drab animals. He found a fawn, but the doe was close by and made an ugly fight for her young. Andoo had to leave the fawn, but as her blood was up she stuck to the attack, and at last he got in a blow of his paw at her nose, and so got hold of her. More meat but less delicacy, and the she-bear, following, had her share. The next afternoon, curiously enough, the very fellow of the first white rock fell, and smashed precisely according to precedent.

The aim of the third, that fell the night after, however, was better. It hit Andoo's unspeculative skull with a crack that echoed up the cliff, and the white fragments went dancing to all the points of the compass. The she-bear coming after him and sniffing curiously at him, found him lying in an odd sort of attitude, with his head wet and all out of shape. She was a young she-bear, and inexperienced, and having sniffed about him for some time and licked him a little, and so forth, she decided to leave him until the odd mood had passed, and went on her hunting alone.

She looked up the fawn of the red doe they had killed two nights ago, and found it. But it was lonely hunting without Andoo, and she returned caveward before dawn. The sky was grey and overcast, the trees up the gorge were black and unfamiliar, and into her ursine mind came a dim sense of strange and dreary happenings. She lifted up her voice and called Andoo by name. The sides of the gorge re-echoed her.

As she approached the caves she saw in the half light, and heard, a couple of jackals scuttle off, and immediately after a hyæna howled and a dozen clumsy bulks went lumbering up the slope, and stopped and yelled derision. "Lord of the rocks and caves—ya-ha!" came down the wind. The dismal feeling in the she-bear's mind became suddenly acute. She shuffled across the amphitheatre.

"Ya-ha!" said the hyænas, retreating. "Ya-ha!"

The cave bear was not lying quite in the same attitude, because the hyænas had been busy, and in one place his ribs showed white. Dotted over the turf about him lay the smashed fragments of the three great lumps of chalk. And the air was full of the scent of death.

The she-bear stopped dead. Even now, that the great and wonderful Andoo was killed was beyond her believing. Then she heard far overhead a sound, a queer sound, a little like the shout of a hyæna but fuller and lower in pitch. She looked up, with her little dawn-blinded eyes, seeing little, her nostrils quivering. And there, on the cliff edge, far above her against the bright pink of dawn, were two little shaggy round dark things, the heads of Eudena and Ugh-lomi, as they shouted derision at her. But though she could not see them very distinctly she could hear, and dimly she began to apprehend. A novel feeling as of imminent strange evils came into her heart.

She began to examine the smashed fragments of chalk that lay about Andoo. For a space she stood still, looking about her and making a low continuous sound that was almost a moan. Then she went back incredulously to Andoo to make one last effort to rouse him.

Thus it was in the dawn of time that the Great Bears, who were the Lords of the Rocks and Caves, began their acquaintance with Man.

STORIES OF THE STONE AGE.

BY H. G. WELLS.

ILLUSTRATED BY COSMO ROWE.

III.—The First Horseman.

OW, in the days when Ugh-lomi killed the great cave bear there was little trouble between the horses and men. Indeed, they lived apart—the men in the river swamps and thickets, the horses on the wide grassy uplands between the chestnuts and the pines. Sometimes a pony would come straying into the clogging marshes to make a flint-hacked meal, and sometimes the tribe would find one, the kill of a lion, and drive off the jackals, and feast heartily while the sun was high. These horses of the old time were clumsy at the fetlock and dun-coloured, with a rough tail and big head. They came every spring-time north-westward into the country, after the swallows and before the hippopotami, as the grass on the wide downland stretches grew long. They came only in small bodies thus far, each herd, a stallion and two or three mares and a foal or so, having its own stretch of country, and they went again when the chestnut trees were yellow and the wolves came down the Wealden mountains.

It was their custom to graze right out in the open, going into cover only in the heat of the day. They avoided the long stretches of thorn and beechwood, preferring an isolated group of trees, void of ambuscade, so that it was hard to come upon them. They were never fighters; their heels and teeth were for one another, but in the clear country, once they were started, no living thing came near them, though perhaps the elephant might have done so, had he felt the need. And in those days man seemed a harmless thing enough. No whisper of prophetic intelligence told the species of the terrible slavery that was to come, of the whip and spur and bearing-rein, the clumsy load and the slippery street, the insufficient food, and the knacker's yard, that was to replace the wide grass-land and the freedom of the earth.

Down in the Wey marshes Ugh-lomi and Eudena had never seen the horses closely, but now they saw them every day as the two of them raided out from their lair on the ledge in the gorge, raiding together in search of food. They had returned to the ledge after the killing of Andoo; for of the she-bear they were not afraid. The she-bear had become afraid of them, and when she winded them she went aside. The two went together everywhere; for since they had left the tribe Eudena was not so much Ugh-lomi's woman as his mate; she learnt to hunt even—as much, that is, as any woman could. She was indeed a marvellous woman. He would lie for hours watching a beast, or planning catches in that shock head of his, and she would stay beside him, with her bright eyes upon him, offering no irritating suggestions—as still as any man. A wonderful woman!

At the top of the cliff was an open grassy lawn and then beechwoods, and going through the beechwoods one came to the edge of the rolling grassy expanse, and in sight of the horses. Here, on the edge of the wood and bracken, were the

And suddenly there was a rustle and a creak.

rabbit-burrows, and here among the fronds Eudena and Ugh-lomi would lie with their throwing-stones ready, until the little people came out to nibble and play in the sunset. And while Eudena would sit, a silent figure of watchfulness, regarding the burrows, Ugh-lomi's eyes were ever away across the greensward at those wonderful grazing strangers.

In a dim way he appreciated their grace and their supple nimbleness. As the sun declined in the evening-time, and the heat of the day passed, they would become active, would start chasing one another, neighing, dodging, shaking their manes, coming round in great curves, sometimes so close that the pounding of the turf sounded like hurried thunder. It looked so fine that Ugh-lomi wanted to join in badly. And sometimes one would roll over on the turf, kicking four hoofs heavenward, which seemed formidable and was certainly much less alluring.

Dim imaginings ran through Ugh-lomi's mind as he watched—by virtue of which two rabbits lived the longer. And sleeping, his brains were clearer and bolder—for that was the way in those days. He came near the horses, he dreamt, and fought, smiting stone against hoof, but then the horses changed to men, or, at least, to men with horses' heads, and he awoke in a cold sweat of terror.

Yet the next day in the morning, as the horses were grazing, one of the mares whinnied, and they saw Ugh-lomi coming up the wind. They all stopped their eating and watched him. Ugh-lomi was not coming towards them, but strolling obliquely across the open, looking at anything in the world but horses. He had stuck three fern-fronds into the mat of his hair, giving him a remarkable appearance, and he walked very slowly. "What's up now?" said the Master Horse, who was capable, but inexperienced.

"It looks more like the first half of an animal than anything else in the world," he said. "Fore-legs and no hind."

"It's only one of those pink monkey things," said the Eldest Mare. "They're a sort of river monkey. They're quite common on the plains."

Ugh-lomi continued his oblique advance. The Eldest Mare was struck with the want of motive in his proceedings.

"Fool!" said the Eldest Mare, in a quick conclusive way she had. She resumed her grazing. The Master Horse and the Second Mare followed suit.

"Look! he's nearer," said the Foal with a stripe.

One of the younger foals made uneasy movements. Ugh-lomi squatted down, and sat regarding the horses fixedly. In a little while he was satisfied that they meant neither flight nor hostilities. He began to consider his next procedure. He did not feel anxious to kill, but he had his axe with him, and the spirit of sport was upon him. How would one kill one of these creatures?—these great beautiful creatures!

Eudena, watching him with a fearful admiration from the cover of the bracken, saw him presently go on all fours, and so proceed again. But the horses preferred him a biped to a quadruped, and the Master Horse threw up his head and gave the word to move. Ugh-lomi thought they were off for good, but after a minute's gallop they came round in a wide curve, and stood winding him. Then, as a rise in the ground hid him, they tailed out, the Master Horse leading, and approached him spirally.

He was as ignorant of the possibilities of a horse as they were of his. And at this stage it would seem he funked. He knew this kind of stalking would make red deer or buffalo charge, if it was persisted in. At any rate Eudena saw him jump up and come walking towards her with the fern plumes held in his hand.

She stood up, and he grinned to show

that the whole thing was an immense lark, and that what he had done was just what he had planned to do from the very beginning. So that incident ended. But he was very thoughtful all that day.

The next day this foolish drab creature with the leonine mane, instead of going about the grazing or hunting he was made for, was prowling round the horses again. The Eldest Mare was all for silent contempt. "I suppose he wants to learn something from us," she said, and "Let him." The next day he was at it again. The Master Horse decided he meant absolutely nothing. But as a matter of fact, Ugh-lomi, the first of men to feel that curious spell of the horse that binds us even to this day, meant a great deal. He admired them unreservedly. There was a rudiment of the snob in him, I am afraid, and he wanted to be near these beautifully-curved animals. Then there were vague conceptions of a kill. If only they would let him come near them! But they drew the line, he found, at fifty yards. If he came nearer than that they moved off—with dignity. I suppose it was the way he had blinded Andoo that made him think of leaping on the back of one of them. But though Eudena after a time came out in the open too, and they did some unobtrusive stalking, things stopped there.

Then one memorable day a new idea came to Ugh-lomi. The horse looks down and level, but he does not look up. No animals look up—they have too much common-sense. It was only that fantastic creature, man, could waste his wits skyward. Ugh-lomi made no philosophical deductions, but he perceived the thing was so. So he spent a weary day in a beech that stood in the open, while Eudena stalked. Usually the horses went into the shade in the heat of the afternoon, but that day the sky was overcast, and they would not, in spite of Eudena's solicitude.

It was two days after that that Ugh-lomi had his desire. The day was blazing hot, and the multiplying flies asserted themselves. The horses stopped grazing before mid-day, and came into the shadow below him, and stood in couples nose to tail, flapping.

The Master Horse, by virtue of his heels, came closest to the tree. And suddenly there was a rustle and a creak, a *thud*. . . . Then a sharp chipped flint bit him on the cheek. The Master Horse stumbled, came on one knee, rose to his feet, and was off like the wind. The air was full of the whirl of limbs, the prance of hoofs, and snorts of alarm. Ugh-lomi was pitched a foot in the air, came down again, up again, his stomach was hit violently, and then his knees got a grip of something between them. He found himself clutching with knees, feet, and hands, careering violently with extraordinary oscillation through the air—his axe gone heaven knows whither. "Hold tight," said Mother Instinct, and he did.

He was aware of a lot of coarse hair in his face, some of it between his teeth, and of green turf streaming past in front of his eyes. He saw the shoulder of the Master Horse, vast and sleek, with the muscles flowing swiftly under the skin. He perceived that his arms were round the neck, and that the violent jerkings he experienced had a sort of rhythm.

Then he was in the midst of a wild rush of tree-stems, and then there were fronds of bracken about, and then more open turf. Then a stream of pebbles rushing past, little pebbles flying sideways athwart the stream from the blow of the swift hoofs. Ugh-lomi began to feel frightfully sick and giddy, but he was not the stuff to leave go simply because he was uncomfortable.

He dared not leave his grip, but he tried to make himself more comfortable. He released his hug on the neck, gripping the mane instead. He slipped his knees forward, and pushing back, came into a sitting position where the quarters broaden.

It was nervous work, but he managed it, and at last he was fairly seated astride, breathless indeed, and uncertain, but with that frightful pounding of his body at any rate relieved.

Slowly the fragments of Ugh-lomi's mind got into order again. The pace seemed to him terrific, but a kind of exultation was beginning to oust his first frantic terror. The air rushed by, sweet and wonderful, the rhythm of the hoofs changed and broke up and returned into itself again. They were on turf now, a wide glade—the beech-trees a hundred yards away on either side, and a succulent band of green starred with pink blossom and shot with silver water here and there, meandered down the middle. Far off was a glimpse of blue valley—far away. The exultation grew. It was man's first taste of pace.

Then came a wide space dappled with flying fallow deer scattering this way and that, and then a couple of jackals, mistaking Ugh-lomi for a lion, came hurrying after him. And when they saw it was not a lion they still came on out of curiosity. On galloped the horse, with his one idea of escape, and after him the jackals, with pricked ears and quickly barked remarks. " Which kills which ? " said the first jackal. " It's the horse being killed," said the second. They gave the howl of following, and the horse answered to it as a horse answers nowadays to the spur.

On they rushed, a little tornado through the quiet day, putting up startled birds, sending a dozen unexpected things darting to cover, raising a myriad of indignant dung-flies, smashing little blossoms, flowering complacently, back into their parental turf. Trees again, and then splash, splash across a torrent ; then a hare shot out of a tuft of grass under the very hoofs of the Master Horse, and the jackals left them incontinently. So presently they broke into the open again, a wide expanse of turfy hillside—the very fellow of the grassy downs that fall northward nowadays from the Epsom Stand.

The first hot bolt of the Master Horse was long since over. He was falling into a measured trot, and Ugh-lomi, albeit bruised exceedingly and quite uncertain of the future, was in a state of glorious enjoyment. And now came a new development. The pace broke again, the Master Horse came round on a short curve, and stopped dead. . . .

Ugh-lomi became alert. He wished he had a flint, but the throwing flint he had carried in a thong about his waist was—like the axe—heaven knows where. The Master Horse turned his head, and Ugh-lomi became aware of an eye and teeth. He whipped his leg into a position of security, and hit at the cheek with his fist. Then the head went down somewhere out of existence apparently, and the back he was sitting on flew up into a dome. Ugh-lomi became a thing of instinct again—strictly prehensile ; he held by knees and feet, and his head seemed sliding towards the turf. His fingers were twisted into the shock of mane, and the rough hair of the horse saved him. The gradient he was on lowered again, and then —" Whup ! " said Ugh-lomi astonished, and the slant was the other way up. But Ugh-lomi was a thousand generations nearer the primordial than man : no monkey could have held on better. And the lion had been training the horse for countless generations against the tactics of rolling and rearing back. But he kicked like a master, and buck-jumped rather neatly. In five minutes Ugh-lomi lived a lifetime. If he came off the horse would kill him, he felt assured.

Then the Master Horse decided to stick to his old tactics again, and suddenly went off at a gallop. He headed down the slope, taking the steep places at a rush, swerving neither to the right nor to the left, and, as they rode down, the wide expanse of valley sank out of sight behind the approaching skirmishers of oak and hawthorn. They skirted a sudden hollow with the pool of a spring, rank weeds and silver bushes. The ground grew softer and the grass taller, and on the right-hand side and the left came scattered bushes of May—still splashed with belated blossom. Presently the bushes thickened until they lashed the passing rider, and little flashes and gouts of blood came out on horse and man. Then the way opened again.

And then came a wonderful adventure. A sudden squeal of unreasonable anger rose amidst the bushes, the squeal of some creature bitterly wronged. And crashing after them appeared a big, grey-blue shape. It was Yaaa the big-horned rhinoceros, in one of those fits of fury of his, charging full tilt, after the manner of his kind. He had been startled at his feeding, and some-one, it did not matter who, was to be ripped and trampled therefore. He was bearing down on them from the left, with his wicked little eye red, and his great horn down, and his little tail like a jury-mast behind him. For a minute Ugh-lomi was minded to slip off and dodge, and then behold! the staccato of the hoofs grew swifter, and the rhinoceros and his stumpy hurrying little legs seemed to slide out at the back corner of Ugh-lomi's eye. In two minutes they were through the bushes of May, and out in the open, going fast. For a space he could hear the ponderous paces in pursuit receding behind him, and then it was just as if Yaaa had not lost his temper, as if Yaaa had never existed.

The pace never faltered, on they rode and on.

Ugh-lomi was now all exultation. To exult in those days was to insult. "Ya-ha! big nose!" he said, trying to crane back and see some remote speck of a pursuer. "Why don't you carry your smiting-stone in your fist?" he ended with a frantic whoop.

But that whoop was unfortunate, for coming close to the ear of the horse, and being quite unexpected, it startled the stallion extremely. He shied violently. Ugh-lomi suddenly found himself uncomfortable again. He was hanging on to the horse, he found, by one arm and one knee.

The rest of the ride was honourable but unpleasant. The view was chiefly of blue sky, and that was combined with the most unpleasant physical sensations. Finally, a bush of thorn lashed him and he let go.

He hit the ground with his cheek and shoulder, and then, after a complicated and extraordinarily rapid movement, hit it again with the end of his backbone. He saw splashes and sparks of light and colour. The ground seemed bouncing about just like the horse had done. Then he found he was sitting on turf, six yards beyond the bush. In front of him was a space of grass, growing greener and greener, and a number of human beings in the distance, and the horse was going round at a smart gallop quite a long way off to the right.

The human beings were on the opposite side of the river, some still in the water, but they were all running away as hard as they could go. The advent of a monster that took to pieces was not the sort of novelty they cared for. For quite a minute Ugh-lomi sat regarding them in a purely spectacular spirit. The bend of the river, the knoll among the reeds and royal ferns, the thin streams of smoke going up to Heaven, were all perfectly familiar to him. It was the squatting-place of the Sons of Uya, of Uya from whom he had fled with Eudena, and whom he had waylaid in the chestnut woods and killed with the First Axe.

He rose to his feet, still dazed from his fall, and as he did so the scattering fugitives turned and regarded him. Some pointed to the receding horse and chattered. He walked slowly towards them, staring. He forgot the horse, he forgot his own bruises, in the growing interest of this encounter. There were fewer of them than there had been—he supposed the others must have hid—the heap of fern

"Hold tight!" said Mother Instinct.

or the night fire was not so high. By the flint heaps should have sat Wau—but then he remembered he had killed Wau. Suddenly brought back to this familiar scene, the gorge and the bears and Eudena seemed things remote, things dreamt of.

He stopped at the bank and stood regarding the tribe. His mathematical abilities were of the slightest, but it was certain there were fewer. The men might be away, but there were fewer women and children. He gave the shout of home-coming. His quarrel had been with Uya and Wau—not with the others. They answered with his name, a little fearfully because of the strange way he had come.

"Children of Uya!" he cried.

For a space they spoke together. Then an old woman lifted a shrill voice and answered him. "Our Lord is a Lion."

Ugh-lomi did not understand that saying. They answered him again several together, "Uya comes again. He comes as a Lion. Our Lord is a Lion. He comes at night. He slays whom he will. But none other may slay us, Ugh-lomi. None other may slay us."

Still Ugh-lomi did not understand.

"Our Lord is a Lion. He speaks no more to men."

Ugh-lomi stood regarding them. He had had dreams—he knew that though he had killed Uya, Uya still existed. And now they told him Uya was a Lion.

The shrivelled old woman, the mistress of the fire-minders, suddenly turned and spoke softly to those next to her. She was a very old woman indeed, she had been the first of Uya's wives, and he had let her live beyond the age to which it is seemly a woman should live. She had been cunning from the first, cunning to please Uya and to get food. And now she was great in counsel. She spoke softly, and Ugh-lomi watched her shrivelled form across the river with a curious distaste. Then she called aloud, "Come over to us, Ugh-lomi."

A girl suddenly lifted up her voice.

"Come over to us, Ugh-lomi," she said. And they all began crying, "Come over to us, Ugh-lomi."

It was strange how their manner changed after the old woman called.

He stood quite still watching them all. It was pleasant to be called, and the girl who had called first was a pretty one. But she made him think of Eudena.

"Come over to us, Ugh-lomi," they cried, and the voice of the shrivelled old woman rose above them all. At the sound of her voice his hesitation returned.

He stood on the river bank, Ugh-lomi —Ugh the Thinker—with his thoughts slowly taking shape. Presently one and then another paused to see what he would do. He was minded to go back, he was minded not to. Suddenly his fear or his caution got the upper hand. Without answering them he turned, and walked back towards the distant thorn-trees, the way he had come. Forthwith the whole tribe started crying to him again very eagerly. He hesitated and turned, then he went on, then he turned again, and then once again, regarding them with troubled eyes as they called. The last time he took two paces back, before his fear stopped him. They saw him stop once more, and suddenly shake his head and vanish among the hawthorn-trees.

Then all the women and children lifted up their voices together, and called to him in one last vain effort.

Far down the river the reeds were stirring in the breeze, where, convenient for his new sort of feeding, the old lion, who had taken to man-eating, had made his lair.

The old woman turned her face that way, and pointed to the hawthorn thickets. "Uya," she screamed, "there goes thine enemy! There goes thine enemy, Uya! Why do you devour us nightly? We have tried to snare him! There goes thine enemy, Uya!

But the lion who preyed upon the tribe was 'taking his siesta. The cry went unheard. That day he had dined on one of the plumper girls, and his mood was a comfortable placidity. He really did not understand that he was Uya or that Ugh-lomi was his enemy.

So it was that Ugh-lomi rode the horse, and heard first of Uya the lion, who had taken the place of Uya the Master, and was eating up the tribe. And as he hurried back to the gorge his mind was no longer full of the horse, but of the thought that Uya was still alive, to slay or be slain. Over and over again he saw the shrunken band of women and children crying that Uya was a lion. Uya was a lion!

And presently, fearing the twilight might come upon him, Ugh-lomi began running.

STORIES OF THE STONE AGE.

BY H. G. WELLS.

ILLUSTRATED BY COSMO ROWE.

IV.—THE REIGN OF UYA THE LION.

HE old lion was in luck. The tribe had a certain pride in their ruler, but that was all the satisfaction they got out of it. He came the very night that Ugh-lomi killed Uya the Cunning, and so it was they named him Uya. It was the old woman, the fire-minder, who first named him Uya. A shower had lowered the fires to a glow, and made the night dark. And as they conversed together, and peered at one another in the darkness, and wondered fearfully what Uya would do to them in their dreams now that he was dead, they heard the mounting reverberations of the lion's roar close at hand. Then everything was still.

They held their breath, so that almost the only sounds were the patter of the rain and the hiss of the raindrops in the ashes. And then, after an interminable time, a crash, and a shriek of fear, and a growling. They sprang to their feet, shouting, screaming, running this way and that, but brands would not burn, and in a minute the victim was being dragged away through the ferns. It was Irk, the brother of Wau. So the lion came.

The ferns were still wet from the rain the next night, and he came and took Click with the red hair. That sufficed for two nights. And then in the dark between the moons he came three nights, night after night, and that though they had good fires. He was an old lion with stumpy teeth, but very silent and very cool; he knew of fires before; these were not the first of mankind that had ministered to his old age. The third night he came between the outer fire and the inner, and he leapt the flint heap, and pulled down Irm the son of Irk, who had seemed like to be the leader. That was a dreadful night, because they lit great flares of fern and ran screaming, and the lion missed his hold of Irm. By the glare of the fire they saw Irm struggle up, and run a little way towards them, and then the lion in two bounds had him down again. That was the last of Irm.

So fear came, and all the delight of spring passed out of their lives. Already there were five gone out of the tribe, and four nights added three more to the number. Food-seeking became spiritless, none knew who might go next, and all day the women toiled, even the favourite women, gathering litter and sticks for the night fires. And the hunters hunted ill: in the warm spring-time hunger came again as though it was still winter. The tribe might have moved, had they had a leader, but they had no leader, and none knew where to go that the lion could not follow them. So the old lion waxed fat and thanked heaven for the race of men. Two of the children and a youth died while the moon was still new, and then it was the shrivelled old fire-minder first bethought herself in a dream of Eudena and Ugh-lomi, and of the way Uya had been slain. She had lived in fear of Uya all her days, and now

That was the last of Irm.

she lived in fear of the lion. That Ugh-lomi could kill Uya for good—Ugh-lomi whom she had seen born—was impossible. It was Uya still seeking his enemy!

And then came the strange return of Ugh-lomi, a wonderful animal seen galloping far across the river, that suddenly changed into two animals, a horse and a man. Following this portent, the vision of Ugh-lomi on the farther bank of the river. . . . Yes, it was all plain to her. Uya was punishing them, because they had not hunted down Ugh-lomi and Eudena.

The men came straggling back to the chances of the night while the sun was still golden in the sky. They were received with the story of Ugh-lomi. She went across the river with them and showed them his spoor hesitating on the farther bank. Siss the Tracker knew the feet for Ugh-lomi's. "Uya needs Ugh-lomi," cried the old woman, standing on the left of the bend, a gesticulating figure of flaring bronze in the sunset. Her cries were strange sounds, flitting to and fro on the borderland of speech, but this was the sense they carried: "The lion needs Eudena. He comes night after night seeking Eudena and Ugh-lomi. When he cannot find Eudena and Ugh-lomi, he grows angry and he kills. Hunt Eudena and Ugh-lomi, Eudena whom he pursued, and Ugh-lomi for whom he gave the death word! Hunt Eudena and Ugh-lomi!"

She turned to the distant reed-bed, as sometimes she had turned to Uya in his life. "Is it not so, my lord?" she cried. And, as if in answer, the tall reeds bowed before a breath of wind.

Far into the twilight the sound of hacking was heard from the squatting-places. It was the men sharpening their ashen spears against the hunting of the morrow. And in the night, early before the moon rose, the lion came and took the girl of Siss the Tracker.

In the morning before the sun had risen, Siss the Tracker, and the lad Wau-

hau, who now chipped flints, and One Eye, and Bo, and the snail-eater, the two red-haired men, and Cat's-skin and Snake, all the men that were left alive of the Sons of Uya, taking their ash spears and their smiting-stones, and with throwing stones in the beast-paw bags, started forth upon the trail of Ugh-lomi through the hawthorn thickets where Yaaa the Rhinoceros and his brothers were feeding, and up the bare downland towards the beechwoods.

That night the fires burnt high and fierce, as the waxing moon set, and the lion left the crouching women and children in peace.

And the next day, while the sun was still high, the hunters returned—all save One Eye, who lay dead with a smashed skull at the foot of the ledge. (When Ugh-lomi came back that evening from stalking the horses, he found the vultures already busy over him.) And with them the hunters brought Eudena bruised and wounded, but alive. That had been the strange order of the shrivelled old woman, that she was to be brought alive—"She is no kill for us. She is for Uya the Lion." Her hands were tied with thongs, as though she had been a man, and she came weary and drooping—her hair over her eyes and matted with blood. They walked about her, and ever and again the Snail-Eater, whose name she had given, would laugh and strike her with his ashen spear. And after he had struck her with his spear, he would look over his shoulder like one who had done an over-bold deed. The others, too, looked over their shoulders ever and again, and all were in a hurry save Eudena. When the old woman saw them coming, she cried aloud with joy.

They made Eudena cross the river with her hands tied, although the current was strong, and when she slipped the old woman screamed, first with joy and then for fear she might be drowned. And when they had dragged Eudena to shore, she could not stand for a time, albeit they beat her sore. So they let her sit with her feet touching the water, and her eyes staring before her, and her face set, whatever they might do or say. All the tribe came down to the squatting-place, even curly little Haha, who as yet could scarcely toddle, and stood staring at Eudena and the old woman, as now we should stare at some strange wounded beast and its captor.

The old woman tore off the necklace of Uya that was about Eudena's neck, and put it on herself—she had been the first to wear it. Then she tore at Eudena's hair, and took a spear from Siss and beat her with all her might. And when she had vented the warmth of her heart on the girl she looked closely into her face. Eudena's eyes were closed and her features were set, and she lay so still that for a moment the old woman feared she was dead until her nostrils quivered. At that the old woman slapped her face and laughed and gave the spear to Siss again, and went a little way off from her and began to talk and jeer at her after her manner.

The old woman had more words than any in the tribe. And her talk was a terrible thing to hear. Sometimes she screamed and moaned incoherently, and sometimes the shape of her guttural cries was the mere phantom of thoughts. But she conveyed to Eudena, nevertheless, much of the things that were yet to come, of the Lion and of the torment he would do her. "And Ugh-lomi! Ha, ha! Ugh-lomi was slain?"

And suddenly Eudena's eyes opened and she sat up again, and her look met the old woman's fair and level. "No," she said slowly, like one trying to remember, "I did not see my Ugh-lomi slain. I did not see my Ugh-lomi slain."

"Tell her," cried the old woman. "Tell her—he that killed him. Tell her how Ugh-lomi was slain."

She looked, and all the women and children there looked, from man to man.

None answered her. They stood shamefaced.

"Tell her," said the old woman. The men looked at one another.

Eudena's face suddenly lit.

"Tell her," she said. "Tell her, mighty men! Tell her the killing of Ugh-lomi."

The old woman rose and struck her sharply across her mouth.

"We could not find Ugh-lomi," said Siss the Tracker, slowly. "Who hunts two, kills none."

Then Eudena's heart leapt, but she kept her face hard. It was as well, for the old woman looked at her sharply, with murder in her eyes.

Then the old woman turned her tongue upon the men because they had feared to go on after Ugh-lomi. She dreaded no one now Uya was slain. She scolded them as one scolds children. And they scowled at her, and began to accuse one another. Until suddenly Siss the Tracker raised his voice and bade her hold her peace.

And so when the sun was setting they took Eudena and went—though their hearts sank within them—along the trail the old lion had made in the reeds. All the men went together. At one place was a group of alders, and here they hastily bound Eudena where the lion might find her when he came abroad in the twilight, and having done so they hurried back until they were near the squatting-place. Then they stopped. Siss stopped first and looked back again at the alders. They could see her head even from the squatting-place, a little black shock under the limb of the larger tree. That was as well.

All the women and children stood watching upon the crest of the mound. And the old woman stood and screamed for the lion to take her whom he sought, and counselled him on the torments he might do her.

Eudena was very weary now, stunned by beatings and fatigue and sorrow, and only the fear of the thing that was still to come upheld her. The sun was broad and blood-red between the stems of the distant chestnuts, and the west was all on fire; the evening breeze had died to a warm tranquillity. The air was full of midge swarms, the fish in the river hard by would leap at times, and now and again a cockchafer would drone through the air. Out of the corner of her eye Eudena could see a part of the squatting-knoll, and little figures standing and staring at her. And—a very little sound but very clear—she could hear the beating of the firestone. Dark and near to her and very still was the reed-fringed thicket of the lair.

She began to weep silently, for this and the gorge was all the life she had known, and life had been a pleasant thing to her.

Presently the firestone ceased. She looked for the sun and found he had gone, and overhead and growing brighter was the waxing moon. She looked towards the thicket of the lair, seeking shapes in the reeds, and then suddenly she began to wriggle and wriggle, weeping and calling upon Ugh-lomi.

But Ugh-lomi was far away. When they saw her head moving with her struggles, they shouted together on the knoll, and then she desisted and was still. And then came the bats, and the star that was like Ugh-lomi crept out of its blue hiding-place in the west. She called to it, but softly, because she feared the lion. And all through the coming of the twilight the thicket was still.

So the dark crept upon Eudena, and the moon grew bright, and the shadows of things that had fled up the hillside and vanished with the evening came back to them short and black. And the dark shapes in the thicket of reeds and alders where the lion lay, gathered, and a faint stir began there. But nothing came out therefrom all through the gathering of the darkness.

She looked at the squatting-place and saw the fires glowing smoky-red, and the men and women going to and fro. The other way, over the river, a white mist was rising. Then far away came the whimpering of young foxes and the yell of a hyæna.

There were long gaps of aching waiting. After a long time some animal splashed in the water, and seemed to cross the river at the ford beyond the lair, but what animal it was she could not see. From the distant drinking-pools she could hear the sound of splashing, and the noise of elephants — so still was the night.

The earth was now a colourless arrangement of white reflections and impenetrable shadows, under the blue sky. The silvery moon was already spotted with the filigree crests of the chestnut woods, and over the shadowy eastward hills the stars were multiplying. The knoll fires were bright red now, and black figures stood waiting against them. They were waiting for a scream. . . . Surely it would be soon.

The night suddenly seemed full of movement. She held her breath. Things were passing—one, two, three—subtly sneaking shadows. . . . Jackals.

Then a long waiting again.

Then, asserting itself as real at once over all the sounds her mind had imagined, came a stir in the thicket, then a vigorous movement. There was a snap. The reeds crashed heavily, once, twice, thrice, and then everything was still save a measured swishing. She heard a low tremulous growl, and then everything was still again. The stillness lengthened— would it never end? She held her breath; she bit her lips to stop screaming. Then something scuttled through the undergrowth. Her scream was involuntary. She did not hear the answering yell from the mound.

Immediately the thicket woke up to vigorous movement again. She saw the grass stems waving in the light of the

For a space he did not move.

setting moon, the alders swaying. She struggled violently—her last struggle. But nothing came towards her. A dozen monsters seemed rushing about in that little place for a couple of minutes, and then again came silence. The moon sank behind the distant chestnuts and the night was dark,

Then an odd sound, a sobbing panting, that grew faster and fainter. Yet another silence, and then dim sounds and the grunting of some animal.

Everything was still again. Far away eastwards an elephant trumpeted, and from the woods came a snarling and yelping that died away.

In the long interval the moon shone out again, between the stems of the trees on the ridge, sending two great bars of light and a bar of darkness across the reedy waste. Then came a steady rustling, a splash, and the reeds swayed wider and wider apart. And at last they broke open, cleft from root to crest. . . . The end had come.

She looked to see the thing that had come out of the reeds. For a moment it seemed certainly the great head and jaw she expected, and then it dwindled and changed. It was a dark low thing, that remained silent, but it was not the lion. It became still — everything became still. She peered. It was like some gigantic frog, two limbs and a slanting body. Its head moved about searching the shadows. . . .

A rustle, and it moved clumsily, with a sort of hopping. And as it moved it gave a low groan.

The blood rushing through her veins was suddenly joy. " *Ugh-lomi !* " she whispered.

The thing stopped. " *Eudena,* " he answered softly with pain in his voice, and peering into the alders.

He moved again, and came out of the shadow beyond the reeds into the moonlight. All his body was covered with dark smears. She saw he was dragging his legs, and that he gripped his axe, the first axe, in one hand. In another moment he had struggled into the position of all fours, and had staggered over to her. " The lion," he said in a strange mingling of exultation and anguish. "Wau !— I have slain a lion. With my own hand. Even as I slew the great bear." He moved to emphasise his words, and suddenly broke off with a faint cry. For a space he did not move.

"Let me free," whispered Eudena. . . .

He answered her no words but pulled himself up from his crawling attitude by means of the alder stem, and hacked at her thongs with the sharp edge of his axe. She heard him sob at each blow. He cut away the thongs about her chest and arms, and then his hand dropped. His chest struck against her shoulder and he slipped down beside her and lay still.

But the rest of her release was easy. Very hastily she freed herself. She made one step from the tree, and her head was spinning. Her last conscious movement was towards him. She reeled, and suddenly fell headlong beside him. Her hand fell upon his thigh. It was soft and wet, and gave way under her pressure ; he cried out at her touch, and writhed and lay still again, with her hand upon him.

Presently a dark dog-like shape came very softly through the reeds. This stopped dead and stood sniffing, hesitated, and at last turned and slunk back into the shadows.

Long was the time they remained there motionless, with the light of the setting moon shining on their limbs. Very slowly, as slowly as the setting of the moon, did the shadow of the reeds towards the mound flow over them. Presently their legs were hidden, and Ugh-lomi was but a bust of silver. The shadow crept to his neck, crept over his face, and so at last the darkness of the night swallowed them up.

The shadow became full of instinctive stirrings. There was a patter of feet, and a faint snarling—the sound of a blow.

There was little sleep that night for the women and children at the squatting-place until they heard Eudena scream. But the men were weary and sat dozing. When Eudena screamed they felt assured of their safety, and hurried to get the nearest places to the fires. The old woman laughed at the scream, and laughed again because Si, the little sister of Eudena, whimpered. Directly the dawn came they were all alert and looking towards the alders. They could see that Eudena had been taken. They could not help feeling glad to think that Uya was appeased. But across the minds of the men the thought of Ugh-lomi fell like a shadow. They could understand revenge, for the world was old in revenge, but they did not think of rescue. Suddenly a hyæna fled out of the thicket, and came galloping across the reed space. His muzzle and paws were dark-stained. At that sight all the men shouted and clutched at throwing-stones and ran towards him, for no animal is so pitiful a coward as the hyæna by day. All men hated the hyæna because he preyed on children, and would come and bite when one was sleeping on the edge of the squatting-place. And Cat's-skin, throwing fair and straight, hit the brute shrewdly, on the flank, whereat the whole tribe yelled with delight.

At the noise they made there came a flapping of wings from the lair of the lion, and three white-headed vultures rose slowly and circled and came to rest amidst the branches of an alder, overlooking the lair. "Our lord is abroad," said the old woman, pointing. "The vultures have their share of Eudena." For a space they remained there, and then first one and then another dropped back into the thicket.

Then over the eastern woods, and touching the whole world to life and colour, poured, with the exaltation of a trumpet blast, the light of the rising sun. At the sight of him the children shouted together, and clapped their hands and began to race off towards the water. Only little Si lagged behind and looked wonderingly at the alders where she had seen the head of Eudena overnight.

But Uya, the old lion, was not abroad but at home, and he lay very still, and a little on one side. He was not in his lair, but a little way from it in a place of trampled grass. Under one eye was a little wound, the feeble little bite of the first axe. But all the ground beneath his chest was ruddy brown with a vivid streak, and in his chest was a little hole that had been made by Ugh-lomi's stabbing-spear. Along his side and at his neck the vultures had marked their claims. For so Ugh-lomi had slain him, lying stricken under his paw and thrusting haphazard at his chest. He had driven the spear in with all his strength and stabbed the giant to the heart. So it was the reign of the lion, of the second incarnation of Uya the Master, came to an end.

From the knoll the bustle of preparation grew, the hacking of spears and throwing-stones. None spake the name of Ugh-lomi for fear that it might bring him. The men were going to keep together, close together, in the hunting for a day or so. And their hunting was to be Ugh-lomi, lest instead he should come a-hunting them.

But Ugh-lomi was lying very still and silent, outside the lion's lair, and Eudena squatted beside him, with the ash spear, all smeared with lion's blood, gripped in her hand.

STORIES OF THE STONE AGE.

BY H. G. WELLS.

ILLUSTRATED BY COSMO ROWE.

V.—THE FIGHT IN THE LION'S THICKET.

UGH-LOMI lay still, his back against an alder, and his thigh was a red mass terrible to see. No civilised man could have lived who had been so sorely wounded, but Eudena got him thorns to close his wounds, and squatted beside him day and night, smiting the flies from him with a fan of reeds by day, and in the night threatening the hyænas who came too near with the first axe in her hand; and in a little while he began to heal. It was high summer, and there was no rain. Little food they had during the first two days his wounds were open. In the low place where they hid were no roots nor little beasts, and the stream, with its water-snails and fish, was in the open a hundred yards away. She could not go abroad by day for fear of the tribe, her brothers and sisters, nor by night for fear of the beasts, both on his account and hers. So they shared the lion with the vultures. But there was a trickle of water near by, and Eudena brought him plenty in her hands.

Where Ugh-lomi lay was well hidden from the tribe by a thicket of alders, and all fenced about with bulrushes and tall reeds. The dead lion he had killed lay near his old lair on a place of trampled reeds fifty yards away, in sight through the reed-stems, and the vultures fought each other for the choicest pieces and kept the jackals off him. Very soon a cloud of flies that looked like bees hung over him, and Ugh-lomi could hear their humming. And when Ugh-lomi's flesh was already healing—and it was not many days before that began—only a few bones of the lion remained scattered and shining white.

For the most part Ugh-lomi sat still during the day, looking before him at nothing, sometimes he would mutter of the horses and bears and lions, and sometimes he would beat the ground with the first axe and say the names of the tribe—he seemed to have no fear of bringing the tribe—for hours together. But chiefly he slept, dreaming little because of his loss of blood and the slightness of his food. During the short summer night both kept awake. All the while the darkness lasted things moved about them, things they never saw by day. For some nights the hyænas did not come, and then one moonless night near a dozen came and fought for what was left of the lion. The night was a tumult of growling, and Ugh-lomi and Eudena could hear the bones snap in their teeth. But they knew the hyæna dare not attack any creature alive and awake, and so they were not greatly afraid.

Of a daytime Eudena would go along the narrow path the old lion had made in the reeds until she was beyond the bend, and then she would creep into the thicket and watch the tribe. She would lie close by the alders where they had bound her to offer her up to the lion, and thence she could see them on the knoll by the fire, little and clear, as she had seen them that night. But she told Ugh-lomi little of what she saw, because she feared to bring them by their names. For so

321

Eudena brought him plenty in her hands.

they believed in those days, that naming called.

She saw the men prepare stabbing-spears and throwing-stones on the morning after Ugh-lomi had slain the lion, and go out to hunt him, leaving the women and children on the knoll. Little they knew how near he was as they tracked off in single file towards the hills, with Siss the Tracker leading them. And she watched the women and children, after the men had gone, gathering fern-fronds and twigs for the night fire, and the boys and girls running and playing together. But the very old woman made her feel afraid. After a long space towards noon, when most of the others were down at the stream by the bend, she came and stood on the hither side of the knoll, a gnarled brown figure, and gesticulated so that Eudena could scarce believe she was not seen. Eudena lay like a hare in its form, with shining eyes fixed on the bent witch away there, and presently she dimly understood it was the lion the old woman was worshipping—the lion Ugh-lomi had slain.

And the next day the hunters came back weary, carrying a fawn, and Eudena watched the feast enviously. And then came a strange thing. She saw—distinctly she heard—the old woman shrieking and gesticulating and pointing towards her. She was afraid, and crept like a snake out of sight again. But presently curiosity overcame her and she was back at her spying-place, and as she peered her heart stopped, for there were all the men, with their weapons in their hands, walking together towards her from the knoll.

She dared not move lest her movement should be seen, but she pressed herself close to the ground. The sun was low and the golden light was in the faces of the men. She saw they carried a piece of rich red meat thrust through by an ashen stake. Presently they stopped. " Go on ! " screamed the old woman. Cat's-skin

grumbled, and they came on, searching the thicket with sun-dazzled eyes. " Here ! " said Siss. And they took the ashen stake with the meat upon it and thrust it into the ground. " Uya !" cried Siss, " behold thy portion. And Ugh-lomi we have slain. Of a truth we have slain Ugh-lomi. This day we slew Ugh-lomi, and to-morrow we will bring his body to you." And the others repeated the words.

They looked at each other and behind them, and partly turned and began going back. At first they walked half turned to the thicket, then facing the mound they walked faster, looking over their shoulders, then faster ; soon they ran, it was a race at last, until they were near the knoll. Then Siss who was hindmost was first to slacken his pace.

The sunset passed and the twilight came, the fires glowed red against the hazy blue of the distant chestnut trees, and the voices over the mound were merry. Eudena lay scarcely stirring, looking from the mound to the meat and then to the mound. She was hungry, but she was afraid. At last she crept back to Ugh-lomi.

He looked round at the little rustle of her approach. His face was in shadow. " Have you got me some food ? " he said.

She said she could find nothing, but that she would seek further, and went back along the lion's path until she could see the mound again, but she could not bring herself to take the meat ; she had the brute's instinct of a snare. She felt very miserable.

She crept back at last towards Ugh-lomi and heard him stirring and moaning. She turned back to the mound again ; then she saw something in the darkness near the stake, and peering distinguished a jackal. In a flash she was brave and angry ; she sprang up, cried out, and ran towards the offering. She stumbled and fell, and heard the growling of the jackal going off.

When she arose only the ashen stake

lay on the ground, the meat was gone. So she went back, to fast through the night with Ugh-lomi; and Ugh-lomi was angry with her, because she had no food for him; but she told him nothing of the things she had seen.

Two days passed and they were near starving, when the tribe slew a horse. Then came the same ceremony, and a haunch was left on the ashen stake; but this time Eudena did not hesitate.

By acting and words she made Ugh-lomi understand, but he ate most of the food before he understood; and then he grew merry with his food. "I am Uya," he said; "I am the Lion. I am the Great Cave Bear, I who was only Ugh-lomi. I am Wau the Cunning. It is well that they should feed me, for presently I will kill them all."

Then Eudena's heart was light, and she laughed with him; and afterwards she ate what he had left of the horseflesh with gladness.

After that it was he had a dream, and the next day he made Eudena bring him the lion's teeth and claws—so much of them as she could find—and hack him a club of alder, and he put the teeth and claws very cunningly into the wood so that the points were outward. Very long it took him, and he blunted two of the teeth hammering them in, and was very angry and threw the thing away; but afterwards he dragged himself to where he had thrown it and finished it—a club of a new sort set with teeth. That day there was more meat for them both, an offering to the lion from the tribe.

It was one day—more than a hand's fingers of days, more than anyone has skill to count—after Ugh-lomi had made the club, that Eudena while he was asleep was lying in the thicket watching the squatting-place. There had been no meat for three days. And the old woman came and worshipped after her manner. Now while she worshipped, Eudena's little sister Si and another, the child of the first

girl Siss had loved, came over the knoll and stood regarding her skinny figure, and presently they began to mock her. Eudena found this entertaining, but suddenly the old woman turned on them quickly and saw them. For a moment she stood and they stood motionless, and then with a shriek of rage she rushed towards them, and all three disappeared over the crest of the knoll.

Presently the children reappeared among the ferns over the shoulder of the hill. Little Si ran first, for she was an active girl, and the other child ran squealing with the old woman close upon her. And over the knoll came Siss with a bone in his hand, and Bo and Cat's-skin obsequiously behind him, each holding a piece of food, and they laughed aloud and shouted to see the old woman so angry. And with a shriek the child was caught and the old woman set to work slapping and the child screaming, and it was very good after-dinner fun for them. Little Si ran on a little way and stopped at last between fear and curiosity.

And suddenly came the mother of the child, with hair streaming, panting, and with a stone in her hand, and the old woman turned about like a wild cat. She was the equal of any woman, was the old chief of the fire-minders, in spite of her years; but before she could do anything Siss shouted to her and the clamour rose loud. Other shock heads came into sight. It seemed the whole tribe was at home and feasting. But the old woman dared not go on wreaking herself on the child Siss befriended. Nevertheless it was a fine row.

Everyone made noises and called names, even little Si. Abruptly the old woman let go of the child she had caught and made a swift run at Si who had no friends; and Si, realising her danger when it was almost upon her, with a faint cry of terror made off headlong, not heeding whither she ran, straight to the lair of the lion. She swerved aside into the reeds presently, not realising whither she went.

But the old woman was a wonderful old woman, as active as she was spiteful, and she caught Si by the streaming hair within thirty yards of Eudena. All the tribe now was running down the knoll and shouting, ready to see the fun.

Then something stirred in Eudena ; and, thinking all of little Si and nothing of her fear, she sprang up from her ambush and ran swiftly forward. The old woman did not see her, for she was busy beating little Si's face with her hand, beating with all her heart, and suddenly something hard and heavy struck her cheek. She went reeling, and saw Eudena with flaming eyes and cheeks between her and little Si. She shrieked with astonishment and terror, and little Si, not understanding, set off towards the gaping tribe. They were quite close now, for the sight of Eudena had driven their fading fear of the lion out of their heads.

In a moment Eudena had turned from the cowering old woman and overtaken Si. " Si!" she cried, " Si!" She caught the child up in her arms as it stopped, pressed the nail-lined face to hers, and turned about to run towards her lair, the lair of the old lion. The old woman stood waist high in the reeds, and screamed foul things and inarticulate rage, but did not dare to intercept her ; and at the bend of the path Eudena looked back and saw all the men of the tribe crying to one another and Siss coming at a trot along the lion's trail.

She ran straight along the narrow way through the reeds to the shady place where Ugh-lomi sat with his healing thigh, just awakened by the shouting and rubbing his eyes. She came to him, a woman, with little Si in her arms. Her heart throbbed in her throat. " Ugh-lomi!" she cried, " Ugh-lomi, the tribe comes !"

Ugh-lomi sat staring in stupid astonishment at her and Si.

She pointed with Si in one arm. She sought among her feeble store of words to explain. She could hear the men calling. Apparently they had stopped outside. She put down Si and caught up the new club with the lion's teeth, and put it into Ugh-lomi's hand, and ran three yards and picked up the first axe.

" Ah !" said Ugh-lomi, waving the new club, and suddenly he perceived the occasion and, rolling over, began to struggle to his feet.

He stood, but clumsily. He supported himself by one hand against the tree, and just touched the ground gingerly with the toe of his wounded leg. In the other hand he gripped the new club. He looked at his healing thigh ; and suddenly the reeds began whispering, and ceased and whispered again, and coming cautiously along the track among the reeds, bending down and holding his fire-hardened stabbing-stick of ash in his hand, appeared Siss. He stopped dead, and his eyes met Ugh-lomi's.

Ugh-lomi forgot he had a wounded leg. He stood firmly on both feet. Something trickled. He glanced down and saw a little gout of blood had oozed out along the edge of the healing wound. He rubbed his hand there to give him the grip of his club, and fixed his eyes again on Siss. The fighting spirit now swiftly and suddenly overflowed.

" Wau !" he cried, and sprang forward, and Siss, still stooping and watchful, drove his stabbing-stick up very quickly in an ugly thrust. It ripped Ugh-lomi's guarding arm and the club came down in a counter that Siss was never to understand. He fell, as an ox falls to the pole-axe, at Ugh-lomi's feet.

To Bo it seemed the strangest thing. He had a comforting sense of tall reeds on either side, and an impregnable rampart, Siss, between him and any danger. Snail-eater was close behind and there was no danger there. He was prepared to shove behind and send Siss to death or victory. That was his place as second

Snail-eater was a readier man.

man. He saw the butt of the spear Siss carried leap away from him, and suddenly a dull whack and the broad back fell away forward, and he looked Ugh-lomi in the face over his prostrate leader. It felt to Bo as if his heart had fallen down a well. He had a throwing-stone in one hand and an ashen stabbing-stick in the other. He did not live to the end of his momentary hesitation which to use.

Snail-eater was a readier man, and besides Bo did not fall forward as Siss had done, but gave at his knees and hips, crumpling up with the toothed club upon his head, smiting him down. The Snail-eater drove his spear forward swift and straight, and took Ugh-lomi in the muscle of the shoulder, and then he drove him hard with the smiting-stone in his other hand, shouting out as he did so. The new club swished ineffectually through the reeds. Eudena saw Ugh-lomi come staggering back from the narrow path into the open space, tripping over Siss and with a foot of ashen stake sticking out of him over his arm, and then the Snail-eater, whose name she had given, had his final injury from her, as his exultant face came out of the reeds after his spear. For she swung the first axe swift and high, and hit him fair and square on the temple ; and down he went on Siss at prostrate Ugh-lomi's feet.

But before Ugh-lomi could get to his feet, the two red-haired men were tumbling out of the reeds, spears and smiting-stones ready, and Snake hard behind them. One she struck on the neck, but not to fell him, and he blundered aside and spoilt his brother's blow at Ugh-lomi's head. In a moment Ugh-lomi dropped his club and had his assailant by the waist, and had pitched him sideways sprawling. He snatched at his club again and recovered it. The man Eudena had hit stabbed at her with his spear as he stumbled from her blow, and involuntarily she gave ground to avoid him. He hesitated between her and Ugh-lomi, half turned, gave a vague

cry at finding Ugh-lomi so near, and in a moment Ugh-lomi had him by the throat, and the club had its third victim. As he went down Ugh-lomi shouted—no words, but an exultant cry.

The other red-haired man was six feet from her with his back to her, and a darker red streaking his head. He was struggling to his feet. She had an irrational impulse to stop his rising. She flung the axe at him, missed, saw his face in profile, and he had swerved beyond little Si, and was running through the reeds. She had a transitory vision of Snake standing in the throat of the path, half turned away from her, and then she saw his back. She saw the club whirling through the air, and the shock head of Ugh-lomi, with blood in the hair and blood upon the shoulder, vanishing below the reeds in pursuit. Then she heard Snake scream like a woman.

She ran past Si to where the handle of the axe stuck out of a clump of fern, and turning, found herself panting and alone with three motionless bodies. The air was full of shouts and screams. For a space she was sick and giddy, and then it came into her head that Ugh-lomi was being killed along the reed-path, and with an inarticulate cry she leapt over the body of Bo and hurried after him. Snake's feet lay across the path, and his head was among the reeds. She followed the path until it bent round and opened out by the alders, and thence she saw all that was left of the tribe in the open, scattering like dead leaves before a gale, and going back over the knoll. Ugh-lomi was hard upon Cat's-skin.

But Cat's-skin was fleet of foot and got away, and so did young Wau-Hau when Ugh-lomi turned upon him, and Ugh-lomi pursued Wau-Hau far beyond the knoll before he desisted. He had the rage of battle on him now, and the wood thrust through his shoulder stung him like a spear. When she saw he was in no danger she stopped running and stood panting, watching the distant active figures run up and vanish one by one over the knoll. In a little time she was alone again. Everything had happened very swiftly. The smoke of Brother Fire rose straight and steady from the squatting-place, just as it had done ten minutes ago, when the old woman had stood yonder worshipping the lion.

And after a long time, as it seemed, Ugh-lomi re-appeared over the knoll, and came back to Eudena, triumphant and breathing heavily. She stood, her hair about her eyes and hot-faced, with the blood-stained axe in her hand, at the place where the tribe had offered her as a sacrifice to the lion. "Wau!" cried Ugh-lomi at the sight of her, his face alight with the fellowship of battle, and he waved his new club, red now and hairy; and at the sight of his glowing face her tense pose relaxed somewhat, and she stood weeping and rejoicing.

Ugh-lomi had a queer unaccountable pang at the sight of her tears; but he only shouted "Wau!" the louder and shook the axe east and west. He called to her to follow him and turned back, striding, with the club swinging in his hand, towards the squatting-place, as if he had never left the tribe; and she stopped weeping and followed as a woman should.

So Ugh-lomi and Eudena came back to the squatting-place from which they had fled many days before from the face of Uya; and by the squatting-place lay a deer half eaten, just as there had been before Ugh-lomi was man or Eudena woman. So Ugh-lomi sat down to eat, and Eudena beside him like a man, and the rest of the tribe watched them from safe hiding-places. And after a time one of the elder girls came back timorously and carrying little Si in her arms, and Eudena called to them by name, and offered them food. But the elder girl was afraid and would not come, though Si struggled to come to Eudena. Afterwards, when Ugh-lomi had eaten, he sat dozing, and at last he

slept, and slowly the others came out of the hiding-places and drew near. And when Ugh-lomi woke, save that there were no men to be seen, it seemed as though he had never left the tribe.

Cat's-skin and the second red-haired man and Wau-Hau, who chipped flints cunningly, as his father had done before him, fled from the face of Ugh-lomi, and none knew where they hid. But two days after they came and squatted among the bracken under the chestnuts a good way off from the knoll and watched. Ugh-lomi's rage had gone, he moved to go against them and did not, and at sundown they went away. That day, too, they found the old woman among the ferns, where Ugh-lomi had blundered upon her when he had pursued Wau-Hau. She was dead and more ugly than ever, but whole. The jackals and vultures had tried her and left her; she was ever a wonderful old woman.

The next day the three men came again and squatted nearer, and Wau-Hau had two rabbits to hold up, and the red-haired man a wood-pigeon, and Ugh-Lomi stood before their women and mocked them.

The next day they sat again nearer—without stones or sticks, and with the same offerings, and Cat's-skin had a trout. It was rare men caught fish in those days, but Cat's-skin would stand silently in the water for hours and catch them with his hand. And the fourth day Ugh-lomi suffered these three to come to the squatting-place in peace, with the food they had with them.

Now, there is a thing strange but true: that all through this fight Ugh-lomi forgot that he was lame, and was not lame, and after he had rested behold! he was a lame man; and he remained a lame man to the end of his days.

So it was Ugh-lomi became Uya and the Lion, and had his will in all things among the children of Uya.

And of his rule among them and of the changing of the squatting-place there is a story still to come.

THE STOLEN BACILLUS

Originally published in *Pearson's Magazine*
June 1905

THE STOLEN BACILLUS

A Tale of Anarchy.

By H. G. Wells.

"This again," said the Bacteriologist, slipping a glass slide under the microscope, "is a preparation of the celebrated bacillus of cholera—the cholera germ."

The pale-faced man peered down the microscope. He was evidently not accustomed to that kind of thing, and held a limp white hand over his disengaged eye. "I see very little," he said.

"Touch this screw," said the Bacteriologist; "perhaps the microscope is out of focus for you. Eyes vary so much. Just the fraction of a turn this way or that."

"Ah! now I see," said the visitor. "Not so very much to see after all. Little streaks and shreds of pink. And yet those little particles, those mere atomies, might multiply and devastate a city! Wonderful!"

He stood up, and releasing the glass slip from the microscope, held it in his hand towards the window. "Scarcely visible," he said, scrutinising the preparation. He hesitated. "Are these—alive? Are they dangerous now?"

"Those have been stained and killed," said the Bacteriologist. "I wish, for my own part, we could kill and stain every one of them in the universe."

"I suppose," the pale man said, with a slight smile, "that you scarcely care to have such things about you in the living—in the active state?"

"On the contrary, we are obliged to," said the Bacteriologist. "Here, for instance—" He walked across the room and took up one of several sealed tubes. "Here is the living thing. This is a cultivation of the actual living disease bacteria." He hesitated. "Bottled cholera, so to speak."

A slight gleam of satisfaction appeared momentarily in the face of the pale man. "It's a deadly thing to have in your possession," he said, devouring the little tube with his eyes. The Bacteriologist watched the morbid pleasure in his visitor's expression. This man who had visited him that afternoon with a note of introduction from an old friend, interested him from the very contrast of their dispositions.

The lank black hair and deep grey eyes, the haggard expression and nervous manner, the fitful yet keen interest of his visitor were a novel change from the phlegmatic deliberations of the ordinary scientific worker with whom the Bacteriologist chiefly associated. It was, perhaps, natural, with a hearer evidently so impressionable to the lethal nature of his topic, to take the most effective aspect of the matter.

He held the tube in his hand thoughtfully. "Yes, here is the pestilence imprisoned. Only break such a little tube as this into a supply of drinking-water, say to these minute particles of life that one must needs stain and examine with the highest powers of the microscope even to see, and that one can neither smell nor taste—say to them, 'Go forth, increase and multiply, and replenish the cisterns,' and death—mysterious, untraceable death, death swift and terrible, death full of pain and indignity—would be released upon this city, and go hither and thither seeking his victims.

"Here he would take the husband from

the wife, here the child from its mother, here the statesman from his duty, and here the toiler from his trouble. He would follow the water-mains, creeping along streets, picking out and punishing a house here and a house there where they did not boil their drinking-water, creeping into the wells of the mineral-water makers, getting washed into salad, and lying dormant in ices. He would wait ready to be drunk in the horse-troughs, and by unwary children in the public fountains. He would soak into the soil, to reappear in springs and wells at a thousand unexpected places. Once start him at the water supply, and before we could ring him in and catch him again, he would have decimated the metropolis."

He stopped abruptly. He had been told rhetoric was his weakness.

"But he is quite safe here, you know—quite safe."

The pale-faced man nodded. His eyes shone.

He cleared his throat. "These Anarchist—rascals," said he, "are fools, blind fools—to use bombs when this kind of thing is attainable. I think——"

A gentle rap, a mere light touch of the finger-nails was heard at the door. The Bacteriologist opened it.

"Just a minute, dear," whispered his wife.

When he re-entered the laboratory his visitor was looking at his watch. "I had no idea I had wasted an hour of your time," he said. "Twelve minutes to four. I ought to have left here by half-past three. But your things were really too interesting. No, positively, I cannot stop a moment longer. I have an engagement at four."

He passed out of the room reiterating his thanks, and the Bacteriologist accompanied him to the door, and then returned thoughtfully along the passage to his laboratory. He was musing on the ethnology of his visitor. Certainly the man was not a Teutonic type nor a common Latin one.

"A morbid product, anyhow, I am afraid," said the Bacteriologist to himself. "How he gloated on those cultivations of disease germs!"

A disturbing thought struck him. He

turned to the bench by the vapour-bath, and then very quickly to his writing-table. Then he felt hastily in his pockets, and then rushed to the door. "I may have put it down on the hall table," he said.

"Minnie!" he shouted hoarsely in the hall.

"Yes, dear," came a remote answer.

"Had I anything in my hand when I spoke to you, dear, just now?"

Pause.

"Nothing, dear, because I remember——"

"Blue ruin!" cried the Bacteriologist, and incontinently ran to the front door and down the steps of his house to the street.

Minnie, hearing the door slam violently, ran in alarm to the window.

Down the street a slender man was getting into a cab. The Bacteriologist, hatless and in his carpet slippers, was running and gesticulating wildly towards this group. One slipper came off, but he did not wait for it. "He has gone *mad!*" said Minnie; "it's that horrid science of his;" and opening the window, would have called after him.

The slender man, suddenly glancing round, seemed struck with the same idea of mental disorder. He pointed hastily to the Bacteriologist, said something to the cabman, the apron of the cab slammed, the whip swished, the horse's feet clattered, and in a moment, cab and Bacteriologist hotly in pursuit, had receded up the vista of the roadway and disappeared round the corner.

Minnie remained straining out of the window for a minute. Then she drew her head back into the room again.

She was dumfounded.

"Of course, he is eccentric," she meditated. "But running about London—in the height of the season, too—in his socks!" A happy thought struck her. She hastily put her bonnet on, seized his shoes, went into the hall, took down his hat and light overcoat from the pegs, emerged upon the doorstep, and hailed a cab that opportunely crawled by.

"Drive me up the road and round Havelock Crescent, and see if we can find a gentleman running about in a velveteen coat and no hat."

"Velveteen coat, ma'am, and no 'at. Very good, ma'am." And the cabman whipped up at once in the most matter-of-fact way, as if he drove to this address every day in his life.

Some few minutes later the little group of cabmen and loafers that collects round the cabmen's shelter at Haverstock Hill were startled by the passing of a cab with a ginger-coloured screw of a horse, driven furiously.

They were silent as it went by, and then as it receded—"That's 'Arry 'Icks. Wot's *he* got?" said the stout gentleman known as Old Tootles.

"He's a-using his whip, he is, *to* rights," said the ostler boy.

"Hullo!" said poor old Tommy Byles; "here's another bloomin' loonatic. Blowed if there ain't."

The Bacteriologist, hatless, and in his carpet slippers, was running and gesticulating wildly towards this group.

"It's old George," said old Tootles, "and he's drivin' a loonatic, *as* you say. Ain't he a-clawin' out of the keb! Wonder if he's after 'Arry 'Icks?"

The group round the cabmen's shelter became animated. Chorus: "Go it, George!" "It's a race." "You'll ketch 'em!" "Whip up!"

"She's a goer, she is!" said the ostler boy.

"Strike me giddy!" cried old Tootles. "Here! *I'm* a-goin' to begin in a minute.

Here's another comin'. If all the kebs in Hampstead ain't gone mad this morning!"

"It's a fieldmale this time," said the ostler boy.

"She's a followin' *him*," said old Tootles. "Usually the other way about."

"What's she got in her 'and?"

"Looks like a 'igh 'at."

"What a bloomin' lark it is! Three to one on old George," said the ostler boy. "Next!"

Minnie went by in a perfect roar of

The Bacteriologist from his cab beamed curiously at him through his spectacles.

applause. She did not like it, but she felt that she was doing her duty, and whirled on down Haverstock Hill and Camden Town High Street with her eyes ever intent on the animated back view of old George, who was driving her vagrant husband so incomprehensibly away from her.

The man in the foremost cab sat crouched in the corner, his arms tightly folded, and the little tube that contained such vast possibilities of destruction gripped in his hand. His mood was a singular mixture of fear and exultation. Chiefly he was afraid of being caught before he could accomplish his purpose, but behind this was a vaguer but larger fear of the awfulness of his crime.

But his exultation far exceeded his fear. No anarchist before him had ever approached this conception of his. Ravachol, Vaillant, all those distinguished persons whose fame he had envied dwindled into insignificance beside him. He had only to make sure of the water supply, and break the little tube into a reservoir. How brilliantly he had planned it, forged the letter of introduction and got into the laboratory, and how brilliantly he had seized his opportunity!

The world should hear of him at last. All those people who had sneered at him, neglected him, preferred other people to him, found his company undesirable, should consider him at last. Death, death, death! They had always treated him as a man of no importance. All the world had been in a conspiracy to keep him under. He would teach them yet what it is to isolate a man.

What was this familiar street? Great St. Andrew Street, of course! How fared the chase? He craned out of the cab. The Bacteriologist was scarcely fifty yards behind. That was bad. He would be caught and stopped yet. He felt in his pocket for money, and found half-a-sovereign. This he

thrust up through the trap in the top of the cab into the man's face. "More," he shouted, "if only we get away."

The money was snatched out of his hand. "Right you are," said the cabman, and the trap slammed, and the lash lay along the glistening side of the horse. The cab swayed, and the Anarchist, half standing under the trap, put the hand containing the little glass tube upon the apron to preserve his balance. He felt the brittle little thing crack, and the broken half of it rang upon the floor of the cab. He fell back into the seat with a curse, and stared dismally at the two or three drops of moisture on the apron.

He shuddered.

"Well! I suppose I shall be the first. *Phew!* Anyhow, I shall be a martyr. That's something; but it is a filthy death, nevertheless. I wonder if it hurts as much as they say."

Presently a thought occurred to him—he

"Vive l' Anarchie! You are too late, my friend. I have drunk it. The cholera is abroad!"

groped between his feet. A little drop was still in the broken end of the tube, and he drank that to make sure. It was better to make sure. At any rate, he would not fail.

Then it dawned upon him that there was no further need to escape the Bacteriologist. In Wellington Street he told the cabman to stop, and got out. He slipped on the step, and his head felt queer. It was rapid stuff this cholera poison. He waved his cabman out of existence, so to speak, and stood on the pavement with his arms folded upon his breast awaiting the arrival of the Bacteriologist. There was something tragic in his pose. The sense of imminent death gave him a certain dignity. He greeted his pursuer with a defiant laugh.

" *Vive l'Anarchie!* You are too late, my friend. I have drunk it. The cholera is abroad!"

The Bacteriologist from his cab beamed curiously at him through his spectacles.

" You have drunk it! An Anarchist! I see now."

He was about to say something more, and then checked himself. A smile hung in the corner of his mouth. He opened the apron of his cab as if to descend, at which the Anarchist waved him a dramatic farewell and strode off towards Waterloo Bridge, carefully jostling his infected body against as many people as possible. The Bacteriologist was so preoccupied with the vision of him that he scarcely manifested the slightest surprise at the appearance of Minnie upon the pavement with his hat and shoes and overcoat.

" Very good of you to bring my things,"

he said, and remained lost in contemplation of the receding figure of the Anarchist.

" You had better get in," he said still staring.

Minnie felt absolutely convinced now that he was mad, and directed the cabman home on her own responsibility.

" Put on my shoes? Certainly, dear," said he, as the cab began to turn, and hid the strutting black figure, now small in the distance, from his eyes.

Then suddenly something grotesque struck him, and he laughed. Then he remarked :

" It is really very serious, though. You see, that man came to my house to see me, and he is an Anarchist. No—don't faint, or I cannot possibly tell you the rest. And I wanted to astonish him, not knowing he was an Anarchist, and took up a cultivation of that new species of Bacterium I was telling you of, that infest, and I think cause, the blue patches upon various monkeys ; and like a fool, I said it was Asiatic cholera. And he ran away with it to poison the water of London, and he certainly might have made things look blue for this civilised city. And now he has swallowed it. Of course, I cannot say what will happen, but you know it turned that kitten blue, and the three puppies—in patches, and the sparrow—bright blue. But the bother is, I shall have all the trouble and expense of preparing some more.

" Put on my coat on this hot day! Why? Because we might meet Mrs. Jabber. My dear, Mrs. Jabber is not a draught. But why should I wear a coat on a hot day because of Mrs. ——? Oh! *very* well."

—11—

IN THE ABYSS

Originally published in *Pearson's Magazine*
August 1896

In The Abyss

By H. G. Wells

THE lieutenant stood in front of the steel sphere and gnawed a piece of pine splinter. "What do you think of it, Steevens?" he asked.

"It's an idea," said Steevens, in the tone of one who keeps an open mind.

"I believe it will smash—flat," said the lieutenant.

"He seems to have calculated it all out pretty well," said Steevens, still impartial.

"But think of the pressure," said the lieutenant. "At the surface of the water it's fourteen pounds to the inch, thirty feet down it's double that; sixty, treble; ninety, four times; nine hundred, forty times; five thousand three hundred—that's a mile—it's two hundred and forty times fourteen pounds; that's—let's see—thirty hundredweight—a ton and a half, Steevens; *a ton and a half* to the square inch. And the ocean where he's going is five miles deep. That's seven and a half——"

"Sounds a lot," said Steevens, "but it's jolly thick steel."

The lieutenant made no answer, but resumed his pine splinter. The object of their conversation was a huge globe of steel, having an exterior diameter of perhaps twenty feet. It looked like the shot for some Titanic piece of artillery. It was elaborately nested in a monstrous scaffolding built into the framework of the vessel, and the gigantic spars that were presently to sling it overboard · gave the stern of the ship an appearance that had raised the curiosity of every decent sailor who had sighted it, from the pool of London to the Tropic of Capricorn. In two places, one above the other, the steel gave place to a couple of circular windows of enormously thick glass, and one of these, set in a steel frame of great solidity, was now partially unscrewed. Both the men had seen the interior of this globe for the first time that morning. It was elaborately padded with air cushions, with little studs sunk between bulging pillows to work the simple mechanism of the affair. Everything was elaborately padded, even the Myer's apparatus which was to absorb carbonic acid and replace the oxygen inspired by its tenant, when he had crept in by the glass manhole, and had been screwed in. It was so elaborately padded that a man might have been fired from a gun in it with perfect safety. And it had need to be, for presently a man was to crawl in through that glass manhole, to be screwed up tightly, and to be flung overboard, and to sink down—down—down, for five miles, even as the lieutenant said. It had taken the strongest hold of his imagination; it made him a bore at mess; and he found Steevens, the new arrival aboard, a godsend to talk to about it, over and over again.

"It's my opinion," said the lieutenant, "that that glass will simply bend in and bulge and smash, under a pressure of that sort. Daubrée has made rocks run like water under big pressures—and, you mark my words——"

"If the glass did break in," said Steevens, "what then?"

"The water would shoot in like a jet of iron. Have you ever felt a straight jet of high pressure water? It would hit as hard as a bullet. It would simply smash him and flatten him. It would tear down his throat, and into his lungs; it would blow in his ears——"

"What a detailed imagination you have," protested Steevens, who saw things vividly.

"It's a simple statement of the inevitable," said the lieutenant.

"And the globe?"

"Would just give out a few little bubbles, and it would settle down comfortably against the day of judgment, among the oozes and the bottom clay—with poor Elstead spread over his own smashed cushions like butter over bread."

He repeated this sentence as though he liked it very much. "Like butter over bread," he said.

"Having a look at the jigger?" said a voice behind them, and Elstead stood behind them, spick and span in white, with a cigarette between his teeth, and his eyes smiling out of the shadow of his ample hat-brim. "What's that about bread and butter, Weybridge? Grumbling as usual about the insufficient pay of naval officers? It won't be more than a day now before I start. We are to get the slings ready to-day. This clean sky and gentle swell is just the kind of thing for swinging off five tons of lead and iron; isn't it?"

"It won't affect you much," said Weybridge.

"No. Seventy or eighty feet down, and I shall be there in a dozen seconds, there's not a particle moving, though the wind shriek itself hoarse up above, and the water lifts halfway to the clouds. No. Down there—" He moved to the side of the ship and the other two followed him. All three leant forward on their elbows and stared down into the yellow-green water.

"*Peace*," said Elstead, finishing his thought aloud.

"Are you dead certain that clockwork will act?" asked Weybridge presently.

"It has worked thirty-five times," said Elstead. "It's bound to work."

"But if it doesn't?"

"Why shouldn't it?"

"I wouldn't go down in that confounded thing," said Weybridge, "for twenty thousand pounds."

"Cheerful chap you are," said Elstead, and spat sociably at a bubble below.

"I don't understand yet how you mean to work the thing," said Steevens.

"In the first place I'm screwed into the sphere," said Elstead, "and when I've turned the electric light off and on three times to show I'm cheerful, I'm swung out over the stern by that crane, with all those big lead sinkers slung below me. The top lead weight has a roller carrying a hundred fathoms of strong cord rolled up, and that's all that joins the sinkers to the sphere, except the slings that will be cut when the affair is dropped. We use cord rather than wire rope because it's easier to cut and more buoyant—necessary points as you will see.

"Through each of these lead weights you notice there is a hole, and an iron rod will be run through that and will project six feet on the lower side. If that rod is rammed up from below it knocks up a lever and sets the clockwork in motion at the side of the cylinder on which the cord winds.

"Very well. The whole affair is lowered gently into the water, and the slings are cut. The sphere floats—with the air in it, it's lighter than water—but the lead weights go down straight and the cord runs out. When the cord is all paid out, the sphere will go down too, pulled down by the cord."

"But why the cord?" asked Steevens. "Why not fasten the weights directly to the sphere?"

"Because of the smash down below. The whole affair will go rushing down, mile after mile, at a headlong pace at last. It would be knocked to pieces on the bottom if it wasn't for that cord. But the weights will hit the bottom, and directly they do the buoyancy of the sphere will come into play. It will go on sinking slower and slower; come to a stop at last and then begin to float upward again.

"That's where the clockwork comes in. Directly the weights smash against the sea bottom, the rod will be knocked through and will kick up the clockwork, and the cord will be rewound on the reel. I shall be lugged down to the sea bottom. There I shall stay for half an hour, with the electric light on, looking about me. Then the clockwork will release a spring knife, the cord will be cut, and up I shall rush again, like a soda water bubble. The cord itself will help the flotation."

"And if you should chance to hit a ship?" said Weybridge.

"I should come up at such a pace, I should go clean through it," said Elstead,

"like a cannon ball. You needn't worry about that."

"And suppose some nimble crustacean should wriggle into your clockwork——"

"It would be a pressing sort of invitation for me to stop," said Elstead, turning his back on the water and staring at the sphere.

*   *   *   *   *

They had swung Elstead overboard by eleven o'clock. The day was serenely bright and calm, with the horizon lost in haze. The electric glare in the little upper compartment beamed cheerfully three times. Then they let him down slowly to the surface of the water, and a sailor in the stern chains hung ready to cut the tackle that held the lead weights and the sphere together. The globe, which had looked so large on deck, looked the smallest thing conceivable under the stern of the ship. It rolled a little, and its two dark windows, which floated uppermost, seemed like eyes turned up in round wonderment at the people who crowded the rail. A voice wondered how Elstead liked the rolling. "Are you ready?" sang out the Commander. "Aye, aye, sir!" "Then let her go!"

The rope of the tackle tightened against the blade and was cut, and an eddy rolled over the globe in a grotesquely helpless fashion. Someone waved a handkerchief, someone else tried an ineffectual cheer, a middy was counting slowly: "Eight, nine, ten!" Another roll, then with a jerk and a splash the thing righted itself.

It seemed to be stationary for a moment, to grow rapidly smaller, and then the water closed over it, and it became visible, enlarged by refraction and dimmer, below the surface. Before one could count three it had disappeared. There was a flicker of white light far down in the water, that diminished to a speck and vanished. Then there was nothing but a depth of water going down into blackness, through which a shark was swimming.

Then suddenly the screw of the cruiser began to rotate, the water was crickled, the shark disappeared in a wrinkled confusion. and a torrent of foam rushed across the crystalline clearness that had swallowed up Elstead. "What's the idee?" said one A.B. to another.

" We're going to lay off about a couple of miles, 'fear he should hit us when he comes up," said his mate.

The ship steamed slowly to her new position. Aboard her almost everyone who was unoccupied remained watching the breathing swell into which the sphere had sunk. For the next half hour it is doubtful if a word was spoken that did not bear directly or indirectly on Elstead. The December sun was now high in the sky, and the heat very considerable.

" He'll be cold enough down there," said Weybridge. " They say that below a certain depth sea water's always just about freezing."

" Where'll he come up ? " asked Steevens. " I've lost my bearings."

" That's the spot," said the Commander, who prided himself on his omniscience. He extended a precise finger south-eastward. " And this, I reckon, is pretty nearly the moment," he said. " He's been thirty-five minutes."

" How long does it take to reach the bottom of the ocean ? " asked Steevens.

" For a depth of five miles, and reckoning —as we did—an acceleration to two foot per second, both ways, is just about three-quarters of a minute.

" Then he's overdue," said Weybridge.

" Pretty nearly," said the Commander. " I suppose it takes a few minutes for that cord of his to wind in."

" I forgot that," said Weybridge, evidently relieved.

And then began the suspense. A minute slowly dragged itself out, and no sphere shot out of the water. Another followed, and nothing broke the low oily swell. The sailors explained to one another that little point about the winding-in of the cord. The rigging was dotted with expectant faces. " Come up, Elstead ! " called one hairy-chested salt impatiently, and the others caught it up, and shouted as though they were waiting for the curtain of a theatre to rise.

The Commander glanced irritably at them.

" Of course, if the acceleration's less than two," he said, " he'll be all the longer. We aren't absolutely certain that was the proper figure. I'm no slavish believer in calculations."

Steevens agreed concisely. No one on the quarter-deck spoke for a couple of minutes. Then Steeven's watch-case clicked.

When, twenty-one minutes after, the sun reached the zenith, they were still waiting for the globe to re-appear, and not a man aboard had dared to whisper that hope was dead. It was Weybridge who first gave expression to that realisation. He spoke while the sound of eight bells still hung in the air. " I always distrusted that window," he said quite suddenly to Steevens.

" Good God !" said Steevens, " you don't think——?"

" Well!" said Weybridge, and left the rest to his imagination.

" I'm no great believer in calculations myself," said the Commander dubiously, " so that I'm not altogether hopeless yet." And at midnight the gunboat was steaming slowly in a spiral round the spot where the globe had sunk, and the white beam of the electric light fled and halted and swept discontentedly onward again over the waste of phosphorescent waters under the little stars.

" If his window hasn't burst and smashed him," said Weybridge, " then it's a cursed sight worse, for his clockwork has gone wrong and he's alive now, five miles under our feet, down there in the cold and dark, anchored in that little bubble of his, where never a ray of light has shone or a human being lived, since the waters were gathered together. He's there without food, feeling hungry and thirsty and scared, wondering whether he'll starve or stifle. Which will it be ? The Myer's apparatus is running out, I suppose. How long do they last?

" Good Heavens !" he exclaimed, " what little things we are ! What daring little devils ! Down there, miles and miles of water—all water, and all this empty water about us and this sky. Gulfs !" He threw his hands out, and as he did so a little white streak swept noiselessly up the sky, travelling more slowly, stopped, became a motionless dot as though a new star had fallen up into the sky. Then it went sliding back again and lost itself amidst the reflections of the stars, and the white haze of the sea's phosphorescence.

Three things like shapes of fire.

At the sight he stopped, arm extended and mouth open. He shut his mouth, opened it again and waved his arms with an impatient gesture. Then he turned, shouted "El-stead ahoy," to the first watch, and went at a run to Lindley and the search light. "I saw him," he said. "Starboard there! His light's on and he's just shot out of the water. Bring the light round, We ought to see him drifting, when he lifts on the swell."

But they never picked up the explorer until dawn. Then they almost ran him down. The crane was swung out and a boat's crew hooked the chain to the sphere. When they had shipped the sphere they unscrewed the manhole and peered into the darkness of the interior (for the electric light chamber was intended to illuminate the water about the sphere, and was shut off entirely from its general cavity).

The air was very hot within the cavity, and the indiarubber at the lip of the manhole was soft. There was no answer to their eager questions and no sound of movement within. Elstead seemed to be lying motionless crumpled up in the bottom of the globe. The ship's doctor crawled in and lifted him out to the men outside. For a moment or so they did not know whether Elstead was alive or dead. His face, in the yellow light of the ship's lamps, glistened with perspiration. They carried him down to his own cabin.

WARWICK GOBLE

He was not dead they found, but in a state of absolute nervous collapse, and besides cruelly bruised. For some days he had to lie perfectly still. It was a week before he could tell his experiences.

Almost his first words were that he was going down again. The sphere would have to be altered, he said, in order to allow him to throw off the cord if need be, and that was all. He had had the most marvellous experience. "You thought I should find nothing but ooze," he said. "You laughed at my explorations, and I've discovered a new world!" He told his story in disconnected fragments and chiefly from the wrong end, so that it is impossible to re-tell it in his words. But what follows is the narrative of his experience.

It began atrociously, he said. Before the cord ran out the thing kept rolling over. He felt like a frog in a football. He could see nothing but the crane and the sky overhead, with an occasional glimpse of the people on the ship's rail. He couldn't tell a bit which way the thing would roll next. Suddenly he would find his feet going up, and try to step, and over he went rolling, head over heels and just anyhow on the padding. Any other shape would have been more comfortable, but no other shape was to be relied upon under the huge pressure of the nethermost abyss.

Suddenly the swaying ceased; the globe righted, and when he had picked himself up, he saw the water all about him greeny-blue, with an attenuated light filtering down from above, and a shoal of little floating things went rushing up past him, as it seemed to him, towards the light. And even as he looked it grew darker and darker, until the water above was as dark as the midnight sky, albeit of a greener shade, and the water below black. And little transparent things in the water developed a faint glint of luminosity, and shot past him in faint greenish streaks.

And the feeling of falling! It was just like the start of a lift, he said, only it kept on. One has to imagine what that means, that keeping on. It was then of all times that Elstead repented of his adventure. He saw the chances against him in an altogether new light. He thought of the big cuttle fish people knew to exist in the middle waters, the kind of things they find half digested in whales at times, or floating dead and rotten and half eaten by fish. Suppose one caught hold and wouldn't leave go. And had the clockwork really been sufficiently tested? But whether he wanted to go on or to go back mattered not the slightest now.

In fifty seconds everything was as black as night outside, except where the beam from his light struck through the waters, and picked out every now and then some fish or scrap of sinking matter. They flashed by too fast for him to see what they were. Once he thought he passed a shark. And then the sphere began to get hot by friction against the water. They had under-estimated this, it seems.

The first thing he noticed was that he was perspiring, and then he heard a hissing growing louder under his feet, and saw a lot of little bubbles—very little bubbles they were—rushing upward like a fan through the water outside. Steam! He felt the window, and it was hot. He turned on the minute glowlamp that lit his own cavity, looked at the padded watch by the studs, and saw he had been travelling now for two minutes. It came into his head that the window would crack through the conflict of temperatures, for he knew the bottom water was very near freezing.

Then suddenly the floor of the sphere seemed to press against his feet, the rush of bubbles outside grew slower and slower, and the hissing diminished. The sphere rolled a little. The window had not cracked, nothing had given, and he knew that the dangers of sinking, at any rate, were over.

In another minute or so he would be on the floor of the abyss. He thought, he said, of Steevens and Weybridge and the rest of them five miles overhead, higher to him than the very highest clouds that ever floated over land are to us, steaming slowly and staring down and wondering what had happened to him.

He peered out of the window. There were no more bubbles now, and the hissing had stopped. Outside there was a heavy blackness—as black as black velvet—except where the electric light pierced the empty water and showed the colour of it—a yellow green.

Then three things like shapes of fire swam into sight, following each other through the water. Whether they were little and near or big and far off he could not tell.

Each was outlined in a bluish light almost as bright as the lights of a fishing smack, a light which seemed to be smoking greatly, and all along the sides of them were specks of this, like the lighted portholes of a ship. Their phosphorescence seemed to go out as

It was a strange vertebrated animal.

they came into the radiance of his lamp, and he saw then that they were indeed fish of some strange sort with huge heads, vast eyes and dwindling bodies and tails. Their eyes were turned towards him, and he judged they were following him down. He supposed they were attracted by his glare.

Presently others of the same sort joined them. As he went on down he noticed that the water became of a pallid colour, and that little specks twinkled in his ray like motes in sunbeam. This was probably due to the clouds of ooze and mud that the impact of his leaden sinkers had disturbed.

By the time he was drawn down to the lead weights he was in a dense fog of white that his electric light failed altogether to pierce for more than a few yards, and many minutes elapsed before the hanging sheets of sediment subsided to any extent. Then, lit by his light and by the transient phosphorescence of a distant shoal of fishes, he was able to see under the huge blackness of the super-incumbent water an undulating expanse of greyish-white ooze, broken here and there by tangled thickets of a growth of sea lilies, waving hungry tentacles in the air.

Farther away were the graceful translucent outlines of a group of gigantic sponges. About this floor there were scattered a number of bristling flattish tufts of rich purple and black, which he decided must be some sort of sea urchin, and small, large-eyed or blind things having a curious resemblance, some to woodlice, and others to lobsters, crawled sluggishly across the track of the light and vanished into the obscurity again, leaving furrowed trails behind them.

Then suddenly the hovering swarm of little fishes veered about and came towards him as a flight of starlings might do. They passed over him like a phosphorescent snow, and then he saw behind them some larger creature advancing towards the sphere.

At first he could see it only dimly, a faintly moving figure remotely suggestive of a walking man, and then it came into the spray of light that the lamp shot out. As the glare struck it, it shut its eyes dazzled. He stared in rigid astonishment.

It was a strange vertebrated animal. Its dark purple head was dimly suggestive of a chameleon, but it had such a high forehead and such a brain-case as no reptile ever displayed before; the vertical pitch of its face gave it a most extraordinary resemblance to a human being.

Two large and protruding eyes projected from sockets in chameleon fashion, and it had a broad reptilian mouth with horny lips beneath its little nostrils. In the position of the ears were two huge gill covers, and out of these floated a branching tree of coralline filaments, almost like the tree-like gills that very young rays and sharks possess.

But the humanity of the face was not the most extraordinary thing about the creature. It was a biped, its almost globular body was poised on a tripod of two frog-like legs and a long thick tail, and its fore limbs, which grotesquely caricatured the human hand much as a frog's do, carried a long shaft of bone, tipped with copper. The colour of the creature was variegated; its head, hands, and legs were purple; but its skin, which

hung loosely upon it, even as clothes might do, was a phosphorescent grey. And it stood there blinded by the light.

At last this unknown creature of the abyss blinked its eyes open, and, shading them with its disengaged hand, opened its mouth and gave vent to a shouting noise, articulate almost as speech might be, that penetrated even the steel case and padded jacket of the sphere. How a shouting may be accomplished without lungs Elstead does not profess to explain. It then moved sideways out of the glare into the mystery of shadow that bordered it on either side, and Elstead felt rather than saw that it was coming towards him. Fancying the light had attracted it, he turned the switch that cut off the current. In another moment something soft dabbed upon the steel, and the globe swayed.

Then the shouting was repeated, and it seemed to him that a distant echo answered it. The dabbing recurred, and the globe swayed and ground against the spindle over which the wire was rolled. He stood in the blackness, and peered out into the everlasting night of the abyss. And presently he saw, very faint and remote, other phosphorescent quasi-human forms hurrying towards him.

Hardly knowing what he did, he felt about in his swaying prison for the stud of the exterior electric light, and came by accident against his own small glow lamp in its padded recess. The sphere twisted, and then threw him down, he heard shouts like shouts of surprise, and when he rose to his feet he saw two pairs of stalked eyes peering into the lower window and reflecting his light.

In another moment hands were dabbing vigorously at his steel casing, and there was a sound, horrible enough in his position, of the metal protection of the clockwork being vigorously hammered. That, indeed, sent his heart into his mouth, for if these strange creatures succeeded in stopping that his release would never occur. Scarcely had he thought as much when he felt the sphere sway violently, and the floor of it press hard against his feet. He turned off the small glow lamp that lit the interior, and sent the ray of the large light in the separate compartment out into the water. The sea floor and the man-like creatures had disappeared, and a couple of fish chasing each other dropped suddenly by the window.

He thought at once that these strange denizens of the deep sea had broken the wire rope, and that he had escaped. He drove up slowly, and rocking, and it seemed to him that it was also being drawn through the water. By crouching close to the window he managed to make his weight effective and roll that part of the sphere downward, but he could see nothing save the pale ray of his light striking down ineffectively into the darkness. It occurred to him that he would see more if he turned the lamp off and allowed his eyes to grow accustomed to the profound obscurity.

In this he was wise. After some minutes the velvety blackness became a translucent blackness, and

The sphere twisted, and then threw him down.

faster and faster, and then stopped with a jerk that sent him flying against the padded roof of his prison. For half a minute perhaps he was too astonished to think.

Then he felt that the sphere was spinning then far away, and as faint as the zodiacal light of an English summer evening, he saw shapes moving below. He judged these creatures had detached his cable and were towing him along the sea bottom.

And then he saw something faint and remote across the undulations of the submarine plain, a broad horizon of pale luminosity that extended this way and that way as far as the range of his little window permitted him to see. To this he was being towed, as a balloon might be towed by men out of the open country into a town. He approached it very slowly, and very slowly the dim irradiation was gathered together into more definite shapes.

It was nearly five o'clock before he came over this luminous area, and by that time he could make out an arrangement suggestive of streets and houses grouped about a vast roofless erection that was grotesquely suggestive of a ruined abbey. It was spread out like a map below him. The houses were all roofless inclosures of walls, and their substance being, as he afterwards saw, of phosphorescent bones, gave the place an appearance as if it were built of drowned moonshine.

Among the inner caves of the place waving trees of crinoid stretched their tentacles, and tall, slender, glassy sponges shot like shining minarets and lilies of filmy light out of the general glow of the city. In the open spaces of the place he could see a stirring movement as of crowds of people, but he was too many fathoms above them to distinguish the individuals in those crowds.

Then slowly they pulled him down, and as they did so the details of the place crept slowly upon his apprehension. He saw that the courses of the cloudy buildings were marked out with beaded lines of round objects, and then he perceived that at several points below him in broad open spaces were forms like the encrusted shapes of ships.

Slowly and surely he was drawn down, and the forms below him became brighter, clearer, were more distinct. He was being pulled down, he perceived, towards the large building in the centre of the town, and he could catch a glimpse ever and again of the multitudinous forms that were lugging at his cord. He was astonished to see that the rigging of one of the ships, which formed such a prominent feature of the place, was crowded with a host of gesticulating figures regarding him, and then the walls of the great building rose about him silently, and hid the city from his eyes.

And such walls they were, of water-logged wood, and twisted wire rope and iron spars, and copper, and the bones and skulls of dead men.

The skulls ran in curious zig-zag lines and spirals and fantastic curves over the building; and in and out of their eye sockets, and over the whole surface of the place, lurked and played a multitude of silvery little fishes.

And now he was at such a level that he could see these strange people of the abyss plainly once more. To his astonishment. he perceived that they were prostrating themselves before him, all save one, dressed as it seemed in a robe of placoid scales, and crowned with a luminous diadem, who stood with his reptilian mouth opening and shutting as though he led the chanting of the worshippers.

They continued worshipping him, without rest or intermission, for the space of three hours.

Most circumstantial was Elstead's account of this astounding city and its people, these people of perpetual night, who have never seen sun or moon or stars, green vegetation, nor any living air-breathing creatures, who know nothing of fire, nor any light but the phosphorescent light of living things.

Startling as is his story, it is yet more startling to find that scientific men, of such eminence as Adams and Jenkins, find nothing incredible in it. They tell me they see no reason why intelligent water-breathing vertebrated creatures inured to a low temperature and enormous pressure, and of such a heavy structure, that neither alive nor dead would they float, might not live upon the bottom of the deep sea, and quite unsuspected by us, descendants like ourselves of the great Theriomorpha of the New Red Sandstone age.

We should be known to them, however, as strange meteoric creatures wont to fall catastrophically dead out of the mysterious blackness of their watery sky. And not only we ourselves, but our ships, our metals, our appliances, would come raining down out of the night. Sometimes sinking things would smite down and crush them, as if it were the judgment of some unseen power above, and sometimes would

WARWICK GOBLE

They were prostrating themselves
before him, all save one.

come things of the utmost rarity or utility or shapes of inspiring suggestion. One can understand, perhaps, something of their behaviour at the descent of a living man, if one thinks what a barbaric people might do, to whom an enhaloed shining creature came suddenly out of the sky.

At one time or another Elstead probably told the officers of the *Ptarmigan* every detail of his strange twelve hours in the abyss. That he also intended to write them down is certain, but he never did, and so unhappily we have to piece together the discrepant fragments of his story from the reminiscences of Commander Simmons, Weybridge, Steevens, Lindley, and the others.

We see the thing darkly in fragmentary glimpses—the huge ghostly building, the bowing, chanting people, with their dark, chameleon-like heads and faintly luminous forms, and Elstead, with his light turned on again, vainly trying to convey to their minds that the cord by which the sphere was held was to be severed. Minute after minute slipped away, and Elstead, looking at his watch, was horrified to find that he had oxygen only for two hours more. But the chant in his honour kept on as remorselessly as if it was the marching song of his approaching death.

The manner of his release he does not understand, but to judge by the end of cord that hung from the sphere, it had been cut through by rubbing against the edge of the altar. Abruptly the sphere rolled over, and he swept up, out of their world, as an ethereal creature clothed in a vacuum would sweep through our own atmosphere back to its native ether again. He must have torn out of their sight as a hydrogen bubble hastens upwards from our air. A strange ascension it must have seemed to them.

The sphere rushed up with even greater velocity than, when weighted with the lead sinkers, it had rushed down. It became exceedingly hot. It drove up with the windows uppermost, and he remembers the torrent of bubbles frothing against the glass. Every moment he expected this to fly. Then suddenly something like a huge wheel seemed to be released in his head, the padded compartment

began spinning about him, and he fainted. His next recollection was of his cabin, and of the doctor's voice.

But that is the substance of the extraordinary story that Elstead related in fragments to the officers of the *Ptarmigan.* He promised to write it all down at a later date. His mind was chiefly occupied with the improvement of his apparatus, which was effected at Rio.

It remains only to tell that on February 2nd, 1896, he made his second descent into the ocean abyss, with the improvements his first experience suggested. What happened we shall probably never know. He never returned. The *Ptarmigan* beat about over the point of his submersion, seeking him in vain for thirteen days. Then she returned to Rio, and the news was telegraphed to his friends. So the matter remains for the present. But it is hardly probable that any further attempt will be made to verify his strange story of these hitherto unsuspected cities of the deep sea.

WARWICK GOBLE

THE VALLEY OF SPIDERS

Originally published in *Pearson's Magazine*
March 1903

THE VALLEY OF SPIDERS

BY H. G. WELLS

Towards mid-day the three pursuers came abruptly round a bend in the torrent bed upon the sight of a very broad and spacious valley. The difficult and winding trench of pebbles along which they had tracked the fugitives for so long, broadened out into a broad talus slope, and with a common impulse the three men left the trail, and rode to a little eminence set with olive dun trees, and there halted, the two others, as became them, a little behind the man with the silver-studded bridle.

For a space they scanned the great expanse below them with eager eyes. It spread remoter and remoter, with only a few ¬lusters of sere thorn bushes here and there, and the dim suggestions of some now water-less ravine to break its desolation of yellow grass. Its purple distances melted at last into the bluish slopes of the further hills— hills it might be of a greener kind—and above them invisibly supported and seeming indeed to hang in the blue were the snowclad summits of mountains—that grew larger and bolder to the north-westward as the sides of the valley drew together. And westward the valley opened until a distant darkness under the sky told where the forests began. But the three men looked neither east nor west, but only steadfastly across the valley.

The gaunt man with the scarred lip was the first to speak. "Nowhere," he said, with a sigh of disappointment in his voice. "But after all, they had a full day's start."

"They don't know we are after them," said the little man on the white horse.

"*She* would know," said the leader bitterly, as if speaking to himself.

"Even then they can't go fast. They've got no beast but the mule, and all to-day the girl's foot has been bleeding——"

The man with the silver bridle flashed a quick intensity of rage on him. "Do you think I haven't seen that?" he snarled.

"It helps, anyhow," whispered the little man to himself.

The gaunt man with the scarred lip stared impassively. "They can't be over the valley," he said. "If we ride hard——"

He glanced at the white horse and paused.

"Curse all white horses!" said the man with the silver bridle, and turned to scan the beast his curse included.

The little man looked down between the melancholy ears of his steed.

"I did my best," he said.

The two others stared again across the

valley for a space. The gaunt man passed the back of his hand across the scarred lip.

" Come up ! " said the man who owned the silver bridle suddenly. The little man started and jerked his rein, and the horse hoofs of the three made a multitudinous faint pattering upon the withered grass as they turned back towards the trail. . . .

They rode cautiously down the long slope before them, and so came through a waste of prickly twisted bushes and strange dry shapes of horny branches that grew amongst the rocks, into the levels below. And there the trail grew faint, for the soil was scanty, and the only herbage was this scorched dead straw that lay upon the ground. Still, by hard scanning, by leaning beside the horse's necks and pausing ever and again, even these white men could contrive to follow after their prey.

There were trodden places, bent and broken blades of the coarse grass, and ever and again the sufficient intimation of a foot-mark. And once the leader saw a brown smear of blood where the half-caste girl may have trod. And at that under his breath he cursed her for a fool.

The gaunt man checked his leader's tracking, and the little man on the white horse rode behind, a man lost in a dream. They rode one after another, the man with the silver bridle led the way, and they spoke never a word. After a time it came to the little man on the white horse that the world was very still. He started out of his dream. Besides the little noises of their horses and equipment, the whole great valley kept the brooding quiet of a painted scene.

Before him went his master and his fellow, each intently leaning forward to the left, each impassively moving with the paces of his horse ; their shadows went before them, still, noiseless, tapering attendants, and nearer a crouched cool shape was his own. He looked about him. What was it had gone? Then he remembered the reverberation from the banks of the gorge and the perpetual accompaniment of shifting, jostling pebbles. And, moreover ——? There was no breeze. That was it ! What a vast, still place it was, a monotonous afternoon slumber. And the sky open and blank, except for a sombre veil of haze that had gathered in the upper valley.

He straightened his back, fretted with his bridle, puckered his lips to whistle, and simply sighed. He turned in his saddle for a time, and stared at the throat of the mountain gorge out of which they had come. Blank ! Blank slopes on either side, with never a sign of a decent beast or tree—much less a man. What a land it was ! What a wilderness ! He dropped again into his former pose.

It filled him with a momentary pleasure to see a wry stick of purple black flash out into the form of a snake, and vanish amidst the brown. After all, the infernal valley *was* alive. And then, to rejoice him still more, came a little breath across his face, a whisper that came and went, the faintest inclination of a stiff black-antlered bush upon a little crest, the first intimations of a possible breeze. Idly he wetted his finger, and held it up.

He pulled up sharply to avoid a collision with the gaunt man who had stopped at fault upon the trail. Just at that guilty moment he caught his master's eye looking towards him.

For a time he forced an interest in the tracking. Then, as they rode on again, he studied his master's shadow and hat and shoulder, appearing and disappearing behind the gaunt man's nearer contours. They had ridden four days out of the very limits of the world into this desolate place, short of water, with nothing but a strip of dried meat under their saddles, over rocks and mountains, where surely none but these fugitives had ever been before—for *that* !

And all this was for a girl, a mere wilful child ! And the man had whole cityfuls of people to do his basest bidding—girls, women ! Why in the name of passionate folly *this* one in particular ? asked the little man, and scowled at the world, and licked his parched lips with a blackened tongue. It was the way of the master, and that was all he knew. Just because she sought to evade him. . . .

His eye caught a whole row of high plumed canes bending in unison, and then the tails of silk that hung before his neck flapped and fell. The breeze was growing stronger. Somehow it took the stiff stillness out of things—and that was well.

"Hullo!" said the gaunt man.

All three stopped abruptly.

"What?" asked the master. "What?"

"Over there," said the gaunt man, pointing up the valley.

"What?"

"Something coming towards us."

And as he spoke a yellow animal crested a rise and came bearing down upon them. It was a big wild dog, coming before the wind, tongue out, at a steady pace, and running with such an intensity of purpose that he did not seem to see the horsemen he approached. He ran with his nose up, clearly following neither scent nor quarry. As he drew nearer the little man felt for his sword. "He's mad," said the gaunt rider.

"Shout!" said the little man and shouted.

The dog came on. Then when the little man's blade was already out, it swerved aside and went panting by them and past. The eyes of the little man followed its flight. "There was no foam," he said. For a space the man with the silver-studded bridle stared up the valley. "Oh, come on!" he cried at last. "What does it matter?" and jerked his horse into movement again.

The little man left the insoluble mystery of a dog that fled from nothing but the wind, and lapsed into profound musings on human character. "Come on!" he whispered to himself. "Why should it be given to one man to say 'Come on!' with that stupendous violence of effect. Always, all his life, the man with the silver bridle has been saying that. If *I* said it——!" thought the little man. But people marvelled when the master was disobeyed even in the wildest things. This half-caste girl seemed to him, seemed to everyone, mad—blasphemous almost. The little man, by way of comparison, reflected on the gaunt rider with the scarred lip, as stalwart as his master, as brave and, indeed, perhaps braver, and yet for him there was obedience, nothing but to give obedience duly and stoutly . . . .

Certain sensations of the hands and knees called the little man back to more immediate things. He became aware of something. He rode up beside his gaunt fellow. "Do you notice the horses?" he said in an undertone.

The gaunt face looked interrogation.

"They don't like this wind," said the little man and dropped behind as the man with the silver bridle turned upon him.

"It's all right," said the gaunt-faced man.

They rode on again for a space in silence. The foremost two rode downcast upon the trail, the hindmost man watched the haze that crept down the vastness of the valley, nearer and nearer, and noted how the wind grew in strength moment by moment. Far away on the left he saw a line of dark bulks—wild hog perhaps, galloping down the valley, but of that he said nothing nor did he remark again upon the uneasiness of the horses.

And then he saw first one and then a second great white ball, a great shining white ball like a gigantic head of thistledown, that drove before the wind athwart the path. These balls soared high in the air, and dropped and rose again and caught for a moment, and hurried on and passed, but at the sight of them the restlessness of the horses increased.

Then presently he saw that more of these drifting globes—and then soon very many more—were hurrying towards him down the valley.

They became aware of a squealing. Athwart the path a huge boar rushed, turning his head but for one instant to glance at them, and then hurling on down the valley again. And at that, all three stopped and sat in their saddles, staring into the thickening haze that was coming upon them.

"If it were not for this thistle-down——" began the leader.

But now a big globe came drifting past within a score of yards of them. It was really not an even sphere at all, but a vast, soft, ragged, filmy thing, a sheet gathered by the corners, an ærial jelly-fish, as it were, but rolling over and over as it advanced, and trailing long, cobwebby threads and streamers that floated in its wake.

"It isn't thistle-down," said the little man.

"I don't like the stuff," said the gaunt man.

And they looked at one another.

"Curse it!" cried the leader. "The air's

An instinctive feeling prompted them to turn their horses to the wind, and stare at that advancing
multitude of floating masses.

full of it up there. If it keeps on at this pace long, it will stop us altogether."

An instinctive feeling, such as lines out a herd of deer at the approach of some ambiguous thing, prompted them to turn their horses to the wind, ride forward for a few paces, and stare at that advancing multitude of floating masses. They came on before the wind with a sort of smooth swiftness rising and falling noiselessly, sinking to earth rebounding high, soaring—all with a perfect unanimity, with a still deliberate assurance.

Right and left of the horsemen the pioneers of this strange army passed. At one that rolled along the ground, breaking shapelessly and trailing out reluctantly into long grappling ribbons and bands, all three horses began to shy and dance. The master was seized with a sudden, unreasonable impatience. He cursed the drifting globes roundly. "Get on!" he cried; "get on! What do these things matter? How *can* they matter? Back

to the trail!" He fell swearing at his horse and sawed the bit across its mouth.

He shouted aloud with rage. "I will follow that trail, I tell you," he cried. "Where is the trail?"

He gripped the bridle of his prancing horse and searched amidst the grass. A long and clinging thread fell across his face, a grey streamer dropped about his bridle arm, some big, active thing with many legs ran down the back of his head. He looked up to discover one of those grey masses anchored as it were above him by these things and flapping out ends as a sail flaps when a boat comes about —but noiselessly.

He had an impression of many eyes, of a dense crew of squat bodies, of long, many-jointed limbs hauling at their mooring ropes to bring the thing down upon him. For a space he stared up, reining in his prancing horse with the instinct born of years of horsemanship. Then the flat of a sword smote his back, and a blade flashed overhead and cut the drifting balloon of spiderweb free and the whole mass lifted softly and drove clear and away.

"Spiders!" cried the voice of the gaunt man. "The things are full of big spiders! Look, my lord!"

The man with the silver bridle still followed the mass that drove away.

"Look, my lord!"

The master found himself staring down at a red smashed thing on the ground that, in spite of partial obliteration, could still wriggle unavailing legs. Then when the gaunt man pointed to another mass that bore down upon them, he drew his sword hastily. Up the valley now it was like a fog bank torn to rags. He tried to grasp the situation.

"Ride for it!" the little man was shouting. "Ride for it down the valley."

What happened then was like the confusion of a battle. The man with the silver bridle saw the little man go past him slashing furiously at imaginary cobwebs, saw him cannon into the horse of the gaunt man and hurl it and its rider to earth. His own horse went a dozen paces before he could rein it in. Then he looked up to avoid imaginary dangers, and then back again to see a horse rolling on the ground, the gaunt man standing and slashing over it at a rent and fluttering mass of grey that streamed and wrapped about them both. And thick and fast as thistledown on waste land on a windy day in July, the cobweb masses were coming on.

The little man had dismounted, but he dared not release his horse. He was endeavouring to lug the struggling brute back with the strength of one arm, while with the other he slashed aimlessly. The tentacles of a second grey mass had entangled themselves with the struggle, and this second grey mass came to its moorings, and slowly sank.

The master set his teeth, gripped his bridle, lowered his head and spurred his horse forward. The horse on the ground rolled over, there was blood and moving shapes upon the flanks, and the gaunt man suddenly leaving it ran forward towards his master, perhaps ten paces. His legs were swathed and incumbered with grey, he made ineffectual movements with his sword. Grey

streamers waved from him; there was a thin veil of grey across his face. With his left hand he beat at something on his body, and suddenly he stumbled and fell. He struggled to rise, and fell again, and suddenly, horribly, began to howl, "Oh—ohoo, ohooh!"

The master could see the great spiders upon him, and others upon the ground.

As he strove to force his horse nearer to this gesticulating, screaming grey object that struggled up and down, there came a clatter of hoofs, and the little man, in act of mounting, swordless, balanced on his belly athwart the white horse, and clutching its mane, whirled past. And again a clinging thread of grey gossamer swept across the master's face. All about him, and over him, it seemed this drifting, noiseless cobweb circled and blew.

· · · ·

To the day of his death he never knew just how the event of that moment happened. Did he, indeed, turn his horse, or did it really of its own accord stampede after its fellow? Suffice it that in another second he was galloping full tilt down the valley with his sword whirling furiously overhead. And all about him on the quickening breeze, the spiders' air-ships, their air bundles and air sheets, seemed to him to hurry in a conscious pursuit.

Clatter, clatter, thud, thud—the man with the silver bridle rode, heedless of his direction, with his fearful face looking up now right, now left, and his sword arm ready to slash. And a few hundred yards ahead of him, with a tail of torn cobweb trailing behind him, rode the little man on the white horse, still but imperfectly in the saddle. The reeds bent before them, the wind blew fresh and strong, over his shoulder the master could see the webs hurrying to overtake.

· · · ·

He was so intent to escape the spiders' webs that only as his horse gathered together for a leap did he realise the ravine ahead. And then he realised it only to misunderstand and interfere. He was leaning forward on his horse's neck and sat up and back all too late.

But if in his excitement he had failed to leap, at any rate he had not forgotten how to fall. He was horseman again in mid-air.

He came off clear with a mere bruise upon his shoulder, and his horse rolled, kicking spasmodic legs, and lay still. But the master's sword drove its point into the hard soil, and snapped clear across, as though Chance refused him any longer as her Knight, and the splintered end missed his face by an inch or so.

He was on his feet in a moment, breathlessly scanning the onrushing spider-webs. For a moment he was minded to run, and then thought of the ravine, and turned back. He ran aside once to dodge one drifting terror, and then he was swiftly clambering down the precipitous sides, and out of the touch of the gale.

And there under the lee of the dry torrent's steeper banks, he might crouch, and watch these strange, grey masses pass and pass in safety till the wind fell, and it became possible to escape. And there for a long time he crouched, watching the strange, grey, ragged masses trail their streamers across his narrowed sky.

And once a stray spider fell into the ravine close beside him—a full foot it measured from leg to leg, and its body was half a man's hand—and after he had watched its monstrous alacrity of search and escape for a little while, and tempted it to bite his broken sword, he lifted up his iron heeled boot and smashed it into a pulp. He swore as he did so, and for a time sought up and down for another.

Then, presently, when he was surer these

There for a long time he crouched, watching the strange, grey, ragged masses trail their streamers across his narrowed sky.

spider swarms could not drop into the ravine, he found a place where he could sit down, and sat and fell into a deep thought and began after his manner to gnaw his knuckles and bite his nails. And from this he was moved by the coming of the man with the white horse.

He heard him long before he saw him, as a clattering of hoofs, stumbling footsteps, and a reassuring voice. Then the little man appeared, a rueful figure, still with a tail of white cobweb trailing behind him. They approached each other without speaking, without a salutation. The little man was fatigued and shamed to the pitch of hopeless bitterness and came to a stop at last, face to face with his seated master. The latter winced a little under his dependant's eye. "Well?" he said at last, with no pretence of authority.

"You left him?"

"My horse bolted."

"I know. So did mine."

He laughed at his master mirthlessly.

"I say my horse bolted," said the man who once had a silver-studded bridle.

"Cowards both," said the little man.

The other gnawed his knuckle through some meditative moments, with his eye on his inferior.

"Don't call me a coward," he said at length.

"You are a coward like myself."

"A coward possibly. There is a limit

beyond which every man must fear. That I have learnt at last. But not like yourself. That is where the difference comes in.''

" I never could have dreamt you would have left him. He saved your life two minutes before. . . . Why are you our lord ? "

The master gnawed his knuckles again, and his countenance was dark.

"No man calls me a coward," he said. " No. . . . A broken sword is better than none. . . . One spavined white horse cannot be expected to carry two men a four days' journey. I hate white horses, but this time it cannot be helped. You begin to understand me ? . . . I perceive that you are minded on the strength of what you have seen and fancy, to taint my reputation. It is men of your sort who unmake kings. Besides which—I never liked you."

" My lord ! " said the little man.

" No," said the master. " *No !* "

He stood up sharply as the little man moved. For a minute perhaps they faced one another. Overhead the spiders' balls went driving. There was a quick movement among the pebbles ; a running of feet, a cry of despair, a gasp and a blow. . . .

Towards nightfall the wind fell. The sun set in a calm serenity and the man who had once possessed the silver bridle came at last very cautiously and by an easy slope out of the ravine again ; but now he led the white horse that once belonged to the little man. He would have gone back to his horse to get his silver mounted bridle again but he feared

After he had stared at the smoke for some time, he mounted the white horse.

night and a quickening breeze might still find him in the valley, and besides he disliked greatly to think he might discover his horse all swathed in cobwebs and perhaps unpleasantly eaten.

And as he thought of those cobwebs and of all the dangers he had been through and the manner in which he had been preserved that day, his hand sought a little reliquary that hung about his neck, and he clasped it for a moment with heartfelt gratitude. As he did so, his eyes went across the valley.

" I was hot with passion," he said, "and now she has met her reward. They also, no doubt——"

And behold ! Far away out of the wooded slopes across the valley, but in the clearness of the sunset distinct and unmistakable, he saw a little spire of smoke.

At that his expression of serene resignation changed to an amazed anger. Smoke ? He turned the head of the white horse about, and hesitated. And as he did so a little rustle of air went through the grass about him. Far away upon some reeds swayed a tattered sheet of grey. He looked at the cobwebs ; he looked at the smoke.

" Perhaps, after all, it is not them," he said at last.

But he knew better.

And after he had stared at the smoke for some time, he mounted the white horse.

And, as he rode, he picked his way amidst stranded masses of web. For some reason there were many dead spiders on the ground, and those that lived feasted guiltily on their fellows. At the sound of his horse's hoofs they fled.

Their time had passed. From the ground, without either a wind to carry them or a winding sheet ready, these things, for all their poison, could do him little evil.

He flicked with his belt at those he fancied came too near. Once, where a number ran together over a bare place, he was minded to dismount, and trample them with his boots, but ~~this~~ impulse he overcame. Ever and again he turned in his saddle, and looked back at the smoke.

" Spiders," he muttered over and over again. " Spiders ! Well, well. . . . The next time *I* will spin a web."

—13—

WHEN THE SLEEPER WAKES

Originally published in *The Graphic*
1898–1899

When the Sleeper Wakes.

BY H.G. WELLS.

ILLUSTRATED BY H. LANOS.

CHAPTER I.

INSOMNIA

ONE afternoon, at low water, Mr. Isbister, a young artist lodging at Boscastle, walked from that place to the picturesque cove of Pentargen, desiring to examine the caves there. Half way down the precipitous path to the Pentargen beach he came round a mass of rock upon a man in an attitude of profound distress. This man was seated on a projecting ledge of slate, his hands hung limply over his knees, his eyes were red, and his face was wet with tears.

At Isbister's footfall he glanced round. Both men were disconcerted, Isbister the more so, and, to override the awkwardness of his involuntary pause, he remarked, with an air of mature conviction, that the weather was hot for the time of year.

"Very," answered the stranger shortly, hesitated a second, and added in a colourless tone, "I can't sleep."

Isbister stopped abruptly. "No?" was all he said, but his bearing conveyed his helpful impulse.

"It may sound incredible," said the stranger, turning weary eyes to Isbister's face and emphasizing his words with a languid hand, "but I have had no sleep—no sleep at all for six nights."

"Had advice?"

"Yes. Bad advice for the most part. Drugs. My nervous system. . . . They are all very well for the run of people. It's hard to explain. I dare not take . . . sufficiently powerful drugs."

"That makes it difficult," said Isbister.

He stood helplessly in the narrow path, perplexed what to do. Clearly the man wanted to talk. An idea natural enough under the circumstances, prompted him to keep the conversation going. "I've never suffered from sleeplessness myself," he said in a tone of commonplace gossip, "but in those cases I have known people have usually found something——"

"I dare make no experiments."

He spoke wearily. He gave a gesture of rejection, and for a space both men were silent.

"Exercise?" suggested Isbister diffidently, with a glance from his interlocutor's face of wretchedness to the touring costume he wore.

"That is what I have tried. Unwisely perhaps. I have followed the coast, day after day—from New Quay. It has only added muscular fatigue to the mental. The cause of this unrest was overwork—trouble. There was something——"

He stopped as if from sheer fatigue. He rubbed his forehead with a lean hand. He resumed speech like one who talks to himself.

"I was a lone wolf, a solitary man, wandering through a world in which I had no part. I was wifeless, childless—who is it speaks of the childless as the dead twigs on the tree of life? I was wifeless, childless—I could find no duty to do. No desire even in my heart. One thing at last I set myself to do.

"I said, I *will* do this, and to do it, to overcome the inertia of this dull body, I resorted to drugs. Great God, I've had enough of drugs! I don't know if *you* feel the heavy inconvenience of the body, its exasperating demand of time from the mind—time—life! Live! We only live in patches. We have to eat, and then come the dull digestive complacencies—or irritations. We have to take the air or else our thoughts grow sluggish, stupid, run into gulfs and blind alleys. A thousand distractions arise from within and without, and then come drowsiness and sleep. Men seem to live for sleep. How little of man's day is his own—even at the best! And then come those false friends, those Thug helpers, the alkaloids that stifle natural fatigue and kill rest—black coffee, cocaine——"

"I see," said Isbister.

"I did my work," said the sleepless man, with a querulous intonation.

"And this is the price?"

"Yes."

For a little while the two remained without speaking.

"You cannot imagine the craving for rest that I feel, a hunger and thirst. For six long days, since my work was done, my mind has been a whirlpool, swift, unprogressive, and incessant, a torrent of thoughts leading nowhere, spinning round swift and steady——"

He paused. "Towards the gulf."

He returned to the motionless seated figure as his astonished landlady entered with the light.

"You must sleep," said Isbister decisively, and with the air of a remedy discovered. "Certainly you must sleep."

"My mind is perfectly lucid. It was never clearer. But I know I am drawing towards the vortex. Presently——"

"Yes?"

"You have seen things go down an eddy? Out of the light of the day, out of this sweet world of sanity——down—"

"But," expostulated Isbister.

The man threw out a hand towards him, and his eyes were wild, and his voice suddenly high. "I shall kill myself. If in no other way— at the foot of yonder dark precipice there, where the waves are green, and the white surge lifts and falls, and that little thread of water patters down. There at any rate is . . . sleep."

"That's unreasonable," said Isbister, startled at the man's hysterical gust of emotion. "Drugs are better than that."

"There at any rate is sleep," repeated the stranger, not heeding him.

Isbister looked at him and wondered transitorily if some complex Providence had indeed brought them together that afternoon. "It's not a cert., you know," he remarked. "There's a cliff like that at Lulworth Cove—as high, anyhow—and a little girl fell from top to bottom. And lives to-day—sound and well."

"But those rocks there——"

"One might lie on them rather dismally through a cold night, broken bones grating as one shivered, chill water splashing over you. Eh?"

Their eyes met. "Sorry to upset your ideals," said Isbister with a sense of devil-may-careish brilliance. "But a suicide over that cliff (or any cliff for the matter of that) really, as an artist——" He laughed. "It's so damned amateurish."

"But the other thing—the other thing. No man can keep sane if night after night——"

"Have you been walking along this coast alone?"

"Yes."

"Silly sort of thing to do. If you'll excuse my saying so. Alone! As you say; body fag is no cure for brain fag. Who told you to? No wonder! Walking! And the sun on your head, heart, fag, solitude, all the day long, and then, I suppose, you go to bed and try very hard—eh?"

Isbister stopped short and looked at the sufferer doubtfully.

"Look at these rocks!" cried the seated man with a sudden force of gesture. "Look at that sea that has shone and quivered there for ever! See the white spume rush into darkness under that great cliff. And this blue vault, with the blinding sun pouring from the dome of it. It is your world. You accept it, you rejoice in it. It warms and supports and delights you. And for me——"

He turned his head and showed a ghastly face, bloodshot pallid eyes and bloodless lips. He spoke almost in a whisper. "It is the garment of my misery. The whole world . . . is the garment of my misery."

Isbister looked at all the wild beauty of the sunlit cliffs about them and back to that face of despair. For a moment he was silent.

He started, and made a gesture of impatient rejection. "You get a night's sleep," he said, "and you won't see much misery out here. Take my word for it."

He was quite sure that this was a providential encounter. Only half an hour ago he had been feeling horribly bored. Here was employment the bare thought of which was righteous self-applause. He took possession forthwith. It seemed to him that the first need of this exhausted being was companionship. He flung himself down on the steeply sloping turf beside the motionless seated figure, and deployed forthwith into a skirmishing line of gossip.

His hearer seemed abruptly to have lapsed into apathy; he stared dismally seaward, and spoke only in answer to Isbister's direct questions—and not to all of those. But he made no sign of objection to this benevolent intrusion upon his despair.

In a helpless way he seemed even grateful, and when presently Isbister, feeling that his unsupported talk was losing vigour, suggested that they should reascend the steep and return towards Boscastle, alleging the view into Blackapit, he submitted quietly. Half-way up he began talking to himself, and abruptly turned a ghastly face on his helper. "What can be happening?" he asked, with a gaunt illustrative hand. "What can be happening? Spin, spin, spin, spin. It goes round and round, round and round for evermore."

He stood with his hand circling.

"It's all right, old chap," said Isbister with the air of an old friend. "Don't worry yourself. Trust to me."

The man dropped his hand and turned again. They went over the brow in single file and to the headland beyond Penally, with the sleepless man gesticulating ever and again, and speaking fragmentary things concerning his whirling brain. At the headland they stood for a space by the seat that looks into the dark mysteries of Blackapit, and then he sat down. Isbister had resumed his talk whenever the path had widened sufficiently for them to walk abreast. He was enlarging upon the complex difficulty of making Boscastle Harbour in bad weather, when suddenly and quite irrelevantly his companion interrupted him again.

"My head is not like what it was," he said, gesticulating for want of expressive phrases. "It's not like what it was. There is a sort of oppression, a weight. No—not drowsiness, would God it were! It is like a shadow, a deep shadow falling suddenly and swiftly across something busy. Spin, spin into the darkness. The tumult of thought, the confusion, the eddy and eddy. I can't express it. I can hardly keep my mind on it—steadily enough to tell you."

He stopped feebly.

"Don't trouble, old chap," said Isbister. "I think I can understand. At any rate, it don't matter very much just at present about telling me, you know."

The sleepless man thrust his knuckles into his eyes and rubbed them. Isbister talked for awhile while this rubbing continued, and then he had a fresh idea. "Come down to my room," he said, "and try a pipe. I can show you some sketches of this Blackapit. If you'd care?" The other rose obediently, and followed him down the steep.

Several times Isbister heard him stumble as they came down, and his movements were slow and hesitating. "Come in with me," said Isbister, "and try some cigarettes and the blessed gift of alcohol. If you take alcohol?"

The stranger hesitated at the garden gate. He seemed no longer clearly aware of his actions. "I don't drink," he said, slowly coming up the garden path, and after a moment's interval repeated absently, "No—I don't drink. It goes round. Spin, it goes—spin——"

He stumbled at the doorstep and entered the room with the bearing of one who sees nothing.

Then he sat down abruptly and heavily in the easy chair, seemed almost to fall into it. He leant forward with his brows on his hands and became motionless.

Presently he made a faint sound in his throat. Isbister moved about the room with the nervousness of an inexperienced host, making little remarks that scarcely required answering. He crossed the room to his portfolio, placed it on the table, and noticed the mantel clock.

"I don't know if you'd care to have supper with me," he said with an unlighted cigarette in his hand—his mind troubled with a design of the furtive administration of chloral. "Only cold mutton, you know, but passing sweet. Welsh. And a tart, I believe." He repeated this after momentary silence.

The seated man made no answer. Isbister stopped, match in hand, regarding him.

The stillness lengthened. The match went out, the cigarette was put down unlit. The man was certainly very still. Isbister took up the portfolio, opened it, put it down, hesitated, seemed about to speak. "Perhaps," he whispered doubtfully. He glanced at the door and back to the figure. Then he stole on tiptoe out of the room, glancing at his companion after each elaborate pace.

He closed the door noiselessly. The house door was standing open, and he went out beyond the porch, and stood where the monkshood rose at the corner of the garden bed. From this point he could see the stranger through the open window, still and dim, sitting head on hand. He had not moved.

A number of children going along the road stopped and regarded the artist curiously. A boatman exchanged civilities with him. He felt that possibly his circumspect attitude and position seemed peculiar and unaccountable. Smoking, perhaps, might seem more natural. He drew pipe and pouch from his pocket, filled the pipe slowly.

"I wonder," he said, with a scarcely perceptible loss of complacency. "At any rate one must give him a chance." He struck a match, and proceeded to light his pipe.

Presently he heard his landlady behind him, coming with his lamp lit from the kitchen. He turned, gesticulating with his pipe, and stopped her at the door of his sitting-room. He had some difficulty in explaining the situation in whispers, for she did not know he had a visitor. She retreated again with the lamp, still a little mystified to judge from her manner, and he resumed his hovering at the corner of the porch, flushed and less at his ease.

Long after he had smoked out his pipe, and when the bats were abroad, his curiosity dominated his complex hesitations, and he stole back into his darkling sitting-room. He paused in the doorway. The stranger was still in the same attitude, dark against the window. Save for the singing of some sailors aboard one of the little slate-carrying ships in the harbour, the evening was very still. Outside, the spikes of monkshood and delphinium stood erect and motionless against the shadow of the hillside. Something flashed into Isbister's mind; he started, and leaning over the table, listened. An unpleasant suspicion grew stronger; became conviction. Astonishment seized him and became—dread.

No sound of breathing came from the seated figure!

He crept slowly and noiselessly round the table, pausing twice to listen. At last he could lay his hand on the back of the armchair. He bent down until the two heads were ear to ear.

Then he bent still lower to look up at his visitor's face. He started violently and uttered an exclamation. The eyes were void spaces of white.

He looked again and saw that they were open and with the pupils rolled under the lids. He was suddenly afraid. Overcome by the strangeness of the man's condition, he took him by the shoulder and shook him. "Are you asleep?" he said, with his voice jumping into alto, and again, "Are you asleep?"

A conviction took possession of his mind that this man was dead. He suddenly became active and noisy, strode across the room, blundering against the table as he did so, and rang the bell.

"Please bring a light at once," he said in the passage. "There is something wrong with my friend."

Then he returned to the motionless seated figure, grasped the shoulder, shook it, and shouted. The room was flooded with yellow glare as his astonished landlady entered with the light. His face was white as he turned blinking towards her. "I must fetch a doctor at once," he said. "It is either death or a fit. Is there a doctor in the village. Where is a doctor to be found?"

CHAPTER II.
THE TRANCE

THE state of rigour into which the man had fallen lasted for an unprecedented length of time, and then he passed on slowly to the flaccid state, to a lax attitude suggestive of profound repose. Then it was his eyes could be closed.

He was removed from the hotel to the Boscastle surgery, and from the surgery, after some weeks, to London. But he still resisted every attempt at reanimation. After a time, for reasons that will appear later, these attempts were discontinued. For a great space he lay in that strange condition, inert and still—neither dead nor living but, as it were, suspended, hanging midway betwen nothingness and existence. His was a darkness unbroken by a ray of thought or sensation, a dreamless inanition, a vast space of peace. The tumult of his mind had swelled and risen to an abrupt climax of silence. Where was the man? Where is any man when insensibility takes hold of him?

"It seems only yesterday," said Isbister. "I remember it all as though it happened yesterday—clearer, perhaps, than if it had happened yesterday."

It was the Isbister of the last chapter, but he was no longer a young man. The hair that had been brown and a trifle in excess of the fashionable length, was iron grey and clipped close, and the face that had been pink and white was buff and ruddy. He had a pointed beard shot with grey. He talked to an elderly man who wore a summer suit of drill (the summer of that year was unusually hot). This was Warming, a London solicitor and next of kin to Graham, the man who had fallen into the trance. And the two men stood side by side in a room in a house in London regarding his recumbent figure.

It was a yellow figure lying lax upon a water bed and clad in a flowing shirt, a figure with a shrunken face and a stubby beard, lean limbs, and lank nails, and about it was a case of thin glass. This glass seemed to mark off the sleeper from the reality of life about him, he was a thing apart, a strange, isolated abnormality. The two men stood close to the glass, peering in.

"The thing gave me a shock," said Isbister. "I feel a queer sort of surprise even now when I think of his white eyes. They were white, you know, rolled up. Coming here again brings it all back to me."

"Have you never seen him since that time?" asked Warming.

"Often wanted to come," said Isbister; "but business nowadays is too serious a thing for much holiday keeping. I've been in America most of the time."

"If I remember rightly," said Warming, "you were an artist?"

"Was. And then I became a married man. I saw it was all up with black and white, very soon—at least for a mediocre man, and I jumped on to process. Those posters on the Cliffs at Dover are by my people."

"Good posters," admitted the solicitor, "though I was sorry to see them there."

"Last as long as the cliffs if necessary," exclaimed Isbister, with satisfaction. "The world changes. When he fell asleep, twenty years ago, I was down at Boscastle, with a box of water-colours and a noble, old-fashioned ambition. I didn't expect that some day my pigments would glorify the whole blessed coast of England from Land's End round again to the Lizard. Luck comes to a man very often when he's not looking."

Warming seemed to doubt the quality of the luck. "I just missed meeting you, if I recollect aright."

"You came back by the trap that took me to Camelford railway station. It was close on the Jubilee, Victoria's Jubilee, because I remember the seats and flags in Westminster, and the row with the cabman at Chelsea."

"The Diamond Jubilee it was," said Warming; "the second one."

"Ah, yes! At the proper Jubilee—the Fifty Year affair—I was down at Wookey—a boy. I missed all that. . . . What a fuss we had with him! My landlady wouldn't take him in, wouldn't let him stay—he looked so queer when he was rigid. We had to carry him in a chair up to the hotel. And the Boscastle doctor—it wasn't the present chap, but the G.P. before him—was at him until nearly two, with me and the landlord holding lights and so forth."

"It was a cataleptic rigour at first, wasn't it?"

"Stiff!—wherever you bent him he stuck. You might have stood him on his head and he'd have stopped. I never saw such stiffness. Of course this"—he indicated the prostrate figure by a movement of his head—"is quite different. And, of course, the little doctor—what was his name?"

"Smithers?"

"Smithers it was—was quite wrong in trying to fetch him round too soon, according to all accounts. The things he did. Even now it makes me feel all—ugh! Mustard, snuff, pricking. And one of those beastly little things, not dynamos——"

"Induction coils."

"Yes. You could see his muscles throb and jump, and he twisted about. There was just two flaring yellow candles, and all the shadows were shivering, and the little doctor nervous and putting on side, and *him*—stark and squirming in the most unnatural ways. Well, it made me dream."

Pause.

"It's a strange state," said Warming.

"It's a sort of complete absence," said Isbister. "Here's the body, empty. Not dead a bit, and yet not alive. It's like a seat vacant and marked 'engaged.' No feeling, no digestion, no beating of the heart—not a flutter. *That* doesn't make me feel as if there was a man present. In a sense it's more dead than death, for these doctors tells me that even the hair has stopped growing. Now with the proper dead, the hair will go on growing——"

"I know," said Warming, with a flash of pain in his expression.

They peered through the glass again. Graham was indeed in a strange state, in the flaccid phase of a trance, but a trance unprecedented in medical history. Trances had lasted for as much as a year before—but at the end of that time it had ever been a waking or a death; sometimes first one and then the other. Isbister noted the marks the physicians had made in injecting nourishment, for that device had been resorted to to postpone collapse; he pointed them out to Warming, who had been trying not to see them.

"And while he has been lying here," said Isbister, with the zest of a life freely spent, "I have changed my plans in life; married, raised a family, my eldest lad—I hadn't begun to think of

sons then—is an American citizen, and looking forward to leaving Harvard. There's a touch of grey in my hair. And this man, not a day older nor wiser (practically) than I was in my downy days. It's curious to think of."

Warming turned. "And I have grown old too. I played cricket with him when he was a boy. And he looks a young man still. Yellow perhaps. But that *is* a young man nevertheless."

"And there's been the War," said Isbister.

"From beginning to end."

"I've understood," asked Isbister, "that he had some moderate property of his own?"

"That is so," said Warming. He coughed primly. "As it happens—I have charge of it."

"Ah!" Isbister thought, hesitated and spoke: "No doubt—his keep here is not expensive—no doubt it will have improved—accumulated?"

"It has. He will wake up very much better off—very much better off—if he wakes—than when he slept."

"As a business man," said Isbister, "that thought has naturally been in my mind. I have, indeed, sometimes thought that, speaking commercially, of course, this sleep may be a very good thing for him. That he knows what he is about, so to speak, in being insensible so long. If he had lived straight on——"

"I doubt if he would have premeditated as much," said Warming. "He was not a far-sighted man. In fact——"

"Yes?"

"We differed on that point. I stood to him somewhat in the relation of a guardian. You have probably seen enough of affairs to recognise that occasionally a certain friction——. But even if that was the case, there is a doubt whether he will ever wake. This sleep exhausts slowly, but it exhausts. Apparently he is sliding slowly, very slowly and tediously, down a long slope, if you can understand me?"

"It will be a pity to lose his surprise. There's been a lot of change these twenty years. It's Rip Van Winkle come real."

"It's Bellamy," said Warming. "There has been a lot of change certainly. And, among other changes, I have changed. I am an old man."

Isbister hesitated, and then feigned a belated surprise. "I shouldn't have thought it."

"I was forty-three when his bankers—you remember you wired to his bankers—sent on to me."

"I got his address from his cheque book in his pocket," said Isbister.

"Well, the addition is not difficult," said Warming.

There was another pause, and then Isbister gave way to an unavoidable curiosity. "He may go on for years yet," he said, and had a moment of hesitation. "We have to consider that. His affairs, you know, may fall some day into the hands of—someone else, you know."

"That, if you will believe me, Mr. Isbister, is one of the problems most constantly before my mind. We happen to be——as a matter of fact, there are no very trustworthy connexions of ours. It is a grotesque and unprecedented position."

"It is," said Isbister. "As a matter of fact, it's a case for a public trustee, if only we had such a functionary."

"It seems to me it's a case for some public body, some practically undying guardian. If he really is going on living—as the doctors, some of them, think. As a matter of fact, I have gone to one or two public men about it. But, so far, nothing has been done."

"It wouldn't be a bad idea to hand him over to some public body—the British Museum Trustees, or the Royal College of Physicians. Sounds a bit odd, of course, but the whole situation is odd."

"The difficulty is to induce them to take him."

"Red tape, I suppose?"

"Partly."

Pause. "It's a curious business, certainly," said Isbister. "And compound interest has a way of mounting up."

"It has," said Warming. "And now the gold supplies are running short there is a tendency towards . . . appreciation."

"I've felt that," said Isbister with a grimace. "But it makes it better for *him*."

"*If* he wakes."

"If he wakes," echoed Isbister. "Do you notice the pinched-in look of his nose, and the way in which his eyelids sink?"

"I doubt if he will wake."

"I never properly understood," said Isbister, "what it was brought this on. He told me something about overstudy. I've often been curious."

"He was a man of considerable gifts, but spasmodic, emotional. He had grave domestic troubles, divorced his wife in fact, and it was a relief from that, I think, that he took up politics of the rabid sort. He was a fanatical Radical—a Socialist. Overwork upon a controversy did this for him. I remember the pamphlet he wrote—a curious production. Wild, whirling stuff. There were one or two prophecies. Some of them are already exploded, some of them are established facts. But for the most part to read such a thesis is to realise how full the world is of unanticipated things. He will have much to learn, much to re-learn when he wakes. If ever a waking comes."

"I'd give anything to be there," said Isbister, "just to hear what he would say to it all."

"So would I," said Warming. "Aye! so would I," with an old man's sudden turn to self pity. "But I shall never see him wake."

He stood looking thoughtfully at the waxen figure. "He will never wake," he said at last. He sighed. "He will never wake again."

CHAPTER III.

THE AWAKENING

WHAT a wonderfully complex thing that simple seeming unity—the self! Who can trace its redintegration as morning after morning we awaken, the flux and confluence of its countless factors interweaving, rebuilding, the dim first stirrings of the soul, the growth and synthesis of the unconscious to the sub-conscious, the subconscious to dawning consciousness, until at last we recognise ourselves again. And as it happens to most of us after the night sleep, so it was with Graham at the end of his vast slumber. A dim cloud of sensation taking shape, a cloudy dreariness, and he found himself vaguely somewhere, recumbent, faint, but alive.

That pilgrimage towards a personal being again seemed to traverse vast gulfs, to occupy epochs. Gigantic dreams that were terrible realities at the time, left vague perplexing memories, strange creatures, strange scenery, as if from another planet. There was a distant impression, too, of a momentous conversation, of a name—he could not tell what name—that was subsequently to recur, of some queer, long-forgotten sensation of vein and muscle, of a feeling of vast hopeless effort, the effort of a man near drowning in darkness. Then came a panorama of dazzling unstable confluent scenes.

The texture that wove at last through the half-light of dreaming to wakefulness, shaped a definite picture of dark masses of cliff, a black shadow of caves at the foot of them, into which the green sea water foamed and vanished, and a cleft in the rocky front and a thin plume of cascade quivering in the wind. There was a sense of intolerable misery linked with this, he was looking down on it, and for some reason he had to fling himself forward, was in fact flinging himself forward, floating down swifter and swifter. A man appeared against the background saying things that were troublesome to hear and in someway arresting that downward swoop. There was a grey distress in this obstruction. The stranger spread out and grew impalpable, and the vision had passed.

Graham became aware that this was either a memory or a phase in a dream, not present at any rate in spite of its vividness, and that his eyes were open and regarding some unfamiliar thing. It was something white, the edge of some-

Looking over his shoulder Graham saw approaching a very short, fat, and thickset beardless man, with aquiline nose and heavy neck and chin. Very thick black and slightly sloping eyebrows that almost met over his nose, and overhung deep grey eyes, gave his face an oddly formidable expression. He scowled momentarily at Graham.

thing, a frame of wood. He moved his head slightly, following the contour of this shape. It went up beyond the top of his eyes. He tried to think where he might be. Did it matter, seeing he was so wretched? The colour of his thoughts was a dark depression. He felt the featureless misery of one who wakes towards the hour of dawn.

He had an uncertain sense of whispers and footsteps hastily receding.

The movements of his head involved a perception of extreme physical weakness. He supposed he was in bed in the hotel at the place in the valley—but he could not recall that white edge. He must have slept. He remembered now that he had wanted to sleep. He recalled the cliff and waterfall again, and then recollected something about talking to a passer-by.

How long had he slept? What was that sound of pattering feet? And that rise and fall, like the murmur of breakers on pebbles? He put out a languid hand to reach his watch from the chair whereon it was his habit to place it, and touched some smooth, hard surface like glass. This was so unexpected that it started him extremely. Quite suddenly he rolled over, stared for a moment, and struggled into a sitting position. The effort was unexpectedly difficult, and it left him giddy and weak—and amazed.

He rubbed his eyes. The riddle of his surroundings was confusing but his mind was quite clear—evidently his sleep had benefited him. He was not in a bed at all as he understood the word, but lying naked on a very soft and yielding mattress, apparently an air mattress, in a trough of dark glass. The mattress was partly transparent, a fact he observed with a strange sense of insecurity, and below it was a mirror reflecting him greyly. About his arm—and he saw with a shock that his skin was strangely dry and yellow—was bound a curious apparatus of rubber, bound so cunningly that it seemed to pass into his skin above and below. And this strange bed was placed in a case of greenish coloured glass (as it seemed to him), a bar in the white framework of which had first arrested his attention. In the corner of the case was a stand of glittering and delicately made apparatus, for the most part quite strange appliances, though a maximum and minimum thermometer was recognisable.

The slightly greenish tint of the glass-like substance which surrounded him on every hand obscured what lay behind, but he perceived it was a vast apartment of spendid appearance, and with a very large and simple white archway facing him. Close to the walls of the cage were articles of furniture, a table covered with a sil-very cloth, silvery like the side of a fish, a couple of black and graceful chairs, and on the table a number of dishes with substances piled on them, a bottle and two glasses. He realised that he was intensely hungry.

He could see no human being, and after a period of hesitation scrambled off the translucent mattress and tried to stand on the clean white floor of his little apartment. He had miscalculated his strength, however, and staggered and put his hand against the glass-like pane before him to steady himself. For a moment it resisted his hand, bending outward like a distended bladder, then it broke with a slight report. He reeled out into the general space of the hall, greatly astonished. He caught at the table to save himself, knocking one of the glasses to the floor—it rang but did not break—and sat down in one of the armchairs.

When he had a little recovered he filled the remaining glass from the bottle and drank—a colourless liquid it was, but not water, with a pleasing faint aroma and taste and a quality of immediate support and stimulus. He put down the vessel and looked about him.

The apartment lost none of its size and magnificence now that the greenish transparency that had intervened was removed. The archway he saw led to a flight of steps, going downward without the intermediation of a door, to a spacious transverse passage. This passage ran between polished pillars of some white-veined substance of deep ultramarine, and along it came the sound of human movements and voices and a deep undeviating droning note. He sat, now fully awake, listening alertly, forgetting the viands in his attention.

Then with a shock he remembered that he was naked, and casting about him for covering, saw a long black robe thrown on one of the chairs beside him. This he wrapped about him and sat down again, trembling.

His mind was still a surging perplexity. Clearly he had slept, and had been removed in his sleep. But where? And who were those people, the distant crowd beyond the deep blue pillars? Boscastle? He poured out and partially drank another glass of the colourless fluid.

What was this place?—this place that to his senses seemed subtly quivering like a thing alive? He looked about him at the clean and beautiful form of the apartment, unstained by ornament, and saw that the roof was broken in one place by a circular shaft full of light, and, as he looked, a steady, sweeping shadow blotted it out and passed, and came again and passed. "Beat, beat," that sweeping shadow had a note of its own in the subdued tumult that filled the air.

He would have called out, but only a little sound came into his throat. Then he stood up, and, with the uncertain steps of a drunkard, made his way towards the archway. He staggered down the steps, tripping on the corner of the black cloak he had wrapped about himself, and saved himself by catching at one of the blue pillars.

The passage ran down a cool vista of blue and purple, and ended remotely in a railed place like a balcony, brightly lit and projecting into a space of haze, a space like the interior of some gigantic building. Beyond and remote were vast and vague architectural forms. The tumult of voices rose now loud and clear, and on the balcony, and with their backs to him, gesticulating, and apparently in animated conversation, were three figures, richly dressed in loose and easy garments of bright soft colourings. The noise of a great multitude of people poured up over the balcony, and once it seemed the top of a banner passed, and once some brightly coloured object, a pale blue cap or garment thrown up into the air perhaps, flashed athwart the space and fell. The shouts sounded like English, there was a reiteration of "Wake!" He heard some indistinct shrill cry, and abruptly these three men began laughing.

"Ha, ha, ha!" laughed one—a red-haired man in a short purple robe. "When the Sleeper wakes—— *When!*"

He turned his eyes full of merriment along the passage. His face changed, the whole man changed, became rigid. The other two turned swiftly at his exclamation, and stood motionless. Their faces assumed an expression of consternation, an expression that deepened to awe.

Suddenly Graham's knees bent beneath him, his arm against the pillar collapsed limply, he staggered forward and fell upon his face.

CHAPTER IV.

THE SOUND OF A TUMULT

GRAHAM'S last impression before he fainted was of a clamorous ringing of bells. He learnt afterwards that he was insensible, hanging between life and death, for the better part of an hour. When he recovered his senses, he was back on his translucent couch, and there was a stirring warmth at heart and throat. The dark apparatus, he perceived, had been removed from his arm, which was bandaged. The white framework was still about him. A man in a deep violet robe, one of those who had been on the balcony, was looking into his face.

Remote but insistent was a clamour of bells and confused sounds, that suggested to his mind the picture of a great number of people shouting together. Something seemed to fall across this tumult like a door suddenly closed.

Graham moved his head. "What does all this mean?" he said slowly. "Where am I?"

He saw the red-haired man who had been first to discover him. A voice seemed to be asking what he had said, and was abruptly stilled.

The man in violet answered in a soft voice, speaking English with a slightly foreign accent, or so at least it seemed to the Sleeper's ears, "You are quite safe. You were brought hither from where you fell asleep. It is quite safe. You have been here some time—sleeping. In a trance."

He said something further that Graham could not hear, and a little phial was handed across to him. Graham felt a cooling spray, a fragrant mist played over his forehead for a moment, and his sense of refreshment increased. He closed his eyes in satisfaction.

"Better?" asked the man in violet, as Graham's eyes re-opened. He was a pleasant-faced man of thirty, perhaps, with a pointed flaxen beard, and a clasp of gold at the neck of his violet robe.

"Yes," said Graham.

"You have been asleep some time. In a cataleptic trance. You have heard? Catalepsy? It may seem strange to you at first, but I can assure you everything is well."

Graham did not answer, but these words served their reassuring purpose. His eyes went from face to face of the three people about him. They were regarding him strangely. He knew he ought to be somewhere in Cornwall, but he could not square these things with that impression.

A matter that had been in his mind during his last waking moments at Boscastle recurred, a thing resolved upon and somehow neglected. He cleared his throat.

"Have you wired my cousin?" he asked. "E. Warming 27, Chancery Lane?"

They were all assiduous to hear. But he had to repeat it. "What an odd *blurr* in his accent!" whispered the red-haired man. "Wire, sir?" said the young man with the flaxen beard, evidently puzzled.

"He means send an electric telegram," volunteered the third, a pleasant-faced youth of nineteen or twenty. The flaxen-bearded man gave a cry of comprehension. "How stupid of me! You may be sure everything shall be done, sir," he said to Graham. "I am afraid it would be difficult to—*wire* to your cousin. He is not in London now. But don't trouble about arrangements yet; you have been asleep a very long time and the important thing is to get over that, sir." (Graham concluded the word was sir, but this man pronounced it "*Sire*.")

"Oh!" said Graham, and became quiet.

It was all very puzzling, but apparently these people in unfamiliar dress knew what they were about. Yet they were odd and the room was odd. It seemed he was in some newly established place. He had a sudden flash of suspicion. Surely this wasn't some hall of public exhibition! If it was he would give Warming a piece of his mind. But it scarcely had that character. And in a place of public exhibition he would not have discovered himself naked.

Then suddenly, quite abruptly, he realised what had happened. There was no perceptible interval of suspicion, no dawn to his knowledge. Abruptly he knew his trance had lasted for a vast interval; as if by some process of thought-reading he interpreted the awe in the faces that peered into his. He looked at them strangely, full of intense emotion. It seemed they read his eyes. He framed his lips to speak and could not. A queer impulse to hide his knowledge came into his mind almost at the moment of his discovery. He looked at his bare feet, regarding them silently. His impulse to speak passed. He was trembling exceedingly.

They gave him some pink fluid with a greenish fluorescence and a meaty taste, and the assurance of returning strength grew.

"That—that makes me feel better," he said hoarsely, and there were murmurs of respectful approval. He knew now quite clearly. He made to speak again, and again he could not.

He pressed his throat and tried a third time. "How long?" he asked in a level voice. "How long have I been asleep?"

"Some considerable time," said the flaxen-bearded man, glancing quickly at the others.

"How long?"

"A very long time."

"Yes—yes," said Graham suddenly testy. "But I want—— Is it—it is—some years? Many years? There was something—I forget what. I feel—confused. But you——" He sobbed. "You need not fence with me. How long——?"

He stopped, breathing irregularly. He squeezed his eyes with his knuckles, and sat waiting for an answer.

They spoke in undertones.

"Five or six?" he asked faintly. "More?"

"Very much more than that."

"More!"

"More."

He looked at them, and it seemed as though imps were twitching the muscles of his face. He looked his question.

"Many years," said the man with the red beard.

Graham struggled into a sitting position. He wiped a rheumy tear from his face with a lean hand. "Many years!" he repeated. He shut his eyes tight, opened them, and sat looking about him from one unfamiliar thing to another.

"How many years?" he asked.

"You must be prepared to be surprised."

"Well?"

"More than a gross of years."

He was irritated at the strange word. "More than a *what?*"

Two of them spoke together. Some quick remarks that were made about "decimal" he did not catch.

"How long did you say?" asked Graham. "How long? Don't look like that. Tell me."

Among the remarks in an undertone, his ear caught six words: "More than a couple of centuries."

"*What?*" he cried, turning on the youth who he thought had spoken. "Who says——? What was that? A couple of *centuries!*"

"Yes," said the man with the red beard. "Two hundred years."

Graham repeated the words. He had been prepared to hear of a vast repose, and yet these concrete centuries defeated him.

"Two hundred years," he said again, with the figure of a great gulf opening very slowly in his mind; and then, "Oh, but——!"

They said nothing.

"You—did you say——?"

"Two hundred years. Two centuries of years," said the man with the red beard.

There was a pause. Graham looked at their faces and saw that what he had heard was indeed true.

"But it can't be," he said querulously. "I am dreaming. Trances. Trances don't last. That is not right—this is a joke you have played upon me! Tell me—some days ago, perhaps, I was walking along the coast of Cornwall——?"

His voice failed him.

The man with the flaxen beard hesitated. "I'm not very strong in history, sir," he said weakly, and glanced at the others.

"That was it, sir," said the youngster. "Boscastle, in the old Duchy of Cornwall—it's in the south-west country beyond the dairy meadows. There is a house there still. I've been there."

"Boscastle!" Graham turned his eyes to the youngster. "That was it—Boscastle. Little Boscastle. I fell asleep—somewhere there. I don't exactly remember. I don't exactly remember."

He pressed his brows and whispered, "More than *two hundred years!*"

He began to speak quickly with a twitching face, but his heart was cold within him. "But if it *is* two hundred years, every soul I know, every human being that ever I saw or spoke to before I went to sleep, must be dead."

They did not answer him.

"The Queen and the Royal Family, her Ministers, Church and State. High and low, rich and poor, one with another——"

"Is there England still?"

"That's a comfort! Is there London?"

"This *is* London, eh? And you are my assistant-custodian? Assistant-custodian. And these——? Eh? Assistant-custodians too!"

He sat with a gaunt stare on his face. "But why am I here? No! Don't talk. Be quiet. Let me——"

He sat silent, rubbed his eyes, and, uncovering them, found another little glass of pinkish fluid held towards him. He took the dose. It was almost immediately sustaining. Directly he had taken it he began to weep naturally and refreshingly.

Presently he looked at their faces, suddenly laughed through his tears, a little foolishly. "But—two—hun—dred—years!" he said. He grimaced hysterically and covered his face again.

After a space he grew calm. He sat up, his hands hanging over his knees in almost precisely the same attitude in which Isbister had found him on the cliff at Pentargen. His attention was attracted by a thick domineering voice, the footsteps of an advancing personage. "What are you doing? Why was I not warned? Surely you could tell? Someone will suffer for this. The man must be kept quiet. Are the doorways closed? All the doorways? He must be kept perfectly quiet. He must not be told. Has he been told anything?"

The man with the fair beard made some inaudible remark, and Graham looking over his shoulder saw approaching a very short, fat, and thickset beardless man, with aquiline nose and heavy neck and chin. Very thick black and slightly sloping eyebrows that almost met over his nose, and overhung deep grey eyes, gave his face an oddly formidable expression. He scowled momentarily at Graham, and then his regard returned to the man with the flaxen beard. "These others," he said in a voice of extreme irritation. "You had better go."

"Go?" said the red-bearded man.

"Certainly—go now. But see the doorways are closed as you go."

The two men addressed turned obediently, after one reluctant glance at Graham, and instead of going through the archway as he expected, walked straight to the dead wall of the apartment opposite the archway. And then came a strange thing; a long strip of this apparently solid wall rolled up with a snap, hung over the two retreating men and fell again, and immediately Graham was alone with the newcomer and the purple-robed man with the flaxen beard.

For a space the thick set man took not the slightest notice of Graham, but proceeded to interrogate the other—obviously his subordinate—upon the treatment of their charge. He spoke clearly, but in phrases only partially intelligible to Graham. The awakening seemed not only a matter of surprise but of consternation and annoyance to him. He was evidently profoundly excited.

"You must not confuse his mind by telling him things," he repeated again and again. "You must not confuse his mind."

His questions answered, he turned quickly and eyed the awakened sleeper with an ambiguous expression.

"Feel queer?" he asked.

"Very."

"The world, what you see of it, seems strange to you?"

"I suppose I have to live in it, strange as it seems."

"I suppose so, now."

"In the first place, hadn't I better have some clothes?"

"They——" said the thickset man and stopped, and the flaxen-bearded man met his eye and went away. "You will very speedily have clothes," said the thickset man.

"Is it true, indeed, that I have been asleep two hundred——?" asked Graham.

"They have told you that, have they? Two hundred and three, as a matter of fact."

Graham accepted the indisputable now with raised eyebrows and depressed mouth. He sat silent for a moment, and then asked a question, "Is there a mill or dynamo near here?" He did not wait for an answer. "Things have changed tremendously, I suppose?" he said.

"What is that shouting?" he asked abruptly.

"Nothing," said the thickset man impatiently. "It's people. You'll understand better later—perhaps. As you say, things have changed." He spoke shortly, his brows were knit, and he glanced about him like a man trying to decide in an emergency. "We must get you clothes and so forth, at any rate. Better wait here until some can come. No one will come near you. You want shaving."

Graham rubbed his chin.

The man with the flaxen beard came back towards them, turned suddenly, listened for a moment, lifted his eyebrows at the older man, and hurried off through the archway towards the balcony. The tumult of shouting grew louder, and the thickset man turned and listened

He went to the railings of the balcony and leant forward.
The place into which he looked was an aisle of Titanic
buildings, curving away in a spacious sweep in
either direction. Gigantic globes of cool white light
shamed the pale sunbeams that filtered down through
the girders and wires.

also. He cursed suddenly under his breath, and turned his eyes upon Graham with an unfriendly expression. It was a surge of many voices, rising and falling, shouting and screaming, and once came a sound like blows and sharp cries, and then a snapping, like the crackling of dry sticks. Graham strained his ears to draw some single thread of sound from the woven tumult.

Then he perceived, repeated again and again, a certain formula. For a time he doubted his ears. But surely these were the words: "Show us the Sleeper! Show us the Sleeper!"

The thickset man rushed suddenly to the archway.

"Wild!" he cried. "How do they know? Do they know? Or is it guessing?"

There was perhaps an answer.

"I can't come," said the thickset man; "I have *him* to see to. But shout from the balcony."

There was an inaudible reply.

"Say he is not awake. Anything! I leave it to you."

He came hurrying back to Graham. "You must have clothes at once," he said. "You cannot stop here—and it will be impossible to——"

He rushed away, Graham shouting unanswered questions after him. In a moment he was back.

"I can't tell you what is happening. It is too complex to explain. In a moment you shall have your clothes made. Yes—in a moment. And then I can take you away from here. You will find out our troubles soon enough."

"But those voices. They were shouting——?"

"Something about the Sleeper—that's you. They have some twisted idea. I don't know what it is. I know nothing. Demology is out of my province."

"Demology?"

"Demology. Ah!"

A shrill bell jetted acutely across the indistinct mingling of remote noises, and this brusque person sprang to a little group of appliances in the corner of the room. He listened for a moment, regarding a ball of crystal, nodded, and said a few indistinct words; then he walked to the wall through which the two men had vanished. It rolled up again like a curtain, and he stood waiting.

Graham lifted his arm, and was astonished to find what strength the restoratives had given him. He thrust one leg over the side of the couch and then the other. His head no longer swam. He could scarcely credit his rapid recovery. He sat feeling his limbs.

The man with the flaxen beard re-entered from the archway, and as he did so the cage of a lift came sliding down in front of the thickset man, and a lean, grey-bearded man, carrying a roll, and wearing a tightly fitting costume of dark green, appeared therein.

"This is the tailor," said the thickset man with an introductory gesture. "It will never do for you to wear that black. I cannot understand how it got here. But I shall. I shall. You will be as rapid as possible?" he said to the tailor.

The man in green bowed, and, advancing, seated himself by Graham on the bed. His manner was calm, but his eyes were full of curiosity. "You will find the fashions altered Sire," he said. He glanced from under his brows at the thickset man.

He opened the roller with a quick movement, and a confusion of brilliant fabrics poured out over his knees. "You lived, Sire, in a period essentially cylindrical—the Victorian. With a tendency to the hemisphere in hats. Circular curves always. Now——" He flicked out a little appliance the size and appearance of a keyless watch, whirled the knob, and behold—a little figure in white appeared kinetoscope fashion on the dial, walking and turning. The tailor caught up a pattern of bluish white satin. "That is my conception of your immediate treatment," he said.

The thickset man came and stood by the shoulder of Graham.

"We have very little time," he said.

"Trust me," said the tailor. "My machine follows. What do you think of this?"

"What is that?" asked the man from the nineteenth century.

"In your days they showed you a fashion plate," said the tailor, "but this is our modern development. See here." The little figure repeated its evolution, but in a different costume. "Or this," and with a click another small figure in a more voluminous type of robe marked on to the dial. The tailor was very quick in his movements, and glanced twice towards the lift as he did these things.

It rumbled again, and a crop-haired, staring, anaemic lad, clad in coarse pale blue canvas, appeared, together with a complicated machine, which he pushed noiselessly on little castors into the room. Incontinently the little kinetoscope was dropped, Graham was invited to stand in front of the machine, and the tailor muttered some instructions to the crop-haired lad, who answered in guttural tones, with words Graham did not recognise. The boy then went to conduct an incomprehensible monologue in the corner, and the tailor pulled out a number of slotted arms terminating in little discs, pulling them out until the discs were flat against the body of

Graham, one at each shoulder blade, one at the elbows, one at the neck and so forth, so that at last there were, perhaps, two score of them upon his body and limbs. At the same time, some other person entered the room by the lift, behind Graham. The tailor set moving a mechanism that initiated a faint-sounding rhythmic movement of parts in the machine, and in another moment he was knocking up the levers, and Graham was released. The tailor replaced his cloak of black, and the man with the flaxen beard proffered him a little glass of some refreshing fluid. Graham saw over the rim of the glass a pale-faced young man regarding him with a singular fixity.

The thickset man had been pacing the room fretfully, and now turned and went through the archway towards the balcony, from which the noise of a distant crowd still came in gusts and cadences. The crop-headed lad handed the tailor a roll of the bluish satin, and the two began fixing this in the mechanism in a manner reminiscent of a roll of paper in a nineteenth century printing machine. Then they ran the entire thing on its easy, noiseless bearings across the room to a remote corner where a twisted cable looped rather gracefully from the wall. They made some connexion and the machine became energetic and swift.

"What is that doing?" asked Graham pointing with the empty glass to the busy figures and trying to ignore the scrutiny of the newcomer. "Is that—some sort of force—laid on?"

"Yes," said the man with the flaxen beard.

"Who is *that?*" He indicated the archway behind him.

The man in purple stroked his little beard, hesitated, and answered in an undertone, "He is Howard, your chief guardian. You see, Sire—it's a little difficult to explain. The Council appoints a guardian and assistants. This hall has under certain restrictions been public—in order that people might satisfy themselves. We have barred the doorways for the first time. But I think—if you don't mind I will leave him to explain."

"Odd!" said Graham. "Guardian? Council?" Then turning his back on the newcomer, he asked in an undertone, "Why is this man *glaring* at me? Is he a mesmerist?"

"Mesmerist! He is a capillotomist."

"Capillotomist!"

"Yes—one of the chief. His yearly fee is six-doz lions."

It sounded sheer nonsense. Graham snatched at the last phrase with an unsteady mind. "Six-doz lions?" he said.

"Didn't you have lions? I suppose not. You

had the old pounds? They are our monetary units."

"But what was that you said—sixdoz?"

"Yes. Six dozen, Sire. Of course things, even these little things, have altered. You lived in the days of the decimal system, the Arab system—tens, and little hundreds and thousands. We have eleven numerals now. We have single figures for both ten and eleven, two figures for a dozen, and a dozen dozen makes a gross, a great hundred, you know, a dozen gross a dozand, and a dozand dozand a myriad. Very simple?"

"I suppose so," said Graham. "But about this cap—what was it?"

The man with the flaxen beard glanced over his shoulder.

"Here are your clothes!" he said. Graham turned round sharply and saw the tailor standing at his elbow smiling, and holding some palpably new garments over his arm. The crop-headed boy, by means of one finger, was impelling the complicated machine towards the lift by which he had arrived. Graham stared at the completed suit. "You don't mean to say——!"

"Just made," said the tailor. He dropped the garments at the feet of Graham, walked to the bed on which Graham had so recently been lying, flung out the translucent mattress, and turned up the looking-glass. As he did so a furious bell summoned the thickset man to the corner. The man with the flaxen beard rushed across to him and then hurried out by the archway.

The tailor was assisting Graham into a dark purple combination garment, stockings, vest, and pants in one, as the thickset man came back from the corner to meet the man with the flaxen beard returning from the balcony. They began speaking quickly in an undertone, their bearing had an unmistakable quality of anxiety. Over the purple under-garment came a complex but graceful garment of bluish white, and Graham was clothed in the fashion once more and saw himself, sallow-faced, unshaven and shaggy still, but at least naked no longer, and in some indefinable unprecedented way graceful.

"I must shave," he said regarding himself in the glass.

"In a moment," said Howard.

The persistent stare ceased. The young man closed his eyes, reopened them, and, with a lean hand extended, advanced on Graham. Then he stopped, with his hand slowly gesticulating, and looked about him.

"A seat," said Howard impatiently: and in a moment the flaxen-bearded man had a chair behind Graham. "Sit down, please," said Howard.

Graham hesitated, and in the other hand of

the wild-eyed man he saw the glint of steel.

"Don't you understand, Sire?" cried the flaxen-bearded man with hurried politness. "He is going to cut your hair."

"Oh!" cried Graham enlightened. "But you called him——"

"A capillotomist—precisely! He is one of the finest artists in the world."

Graham sat down abruptly. The flaxen-bearded man disappeared. The capillotomist came forward with graceful gestures, examined Graham's ears and surveyed him, felt the back of his head, and would have sat down again to regard him but for Howard's audible impatience. Forthwith with rapid movements and a succession of deftly handled implements he shaved Graham's chin, clipped his moustache, and cut and arranged his hair. All this he did without a word, with something of the rapt air of a poet inspired. And as soon as he had finished Graham was handed a pair of shoes.

Suddenly a loud voice shouted—it seemed from a piece of machinery in the corner—"At once—at once. The people know all over the city. Work is being stopped. Work is being stopped. Wait for nothing, but come."

This shout appeared to perturb Howard exceedingly. By his gestures it seemed to Graham that he hesitated between two directions. Abruptly he went towards the corner where the apparatus stood about the little crystal ball. As he did so the undertone of tumultuous shouting from the archway that had continued during all these occurrences rose to a mighty sound, roared as if it were sweeping past, and fell again as if receding swiftly. It drew Graham after it by an irresistible attraction of amazement and curiosity. He glanced at the thickset man, and then obeyed his natural impulse. In two strides he was down the steps and in the passage, and in a score he was out upon the balcony upon which the three men had been standing.

CHAPTER V.

THE MOVING WAYS

HIS first impression was one of overwhelming astonishment at the greatness of the architecture that opened out as he came down the passage. He went to the railings of the balcony and leant forward. An exclamation of surprise at his appearance, and the movements of a number of people came up from the spacious area below.

The place into which he looked was an aisle of Titanic buildings, curving away in a spacious sweep in either direction; overhead mighty cantilevers sprang together across the huge width of the place, and a tracery of some translucent material shut out the sky. Gigantic globes of cool white light shamed the pale sunbeams that filtered down through the girders and wires. Here and there a gossamer suspension bridge dotted with foot-passengers flung across the chasm and the air was webbed with slender cables. A cliff of edifice hung above him, he perceived as he glanced upward, and the opposite façade was grey and dim and broken by great archings, circular perforations, balconies, buttresses, turret projections, myriads of vast windows, and an intricate scheme of architectural relief. Athwart these horizontally and obliquely ran inscriptions in an unfamiliar lettering. Here and there close to the roof cables of a peculiar stoutness were fastened, and drooped in a steep curve to circular openings on the opposite side of the space, and even as Graham looked at them a remote and tiny figure of a man clad in pale blue arrested his attention. He was far overhead across the space beside the higher fastening of one of these festoons, hanging forward from a little ledge of masonry and handling some well-nigh invisible strings dependent from the line. Then suddenly, with a swoop that sent Graham's heart into his mouth, this man had rushed down the curve and vanished through a round opening on the hither side of the way.

Graham had been looking up as he came out upon the balcony, and the things he saw above and opposed to him had at first seized his attention to exclusion of anything else. But suddenly he discovered the roadway! It was not a roadway at all, as Graham understood such things, for in the nineteenth century the only roads and streets were beaten tracks of motionless earth, jostling rivulets of vehicles between narrow footways. But this roadway was three hundred feet across, and it moved; it moved all save the middle, the lowest part. For a moment, the motion dazzled his mind. Then he understood.

Under the balcony this extraordinary roadway ran swiftly to Graham's right, an endless flow rushing along as fast as a nineteenth century express train, an endless platform of narrow transverse overlapping rods with little interspaces that permitted it to follow the curvature of the street. Upon it were seats, and here and there little kiosks, but they swept by too swiftly for him to see what might be therein. From the nearest and swiftest platform a series of others descended to the centre. Each moved to the right, each perceptibly slower than the one above it, but the difference in pace was small enough to permit anyone to step from any platform to the one adjacent, and so to walk, uninterruptedly from the swiftest to the motionless middle space. Beyond the middle space were another series of endless platforms rushing with varying pace to Graham's left. And seated in crowds upon the two widest and swiftest platforms, or stepping from one to another down the steps, or swarming over the central space, was an innumerable and wonderfully diversified multitude of people.

"You must not stop here," shouted Howard suddenly at his side. "You must come away. You must come away."

Graham made no answer. He heard without hearing. The current on the platforms ran with a roar and the people were shouting. He perceived women and girls with flowing hair, beautifully robed, with bands crossing between the breasts. These first came out of the confusion. Then he perceived that the dominant note in that kaleidoscope of costume was the pale blue that the tailor's boy had worn. He became aware of cries of "The Sleeper. What has happened to the Sleeper?" and it seemed as though the rushing platforms before him were suddenly spattered with the pale buff of human faces, and then still more thickly. He saw pointing fingers. He perceived that the motionless central area of this huge arcade was densely crowded with pallid blue-clad people just opposite to the balcony. Some sort of struggle had sprung into life. People seemed to be pushed up the running platforms on either side, and carried away against their will. They would spring off so soon as they were beyond the thick of the confusion, and run back towards the conflict.

"It is the Sleeper! Verily, it is the Sleeper!" shouted voices. "That is never the Sleeper," shouted others. More and more faces were turned to him. At intervals along this central area Graham noted openings, pits, the heads of staircases going down apparently, with people ascending out of them and descending into them. The struggle it seemed centred about one of these. People would come running down the moving platforms to this, and would run up again and return, leaping dexterously from platform to platform. The clustering people on the higher platforms seemed to divide their interest between this point and the balcony. A number of sturdy little figures clad in a uniform of bright red, and working methodically together, were employed, it seemed, in preventing access to this descending staircase. Their brilliant colour contrasted vividly with the whitish-blue of their antagonists, for the struggle was indisputable.

He saw these things with Howard shouting in his ear and shaking his arm. And then suddenly Howard was gone and he stood alone.

He perceived that the cries of "The Sleeper!" grew in volume, and that the people on the nearer platform were now standing up, and many of them running obliquely across the slower moving platforms. The nearer swifter platform he perceived was empty to the right of him, and far across the space the platform running in the opposite direction was coming crowded and passing away bare. With incredible swiftness a vast crowd gathered in the central space before his eyes; it became a swaying mass of people, and the shouts grew from a fitful crying to a voluminous, incessant clamour: "The Sleeper! The Sleeper!" and yells and cheers, a waving of garments and cries of "Stop the ways!" They were also crying another name strange to Graham. It sounded like "Ostrog." The slower platforms were thick with active people, running against the movement so as to keep themselves opposite to him.

"Stop the ways," they cried. Agile figures ran up swiftly from the centre to the swift road nearest him, were borne rapidly past him, shouting strange, unintelligible things, and ran back obliquely to the central way. One thing he distinguished: "It is indeed the Sleeper. It is indeed the Sleeper," they testified.

For a space Graham stood without a movement. Then he became vividly aware that all this concerned him. He was pleased at his wonderful popularity, he bowed, and, seeking a gesture of longer range, waved his arm. He was astonished at the violence of uproar that this provoked. The tumult about the descending stairway rose to furious violence. He became aware of crowded balconies, of men sliding along ropes, of men in trapeze-like seats hurling athwart the space. He heard voices behind him, a number of people descending the steps through the archway; he suddenly perceived that his guardian Howard was back again and gripping his arm painfully, and shouting inaudibly in his ear.

He turned and Howard's face was white. "Come back," he heard. "They will stop the ways. The whole city will be in confusion."

He perceived a number of men hurrying along the passage of blue pillars behind Howard, the red-haired man, the man with the flaxen beard, a tall man in vivid vermilion, a crowd of others in red carrying staves, and all these people had anxious, eager faces.

"Get him away," cried Howard.

"But why?" said Graham. "I don't see――"

"You must come away!" said the man in red in a resolute voice. His face and eyes were resolute too. Graham's glances went from face to face, and he was suddenly aware of that most disagreeable flavour in life, compulsion. Someone gripped his arm. He was being dragged away. It seemed as though the tumult became two, as if half the shouts that had come in from this wonderful roadway had sprung into the passages of the great building behind him. Marvelling and confused, feeling an impotent desire to resist, Graham was half led, half thrust, along the passage of blue pillars, and suddenly he found himself alone with Howard in a lift and moving swiftly upward.

Howard's face was flushed deep, his brows were knit, and his lips opened and shut without a sound.

CHAPTER VI.

THE HALL OF THE ATLAS

FROM the moment when the tailor had bowed his farewell to the moment when Graham found himself in the lift, was altogether barely five minutes. And as yet the haze of his vast interval of sleep hung about him, as yet the initial strangeness of his being alive at all in this remote age touched everything with wonder, with a sense of the irrational, with something of the quality of a realistic dream. He was still detached, an astonished spectator, still but half involved in life. What he had seen, and especially the last crowded tumult, framed in the setting of the balcony, had a spectacular turn, like a thing witnessed from the box of a theatre, "I don't understand," he said. "What was the trouble? My mind is in a whirl. Why were they shouting? What is the danger?"

Howard looked at him keenly. "We have our troubles," he said with shifty eyes. "This is a time of unrest. And, in fact, your appearance, your waking just now, has a sort of connexion——"

He spoke jerkily like a man not quite sure of his breathing. He stopped abruptly.

"I don't understand," said Graham.

"It will be clearer later," said Howard.

He glanced uneasily upward as though he found the progress of the lift slow.

"I shall understand better no doubt when I have seen my way about a little," said Graham, puzzled. "It will be—it is bound to be—perplexing. At present it is all so strange. Anything seems possible. Anything. In the details even. Your counting I understand is different."

The lift stopped, and they stepped out into a narrow but very long passage between high walls, along which ran an extraordinary number of tubes and big cables.

"What a huge place this is!" said Graham. "Is it all one building? What place is it?"

"This is one of the city ways for various public services. Light and so forth."

"Was it a social trouble—that—in the great roadway place? How are you governed? Have you still a police?"

"Several," said Howard.

"Several?"

"About fourteen."

"I don't understand."

"Very probably not. Our social order will probably seem very complex to you. To tell you the truth, I don't understand it myself very clearly. Nobody does. You will perhaps—by and by. We have to go to the Council."

Graham's attention was divided between the urgent necessity of his inquiries and the people in the passages and halls they were traversing. For a moment his mind would be concentrated upon Howard and the halting answers he made, and then he would lose the thread in response to some vivid unexpected impression. Along the passages, in the halls, half the people seemed to be men in the red uniform. The pale blue canvas that had been so abundant in the aisle of moving ways did not appear. Invariably these men looked at him, and saluted him and Howard as they passed.

He had a clear vision of entering a long corridor, and there were a number of girls sitting on low seats, and as though in a class. He saw no teacher, but only a novel apparatus from which he fancied a voice proceeded. The girls regarded him and his conductor, he thought, with curiosity and astonishment. But he was hurried on before he could form a clear idea of the gathering. He judged they knew Howard but not himself, and that they wondered who he was. This Howard, it seemed, was a person of importance. But then he was also merely Graham's guardian. That was odd.

There came a passage in twilight, and into this passage a footway hung so that he could see the feet and ankles of people going to and fro thereon, but no more of them. Then vague impressions of galleries and of casual astonished passers-by turning round to stare after the two of them with their red-clad guard.

The stimulus of those clear fluids he had taken was only temporary. He was speedily fatigued by this excessive haste. He asked Howard to slacken his speed. Presently he was in a lift that had a window upon the great street space, but this was glazed and did not open, and they were too high for him to see the moving platforms below. But he saw people going to and fro along cables and strange, frail-looking bridges.

And thence they passed across the street and at a vast height above it. They crossed by means of a narrow bridge closed in with glass, so clear that it made him giddy even to remember it. The floor of it also was of glass. From his memory of the cliffs between New Quay and Boscastle, so remote in time, and so recent in his experience, it seemed to him that they must be near four hundred feet above the moving ways. He stopped, looked down between his legs upon the swarming blue and red multitudes, minute and foreshortened, struggling and gesticulating still towards the little balcony far below, a little toy balcony it seemed, where he had so recently been standing. A thin haze and the glare of the mighty globes of light obscured everything. A man seated in a little openwork cradle shot by from some point still higher than the little narrow bridge, rushing down a cable as swiftly almost as if he were falling. Graham stopped involuntarily to watch this strange passenger vanish in a great circular opening below, and then his eyes went back to the tumultuous struggle.

Along one of the swifter ways rushed a thick crowd of red spots. This broke up into individuals as it approached the balcony, and went pouring down the slower ways towards the dense struggling crowd on the central area. These men in red appeared to be armed with sticks or truncheons; they seemed to be striking and thrusting. A great shouting, cries of wrath, screaming, burst out and came up to Graham faint and thin. "Go on," cried Howard, laying hands on him.

Another man rushed down a cable. Graham suddenly glanced up to see whence he came, and beheld through the glassy roof and the network of cables and girders, dim rhythmically passing forms like the vans of windmills, and between them glimpses of a remote and pallid sky. Then Howard had thrust him forward across the bridge, and he was in a little narrow passage decorated with geometrical patterns.

"I want to see more of that," cried Graham, resisting.

"No, no," cried Howard, still gripping his arm. "This way. You must go this way." And the men in red following them seemed ready to enforce his orders.

Some men in a curious wasp-like uniform of black and yellow appeared down the passage, and one hastened to throw up a sliding shutter that had seemed a door to Graham, and led the way through it. Graham found himself in a gallery overhanging the end of a great chamber. The attendant in black and yellow crossed this, thrust up a second shutter, and stood waiting.

This place had the appearance of an anteroom. He saw a number of people in the central space, and at the opposite end a large and imposing doorway at the top of a flight of steps, heavily curtained but giving a glimpse of some

still larger hall beyond. He perceived men in red and other men in blaack and yellow standing stiffly about those portals.

As they crossed the gallery he distinctly heard a whisper from below, "The Sleeper," and was aware of a sudden turning of heads, a hum of observation. They entered another little passage in the wall of this ante-chamber, and then he found himself on an iron-railed gallery of metal that passed round the side of the great hall he had already seen through the curtains. He entered the place at the corner, so that he received the fullest impression of its huge proportions. The man in the wasp uniform stood aside like a well-trained servant, and closed the valve behind him.

Compared with any of the places Graham had so far seen, this second hall appeared to be decorated with extreme richness. On a pedestal at the remoter end, and more brilliantly lit than any other object was a huge white figure of Atlas, strong and strenuous, the globe upon his bowed shoulders. It was the first thing to strike his attention, it was so vast, so white and simple. Save for this figure and for a daïs in the center the wide floor of the place was a shining vacancy. The daïs was remote in the greatness of the area; it would have looked a mere slab of metal had it not been for the group of seven men who stood about a table upon it, and gave an inkling of its proportions. They were all dressed in white robes, they seemed to have arisen that moment from their seats, and they stood steadfastly regarding Graham. At the end of the table he perceived the glitter of some mechanical appliances, and across it all the shadow of the Atlas fell.

Howard led him along the end gallery until they were opposite this mighty labouring figure. Then he stopped. The two men in red who had followed them into the gallery came and stood on either hand of Graham.

"You must remain here," murmured Howard, "for a few moments," and, without waiting for a reply, hurried away along the gallery.

"But, *why*———?" began Graham.

He moved as if to follow Howard, and found his path obstructed by one of the men in red. "You have to wait here, Sire," said the man in red.

"*Why?*"

"Orders, Sire."

"Whose orders?"

"Our orders, Sire."

Graham looked his exasperation.

"What place is this?" he said presently. "Who are those men?"

"They are Lords of the Council, Sire."

"What council?"

"*The* Council."

"Oh!" said Graham, and after an equally ineffectual attempt at the other man, went to the railing and stared at the distant men in white, who stood watching him and whispering together.

The Council? He perceived there were now eight, though how the newcomer had arrived he had not observed. They made no gestures of greeting; they stood regarding him as in the nineteenth century a group of men might have stood in the street regarding a distant balloon that had suddenly floated into view. What council could it be that gathered there, that little body of men beneath the significant white Atlas, secluded from every eavesdropper in this impressive spaciousness? And why should he be brought to them and looked at strangely and spoken of inaudibly? Howard appeared beneath, walking quickly across the polished floor towards them. As he drew near he bowed and performed certain peculiar movements, apparently of a ceremonial nature. Then he ascended the steps of the daïs, and stood by the apparatus at the end of the table.

Graham watched that visible inaudible conversation. Occasionally, one of the white-robed men would glance towards him. He strained his ears in vain. The gesticulation of two of the speakers became animated. He glanced from them to the passive faces of his attendants. When he looked again Howard was extending his hands and moving his head like a man who protests. He was interrupted, it seemed, by one of the white-robed men rapping the table.

The conversation lasted an interminable time to Graham's sense. His eyes rose to the still giant at whose feet the Council sat. Thence they wandered at last to the walls of the hall. It was decorated in long painted panels of a quasi-Japanese type, many of them very beautiful. Those panels were grouped in a great and elaborate framing of dark wood or metal, which passed into the metallic caryatidæ of the galleries, and the great structural lines of the interior. The facile grace of these panels enhanced the mighty white effort that laboured in the centre of the scheme. Graham's eyes came back to the Council, and Howard was descending the steps. As he drew nearer his features could be distinguished, and Graham saw that he was flushed and blowing out his cheeks. His countenance was still disturbed when presently he reappeared along the gallery.

"This way," he said concisely, and they went on in silence to a little door that opened at their approach. The two men in red stopped on either side of this door. Howard and Graham passed in, and Graham, glancing back, saw the white-robed Council still standing in a close group and looking at him. Then the door closed behind him with a heavy thud, and for the first time since his awakening he was in silence. The floor even was noiseless to his feet.

Howard opened another door, and they were in the first of two contiguous little chambers furnished in white and green. "What Council was that?" began Graham. "What were they discussing? What have they to do with me?" Howard closed the door carefully, heaved a huge sigh, and said something in an undertone. He walked slantingways across the room and turned, blowing out his cheeks again. "Ugh!" he grunted, a man relieved.

Graham stood regarding him.

"You must understand," began Howard abruptly, avoiding Graham's eyes, "that our social order is very complex. A half explanation, a bare unqualified statement would give you false impressions. As a matter of fact—it is a case of compound interest partly—your small fortune, and the fortune of your cousin Warming which was left to you—and certain other beginnings—have become very considerable. And in other ways that will be hard for you to understand, you have become a person of significance—of very considerable significance—involved in the world's affairs."

He stopped.

"Yes?" said Graham.

"We have grave social troubles."

"Yes?"

"Things have come to such a pass that, in fact, it is advisable to seclude you here."

"Keep me prisoner!" exclaimed Graham.

"Well—to ask you to keep in seclusion."

Graham turned on him. "This is strange!" he said.

"No harm will be done you."

"No harm!"

"But you must be kept here——"

"While I learn my position, I presume."

"Precisely."

"Very well then. Begin. Why *harm?*"

"Not now."

"Why not!"

"It is too long a story, Sire."

"All the more reason I should begin at once. You say I am a person of importance. What was that shouting I heard? Why is a great multitude shouting and excited because my trance is over, and who are the men in white in that huge council chamber?"

"All in good time, Sire," said Howard. "But not crudely, not crudely. This is one of those

*Graham, glancing back, saw the white-robed
Council still standing in a close group
and looking at him.*

flimsy times when no man has a settled mind. Your awakening. No one expected your awakening. The Council is consulting."

"What Council?"

"The Council you saw."

Graham made a petulant movement. "This is not right," he said. "I should be told what is happening."

"You must wait. Really you must wait."

Graham sat down abruptly.

"I suppose since I have waited so long to resume life," he said shortly, "that I must wait a little longer."

"That is better," said Howard. "Yes, that is much better. And I must leave you alone. For a space. While I attend the discussion in the Council. . . . I am sorry."

He went towards the noiseless door, hesitated and vanished.

Graham walked to the door, tried it, found it securely fastened in some way he never came to understand, turned about, paced the room restlessly, made the circuit of the room, and sat down. He remained sitting for some time with folded arms and knitted brow, biting his finger nails and trying to piece together the kaleidoscopic impressions of this first hour of awakened life; the vast mechanical spaces, the endless series of chambers and passages, the great struggle that roared and splashed through these strange ways, the little group of remote unsympathetic men beneath the colossal Atlas, Howard's mysterious behaviour. There was an inkling of some vast inheritance already in his mind—a vast inheritance perhaps misapplied—of some unprecedented importance and opportunity. What had he to do? And this room's secluded silence was eloquent of imprisonment!

It came into Graham's mind with irresistible conviction that this series of magnificent impressions was a dream. He tried to shut his eyes and succeeded, but that time-honoured device led to no awakening.

Presently he began to touch and examine all the unfamiliar appointments of the two contiguous chambers in which he found himself.

In a long oval panel of mirror he saw himself and stopped astonished. He was clad now in a graceful costume of purple and bluish white, with a little greyshot beard trimmed to a point, and his hair, its black streaked now with bands of grey, arranged over his forehead in an unfamiliar but graceful manner. He seemed a man of five-and-forty perhaps. For a moment he did not perceive this was himself.

A flash of laughter came with the recognition.

"To call on old Warming like this!" he exclaimed, "and make him take me out to lunch!"

Then he thought of meeting first one and then another of the few familiar acquaintances of his early manhood, and in the midst of his amusement realised that every soul with whom he might jest had died many scores of years ago. The thought smote him abruptly and keenly; he stopped short, the expression of his face changed to a white consternation.

The tumultuous memory of the moving platforms and the huge façade of that wonderful street reasserted itself. The shouting multitudes came back clear and vivid, and those remote, inaudible, unfriendly councillors in white glancing towards him. He felt himself a little figure, very small and ineffectual, pitifully conspicuous. And all about him, the world was—strange.

CHAPTER VII.

IN THE SILENT ROOMS

PRESENTLY Graham resumed his examination of his apartments. Curiosity kept him moving in spite of his fatigue. The inner room, he perceived, was high, and its ceiling dome shaped, with an oblong aperture in the centre, opening into a funnel in which a wheel of broad vans seemed to be rotating, apparently driving the air up the shaft. The faint humming note of its easy motion was the only clear sound in that quiet place. As these vans sprang up one after the other, Graham could get transient glimpses of the sky. He was surprised to see a star.

This drew his attention to the fact that the bright lighting of these rooms was due to a multitude of very faint glow-lamps set about the cornices. There were no windows. And he began to recall that along all the vast chambers and passages he had traversed with Howard he had observed no windows at all. Had there been windows? There were windows on the street indeed, but were they for light? Or was the whole city lit day and night for evermore, so that there was no night there? He could not clearly determine this at the time, but afterwards he found the latter alternative was the case.

And another thing dawned upon him. There was no fireplace in either room. Was the season summer, and were these merely summer apartments, or was the whole city uniformly heated or cooled? He became interested in these questions, began examining the smooth texture of the walls, the simply constructed bed, the ingenious arrangements by which the labour of bedroom service was practically abolished. The air was sweet and pleasing and free from any sense of dust. And over everything was a curious absence of deliberate ornament, a bare grace of form and colour, that he found very pleasing to the eye. There were several comfortable chairs, a light table on silent runners carrying bottles of fluid and glasses, and two plates bearing a clear substance like jelly. Then he noticed there were no books, no newspapers, no writing materials. "The world has changed indeed," he said.

He observed one entire side of the outer room was set with rows of peculiar double cylinders in racks inscribed with green lettering on white that harmonised with the decorative scheme of the room, and in the centre of this side projected a little apparatus about a yard square and having a white smooth face to the room. A chair faced this. He had a transitory idea that these cylinders might be books, or a modern substitute for books, but at first it did not seem so.

The lettering on the cylinders puzzled him. At first sight it seemed like Russian. Then he noticed a suggestion of mutilated English about certain of the words.

"θi Man huwdbi Kiŋ,"

forced itself on him as "The Man who would be King." "Phonetic spelling," he said. He remembered reading a story with that title, then he recalled the story vividly, one of the best stories in the world. But this thing before him was not a book as he understood it.

He puzzled over the peculiar cylinder for some time and replaced it. Then he turned to the square apparatus and examined that. He opened a sort of lid and found one of the double cylinders within, and on the upper edge a little stud like the stud of an electric bell. He pressed this and a rapid clicking began and ceased. He became aware of voices and music, and noticed a play of colour on the smooth front face. He suddenly realised what this might be, and stepped back to regard it.

On the flat surface was now a little picture, very vividly coloured, and in this picture were figures that moved. Not only did they move, but they were conversing in clear small voices. It was exactly like reality viewed through an inverted opera glass and heard through a long tube. His interest was seized at once by the situation, which presented a man pacing up and down and vociferating angry things to a pretty but petulant-looking woman. Both were in the picturesque costume that seemed so strange to Graham. "I have worked," said the man, "but what have you been doing?"

"Ah!" said Graham. He forgot everything else, and sat down in the chair. Within five minutes he heard himself named, heard "when the Sleeper wakes," used jestingly as a proverb for remote postponement, and passed himself by, a thing remote and incredible. But in a little while he knew those two people like intimate friends.

At last the miniature drama came to an end, and the square face of the apparatus was blank again.

It was a strange world into which he had been permitted to see, unscrupulous, pleasure-seeking, energetic, subtle, a world too of dire economic struggle; there were allusions he did not understand, incidents that conveyed strange suggestions of altered moral ideals, flashes of dubious enlightenment. The blue canvas that bulked so largely in his first impression of the city ways appeared again and again as the costume of the common people. He had no doubt the story was contemporary, and its intense realism was undeniable. And the end had been a tragedy that oppressed him. He sat staring at the blankness.

He started and rubbed his eyes. He had been so absorbed in the latter-day substitute for a novel, that he awoke to the little green and white room with more than a touch of the surprise of his first awakening.

He stood up, and abruptly he was back in his own wonderland. The clearness of the kinetoscope drama passed, and the struggle in the vast place of streets, the ambiguous Council, the swift phases of his waking hour, came back. These people had spoken of the Council with suggestions of a vague universality of power. And they had spoken of the Sleeper; it had really not struck him vividly at the time that he was the Sleeper. He had to recall precisely what they had said . . .

He walked in the bedroom and peered up through the quick intervals of the revolving fan. As the fan swept round, a dim turmoil like the noise of machinery came in rhythmic eddies. All else was silence. Though the perpetual day still irradiated his now apartments, he perceived the little intermittent strip of sky was deep blue— black almost, and set with faint stars. He concluded the time must be far on in the night.

But he was neither hungry nor sleepy. He resumed his examination of the rooms. He could find no way of opening the padded door, no bell nor other means of calling for attendance. His feeling of wonder was in abeyance; but he was curious, anxious for information. He wanted to know exactly how he stood to these new things. He tried to compose himself to wait until someone came to him. Presently he became restless and eager for information, for distraction, for fresh sensations.

He went back to the apparatus in the other room, and had soon puzzled out the method of replacing the cylinders by others. As he did so, it came into his mind that it was these little appliances had fixed the language so that it was still clear and understandable after two hundred years. The haphazard cylinders he substituted displayed a musical fantasia. At first it was beautiful, and then it was sensuous. He presently recognised what appeared to him to be an altered version of the story of Tannhauser. The music was unfamiliar. But the rendering was realistic, and with a contemporary unfamiliarity. Tannhauser did not go to a Venusberg, but to a Pleasure City. What was a Pleasure City? A dream, surely, the fancy of a fantastic, voluptuous writer.

He became interested, curious. The story developed with a flavour of strangely twisted sentimentality. Suddenly he did not like it. He liked it less as it proceeded.

He had a revulsion of feeling. There were no pictures, no idealisations, but photographed realities. He wanted no more of the twenty-second century Venusberg. He forgot the part played by the model in nineteenth century art, and gave way to an archaic indignation. He rose, angry and half-ashamed at himself for witnessing this thing even in solitude. He pulled forward the apparatus, and with some violence sought for a means of stopping its action. Something snapped. A violet spark stung and convulsed his arm and the thing was still. When he attempted next day to replace these Tannhauser cylinders by another pair he found the apparatus broken . . .

He had come upon strange times. He struck out a path oblique to the room and paced to and fro, struggling with intolerable vast impressions. The things he had derived from the cylinders and the things he had seen conflicted, confused him. It seemed to him the most amazing thing of all that in his thirty years of life he had never tried to shape a picture of these coming times. "We were making the future," he said, "and hardly any of us trouble to think what future we were making. And here it is!"

"What have they got to, what has been done? How do I come into the midst of it all?" The vastness of street and house he was prepared for, the multitudes of people. But conflicts in the city ways! And the systematised sensuality of a class of rich men!

He thought of Bellamy, the hero of whose Socialistic Utopia had so oddly anticipated this actual experience. But here was no Utopia, no Socialistic state. He had already seen enough to realise that the ancient antithesis of luxury, waste and sensuality on the one hand and abject poverty on the other, still prevailed. He knew enough of the essential factors of life to understand that correlation. And not only were the buildings of the city gigantic and the crowds in the street gigantic, but the voices he had heard in the ways, the uneasiness of Howard, the very atmosphere spoke of gigantic discontent. What country was he in? Still England it seemed, and yet strangely "un-English." His mind glanced at the rest of the world, and saw only an enigmatical veil.

He prowled about his apartment, examining everything as a caged animal might do. He felt very tired, felt that feverish exhaustion that does not admit of rest. He listened for long spaces under the ventilator to catch some distant echo of the tumults he felt must be proceeding in the city.

The strangeness of his experience came to dominate his mind. He began to talk to himself. "Two hundred and three years!" he said to himself over and over again, laughing stupidly. "Then I am two hundred and thirty-three years old! The oldest inhabitant! Surely they haven't reversed the tendency of our time and gone back to the rule of the oldest. My claims are indisputable. Mumble, mumble. I remember the Armenian atrocities as though it was yesterday. 'Tis a great age! Haha!" He was surprised at first to hear himself laughing, and then laughed again deliberately and louder. Then he realised that he was behaving foolishly. "Steady," he said. "Steady!"

His pacing became more regular. "This new world," he said "I don't understand it. *Why?* But it is all *why!*"

"I suppose they can fly and do all sorts of things."

"Let me try and remember just how it began."

He was surprised at first to find how vague the memories of his first thirty years had become. He remembered fragments, for the most part trivial moments, things of no great importance that he had observed. His boyhood seemed the most accessible at first, he recalled school books and certain lessons in chemistry. Then he revived the more salient features of his life, memories of the wife long since dead, her magic influence now gone beyond corruption, of his rivals and friends and betrayers, of the swift decision of this issue and that, and then of his last years of misery, of fluctuating resolves, and at last of his strenuous studies. In a little while he perceived he had it all again; dim perhaps, like metal long laid aside, but in no way defective or injured, capable of re-polishing? And the hue of it was a deepening misery. Was it worth re-polishing? By a miracle he had been lifted out of a life that had become intolerable . . .

He reverted to his present condition. He wrestled with the facts in vain. It became an inextricable tangle. He saw the sky through the ventilator pink with dawn. An old persuasion came out of the dark recesses of his memory. "I must sleep," he said. It appeared as a delightful relief from this mental distress and from the growing pain and heaviness of his limbs. He went to the strange little bed, lay down and was presently asleep. . .

He was destined to become very familiar indeed with these apartments before he left them, for he remained imprisoned for three days. During that time no one, except Howard, entered his prison. The marvel of his fate mingled with and in some way minimised the marvel of his survival. He had awakened to mankind it seemed only to be snatched away into this unaccountable solitude. Howard came regularly with subtly sustaining and nutritive fluids, and light and pleasant foods, quite strange to Graham. He always closed the door carefully as he entered. On matters of detail he was increasingly obliging, but the bearing of Graham on the great issues that were evidently being contested so closely beyond the sound-proof walls that enclosed him, he would not elucidate. He evaded, as politely as possible, every question of the position of affairs in the outer world.

And in those three days Graham's incessant thoughts went wide and far. All that he had seen, all this elaborate contrivance to prevent him seeing, worked together in his mind. Almost every possible interpretation of his position was debated in his mind—even as it chanced, the right interpretation. Things that presently happened to him, came to him at least credible, by virtue of this seclusion. When at last the moment of his release arrived, it found him prepared. He was no longer passive and enfeebled but alert, and very speedily a participator in the great drama that played about him.

Howard's bearing went far to deepen Graham's impression of his own strange importance; the door between its opening and closing seemed to admit with him a breath of momentous happening. His inquiries became more definite and searching. Howard retreated through protests and difficulties. The awakening was unforeseen, he repeated; it happened to have fallen in with the trend of a social convulsion. "To explain it I must tell you the history of a gross and a half of years," protested Howard.

"The thing is this," said Graham. "You are afraid of something I shall do. In some way I am arbitrator—I might be arbitrator."

"It is not that. But you have—I may tell you this much—the automatic increase of your property puts great possibilities of interference in your hands. And in certain other ways you have influence, with your eighteenth century notions."

"Nineteenth century," corrected Graham.

"With your old world notions, anyhow, ignorant as you are of every feature of our State."

"Am I a fool?"

"Certainly not."

"Do I seem to be the sort of man who would act rashly?"

"You were never expected to act at all. No one counted on your awakening. No one dreamt you would ever wake. The Council had surrounded you with antiseptic conditions. As a matter of fact, we thought that you were dead—a mere arrest of decay. And—but it is too complex. We dare not suddenly—while you are still half awake."

"It won't do," said Graham. "Suppose it is as you say—why am I not being crammed night and day with facts and warnings and all the wisdom of the time to fit me for my responsibilities? Am I any wiser now than two days ago, if it is two days, when I awoke?"

Howard pulled his lip.

"I am beginning to feel—every hour I feel more clearly—a sense of complex concealment of which you are the salient point. Is your precious Council, or committee, or whatever they are, cooking the accounts of my estate? Is that it?"

"That note of suspicious——" said Howard.

"Ugh!" said Graham. "Now, mark my words, it will be ill for those who have put me here. It will be ill. I am alive. Make no doubt of it, I am alive. Every day my pulse is stronger and my mind clearer and more vigorous. No more quiescence. I am a man come back to life. And I want to *live*——"

"*Live!*"

Howard's face lit with an idea. He came towards Graham and spoke in an easy confidential tone.

"The Council secludes you here—for your good. You are restless. Naturally—an energetic man! You find it dull here. But we are anxious that everything you may desire—every desire— every sort of desire. There may be something. Is there any sort of company?"

He paused meaningly.

"Yes," said Graham thoughtfully. "There is."

"Ah! *Now!* We have treated you neglectfully."

"The crowds in yonder streets of yours."

"That," said Howard, "I am afraid——, But ——"

Graham began pacing the room.

"Everything you say, everything you do, convinces me—of some great issue in which I am concerned. Yes, I know. Desires and indulgence arc life in a sense—and Death! Extinction! In my life before I slept I had worked out that pitiful question. I will not begin again. There is a city, a multitude—— And meanwhile I am here like a rabbit in a bag."

His rage surged high. He choked for a moment and began to wave his clenched fists. He gave way to an anger fit, he swore archaic curses. His gestures had the quality of physical threats.

"I do not know who your party may be. I am in the dark, and you keep me in the dark. But I know this, that I am secluded here for no good purpose. For no good purpose. I warn you, I warn you of the consequences. Once I come at my power——"

He realised that to threaten thus might be a danger to himself. He stopped. Howard stood regarding him with a curious expression.

"I take it this is a message to the Council," said Howard.

Graham had a momentary impulse to leap upon the man, fell or stun him. It must have shown upon his face; at any rate Howard's movement was quick. In a second the noiseless door had closed again, and the man from the nineteenth century was alone.

For a moment he stood rigid, with clenched hands half raised. Then he flung them down. "What a fool I have been!" he said, and gave way to his anger again, stamping about the room and shouting curses. For a long time he kept himself in a sort of frenzy, raging at his position, at his own folly, at the knaves who had imprisoned him. He did this because he did not want to look calmly at his position. He clung to his anger—because he was afraid of Fear.

Presently he found himself reasoning with himself. This imprisonment was unaccountable, but no doubt the legal forms—new legal forms—of the time permitted it. It must, of course, be legal. These people were two hundred years further on in the march of civilisation than the Victorian generation. It was not likely they would be less—humane. His imagination set to work to suggest things that might be done to him. The attempts of his reason to dispose of these suggestions, though for the most part logically valid, were quite unavailing. "Why should anything be done to me?"

"If the worst comes to the worst," he found himself saying at last, "I can give up what they want. But what do they want? And why don't they ask me for it instead of cooping me up?"

He returned to his former preoccupation with the Council's possible intentions. He began to reconsider the details of Howard's behaviour, sinister glances, inexplicable hesitations. Then, for a time, his mind circled about the idea of escaping from these rooms; but whither could he escape into this vast, crowded, world? He would be worse off than a Saxon yeoman suddenly dropped into nineteenth century London. And besides, how could anyone escape from these rooms?

"How can it benefit anyone if harm should happen to me?"

He thought of the tumult, the great social trouble of which he was so unaccountably the axis. A text, irrelevant enough and yet curiously insistent, came floating up out of the darkness of his memory. This also a Council had said:

"It is expedient for us that one man should die for the people."

CHAPTER VIII.

THE ROOF SPACES

AS the fans in the circular aperture of the inner room rotated and permitted glimpses of the night, dim sounds drifted in thereby. And Graham, standing underneath, wrestling darkly with the unknown powers that imprisoned him, and which he had now deliberately challenged, was startled by the sound of a voice.

He peered up and saw in the intervals of the rotation, dark and dim, the face and shoulders of a man regarding him. Then a dark hand was extended, the swift fan struck it, swung round and beat on with a little brownish patch on the edge of its thin blade, and something began to fall therefrom upon the floor, dripping silently.

Graham looked down, and there were spots of blood at his feet. He looked up again in a strange excitement. The two figures had gone.

He remained motionless—his every sense intent upon the flickering patch of darkness, for outside it was high night. He became aware of some faint, remote, dark specks floating lightly through the outer air. They came down towards him, fitfully, eddyingly, and passed aside out of the uprush from the fan. A gleam of light flickered, the specks flashed white, and then the darkness came again. Warmed and lit as he was, he perceived that it was snowing within a few feet of him.

Graham walked across the room, and came back to the ventilator again. He saw the head of a man pass near. There was a sound of whispering. Then a smart blow on some metallic substance, effort, voices, and the fans stopped. A gust of snowflakes whirled into the room, and

Far below, mere stirring specks and dots, went the people of the unsleeping city in their perpetual daylight. . . . It was like peering into a gigantic glass hive, and it lay vertically below him with only a tough glass of unknown thickness to save him from a fall.

vanished before they touched the floor. "Don't be afraid," said a voice.

Graham stood under the fan. "Who are you?" he whispered.

For a moment there was nothing but a swaying of the fan, and then the head and shoulders of a man were thrust cautiously into the opening. His face appeared nearly inverted to Graham; his dark hair was wet with dissolving flakes of snow upon it. His arm went up into the darkness holding something unseen. He had a youthful face and bright eyes, and the veins on his forehead were swollen. He seemed to be exerting himself to maintain his position.

For several seconds neither he nor Graham spoke.

"You were the Sleeper?" said the stranger at last.

"Yes," said Graham. "What do you want with me?"

"I come from Ostrog, Sire."

"Ostrog?"

The man in the ventilator twisted his head round so that his profile was towards Graham. He appeared to be listening. Suddenly there was a hasty exclamation, and the intruder sprang back just in time to escape the sweep of the released fan. And when Graham peered up there was nothing visible but the slowly falling snow.

It was, perhaps, a quarter of an hour before anything returned to the ventilator. But at last came the same metallic interference again; the fans stopped and the face reappeared. Graham had remained all this time in the same place, alert and tremulously excited.

"Who are you? What do you want?" he said.

"We want to speak to you, Sire," said the intruder. "We want—I can't hold the thing. We have been trying to find a way to you—three days."

"Is it rescue?" Whispered Graham. "Escape?"

"Yes, Sire. If you will."

"You are my party—the party of the Sleeper?"

"Yes, Sire."

"What am I to do?" said Graham.

There was a struggle. The stranger's arm appeared, and his hand was bleeding. His knees came into view over the edge of the funnel. "Stand away from me," he said, and he dropped rather heavily on his hands and one shoulder at Graham's feet. The released ventilator whirled noisily. The stranger rolled over, sprang up nimbly and stood panting, hand to a bruised shoulder, and with his bright eyes on Graham.

"You are, indeed, the Sleeper," he said. "I saw you asleep. When it was the law that anyone might see you."

"I am the man who was in the trance," said Graham. "They have imprisoned me here. I have been here since I awoke—at least three days."

The intruder seemed about to speak, heard something, glanced swiftly at the door, and suddenly left Graham and ran towards it, shouting quick, incoherent words. A bright wedge of steel flashed in his hand, and he began tap, tap, a quick succession of blows upon the hinges. "Mind!" cried a voice. "Oh!" The voice came from above.

Graham glanced up, saw the soles of two feet, ducked, was struck on the shoulder by one of them, and a heavy weight bore him to the earth. He fell on his knees and forward, and the weight went over his head. He knelt up and saw a second man from above seated before him.

"I did not see you, Sire," panted the man. He rose and assisted Graham to rise. "Are you hurt, Sire?" he panted. A succession of heavy blows on the ventilator began, something fell close to Graham's face, and a shivering edge of white metal danced, fell over, and lay flat upon the floor.

"What is this?" cried Graham, confused and looking at the ventilator. "Who are you? What are you going to do? Remember I understand nothing."

"Stand back," said the stranger, and drew him from under the ventilator as another fragment of metal fell heavily.

"We want you to come, Sire," panted the newcomer, and Graham, glancing at his face again, saw a new cut had changed from white to red on his forehead, and a couple of little trickles of blood starting therefrom. "Your people call for you."

"Come where? My people!"

"To the hall about the markets. Your life is in danger here. We have spies. We learned but just in time. The Council has decided—this very day—either to drug or kill you. And everything is ready. The people are drilled, the wind-vane police, the engineers, and half the way-gearers are with us. We have the halls crowded—shouting. The whole city shouts against the Council. We have arms." He wiped the blood with his hand. "Your life here is not worth——"

"But why arms?"

"The people have risen to protect you, Sire. What?"

He turned quickly as the man who had first come down made a hissing with his teeth, and looking through the intervening archway,

Graham saw the latter start back, gesticulate to them to conceal themselves, and move as if to hide behind the opening door.

As he did so, Howard appeared, a little tray in one hand and his heavy face downcast. He started, looked up, the door slammed behind him, the tray tilted sideways, and the steel wedge struck him behind the ear. He went down like a felled tree, and lay as he fell athwart the floor of the outer room. The man who had struck him bent hastily, studied his face for a moment, rose, and returned to work at the door.

"Your poison," said a voice in Graham's ear.

Then abruptly they were in darkness. The innumerable cornice lights had been extinguished. Graham saw the aperture of the ventilator, with ghostly snow whirling above it and dark figures moving hastily. Three knelt on the vane. Some dim thing—a ladder—was being lowered through the opening, and a hand appeared holding a fitful yellow light.

He had a moment of hesitation. But the manner of these men, the swift alacrity, their words, marched so completely with his own fears of the Council, with his idea and hope of a rescue, that it lasted not a moment. And his people awaited him!

"I do not understand," he said, "but I trust you. Tell me what to do."

The man with the cut brow gripped Graham's arm. "Clamber up the ladder," he whispered. "Quick. They will have heard——"

Graham felt for the ladder with extended hands, put his foot on the lower rung, and, turning his head, saw over the shoulder of the nearest man, in the yellow flicker of light, the first-comer astride over Howard and still working at the door. Graham turned to the ladder again, and was thrust by his conductor and helped up by those above, and then he was standing on something hard and cold and slippery outside the ventilating funnel.

He shivered. He was aware of a great difference in the temperature. Half a dozen men stood about him, and light flakes of snow touched hands and face and melted. For a moment it was dark, then for a flash a ghastly violet white, and then everything was dark again.

He saw he had come out upon the roof of the vast city structure which had replaced the miscellaneous houses, streets and open spaces of Victorian London. The place upon which he stood was level, with serpentine cables lying athwart it in every direction. The circular wheels of a number of windmills loomed indistinct and gigantic through the darkness and snowfall, and roared with a varying loudness as the fitful wind rose and fell. Some way off an intermittent white light smote up from below, touched the snow eddies with a transient glitter, and made an evanescent spectre in the night; and here and there, low down, some vaguely outlined wind-driven mechanism flickered with livid sparks.

All this he appreciated in a fragmentary manner as his rescuers stood about him. Someone threw a thick soft cloak of fur-like texture about him, and fastened it by buckled straps at waist and shoulders. Things were said briefly, decisively. Someone thrust him forward.

Before his mind was yet clear a dark shape gripped his arm. "This way," said this shape, urging him along, and pointed Graham across the flat roof in the direction of a dim semicircular haze of light. Graham obeyed.

"Mind!" said a voice, as Graham stumbled against a cable. "Between them, not across them," said the voice. And, "We must hurry."

"Where are the people?" said Graham—"the people you said awaited me?"

The stranger did not answer. He left Graham's arm as the path grew narrower, and led the way with rapid strides. Graham followed blindly. In a minute he found himself running. "Are the others coming?" he panted, but received no reply. His companion glanced back and ran on. They came to a sort of pathway of open metal-work, transverse to the direction they had come, and they turned aside to follow this. Graham looked back, but the snowstorm had hidden the others.

"Come on!" said his guide. Running now, they drew near a little windmill spinning high in the air. "Stoop," said Graham's guide, and they avoided an endless band running roaring up to the shaft of the vane. "This way!" and they were ankle deep in a gutter full of drifted thawing snow, between two low walls of metal that presently rose waist high. "I will go first," said the guide. Graham drew his cloak about him and followed. Then suddenly came a narrow abyss across which the gutter leapt to the snowy darkness of the further side. Graham peeped over the side once and the gulf was black. For a moment he regretted his flight. He dared not look again, and his brain spun as he waded through the half liquid snow.

Then out of the gutter they clambered and hurried across a wide flat space damp with thawing snow, and for half its extent dimly translucent to lights that went to and fro underneath. He hesitated at this unstable-looking substance, but his guide ran on unheeding, and so they came to and clambered up slippery steps to the rim of a great dome of glass. Round this they went. Far below a number of people seemed to be dancing, and music filtered through the dome. Graham fancied he heard a shouting through the snowstorm, and his guide hurried him on with a new spurt of haste. And then an ascent to a space of windmills, one so vast that only the lower edge of its fans came rushing into sight and rushed up again and was lost in the night and the snow. They hurried for a time through the metallic tracery of its supports, and came at last above a place of moving platforms like the place into which Graham had looked from the balcony.

They crawled across the sloping transparency that covered this street of platforms, crawling on hands and knees because of the slipperiness of the snowfall.

For the most part the glass was bedewed, and Graham saw only hazy suggestions of the forms below, but near the pitch of the transparent roof the glass was clear, and he found himself looking sheerly down upon it all. For awhile, in spite of the urgency of his guide, he gave way to vertigo and lay spread-eagled on the glass, sick and paralysed. Far below, mere stirring specks and dots, went the people of the unsleeping city in their perpetual daylight, and the moving platforms ran on their incessant journey. Messengers and men on unknown businesses shot along the drooping cables, and the frail bridges were crowded with men. It was like peering into a gigantic glass hive, and it lay vertically below him with only a tough glass of unknown thickness to save him from a fall. The street showed warm and lit, and Graham was wet now to the skin with thawing snow, and his feet were numbed with cold. For a space he could not move. "Come on!" cried his guide, with terror in his voice. "Come on!"

Graham reached the pitch of the roof by an effort.

Over the ridge, following his guide's example, he turned about and slid backward, amid a little avalanche of snow. While he was sliding he thought of what would happen if some broken gap should come in his way. At the edge he stumbled to his feet ankle deep in slush, thanking heaven for an opaque footing again. His guide was already clambering up a metal screen to a level expanse.

Through the spare snowflakes above this loomed another line of windmills, and then suddenly the amorphous tumult of the rotating wheels was pierced with a deafening sound. It was a mechanical shrilling of extraordinary intensity that seemed to come simultaneously from every point of the compass.

"They have missed us already!" cried Graham's guide in an accent of terror, and suddenly, with a blinding flash, the night became day.

Above the driving snow, from the summits of the wind wheels, appeared vast masts carrying globes of livid light. They receded in illimitable vistas in every direction. As far as his eye could penetrate the snowfall they glared.

"Get on this," cried Graham's conductor, and thrust him forward to a long grating of metal, snowless metal that ran like a band between two slightly sloping expanses of snow. It felt warm to Graham's benumbed feet, and a faint eddy of steam rose from it.

"Come on!" shouted his guide ten yards off, and, without waiting, ran swiftly through the incandescent glare towards the iron supports of the next range of wind wheels. Graham, recovering from his astonishment, followed as fast, convinced of his imminent capture . . .

In a score of seconds they were within a tracery of glare and black shadows shot with moving bars beneath the monstrous wheels. Graham's conductor ran on for some time, and suddenly darted sideways and vanished into a black shadow in the corner of the foot of a huge support. In another moment Graham was beside him.

They cowered panting, and stared out.

The scene upon which Graham looked was very wild and strange. The snow had now almost ceased; only a belated flake passed now and again across the picture. But the broad stretch of level before them was a glastly white, broken only by gigantic masses and moving shapes and lengthy strips of impenetrable darkness, vast ungainly Titans of shadow. All about them, huge metallic structures, iron girders, inhumanly vast as it seemed to him, interlaced, and the edges of wind wheels, scarcely moving in the lull, passed in great shining curves steeper and steeper up into a luminous haze. Wherever the snow-spangled light struck down, beams and girders, and incessant bands running with a halting, indomitable resolution, passed upward and downward into the black. And with all that mighty activity, with an omnipresent sense of motive and design, this snow-clad desolation of mechanism was void of all human presence save themselves, and seemed as trackless and deserted and unfrequented by men as some inaccessible Alpine snowfield.

"They will be chasing us," cried the leader. "We are scarcely halfway there yet. Cold as it is we must hide here for a space—at least until it snows more thickly again.

His teeth chattered in his head.

"Where are the markets?" asked Graham, staring out. "Where are all the people?"

The other made no answer.

"*Look!*" whispered Graham, as he crouched close, and became still.

The snow had suddenly become thick again, and sliding with the whirling eddies out of the black pit of the sky came something, vague and large and very swift. It came down in a steep curve and swept round, wide wings extended and a trail of condensing white vapour behind it, rose with an easy swiftness and went gliding up the air, swept horizontally forward in a wide curve, and vanished again in the steaming specks of snow. And, under the ribs of its body, Graham saw two little men, very minute and active, searching the snowy areas about him, as it seemed to him, with field glasses. For a second they were clear, then hazy through a thick whirl of snow, then small and distant, and in a minute they were gone.

"*Now!*" cried his companion. "Come!"

He pulled Graham's sleeve, and incontinently the two were running headlong down the arcade of ironwork beneath the wind wheels. Graham, running blindly, collided with his leader, who had turned back on him suddenly. He found himself within a dozen yards of a black chasm. It extended as far as he could see right and left. It seemed to cut off their progress in either direction.

"Do as I do," whispered his guide. He lay down and crawled to the edge, thrust his head over and twisted until one leg hung. He seemed to feel for something with his foot, found it, and went sliding over the edge into the gulf. His head reappeared. "It is a ledge," he whispered. "In the dark all the way along. Do as I did."

Graham hesitated, went down upon all fours, crawled to the edge, and peered into a velvety blackness. For a sickly moment he had courage neither to go on nor retreat, then he sat and hung his leg down, felt his guide's hands pulling at him, had a horrible sensation of sliding over the edge into the unfathomable, splashed, and felt himself in a slushy gutter, impenetrably dark.

"This way," whispered the voice, and he began crawling along the gutter through the trickling thaw, pressing himself against the wall. They continued along it for some minutes. He seemed to pass through a hundred stages of misery, to pass minute after minute through a hundred degrees of cold, damp, and exhaustion. In a little while he ceased to feel his hands and feet.

The gutter sloped downwards. He observed that they were now many feet below the edge of the buildings. Rows of spectral white shapes like the ghosts of blind-drawn windows rose above them. They came to the end of a cable, fastened above one of these white windows, dimly visible and dropping into impenetrable shadows. Suddenly his hand came against his guide's. "*Still!*" whispered the latter very softly.

He looked up with a start and saw the huge wings of the flying machine gliding slow and noiselessly overhead athwart the broad band of snow-flecked grey-blue sky. In a moment it was hidden again.

"Keep still; they were just turning."

For a while both were motionless, then Graham's companion stood up, and reaching towards the fastenings of the cable fumbled with some indistinct tackle.

"What is that?" asked Graham.

The only answer was a faint cry. The man became motionless. Graham peered and saw his face dimly. He was staring down the long ribbon of sky, and Graham, following his eyes, saw the flying machine small and faint and remote. Then he saw that the wings spread on either side, that it headed toward them, that every moment it grew larger. It was following the edge of the chasm towards him.

The man's movements became convulsive. He thrust two cross bars into Graham's hand. Graham could not see them, he ascertained their form by feeling. They were slung by thin cords to the cable. On the cord were hand grips of some soft elastic substance. "Put the cross between your legs," whispered the guide hysterically, "and grip the holdfasts. Grip tightly! Grip!"

Graham did as he was told.

"Jump," said the voice. "In Heaven's name, jump!"

For one momentous second Graham could not speak. He was glad afterwards that darkness hid his face. He said nothing. He began to tremble violently. He looked sideways at the swift shadow, that swallowed up the sky, as it rushed upon him.

"Jump! Jump—in God's name. Or they will have us!" cried Graham's guide, and in the violence of his passion thrust him forward.

Graham tottered convulsively, gave a sobbing cry, a cry in spite of himself, and then, as the flying machine swept over them, fell forward into a pit of that darkness, seated on the cross wood and holding the ropes. Something cracked, something rapped smartly against a wall. He heard the pulley of the cradle hum on its rope. He heard the aeronauts shout. He felt a pair of knees digging into his back. He was sweeping headlong through the air, falling through the air, all his strength was in his hands.

He would have screamed, but he had no breath.

He shot into a blinding light that made him grip the tighter. He recognised the great passage with the running ways, the hanging lights and interlacing girders. They rushed upward and by him. He had a momentary impression of a great circular aperture yawning to swallow him up.

He was in the dark again, falling, falling, gripping with aching hands, and behold! a clap of sound, a burst of light, and he was in a brightly lit hall with a roaring multitude of people beneath his feet. The people! His people! A proscenium, a stage rushed up towards him, and his cable swept down to a circular aperture to the right of this. He felt he was travelling slower, and suddenly very much slower. He distinguished shouts of "Saved!" "The Master. He is safe." The stage rushed towards him with rapidly diminishing swiftness. Then——.

He heard the man clinging behind him shout as if suddenly terrified, and this shout was echoed by a shout from below. He felt that he was no longer gliding along the cable but falling with it. There was a tumult of yells, screams and cries. He felt something soft against his extended hand, and the impact of a broken fall quivering through his arm. . . .

He wanted to be still and people were lifting him. He believed afterwards he was carried to the platform and given some drink, but he was never sure. He did not notice what became of his guide. When his mind was clear again he was on his feet; eager hands were assisting him to stand. He was in a big alcove, occupying the position that in his previous experience had been devoted to the lower boxes. If this was, indeed, a theatre.

A mighty tumult was in his ears, a thunderous roar, the shouting of a countless multitude. "It is the Sleeper! The Sleeper is with us!"

"The Sleeper is with us! The Master—the Owner! The Master is with us. He is safe."

Graham had a surging vision of a great hall crowded with people. He saw no individuals, he was conscious of a froth of pink faces, of waving arms and garments, he felt the occult influence of a vast crowd pouring over him, buoying him up. There were balconies, galleries, great archways giving remoter perspectives, and everywhere people, a vast area of people, densely packed and cheering. Across the nearer space, like a huge snake, lay the collapsed cable. It had been cut by the men of the flying machine at its upper end, and had crumpled down into the hall. Men seemed to be hauling this out of the way. But the whole effect was vague, the very buildings throbbed and leapt with the roar of the voices.

He stood unsteadily, and looked at those about him. Someone supported him by one arm. "Let me go into a little room," he said; "a little room," And could say no more. A man in black stepped forward, took his disengaged arm. He was aware of officious men opening a door before him. Someone guided him to a seat. He sat down heavily and covered his face with his hands; he was trembling violently, his nervous control was at an end. He was relieved of his cloak, he could not remember how; his purple hose he saw were black with wet. People were running about him, things were happening, but for some time he gave no heed to them.

He had escaped. A myriad cries told him that. He was safe. These were the people who were on his side. For a space he sobbed for breath, and then he sat still with his face covered. The air was full of the shouting of innumerable men.

CHAPTER IX.

THE PEOPLE MARCH

HE became aware of someone urging a glass of clear fluid upon his attention, looked up and discovered this someone to be a dark young man in a yellow garment. He took the dose forthwith, and in a moment he was glowing. A tall man in a black robe stood by his shoulder, and pointed to the half open door into the hall. This man was shouting close to his ear, and yet what was said was indistinct, because of the tremendous uproar from the great theatre. Behind the man was a girl in a silvery grey robe, whom Graham, even in this confusion, perceived to be beautiful. Her dark eyes, full of wonder and curiosity, were fixed on him, her lips trembled apart. A partially opened door gave a glimpse of the crowded hall, and admitted a vast, uneven tumult, a hammering, clapping, and shouting that died away and began again, and rose to a thunderous pitch, and so continued intermittently all the time that Graham remained in the little room. He watched the lips of the man in black and gathered that he was making some clumsy explanation.

He stared stupidly for some moments at these things and then stood up abruptly; he grasped the arm of this shouting person.

"Tell me!" he cried. "Who am I? Who am I?"

The others came nearer him to hear his words. "Who am I?" His eyes searched their faces.

"They have told him nothing!" cried the girl.

"Tell me, tell me!" cried Graham.

"You are Master of the Earth. You are owner of half the world."

He did not believe he heard aright. He resisted the persuasion. He pretended not to un-

*Graham's instinct of self-preservation overcame the
paralysis of his incredulous astonishment. He became
for a time the blind creature of the fear of death. He ran,
stumbling, blundered into his guards as they turned
to run with him. Haste was his one desire, to escape
this perilous gallery upon which he was exposed.*

derstand, not to hear. He lifted his voice again. "I have been awake three days—a prisoner three days. I judge there is some struggle between a number of people in this city—it is London?"

"Yes," said the younger man.

"And those who meet in the great hall with the White Atlas. How does it concern me? In some way it has to do with me. *Why*, I don't know. Drugs? It seems to me that while I have slept the world has gone mad. I have gone mad. Who are those Councillors under the Atlas? Why should they try to drug me?"

"To keep you insensible," said the man in yellow. "To prevent your interference."

"But *why?*"

"Because *you* are the Atlas, Sire," said the man in yellow. "The world is on your shoulders. They rule it in your name."

The sounds from the hall had died into a silence threaded by one monotonous voice. Now suddenly, trampling on these last words, came a deafening tumult, a roaring and thundering, cheer crowded on cheer, voices hoarse and shrill, beating, overlapping, and while it lasted the people in the little room could not hear each other shout.

Graham stood, his intelligence clinging helplessly to the thing he had just heard. "The Council," he repeated blankly, and then snatching at a name that had struck him: "But who is Ostrog?" he said.

"He is the organiser—the organiser of the revolt. Our Leader—in your name."

"In my name. And you? Why is he not here?"

"He has deputed us. I am his brother—his half-brother Lincoln. He wants you to show yourself to these people and then come on to him. That is why he has sent. He is at the wind vane offices directing. The people are marching."

"In your name," shouted the younger men. "They have ruled, crushed, tyrannised. At last even——"

"In my name! My name! Master?"

The younger man suddenly became audible in a pause of the outer thunder, indignant and vociferous, a high penetrating voice under his red aquiline nose and bushy moustache. "No one expected you to wake. No one expected you to wake. They were cunning. Damned tyrants! But they were taken by surprise. They did not know whether to drug you, hypnotise you, kill you."

Again the hall dominated everything.

"Ostrog is at the wind vane offices ready——Even now, there is a rumour of fighting beginning."

The man who had called himself Lincoln came close to him. "Ostrog has it planned. Trust him. We have our organisations ready. We shall seize the flying stages—— Even now, he may be doing that. Then——"

"This public theatre," bawled the man in yellow, "is only a contingent. We have five myriads of drilled men——"

"We have arms," cried Lincoln. "We have plans. A leader. Their police have gone from the streets, and are massed in the——" (inaudible). "It is now or never. The Council is rocking—— They cannot trust even their drilled men——"

"Hear the people calling to you!"

Graham's mind was like a night of moon and swift clouds, now dark and hopeless, now clear and ghastly. He was Master of the Earth, he was a man sodden with thawing snow. Of all his fluctuating impressions the dominant ones presented an antagonism; on the one hand was the White Council, powerful, disciplined, few, the White Council from which he had just escaped; and on the other, monstrous crowds, packed masses of indistinguishable people clamouring his name, hailing him Master. The other side had imprisoned him, debated his death. These shouting thousands beyond the little doorway had rescued him. But why these things should be so he could not understand.

The door opened, Lincoln's voice was swept away and drowned, and a rush of people followed on the heels of the tumult. These intruders came towards him and Lincoln gesticulating. The voices without explained their soundless lips. "Show us the Sleeper! Show us the Sleeper!" was the burden of the uproar. Men were bawling for "Order! Silence!"

Graham glanced towards the open doorway, and saw a tall, oblong picture of the hall beyond, a waving, incessant confusion of crowded, shouting faces, men and women together, waving pale blue garments, extended hands. Many were standing. One man in rags of dark brown, a gaunt figure, stood on the seat and waved a black cloth. He met the wonder and expectation of the girl's eyes. What did these people expect from him? He was dimly aware that the tumult outside had changed its character, was in some way beating, marching. His own mind, too, changed. For a space he did not recognise the influence that was transforming him. But a moment that was near to panic passed. He tried to make audible inquiries of what was required of him.

Lincoln was shouting in his ear, but Graham was deafened to that. All the others save the woman gesticulated towards the hall. He perceived what had happed to the uproar. The whole mass of people was chanting together. It was not simply a song, the voices were gathered together and upborne by a torrent of instrumental music, music like the music of an organ, a woven texture of sounds, full of trumpets, full of flaunting banners, full of the march and pageantry of opening war. And the feet of the people were beating time—tramp, tramp.

He was urged towards the door. He obeyed mechanically. The rhythm of that chant took hold of him, stirred him, emboldened him. The hall opened to him, a vast welter of fluttering colour swaying to the music.

"Wave your arm to them," said Lincoln. "Wave your arm to them."

"This," said a voice on the other side—"he must have this."

Arms were about his neck detaining him in the doorway, and a black, subtly-folding mantle hung from his shoulder. He threw his arm free of this and followed Lincoln. He perceived the girl in grey close to him, her face lit, her gesture onward. For the instant she became to him, flushed and eager as she was, an embodiment of the song. He emerged in the alcove again. Incontinently the mounting waves of the song broke upon his appearing, and flashed up into a foam of shouting. Guided by Lincoln's hand he marched obliquely across the centre of the stage facing the people.

The hall was a vast and intricate space—galleries, balconies, broad spaces of amphitheatrical steps, and great archways. Far away, high up, seemed the mouth of a huge passage full of struggling humanity. The whole multitude was swaying in congested masses. Individual figures sprang out of the tumult, impressed him momentarily, and lost definition again. Close to the platform a beautiful fair woman, her hair across her face, swayed, carried by three men, and brandished a green staff. Next this group an old careworn man in blue canvas maintained his place in the crush with difficulty, and behind shouted a hairless face, a great cavity of toothless mouth. A voice called that enigmatical word "Ostrog." All his impressions were vague save the massive emotion of that trampling song. The multitude was beating time with their feet—marking time: tramp, tramp, tramp, tramp. The green weapons waved, flashed, and slanted. Then he saw those nearest to him on a level space before the stage were marching in front of him, passing towards a great archway, shouting, "To the Council!" Tramp, tramp, tramp, tramp. He raised his arm, and the roaring was redoubled. He remembered he had to shout "March!" His mouth shaped inaudible heroic words. He waved his arm again and pointed to the archway, shouting "Onward!" They were no longer marking time, they were marching: tramp, tramp, tramp, tramp. Those passing him looked at him and shouted their utmost: tramp, tramp, tramp, tramp. In that host were bearded men, old men, youths, fluttering-robed bare-armed women, girls. Men and women of the new age! Rich robes, grey rags fluttered together in the whirl of their movement amidst the dominant blue. A monstrous black banner jerked its way to the right. He perceived a blue-clad negro, a shrivelled woman in yellow, then a group of tall, fair-haired, white faced, blue-clad men pushed theatrically past him. A tall, sallow, dark-haired, shiny-eyed youth, white-clad from top to toe, clambered up towards the platform shouting loyally, and sprang down again and receded, looking backward. Heads, shoulders, hands clutching weapons, all were swinging with those marching cadences.

Faces came out of the confusion to him as he stood there, eyes met his, and passed and vanished. Men gestured to him, shouted inaudible personal things. Most of the faces were flushed, but many were ghastly white. And disease was there, and many a hand that waved to him was gaunt and lean. Men and women of the new age! Strange and incredible meeting! As the broad stream passed before him to the right, tributary gangways from the remote uplands of the hall thrust downward in an incessant replacement of people: tramp, tramp, tramp, tramp. The unison of the song was enriched and complicated by the massive echoes of arches and passages. Men and women mingled in the ranks: tramp, tramp, tramp, tramp. The whole world seemed marching. Tramp, tramp, tramp, tramp; his brain was tramping. The garments waved onward, the faces poured by more abundantly.

Tramp, tramp, tramp, tramp. At Lincoln's pressure he turned towards the archway, walking unconsciously in that rhythm, scarely noticing his movement for the melody and stir of it. The multitude, the gesture and song, all moved in that direction, the flow of people smote downward until the upturned faces were below the level of his feet. He was aware of a path before him, of a suite about him, of guards and dignities, and Lincoln on his right hand. Attendants intervened, and ever and again blotted out the sight of the multitude to the right. Before him went the backs of the guards in black—three and three and three. He was marched along a little railed way, and crossed above the archway, with the torrent dipping to flow beneath, and shouting up to him. He did not know whither he went; he did not want to know. He glanced back across a flaming spaciousness of hall. Tramp, tramp, tramp, tramp.

CHAPTER X.

THE BATTLE OF THE DARKNESS

HE was no longer in the hall. He was marching along a gallery overhanging one of the great streets of moving platforms that traversed the city. Before him and behind him tramped his guards. The whole concave of the moving ways below was a congested mass of people marching, tramping to the left, shouting, waving hands and arms, pouring along a huge vista, shouting as they came into view, shouting as they passed, shouting as they receded, until the globes of electric light dropped down the perspective, and hid the swarming bare heads.

The song roared up to Graham now, no longer upborne by music, but coarse and noisy, and the beating of the marching feet, tramp, tramp, tramp, tramp, interwove with a thunderous irregularity of footsteps from the undisciplined rabble that poured along the higher ways.

Abruptly he noted a contrast. The buildings on the opposite side of the way seemed deserted, the cables and bridges that laced across the aisle were empty and shadowy. It came into Graham's mind that these also should have swarmed with people.

He felt a curious emotion—throbbing—very fast! He stopped again. The guards before him marched on; those about him stopped as he did. He saw the direction of their faces. The throbbing had something to do with the lights. He too looked up.

At first it seemed to him a thing that affected the lights simply, an isolated phenomenon, having no bearing on the things below. Each huge globe of blinding whitness was as it were clutched, compressed in a systole that was followed by a transitory diastole, and again a systole like a tightening grip, darkness, light, darkness, in rapid alternation.

Graham became aware that this strange behaviour of the lights had to do with the people below. The appearance of the houses and ways, the appearance of the packed masses changed, became a confusion of vivid lights and leaping shadows. He saw a multitude of shadows had sprung into aggressive existence, seemed rushing up, broadening, widening, growing with steady swiftness—to leap suddenly back and return reinforced. The song and the tramping had ceased. The unanimous march, he discovered, was arrested, there were eddies, a flow sideways, shouts of "The lights!" Voices were crying together one thing. "The lights!" cried these voices. "The lights!" He looked down. In this dancing death of the lights the area of the street had suddenly become a monstrous strug-

gle. The huge white globes became purple white, purple with reddish glow, flickered, flickered faster and faster, fluttered between light and extinction, ceased to flicker and became mere fading specks of glowing red in a vast darkness. In ten seconds the extinction was accomplished, and there was only that vast darkness—a vast darkness whose coming had almost the shock of a blow, a black thing that had suddenly swallowed up those glittering myriads of men.

He felt invisible forms about him; his arms were gripped. Something rapped sharply against his shin. A voice bawled in his ear, "It is all right—all right."

Graham shook off the paralysis of his first astonishment. He struck his forehead against Lincoln's and bawled, "What is this darkness?"

"The Council has cut the currents that light the city. We must wait—stop. The people will go on. They will——"

His voice was drowned. Voices were shouting, "Save the Sleeper. Take care of the Sleeper." A guard stumbled aginst Graham and hurt his hand by an inadvertent blow of his weapon. A wild tumult tossed and whirled about him, growing, as it seemed, louder, denser, more furious each moment. Fragments of recognisable sounds drove towards him, were whirled away from him as his mind reached out to grasp them. Voices seemed to be shouting conflicting orders, other voices answered. There were suddenly a succession of piercing screams close beneath them.

A voice bawled in his ear, "The red police," and receded forthwith beyond his questions.

A crackling sound grew to distinctness, and therewith a leaping of faint flashes along the edge of the further ways. By their light Graham saw the heads and bodies of a number of men, armed with weapons like those of his guards, leap into an instant's dim visibility. The whole area suddenly began to crackle, to flash with little instantaneous streaks of light, and abruptly the darkness rolled back like a curtain.

A glare of light dazzled his eyes, a vast seething expanse of struggling men confused his mind. A shout, a burst of cheering, came across the ways. He looked up to see the source of the light. A man hung far overhead from the upper part of a cable, holding by a rope the blinding star that had driven the darkness back. He wore a red uniform.

Graham's eyes fell to the ways again. A wedge of red a little way along the vista caught his eye. He saw it was a dense mass of red-clad men jammed on the higher further way, their backs against the pitiless cliff of building, and surrounded by a dense crowd of antagonists. They were fighting. Weapons flashed and rose and fell, heads vanished at the edge of the contest, and other heads replaced them, the little flashes from the green weapons became little jets of smoky grey while the light lasted.

Abruptly the flare was extinguished and the ways were an inky darkness one more, a tumultuous mystery.

He felt something thrusting against him. He was being pushed back along the gallery. Some-one was shouting—it might be at him. He was too confused to hear. He was thrust against the wall, and a number of people blundered past him. It seemed to him that his guards were struggling with another.

Suddenly the cable-hung star-holder appeared again, and the whole scene was white and dazzling. The band of red-coats seemed broader and nearer; its apex was half-way down the ways towards the central aisle. And raising his eyes Graham saw that a number of these men had also appeared now in the darkened lower galleries of the opposite building, and were firing over the heads of their fellows below into the boiling confusion of people on the lower ways. The meaning of these things dawned upon him. The march of the people had come upon an ambush at the very outset. Thrown into confusion by the extinction of the lights they were now being attacked by the red police. Then he became aware that he was standing alone, that his guards and Lincoln were along the gallery in the direction along which he had come before the dark-ness fell. He saw they were gesticulating to him wildly, running back towards him. A great shouting came from across the ways. Then it seemed as though the whole face of the darkened building opposite was lined and speckled with red-clad men. And they were pointing over to him and shouting. "The Sleeper! Save the Sleeper!" shouted a multitude of throats.

Something struck the wall above his head. He looked up at the impact and saw a star-shaped splash of silvery metal. He saw Lincoln near him. Felt his arm gripped. Then pat, pat; he had been missed twice.

For a moment he did not understand this. The street was hidden, everything was hidden, as he looked. The second flare had burned out.

Lincoln had gripped Graham by the arm, was lugging him along the gallery. "Before the next light!" he cried. His haste was contagious. Graham's instinct of self-preservation overcame the paralysis of his incredulous astonishment. He became for a time the blind creature of the fear of death. He ran, stumbling because of the uncertainty of the darkness, blundered into his guards as they turned to run with him. Haste was his one desire, to escape this perilous gallery upon which he was exposed. A third glare came close on its predecessors. With it came a great shouting across the ways, an answering tumult from the ways. The red-coats below, he saw, had now gained the central passage. Their countless faces turned towards him, and they shouted. The white façade opposite was densely stippled with red. All these wonderful things concerned him, turned upon him as upon a pivot. These were the guards of the Council attempting to recapture him.

Lucky it was for him that these shots were the first fired in anger for a hundred and fifty years. He heard bullets whacking over his head, felt a splash of molten metal sting his ear, and per-ceived without looking that the whole opposite façade, an unmasked ambuscade of red police, was crowded and bawling and firing at him. Down went one of his guards before him, and Graham, unable to stop, leapt the writhing body.

In another second he had plunged, unhurt, into a black passage, and incontinently someone, coming, it may be, in a transverse direction, blundered violently into him. He was hurling down a staircase in absolute darkness. He reeled, and was struck again, and came against a wall with his hands. For a moment he was crushed by a weight of struggling bodies, whirled round, and thrust to the right. For a moment a vast pressure pinned him. He screamed, and then the whole mass of people moving together, bore him back towards the great theatre from which he had so recently come. There were shouts of "They are coming!" and a muffled cry close to him. His foot blun-dered against something soft, he heard a hoarse scream underfoot. He heard shouts of "The Sleeper!" but he was too confused to answer. He heard the green weapons crackling. For a space he lost his individual will, became an atom in a panic, blind, unthinking, mechanical. He thrust and pressed back and writhed in the pressure, kicked presently against a step, and found him-self ascending a slope. And abruptly the faces all about him leapt out of the black, ghastly white and visible, astonished, terrified, perspiring in a livid glare. One face—a young man's—was very near to him. At the time it was but a passing incident, of no emotional value, but afterwards it came back to him in his dreams. For this young man, wedged upright in the crowd for a time had been shot and was already dead.

A fourth white star must have been lit by the man on the cable. Its light came glaring in through vast windows and arches and showed

Graham that he was now one of a dense mass of flying black figures pressed back across the lower area of the great theatre. This time the picture was livid and fragmentary, slashed and barred with black shadows. He saw that quite near to him the red guards were fighting their way through the people. He could not tell whether they saw him. He looked for Lincoln and his guards. He saw Lincoln near the stage of the theatre surrounded in a crowd of black-badged revolutionaries, lifted up and staring to and fro as if seeking him. Graham perceived that he himself was near the opposite edge of the crowd, that behind him, separated by a barrier, sloped the now vacant seats of the theatre. A sudden idea came to him, and he began fighting his way towards the barrier. As he reached it the glare came to an end.

In a moment he had thrown off the great cloak that not only impeded his movements but made him conspicuous, had slipped it from his shoulders. He heard someone trip in its folds. In another he was scaling the barrier and had dropped into blackness on the further side. Then feeling his way he came to the lower end of an ascending gangway. In the darkness the sound of firing ceased and the roar of feet and voices lulled. Then suddenly he came to an unexpected step and tripped and fell. As he did so pools and islands amidst the darkness about him leapt to vivid light again, and the glare of the fifth white star shone through the vast fenestrations of the theatre walls.

He rolled over among some seats, heard a shouting and the whirring rattle of weapons, struggled up and was knocked back again, perceived that a number of black-badged men were all about him firing at the reds below, leaping from seat to seat, crouching among the seats to re-load. Instinctively he crouched amidst the seats as stray shots ripped the pneumatic cushions and cut bright slashes on their soft metal frames. Instinctively he marked the direction of the gangways, the most plausible way of escape for him so soon as the veil of darkness fell again.

A young man in faded blue garments came vaulting over the seats. "Hullo!" he said, with his flying feet within six inches of the crouching Sleeper's face.

He stared without any sign of recognition, turned to fire, fired, and, shouting "To hell with the Council!" was about to fire again. Then it seemed to Graham that the half of this man's neck had vanished. A drop of moisture fell on Graham's cheek. The green weapon stopped half raised. For a moment the man stood still with his face suddenly expressionless, then he began to slant forward. His knees bent. Man and darkness fell together.

At the sound of his fall Graham rose up and ran for his life until a step down to the gangway tripped him. He scrambled to his feet, turned up the gangway and ran on.

When the sixth star glared he was already close to the yawning round throat of a passage. He ran on the swifter for the light, entered the passage, and turned a corner into absolute night again. He was knocked sideways, rolled over, and recovered his feet. He found himself one of a crowd of invisible fugitives pressing in one direction. His one thought now was their thought also—to escape out of this fighting.

For some minutes he was running through the darkness along a winding passage, and then he crossed some wide and open space, passed down a long incline, and came at last down a flight of steps to level place. Many people were shouting, "They are coming. The guards are coming. They are firing. Get out of the fighting. The guards are firing. It will be safe in Seventh Way. Along here to Seventh Way!" There were women and children in the crowd as well as men. Men called names to him. The crowd converged on an archway, passed through a short throat and emerged on a wider space again, lit dimly. The black figures about him spread out and ran up what seemed in the twilight to be a gigantic series of steps. He followed. The people dispersed to the right and left. He perceived that he was no longer in a crowd. He stopped near the highest step. Before him, on that level, were groups of seats and a little kiosk. He went up to this and, stopping in the shadow of its eaves, looked about him panting.

Everything was vague and grey, but he recognised that these great steps were a series of the platforms of the "ways," now motionless again. The platform slanted up on either side, and the tall buildings rose beyond, vast dim ghosts, their inscriptions and advertisements indistinctly seen, and up through the girders and cables was a faint interrupted ribbon of pallid sky. A number of people hurried by. From their shouts and voices, it seemed they were hurrying to join the fighting. Other less noisy figures flitted timidly among the shadows.

From very far away down the street he could hear the sound of a struggle. But it was evident to him that this was not the street into which the theatre opened. That former fight, it seemed, had suddenly dropped out of sound and hearing. And—grotesque thought!—they were fighting for him!

For a space he was like a man who pauses in the reading of a vivid book, and suddenly doubts what he has been taking unquestioningly. At that time he had little mind for details; the whole effect was a huge astonishment. Oddly enough,

He was startled by a cough close at hand. He turned sharply, and peering saw a small, hunched-up figure sitting a couple of yards off in the shadow of the enclosure.

while the light from the Council prison, the great crowd in the hall, and the attack of the red police upon the swarming people were clearly present in his mind, it cost him an effort to piece in his awakening and to revive to meditative intervals of the Silent Rooms. At first his memory leapt these things and took him back to the cascade at Pentargen quivering in the wind, and all the sombre splendours of the sunlit Cornish coast. And then the gap filled, and he began to comprehend his position.

It was no longer absolutely a riddle as it had been in the Silent Rooms. At least he had the strange, bare outline now. He was in some way the owner of half the world, and great political parties were fighting to possess him. On the one hand was the White Council, with its red police, set resolutely it seemed on the usurpation of his property and perhaps his murder; on the other, the revolution that had liberated him, with this unseen "Ostrog" as its leader. And the whole of this gigantic city was convulsed by their struggle. Strange development of his world!

He had slipped out between them into this liberty of the twilight. What would happen next? What was happening? He figured the red-clad men as busily hunting him, driving the black-badged revolutionists before them.

At any rate chance had given him a breathing space. He could lurk, unchallenged by the passers-by, and watch the course of things. His eye followed up the intricate dim immensity of the twilight buildings, and it came to him as a thing infinitely wonderful, that on above there, four hundred feet above there, the sun was rising, and the world was lit and glowing with the old familiar light of day. In a little while he had recovered his breath. His clothing had already dried upon him from the snow.

He wandered for miles along these twilight ways, speaking to no one, accosted by no one—a dark figure among dark figures—the inestimable, unintentional owner of half the world, the coveted man out of the past. Wherever there were lights or dense crowds or exceptional excitement he was afraid of recognition, and watched and turned back or went up and down by the middle stairways, into some transverse system of ways at a lower or higher level. And though he came on no more fighting, the whole city stirred with battle. Once he had to run to avoid a marching multitude of men that swept the street. Everyone abroad seemed involved. For the most part they were men, and they carried what he judged were weapons. It seemed as though the struggle was concentrated mainly in the quarter of the city from which he came. Ever and again a distant roaring, the remote

suggestion of that conflict, reached his ears. Then his caution and his curiosity struggled together. But his caution prevailed, and he continued wandering away from the fighting—so far as he could judge. He went unmolested, unsuspected through the dark. After a time he ceased to hear even a remote echo of the battle, fewer and fewer people passed him, until at last the Titanic streets became deserted. The frontage of the buildings grew plain and harsh; he seemed to have come to a deserted district of warehouses. Solitude crept upon him—his pace slackened.

He became aware of a growing fatigue. At times he would turn aside and seat himself on one of the numerous seats of the upper ways. But a feverish restlessness, the knowledge of his vital implication in this struggle, would not let him rest in any place for long. Was the struggle on his behalf alone?

And then in a desolate place came the shock of an earthquake—a roaring and thundering—a mighty wind of cold air pouring through the city, the smash of glass, the slip and thud of falling masonry—a series of gigantic concussions. A mass of glass and ironwork fell from the remote roofs into the middle gallery not a hundred yards away from him, and in the distance were shouts and running. He, too, was startled to an aimless activity, and ran first one way and then as aimlessly back.

A man came running towards him. His self-control returned.

"What have they blown up?" asked the man breathlessly. "That was an explosion," and before Graham could speak he had hurried on.

The great buildings rose dimly above Graham everywhere, veiled by a perplexing twilight, albeit the rivulet of sky above was now bright with day. He noted many strange features, understanding none at the time; he even spelt out many of the inscriptions in Phonetic lettering. But what profits it to decipher a confusion of odd-looking letters resolving itself, after painful strain of eye and mind, into "Here is Eadhamite," or "Labour Bureau—Little Side"? Grotesque thought, that in all probability some or all of these cliff-like houses were his!

The perversity of his experience came to him vividly. In actual fact he had made such a leap in time as romancers have imagined again and again. And that fact realised, he had been prepared, his mind had, as it were, seated itself for a spectacle. And no spectacle, but a great vague danger, unsympathetic shadows and veils of darkness. Somewhere through the labyrinthine obscurity his death sought him. Would he, after all, be killed before he saw? It might be that even at the next shadowy corner his destruction ambushed. A great desire to see, a great longing to know, arose in him.

He became fearful of corners. It seemed to him that there was safety in concealment. Where could he hide to be inconspicuous when the lights returned?

At last he sat down upon a seat in a recess on one of the higher ways, conceiving he was alone there.

He squeezed his knuckles into his weary eyes. Suppose when he looked again he found the dark trough of parallel ways, and that intolerable altitude of edifice gone. Suppose he were to discover the whole story of these last few days, the awakening, the shouting multitudes, the darkness and the fighting, a phantasmagoria, a new and more vivid sort of dream. It must be a dream; it was so inconsecutive, so reasonless. Why were the people fighting for him? Why should this saner later world regard him as Owner and Master?

So he thought, sitting blinded, and then he looked again, half hoping in spite of his ears to see some familiar aspect of the life of the nineteenth century, to see perhaps the little harbour of Boscastle about him, the cliffs of Pentargen, or the bedroom of his home. But fact takes no heed of human hopes. A squad of dim men with a black banner tramped athwart the nearer shadows, intent on conflict, and beyond rose that giddy wall of frontage, vast and dark, with the dim incomprehensible lettering showing faintly on its face.

"It is no dream," he said, "no dream." And he bowed his face upon his hands.

CHAPTER XI.

THE OLD MAN WHO KNEW EVERYTHING

HE was started by a cough close at hand.

He turned sharply, and peering saw a small, hunched-up figure sitting a couple of yards off in the shadow of the enclosure.

"Have ye any news?" asked the high-pitched wheezy note of a very old man.

Graham hesitated. "None," he said.

"I stay here till the lights come again," said the old man.

"These blue scoundrels are everywhere—everywhere."

Graham's answer was inarticulate assent. He tried to see the old man but the darkness hid his face. He wanted very much to respond, to talk, but he did not know how to begin.

"Dark and damnable," said the old man suddenly. "Dark and damnable. Turned out of my room among all these dangers."

"That's hard," ventured Graham. "That's hard on you."

"Darkness. An old man lost in the darkness. And all the world gone mad. War and fighting. The police beaten and rogues abroad. No more dark passages for me. I fell over a dead man."

"You're safe out here," said Graham.

"One's safer with company," answered the old man, "if it's company of the right sort," and peered frankly. He rose suddenly and came towards Graham.

Apparently the scrutiny was satisfactory. The old man sat down as if relieved to be no longer alone. "Eh!" he said, "but this is a terrible time! War and fighting, and the dead lying there—men, strong men, dying in the dark. Sons! I have three sons. God knows where they are to-night."

The voice ceased. Then repeated quavering: "God knows where they are to-night."

Graham stood revolving a question that should not betray his ignorance. Again the old man's voice ended the pause.

"This Ostrog will win," he said. "He will win. And what the world will be like under him no one can tell. My sons are under the wind-vanes, all three. One of my daughters-in-law was his sweetheart for a while. His mistress! We're not common people. Though they've set me to wander to-night and take my chance. . . . I knew what was going on. Before most people. But this darkness! And to fall over a dead body suddenly in the dark!"

His wheezy breathing could be heard.

"Ostrog!" said Graham.

"The greatest Boss the world has ever seen," said the voice.

Graham ransacked his mind. "The Council has few friends among the people," he hazarded.

"Few friends. And poor ones at that. They've had their time. Eh! They should have kept to the clever ones. But twice they held election. And Ostrog——. And now it has burst out and nothing can stay it, nothing can stay it. Twice they rejected Ostrog—Ostrog the Boss. I heard of his rages at the time—he was terrible. Heaven save them! For nothing on earth can now he has raised the Labour Companies upon them. No one else would have dared. All the blue canvas armed and marching! He will go through with it. He will go through."

He was silent for a little while. "This Sleeper," he said, and stopped.

"Yes," said Graham. "Well?"

The senile voice sank to a confidential whisper, the dim, pale face came close. "The real Sleeper——"

"Yes?" said Graham.

"Died years ago."

"What?" said Graham sharply.

"Years ago. Died. Years ago."

"You don't say so?" said Graham.

"I do. I do say so. He died. This Sleeper who's woke up. They changed in the night. A poor, drugged insensible creature. But I mustn't tell all I know. I mustn't tell all I know."

For a little while he muttered inaudibly. His secret was too much for him. "I don't know the ones that put him to sleep—that was before my time—but I know the man who injected the stimulants and woke him again. It was ten to one—wake or kill. Wake or kill. Ostrog's way."

Graham was so astonished at these things that he had to interrupt, to make the old man repeat his words, to re-question vaguely, before he was sure of the meaning and folly of what he heard. And his awakening had not been natural! Was that an old man's senile superstition too, or had it any truth in it? Feeling in the dark corners of his memory, he presently came on something that might conceivably be an impression of some such stimulating effect. It dawned upon him that he had happened upon a lucky encounter, that at last he might learn something of the new age. The old man wheezed awhile and spat, and then the piping, reminiscent voice resumed:

"The first time they rejected him. I've followed it all!"

"Rejected whom?" said Graham. "The Sleeper?"

"Sleeper! *No.* Ostrog. He was terrible—terrible! And he was promised then, promised certainly the next time. Fools they were—not to be more afraid of him. Now all the city's his millstone, and such as we dust ground between 'em. Dust ground between 'em. Until he set to work—the workers cut each other's throats, and murdered a Labour policeman at times, and left the rest of us at peace. Dead bodies! Robbing! Darkness! Such a thing hasn't been this gross of years. Eh—but 'tis ill on small folks when the great fall out! It's ill."

"Did you say—there had not been—what?—for a gross of years."

"Eh?" said the old man.

The old man said something about clipping his words, and made him repeat this a third time. "Fighting and slaying, and weapons in hand, and fools bawling freedom and the like," said the old man. "Now in all my life has there been that. These are like the old days—for sure—when the Paris people broke out—three gross of years ago. That's what I mean hasn't been. But it's the world's way. It had to come back. I know. I know. This five years Ostrog has

been working, and there has been trouble and trouble and hunger and threats and high talk and arms. Blue canvas and murmurs! No one safe. Everything sliding and slipping. And now here we are! Revolt and fighting, and the Council come to its end."

"You are rather well informed on these things," said Graham.

"I know what I hear. It isn't all Babble Machine with me."

"No," said Graham, wondering what Babble Machine might be. "And you are certain this Ostrog—you are certain Ostrog organised this rebellion and arranged for the waking of the Sleeper? Just to assert himself—because he was not elected to the Council?"

"Everyone knows that, I should think," said the old man. "Except—just fools. He meant to be master somehow. In the Council or out. Everyone who knows anything knows that. And here we are with dead bodies lying in the dark! Why, where have you been if you haven't heard all about the trouble between Ostrog and the Verneys? And what do you think the troubles are about? The Sleeper? Eh? You think the Sleeper's real and woke of his own accord—eh?"

"I'm a dull man, older than I look, and forgetful," said Graham. "Lots of things that have happened—especially of late years—— If I was the Sleeper, to tell you the truth, I couldn't know less about them."

"Eh!" said the voice. "Old, are you? You don't sound so very old! But it's not everyone keeps his memory to my time of life—truly. But these notorious things? But you're not so old as me—not nearly so old as me. Well! I ought not to judge other men by myself, perhaps. I'm young—for so old a man. Maybe you're old for so young."

"That's it," said Graham. "And I've a queer history. I know very little. And history! Practically I know no history. The Sleeper and Julius Caesar are all the same to me. It's interesting to hear you talk of these things."

"I know a few things," said the old man. "I know a thing or two. But—— Hark!"

The two men became silent, listening. There was a heavy thud, a concussion that made their seat shiver. The passers-by stopped, shouted to one another. The old man was full of questions; he shouted to a man who passed near. Graham, emboldened by his example, got up and accosted others. None knew what had happened.

He returned to the seat and found the old man muttering vague interrogations in an undertone. For a while they said nothing to one another.

The sense of this gigantic struggle, so near and so remote, oppressed Graham's imagination.

Was this old man right, was the report of the people right, and were the revolutionaries winning? Or were they all in error, and were the red guards driving all before them? At any time the flood of warfare might pour into this silent quarter of the city and seize upon him again. It behoved him to learn all he could while there was time. He turned suddenly to the old man with a question and left it unsaid. But his motion moved the old man to speak again.

"Eh! but how things work together," said the old man. "This Sleeper that all the fools put their trust in! I've the whole history of it—I was always a good one for histories. When I was a boy—I'm that old—I used to read printed books. You'd hardly think it. Likely you've seen none—they rot and dust so—and the sanitary company burns them to make ashlarite. But they were convenient in their dirty way. One learnt a lot. These new-fangled Babble Machines—they don't seem new-fangled to you, eh?—they're easy to hear, easy to forget. But I've traced all the Sleeper business from the first."

"You will scarcely believe it," said Graham slowly, "I'm so ignorant—I've been so preoccupied in my own little affairs, my circumstances have been so odd—I know nothing of this Sleeper's history. Who was he?"

"Eh!" said the old man. "I know. I know. He was a poor nobody, and set on a playful woman, poor soul! And he fell into a trance. There's the old things they had, those brown things—silver photographs—still showing him as he lay, a gross and a half of years ago—a gross and a half of years."

"Set on a playful woman, poor soul," said Graham softly to himself, and then aloud, "Yes—well? Go on."

"You must know he had a cousin named Warming, a solitary man without children, who made a big fortune speculating in roads—the first Eadhamite roads. But surely you've heard? No? Why? He bought all the patent rights and made a big company. In those days there were grosses of grosses of separate businesses and business companies. Grosses of grosses! His roads killed the railroads—the old things—in two dozen years; he bought up and Eadhamited the tracks. And because he didn't want to break up his great property or let in shareholders, he left it all to the Sleeper, and put it under a Board of Trustees that he had picked and trained. He knew then the Sleeper wouldn't wake, that he would go on sleeping, sleeping till he died. He knew that quite well! And plump. A man in the United States, who had lost two sons in a boat accident, followed that up with another great bequest. His trustees found themselves with a

dozen myriads of Lions' worth or more of property at the very beginning."

"What was his name?"

"Graham."

"No—I mean—that American's."

"Isbister."

"Isbister!" cried Graham. "Why, I don't even know the name."

"Of course not," said the old man. "Of course not. People don't learn much in the schools nowadays. But I know all about him. He was a rich American who went from England, and he left the Sleeper even more than Warming. How he made it? That I don't know. Something about pictures by machinery. But he made it and left it, and so the Council had its start. It was just a council of trustees at first."

"And how did it grow?"

"Eh!—but you're not up to things. Money attracts money—and twelve brains are better than one. They played it cleverly. They worked politics with money, and kept on adding to the money by working currency and tariffs. They grew—they grew. And for years the twelve trustees hid the growing of the Sleeper's estate, under double names and company titles and all that. The Council spread by title deed, mortgage—share, every political party, every newspaper, they bought. If you listen to the old stories you will see the Council growing and growing. Billions and billions of Lions at last— the Sleeper's estate. And all growing out of a whim—out of this Warming's will, and an accident to Isbister's sons.

"Men are strange," said the old man. "The strange thing to me is how the Council worked together so long. As many as twelve. But they worked in cliques from the first. And they've slipped back. In my young days speaking of the Council was like an ignorant man speaking of God. We didn't think they could do wrong. We didn't know of their women and all that! Or else I've got wiser.

"Men are strange," said the old man. "Here are you, young and ignorant, and me—sevendy years old, and I might reasonably be forgetting—explaining it all to you, short and clear.

"Sevendy," he said, "sevendy, and I hear and see—hear better than I see. And reason clearly, and keep myself up to all the happenings of things. Sevendy!

"Life is strange. I was twaindy before Ostrog was a baby. I remember him long before he'd pushed his way to the head of the Wind Vanes Control. I've seen many changes. Eh! I've worn the blue. And at last I've come to see this crush and darkness and tumult and dead men carried by in heaps on the ways. And all his doing! All his doing!"

His voice died away in scarcely articulate praises of Ostrog.

Graham thought. "Let me see," he said, "if I have it right."

He extended a hand and ticked off points upon his fingers.

"The Sleeper has been asleep——"

"Changed," said the old man.

"Perhaps. And meanwhile the Sleeper's property grew in the hands of Twelve Trustees, until it swallowed up nearly all the great ownership of the world. The Twelve Trustees——by virtue of this property have become practically masters of the world. Because they are the paying power—just as the old English Parliament used to be——"

"Eh!" said the old man. "That's so—that's a good comparison. You're not so——"

"And now this Ostrog—has suddenly revolutionised the world by waking the Sleeper—whom no one but the superstitious, common people had ever dreamt would wake again—raising the Sleeper to claim his property from the Council, after all these years."

The old man endorsed this statement with a cough. "It's strange," he said, "to meet a man who learns these things for the first time to-night."

"Aye," said Graham, "it's strange."

"Have you been in a Pleasure City?" said the old man. "All my life I've longed——" He laughed. "Even now," he said, "I could enjoy a little fun. Enjoy seeing things, anyhow." He mumbled a sentence Graham did not understand.

"The Sleeper—when did he awake?" said Graham suddenly.

"Three days ago."

"Where is he?"

"Ostrog has him. He escaped from the Council not four hours ago. My dear Sir, where were you at the time? He was in the hall of the markets—where the fighting has been. All the city was screaming about it. All the Babble Machines. Everywhere it was shouted. Even the fools who speak for the Council were admitting it. Everyone was rushing off to see him—everyone was getting arms. Were you drunk or asleep? And even then! But you're joking! Surely you're pretending. It was to stop the shouting of the Babble Machines and prevent the people gathering that they turned off the electricity—and put this damned darkness upon us. Do you mean to say——?"

"I had heard the Sleeper was rescued," said Graham. "But—to come back a minute. Are you sure Ostrog has him?"

"He won't let him go," said the old man.

"And the Sleeper. Are you sure he is not genuine? I have never heard——."

"So all the fools think. So they think. As if there wasn't a thousand things that were never heard. I know Ostrog too well for that. Did I tell you? In a way I'm a sort of relation of Ostrog's. A sort of relation. Through my daughter-in-law."

"I suppose——"

"Well?"

"I suppose there's no chance of this Sleeper asserting himself? I suppose he's certain to be a puppet—in Ostrog's hands or the Council's as soon as the struggle is over?"

"In Ostrog's hands—certainly. Why shouldn't he be a puppet? Look at his position. Everything done for him, every pleasure possible. Why should he want to assert himself?"

"What are these Pleasure Cities?" said Graham abruptly.

The old man made him repeat the question. When at last he was assured of Graham's words, he nudged him violently. "That's *too* much," said he. "You're poking fun at an old man. I've been suspecting you know more than you pretended."

"Perhaps I do," said Graham. "But no. Why should I go on acting? No, I do not know what a Pleasure City is."

The old man laughed in an intimate way.

"What is more, I do not know how to read your letters, I do not know what money you use, I do not know what foreign countries there are. I do not know where I am. I cannot count. I do not know where to get food, nor drink, nor shelter."

"Come, come," said the old man, "If you had a glass of drink, now, would you put it in your ear or your eye?"

"I want you to tell me all these things."

"He, he! Well, gentlemen who dress in silk must have their fun." A withered hand caressed Graham's arm for a moment. "Silk. Well, well! But, all the same, I wish I was the man who was put up as the Sleeper. He'll have a fine time of it. All the pomp and pleasure. He's a queer-looking face. When they used to let anyone go to see him, I've got tickets and been. The image of the real one, as the photographs show him, this substitute used to be. Yellow. But he'll get fed up. It's a queer world. Think of the luck of it. The luck of it. I expect he'll be sent to Capri. It's the best fun for a greener."

His cough overtook him again. Then he began mumbling enviously of pleasures and strange delights. "The luck of it, the luck of it! All my life I've been in London, hoping to get my chance."

"But you don't know that the Sleeper died," said Graham suddenly.

The old man made him repeat his words.

"Men don't live beyond ten dozen. It's not in the order of things," said the old man. "I'm not a fool. Fools may believe it, but not me."

Graham became angry with the old man's assurance. "Whether you are a fool or not," he said, "It happens you are wrong about the Sleeper."

"Eh?"

"You are wrong about the Sleeper. I haven't told you before, but I will tell you now. You are wrong about the Sleeper."

"How do you know? I thought you didn't know anything—not even about Pleasure Cities."

Graham paused.

"You don't know," said the old man. "How are you to know? It's very few men——"

"I *am* the Sleeper."

He had to repeat it.

There was a brief pause. "There's a silly thing to say, sir, if you'll excuse me. It might get you into trouble in a time like this," said the old man.

Graham, slightly dashed, repeated his assertion.

"I was saying I was the Sleeper. That years and years ago I did indeed fall asleep, in a little stone-built village, in the days when there were hedgerows, and villages, and inns, and all the countryside cut up into little pieces, little fields. Have you never heard of those days? And it is I—I who speak to you—who awakened again these four days since."

"Four days since!—the Sleeper! But they've *got* the Sleeper. They have him, and they won't let him go. Nonsense! You've been talking sensibly enough up to now. I can see it as though I was there. There will be Lincoln like a keeper just behind him; they won't let him go about alone. Trust them. You're a queer fellow. One of these fun pokers. I see now why you have been clipping your words so oddly, but——"

He stopped abruptly, and Graham could see his gesture.

"As if Ostrog would let the Sleeper run about alone! No, you're telling that to the wrong man altogether. Eh! as if I should believe. What's your game? And besides, we've been talking of the Sleeper."

Graham stood up. "Listen," he said. "I am the Sleeper."

"You're an odd man," said the old man, "to sit here in the dark, talking clipped, and telling a lie of that sort. But——"

Graham's exasperation fell to laughter. "It is preposterous," he cried. "Preposterous. The dream must end. It gets wilder and wilder. Here am I—in this damned twilight—I never knew a dream in twilight before—trying to persuade an old fool that I am myself, and meanwhile—— Ugh!"

He moved in gusty irritation and went striding. In a moment the old man was pursuing him. "Eh! but don't go!" cried the old man. "I'm an old fool, I know. Don't go. Don't leave me in all this darkness."

Graham hesitated, stopped. Suddenly the folly of telling his secret flashed into his mind.

"I didn't mean to offend you—disbelieving you," said the old man coming near. "It's no manner of harm. Call yourself the Sleeper if it pleases you. 'Tis a foolish trick——"

Graham hesitated, turned abruptly and went on his way.

For a time he heard the old man's hobbling pursuit and his wheezy cries receding. But at last the darkness swallowed him, and Graham saw him no more.

CHAPTER XII.
OSTROG

BUT now Graham could take a clearer view of his position. For a long time yet he wandered before he could determine to seek this Ostrog, this leader and organiser of his awakening, but after the talk of the old man his return was clear in his mind as the final inevitable decision. One thing became clear to him, those who were at the headquarters of the revolt had succeeded very admirably in suppressing the news of his disappearance. But every moment he expected to hear the news of his death or recapture by the Council.

Presently a man stopped before him. "Have you heard?" he said.

"No!" said Graham, starting.

"Near a dozand," said the man, "a dozand men!" and hurried on.

A number of men and a girl passed in the darkness, gesticulating excitedly and shouting, "Capitulated! Given up." "A dozand of men." "Two dozand of men." "Goodle Ostrog." "Goodle Ostrog." These cries receded, became indistinct. "Goodle!" said Graham, and recognised a familiar vulgarism of his own time.

Other shouting men followed. For a time his attention was absorbed in the attempt to understand the fragments of speech he heard. He had a

Ostrog stepped across the room, something clicked, and suddenly they were in darkness, save for an oval glow. For a moment Graham was puzzled. Then he saw that the cloudy grey disc had taken depth and colour, had assumed the appearance of an oval window looking out upon a strange unfamiliar scene.

doubt whether all were speaking English. He dared accost no one with questions. The impression the people gave him jarred altogether with his preconceptions of the struggle, and confirmed the old man's faith in Ostrog. It was only slowly he could bring himself to believe that all these people were rejoicing at the defeat of the Council, that the Council which had pursued him with such power and vigour was after all the weaker of the two sides in conflict. And if that were so, how did it affect him? Several times he hesitated on the verge of fundamental questions. Once he turned and walked for a long way after a little man of rotund, inviting outline, but he was unable to master enough confidence to address him.

It was only slowly that it came to him that he might ask for the "wind-vane offices," whatever the "wind-vane offices" might be. His first inquiry simply resulted in a direction to go on towards Westminster. His second led to the discovery of a short cut in which he was speedily lost. He was told to leave the ways to which he had hitherto confined himself—knowing no other means of transit—and to plunge down one of the middle staircases into the blackness of a crossway. Thereupon came some trivial adventures; chief of these an ambiguous encounter with a gruff-voiced invisible creature speaking in a strange dialect that at first seemed a strange tongue, a thick flow of speech with the drifting corpses of English words therein, the dialect of the latter-day vile. Then another voice, a girl's voice calling, drew near. She spoke English touched with something of the same quality. She professed to have lost her sister, she blundered needlessly into him, he thought, caught hold of him and laughed. But a word of vague remonstrance sent her into the unseen again.

Then abruptly the sound of voices increased. Other unseen stumbling people passed them speaking excitedly. "They have surrendered!" "The Council! Surely not the Council!" "They are saying so on the ways." The passage seemed wider. Suddenly the wall fell away. They were in a great space and people were stirring remotely. He inquired his way. "Strike straight across," said a woman's voice. He left his guiding wall, and in a moment was stumbling over a little table on which were utensils of glass. Graham's eyes, now attuned to darkness, made out a long vista of pallid tables. He went down this. At one or two of the tables he heard a clang of glass and a sound of eating. There were people cool enough to dine, or daring enough to steal a meal in spite of social convulsion and darkness. Far off and high up he presently saw a pallid light of a semicircular shape. As he approached

this, a black edge came up and hid it. He stumbled at steps and found himself in a gallery. He heard a sobbing, and found two scared little girls crouching by a railing. These children became silent at the near sound of feet. He tried to console them, but they were very still until he left them.

Presently he found himself at the foot of a staircase and near a wide opening. He saw a dim twilight above this and ascended out of the blackness into a street again. He found a disorderly swarm of people marching and shouting. He perceived they were singing snatches of the song of the revolt, most of them out of tune. Here and there torches flared creating brief hysterical shadows. He asked his way and was twice puzzled by that same thick dialect. His third attempt won an answer he could understand. He was two miles from the wind-vane offices in Westminster, but the way was easy to follow.

When at last he did approach the district of the wind-vane offices it seemed to him, from the cheering procession that came marching along the ways, from the tumult of rejoicing, and finally from the restoration of the lighting of the city, that the overthrow of the Council must already be accomplished. And still no news of his absence came to his ears.

The re-illumination of the city came with startling abruptness. Suddenly he stood blinking, and all about him men halted dazzled, and the world was incandescent. The light found him already upon the outskirts of the excited crowds that choked the ways near the wind-vane offices, and the sense of visibility and exposure that came with it turned his colourless intention of joining Ostrog to a keen anxiety.

For a time he was jostled, obstructed, and endangered by men hoarse with cheering his name, weary, and some of them bandaged and bloody in his cause. The frontage of the wind-vane offices was illuminated by some moving picture, but what it was he could not see, because in spite of his strenuous attempts the density of the crowd prevented his approaching it. From the fragments of speech he caught, he judged it conveyed news of the fighting about the Council House. Ignorance and indecision made him slow and ineffective in his movements. For a time he could not conceive how he was to get within the broken façade of this place, drove helplessly with the currents of this mass of people, until he realised that the descending staircase of the central way led to the interior of the buildings. It was long before he could reach one. And even then he encountered intricate obstruction, and had an hour of vivid argument first with this guard and then with that before he could get a note taken to the one man of all men who was most eager to see him. His story was laughed to scorn at one place, and wiser for that, when at least he reached a second stairway he professed simply to have news of extraordinary importance for Ostrog. What it was he would not say. They sent his note reluctantly. For a long time he waited in a little room at the foot of the lift shaft, and thither at last came Lincoln, eager, apologetic, astonished. He stopped in the doorway scrutinising Graham, then rushed forward effusively.

"Yes," he cried. "It is you. And you are not dead!"

Graham made a brief explanation.

"My brother is waiting," explained Lincoln. "He is alone is the wind-vane offices. He doubted—and things are very urgent still in spite of what we are telling them *there*—or he would have come to you."

They ascended a lift, passed along a narrow passage, crossed a great hall, empty save for two hurrying messengers, and entered a comparatively little room, whose only furniture was a sort of long settee and a large oval disc of cloudy, shifting grey, hung by cables from the wall. There Lincoln left Graham for a space, and he remained alone watching without understanding the shifty smoky shapes that drove slowly across this disc.

His attention was arrested by a sound that began abruptly. It was cheering, the frantic cheering of a vast but very remote crowd, a roaring exultation. This ended as sharply as it had begun, like a sound heard between the opening and shutting of a door. In the outer room was a noise of hurrying steps and a clinking like a chain running over the teeth of a wheel.

Then he heard the voice of a woman, the rustle of unseen garments. "It is Ostrog!" he heard her say. A little bell rang fitfully, and then everything was still again.

Presently came voices, footsteps and movement without. The footsteps of some one person detached itself from the other sounds and drew near, firm, evenly measured footsteps.

The curtain lifted, and a tall, white-haired man, clad in garments of cream-coloured silk, stood regarding Graham.

For a moment the white form remained holding the curtain, then dropped it and stood before it. Graham's first impression was of a very broad forehead, very pale blue eyes deep sunken under white brows, an aquiline nose, and a heavily lined, resolute mouth. The folds of flesh over the eyes, the drooping of the corners of the mouth contradicted the upright bearing, and said the man was old. Graham knew that this was Os-

trog. He rose to his feet instinctively, and for a moment the two men stood in silence, steadfastly regarding each other.

"You are Ostrog?" said Graham.

"I am Ostrog."

"The Boss?"

"So I am called."

Graham felt the inconvenience of the silence. "I have to thank you chiefly, I understand, for my safety," he said presently.

"We were afraid you were killed," said Ostrog. "Or sent to sleep again—for ever. We have been doing everything to keep our secret—the secret of your disappearance. Where have you been? How did you get here?"

Graham told him briefly.

Ostrog listened in silence.

He smiled faintly. "Do you know what I was doing when they came to tell me you had come?"

"How can I guess?"

"We were preparing your double."

"My double?"

"A man as much like you as we could find. We were going to hypnotise him, to save him the difficulty of acting. It was imperative. The whole of this revolt depends on the idea that you are awake, alive, and with us. Even now a great multitude of people is clamouring to see you. You know, of course—something of your position."

"Very little," said Graham.

"It is like this." Ostrog walked a pace or two into the room and turned. Graham watched him. "Practically," said Ostrog, "you are absolute owner of more than half of this new world into which your sleep has brought you. As a result of that you are practically King. Your powers are limited in many intricate ways, but you are the figure-head, the popular symbol of government. This White Council, the Council of Trustees as it is called——"

"I have heard the vague outline of these things."

"I wondered."

"I came upon a garrulous old man."

"I see. Our masses—the word comes from your days—you know, of course, that we still have masses—regard you as our actual ruler. Just as a great number of people in your days regarded the Crown as the ruler. They are discontented—the masses all over the earth—with the rule of your Trustees. For the most part it is the old discontent, the old quarrel of the common man with his commonness—the misery of work and discipline and unfitness. But your Trustees have ruled ill. In certain matters, in the administration of the Labour Companies, for example, they have been unwise. They have given endless opportunities. Already we of the popular party were agitating for reforms— when your waking came. Came! If it had been contrived it could not have come more opportunely." He smiled. "The public mind, making no allowance for your years of quiescence, had already hit on the thought of waking you and appealing to you, and—Flash!"

He indicated the outbreak by a gesture, and Graham moved his head to show that he understood.

"The Council muddled—quarrelled. They always do. They could not decide what to do with you. You know how they imprisoned you?"

"I see. I see. And now—we win?"

"We win. Indeed we win. To-night, in five swift hours. Suddenly we struck everywhere. The wind-vane people, the Labour Company and its millions, burst the bonds. We got the pull of the acropiles."

He paused.

"Yes," said Graham, guessing that aeropile meant flying machine.

"That was, of course, essential. Or they could have got away. All the city rose, every third man almost was in it! All the blue, all the public services, save only just a few aeronauts and about half the red police. You were rescued, and their own police of the ways—not half of them could be massed at the Council House—have been broken up, disarmed or killed. All London is ours—practically now. Only the Council House remains.

"Half of those who remain to them of the red police were lost in that foolish attempt to recapture you. They flung all they had at the theatre. We cut them off there. Truly to-night has been a night of victory. Everywhere your star has blazed. A day ago—the White Council ruled as it has ruled for a gross of years, for a century and a half of years, and then with only a little whispering, a covert arming here and there, suddenly—So!"

"I am very ignorant," said Graham. "I suppose—I do not clearly understand the conditions of this fighting. If you could explain. Where is the Council? Where is the fight?"

Ostrog stepped across the room, something clicked, and suddenly they were in darkness, save for an oval glow. For a moment Graham was puzzled.

Then he saw that the cloudy greywydisc had taken depth and colour, had assumed the appearance of an oval window looking out upon a strange unfamiliar scene.

At the first glance he was unable to guess what this scene might be. It was a daylight scene, the daylight of a wintry day, grey and clear. Across the picture and halfway as it seemed between him and the remoter view, a stout cable of twisted white wire stretched vertically. Then he perceived that the rows of great wind wheels he saw, the wide intervals, the occasional gulfs of darkness, were akin to those through which he had fled from the Council House. He distinguished an orderly file of red figures marching across an open space between files of men in black, and realised before Ostrog spoke that he was looking down as it were on the upper surface of latter-day London. The overnight snows had gone. He judged that this mirror was some modern replacement of the camera obscura, but that matter was not explained to him. He saw that though the file of red figures were trotting from left to right, yet they were passing out of the picture to the left. He wondered momentarily, and then saw that the picture was passing slowly panorama fashion across the oval.

"In a moment you will see the fighting," said Ostrog at his elbow. "Those fellows in red you notice are prisoners. This is the roof space of London—all the houses are practically continuous now. The streets and public spaces are covered in. The gaps and chasms of your time have disappeared."

Something out of focus obliterated half the picture. Its form suggested a man. There was a gleam of metal, a flash, something that swept across the oval, as the eyelid of a bird sweeps across its eye, and the picture was clear again. And now Graham beheld men running down among the wind-wheels, pointing weapons from which jetted out little smoky flashes. They swarmed thicker and thicker to the right, gesticulating—it might be they were shouting, but of that the picture told nothing. They and the windwheels passed slowly and steadily across the field of the mirror.

"Now," said Ostrog, "comes the Council House," and slowly a black edge crept into view and gathered Graham's attention. Soon it was no longer an edge but a cavity, a huge blackened space amidst the clustering edifices, and from it thin spires of smoke rose into the pallid winter sky. Gaunt ruinous masses of building, mighty truncated piers and girders, rose dismally out of this cavernous darkness. And over these vestiges of some splendid place, countless minute men were clambering, leaping, swarming.

"This is the Council House," said Ostrog. "Their last stronghold. And the fools wasted enough ammunition to hold out for a month in blowing up the buildings all about them—to stop our attack. You heard the smash? It shattered half the brittle glass in the city."

And while he spoke, Graham saw that beyond this area of ruins, overhanging it and rising to a great height, was a ragged mass of white building. Apparently this mass had been isolated by the ruthless destruction of its surroundings. Black gaps marked the passages the disaster had torn apart; big halls had been slashed open and the decoration of their interiors showed dismally in the wintry dawn, and down the jagged walls hung festoons of divided cables and twisted ends of lines and metallic rods. And amidst all the vast details moved little red specks, the red-clothed defenders of the Council. Every now and then faint flashes illuminated the bleak shadows. At the first sight it seemed to Graham that an attack upon this isolated white building was in progress, but then he perceived that the party of the revolt was not advancing, but apparently sheltering amidst the colossal wreckage that encircled this last ragged stronghold of the red-garbed men.

And not ten hours ago he had stood beneath the ventilating fans in a little chamber within that remote building wondering what was happening in the world!

Looking more attentively as this warlike episode moved silently across the centre of the mirror, Graham saw that the white building was surrounded on every side by ruins, and Ostrog proceeded to describe in concise phrases how its defenders had sought by such destruction to isolate themselves from a storm. He spoke of the loss of men that huge downfall had entailed in an indifferent tone. He indicated an improvised mortuary among the wreckage, showed ambulances swarming like cheese mites along a ruinous groove that had once been a street of moving ways. He was more interested in pointing out the parts of the Council House, the distribution of the besiegers. In a little while the civil contest that had convulsed London was no longer a mystery to Graham. It was no tumultuous revolt had occurred that night, no equal warfare, but a spendidly organised *coup d'ètat*. Ostrog's grasp of details was astonishing; he seemed to know the business of even the smallest knot of black and red specks that crawled amidst these places.

He stretched a huge black arm across the luminous picture, and showed the room whence Graham had escaped, and across the chasm of ruins the course of his flight. Graham recognised the gulf across which the gutter ran, and the wind wheels where he had crouched from the flying machine. The rest of his path had succumbed to the explosion. He looked again at the Council House, and it was already half hidden, and on the right a hillside with a cluster of domes

and pinnacles amidst the ubiquitous wind wheels, hazy, dim and distant, was gliding into view.

"And the Council is really overthrown?" he said.

"Overthrown," said Ostrog.

"And I——Is it indeed true that I——?"

"You are Master of the World."

"But that white flag—"

"That is the flag of the Council—the flag of the Rule of the World. It will fall. The fight is over. Their attack on the theatre was their last frantic struggle. They have only a thousand men or so, and some of these men will be disloyal. They have little ammunition. And we are reviving the ancient arts. We are casting guns."

"But—help. Is this city the world?"

"Practically this is all they have left to them of their empire. Abroad the cities have either revolted with us or wait the issue. Your awakening has perplexed them, paralysed them."

"But haven't the Council flying machines? Why is there no fighting with those?"

"They had. But the greater part of the aeronauts were in it with us. They wouldn't take the risk of fighting with us, but they would not stir against us. We had to get a pull with the aeronauts. Quite half were with us, and the others knew it. Directly they knew you had got away, those that were out looking for you dropped. We hung the man who shot at you an hour ago. And we occupied the flying stages at the outset in every city we could, and so stopped and captured the aeroplanes, and as for the little flying machines that turned out—for some did—we kept up too straight and steady a fire for them to get near the Council House. If they dropped they couldn't rise again, because there's no clear space about there for them to get up. Several we have smashed, several others have dropped and surrendered, the rest have gone off to the Continent to find a friendly city if they can before their fuel runs out. Most of these men were only too glad to be taken prisoner and kept out of harm's way. Upsetting in a flying machine isn't a very attractive prospect. There's no chance for the Council that way. Its days are done."

He laughed and turned to the oval reflection again to show Graham what he meant by flying stages. Even the four nearer ones were remote and obscured by a thin morning haze. But Graham could perceive they were very vast structures, judged even by the standard of the things about him.

And then as these dim shapes passed to the left there came again the sight of the expanse across which the disarmed men in red had been marching. And then the black ruins, and then again the beleaguered white fastness of the Council. It appeared no longer a ghostly pile, but glowing amber in the sunlight, for a cloud shadow had passed. About it the pigmy struggle still hung in suspense, but now the red defenders were no longer firing.

So, in the dusky stillness, the man from the nineteenth century saw the closing scene of the great revolt, the forcible establishment of his rule. With a quality of startling discovery it came to him that this was his world, and not that other he had left behind; that this was no spectacle to culminate and cease; that in this world lay whatever life was still before him, lay all his duties and dangers and responsibilities. He turned with fresh questions. Ostrog began to answer them, and then broke off abruptly. "But these things I must explain more fully later. At present there are things to do. The people are coming by the moving ways towards this ward from every part of the city—the markets and theatres are densely crowded. You are just in time for them. They are clamouring to see you. And abroad they want to see you. Paris, New York, Chicago, Denver, Capri—thousands of cities are up and in a tumult, undecided, and clamouring to see you."

"But surely—I can't go."

Ostrog answered from the other side of the room, and the picture on the oval disc paled and vanished as the light jerked back again. "There are kineto-tele-photographs," he said. "As you bow to the people here—all over the world myriads of myriads of people, packed and still in darkened halls, will see you also. In black and white, of course—not like this. And you will hear their shouts reinforcing the shouting in the hall.

"There is an optical contrivance," said Ostrog, "used by some of the posturers and women dancers. It may be novel to you. You stand in a very bright light, and they see not you but a magnified real image of you thrown on a screen—so that even the furtherest man in the remotest gallery can count your eyelashes."

Graham clutched desperately at one of the questions in his mind. "What is the population of London?" he said.

"Eight and twaindy myriads."

"Eight and what?"

"More than thirty-three millions."

These figures went beyond Graham's imagination.

"You will be expected to say something," said Ostrog. "Not what you used to call a Speech, but what our people call a Word—just one sentence, six or seven words. Something formal. If I might suggest—'I have awakened and my heart is with you.' That is what they want."

"What was that?" asked Graham.

" 'I am awakened and my heart is with you.' And bow—bow royally. But first we must get you black robes—for black is your colour. Do you mind? And then they will disperse to their homes."

Graham hesitated. "I am in your hands," he said.

Ostrog was clearly of that opinion. He thought for a moment, turned to the curtain, and called brief directions to some unseen attendants. Almost immediately a black robe, the very fellow of the black robe Graham had worn in the theatre, was brought. And as he threw it about his shoulders there came from the room without the shrilling of a high-pitched bell. Ostrog turned in interrogation to the attendant, then suddenly seemed to change his mind, pulled the curtain aside and disappeared.

For a moment Graham stood with the deferential attendant listening to his retreating steps. There was a sound of quick question and answer and footsteps running. The curtain was snatched back and Ostrog reappeared, his massive face glowing with excitement. He crossed the room in a stride, clicked the room into darkness, and came and gripped Graham's arm.

"Even as we turned away," he said.

Graham saw his index finger, black and colossal, pointing to the Council House that was gliding slowly into the field of view once more. For a moment he did not understand. And then he perceived that the flagstaff that had carried the white banner was bare.

"Do you mean—?" he began.

"The Council has surrendered. Its rule is at an end for evermore."

"Its rule is at an end for evermore."

"Look!" said Ostrog, and pointed to a coil of black that crept in little jerks up the vacant flagstaff, unfolding as it rose.

The oval picture paled as Lincoln pulled the curtain aside and entered.

"They are clamorous," he said.

Ostrog kept his grip of Graham's arm.

"We have raised the people," he said. "We have given them arms. For to-day at least their wishes must be law."

Lincoln held the curtain open for Graham and Ostrog to pass through.

On his way to the markets Graham had a transitory glance of a long narrow white-walled room in which men in the universal blue canvas were carrying covered things like biers, and about which men in medical purple hurried to and fro. From this room came groans and wailing. He had an impression of an empty bloodstained couch, of men on other couches, bandaged and bloodstained. It was just a glimpse from a railed footway and then a buttress hid the place and they were going on towards the markets.

The roar of the multitude was near now: it leapt to thunder. And, arresting his attention, a fluttering of black banners, the waving of blue canvas and brown rags, and the swarming vastness of the theatre near the public markets came into view down a long passage. The picture opened out. He perceived they were entering the great theatre of his first appearance, and which he had last seen a chequer-work of glare and blackness when he had fled from the red police. This time he entered it along a gallery at a level high above the stage. The place was now brightly lit again. He sought the gangway up which he had fled, but he could not tell it from among its dozens of fellows; nor could he see anything of the smashed seats, deflated cushions, and suchlike traces of the fight because of the density of the people. Except the stage the whole place was closely packed, and looked down the effect was a vast area of stippled pink, each dot a still upturned face regarding him. At his appearance with Ostrog the cheering died away, the singing died away, a common interest stilled and unified the disorder. It seemed as though every individual of those myriads was watching his progress.

CHAPTER XIII.
THE END OF THE OLD ORDER

SO far as Graham was able to judge, it was near midday when the white banner of the Council fell. But some hours elapsed before it was possible to effect the formal capitulation, and after he had spoken his "Word" before the enthusiastic disorder of that same vast theatre across which he had fled for his life not eight hours since, he rested and took refreshment in the apartments of the Wind Vane offices that had been assigned him until the surrender was prepared. The continuous excitement of the last twelve hours had left him inordinately fatigued, even his curiosity was exhausted; for a space he sat inert and passive with open eyes, and for a space he slept. He was roused by two medical attendants, come prepared with stimulants to sustain him through the next occasion. After he had taken their drugs and bathed by their advice in cold water, he felt a rapid return of interest and energy, and was presently able and willing to accompany Ostrog through several miles (as it seemed) of passages, lifts, and slides to the closing scene of the White Council's rule.

The way ran deviously through a maze of buildings. They came at last to a passage that curved about, and suddenly broadening before him he saw an oblong opening, clouds hot with sunset, and the ragged skyline of the ruinous Council House. A tumult of shouts came drifting to him. In another moment they had come out high up on the brow of the cliff of torn buildings that overhung the wreckage. The vast area opened to Graham's eyes, none the less strange and wonderful for the remote view he had had of it in the oval mirror.

This rudely amphitheatral space seemed now the better part of a mile to its outer edge. It was gold-lit on the left hand, catching the sunlight, and below and to the right clear and cold in the shadow. Above the shadowy grey Council House that stood in the midst of it, the great banner of the surrender still hung in sluggish folds against the blazing sunset. Severed rooms, halls and passages gaped strangely, broken masses of metal projected dismally from the complex wreckage, vast masses of twisted cable dropped like tangled seaweed, and from its base came a tumult of innumerable voices, violent concussions, and the sound of trumpets. All about this great white pile was a ring of desolation; the smashed and blackened masses, the gaunt foundations and ruinous lumber of the fabric that had been destroyed by the Council's orders, skeletons of girders, Titanic masses of wall, forests of stout pillars; the thunderous concussion of their downfall he had heard that morning in the darkened ways. Amongst the sombre wreckage beneath, running water flashed and glistened, and far away across the space, out of the midst of a vague vast mass of buildings, the twisted end of a water-main, two hundred feet in the air, thunderously spouted a shining cascade. And everywhere great multitudes of people.

Wherever there was space and foothold, people swarmed, little people, small and minutely clear, except where the sunset touched them to indistinguishable gold. They clambered up the tottering walls, they clung in wreaths and groups about the high-standing pillars. They swarmed along the edges of the circle of ruins. The air was full of their shouting, and they were pressing and swaying towards the central space.

The upper stories of the Council House seemed deserted, not a human being was visible. Only the drooping banner of the surrender hung heavily against the light. The dead were within the Council House, or hidden by the swarming people, or carried away. Graham could see only a few neglected bodies in gaps and corners of the ruins, and amidst the flowing water.

"Will you let them see you, Sire?" said Os-

Broken masses of metal projected dismally from the complex wreckage, vast masses of twisted cable dropped like tangled seaweed. All about this great white pile was a ring of desolation; the smashed and blackened masses, the gaunt foundations and ruinous lumber of the fabric that had been destroyed by the Council's orders, skeletons of girders, Titanic masses of wall, forests of stout pillars, and everywhere great multitudes of people.

trog. "They are very anxious to see you."

Graham hesitated, and then walked forward to where the broken verge of wall dropped sheer. He stood looking down, a lonely, tall, black figure against the sky.

Very slowly the swarming ruins became aware of him. And as they did so little bands of black-uniformed men appeared remotely, thrusting through the crowd towards the Council House. He saw little black heads become pink, looking at him, saw by that means a wave of recognition sweep suddenly across the space. It occurred to them that he should accord them some recognition. He held up his arm, then pointed to the Council House and dropped his hand. The voices below became unanimous, gathered volume, came up to him as multitudinous pin-point cheers.

The sun had long since vanished, the western sky was a pallid bluish green, and Jupiter shone high in the south, before the capitulation was accomplished. Above was a slow insensible change, the advance of night serene and beautiful; below was hurry, excitement, conflicting orders, pauses, spasmodic developments of organisation, a vast ascending clamour and confusion. Before the Council came out, toiling, perspiring men, directed by a conflict of shouts, carried forth hundreds of those who had perished in the hand-to-hand conflict within those long passages and chambers. The Twelve Trustees came out at last, preceded by the disarmed guards in red, and by the black and yellow lackeys; they came along a wooden footway that had been hurriedly made to bridge a streaming torrent of water, along an avenue of improvised lights, to the place Ostrog had chosen to receive them. A perpetual hammering drowned the sound of their approach.

Guards in black lined the way, and as far as the eye could reach into the hazy blue twilight of the ruins, and swarming now at every possible point in the captured Council House and along the shattered cliff of its circumadjacent buildings, were innumerable people, and their voices even when they were not cheering were as the soughing of the sea upon a pebble beach. Ostrog had chosen a huge commanding pile of overthrown masonry, and on this a stage of timbers and metal girders was being hastily constructed. Its essential parts were complete, and Graham stood in his place, but humming and clangorous machinery still glared fitfully in the shadows beneath this edifice.

The stage had a small higher portion on which Graham stood with Ostrog and Lincoln close beside him, a little in advance of a group of minor officers. A broader lower stage surrounded this quarter-deck, and on this were the black-uniformed guards of the revolt armed with little green weapons, whose very names Graham still did not know. Those standing about him perceived that his eye wandered perpetually from the swarming people in the dusky ruins about him to the mass of the White Council House, whence the Trustees would presently come, and to the gaunt cliffs of ruin that encircled him, and so back to the people.

The voices of the crowd swelled to a tumult.

He saw the Councillors first afar off in the glare of one of the lights, a little group of white figures blinking in a black archway. In the Council House they had been in darkness. He watched them slowly approaching, drawing nearer, past first this blazing electric star and then that; the minatory roar of the crowd over whom their power had lasted for a hundred and fifty years marched along beside them. As they drew still nearer their faces came out weary and white and anxious. He saw them blinking up at the glare to see him and Ostrog. He contrasted his memory of their strange cold looks in the Hall of the Atlas. Presently he could recognise several of them; the man who had rapped the table at Howard, a burly man with a red beard, and one delicate-featured, short, dark man with a peculiarly long skull. He noted that two were whispering together and looking behind him at Ostrog. Next there came a tall, dark, and handsome man, walking downcast. Abruptly he glanced up, his eyes touched Graham for a moment, and passed beyond him to Ostrog.

"The Master, the Master! God and the Master!" shouted the people. "To hell with the Council!" Graham looked at their multitudes, receding beyond counting into a shouting haze, and then at Ostrog beside him, white and steadfast and still. His eye went to the little patch of White Councillors. The way that had been made for them was so contrived that they had to march past and curve about before they came to the sloping path of planks that ascended to the stage where their surrender was to be made. And then he looked up at the familiar quiet stars overhead. The marvellous element in his fate was suddenly vivid. Could that be his, indeed, that little life in his memory two hundred years ago by—and this as well?

CHAPTER XIV.
FROM THE CROW'S NEST

AND so, after strange delays and through an avenue of battle and doubt and struggle, this man from the nineteenth century came at last to his position at the head of that new world.

At first, when he rose from the long deep sleep that followed his rescue and the surrender of the Council, he did not recognise his surroundings. By an effort he gained a clue in his mind, and all that had happened came back to him, at first with a quality of insincerity like a story heard, like something read out of a book. And even before his memories were clear, the exultation of his escape, the wonder of his prominence were back in his mind. He was owner of half the world, Master of the Earth. This new great age was in the completest sense his. He no longer hoped to discover his experiences a dream; he became anxious now to convince himself that they were real.

An obsequious valet assisted him to dress under the direction of a dignified chief attendant, a little man whose face proclaimed him Japanese, albeit he spoke English like an Englishman. From the latter he learnt something of the state of affairs. Already the revolution was an accepted fact; already business was being resumed throughout the City. Abroad the downfall of the Council had been received for the most part with delight. Nowhere was the Council popular, and the thousand cities of Western America, after two hundred years, still bitterly jealous of New York, London, and the East, had risen almost unanimously two days before at the news of Graham's imprisonment. Paris was fighting within itself. The rest of the world hung in suspense.

While he was breaking his fast, the sound of a telephone bell jetted from a corner, and his chief attendant called his attention to the voice of Ostrog making polite inquiries. Graham interrupted his refreshment to reply. Very shortly Lincoln arrived, and Graham at once expressed a strong desire to talk to people and to be shown more of the new life that was opening before him. Lincoln informed him that in three hours' time a representative gathering of officials and their wives would be held in the state apartments of the wind-vane Chief. Graham's desire to traverse the ways of the city was, however, at present impossible, because of the enormous excitement of the people. It was, however, quite possible for him to take a bird's-eye view of the city from the crow's nest of the wind-vane keeper. To this accordingly Graham was conducted by his attendant. Lincoln, with a graceful compliment to the attendant, apologised for not accompanying them on account of the present pressure of administrative work.

Higher even than the most gigantic wind wheels hung this crow's nest, a clear thousand feet above the roofs, a little disc-shaped speck on a spear of metallic filigree, cable stayed. To its summit Graham was drawn in a little cradle, wire-hung. Halfway down the frail-seeming stem was a light gallery about which hung a cluster of tubes—minute they looked from above—rotating slowly on the ring of its outer rail. These were the specula, *en rapport* with the wind-vane keeper's mirrors, in one of which Ostrog had shown him the coming of his rule. His Japanese attendant ascended before him, and they spent nearly an hour asking and answering questions.

It was a day full of the promise and quality of spring. The touch of the wind warmed. The sky was an intense blue and the vast expanse of London shone dazzling under the morning sun. The air was clear of smoke and haze, sweet as the air of a mountain glen.

Save for the irregular oval of ruins about the House of the Council and the black flag of the surrender that fluttered there, the mighty city seen from above showed few signs of the swift revolution that had, to his imagination, in one night and one day, changed the destinies of the world. A multitude of people still swarmed over these ruins, and the huge openwork stagings in the distance at which the still interrupted service of aeroplanes to the various great cities of Europe and America started, were also black with the victors. Across a narrow way of planking raised on trestles that crossed the ruins a crowd of workmen were busy restoring the connection between the cables and wires of the Council House and the rest of the city, preparatory to the transfer thither of Ostrog's headquarters from the wind-vane buildings.

For the rest, the luminous expanse was undisturbed. So vast was its serenity in comparison with the areas of disturbance, that presently Graham, looking beyond them, could almost forget the thousands of men lying out of sight in the artificial glare within the quasi-subterranean labyrinth, dead or dying of the overnight wounds, forget the improvised wards with the hosts of surgeons, nurses, and bearers feverishly busy, forget, indeed, all the wonder, consternation and novelty under the electric lights. Down there in the hidden ways of the ant-hill he knew that the revolution triumphed, that black everywhere carried the day, black favours, black banners, black festoons across the streets. And out here, under the fresh sunlight, beyond the crater of the fight, as if nothing was happening to the earth, the forest of wind-vanes that had grown from one or two while the Council had ruled, roared peacefully upon their incessant duty.

Far away, spiked, jagged, and indented by the

wind-vanes, the Surrey hills rose blue and faint, to the north and nearer, the sharp contours of Highgate and Muswell Hill were similarly jagged. And all over the countryside, he knew, on every crest and hill, where once the hedges had interlaced, and cottages, churches, inns, and farmhouses had nestled among their trees, wind wheels similar to those he saw, and bearing like them vast advertisements, gaunt and distinctive symbols of the new age, cast their whirling shadows and stored incessantly the energy that flowed away incessantly through all the arteries of the city. And underneath these wandered the countless flocks and herds of the British Food Trust with their lonely guards and keepers.

Not a familiar outline anywhere broke the cluster of gigantic shapes below. St. Paul's he knew survived, and many of the old buildings in Westminster, embedded out of sight, arched over and covered in among the giant growths of this great age. The Thames, too, made no fall and gleam of silver to break the wilderness of the city; it ran a dark stream of clarified sewage beneath the foundations of houses, and a race of grimy bargemen brought the heavy materials of trade from the Pool thereby to the very feet of the workers. Faint and dim in the eastward between earth and sky hung the clustering masts of the colossal shipping in the Pool. For all the heavy traffic, for which there was no need of haste, came in gigantic sailing ships from the ends of the earth, and the heavy goods for which there was urgency in mechanical ships of a smaller, swifter sort.

And to the south over the hills, in three separate directions, ran pallid lines—the road, stippled with moving grey specks. He tried to imagine these roads. On the first occasion that offered he was determined to go out and see them. That would come after the flying ship he was presently to try. His attendant officer described them as a pair of gently curving surfaces a hundred yards wide, each one for the traffic going in one direction, and made of a substance called Eadhamite—an artificial substance, so far as he could gather, resembling toughened glass. Along this shot a strange traffic of rubber-shod vehicles, great single wheels, two and four wheeled vehicles, sweeping along at velocities of from one to six miles a minute. Railroads had vanished; a few embankments remained as rust-crowned trenches here and there. Some few formed the cores of Eadhamite ways.

Among the first things to strike his attention had been the great fleets of advertisement balloons and kites that receded in irregular vistas northward and southward along the lines of the aeroplane journeys. No aeroplanes were to be seen. Their passages had ceased, and only one little-seeming aeropile circled high in the blue distance above the Surrey Hills, an unimpressive soaring speck.

A thing Graham had already learnt, and which he found very hard to imagine, was that nearly all the towns in the country, and almost all the villages, had disappeared. Here and there only, he understood, some gigantic hotel-like edifice stood amid square miles of some single cultivation and preserved the name of a town—as Bournemouth, Wareham, or Swanage. Yet the officer had speedily convinced him how inevitable such a change had been. The old order had dotted the country with farm houses, and every two or three miles was the ruling landlord's estate, and the place of the inn and cobbler, the grocer's shop and church—the village. Every eight miles or so was the country town, where lawyer, corn merchant, wool-stapler, saddler, veterinary surgeon, doctor, draper, milliner, and so forth lived. Every eight miles—simply because that eight-mile marketing journey, four back and home, was as much as was comfortable for the farmer. But directly the railways came into play, and after them the light railways, and all the swift new motor-cars that had replaced waggons and horses, and so soon as the high roads began to be made of wood, and rubber, and Eadhamite, and all sorts of elastic durable substances—the necessity of having such frequent market towns disappeared. And the big towns grew. They drew the worker with the gravitational force of seemingly endless work, the employer with their suggestions of an infinite ocean of labour.

And as the standard of comfort rose, as the complexity of the mechanism of living increased, life in the country had become more and more costly, or narrow and impossible. The disappearance of vicar and squire, the extinction of the general practitioner by the city specialist, had robbed the village of its last touch of culture. After telephone, kinematograph and phonograph had replaced newspaper, book, schoolmaster, and letter, to live outside the range of the electric cables was to live an isolated savage. In the country were neither means of being clothed nor fed (according to the refined conceptions of the time), no efficient doctors for an emergency, no company and no pursuits.

Moreover, mechanical appliances in agriculture made one engineer the equivalent of thirty labourers. So, inverting the condition of the city clerk in the days when London was scarce inhabitable because of the coaly foulness of its air, the labourers now came hurrying by road or air to the city and its life and delights at night to leave it again in the morning. The city had swallowed up humanity; man had entered upon a new stage in his development. First had come the nomad, the hunter, then had followed the agriculturalist of the agricultural state, where towns and cities and ports were but the headquarters and markets of the countryside. And now, logical consequence of an epoch of invention was this huge new aggregation of men. Save London, there were only four other cities in Britain—Edinburgh, Portsmouth, Manchester, and Shrewsbury. Such things as these, simple statements of fact though they were to contemporary men, strained Graham's imagination to picture. And when he glanced "over beyond there" at the strange things that existed on the Continent, it failed him altogether.

He had a vision of city beyond city, cities on great plains, cities beside great rivers, vast cities along the sea margin, cities girdled by snowy mountains. Over a great part of the earth the English tongue was spoken; taken together with its Spanish-American and Hindoo and Negro and Pigeon dialects, it was the everyday language of two-thirds of the people of the earth. On the Continent, save as remote and curious survivals, three other languages alone held sway—German which reached to Salonica and Genoa and jostled Spanish-English at Cadiz, a Gallicised Russian which had spread to Syria and met the Indian English at Ormuz, and French, still clear and brilliant, the language of lucidity, which circled the Mediterranean, and reached through a negro dialect to the Congo.

And everywhere now, through the city-set earth, save in the administered "black belt" territories of the tropics, the same cosmopolitan social organisation prevailed, and everywhere from Pole to Equator his property and his responsibilities extended. The whole world was civilised; the whole world dwelt in cities; the whole world was property. Over the British Empire and throughout America his ownership was scarcely disguised, Congress and Parliament were usually regarded as antique, curious gatherings. And even in the two Empires of Russia and Germany, the influence of his wealth was conceivably of enormous weight. There, of course, came problems—possibilities, but, uplifted as he was, even Russia and Germany seemed sufficiently remote. And of the quality of the black belt administration, and of what that might mean for him after the fashion of his former days, he thought not at all.

Out of the dim south-west, glittering and strange, voluptuous, and in some way terrible, shone those Pleasure Cities, too, of which the kinematograph-phonograph and the old man in the street had spoken. Strange places reminiscent of the legendary Sybaris, cities of art and beauty, mercenary art and mercenary beauty, sterile, wonderful cities of motion and music, whither repaired all who profited by the fierce, inglorious, economical struggle that went on in the glaring labyrinth below.

Fierce he knew it was. How fierce he could judge from the fact that these latter-day people referred back to the England of the nineteenth century as the figure of an idyllic, easy-going life. He turned his eyes to the scene immediately before him again, trying to conceive the big factories of that intricate maze.

Northward he knew were the potters, makers not only of earthenware and china, but of the kindred pastes and compounds a subtler mineralogical chemistry had devised; there were the makers of statuettes and wall ornaments and much intricate furniture; there too were the factories where feverishly competitive authors devised their phonograph discourses and advertisements and arranged the groupings and developments for their perpetually startling and novel kinematographic dramatic works. Thence too flashed the worldwide messages, the world-wide falsehoods of the news-tellers, the chargers of the telephonic machines that had replaced the newspapers of the past.

To the westward beyond the smashed Council House were the voluminous offices of municipal control and government; and to the eastward, towards the port, the trading quarters, the huge public markets, the theatres, houses of resort, betting palaces, miles of billiard saloons, baseball and football circuses, wild beast rings and the innumerable temples of the Christian and quasi-Christian sects, the Mahomedans, Buddhists, Gnostics, Spook Worshippers, the Incubus Worshippers, the Furniture Worshippers, and so forth; and to the south again a vast manufacture of textiles, pickles, wines and condiments. And from point to point tore the countless multitudes along the roaring mechanical ways. A gigantic hive, of which the winds were tireless servants, and the ceaseless wind vanes an appropriate crown and symbol.

He thought of the unprecedented population that had been sucked up by this sponge of halls and galleries—the thirty-three million lives that were playing out each its own brief ineffectual drama below him, and the complacency that the brightness of the day and space and splendour of the view, and above all the sense of his own importance had begotten, dwindled and perished. Looking down from the height over the city it became at last possible to conceive this overwhelming multitude of thirty-three millions, the reality of the responsibility he would take upon himself, the vastness of the human Maelstrom over which his slender kingship hung.

He tried to figure the individual life. It astonished him to realise how little the common man had changed in spite of the visible change in his conditions. Life and property, indeed, were secure from violence over almost all the world, zymotic diseases, bacterial diseases of all sorts had practically vanished, everyone had a sufficiency of food and clothing, was warmed in the city ways and sheltered from the weather—so much the almost mechanical progress of science and the physical organisation of society had accomplished. But the crowd, he was already beginning to discover, was a crowd still, helpless in the hands of demagogue and organiser, individually cowardly, individually swayed by appetite, collectively incalculable. The memory of countless figures in pale blue canvas came before his mind. Millions of such men and women below him, he knew, had never been out of the city, had never seen beyond the little round of unintelligent grudging participation in the world's business, and unintelligent dissatisfied sharing of its tawdrier pleasures. He thought of the hopes of his vanished contemporaries, and for a moment the dream of London in Morris's quaint old *News from Nowhere*, and the perfect land of Hudson's beautiful *Crystal Age* appeared before him in an atmosphere of infinite loss. He thought of his own hopes.

For in the latter days of that passionate life that lay now so far behind him, the conception of a free and equal manhood had become a very real thing to him. He had hoped, as indeed his age had hoped, rashly taking it for granted, that the sacrifice of the many to the few would some day cease, that a day was near when every child born of woman should have a fair and assured chance of happiness. And here, after two hundred years, the same hope, still unfulfilled, cried passionately through the city. After two hundred years, he knew, greater than ever, grown with the city to gigantic proportions, were poverty and hopeless labour and all the sorrows of his time.

Already he knew something of the history of the intervening years. He had heard now of the moral decay that had followed the collapse of supernatural religion in the minds of ignoble man, the decline of public honour, the ascendency of wealth. For men who had lost their belief in God had still kept their faith in Property, and wealth ruled a venial world.

His Japanese attendant, Asano, in expounding the history of the intervening two centuries,

drew an apt image from a seed eaten by insect parasites. First there is the original seed, ripening vigorously enough. And then comes some insect and lays an egg under the skin, and behold! in a little while the seed is a hollow shape with an active grub inside that has eaten out its substance. And then comes some secondary parasite, some ichneumon fly, and lays an egg within this grub, and behold! that, too, is a hollow shape, and the new living thing is inside its predecessor's skin which itself is snug within the seed coat. And the seed coat still keeps its shape. Most people think it a seed still, and for all one knows it may still think itself a seed, vigorous and alive. "Your Victorian kingdom," said Asano, "was like that—kingship with the heart eaten out." The landowners—the barons and gentry—began ages ago with King John; there were lapses, but they beheaded King Charles, and ended practically with King George, a mere husk of a king . . . the real power in the hands of their Parliament. But the Parliament—the organ of the landholding tenant-ruling gentry—did not keep its power long. The change had already come in the nineteenth century. The franchise had been broadened until it included masses of ignorant men, "urban myriads," who went in their featureless thousands to vote together. And the natural consequence of a swarming constituency is the rule of the party organisation. Power had passed even in the Victorian time to the party machinery, secret, complex, and corrupt. Very speedily power was in the hands of great men of business who financed the machines. Parliament became a shadow—a sham. A time came when the real power and interest of the Empire rested visibly between the two party councils, ruling by newspapers and electoral organisations—two small groups of rich and able men, working at first in opposition, then presently together.

There was a reaction of a genteel, ineffectual sort. There were numberless books in existence, Asano said, to prove that—the publication of some of them was as early as Graham's sleep—a whole literature of reaction in fact. The party of the reaction seems to have locked itself into its study and rebelled, with unflinching determination—on paper. The urgent necessity of either capturing or depriving the party councils of power is a common suggestion underlying all the thoughtful work of the early twentieth century, both in America and England. In most of these things America was a little earlier than England, though both countries drove the same way.

That counter revolution never came. It could never organise and keep pure. There was not

"I remember you," said Graham. *"You were in that little room."*

enough of the old sentimentality, the old faith in righteousness, left among men. Any organisation that became big enough to influence the polls became complex enough to be undermined, broken up, or bought outright by capable rich men. Socialistic and Popular, Reactionary and Purity Parties were all at last mere Stock Exchange counters, selling their principles to pay for their electioneering. And the great concern of the rich was naturally to keep property intact, the board clear for the game of trade. Just as the feudal concern had been to keep the board clear for hunting and war. The whole world was exploited, a battlefield of business; and financial convulsions, the scourge of currency manipulation, tariff wars, made more human misery during the twentieth century—because the wretchedness was dreary life instead of speedy death—than had war, pestilence, famine, in the darkest hours of earlier history.

His own part in the development of this time he now knew clearly enough. Through the successive phases in the development of this mechanical civilisation, aiding and presently directing its development, there had grown a new power, the Council, the board of his trustees. At first it had been a mere chance union of the millions of Isbister and Warming, a mere property-holding company, the creation of two childless testators' whims, but the collective talent of its first constitution had speedily guided it to a vast influence, until, by title deed, loan and share, under a hundred disguises and pseudonyms it had ramified through the fabric of the American and English States.

Wielding an enormous influence and patronage, the Council had early assumed a political aspect; and in its development it had continually used its wealth to tip the beam of political decisions and its political advantages to grasp yet more and more wealth. At last the party organisations of two hemispheres were in its hands; it became an inner council of political control. Its last struggle was with the tacit alliance of the great Jewish families. But these families were linked only by a feeble sentiment, at any time inheritance might fling a huge fragment of their resources to a minor, a woman or a fool, marriages and legacies alienated hundreds of thousands at one blow. The Council had no such breach in its continuity. Steadily, steadfastly it grew.

The original Council was not simply twelve men of exceptional ability; they fused, it was a council of genius. It struck boldly for riches, for political influence, and the two subserved each other; with amazing foresight it spent great sums of money on the art of flying, holding that invention back against an hour foreseen. It used the

patent laws, and a thousand half-legal expedients, to hamper all investigators who refused to work with it. In the old days it never missed a capable man. It paid his price. Its policy in those days was vigorous—unerring, and against it as it grew steadily and incessantly was only the chaotic selfish rule of the casually rich. In a hundred years Graham had become almost exclusive owner of Africa, of South America, of France, of London, of England and all its influence—for all practical purposes that is—a power in North America—then the dominant power in America. The Council bought and organised China, drilled Asia, crippled the Old World empires, undermined them financially, fought and defeated them.

And this spreading usurpation of the world was so dexterously performed—a Proteus—hundreds of banks, companies, syndicates, masked their operations—that it was already far advanced before common men suspected the tyranny that had come. The Council never hesitated, never faltered. Means of communication, land, buildings, governments, municipalities, the territorial companies of the tropics, every human enterprise, it gathered greedily. And it drilled and marshalled its men, its railway police, its roadway police, its house guards, and drain and cable guards, its hosts of landworkers. Their unions it did not fight, but it undermined and betrayed and bought them. It bought the world at last. And, finally, its culminating stroke was the introduction of flying.

When the Council, in conflict with the workers in some of its huge monopolies, did something flagrantly illegal, the old Law looked about it for weapons. There were no more armies, no navies, the age of Peace had come. The only navies were the great steamships of the Council's Navigation Trust. The police forces they controlled, the police of the railways, of the ships, of their agricultural estates, their time-keepers and order-keepers, outnumbered the neglected little forces of the old country and municipal organisations ten to one. And they produced flying machines. There were men alive still who could remember the last great debate in the London House of Commons—the party against the Council was in a minority, but it made a desperate fight—and how the members came crowding out upon the terrace to see the great and unfamiliar winged shapes circling quietly overhead. The Council had soared to its power. The last pretence of democracy was at an end.

Within one hundred and fifty years of Graham's falling asleep, it had thrown off its disguises and ruled supreme in his name. Elections had become a cheerful formality, a septennial folly, an ancient unmeaning custom; a social

Parliament as ineffectual as the convocation of the Established Church in Victorian times assembled now and then, and a legitimate King of England, disinherited, drunken and witless, played foolishly in a second-rate music-hall. So the magnificient dream of the nineteenth century, the noble project of universal individual liberty and universal happiness, touched by a disease of honour, crippled by a superstition of absolute property, had worked itself out in the face of invention and ignoble enterprise, first to a warring plutocracy, and finally to the rule of a supreme plutocrat. His Council at last had ceased even to trouble to have its decrees endorsed by the constitutional authorities, and he a motionless, sunken, yellow-skinned figure had lain, neither dead nor living, recognisably and immediately Master of the earth. And awoke at last to find himself—Master of that inheritance! Awoke to stand under the cloudless, empty sky and gaze down upon the greatness of his dominion. And now indeed he was face to face with the riddle of his fate.

To what end had he awakened? Was this city, this hive of hopeless toilers, the final refutation of his hope? Or was the fire of liberty, the fire that had blazed and waned in the years of his past life, still smouldering below there? He thought of the stir and impulse of the song of the revolution. Was that song merely the trick of a demagogue, to be forgotten when its purpose was served? Was the hope that still stirred within him only the memory of abandoned things, the vestige of a creed outworn? Or had it a wider meaning, an import interwoven with the destiny of man? To what end had he awakened? What things lay before him for him to do? Was his sleep, and this great city, and the miracle of his suspended life after all but the work of chance, the casual shaping of unmeaning things?

So this man from the nineteenth century wandered in the doubt-choked desert of his faith, seeking a refuge of belief, were it but a hiding place from his inexorable impossible sense of duty, and finding none. So he wandered, pursued by the greatness of his charge, by the knowledge of his own inadequacy. He knew too well the fluctuations of his will, the shifting sands of motive on which he had to build. And God was silent. "Could he be silent—"he cried, "could he be silent—and exist?" Yet at last his weakness overwhelmed him. He lifted his hands to heaven for strength, and doubting, desiring, denying, he prayed that ultimate last prayer of men, that hopeless prayer, that apology for the heart that fails, the prayer to the Unknown God.

A man and a woman were far below on a roof space to the southward enjoying the freshness of the morning air. The man had brought out a perspective glass to spy upon the Council House and he was showing her how to use it. Presently their curiosity was satisfied, they could see no traces of bloodshed from their position, and after a survey of the empty sky she came round to the crow's nest. And there she saw two little black figures, so small it was hard to believe they were men, one who watched and one who gesticulated with hands outstretched to the silent emptiness of Heaven.

She handed the glass to the man. He looked and exclaimed:

"I believe it is the Master. Yes. I'm sure. It *is* the Master!"

He lowered the glasses and looked at her. "Waving his hands about almost as if he was worshipping. I wonder what he is up to. There weren't Parsees in this country in *his* time, were there?"

He looked again. "He's stopped it now. It was just a chance attitude, I suppose." He put down the glass and became meditative. "He won't have anything to do but enjoy himself. Ostrog will boss the show of course. Ostrog will have to, because of keeping all these Labourer fools in bounds. They and their song! And got it all by sleeping, dear eyes—just sleeping. It's a wonderful world."

CHAPTER XV.

PROMINENT PEOPLE

THE state apartments of the Wind-Vane Keeper would have seemed astonishingly intricate to Graham had he entered them fresh from his nineteenth-century life, but already he was growing accustomed to the scale of the new time. They can scarcely be described as halls and rooms, seeing that a complicated system of arches, bridges, passages, and galleries divided and united every part of the great space. He came out through one of the now familiar sliding panels upon a plateau of landing at the head of a flight of very broad and gentle steps, with men and women far more brilliantly dressed than any he had hitherto seen ascending and descending. From this position he looked down a vista of intricate ornament in lustreless white and mauve and purple, spanned by bridges that seemed wrought of porcelain and filigree, and terminating far off in a cloudy mystery of perforated screens.

Glancing upward, he saw tier above tier of ascending galleries, with faces looking down upon him. The air was full of the babble of innumerable voices and of a music that descended from above, a gay and exhilarating music whose source he never discovered.

The central aisle was thick with people, but by no means uncomfortably crowded; altogether that assembly must have numbered many thousands. They were brilliantly, even fantastically dressed, the men as fancifully as the women, the sobering influence of the Puritan conception of dignity upon masculine dress had at last passed altogether away. The hair of the man too, though it was rarely worn long, was commonly curled in a manner that suggested the barber, and baldness had vanished from the earth. Frizzy straight-cut masses that would have charmed Rossetti abounded, and one gentleman, who was pointed out to Graham under the mysterious title of an "amorist," wore his hair in two becoming plaits *à la* Marguerite. There was little uniformity of fashion apparent in the forms of clothing worn. The more shapely men displayed their symmetry in trunk hose, and here were puffs and slashes, and there a cloak and there a robe. The fashions of the days of Leo the Tenth were perhaps the prevailing influence. Masculine embonpoint, which, in Victorian times, would have been subjected to the tightly buttoned perils, the ruthless exaggeration of tight-legged, tight-armed evening dress, now formed but the basis of a wealth of dignity and drooping folds. Graceful slenderness abounded also. To Graham, a typically stiff man from a typically stiff period, not only did these men seem altogether too graceful in person, but altogether too expressive in their vividly expressive faces. They gesticulated, they expressed surprise, interest, amusement, above all, they expressed the emotions excited in their minds by the ladies about them with astonishing frankness. Even at the first glance it was evident that women were in a great majority.

The ladies in the company of these gentlemen displayed in dress, bearing and manner alike, less emphasis and more intricacy. Some affected a classical simplicity of robing and subtlety of fold, and flashed conquering arms and shoulders as Graham passed. Others had closely fitting dresses without seam or belt at the waist, sometimes with long folds falling from the shoulders. The delightful confidences of *décolleté* costume had not been diminished by the passage of two centuries, nor had the hygienic divided skirt prevailed.

Everyone's movements seemed graceful. Graham remarked to Lincoln that he saw men as Raphael's cartoons walking, and Lincoln told him that the attainment of an appropriate set of gestures was part of every rich person's education. The Master's entry was greeted with a sort of tittering applause, but these people showed their distinguished manners by not crowding upon him nor annoying him by any persistent scrutiny, as he descended the steps towards the floor of the aisle.

He had already learnt from Lincoln that these were the leaders of existing London society; almost every person there that night was either a powerful official or the immediate connexion of a powerful official. Many had returned from the European Pleasure Cities expressly to welcome him. The aeronautic authorities, whose defection had played a part in the overthrow of the Council only second to Graham's, were very prominent, and so, too, was the Wind Vane Control. Amongst others there were several of the more prominent officers of the Food Trust; the controller of the European Piggeries had a particularly melancholy and interesting countenance and a daintily cynical manner. A bishop in full canonicals passed athwart Graham's vision, conversing with a gentleman dressed exactly like the traditional Dante, including even the laurel wreath.

"Who is that?" he asked almost involuntarily.

"The Bishop of London," said Lincoln.

"No—the other, I mean."

"Poet Laureate."

"You still—?"

"He doesn't write poetry, of course. He's a cousin of Wotton—one of the Councillors. But he's one of the Red Rose Royalists—a delightful club—and they keep up the tradition of these things."

"Asano told me there was a King."

"The King doesn't belong. They had to expel him. It's the Stuart blood, I suppose; but really—"

"Too much?"

"Far too much."

Graham did not quite follow all this, but it seemed part of the general inversion of the new age. He bowed condescendingly to his first introduction. It was evident that subtle distinction of class prevailed even in this assembly, that only to a small proportion of the guests, to an inner group, did Lincoln consider it appropriate to introduce him. This first introduction was the Master Aeronaut, a man whose sun-tanned face contrasted oddly with the delicate complexions about him. Just at present his critical defection from the Council made him a very important person indeed.

His manner contrasted very favourably, according to Graham's ideas, with the general bearing. He made a few commonplace remarks, assurances of loyalty and frank inquiries about the Master's health. His manner was breezy, his accent lacked the easy staccato of latter-day English. He made it admirably clear to Graham that he was a bluff "aerial dog"—he used that phrase—that there was no nonsense about him, that he was a thoroughly manly fellow and old-fashioned at that, that he didn't profess to know much, and that what he did not know was not worth knowing. He made a manly bow, ostentatiously free from obsequiousness, and passed.

"I am glad to see that type endures," said Graham.

"Phonographs and kinematographs," said Lincoln a little spitefully. "He has studied from the life." Graham glanced at the burly form again. It was oddly reminiscent.

"As a matter of fact we bought him," said Lincoln. "Partly. And partly he was afraid of Ostrog."

He turned sharply to introduce the Surveyor-General of the Public School Trust. This person was a willowy figure in a blue-grey academic gown. He beamed down upon Graham through *pince-nez* of a Victorian pattern, and illustrated his remarks by gestures of a beautifully manicured hand. Graham was immediately interested in this gentlemen's functions, and asked him a number of singularly direct questions. The Surveyor-General seemed quietly amused at the Master's fundamental bluntness. He was a little vague as to the monopoly of education his Company possessed; it was done by contract with the syndicate that ran the numerous London Municipalities, but he waxed enthusiastic over educational progress since the Victorian times. "We have conquered Cram," he said, "completely conquered Cram—there is not an Examination left in the world. Aren't you glad?"

"How do you get the work done?" asked Graham.

"We make it attractive—as attractive as possible. And if it does not attract then—we let it go. We cover an immense field."

He proceeded to details, and they had a lengthy conversation. The Surveyor-General mentioned the names of Pestalozzi and Froebel with profound respect, although he displayed no intimacy with their epoch-making works. Graham learnt that University Extension still existed in a modified form. "There is a certain type of girl, for example," said the Surveyor-General, dilating with a sense of his usefulness, "with a perfect passion for severe studies—when they are not too difficult. We cater for them by the thousand. At this moment," he said with a Napoleonic touch, "nearly five hundred phonographs are lecturing in different parts of London on the influence exercised by Plato and Swift on the love affairs of Shelley, Hazlitt, and Burns. And afterwards they write essays on the

lectures, and the names in order of merit are put in conspicuous places. You see how your little germ has grown? The illiterate middle-class of your days has quite passed away."

"About the public elementary schools," said Graham. "Do you control them?"

The Surveyor-General did "entirely." Now, Graham, in his later democratic days, had taken a keen interest in these and his questioning quickened. Certain casual phrases that had fallen from the old man with whom he had talked in the darkness recurred to him. The Surveyor-General, in effect, endorsed the old man's words. "We have abolished Cram," he said, a phrase Graham was beginning to interpret as the abolition of all sustained work. The Surveyor-General became sentimental. "We try and make the elementary schools very pleasant for the little children. They will have to work so soon. They have to work so soon. Just a few simple principles—obedience—industry."

"You teach them very little?"

"Why should we?" It only leads to trouble and discontent. We amuse them. Even as it is— there are troubles—agitations. Where the labourers get the ideas, one cannot tell. They tell one another. There are socialistic dreams— anarchy even! Agitators *will* get to work among them. I take it—I have always taken it—that my foremost duty is to fight against popular discontent. Why should people be made unhappy?"

"I wonder," said Graham thoughtfully. "But there are a great many things I want to know."

Lincoln, who had stood watching Graham's face throughout the conversation, intervened. "There are others," he said in an undertone.

The Surveyor-General of schools gesticulated himself away. "Perhaps," said Lincoln, intercepting a casual glance, "you would like to know some of these ladies?"

The daughter of the Manager of the Piggeries of the European Food Trust was a particularly charming little person with red hair and animated blue eyes. Lincoln left him awhile to converse with her, and she displayed herself as quite an enthusiast for the "dear old times," as she called them, that had seen the beginning of his trance. As she talked she smiled, and her eyes smiled in a manner that demanded reciprocity.

"I have tried," she said, "countless times—to imagine those old romantic days. And to you— they are memories. How strange and crowded the world must seem to you! I have seen photographs and pictures of the old times, the little isolated houses built of bricks made out of burnt mud and all black with soot from your fires, the railway bridges, the simple advertisements, the solemn savage men in strange black coats and those tall hats of theirs, iron railway trains on iron bridges overhead, horses and cattle, and even dogs running half wild about the streets. And suddenly, you have come into this!"

"Into this," said Graham.

"Out of your life—out of all that was familiar."

"The old life was not a happy one," said Graham. "I do not regret that."

She looked at him quickly. There was a brief pause. She sighed encouragingly. "No?"

"No," said Graham. "It was a little life—and unmeaning. But this—. We thought the world complex and crowded and civilised enough. Yet I see—although in this world I am barely four days old—looking back on my own time, that it was a queer, barbaric time—the mere beginning of this new order. The mere beginning of this new order. You will find it hard to understand how little I know."

"You may ask me what you like," she said, smiling at him.

"Then tell me who these people are. I'm still very much in the dark about them. It's puzzling. Are there any generals?"

"Men in armour?"

"Of course not. No. I suppose they are the men who control the great public businesses. Who is that distinguished-looking man?"

"That? He's a most important officer. That is Morden. He is managing director of the Antibilious Pill Company. I have heard that his workers sometimes turn out a myriad myriad of pills a day in the twenty-four hours. Fancy a myriad myriad!"

"A myriad myriad. No wonder he looks proud," said Graham. "Pills! What a wonderful time it is! That man in purple?"

"He is not quite one of the inner circle, you know. But we like him. He is really clever, and very amusing. He is one of the heads of the Medical Faculty of our London University. All medical men, you know, are shareholders in the Medical Faculty Company, and wear that purple. You have to be—to be qualified. But, of course, people who are paid by fees for doing something—" She smiled away the pretensions of all such people.

"Are any of your great artists or authors here?"

"No authors. They are mostly such queer little women—and so preoccupied about themselves. And they quarrel so dreadfully! But I think Wraysbury, the fashionable capillotomist, is here. From Capri."

"Capillotomist," said Graham. "Ah, I remember. An artist! Why not?"

"We have to cultivate him," she said apologetically. "Our heads are in his hands." She smiled.

Graham hesitated at the invited compliment, but his glance was expressive. "Have the arts grown with the rest of civilised things?" he said. "Who are your great painters?"

She looked at him doubtfully. Then laughed. "For a moment," she said, "I thought you meant—" She laughed again. "You mean, of course, those good men you used to think so much of because they could cover great spaces of canvas with oil-colours? Great oblongs. And people used to put the things in gilt frames and hang them up in rows in their square rooms. We haven't any. People grew tired of that sort of thing."

"But what did you think I meant?"

She put a finger significantly on a cheek whose glow was above suspicion, and smiled and looked very arch and pretty and inviting.

"And here," and she indicated her eyelid.

Graham had an adventurous moment. Then a grotesque memory of a picture he had somewhere seen of Uncle Toby and the Widow flashed across his memory. An archaic shame came upon him. He became acutely aware that he was visible to a great number of interested people. "I see," he remarked inadequately. He turned awkwardly away from her fascinating facility. He looked about him to meet a number of eyes that immediately occupied themselves with other things. Possibly he coloured a little. "Who is that talking with the lady in saffron?" he asked, avoiding her eyes.

The person in question he learnt was one of the great organisers of the American theatres just fresh from a gigantic production at Mexico. His face reminded Graham of a bust of Caligula. The little lady, in no degree embarrassed, pointed out to him a charming little woman beyond as one of the subsidiary wives of the aeronautic chief.

Graham was on the verse of hesitating inquiries about the status of a "subsidiary wife," apparently an euphemistic phrase, when Lincoln's return broke off this very suggestive and interesting conversation. They crossed the aisle to where a tall man in crimson, and two charming persons in Burmese costume (as it seemed to him) awaited him diffidently. From their civilities he passed to other presentations.

In a little while his multitudinous impressions began to organise themselves into a general effect. At first the glitter of the gathering had raised all the democrat in Graham; he had felt hostile and satirical. But it is not in human nature to resist an atmosphere of courteous regard. Soon the music, the light, the play of colours, the shining arms and shoulders about him, the touch of hands, the transient interest of smiling faces, the frothing sound of skillfully modulated voices, the atmosphere of compliment, interest and respect, had woven together into a fabric of indisputable pleasure. Graham for a time forgot his spacious resolutions. He gave way slowly to the intoxication of the position that was conceded him, his manner became less conscious, more convincingly regal, his feet walked assuredly, the black robe fell with a bolder fold, and pride ennobled his voice. After all this was a brilliant, interesting world.

His glance went approvingly over the shifting colours of the people, it rested here and there in kindly criticism upon a face. Presently it occurred to him that he owed some apology to the charming little person with the red hair and blue eyes. He felt guilty of a clumsy snub. It was not princely to ignore her advances, even if his policy necessitated their rejection. He wondered if he should see her again. And suddenly a little thing touched all the glamour of this brilliant gathering and changed its quality.

He looked up and saw passing across a bridge of porcelain and looking down upon him, a face that was almost immediately hidden, the face of the girl he had seen overnight in the little room beyond the theatre after his escape from the Council. And she was looking with much the same expression of curious expectation, of uncertain intentness, upon his proceedings. For the moment he did not remember when he had seen her, and then with recognition came a vague memory of the stirring emotions of their first encounter. But the dancing web of melody about him kept the air of that great marching song from his memory.

The lady to whom he was talking repeated her remark, and Graham recalled himself to the quasi-regal flirtation upon which he was engaged.

But from that moment a vague restlessness, a feeling that grew to dissatisfaction, came into his mind. He was troubled as if by some half-forgotten duty, by the sense of things important slipping from him amidst this light and brilliance. The attraction that these bright ladies who crowded about him were beginning to exercise ceased. He no longer made vague and clumsy responses to the subtly amorous advances that he was now assured were being made to him, and his eyes wandered for another sight of that face that had appealed so strongly to his sense of beauty. But he did not see her again until he was awaiting Lincoln's return to leave this assembly. In answer to his request Lincoln had promised that an attempt should be made to

fly that afternoon, if the weather permitted. He had gone to make certain necessary arrangements.

Graham was in one of the upper galleries in conversation with a bright-eyed lady on the subject of Eadhamite—the subject was his choice and not hers. He had interrupted her warm assurances of personal devotion with a matter-of-fact inquiry. He found her, as he had already found several other latter-day women that night, less well informed than charming. Suddenly, struggling against the eddying drift of nearer melody, the song of the Revolt, the great song he had heard in the Hall, hoarse and massive, came beating down to him.

He glanced up startled, and perceived above him an *oeil de boeuf* through which this song had come, and beyond the upper courses of cable, the blue haze, and the pendant fabric of the lights of the public ways. He heard the song break into a tumult of voices and cease. But now he perceived quite clearly the drone and tumult of the moving platforms and a murmur of many voices. He had a vague persuasion that he could not account for, a sort of instinctive feeling that outside in the ways a huge crowd must be watching this place in which their Master amused himself. He wondered what they might be thinking of him.

Though the song had stopped so abruptly, though the special music of this gathering reasserted itself, the *motif* of the marching song, once it had begun, lingered in his mind.

The bright-eyed lady was still struggling with the mysteries of Eadhamite when he perceived the girl he had seen in the theatre again. She was coming now along the gallery towards him; he saw her first before she saw him. She was dressed in a faintly luminous grey, her dark hair about her brows was like a cloud, and as he saw her the cold light from the circular opening into the ways fell upon her downcast face.

The lady in trouble about the Eadhamite saw the change in his face, and grasped her opportunity. "Would you care to know that girl, Sire?" she asked boldly. "She is Helen Wotton—a niece of Ostrog's. She knows a great many serious things. She is one of the most serious persons alive. I am sure you will like her."

In another moment Graham was talking to the girl, and the bright-eyed lady had fluttered away.

"I remember you," said Graham. "You were in that little room. When all the people were singing and beating time with their feet. Before I walked across the hall."

Her momentary embarrassment passed. She

looked up at him, and her face was steady. "It was wonderful," she said, hesitated, and spoke with a sudden effort. "All those people would have died for you, Sire. Countless people did die for you that night."

Her face glowed. She glanced swiftly aside to see that no other heard her words.

Lincoln appeared some way off along the gallery, making his way through the press towards them. She saw him, and turned to Graham strangely eager, with a swift change to confidence and intimacy. "Sire," she said quickly, "I cannot tell you now and here. But the common people are very unhappy; the common people are very unhappy. They are oppressed—they are misgoverned. Do not forget the people, who faced death—death that you might live."

"I know nothing—" began Graham.

"I cannot tell you now."

Lincoln's face appeared close to them.

"You find the new world pleasant, Sire?" asked Lincoln, with smiling deference, and indicating the space and splendour of the gathering by one comprehensive gesture. "At any rate, you find it changed?"

"Yes," said Graham, "changed. And yet, after all, not so greatly changed."

"Wait till you are in the air," said Lincoln. "The wind has fallen; even now the aëropile awaits you."

Graham glanced at the girl, was on the verge of a question, found a warning in her expression, bowed to her and turned to accompany Lincoln.

CHAPTER XVI.

THE AËROPILE

FOR a while, as Graham went through the passages of the Wind-Vane offices with Lincoln, he was preoccupied. But, by an effort, he attended to the things which Lincoln was saying. Soon his preoccupation vanished. Lincoln was talking of flying. Graham had a strong desire to know more of this new human attainment. He began to ply Lincoln was questions. He had followed the crude beginnings of aërial navigation very keenly in his previous life; he was delighted to find the familiar names of Maxim and Pilcher, Langley and Chanute, and above all of the aërial proto-martyr Lillienthal still honoured by men.

Even during his previous life two lines of investigation had pointed clearly to two distinct types of contrivance as possible, and both of these had been realised. On the one hand was the great engine-driven aëroplane, a double row of horizontal floats with a big aërial screw behind, and on the other the nimbler aëropile. The aëroplanes flew safely only in a calm or moderate

wind, and sudden storms, occurrences that were now accurately predictable, rendered them for all practical purposes useless. They were built of enormous size—the usual stretch of wing being six hundred feet or more, and the length of the fabric a thousand feet. They were for passenger traffic alone. The lightly swung car they carried was from a hundred to a hundred and fifty feet in length. It was hung in a peculiar manner in order to minimise the complex vibration that even a moderate wind produced, and for the same reason the little seats within the car—each passenger remained seated during the voyage—were slung with great freedom of movement. The starting of the mechanism was only possible from a gigantic car on the rail of a specially constructed stage. Graham had seen these vast stages, the flying stages, from the crow's nest very well. Six huge blank areas they were, with a giant "carrier" stage on each.

The choice of descent was equally circumscribed, an accurately plane surface being needed for safe grounding. Apart from the destruction that would have been caused by the descent of this great expanse of sail and metal, and the impossibility of its rising again, the concussion of an irregular surface, a tree-set hillside, for instance, or an embankment, would be sufficient to pierce or damage the framework, to smash the ribs of the body, and perhaps kill those aboard.

At first Graham felt disappointed with these cumbersome contrivances, but he speedily grasped the fact that smaller machines would have been unremunerative, for the simple reason that their carrying power would be disproportionately diminished with diminished size. Moreover, the huge size of these things enabled them—and it was a consideration of primary importance—to traverse the air at enormous speeds, and so run no risks of unanticipated weather. The briefest journey performed, that from London to Paris, took about three-quarters of an hour, but the velocity attained was not high; the leap to New York occupied about two hours, and by timing one's self carefully at the intermediate stations it was possible in quiet weather to go round the world in a day.

The little aëropiles (as for no particular reason they were distinctively called) were of an altogether different type. Several of these were going to and fro in the air. They were designed to carry only one or two persons, and their manufacture and maintenance was so costly as to render them the monopoly of the richer sort of people. Their sails, which were brilliantly coloured, consisted only of two pairs of lateral air floats in the same plane, and of a screw behind.

Its lateral supporting sails braced and stayed with metal nerves almost like the nerves of a bee's wing, and made of some sort of glassy artificial membrane, cast their shadow over many hundreds of square yards. The chairs for the engineer and his passengers hung free to swing by a complex tackle, within the protecting ribs of the frame and well abaft the middle. The passenger's chair was protected by a wind-guard and guarded about with metallic rods carrying air cushions. It could, if desired, be completely closed in, but Graham was anxious for novel experiences, and desired that it should be left open. The aëronaut sat behind a glass that sheltered his face.

Their small size rendered a descent in any open space neither difficult nor disagreeable, and it was possible to attach pneumatic wheels or even the ordinary motors for terrestrial traffic to them, and so carry them to a convenient starting place. They required a special sort of swift car to throw them into the air, but such a car was efficient in any open place clear of high buildings or trees. Human aëronautics, Graham perceived, were evidently still a long way behind the instinctive gift of the albatross or the fly-catcher. One great influence that might have brought the aëropile to a more rapid perfection had been withheld; these inventions had never been used in warfare. The last great international struggle—the raiding of the wheat districts of Canada by the American subjects of the Wheat and Oil Trusts—had occurred before the usurpation of the Council.

The flying stages of London were collected together in an irregular crescent on the southern side of the river. They formed three groups of two each and retained the names of ancient suburban hills or villages. They were named in order, Roehampton, Wimbledon Park, Streatham, Norwood, Blackheath, and Shooter's Hill. They were uniform structures rising high above the general roof surfaces. Each was about four thousand yards long and a thousand broad, and constructed of the compound of aluminum and iron that had replaced iron in architecture. Their higher tiers formed an openwork of girders through which lifts and staircases ascended. The upper surface was a uniform expanse, with portions—the starting carriers—that could be raised and were then able to run on very slightly inclined rails to the end of the fabric. Save for any aëropiles or aëroplanes that were in port these open surfaces were kept clear for arrivals.

During the adjustment of the aëroplanes it was the custom for passengers to wait in the system of theatres, restaurants, newsrooms, and places of pleasure and indulgence of various sorts that interwove with the prosperous shops below. This portion of London was in consequence commonly the gayest of all its districts, with something of the meretricious gaiety of a seaport or city of hotels. And for those who took a more serious view of aëronautics, the religious quarters had flung out an attractive colony of devotional chapels, while a host of brilliant medical establishments competed to supply physical preparatives for the journey. At various levels through the mass of chambers and passages beneath these ran, in addition to the main moving ways of the city which laced and gathered here, a complex system of special passages and lifts and slides, for the convenient interchange of people and luggage between stage and stage. And a distinctive feature of the architecture of this section was the ostentatious massiveness of the metal piers and girders that everywhere broke the vistas and spanned the halls and passages, crowding and twining up to meet the weight of the stages and the weighty impact of the aëroplanes overhead.

Graham went to the flying stages by the public ways. He was accompanied by Asano, his Japanese attendant. Lincoln was called away by Ostrog, who was busy with his administrative concerns. A strong guard of the Wind-Vane police awaited the Master outside the Wind-Vane offices, and they cleared a space for him on the upper moving platform. His passage to the flying stages was unexpected, nevertheless a considerable crowd gathered and followed him to his destination. As he went along, he could hear the people shouting his name, and saw numberless men and women and children in blue come swarming up the staircases in the central path, gesticulating and shouting. He could not hear what they shouted. He was struck again by the evident existence of a vulgar dialect among the poor of the city. When at last he descended, his guards were immediately surrounded by a dense excited crowd. He believed that some tried to reach him with petitions. His guards cleared a passage for him with some difficulty.

He found an aëropile in charge of an aëronaut awaiting him on the westward stage. Seen closely this mechanism was no longer small. As it lay on its launching carrier upon the wide expanse of the flying stage, its aluminum body skeleton was as big as the hull of a twenty-ton yacht. Its lateral supporting sails braced and stayed with metal nerves almost like the nerves of a bee's wing, and made of some sort of glassy artificial membrane, cast their shadow over many hundreds of square yards. The chairs for the engineer and his passenger hung free to swing by a complex tackle, within the protecting ribs of the frame and well abaft the middle. The passenger's chair was protected by a wind-guard and guarded about with metallic rods carrying air cushions. It could, if desired, be completely closed in, but Graham was anxious for novel experiences, and desired that it should be left open. The aëronaut sat behind a glass that sheltered his face. The passenger could secure himself firmly in his seat, and this was almost unavoidable on landing, or he could move along by means of a little rail and rod to a locker at the stem of the machine, where his personal luggage, his wraps and restoratives were placed, and which also with the seats, served as a makeweight to the parts of the central engine that projected to the propeller at the stern.

The engine was very simple in appearance. Asano, pointing out the parts of this apparatus to him, told him that, like the gas-engine of Victorian days, it was of the explosive type, burning a small drop of a substance called "fomile" at each stroke. It consisted simply of reservoir and piston about the long fluted crank of the propeller shaft. So much Graham saw of the machine.

The flying stage about him was empty save for Asano and their suite of attendants. Directed by the aëronaut he placed himself in his seat. He then drank two prescriptions, one containing strychnine, the other ergot—doses, he learnt, invariably administered to those about to fly, and designed to counteract the possible effect of diminished air pressure upon the system. Having done so, he declared himself ready for the journey. Asano took the empty glasses from him, stepped through the bars of the hull, and stood below on the stage waving his hand. Suddenly he seemed to slide along the stage to the right and vanish.

The engine was beating, the propeller spinning, and for a second the stage and the buildings beyond were gliding swiftly and horizontally past Graham's eye; then these things seemed to tilt up abruptly. He gripped the little rods on either side of him instinctively. He felt himself moving upward, heard the air whistle over the top of the wind screen. The propeller screw moved round with powerful rhythmic impulses—one, two, three, pause; one, two three—which the engineer controlled very delicately. The machine began a quivering vibration in sympathy that continued throughout the flight, and the roof areas seemed running away to starboard very quickly and growing rapidly smaller. He looked from the face of the engineer through the ribs of the machine. Looking sideways, there was nothing very startling in what he saw—a rapid funicular railway might have given the same sensations. He recognised the Council House and the Highgate Ridge. And then he looked straight down between his feet.

For a moment physical terror possessed him, a passionate sense of insecurity. He held tight. For a second or so he could not lift his eyes. Some hundred feet or more sheer below him was one of the big wind-vanes of south-west London, and beyond it the southernmost flying stage crowded with little black dots. These things seemed to be falling away from him. For a second he had an impulse to pursue the earth. He set his teeth, he lifted his eyes by a muscular effort, and the moment of panic passed.

He remained for a space with his teeth set hard, his eyes staring into the sky. Throb, throb, throb—beat, went the engine; throb, throb, throb—beat. He gripped his bars tightly, glanced at the aëronaut, and saw a smile upon his sun-tanned face. He smiled in return—perhaps a little artificially. "A little strange at first," he said, before he recalled his dignity. But he dared not look down again for some time. He looked over the aëronaut's head to where a rim of vague blue horizon crept up the sky. For a little while he could not banish the thought of possible accidents from his mind. Throb, throb, throb—beat; suppose some trivial screw went wrong in that supporting engine! Suppose—! He made a grim effort to dismiss all such suppositions. After a while they did at least abandon the foreground of his thoughts. And up he went steadily, higher and higher into the clear air.

Once the mental shock of moving unsupported through the air was over, his sensations ceased to be unpleasant, became very speedily pleasurable. He had been warned of air sickness. But he found the pulsating movement of the aëropile as it drove up the faint south-west breeze was very little in excess of the pitching of a boat head on to broad rollers in a moderate gale, and he was constitutionally a good sailor. And the keenness of the more rarefied air into which they ascended produced a sense of lightness and exhilaration. He looked up and saw the blue sky above fretted with cirrus clouds. His eye came cautiously down through the ribs and bars to a shining flight of white birds that hung in the lower sky. For a space he watched these. Then going lower and less apprehensively, he saw the slender filigree of the Wind-Vane keeper's crow's nest shining golden in the sunlight and growing smaller every moment. As his eye fell with more confidence now, there came a blue line of hills, and then London, already to leeward, an intricate space of roofing. Its near edge came sharp and clear, and banished his last apprehensions in a shock of surprise. For the boundary of London was like a wall, like a cliff, a steep fall of three or four hundred feet, a frontage broken only by terraces here and there, a complex decorative façade.

That gradual passage of town into country through an extensive sponge of suburbs, which was so characteristic a feature of the great cities of the nineteenth century, existed no longer. Nothing remained of it but a waste of ruins here, variegated and dense with thickets of the heterogeneous growths that had once adorned the gardens of the belt, interspersed among levelled brown patches of sown ground, and verdant stretches of winter greens. The latter even spread among the vestiges of houses. But for the most part the reefs and skerries of ruins, the wreckage of suburban villas, stood along their street and roads, queer islands amidst the levelled expanses of green and brown, abandoned indeed by the inhabitants years since, but too substantial, it seemed, to be cleared out of the way of the wholesale horticultural mechanisms of the time.

The vegetation of this waste undulated and frothed amidst the countless cells of crumbling house walls, and broke along the foot of the city wall in a surf of bramble and holly and ivy and teazle and tall grasses. Here and there gaudy pleasure places towered amidst the puny remains of Victorian times, and cable ways slanted to them from the city. That winter day they seemed deserted. Deserted, too, were the artificial gardens among the ruins. The city limits were indeed as sharply defined as in the ancient days when the gates were shut at nightfall and the robber foreman prowled to the very walls. A huge semicircular throat swallowed the shining curves of the Thames, and from one of the archways came and went a vigorous traffic along the Eadhamite Bath Road. So the first prospect of the world beyond the city flashed on Graham, and ran past and dwindled. And when at last he could look vertically downward again, he saw below him the leafless woods of the Thames valley—a froth of ruddy brown.

His exhilaration increased rapidly, became a sort of intoxication. He found himself drawing deep breaths of air, laughing aloud, desiring to shout. After a time that desire became too strong for him, and he shouted.

The machine had now risen as high as was customary with aëropiles, and they began to curve about towards the south. Steering, Graham perceived, was effected by the opening or closing of one or two thin strips of membrane in one or other of the otherwise rigid wings, and by the movement of the whole engine backward or forward along its supports. The aëronaut set the engine gliding slowly forward along its rail and opened the valve of the leeward wing until the stem of the aëropile was horizontal and pointing southward. And in that direction they soared with a slight list to leeward, and with a slow alternation of movement, first a short, sharp ascent and then a long gradual downward glide that was very steady and pleasing. During these downward glides the propeller was inactive altogether. These ascents gave Graham a glorious sense of successful effort; the descents through the rarefied air were beyond all experience. He wanted never to leave the upper air again.

For a time he was intent upon the minute details of the landscape that ran swiftly northward from beneath. Its minute, clear detail pleased him exceedingly. He was impressed by the ruin of the houses that had once dotted the country, by the vast treeless expanse of country from which all farms and villages had gone, save for crumbling ruins. He had known the thing was so, but seeing it so was an altogether different matter. He tried to make out places he had known, within the hollow basin of the world below, but at first he could distinguish no data now that the Thames was left behind. Soon, however, they were driving over a sharp chalk hill that he recognised as the Guildford Hog's Back, because of the familiar outline of the gorge at its eastward end, and because of the ruins of the town that rose steeply on either lip of this gorge. And from that he made out other points, Leith Hill, the sandy wastes of Aldershot, and so forth. The Down escarpment was set with gigantic slow-moving wind-wheels. Save where the broad Eadhamite Portsmouth Road, thickly dotted with rushing shapes, followed the course of the old railway, the gorge of the Wey was choked with thickets.

The whole expanse of the Downs escarpment, so far as the grey haze permitted him to see, was set with wind-wheels to which the largest of the city was but a younger brother. They stirred with a stately motion before the south-west wind. And here and there were vast patches dotted with the sheep of the British Food Trust, and here and there a mounted shepherd made a spot of black. Then rushing under the stern of the aëropile came the Wealden Heights, the line of Hindhead, Pitch Hill, and Leith Hill, with a second row of wind-wheels that seeemed striving to rob the Downland whirlers of their share of breeze. The purple heather was speckled with gold, and on the further side a vast drove of black oxen stampeded before a couple of mounted men. Swiftly these swept behind, and dwindled and lost colour, and became little scarce moving specks that were swallowed up in blue haze.

And when these had vanished in the distance Graham heard a peewit wailing close at hand. He answered it by a loud cry. He perceived he was now above the South Downs, and staring over his shoulder saw the battlements of Portsmouth towering over the ridge of Portsdown Hill. In another moment there came into sight a spread of shipping like floating cities, the little white cliffs of the Needles dwarfed and sunlit, and the grey and glittering waters of the narrow sea. They seemed to leap the Solent in a moment, in a few seconds the Isle of Wight was running past, and then beneath him spread a wider and wider extent of sea, here purple with the shadow of a cloud, here grey, here a burnished mirror, and here a spread of cloudy greenish blue. The Isle of Wight grew smaller and smaller. In a few more minutes a strip of grey haze detached itself from other strips that were clouds, descended out of the sky and became a coast-line—sunlit and pleasant—the coast of Northern France. It rose, it took colour, became definite and detailed, and the counterpart of the Downland of England was speeding by below.

In a little time, as it seemed, Paris came above the horizon, and hung there for a space, and sank out of sight again as the aëropile circled about to the north again. But he perceived the Eiffel Tower still standing, and beside it a huge dome surmounted by a pin-point Colossus. And he perceived, too, though he did not understand it at the time, a slanting drift of smoke. But he marked the minarets and towers and slender masses that streamed skyward along the city wind-vanes, and knew that in the matter of grace at least Paris still kept in front of her larger rival. And even as he looked a pale blue shape ascended very swiftly from the city like a dead leaf driving up before a gale. It curved round and soared towards them, growing rapidly larger and larger. The aëronaut was saying something. "What?" said Graham, loth to take his eyes from this. "Aëroplane, Sire," bawled the aëronaut pointing.

They rose and curved about northward as it drew nearer. Nearer it came and nearer, growing, growing. The throb, throb, throb—beat, of the aëropile's flight, that had seemed so potent and so swift, suddenly appeared slow by comparison with this tremendous rush. How great the monster seemed, how swift and steady! It passed quite closely beneath them, a vast spread of netted translucent wing, soaring silently, a thing alive. Graham had a momentary glimpse of the rows and rows of wrapped-up passengers, slung in their little cradles behind wind-screens, of a white-clothed engineer crawling against the gale along a ladder way, of spouting engines beating together, of the whirling wind-screw, and of a wide waste of wing. He whooped in exultation of the sight. And in an instant the thing had passed.

It rose slightly and their own little wings swayed in the rush of its flight. It fell and grew smaller. Scarcely had they moved, as it seemed, before it was again only a flat blue thing that dwindled in the sky. This was the aëroplane that went to and fro between London and Paris. In fair weather it came and went four times a day.

They beat across the Channel, slowly as it seemed now, to Graham's enlarged ideas, and Beachy Head rose greyly to the left of them.

"Land," said the aëronaut.

"Not yet," said Graham, laughing. "Not land yet. I want to learn more of this machine."

"I meant—" said the aëronaut.

"I want to learn more of this machine," repeated Graham.

"I'm coming to you," he said, and had flung himself free of his chair and taken a step along the guarded rail between them. He stopped for a moment, and his colour changed and his hands tightened. Another step and he was clinging close to the aëronaut. He felt a weight on his shoulder, the pressure of the air. The wind came in gusts over his wind screen and blew his hair in streamers past his cheek. The aëronaut made some hasty adjustments for the shifting of the centres of gravity and pressure.

"I want to have these things explained," said Graham. "What do you do when you move that engine forward?"

The aëronaut hesitated. Then he answered, "They are complex, Sire."

"I don't mind," said Graham. "I don't mind."

There was a moment's pause. "Aëronautics is the secret—the privilege—"

"I know. But I'm the Master, and I mean to know." He laughed, full of this novel realisation of power that was his gift from the upper air.

The aëropile curved about, and the keen fresh wind cut across Graham's face and his garment lugged at his body as the stem pointed round to the west. The two men looked into each other's eyes.

"Sire, there are rules—"

"Not where I am concerned," said Graham. "You seem to forget."

The aëronaut scrutinised his face. "No," he said. "I do not forget, Sire. But in all the earth—no man who is not a sworn aëronaut—has ever a chance. They come as passengers—"

"I have heard something of the sort. But I'm not going to argue these points. Do you know why I have slept two hundred years? To fly!"

"Sire," said the aëronaut, "the rules—if I break the rules—"

Graham waved the penalties aside.

"Then if you will watch me—"

"No," said Graham, swaying and gripping tight as the machine lifted its nose again for an ascent. "That's not my game. I want to do it myself. Do it myself if I smash for it! No! I will. See. I am going to clamber by this—to come and share your seat. Steady! I mean to fly of my own accord if I smash at the end of it. I will have something to pay for my sleep. Of all other things— In my past it was my dream to fly. Now—keep your balance."

"A dozen spies are watching me, Sire!"

Graham's temper was at an end. Perhaps he

chose it should be. He swore. He swung himself round the intervening mass of levers and the aëropile swayed.

"Am I Master of the earth?" he said. "Or is your Society? Now. Take your hands off those levers, and hold my wrists. Yes—so. And now, how do we turn her nose down to the glide?"

"Sire," said the aëronaut.

"What is it?"

"You will protect me?"

"Lord! Yes! If I have to burn London. Now!"

And with that promise Graham bought his lesson in aërial navigation. "It's clearly to your advantage, this journey," he said with a loud laugh—for the air was like strong wine, "to teach me quickly and well. So I pull this? Ah! So! Hullo!"

"Back, Sire! Back!"

"Back—right.   One—two—three—good God! Ah! Up she goes! But this is living!"

And now the machine began to dance the strangest figures in the air. Now it would sweep round a spiral of scarcely a hundred yards diameter, now it would rush up into the air and swoop down again, steeply, swiftly, falling like a hawk, to recover in a rushing loop that swept it high again. In one of these descents it seemed driving straight at the drifting park of balloons in the south-east, and only curved about and cleared them by a sudden recovery of dexterity. The extraordinary swiftness and smoothness of the motion, the extraordinary effect of the rarefied air upon his constitution, made Graham a different man. In spite of the protests of the aëronaut he attempted more and more daring things.

But at last a queer little incident came to sober him, and send him down once more to the crowded life and all its dark riddles below. As he swooped, came a tap and something flying past, and a drop like a drop of rain. Then as he went on down he saw something like a white rag whirling down in his wake. "What was that?" he asked. "I did not see."

The aeronaut glanced, and then clutched at the lever to recover, for they were driving low. When the aëropile was rising again he drew a deep breath and replied. "That," and he indicated the white thing still fluttering down, " was a swan."

"I never saw it," said Graham.

The aëronaut made no answer, and Graham saw that, spite of the keen air, there were little drops upon the man's forehead.

They drove horizontally while Graham went back to the passenger's place out of the lash of the wind. And then came a swift rush down, with the windscrew whirling now to check their fall,

and the flying stage growing broad and dark before them. The sun, sinking over the chalk hills in the west, fell with them, and left the sky a blaze of gold.

He heard a noise coming up to meet him, a noise like the sound of waves upon a pebbly beach, and looking, saw the roofs about the flying stage were dark with his people applauding his safe return. A dark mass it was, stippled with faces, and quivering with the minute oscillation of waved white handkerchiefs and waving hands.

CHAPTER XVII.

THREE DAYS

LINCOLN awaited Graham in a suite of apartments beneath the flying stages. He seemed curious to learn all that had happened, pleased to hear of the extraordinary delight and interest which Graham took in flying. Graham was in a mood of enthusiasm. "I must learn to fly," he cried. "I must master that. I pity all poor souls who have died without this opportunity. The sweet swift air! It is the most wonderful experience in the world."

"You will find our new times full of wonderful experiences," said Lincoln. "I do not know what you will care to do now. We have music that may seem novel."

"For the present," said Graham, "flying holds me. Let me learn more of that. Your aëronaut was saying there is some trades union objection to one's learning."

"There is, I believe," said Lincoln. "But for you—! If you would like to occupy yourself with that, we can make you a sworn aëronaut to-morrow."

Graham expressed his wishes vividly and talked of his sensations for a while. "And as for affairs," he asked abruptly. "How are things going?"

Lincoln waved affairs aside. "Ostrog will tell you that to-morrow," he said. "Everything is settling down. The Revolution accomplishes itself all over the world. Friction is inevitable here and there, of course; but your rule is assured. You may rest secure with things in Ostrog's hands."

"Would it be possible for me to be made a sworn aëronaut, as you call it, forthwith— before I sleep?" said Graham, pacing. "Then I could be at it the very first thing to-morrow again . . . This is a wonderful time."

"It would be possible," said Lincoln thoughtfully. "Quite possible. Indeed, it shall be done." He laughed. "I came prepared to suggest amusements, but you have found one for yourself. I will telephone to the aëronautical offices

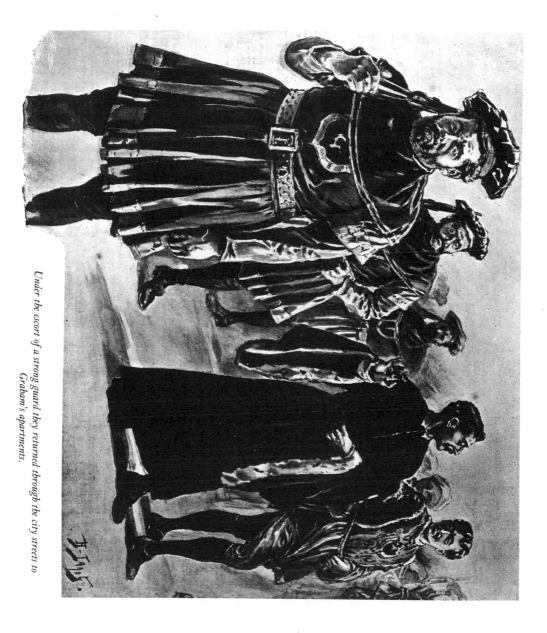

Under the escort of a strong guard they returned through the city streets to Graham's apartments.

from here and we will return to your apartments in the Wind-Vane Control. By the time you have dined the aëronauts will be able to come. You don't think that after you have dined you might prefer—" He paused.

"Yes?" said Graham.

"We had prepared a show of dancers—they have been brought from the Capri theatre."

"I hate ballets," said Graham shortly. "Always did. That's not what I want to see. We had dancers in the old days. For the matter of that, they had them in ancient Egypt. But flying—"

"True," said Lincoln. "Though our dancers—"

"They can afford to wait," said Graham. "There's questions I want to ask some expert—about your machinery. I'm keen, I want no distractions."

"You have the world to choose from," said Lincoln; "whatever you want is yours."

Asano appeared, and under the escort of a strong guard they returned through the city streets to Graham's apartments. Far larger crowds had assembled to witness his return than his departure had gathered, and the shouts and cheering of these masses of people sometimes drowned Lincoln's answers to the endless questions Graham's aërial journey had suggested. At first Graham had acknowledged the cheering and cries of the crowd by bows and gestures, but Lincoln warned him that such a recognition would be considered incorrect behaviour. Graham, already a little wearied by his civilities, ignored his subjects for the remainder of his public progress.

Directly they arrived at his apartments, Asano departed in search of kinematographic renderings of machinery in motion, and Lincoln despatched Graham's commands for models of machines and small machines to illustrate the various mechanical advances of the last two centuries. The little group of appliances for telegraphic communication attracted the Master so strongly that his delightfully prepared dinner, served by a number of charmingly dexterous girls, waited for a space. The habit of smoking had almost ceased from the face of the earth, but when he expressed a wish for that indulgence, inquiries were made and some excellent cigars were discovered in Florador, and sent to him by pneumatic despatch while the dinner was still in progress. Afterwards came the aëronauts, and a feast of ingenious wonders in the hands of a latter-day engineer. For the time, at any rate, the neat dexterity of counting and numbering machines, building machines, spinning engines, patent doorways, explosive motors, grain and water elevators, slaughter-house machines and harvesting appliances, was more fascinating to Graham than any bayadere. "We were savages," was his refrain, "we were savages. We were in the Stone Age compared with this . . . And what else have you?"

There came also practical psychologists with some very interesting developments of the art of hypnotism. Their science was now in general use; it had largely superseded drugs, antiseptics, and anaesthetics in medicine; was employed by almost all who had any need of mental concentration. A real enlargement of human faculty seemed to have been effected in this direction. The feats of "calculating boys," the wonders, as Graham had been wont to regard them, of mesmerisers were now within the range of anyone who could afford the services of a skilled hypnotist. Long ago the old examination methods in education had been destroyed by these expedients. Instead of years of study, candidates had substituted a few weeks of trances, and during the trances expert coaches had simply repeated over all the points necessary for adequate answering, together with the suggestion of a post hypnotic recollection of these points. In process mathematics particularly, this aid had been of singular service, and it was now invariably invoked by such players of chess and of games of manual dexterity, as were still to be found. In fact all operations conducted under finite rules, of a quasi-mechanical sort that is, were now systematically relieved from the wanderings of imagination and emotion, and brought to an unexampled pitch of accuracy. Little children of the labouring classes, so soon as they were of sufficient age to be hypnotised, were thus converted into beautifully punctual and trustworthy machine minders, and released forthwith from the long, long thoughts of youth. Aëronautical pupils, who gave way to giddiness, could be relieved from their imaginary terrors. In every street were hypnotists ready to print permanent memories upon the mind. If anyone desired to remember a name, a series of numbers, a song or a speech, it could be done by this method, and conversely memories could be effaced, habits removed, and desires eradicated—a sort of psychic surgery was, in fact, in general use. Indignities, humbling experiences, were thus forgotten, amorous widows would obliterate their previous husbands, angry lovers release themselves from their slavery. To graft desires, however, was still impossible, and the facts of thought transference were yet unsystematised. The psychologists illustrated their expositions with some astounding experiments in mnemonics made through the agency of a troupe of pale-faced children in blue.

Graham, like most of the people of his former time, distrusted the hypnotist, or he might then and there have eased his mind of many painful preoccupations. But in spite of Lincoln's assurances he held to the old theory that to be hypnotised was in some way the surrender of his personality, the abdication of his will. At the banquet of wonderful experiences that was beginning he wanted very keenly to remain absolutely himself.

The next day, and another day, and yet another day passed in such interests as these. Each day Graham spent many hours in the glorious entertainment of flying. On the third day he soared across middle France, and within sight of the snow-clad Alps. These vigorous exercises gave him restful sleep, and each day saw a great stride in his health from the spiritless anaemia of his first awakening. And whenever he was not in the air, and awake, Lincoln was assiduous in the cause of his amusement; all that was novel and curious in contemporary invention was brought to him, until at last his appetite for novelty was well-nigh glutted. One might fill a dozen inconsecutive volumes with the strange things they exhibited. Each afternoon he held his court for an hour or so. He speedily found his interest in his contemporaries becoming personal and intimate. At first he had been alert chiefly for unfamiliarity and peculiarity; any foppishness in their dress, any discordance with his preconceptions of nobility in their status and manners had jarred upon him, but it was remarkable to him how soon that strangeness and the faint hostility that arose from it, disappeared; how soon he came to appreciate the true perspective of his position, and see the old Victorian days remote and quaint. He found himself particularly amused by the red-haired daughter of the Manager of the European Piggeries. And after that, more hypnotic wonders. On the third day Lincoln was moved to suggest that the Master should remove to a Pleasure City, but this Graham declined, nor would he accept the services of the hypnotists in his aëronautical experiments. The link of locality held him to London; he found a perpetual wonder in topographical identifications that he would have missed abroad. "Here—or a hundred feet below here," he could say, "I used to eat my midday cutlets during my London University days. Underneath here was Waterloo and the perpetual hunt for confusing trains. Often have I stood waiting down there, bag in hand, and stared up into the sky above the forest of signals, little thinking I should walk some day a hundred yards in the air. And now in that very sky that was once a grey smoke canopy, I circle in an aëropile."

During those three days Graham was so occupied with such interests that the vast political movements in progress outside his quarters had but a small share of his attention. Those about him told him little. Daily came Ostrog, the Boss, his Grand Vizier, his mayor of the palace, to report in vague terms the steady establishment of his rule; "a little trouble" soon to be settled in this city, "a slight disturbance" in that. The song of the social revolt came to him no more; he never learned that it had been forbidden in the municipal limits; and all the great emotions of the crow's nest slumbered in his mind. But on the second and third of the three days he found himself, in spite of his interest in the daughter of the Pig Manager, or it may be by reason of the thoughts her conversation suggested, thinking of the girl Helen Wotton, who had spoken to him so oddly at the Wind-Vane Keeper's gathering. Her beauty came compellingly between him and certain immediate temptations of ignoble passion. The thought of her revived in this disillusioned man something of the noble emotions of his lost adolescence. He wondered what she had meant by those broken half-forgotten sentences; his memory of her eyes and the earnest passion of her face, became more vivid as his mechanical interests faded. But he did not see her again until three full days were past.

CHAPTER XVIII.
THE GIRL WITH THE EAGER FACE

IT was in the little gallery that ran from the Wind-Vane offices towards his State apartments that Graham spoke to Helen Wotton for the second time. The gallery was long and narrow, with a series of faithful reproductions of the Briar Rose and Perseus series of Burne-Jones on the right-hand side, and on the left arched fenestrations, a recess with seats below each, looking out upon a large hall wherein a slender fountain played incessantly amidst the fronds and palms. Graham came upon her suddenly. She was seated in one of the recesses, and she had turned at the sound of his footsteps. She started when she saw him.

He stopped, then advanced, and seated himself beside her. "I have wanted to see you," he said as he did so. "A few days ago you wanted to tell me something—you wanted to tell me of the people. What was it you had to tell me?"

She looked at him with troubled eyes.

"You said the people were unhappy?"

For a moment she was silent still.

"It must have seemed strange to you," she said abruptly.

"It did. And yet—"

"It was an impulse."

"Well?"

"That is all."

She looked at him with a face of hesitation. She spoke with an effort. "You forget," she said, drawing a deep breath.

"What?"

"The people—"

"Do you mean—?"

"You forget the people."

He looked interrogative.

"Yes. I know you are surprised. For you do not understand what you are. You do not know the things that are happening."

"Well?"

"You do not understand."

"Not clearly perhaps. But—tell me."

She turned to him with sudden resolution. "It is so hard to explain. And I am not ready with words. But about you—there is something. It is Wonder. Your sleep—your awakening. These things are miracles. To me at least—and to all the common people. You who lived and suffered and died, you who were a common citizen, wake again, live again, to find yourself Master almost of the earth."

"Master of the earth," he said. "So they tell me. But try and imagine how little I know of it."

"Cities—Trusts—the Labour Company—"

"Principalities, powers, dominions—the power and the glory. Yes. I have heard them shout. I know. I am Master. King if you wish. With Ostrog, the great Boss—"

He paused.

She turned upon him and surveyed his face with a curious scrutiny. "Well?"

He smiled. "To take the responsibility."

"That is what I have begun to fear." For a moment she said no more. "No," she said slowly. "*You* will take the responsibility. You will take the responsibility. The people look to you."

She spoke softly. "Listen! For at least half the years of your sleep—in every generation—multitudes of people, in every generation greater multitudes of people, have prayed that you might awake—*prayed.*"

Graham moved to speak and did not.

She hesitated, and a faint colour crept into her cheek. "Do you know that you have been to myriads—King Arthur, Barbarossa—the King who would come in his own good time and put the world right for them?"

"I suppose the imagination of the people—"

"Have you not heard our proverb, 'When the Sleeper wakes.' While you lay insensible and motionless there—thousands came. Thousands. Every first of the month you lay in state

with a white robe upon you and the people filed by you. When I was a little girl I saw you like that, with your face white and calm."

She turned her face from him and looked stedfastly at the painted wall before her. Her voice fell. "When I was a little girl I used to look at your face . . . it seemed to me fixed and waiting, like the patience of God.

"That is what we thought of you," she said. "That is how you seemed to us."

She turned shining eyes to him, her voice was clear and strong. "In the city, in the earth, a myriad myriad men and women are waiting to see what you will do, a myriad myriad children are lisping strange expectations."

"Yes?"

"Ostrog—no one—can take that responsibility."

"Do you think," she said, "that you who have lived that little life so far away in the past, you who have fallen into and risen out of this miracle of sleep—do you think that the wonder and reverence and hope of half the world has gathered about you only that you may live another little life? . . . That you may shift the responsibility to any other man?"

Graham looked at her in surprise, at her face lit with emotion. She seemed at first to have spoken with an effort, and to have fired herself by speaking. Now she was eloquent.

"I know how great this kingship of mine is," he said haltingly. "I know how great it seems. But is it real? Is it incredible—dreamlike. Is it real, or is it only a great delusion?"

"It is real," she said; "if you dare."

"After all, like all kingship, my kingship is belief. It is an illusion in the minds of men."

"If you dare!" she said.

"But—"

"Countless men," she said, "and while it is in their minds—they will obey."

"But I know nothing. That is what I had in mind. I know nothing. And these others—the Councillors, Ostrog. They are wiser, cooler, they know so much, every detail. And, indeed, what are these miseries of which you speak? What am I to know? Do you mean—?"

He stopped blankly.

"I am still hardly more than a girl," she said. "But to me the world seems full of wretchedness and oppression. The world has altered since your days, altered very strangely. I have prayed that I might see you and tell you these things. The world has changed. As if a canker had seized it—and robbed life of honour and freedom."

She turned a flushed face upon him, moving suddenly. "Your days were the days of freedom.

Yes—I have thought. I have been made to think, for my life—has not been happy. Men are no longer free—no greater, no better than the men of your time. That is not all. This city—is a prison. Every city now is a prison. Mammon grips the key in his hand. Myriads, countless myriads, toil from the cradle to the grave. Is that right? Is that to be—for ever? Yes, far worse than in your time. All about us, beneath us, is sorrow and pain, and the perpetual tragedy of ineffectual lives. The light, the space, the music, all the beauty and splendour and shallow delight of such life as you find about you, is separated by just a little from a life of wretchedness beyond any telling. Yes, the poor know it—they know they suffer. These countless multitudes who faced death for you two nights since—for you and hope! You owe your life to them."

"Yes," said Graham slowly. "Yes. I owe my life to them."

"You come," she said, " from the days when this new tyranny of the cities and of the rich man was scarcely beginning. It is a tyranny-tyranny. The feudal war lords had gone, and the new lordship of wealth had still to come. Half the men in the world still lived out upon the free countryside, as men have lived for endless years. The cities had still to devour them. I have heard the stories out of the old books—there was nobility! Common men and lives of love and faithfulness then—they did a thousand things for love of honour and love of country. And you—you come from that time."

"And now?"

"Gain and the Pleasure Cities! Or slavery—unthanked, unhonoured, grudging slavery."

"Slavery!" he said.

"Slavery."

"You don't mean to say that human beings are chattels?"

"Worse. That is what I want you to know, what I want you to see. I know you do not know. They will keep things from you, they will take you presently to a Pleasure City. But you have noticed men and women and children in pale blue canvas, with thin yellow faces and dull eyes?"

"Everywhere."

"Speaking a dull dialect, coarse and weak—the English of their misery."

"I have heard it."

"They are the slaves—your slaves. They are the slaves of the Labour Company you own."

"The Labour Company! In some way—that is familiar. Ah! now I remember. I saw it when I was wandering about the city, after the lights returned, great fronts of buildings coloured pale blue. Do you really mean——?"

"Yes. How can I explain it to you? Of course the blue uniform struck you. Nearly a third of our people wear it—more assume it now every day. This Labour Company has grown imperceptibly."

"What *is* this Labour Company?" asked Graham.

"In the old times, how did you manage with starving people?"

"There was the workhouse—which the parishes maintained."

"Workhouse! Yes—there was something. In our history lessons. I remember now. The Labour Company ousted the workhouse. It grew—partly—out of something—you perhaps may remember it—an emotional religious organisation called the Salvation Army—that became a business company. In the first place it was almost a charity. To save people from workhouse rigours. Now I come to think of it, it was one of the earliest properties your Trustees acquired. They bought the Salvation Army and reconstructed it as this. The idea in the first place was to give work to starving homeless people."

"Yes. "

"Nowadays there are no workhouses, no refuges and charities, nothing but that Company. Its offices are everywhere. That blue is its colour. And any man, woman or child who comes to be hungry and weary and with neither home nor friend nor resort, must go to the Company in the end—or seek some way of death. The Euthanasy is beyond their means—for the poor there is no easy death. And at any hour in the day or night there is food, shelter, and a blue uniform for all comers—that is the first condition of the Company's incorporation—and in return for a day's shelter the Company extracts a day's work, and then returns the visitor's proper clothing and sends him or her out again."

"Yes."

"Perhaps that does not seem so terrible to you. In your days men starved in your streets. That was bad. But these people in blue—The proverb runs: 'Blue canvas once and ever.' The Company trades in their labour, and it has taken care to assure itself of a supply of that labour. People came to it starving and helpless—they eat and sleep for a night and day, they work for a day, and at the end of the day they go out again. If they have worked well they have a penny or so—enough for a theatre or a cheap dancing place, or a kinematograph story, or a dinner or a bet. They wander about after that is spent. Begging is prevented by the police of the ways. Besides, no one gives. They come back again the next day or the day after—brought back by the same incapacity that brought them first. At last their proper clothing wears out, or their rags get so shabby that they are ashamed. Then they must work for months to get fresh. If they want fresh. A great number of children are born under the Company's care. The mother owes them a month thereafter—the children they cherish and educate until they are fourteen, and they pay two years' service. You may be sure these children are educated for the blue canvas. And so it is the Company works. "

"And none are destitute in the city."

"None. They are either in blue canvas or in prison."

"If they will not work?"

"Most people will work at that pitch, and the Company has powers. There are stages of unpleasantness in the work—stoppage of food—and a man or woman who has refused to work once is known by a thumb-marking system in the Company's offices all over the world. Besides, who can leave the city who is poor? To go to Paris costs two Lions. And for insubordination there are the prisons—dark and miserable—out of sight below. There are prisons now for many things."

"And a third of the people wear this blue canvas?"

"More than a third. Toilers, living without pride or delight or hope, with the stories of the Pleasure Cities ringing in their ears, mocking their shameful lives, their privations and hardships. Too poor even for the Euthanasy that opens its doors as the rich man's refuge from life. Dumb, crippled millions, countless millions, all the world about, ignorant of anything but limitations and unsatisfied desires. They are born, they are thwarted, and they die. That is the state to which we have come."

For a space Graham sat downcast, overwhelmed by this sudden darkening of the spacious vision of the crow's nest. Presently he had a thought.

"But there has been a revolution," he said. "All these things will be changed. Ostrog—"

"That is our hope. That is the hope of the world. But Ostrog will not do it. He is a politician. To him it seems things must be like this. He does not mind. He takes it for granted. All the rich, all the influential, all who are happy, come at last to take these miseries for granted. They use the people in their politics, they live in ease by their degradation. But you—you who come from a happier age—it is to you the people look. You are the last hope left to common men."

He looked at her face. Her eyes were bright with unshed tears. He felt a rush of emotion. For a moment he forgot this city, he forgot the race, and all those vague remote voices, in the immediate humanity of her beauty.

"But what am I to do?" he said with his eyes upon her.

"Rule," she answered. "Rule the world as it has never been ruled, for the good and happiness of men. For you might rule it—you could rule it."

She rose up and stood before him, appealing and beautiful. "The people are fermenting," she said. "All over the world the people are stirring. It wants but a word—but a word from you—to bring them all together. Even the middle sort of people are restless—unhappy.

"They are not telling you the things that are happening. The people will not go back to their drudgery—they refuse to be disarmed. Ostrog has awakened something greater than he dreamt of—he has awakened hopes."

His heart was beating fast. He tried to seem judicial, to weigh considerations. But he found it impossible to resist her expectation. He stood up before her. "I will not forget these hopes," he said. "I am waiting, I am learning. In the end I will surely take the power God has offered me and rule. Even now—I was on my way—"

CHAPTER XIX.
OSTROG'S POINT OF VIEW

GRAHAM returned at last to his apartments in a mood of sombre earnestness. The intense persuasion of his responsibility that had come to him in the crow's nest brooded once more upon his mind, touched with emotions of a keener kind. He saw himself in Helen's eyes. He reproached himself bitterly for his three days of aërial pleasure, for the idle occupation of his time. He wanted very greatly to go abroad at once and see the ways and habitations of the common people, to demonstrate in some way to himself that his promise to rule was no mere emotional flourish. But how was he to begin?

After a time Ostrog came to him, after his fashion, to give a formal vague account of the day's affairs. An instinct of distrust kept Graham from the mention of his conversation with Helen Wotton, but its import hung like a cloud upon his mind. On previous occasions Graham had passed over this ceremony as speedily as possible, in order to resume his aërial experiences, but now he asked questions. Ostrog brought flattering reports of the development of affairs abroad. In Paris and Berlin there had been trouble, not resistance to Graham, indeed, but insubordinate proceedings. "After all these years," said Ostrog, when Graham demanded particulars, "the Commune has lifted its

It was covered with inscriptions from top to base, in vivid white and blue, save where a vast and glaring kinematograph transparency presented a realistic crucifixion, and where a vast festoon of black to show that the popular religion followed the popular politics, hung across the lettering. Graham had already become familiar with the phonotype writing and these inscriptions arrested him, being to his sense for the most part almost incredible blasphemy. Among the less offensive were "Salvation on the Third Floor and turn to the Right." "The Sharpest Conversion in London, Expert Operators! Look Slippy!"

head again." But order had been restored in these cities. Graham, the more deliberately judicial for the stirring emotions he felt, asked if there had been any fighting. "A little," said Ostrog. "But the Soudanese division of our African agricultural police—the Consolidated African Companies have a very well-drilled police—was ready, and so were aëroplanes. We expected a little trouble in the continental cities, and in America. But things are very quiet in America. They are satisfied with the overthrow of the Council."

"Why should you expect trouble?" asked Graham abruptly.

"There is a lot of discontent—social discontent."

"The Labour Company?"

"You are learning," said Ostrog, with a touch of surprise. "Yes. It is chiefly the discontent with the Labour Company. It was that discontent supplied the motive force of this overthrow—that and your awakening."

"Yes?"

Ostrog smiled. "We had to stir up their discontent, we had to revive the old ideas of universal happiness—all men equal—all men happy—no luxury that everyone may not share—ideas that have slumbered for two hundred years. You know them? We had to revive these ideals, impossible as they are, in order to overthrow the Council. And now—"

"Well?"

"Our revolution is accomplished, and the Council is overthrow, and people whom we have stirred up—remain surging. There was scarcely enough fighting . . . We made promises, of course. It is extraordinary how violently and rapidly this vague out-of-date Humanitarianism has revived and spread. We who sowed the seed even have been astonished. In Paris, as I say—we have had to call in external help.

"And here?"

"There is trouble. Multitudes will not go back to work. There is a general strike. Half the factories are empty and the people are swarming in the ways. They are talking of a Commune. Men in silk and satin have been insulted in the streets. The blue canvas is expecting all sorts of things from you. Of course there is no need for you to trouble. We are setting the Babble Machines to work with counter suggestions in the cause of law and order. We must keep the grip tight; that is all."

Graham thought.

"Even to the pitch of bringing a negro police," he said.

"They are useful," said Ostrog. "They are fine loyal brutes, with no wash of ideas in their heads—such as our rabble has. The Council should have had them as a police of the ways, and things might have been different. Of course, there is nothing to fear excepting rioting and wreckage. You can manage your own wings now, and you can soar away to Capri if there is any smoke or fuss. We have the pull of all the great things; the aëronauts are privileged and rich, the closest trades union in the world, and so are the engineers of the wind-vanes. We have the air, and the mastery of the air is the mastery of the earth. No one of any ability is organising against us. They have no leaders—only the sectional leaders of the secret society we organised before your very opportune awakening. But none of these is man enough for a central figure. The only trouble will be a disorganised upheaval. To be frank—that may happen. But it won't interrupt your aëronautics. The days when the people could make revolutions are past."

"I suppose they are," said Graham. "I suppose they are. This world of yours has been full of surprises to me. In the old days we dreamt of a wonderful democratic life, of a time when all men would be equal and happy."

Ostrog looked at him keenly. "The day of democracy is past," he said. "Past for ever. That day began with the bowmen of Creçy, it ended when marching infantry, when common men in masses ceased to win the battles of the world, when costly cannon, great ironclads, and strategic railways became the means of power. To-day is the day of wealth. Wealth now is power as it never was power before—it commands earth and sea and sky. All power is for those who can handle wealth. You must accept facts, and these are facts. The world for the Crowd! The Crowd as Ruler! Even in your days that creed had been tried and condemned. To-day it has only one believer—a multiplex, feeble one—the man in the Crowd."

Graham did not answer immediately. He stood lost in sombre preoccupations.

"No," said Ostrog. "The day of the common man is past. On the open countryside one man is as good as another, or nearly as good. The old aristocracy had a precarious tenure of strength and audacity. The first real aristocracy came in with castles and armour, and vanished before the musket and bow. But in these new days we have this great machine of the city, and an organisation complex beyond a common man's understanding."

"Yet," said Graham, "there is something you

are holding down—something that stirs and presses."

"You will see," said Ostrog with a smile that brushed these difficult questions aside. "I have not roused the force to destroy myself—trust me."

"I wonder," said Graham.

Ostrog glanced at him again very keenly.

"Must the world go this way?" said Graham.

"What do you mean?" said Ostrog.

"I came from a democratic age. To find an aristocratic tyranny."

"Aristocracy, the prevalence of the best—the suffering and extinction of the unfit. And so to better things. It is the way that change has always travelled," said Ostrog.

"But aristocracy! those people I met—"

"Oh! not those!" said Ostrog. "But for the most part they go to their death. Vice and pleasure! They have no children. That sort of stuff will die out. If the world keeps to one road, if there is no turning back. An easy road to excess, convenient Euthanasia for the pleasure-seekers singed in the flame, that is the way to improve the race!"

"Pleasant extinction," said Graham. "But there is that other thing—the Crowd, the great mass of poor men. Will that die out? And it suffers, its suffering is a force that even you—"

Ostrog moved impatiently, and when he spoke he spoke rather less evenly than before.

"Don't you trouble about these things," he said. "Everything will be settled in a few days now. The Crowd is a fool, hysterical and illogical. What if it does not die out? You heard those people shouting and singing two nights ago. They were taught that song. If you had taken any man there in cold blood and asked why he shouted, he could not have told you. They think they are shouting for you, that they are loyal and devoted to you. Just then they were ready to slaughter the Council. To-day—they are already murmuring against them that have overthrown the Council. The Crowd is a huge foolish beast. Even if it does not die, it can still be tamed and driven."

"They shouted," said Graham, "because their lives were dreary, without joy or pride, and because in me—in me—they hoped."

"And what was their hope? What is their hope? What right have they to hope? They work ill and they want the reward of those who work well. The hope of mankind—what is it? That some day the Over-man may come, that some day the inferior, the weak, and the bestial may be subdued or eliminated. The world is no place for the bad, the stupid, the enervated. Their

duty—it's a fine duty too!—is to die. The death of the failure! That is the path by which the beast rose to manhood, by which man goes on to higher things."

Ostrog took a pace, seemed to think, and turned on Graham. "I can imagine how this great world state of ours seems to a Victorian Englishman. You regret all the old forms of representative government—their spectres still haunt the world, the voting councils and parliaments and all that eighteenth century tomfoolery. You feel moved against our Pleasure Cities. I might have thought of that—had I not been busy. But you will learn better. The people are mad with envy—they would be in sympathy with you. Even in the streets now, they clamour to destroy the Pleasure Cities. But the Pleasure Cities are the excretory organs of the State, attractive places that year after year draw together all that is weak and vicious, all that is undisciplined and lazy, all the eager roguery of the world, to a graceful destruction. They go there, they have their time, they die childless, all the pretty silly women die childless and mankind is the better. And you would emancipate the silly brainless workers that we have enslaved, and try to make their lives easy and pleasant again. Now their lot is just tolerable if they abstain from child-bearing—but you would try to make life easy for them too, and so their dreary breed would continue." He smiled a smile of superiority that irritated Graham, oddly. "You will learn better. I know those ideas; in my boyhood days I read your Shelly and dreamt of Liberty. There is no Liberty, save wisdom and self-control. Liberty is within—not without. It is each man's own affair. Suppose—which is impossible—that these swarming yelping fools in blue get the upper hand of us, what then? It would mean but a few hundred years delay. The coming of the aristocrat is as certain as fate. The end will be the Over-man—for all the mad protests of humanity. The end will be the same."

"I wonder," said Graham, doggedly.

For a moment he stood downcast.

"But I must see these things for myself," he said. "Only by seeing can I understand. I must learn. That is what I want to tell you, Ostrog. I do not want to be King in a Pleasure City; that is not my pleasure. I have spent enough time with aëronautics—and these other things. I must learn how people live, how the common life has developed. Then I shall understand these things better. I must learn how common people live—the labour people more especially—how they work, marry, bear children, die—"

"Our realistic novelists," suggested Ostrog, suddenly preoccupied.

"I want reality," said Graham, "not realism."

"There are difficulties," said Ostrog, and thought. "On the whole, perhaps—

"I did not expect—.

"I had thought—. And yet, perhaps—. Things are almost completed."

Suddenly he came to some conclusion. "You would need to go disguised," he said. "The city is intensely excited, and the discovery of your presence among them might create a fearful tumult. Still this wish of yours to go into this city—this idea of yours—. Yes, now I think the thing over it seems to me not altogether—. Yes, it may be done. It can be contrived. If you would really find an interest in that! You are, of course, Master. You are Master. Shall I tell Asano? For my own part, there is a matter I have to do. A matter of detail. Details! This evening. I see no reason—. Would you care to go soon? A disguise for this excursion Asano will be able to manage. He might go with you. I daresay you could go soon if you cared."

"You will not want to consult me in any matter?" asked Graham suddenly.

"Oh, dear no! No. I think you may trust affairs to me for a time," said Ostrog, following out some train of thought. "Even if we differ—"

Graham glanced at him sharply.

"There is no struggle likely to happen soon?" he asked abruptly.

"No."

"I have been thinking about these negroes. I don't believe the people intend any hostility to me, and, after all, I am the Master. I do not want any negroes brought to London. It is an archaic prejudice perhaps, but I have peculiar feelings about Europeans and the subject races. Even about Paris—"

Ostrog stood watching him from under his drooping brows.

"You are not to bring armed negroes to London, whatever happens," said Graham. "In that matter I am quite decided."

Ostrog bowed deferentially.

CHAPTER XX.

IN THE CITY WAYS

AND that night, unknown and unsuspected, Graham, dressed in the costume of an inferior wind-vane official keeping holiday, and accompanied by Asano in Labour Company canvas, surveyed the city through which he had wandered when it was veiled in darkness. But now he saw it lit and waking, a whirlpool of life. In spite of the surging and swaying of the forces of revolution, in spite of the unusual discontent, the mutterings of the greater struggle of which the first revolt was but the prelude, the myriad streams of commerce still flowed wide and strong. He knew now something of the dimensions and quality of the new age, but he was not prepared for the infinite surprise of the detailed view, for the torrent of colour and vivid impressions that poured past him.

This was his first real contact with the people of these latter days. He realised that all that had gone before, saving his glimpses of the public theatres and markets, had had its element of seclusion, had been a movement within the comparatively narrow official quarter, that all his previous experiences had revolved immediately about the question of his own position. But here was the city at the busiest hours of night, the people to a large extent returned to their own immediate interests, the resumption of the real informal life, the common habits, of the new time.

They emerged at first into a street whose opposite ways were crowded with the blue canvas liveries. This swarm Graham saw was a portion of a procession—it was odd to see a procession parading the city *seated*. They carried banners, coarse red stuff with black letters. "No disarmament," said the banners, for the most part in crudely daubed letters and with variant spellings, and "Why should we disarm?" "No disarming." "No disarming." Banner after banner went by, a stream of banners flowing past, and at last at the end, the song of the revolt and a noisy band of strange instruments. "They all ought to be at work," said Asano. "They have had no food these two days, or they have stolen it."

Presently Asano made a detour to avoid the congested crowd that gaped upon the occasional passage of dead bodies from hospital to a mortuary, the gleanings after death's harvest of the first revolt.

That night few people were sleeping, everyone was abroad. A vast excitement, perpetual crowds perpetually changing, surrounded Graham; his mind was confused and darkened by an incessant tumult, by the cries and enigmatical fragments of the social struggle that was as yet only beginning. Everywhere festoons and banners of black and coloured lights and strange decorations, intensified the quality of his popularity. Everywhere he caught snatches of that crude thick dialect that served the illiterate class, the class, that is, beyond the reach of phonographic culture, in their commonplace intercourse. Everywhere this trouble of disarmament was in the air, with a quality of immediate stress of which he had no inkling during his seclusion in the Wind-Vane quarter. He perceived that as soon as he returned he must discuss this with Ostrog , this and the greater issues of which it was the expression, in a far more conclusive way than he had so far done. Perpetually that night, even in the earlier hours of their wanderings about the city, the spirit of unrest and revolt swamped his attention, to the exclusion of countless strange things he might otherwise have observed.

This preoccupation made his impressions fragmentary. Yet amidst so much that was strange and vivid, no subject, however personal and insistent, could exert undivided sway. There were spaces when the revolutionary movement passed clean out of his mind, was drawn aside like a curtain from before some startling new aspect of the time. Helen had swayed his mind to this intense earnestness of inquiry, but there came a time even when her figure receded beyond his concious thoughts. At one moment, for example, he found they were traversing the religious quarter, for the easy transit about the city afforded by the moving ways rendered sporadic churches and chapels no longer necessary—and his attention was vividly arrested by the façade of one of the Christian sects.

They were travelling seated on one of the swift upper ways, the place leapt upon them at a bend and advanced rapidly towards them. It was covered with inscriptions from top to base, in vivid white and blue, save where a vast and glaring kinematograph transparency presented a realistic crucifixion, and where a vast festoon of black to show that the popular religion followed the popular politics, hung across the lettering. Graham had already become familiar with the phonotype writing and these inscriptions arrested him, being to his sense for the most part almost incredible blasphemy. Among the less offensive were "Salvation on the Third Floor and turn to the Right." "The Sharpest Conversion in London, Expert Operators! Look Slippy!" "Be a Christian—without hindrance to your present Occupation." "Brisk Blessing for Busy Business Men."

"But this is appalling!" said Graham as that deafening scream of mercantile piety towered above them.

"What is appalling?" asked his little officer, apparently seeking vainly for anything unusual in this shrieking enamel.

"*This!* Surely the essence of religion is reverence."

"Oh, *that!*" Asano looked at Graham. "Does it shock you?" he said in the tone of one who makes a discovery. "I suppose it would, of course. I had forgotten. Nowadays the competition for attention is so keen, and people simply haven't the leisure to attend to their souls, you know, as they used to do." He smiled. "In the old days you had quiet Sabbaths and the countryside. Though somewhere I've read of Sunday afternoons that—"

"But, *that*," said Graham, glancing back at the receding blue and white. "That is surely not the only—"

"There are hundreds of different ways. But, of course, if a sect doesn't *tell* it doesn't pay. Worship has moved with the times. There are high-class sects with quieter ways—costly incense and personal attentions and all that. These people are extremely popular and prosperous. They pay several dozen lions for those apartments to the Council—to you I should say."

Graham still felt a difficulty with the coinage, and this mention of a dozen lions brought him abruptly to that matter. In a moment the screaming temples and their swarming touts were forgotten in this new interest. A turn of a phrase suggested, and an answer confirmed the idea that gold and silver were both demonetised, that stamped gold which had begun its reign amidst the merchants of Phoenicia was at last dethroned. The change had been graduated but swift, brought about by an extension of the system of cheques that had even in his previous life already practically superseded gold in all the larger business transactions. The common traffic of the city, the common currency indeed of all the world, was conducted by means of the little brown, green and pink council cheques for small amounts, printed with a blank payee. Asano had several with him, and at the first opportunity he supplied the gaps in his set. They were printed not on tearable paper, but on a semi-transparent fabric of silken flexibility, interwoven with silk. Across them all sprawled a facsimile of Graham's signature, his first encounter with the curves and turns of that familiar autograph for two hundred and three years.

Some intermediary experiences made no impression sufficiently vivid to prevent the matter of the disarmament claiming his thoughts again; a blurred picture of a Theosophist temple that promised MIRACLES in letters of unsteady fire was least submerged perhaps, but then came the view of the dining-hall in Northumberland Avenue. That interested him very greatly.

By the energy and thought of Asano, he was able to view this place from a little screened gallery reserved for the attendants of the tables. The building was pervaded by a distant muffled hooting, piping and bawling, of which he did not at first understand the import, but which recalled a certain mysterious leathery voice he had heard after the resumption of the lights towards the end of his solitary wandering on the night of the great revolt.

He had grown accustomed now to vastness and great numbers of people, nevertheless this spectacle held him for a long time. It was as he watched the table service more immediately beneath, and interspersed with many questions and answers concerning details, that the realisation of the full significance of the feast of several thousand people came to him.

It was his constant surprise to find that points that one might have expected to strike vividly at the very outset never occurred to him until some trivial detail suddenly shaped as a riddle and pointed to the obvious thing he had overlooked. In this matter, for instance, it had not occurred to him that this continuity of the city, this exclusion of weather, these vast halls and ways, involved the disappearance of the household; that the typical Victorian "Home," the little brick cell containing kitchen and scullery, living-rooms and bedrooms, had, save for the ruins that diversified the countryside, vanished as surely as the wattle hut. But now he saw what had indeed been manifest from the first, that London, regarded as a living place, was no longer an aggregation of houses but a prodigious hotel, an hotel with a thousand classes of accommodation, thousands of dining halls, chapels, theatres, markets and places of assembly, a synthesis of enterprises, of which he chiefly was the owner. People had their sleeping rooms, with, it might be, antechambers, rooms that were always sanitary at least whatever the degree of comfort and privacy, and for the rest they lived much as many people had lived in the new-made giant hotels of the Victorian days, eating, reading, thinking, playing, conversing, all in places of public resort, going to their work in the industrial quarters of the city or doing business in their offices in the trading section.

He perceived at once how necessarily this state of affairs had developed from the Victorian city. The fundamental reason for the modern city had ever been the economy of cooperation. The chief thing to prevent the merging of the separate households in his own generation was simply the still imperfect civilisation of the people, the strong barbaric pride, passions, and prejudices, the jealousies, rivalries, and violence of the middle and lower classes, which had necessitated the entire separation of contiguous households. But the change, the taming of the people, had been in rapid progress even then. In his brief thirty years of previous life he had seen

an enormous extension of the habit of consuming meals from home, the casually patronised horse-box coffee-house had given place to the open and crowded Aërated Bread Shop for instance, women's clubs had had their beginning, and an immense development of reading rooms, lounges and libraries had witnessed to the growth of social confidence. These promises had by this time attained to their complete fulfillment. The locked and barred household had passed away.

These people below him belonged, he learnt, to the lower middle class, the class just above the blue labourers, a class so accustomed in the Victorian period to feed with every precaution of privacy that its members, when occasion confronted them with a public meal, would usually hide their embarrassment under horseplay or a markedly militant demeanour. But these gaily, if lightly dressed people below, albeit vivacious, hurried and uncommunicative, were dexterously mannered and certainly quite at their ease with regard to one another.

He noted a slight significant thing. The table, so far as he could see, was and remained delightfully neat, there was nothing to parallel the confusion, the broadcast crumbs, the splashes of viand and condiment, the overturned drink and displaced ornaments, which would have marked the stormy progress of the Victorian meal. The table furniture was very different. There were no ornaments, no flowers, and the table was without a cloth, being made, he learnt, of a solid substance having the texture and appearance of damask. He discerned that this damask substance was patterned with gracefully designed trade advertisements

In a sort of recess before each diner was a complex apparatus of porcelain and metal. There was one plate of white porcelain, and by means of taps for hot and cold volatile fluids the diner washed this himself between the courses; he also washed his elegant white metal knife and fork and spoon as occasion required.

Soup and the chemical wine that was the common drink were delivered by similar taps, and the remaining covers travelled automatically in tastefully arranged dishes down the table along silver rails. The diner stopped these and helped himself at his discretion. They appeared at a little door at one end of the table, and vanished at the other. That turn of democratic sentiment in decay, that ugly pride of menial souls, which renders equals loth to wait on one another, was very strong he found among these people. He was so preoccupied with these details that it was only just as he was leaving the place that he remarked the huge advertisement

Altogether, great and small, there must have been nearly a thousand of these erections,
piping, hooting, bawling, and gabbling in that great space, each with its crowd of excited listeners,
the majority of them men dressed in blue canvas. There were all sizes of machines, from the little
gossiping mechanisms that chuckled out mechanical sarcasm in odd corners, through a number of
grades to such fifty-foot giants as that which had first hooted over Graham.

dioramas that marched majestically along the upper walls and proclaimed the most remarkable commodities.

Beyond this place they came into a crowded hall, and he discovered that cause of the noise that had perplexed him. They paused at a turnstile at which a payment was made.

Graham's attention was immediately arrested by a violent, loud hoot, followed by a vast leathery voice. "The Master is sleeping peacefully," it vociferated. "He is in excellent heath. He is going to devote the rest of his life to Aëronautics. He says women are more beautiful than ever. Haha! Our wonderful civilisation astonishes him beyond measure. Beyond all measure. Haha! He puts great trust in Boss Ostrog, absolute confidence in Boss Ostrog. Ostrog is to be his chief minister; is authorised to remove or reinstate public officers—all patronage will be in his hands. All patronage in the hands of Boss Ostrog! The Councillors have been sent back to their own prison above the Council House."

Graham stopped at the first sentence, and, looking up, beheld a foolish trumpet face from which this was brayed. This was the General Intelligence Machine. For a space it seemed to be gathering breath, and a regular throbbing from its cylindrical body was audible. Then it trumpeted "Galloop, Galloop," and broke out again.

"Paris is now pacified. All resistance is over. Haha! The black police hold every position of importance in the city. They fought with great bravery, singing songs written in praise of their ancestors by the poet Kipling. Once or twice they got out of hand, and tortured and mutilated wounded and captured insurgents, men and women. Moral—don't go rebelling. Haha! Galloop, Galloop. They are lively fellows. Let this be a lesson to the disorderly banderlog of the city. Galloop, Galloop."

The voice ceased. There was a confused murmur of disapproval among the crowd. "Damned niggers." A man began to harangue near them. "Is this the Master's doing, brothers? Is this the Master?"

"Black police!" said Graham. "What is that? You don't mean——"

Asano touched his arm and gave him a warning look, and forthwith another of these mechanisms screamed deafeningly and gave tongue in a shrill voice. "Yahahah, Yahah, Yap! Hear a live paper yelp! Live paper. Yaha! Shocking outrage in Paris. Yahahah! The Parisians exasperated by the black police to the pitch of assassinating them. Dreadful reprisals. Savage times come again. Yaha!" The nearer Babble Machine hooted stupendously, "Galloop, Galloop," drowned the end of the sentence, and proceeded

in a rather flatter note than before with novel comments on the horrors of disorder. "Law and order must be maintained," said the nearer Babble Machine.

"But," began Graham.

"Don't ask questions here," said Asano, "or you will be involved in an argument."

"Then let us go on," said Graham, "for I want to know more of this."

As he and his companion pushed their way through the excited crowd that swarmed beneath these voices, towards the exit, Graham conceived more clearly the proportion and features of this room. Altogether, great and small, there must have been nearly a thousand of these erections, piping, hooting, bawling and gabbling in that great space, each with its crowd of excited listeners, the majority of them men dressed in blue canvas. There were all sizes of machines, from the little gossiping mechanisms that chuckled out mechanical sarcasm in odd corners, through a number of grades to such fifty-foot giants at that which had first hooted over Graham.

This place was unusually crowded, because of the intense public interest in the course of affairs in Paris. Evidently the struggle had been much more savage than Ostrog had represented it. All the mechanisms were discoursing upon that topic, and the repetition of the people made the huge hive buzz with such phrases as "Lynched policemen," "Women burnt alive," "Fuzzy wuzzy." "But does the Master allow such things?" asked a man near him. "Is *this* the beginning of the Master's rule?"

Is *this* the beginning of the Master's rule? For a long time after he had left the place, the hooting, whistling and braying of the machines pursued him, "Galloop, Galloop, Yahaha, Yaha, Yap!"

Directly they were out upon the ways he began to question Asano closely on the nature of the Parisian struggle. "This disarmament! What was their trouble? What does it all mean?"

Asano seemed chiefly anxious to reassure him that it was "all right."

"But these outrages!"

"You cannot have an omelet," said Asano, "without breaking eggs. It is only the rough people. Only in one part of the city. All the rest is all right. The Parisian labourers are the wildest in the world, except ours."

"What! the Londoners?"

"No, the Japanese. They have to be kept in order."

"But burning women alive!"

"A Commune!" said Asano. "They would rob you of your property. They would do away with property and give the world over to mob rule. You are Master, the world is yours. But there will be no Commune here. There is no need for black police here."

"I did not think," began Graham, and stopped abruptly. He went off at a tangent to ask for information about these Babble Machines. For the most part, the crowd present had been shabbily or even raggedly dressed, and Graham learnt that so far as the more prosperous classes were concerned, in all the more comfortable private apartments of the city were fixed Babble Machines that would speak directly a lever was pulled. The tenant of the apartment could connect this with the cables of any of the great News Syndicates that he preferred. When he learnt this presently, he demanded the reason of their absence from his own suite of apartments. Asano stared. "I never thought," he said. "Ostrog must have had them removed."

"They must be replaced directly I return," said Graham.

He found a certain difficulty in understanding that both this news-room and the dining-hall were not great central places, that such establishments were repeated almost beyond counting all over the city. But ever and again during the night's expedition his ear, in some new quarter, would pick out from the tumult of the ways the peculiar hooting of the organ of Boss Ostrog, "Galloop, Galloop!" or the shrill "Yahaha, Yaha, Yap!—Hear a live paper yelp!" of its chief rival.

Repeated too, everywhere, were such *crèches* as the one he now entered. It was reached by a lift, and by a glass bridge that flung across the dining-hall and traversed the ways at a slight upward angle. To enter the first section of the place necessitated the use of his solvent signature under Asano's direction. They were immediately attended to by a man in a violet robe and gold clasp, the insignia of practising medical men. He perceived from this man's manner that his identity was known, and proceeded to ask questions on the strange arrangements of the place without reserve.

On either side of the passage, which was silent and padded, as if to deaden the footfall, were narrow little doors, their size and arrangement suggestive of the cells of a Victorian prison. But the upper portion of each door was of the same greenish transparent stuff that had enclosed him at his awakening, and within, dimly seen, lay, in every case, a very young baby in a little nest of wadding. Elaborate apparatus watched the atmosphere and rang a bell far away in the central office at the slightest departure from the optimum of temperature and moisture. A system

of such *crèches* had almost entirely replaced the hazardous adventures of the old-world nursing. The attendant presently called Graham's attention to the wet nurses, a vista of mechanical figures, with arms, shoulders, and breasts of astonishingly realistic modelling, articulation, and texture, but mere brass tripods below, and having in the place of features a flat disc bearing advertisements likely to be of interest to mothers.

Of all the strange things that Graham came upon that night, none jarred more upon his habits of thought than this place. The spectacle of the little pink creatures, their feeble limbs swaying uncertainly in vague first movements, left alone, without embrace or endearment, was wholly repugnant to him. The attendant doctor was of a different opinion. His statistical evidence showed beyond dispute that in the Victorian time that most dangerous passage of life was in the arms of the mother, that there human mortality had ever been most terrible. On the other hand this *crèche* company, the International Crèche Syndicate, lost not one-half per cent of the million babies or so that formed its peculiar care. But Graham's prejudice was too strong even for these figures.

Along one of the many passages of the place they presently came upon a young couple in the usual blue canvas peering through the transparency and laughing hysterically at the bald head of their first-born. Graham's face must have showed his estimate of them, for their merriment ceased and they looked abashed. But this little incident accentuated his sudden realisation of the gulf between his habits of thought and the ways of the new age. He passed on to the crawling-rooms and the Kindergarten, perplexed and distressed. He found the endless long playrooms were empty! the latter-day children at least still spent their nights in sleep. As they went through these the little officer pointed out the character of the toys, developments of those devised by that inspired sentimentalist Froebel. There were nurses here, but much was done by machines that sang and danced and dandled.

Graham was still not clear upon many points. "But so many orphans, " he said perplexed, reverting to a first misconception, and learnt again that they were not orphans.

So soon as they had left the *crèche* he began to speak of the horror the babies in their incubating cases had caused him. "Is motherhood gone?" he said. "Was it a cant? Surely it was an instinct. This seems so unnatural—abominable almost."

"Along here we shall come to the dancing place," said Asano, by way of reply. "It is sure to be crowded. In spite of all the political unrest it will be crowded. The women take no great interest in politics—except a few here and there. You will see the mothers—most young women of the middle class in London are mothers. It is considered a creditable thing to have a child—a proof of animation. As for motherhood! They still take an immense pride in the children—if they are nice. They come here to look at them quite often."

The air was suddenly dancing with music, and down a way they approached obliquely, set with gorgeous pillars as it seemed of clear amethyst, flowed a concourse of gay people and a tumult of merry cries and laughter. He saw curled heads, wreathed brows, and a happy, intricate flutter of gamboge passed triumphant across the picture.

"You will see," said Asano with a faint smile. "The world has changed. In a moment you will see the mothers of the new age. Come this way. We shall see them yonder again very soon."

They ascended a certain height in a swift lift, and changed to a slower one. As they went on the music grew upon them, until it was near and full and splendid, and, moving with its glorious intricacies, they could distinguish the beat of innumerable dancing feet. They made a payment at a turnstile, and emerged upon the wide gallery that overlooked the dancing place, and upon the full enchantment of sound and sight.

"Here," said Asano, "are the fathers and mothers of the little ones you saw."

The hall was not so richly decorated as that of the Atlas, but saving that, it was, for its size, the most splendid Graham had seen. The beautiful white-limbed figures that supported the galleries reminded him once more of the restored magnificence of sculpture; they seemed to writhe in engaging attitudes, their faces laughed. The source of the music that filled the place was hidden, and the whole vast shining floor was thick with dancing couples. "Look at them," said the little officer. "See how much they show of motherhood."

The gallery they stood upon ran along the upper edge of a huge screen that cut the dancing hall on one side from a sort of outer hall that showed through broad arches the incessant onward rush of the city ways. In this outer hall was a great crowd of less brilliantly dressed people, as numerous almost as those who danced within, the great majority wearing the blue uniform of the Labour Company that was now so familiar to Graham. Unable to pass the turnstiles to the festival, they were yet unable to keep away from the sound of its seductions. Some of them even had cleared spaces, and were dancing also, flut-

tering their rags in the air. Some shouted as they danced, jests and odd allusions Graham did not understand. Once someone began whistling the refrain of the revolutionary song, but it seemed as though that beginning was promptly suppressed. The corner was dark and Graham could not see. He turned to the hall again. Great black festoons and eloquent sentiments reinforced the huge inscription that partially defaced the upper end of the dancing place, and asserted that "The Festival of the Awakening" was in progress.

"Myriads are taking holiday or staying from work because of that, quite apart from the labourers who refuse to go back," said Asano. "These people are always ready for holidays. And, of course, no one blames them. What is life for but pleasure?"

Graham walked to the parapet and stood leaning over, looking down at the dancers. Save for two or three remote whispering couples, who had stolen apart, he and his guide had the gallery to themselves. A warm breath of scent and vitality came up to him. Both men and women below were lightly clad, bare-armed, open-necked, as the universal warmth of the city permitted. Many of the women were pretty, and all were dressed with elaborate coquetry.

"What sort of people are these?" he asked abruptly.

"Workers—prosperous workers. What you would have called the middle class. Independent tradesmen with little separate businesses have vanished long ago, but there are store servers, managers, engineers of a hundred sorts. To-night is a holiday, of course, and every dancing place in the city will be crowded, and every place of worship."

"But—the women?"

"The same. There's a thousand forms of work for women now. But you had the beginning of the independent working woman in your days. Most women are independent now. Most of these are married more or less, and that gives them more money, and enables them to enjoy such delights as these."

"I see," said Graham looking at the flushed faces, the flash and swirl of movement, and still thinking of that nightmare of pink, helpless limbs. "And these are—mothers."

"Most of them."

Graham stood looking down.

"The more I see of these things," he said, "the more complex I find your problems. This, for instance, is a surprise. That news from Paris was a surprise."

In a little while he spoke again:

"These are mothers. Presently, I suppose, I shall get into the modern way of seeing things. I have old habits of mind clinging about me — habits based, I suppose, on needs that are over and done with. Of course, in our time, a woman was supposed not only to bear children, but to cherish them, to devote herself to them, to educate them — all the essentials of moral and mental education a child owed to its mother. Or went without. Quite a number, I admit, went without. Nowadays, clearly, there is no more need for such care than if they were butterflies. I see that! Only there was an ideal — that figure of a grave, patient woman, silently and serenely mistress of home, mother and maker of men — to love her was a sort of worship——"

He stopped, and repeated, "A sort of worship."

"Ideals change," said the little man, "as needs change."

Graham awoke from an instant reverie, and Asano repeated his words. Graham's mind returned to the things at hand.

"Of course, I see the perfect reasonableness of this. Restraint, soberness, the matured thought, the unselfish act, they are necessities of the barbarous state, the life of dangers. Dourness is man's tribute to unconquered nature. But man has conquered nature now for all practical purposes, his political affairs are managed by Bosses with a black police — and life is joyous."

He looked at the dancers again. "Joyous," he said.

"There are weary moments," said the little officer reflectively.

"They all look young. Down there I should be visibly the oldest man. And in my own time I should have passed as middle-aged."

"They are young. There are few old people in this class in the work cities."

"How is that?"

"Old people's lives are not so pleasant as they used to be, unless they are rich to hire lovers and helpers. And we have an institution called Euthanasy."

"Euthanasy!" said Graham. "The easy death?"

"The easy death. It is the last pleasure. The Euthanasy Company does it well. People will pay the sum — it is a costly thing — long beforehand, go off to some pleasure city and return impoverished and weary, very weary."

"There is a lot left for me to understand," said Graham, after a pause. "Yet I see the logic of it. I see the logic of it all. As you say, what pleasure is there in life but pleasure? It's clear — and it's unsympathetic. All our array of angry virtues and sour restraints was the offspring of danger and insecurity. The Stoic, the Puritan, even in my time, were vanishing types. In the old days

man was armed against Pain, now he is eager for Pleasure. There lies the difference. Civilization has driven Pain and Danger so far off — for well-to-do people. And only well-to-do people matter. I have been asleep two hundred years."

For a minute they leant on the balustrading, following the intricate evolutions of the dance, and indeed the scene was very beautiful.

"I am King of this world," said Graham suddenly. "And before God, I would rather be a wounded sentinel freezing in the snow than one of these dancing fools!"

He turned abruptly on the little officer and was half surprised to meet an answering light in the sloping eyes. "When one is grieved," said Asano thoughtfully, "one thinks like that — even in these days."

"I am uncivilised," said Graham. "That is the trouble. I am primitive — Palaeolithic. *Their* fountain of rage and fear and anger is sealed and closed, the habits of a lifetime make them cheerful and easy and delightful. You must bear with my nineteenth century shocks and disgusts. These people, you say, are skilled workers and so forth. And while these dance, men are fighting — men are dying in Paris to keep the world — that they may dance."

"For that matter, men are dying in London," said Asano.

There was a moment's silence.

"Where do these sleep?" asked Graham.

"Above and below — an intricate warren."

"And where do they work? This is — the domestic life."

"You will see little work to-night. Half the workers are out or under arms. Half these people are keeping holiday. But we will go to the work places if you wish it."

For a time Graham watched the dancers, then suddenly turned away. "I want to see the workers. I have seen enough of these," he said.

Asano led the way along the gallery across the dancing hall. Presently they came to a transverse passage that brought a breath of fresher, colder air.

Asano glanced at this passage as they went past, stopped, went back to it, and turned to Graham with a faint smile. "Here, Sire," he said, " is something — will be familiar to you at least — and yet —— But I will not tell you. Come!"

He led the way along a closed passage that presently became cold. The reverberation of their feet told that this passage was a bridge. They came into a circular gallery that was glazed in from the outer weather, and so reached a circular chamber which seemed familiar, though Graham could not recall distinctly when he had entered it before. In this was a ladder—the first ladder he had seen since his awakening—up which they went, and came into a high, dark, cold place in which was another almost vertical ladder. This they ascended, Graham still perplexed. But at the top he understood, and recognised the metallic bars to which he clung. He was in the cage under the ball of St. Paul's. The dome rose but a little way above the general contours of the city into the still twilight, and sloped away, shining greasily under a few distant lights, into a circumambient ditch of darkness.

Out between the bars he looked upon the wind-clear northern sky and saw the starry constellations all unchanged. Capella hung in the west, Vega was rising, and the seven glittering points of the Great Bear swept overhead in their stately circle about the Pole.

He saw these stars in a clear gap of sky. To the east and south the great circular shapes of complaining wind-wheels blotted out the heavens, so that the glare about the Council House was hidden. To the south-west he saw Orion like a pallid ghost through the tracery of ironwork and interlacing shapes, overhanging a dazzling coruscation of lights about the aëroplane stages. A bellowing and siren screaming that came therefrom warned the world that one of these appliances was ready to start. He remained for a space gazing towards that brilliance. Then his eyes went back to the northward constellations.

For a long time he was silent. "This," he said at last, smiling in the shadow, "seems the strangest thing of all. These old, familiar, silent, shining stars!"

And thence Graham was taken along devious ways to the great gambling and business quarters where the bulk of the fortunes in the city were lost and made. It impressed him as a wellnigh interminable series of very high halls, surrounded by tiers upon tiers of galleries into which opened thousands of offices, and traversed by a complicated multitude of bridges, footways, aërial motor rails, and trapeze and cable leaps. And here more than anywhere the note of vehement vitality, of uncontrollable, hasty activity, rose high. Everywhere was violent advertisement, until his brain swam at the tumult of light and colour. And Babble Machines of a peculiarly rancid tone were abundant and filled the air with strenuous squealing and an idiotic slang. "Skin your eyes and slide!" "Gewhoop, Bonanza!" "Gollipers come and hark!" The place seemed to him to be dense with people either dreadfully agitated or swelling with obscure cunning, yet he learnt that the place was comparatively empty, that the great

political convulsion of the last few days had reduced transactions to an unprecedented minimum. In one huge place were long avenues of roulette tables, each with an excited, undignified crowd about it; in another a yelping Babel of white-faced women and red-necked leathery-lunged men bought and sold the shares of an absolutely fictitious business undertaking which, every five minutes, paid a dividend of ten per cent, and cancelled a certain proportion of its shares by means of a lottery wheel. These business activities were prosecuted with an energy that readily passed into violence, and Graham approaching a dense crowd found at its centre a couple of prominent merchants in violent controversy with teeth and nails on some delicate point of business etiquette. Something still remained in life to be fought for. Further he had a shock at a vehement announcement in phonetic letters of scarlet flame, each twice the height of a man, that "WE ASSURE THE PROPRIETOR. WE ASSURE THE PROPRIETOR."

"Who's the proprietor?" he asked.

"You."

"But what do they assure me?" he asked. "What do they assure me?"

"Didn't you have assurance?"

Graham thought. "Insurance?"

"Yes—Insurance—I remember that was the older word. They are insuring your life. Dozands of people are taking out policies, myriads of lions are being put on you. And further on other people are buying annuities. They do that on everybody who is at all prominent. Look there!"

A crowd of people surged and roared, and Graham saw a vast black screen suddenly illuminated in still larger letters of burning purple. "Anuetes on the Propraitor—†5 pr. G." The people began to boo and shout at this, a number of hardbreathing, wild-eyed men came running past, clawing with hooked fingers at the air. There was a furious crush about a little doorway.

Asano did a brief calculation. "Seventeen per cent. per annum is their annuity on you. They would not pay so much per cent. if they could see you now, Sire. But they do not know. Your own annuities used to be a very safe investment, but now you are sheer gambling, of course. This is probably a desperate bid. I doubt if people will get their money."

The crowd of would-be annuitants grew so thick about them that for some time they could move neither forward nor backward. Graham noticed what appeared to him to be a high proportion of women among the speculators, and was reminded again of the economic independence of their sex. They seemed remarkably well able to take care of themselves in the crowd, using their elbows with particular skill, as he learnt to his cost. One curly-headed person caught in the pressure for a space, looked steadfastly at him several times, almost as if she recognised him, and then, edging deliberately twoards him, touched his hand with her arm in a scarcely accidental manner, and made it plain by a look as ancient as Chaldea, that he had found favour in her eyes. And then a lank, grey-bearded man, perspiring copiously in a noble passion of self-help, thrust between them in a cataclysmal rush towards that alluring "†pr. G."

"I want to get out of this," said Graham to Asano. "This is not what I came to see. Show me the workers. I want to see the people in blue. These parasitic lunatics——"

He found himself wedged in a struggling mass of people, and this hopeful sentence went unfinished.

CHAPTER XXI.

THE UNDER SIDE

AND from the Middle Class Quarter they presently passed by the running ways into a remote quarter of the city, where the bulk of the manufactures was done. On their way the platforms crossed the Thames twice, and passed in a broad viaduct across one of the great roads that entered the city from the North. In both cases his impression was swift and in both very vivid. The river was a broad wrinkled glitter of black water, over-arched by buildings, and vanishing either way into a blackness starred with receding lights. A string of black barges passed seaward, manned by blue-clad men. The road was a long and very broad and high tunnel along which big-wheeled machines drove noiselessly and swiftly. Here, too, the distinctive blue of the Labour Company was in abundance. The smoothness of the double tracks, the largeness and the lightness of the big pneumatic wheels in proportion to the vehicular body, struck Graham most vividly. One lank and very high carriage with longitudinal metallic rods hung with the carcases of many hundred sheep arrested his attention unduly. Abruptly the edge of the archway cut and blotted out the picture.

Presently they left the way and descended by a lift and traversed a passage that sloped downward, and so came to a descending lift again. The appearance of things changed. Even the pretence of architectural ornament disappeared, the lights diminished in number and size, as the factory quarters were reached. And in the dusty biscuit-making place of the potters, among the

felspar mills, in the furnace rooms of the metal workers, among the incandescent lakes of crude Eadhamite, the blue canvas clothing was on men, women, and children.

Many of these great and dusty galleries were silent avenues of machinery, endless ashen furnaces testified to the revolutionary dislocation, but wherever there was work it was being done by slow-moving workers in blue canvas. The only people not in blue canvas were the overlookers of the work-places and the orange-clad Labour Police. And fresh from the flushed faces of the dancing halls, the voluntary vigours of the business quarters, Graham could note the pinched faces, the feeble muscles, and weary eyes of many of the latter-day workers. Such as he saw at work were noticeably inferior in physique to the few gaily dressed managers and forewomen who were directing their labours. The burly labourers of the old Victorian times had followed the dray horse and all such living force producers to extinction; the place of his costly muscles was taken by some dexterous machine. The latter-day labourer, male as well as female, was essentially a machine minder and feeder, a servant and attendant, or an artist—under direction. The women, in comparison with those Graham remembered, were as a class distinctly plain and flat-chested. Two hundred years of emancipation from the moral restraints of Puritanical religion, two hundred years of city life, had done their work in eliminating the strain of feminine beauty and vigour from the blue canvas myriads. To be brilliant physically or mentally, to be in any way attractive or exceptional, had been and was still a certain way of emancipation to the drudge, a line of escape to the Pleasure City and its splendours and delights, and at last to the Euthanasy and peace. In the young cities of his former life, the newly aggregated labouring mass had been a diverse multitude, still stirred by the tradition of personal honour and a high morality; now it was differentiating into a distinct class, with a physical difference of its own—even with a dialect of its own.

They penetrated downwards towards the working places. Presently they passed underneath one of the streets of the moving ways, and saw its platforms running on their rails far overhead, and chinks of white light between the transverse slits. The factories that were not working were sparsely lighted; to Graham they and their shrouded aisles of giant machines seemed plunged in gloom, and even where work was going on the illumination was far less brilliant than upon the public ways.

Beyond the blazing lakes of Eadhamite he

Graham hears with horror the people shouting on the ways, "Ostrog has ordered the Black Police to London."

came to the warren of the jewellers, and, with some difficulty and by using his signature, obtained admission to these galleries. They were high and dark, and rather cold. In the first men were making ornaments of gold filigree, each man at a little bench by himself, and with a little shaded light. The long vista of light patches, with the nimble fingers brightly lit and moving among the gleaming yellow coils, and the intent face, like the face of a ghost, in each shadow, had the oddest effect. The work was beautifully executed, but without any strength of modelling or drawing, for the most part intricate grotesques or the ringing of the changes on a geometrical *motif.* These workers wore a peculiar white uniform without pockets or sleeves. They assumed this on coming to work, but at night they were stripped and examined before they left the premises of the company. In spite of every precaution, the Labour policeman told them in a depressed tone, the company was not infrequently robbed.

Beyond was a gallery of women busied in cutting and setting slabs of artificial ruby, and next these were men and women busied together upon the slabs of copper net that formed the basis of *cloisonné* tiles. Many of these workers had lips and nostrils a livid white, due to a disease caused by a peculiar purple enamel that chanced to be much in fashion. Asano apologised to Graham for the offence of their faces, but excused himself on the score of the convenience of this route. "This is what I wanted to see," said Graham; "this is what I wanted to see," trying to avoid a start at a particularly striking disfigurement that suddenly stared him in the face.

They continued along one of the lower galleries of this *cloisonné* factory, and came to a little bridge that spanned a vault. Looking over the parapet, Graham saw that beneath was a wharf under tremendous archings, archings like those of a Gargantuan cellar. Three barges, smothered in floury dust, were being unloaded of their cargoes of powdered felspar by a multitude of coughing men, each guiding a little truck; the dust filled the place with a choking mist, and turned the electric glare yellow. The vague shadows of these workers gesticulated about their feet, and rushed to and fro against a long stretch of whitewashed wall. A shadowy, huge mass of masonry rising out of the inky water, brought to Graham's mind the thought of the multitude of ways and galleries and lifts, that rose floor above floor overhead between him and the sky. The men worked in silence under the supervision of two of the Labour Police; their feet made a hollow thunder on the planks along which they went to and fro. And as he looked at

this scene, some voice hidden in the darkness began to sing.

"Stop that!" shouted one of the policemen, but the order was disobeyed, and first one and then all the white-stained men who were working there had taken up the beating refrain, singing it defiantly, the Song of the Revolt. The feet upon the planks thundered now to the rhythm of the song, tramp, tramp, tramp. The policeman who had shouted glanced at his fellow, and Graham saw him shrug his shoulders. He made no further effort to stop the singing.

And so they went through these factories and places of toil, seeing many painful and grim things. But why should the gentle reader be depressed? Surely to a refined mind our present world is distressing enough without bothering ourselves about the miseries to come. That walk left on Graham's mind a maze of memories, fluctuating pictures of swathed halls, and crowded vaults seen through clouds of dust, of intricate machines, the racing threads of looms, the heavy beat of stamping machinery, the roar and rattle of belt and armature, of ill-lit subterranean aisles of sleeping places, illimitable vistas of pin-point lights. And here the smell of tanning, and here the reek of a brewery. And everywhere were pillars and cross archings of such a massiveness as Graham had never before seen, thick Titans of greasy shining brickwork crushed beneath the vast weight of that complex city world, even as these anaemic millions were crushed by its complexity. And everywhere were pale features, lean limbs, disfigurement and degradation.

Once and again, and again a third time, Graham heard the song of the revolt during his long unpleasant research in these places, and once he saw a confused struggle down a passage, and learnt that a number of these serfs had seized their bread before their work was done. Graham was ascending towards the ways again when he saw a number of blue-clad children running down a transverse passage, and presently perceived the reason of their panic in a company of the Labour Police armed with clubs, trotting towards some unknown disturbance. And then came a remote disorder. But for the most part this remnant that worked hopelessly. All the spirit that was left in fallen humanity was above in the streets that night, calling for the Master, and valiantly and noisily keeping its arms.

They emerged from these wanderings and stood blinking in the bright light of the middle passage of the platforms again. They became aware of the remote hooting and yelping of the machines of one of the General Intelligence Offices, and suddenly came men running, and along the platforms and about the ways everywhere was a shouting and crying. "What has happened now?" said Graham puzzled, for he could not understand their thick speech. But the thing that everyone was shouting, that men yelled to one another, that women took up screaming, that was passing like the first breeze of a thunderstorm, chill and sudden through the city, was this: "Ostrog has ordered the Black Police to London. The Black Police are coming from South Africa. The Master is to be guarded by the Black Police." Asano hesitated, came to some swift decision, and told him the thing they cried.

Graham heard someone shouting, "Stop all work! Stop all work!" and a swarthy hunchback, ridiculously gay in green and gold, came leaping down the platforms towards him, bawling again and again in good English, "This is Ostrog's doing, Ostrog, the Knave! The Master is betrayed."

For a moment Graham stood still, for it came upon him that these things were a dream. He looked up at the great cliff of buildings on either side, vanishing into blue haze at last above the lights, and down to the roaring tiers of platforms, and the shouting running people who were gesticulating past. "The Master is betrayed!" they cried. "The Master is betrayed!" Suddenly the situation shaped itself in his mind; Ostrog had disobeyed. His heart began to beat fast and strong.

"It has come," he said. "I might have known. The hour has come."

He looked at Asano in sudden doubt.

"I did not know," said Asano simply; "or I would have told you. For I am on your side, Master, and not on Ostrog's. I have made my choice. I am on your side."

Graham thought swiftly. "If you are against me——" he said, and left the sentence unfinished. "What am I to do?"

"Go back to the Council House," said Asano.

"Why not appeal——? The people are here."

"You will lose time. They will doubt if it is you. But they will mass about the Council House. There you will find their leaders. Your strength is there—with them."

"Suppose this is only a rumour?"

"It sounds true," said Asano.

"Let us have the facts," asked Graham.

Asano shrugged his shoulders. "We had better get towards the Council House," he cried. "That is where they will swarm. Even now the ruins may be impassable."

They went up the stepped platforms to the swifter one, and there Asano accosted a labourer. The answers to his questions were in the thick vulgar speech.

"What did he say?" asked Graham.

"He knows little, but he told me that the Black Police would have arrived here before the people knew—had not someone in the Wind-Vane Offices learnt. He said a girl."

"A girl? Not——?"

"He said a girl. Who came out from the Council House crying aloud, and told the men at work among the ruins."

CHAPTER XXII.
IN THE ATLAS CHAMBER

AS Asano and Graham hurried along the ways to the ruins about the Council House, they saw everywhere the excitement of the people rising. Everywhere men and women in blue were hurrying from unknown subterranean employments, up the staircases of the middle path; at one place Graham saw an arsenal of the revolutionary committee besieged by a crowd of shouting men, at another a couple of men in the hated yellow uniform of the Labour Police, pursued by a gathering crowd, fled precipitately along the swift way that went in the opposite direction.

The cries of "No niggers!" "Curse the niggers!" and "The Master is betrayed!" became at last a continuous shouting as they drew near the Government quarter. Many of the shouts were unintelligible. "Ostrog has betrayed us!" one man bawled in a hoarse voice, again and again, dinning that refrain into Graham's ear until it haunted him. This person stayed close beside Graham and Asano on the swift way, shouting to the people who swarmed on the lower platforms as he rushed past them. Presently he went leaping down and disappeared.

The way to the Council House across the ruins was impassable, but Asano met that difficulty and took Graham into the premises of the central post office. The post office was nominally at work, but the blueclothed porters moved sluggishly or had stopped to stare through the arches of their galleries at the shouting men who were going by outside. Here, by Asano's advice, Graham revealed his identity. They crossed at once to the Council House by a cable cradle. Already, in the brief interval since the capitulation of the Councillors a great change had been wrought in the appearance of the ruins. The spurting cascades of the ruptured watermains had been captured and tamed, and huge temporary pipes ran overhead along a flimsy-looking fabric of girders. The sky was laced with the cables and wires that served the Council House, and a mass of new fabric, with great cranes and other building machines going to and fro upon it, projected to the left of the white pile.

The moving ways that ran across this area had been restored, albeit for once running under the open sky. These were the ways that Graham had seen from the little balcony in the hour of his awakening, not nine days since, and the hall of his Trance had been on the further side where shapeless piles of smashed and shattered masonry were how heaped together.

It was already high day and the sun was shining brightly. Out of their tall caverns of blue electric light came the swift ways, crowded with multitudes of people who poured off them and gathered ever denser over the wreckage and confusion of the ruins. The air was full of their shouting, and they were pressing and swaying towards the central building. For the most part that shouting blue mass consisted of shapeless swarms, but here and there Graham could see that a rude discipline struggled to establish itself.

The cable carried them into a hall which Graham recognised as the ante-chamber to the Hall of the Atlas, about the gallery of which he had walked days ago with Howard to show himself to the vanished Council, an hour from his awakening. Now the place was empty except for two cable attendants who seemed hugely astonished to recognise the Sleeper in the man who swung down from the cross seat. "Where is Helen Wotton?" he demanded. "Where is Helen Wotton?" They did not know. "Then where is Ostrog? I must see Ostrog forthwith. He has disobeyed me. I have come back to take things out of his hands." Without waiting for Asano, he went straight across the place, ascended the steps at the further end, and, pulling the curtain aside, found himself facing the white Titan.

The hall was empty. Its appearance had changed very greatly since his first sight of it. It had suffered serious injury in the violent struggle of the first outbreak. On the right-hand side of the great figure the upper half of the wall had been torn away for nearly two hundred feet of its length, and a sheet of the same glassy green film that had enclosed Graham at his awakening had been drawn across the gap. This deadened but did not altogether exclude the roar of the people outside. Through it there were visible the beams and supports of metal scaffoldings that rose and fell according to the requirements of a great crowd of workmen. A dexterous, loud-hissing building machine, with lank arms of red painted metal that caught the still plastic blocks of mineral paste and swung them neatly into position, moved at intervals across this green-tinted picture. For a moment he stood regarding these things, and Asano overtook him.

"Ostrog," said Asano, "will be in the small offices beyond there." They had scarcely advanced ten paces from the curtain before a little panel to the left of the Atlas rolled up, and Ostrog, accompanied by Lincoln and followed by two black and yellow attendants, appeared crossing the remote corner of the hall, towards a second panel that was raised and open. "Ostrog," shouted Graham, and at the sound of his voice the little party turned. Ostrog said something to Lincoln and advanced alone.

Graham was the first to speak. "What is this I hear?" he asked. "Are you bringing negroes here—to keep the people down?"

"It is none too soon," said Ostrog. "They have been getting out of hand more and more, since the revolt. I underestimated——"

"Do you mean that these negroes are on the way?"

"They may be starting now. As it is, you have seen the people —outside?"

"No wonder! But—after what was said. You have taken too much on yourself, Ostrog."

Ostrog said nothing.

"These negroes must not come to London," said Graham.

Ostrog glanced at Lincoln, who at once came towards them, with his two attendants close behind him. Asano drew close to Graham. "Why not?" asked Ostrog.

"White men must be mastered by white men."

"The negroes are only an instrument."

"But that is not the question. I am the Master. I mean to be the Master. And I say these negroes shall not come."

"The people——"

"I believe in the people."

"Because you are an anachronism. You are a man out of the Past—an accident. You are Owner perhaps of half the property in the world. But you are not Master. You do not know enough to be Master."

Ostrog glanced at Lincoln again. "I know now what you think—I can guess something of what you mean to do. Even now it is not too late to warn you. You dream of human equality—of a socialistic order—you have all those worn out dreams of the nineteenth century fresh and vivid in your mind, and you would rule this age that you do not understand."

"Listen!" said Graham. "You can hear it—a sound like the sea. Not voices—but a voice. Do *you* altogether understand?"

"We taught them that song," said Ostrog.

"Perhaps. Can you teach them to forget it? But enough of this! These negroes must not come."

There was a pause, and Ostrog looked him in the eyes.

"They will," he said.

"I forbid it," said Graham.

"No," said Ostrog. "Sorry as I am to follow the method of the Council—— For your own good—you must not side with—Disorder."

Lincoln laid his hand on Graham's shoulder. Then Asano had stepped forward and thrown Lincoln's arm aside. Something flashed, and Graham saw this something was a razor like blade, fantastically engraved, that the little Japanese had drawn. Lincoln recoiled, the attendants seemed to hesitate.

"Go back!" said Asano very quickly to Graham. "Go back. You are in his hands here. Get back to the people."

For a moment Graham did not understand. Then he saw Ostrog's face. "Look!" he said, and Asano half turned as Ostrog gripped the wrist and throat of the Japanese.

Graham suddenly understood Asano. He turned towards the curtains that separated the hall from the ante-chamber. The clutching hand of one of the black and yellow attendants intervened. In another moment Lincoln had grasped his cloak. He turned and struck at Lincoln's face, and incontinently an attendant had him by collar and arm. He wrenched himself away, his sleeve tore noisily, and he stumbled back, to be tripped by the other man. As he went down he saw Asano's knife descend on Ostrog's wrist, and then he was staring at the distant ceiling of the hall.

He rolled over, struggling fiercely, and suddenly one of the attendants shrieked and went down under Asano with the knife driving the blood before it through the side of the neck. The other attendant sprang to secure the blade, and Graham struggled to his feet.

Lincoln appeared before him, and went down heavily again with a blow under the point of the jaw. Graham made two strides, stumbled. And then Ostrog's arm, dripping blood, was round his neck, he was pulled over backward, fell heavily, and his arms were pinned to the ground. After a few violent efforts he ceased to struggle and lay staring at Ostrog's heaving throat and wondering what had become of Asano.

"You—are—a prisoner," panted Ostrog.

Graham tried to see what had happened to Asano, and turning his head perceived through the irregular green window in the walls of the hall the men who had been working the building cranes gesticulating excitedly to people unseen. A bullet smashed among the mouldings above the Atlas. The two sheets of transparent matter that had been stretched across this gap were rent, the edges of the torn aperture darkened, curved, ran rapidly towards the framework, and in a moment the Council chamber stood open to the air. A chilly gust blew in by the gap, bringing with it a war of voices from the ruinous spaces without, an elvish babblement, "Save the Master!" "What are they doing?" "The Master is betrayed!"

And then he realised that Ostrog's attention was distracted, that Ostrog's grip had relaxed, and, wrenching his arms free, he struggled to his knees. In another moment he had thrust Ostrog back, and he was on one foot, his hand gripping Ostrog's throat, and Ostrog's hands clutching the silk about his neck.

But now men were coming towards them from beyond the dais—men whose intentions he misunderstood. He had a glimpse of someone running in the distance towards the curtains of the antechamber, and then Ostrog had slipped from him and these newcomers were upon him. They thrust and pulled him to his infinite astonishment. They obeyed the shouts of Ostrog.

He was lugged a dozen yards before he realised that they were dragging him towards the open panel. When he saw this he pulled back, he tried to fling himself down, he shouted for help with all his strength. There were answering cries.

The grip upon his neck relaxed, and behold! in the lower corner of the rent upon the wall, first one and then a number of little black figures appeared shouting and waving arms. They came leaping down from the gap into the light gallery that had led to the Silent Rooms. They ran along it, so near that Graham could see the weapons in their hands. Then Ostrog was shouting in his ear to the men who held him, and once more he was struggling with all his strength against their endeavours to thrust him towards the opening that yawned to receive him. "They can't come down," shouted Ostrog. "They daren't fire. It's all right. We'll save him from them yet."

For long minutes as it seemed to Graham that inglorious struggle continued. He flung himself down to gain time. His clothes were rent in a dozen places, he was covered in dust, one hand had been trodden upon. He could hear the shouts of his supporters, and once he heard shots. He was dragged along the floor.

He could feel his strength giving way, feel his efforts wild and aimless. But no help came, and surely, irresistibly, that black, yawning opening came nearer.

The pressure upon him relaxed, and he struggled up. He saw Ostrog's grey head receding and perceived that he was no longer held. He turned about and came full into a man in black. One of the green weapons cracked close to him, a drift of pungent smoke came into his face, and a steel blade flashed. He saw a man in pale blue stabbing one of the black and yellow attendants not three yards from his face. Then hands were upon him again. He was being pulled in two directions now. It seemed as though people were shouting indistinguishable things to him. Someone was clutching about his thighs, he was being hoisted in spite of his earnest efforts. He understood suddenly, he ceased to struggle. He was lifted up on men's shoulders and carried away from that devouring panel. A thousand throats were cheering.

He saw men in blue and black hurrying towards this—and firing after the retreating Ostrogites. Lifted up, he saw now across the whole expanse of the hall beneath the Atlas image, saw that he was being carried towards the raised platform in the centre of the place. The far end of the hall was already full of people running towards him. They were looking at him and cheering.

He became aware that a sort of bodyguard surrounded him. Active men about him shouted vague orders. He saw close at hand the black-moustached man in yellow who had been among those who had greeted him in the public theatre, shouting directions. The hall was already densely packed with swaying people, the little metal gallery sagged with a shouting load, the curtains at the end had been torn away, and the antechamber was revealed densely crowded. He could scarcely make the man near him hear for the tumult all about them. "Where is Ostrog?" he asked.

The man he questioned pointed over the heads towards the lower panels about the hall on the side opposite the gap. They stood open and armed men were running through them and vanishing into the chambers and passages beyond. It seemed to Graham that a sound of firing drifted through the riot. He was carried in a staggering curve across the great hall towards an opening beneath the gap.

He perceived men working with a sort of rude discipline to keep the crowd off him, to make a space clear about him. He passed out of the hall, and saw a crude, new wall rising blankly before him topped by blue sky. He was swung down to his feet; someone gripped his arm and guided him. He found the man in yellow close at hand. They were taking him up a narrow stairway of brick, and close at hand rose the great red painted masses, the cranes and levers and the throbbing engines of the now inactive building machine.

He was at the top of the steps. He was hurried across a narrow railed footway, and suddenly with a vast shouting the amphitheatre of ruins opened again before him. "The Master is with

us! The Master! The Master!" The shout swept athwart the lake of faces like a wave, broke against the distant cliff of ruins, and came back in a welter of cries. "The Master is on our side!"

Graham perceived that he was no longer encompassed by people, that he was standing upon a little temporary platform of white metal, part of a flimsy-seeming scaffolding that laced about the great mass of the Council House. Over all the huge expanse of the ruins, swayed and eddied the shouting people; and here and there the black banners of the revolutionary societies ducked and swayed and formed rare nuclei of organisation in the chaos. Up the steep stairs of wall and scaffolding by which his rescuers had reached the opening in the Atlas Chamber, clung a solid crowd, and little energetic black figures, clinging to pillars and projections, were strenuous to induce these congested masses to stir. Behind him, at a higher point on the scaffolding, a number of men struggled upwards with the flapping folds of a huge black standard. Through the yawning gap in the walls below him he could look down upon the packed attentive multitudes in the Hall of the Atlas.

The distant flying stages to the south came out bright and vivid, brought nearer as it seemed by an unusual translucency of the air. A solitary aëropile beat up from the central stage.

"What became of Ostrog?" asked Graham, and even as he spoke he saw that all eyes were turned from him towards the crest of the Council House building. He looked also in this direction of universal attention. For a moment he saw nothing but the jagged corner of a wall, hard and clear against the sky. Then in the shadow he perceived the interior of a room and recognised with a start the green and white decorations of his former prison. And coming quickly across this opened room to the very verge of the cliff of the ruin came a little white grey-headed figure followed by two other smaller-seeming figures in black and yellow. He heard the man beside him exclaim "Ostrog," and turned to ask a question. But he never did, because of the startled exclamation of another of those who were with him and a lank finger suddenly pointing. He looked, and beheld the aëropile that had been rising from the flying stage when last he had looked in that direction, was driving towards them. That swift, steady flight was still novel enough to hold his attention.

Nearer it came, growing rapidly larger and larger, until it had swept over the further edge of the ruins and into view of the dense multitudes below. It dropped across the space and rose and passed overhead, rising to clear the mass of the Council House, a filmy translucent shape with

The huge ears of a phonographic mechanism gaped in a battery for his words, the black eyes of great photographic cameras awaiting his beginning, beyond metal rods and coils glittered dimly, and something span with a droning hum. He walked into the centre of the square, and his shadow drew together black and sharp to a little blot at his feet. . . .

"Here and now," he cried, "I make my will. All that is mine in the world I give to the people of the world. All that is mine in the world I give to the people of the world. I give it to you, and myself I give to you. For as God wills I will live for men, or I will die."

the solitary aëronaut peering down through its ribs. It vanished beyond the skyline of the ruins. Graham glanced at Ostrog and saw him signalling with his hands, and his attendants busy breaking down the wall beside him. In another moment the aëropile came into view again, a little thing far away, coming round in a wide curve and going slower.

Then suddenly the man in yellow shouted, "What are they doing? What are the people doing? Why is Ostrog left there? Why is he not captured? They will lift him—the aëropile will lift him! Ah!"

The exclamation was echoed by a shout from the ruins. The rattling sound of the green weapons drifted across the intervening gulf to Graham, and, looking down, he saw a number of black and yellow uniforms running along one of the galleries that lay open to the air below the promontory upon which Ostrog stood. They fired as they ran at men unseen, and then emerged a number of pale blue figures in pursuit. These minute fighting figures had the oddest effect; they seemed as they ran like little model soldiers as a toy. This queer appearance of a house cut open gave that struggle amidst furniture and passages a quality of unreality. It was perhaps two hundred yards away from him, and very nearly fifty above the heads in the ruins below. The black and yellow men ran into an open archway, and turned and fired a volley. One of the blue pursuers striding forward close to the edge, flung up his arms, staggered sideways, seemed to Graham's sense to hang over the edge for several seconds, and fell headlong down. Graham saw him strike a projecting corner, fly out head over heels, and vanish behind the red arm of the nearest building machine.

And then a shadow came between him and the sun. He looked up and the sky was clear, but he knew the aëropile had passed. Ostrog had vanished.

"They are grounding!" cried the man in yellow. "They are grounding. Tell the people to fire at him. Tell them to fire at him!"

Graham could not understand. He heard loud voices repeating these enigmatical orders. Suddenly over the edge of the ruins came the prow of the aëropile and stopped with a jerk. In a moment Graham understood that the thing had grounded in order that Ostrog might escape by it. He saw a blue haze climbing out of the gulf, perceived that the people below him were firing up at the projecting corners of the vanes. A man beside him cheered hoarsely, and he saw that the blue rebels had gained the archway that had been contested by the men in black and yellow a moment before, and were running in a continual stream along the open passage.

And suddenly the aëropile came sliding over the edge of the Council House and fell. It dropped, tilting at an angle of forty-five degrees, and drooping so steeply that it seemed to Graham—it seemed perhaps to most of those below—that it could not possibly rise again. It came so closely past him that he could see Ostrog clutching the guides of the seat, with his grey hair streaming; see the white-faced aëronaut wrenching over the lever that drove the engine along its guides. He heard the apprehensive, vague cry of innumerable men.

Graham clutched the railing before him. The lower vane of the aëropile seemed within an ace of touching the people, who yelled and screamed and trampled one another below. And then it was rising. For a moment it looked as if it could not possibly clear the opposite cliff, that it could not possibly clear the wind-wheel that rotated beyond. And behold! it was clear and soaring, still heeling sideways, upward, upward into the wind-swept sky.

The suspense of the moment gave place to a fury of exasperation as the swarming people realised that Ostrog had escaped them. With belated activity they began to fire, until the rattling wove into a roar, until the whole area became dim and blue and the air pungent with the thin smoke of their weapons. Too late! The little aëropile dwindled smaller and smaller, and curved about and swept downward to the flying stage from which it had so lately arisen.

For a while a confused babblement arose from the ruins, and then the universal attention came back to Graham, perched high among the scaffolding. He saw the faces of the people turned towards him, heard their exultant shouts at his rescue. From the throat of the ways the song came spreading like a breeze across that swaying sea of men. The little group of men about him shouted congratulations on his escape. The man in yellow was close to him, with a set face and shining eyes. And the song was rising. Slowly the realisation came to the full meaning of these things to him, the perception of the swift change in his position. Ostrog, who had stood beside him whenever he had faced that shouting multitude before, was beyond there—the antagonist. There was no one to rule for him any longer. Even the people about him, the leaders and organisers of the multitude, looked to see what he would do, looked to him to act, awaited his orders. He was King indeed. His puppet reign was at an end.

CHAPTER XXIII.

GRAHAM AS KING

HE was very intent to do the thing that was expected of him. His nerves and muscles were quivering, his mind was perhaps a little confused, but he felt neither fear nor anger. His hand that had been trodden upon throbbed and was hot. He was a little nervous about his bearing. He knew he was not afraid, but he was anxious not to seem afraid. In his former life he had often been more excited in playing games of skill. He was desirous of immediate action, he knew he must not think too much in detail of the huge complexity of the struggle about him lest he should be paralysed by the sense of its intricacy. Over there those square blue shapes, the flying stages, meant Ostrog; against Ostrog he was fighting for the world.

One idea was very clear in his mind. He turned to the men, who crowded on the narrow bridge that led to his little stage and who clung all down the crude brick stairway. He pointed to the distant flying stages. "We must take those," he said. "We must take the flying stages before those negroes come."

He turned his head to the chaos below. "These people, have they no drill, no order?"

He understood the man in yellow to say he was a master of the ward societies, the secret societies by which the insurrection had been organised. "They have no order here. They have come on the impulse," he said, "each man by himself."

"How can we get them in order? And quick! Can they march as they are, a crowd, a tumult?"

"No," said the man in yellow. "If the ways are not stopped, if the way-men keep them going we can do better than that." He searched his mind, full of the knowledge of things that were beyond Graham's understanding.

"I have it!" he said. He thrust his way towards the little bridge.

"Pass the word!" he shouted to the men on the stairway. "Pass the word! Each man go back to his ward. Each man to his ward leaders. Get in order there at the ward centres, fall in, and march to the flying stages."

He shouted this again, and incontinently all the men on the narrow stairs were thrusting their way down and shouting. The tumult in the Atlas Chamber sank to hear, and rose again repeating Graham's order. The workmen clinging up the face of the scaffolding caught the words and shouted them down. In a few seconds the whole multitude had it. "The Master's Word—each man to his ward; each man to his ward leaders. The flying stages are to be taken!

The Master's word. Each man to his ward to fall in there!"

The man in yellow thrust his way back to Graham. "It is the only way. They are hampered here—no rallying points—no order. It is their only chance of finding their ward captains, to go back. See! They are already swarming back on the ways. The city is a crowd now—in a little while it will be an army."

"But orders! If they go from here, how am I to give them orders?"

"Here, across the Hall of the Atlas, are the telephones to the Public Intelligence Centres. And I will send men to hold up all the central voices of the Babble Machines for you."

Graham made no answer save a gesture of assent, and moved towards the little bridge. The men about him began to thrust and shout to clear his path. "Way for the Master, the Master is coming!"

As Graham crossed the great hall on his way to the central office, he saw the people in that place still in a dense disorder, in spite of the efforts of the black-badged Society Marshals. The men about him hurried him along a gallery behind the Atlas. Graham scanned the tumult. He hesitated as if he would speak to the mass below, exhort them to battle. "It is no good," he said. "It is no good. And they would not hear me," and he hurried on.

"There is no time. I must speak to the whole world," he said. "I must make a sort of proclamation. And then. Those flying stages."

They took him first into the little chamber from which they communicated with the General Intelligence Machines and with certain of the ward leaders. There an informal Council of War had assembled—a portion of the committee of ward organisers that Ostrog had created. "We must capture the flying stages," he repeated. He was vaguely aware of the ward leaders about him, talking with one another, offering conflicting counsels. They were all excited, all fragmentary, all in that state of mind when men seek emphasis in repetition and vociferation. Some appeared to be entirely engaged in keeping up a creditable appearance under the crisis. None seemed to grasp the situation in its entirety; each clung to some partial inadequate proposal, each looked to Graham for the final decisions. He was King indeed. The man in yellow showed him a plan of the city spread upon a table and coloured to divide it into sections, and with little numbers to show how many men could bear arms in each ward. "All this was Ostrog's planning," said the man in yellow extending a comprehensive hand. "He calculated everything. Except——" He indicated the people without by a movement of the hand. "*That.*"

"How about the flying machines? " cried Graham. "The flying machines?" A ward leader repeated his question.

"They are all against us—all with Ostrog," said the man in yellow.

"Have we none—not one on our side?"

"Not an aëronaut is with us."

"If there was one—there are no machines."

He began to point out the strategic qualities of the city ways about the Roehampton stage.

While Graham was bending over the unfamiliar symbolism of the map asking eager questions, came men to say that the body of Ostrogites cooped up in the corner of the Council House above, had capitulated, that Lincoln was a prisoner. Graham did not understand for a moment. When he did he reverted to the map. "Never mind our prisoners," he said. "We have to capture those flying stages. Get the people marching—get the people marching."

Then a stir, and through an open panel he heard in the adjacent apartment the click of a lever followed by the murmur of a Babble Machine. Presently one of the committee came to tell him that the General Intelligence Machines were with him, that the people were massing in their Wards all over the city, that everywhere the Londoners, even many of the middle-class Londoners, had risen against the coming of the black police. "Ostrog has miscalculated," said the committee-man.

"There are the flying machines against us—the flying machines," said Graham. "We must capture the flying stages."

He returned to the map, looked up with a question and missed Asano for the first time. He asked what had become of him. None of these strangers present knew Asano's name. "There were three or four men killed in the Atlas Chamber," said one. "Killed!" Graham understood only slowly. He stared vaguely at the moving figures about him. The little active man in black, intervening to protect him, was very vivid for an instant.

The man in yellow came pushing his way towards him to report the orders given, the Wards gathering rapidly, the people of the Westminster quarter already in motion towards the Roehampton flying stage. "Good," exclaimed Graham. "But about the flying machines. What is Ostrog doing with the flying machines?"

"The sky is clear," said the man in yellow.

"The flying machines are our danger," said Graham. "It cannot be long. They are Ostrog's strength. Very soon he will be launching aëropiles at us. What are we to do!"

"In our last fight——" said one of the committee-men.

"In your last fight they were for Ostrog. They are for Ostrog still."

He suddenly remembered a remark of Ostrog's. "Ah! There are guns. On the night of the revolt they were casting heavy guns!"

The men about him looked at one another. One volunteered inconclusive information. Two others began a private argument. Their voices bubbled about him.

"Someone must find out about those guns," shouted Graham, pacing. "Even now aëropiles may be soaring overhead. They can drop explosives."

"The sky was clear not three minutes since," said the man in yellow; "and they have no explosives. Bombs, grenades, torpedoes—there are none in Europe. Until the aëroplanes arrive from Africa they can do nothing. In Africa they use such things still—in the native villages. But not here—not here."

"We must have those guns," Graham repeated. "We must have those guns." He scarcely noticed the shrill bell of the neighbouring Babble Machine until one of his committee-men was back with the news. "The black police are starting," he said. "Twenty aëroplanes are starting one after the other from the flying stages at Kimberley, and those from the stage at Stanley Falls, and others from Asia are circling over the Say stage, waiting their turn. Fancy their being prepared! They are starting! They——"

"I have it," interrupted Graham, gesticulating. "One thing at any rate—get men who can shoot well. They must push across the roof spaces towards the delivery end of the stages, pick off Ostrog's aëronauts if they attempt to start. Get that done now. See that is done now. Telephone to the nearest centre and send these men at once."

He continued pacing excitedly. "As for those aëroplanes! There is only one thing. We must capture the flying stages. We must capture those flying stages before they get here. If only we had an aëropile or so. If only we had an aëropile! Tell me! Are the people getting in order? Once the aëropiles are launched they can ruin the city. Every moment is vital."

And then, to exasperate his gathering impatience, came delay, the inevitable pause before the battle began. There came no news from the foundries of Ostrog's lost guns, no news of the starting of the sharpshooters. The ward leaders dispersed on various commissions. His shadow went to and fro, to and fro, as the dilatory news of concentration came trickling to him. He wondered why Helen did not come to him; wondered where she might be in that labyrinthine city. Did she know what he was doing? He asked himself what he was doing. Suddenly he remembered his intention of a proclamation to the world. It might be advisable to make that before the battle joined. Of course it was absolutely necessary. Something stirring was needed, something Napoleonic. For a time he paced, meditating exuberant phrases, then he became active, announced his intention, inquired the means for its fulfillment, "There are the people abroad," he said. "The people all over the earth. I must speak to them. Speak."

The room to which Graham was taken in order to make his proclamation was grotesquely latter-day in its appointments. In the centre was a square area of grey marked out in the midst of a bright oval lit by shaded electric lights from above. The rest was in shadow, and the double finely fitting doors through which he came from the Hall of the Atlas made the place very still. The dead thud of the closing doors, the sudden cessation of the tumult in which he had been living for hours, the quivering circle of light, the whispers and quick noiseless movements of vaguely visible attendants in the shadows, had a strange effect upon Graham. For the last time came that doubt of reality, that distrust of all the fabric of space and time. Might he not be dreaming all this in Boscastle even now? The huge ears of a phonographic mechanism gaped in a battery for his words, the black eyes of great photographic cameras awaiting his beginning, beyond metal rods and coils glittered dimly, and something span with a droning hum. He walked into the centre of the square, and his shadow drew together black and sharp to a little blot at his feet.

Now some such occasion as this he had been prepared for, the vague shape of the thing he meant to say, the thing he meant to do, was in his mind. But this silence, this isolation, the sudden withdrawal from that contagious crowd, this silent audience and these gaping, glaring machines had not been in his anticipation. For a while he was paralysed, incompetent. He feared to be inadequate, he feared to be theatrical, he feared the quality of his voice, the quality of his wit, he turned to the man in yellow with a gesture. "For a moment," he said, "I must wait. And meanwhile—What is being done beyond there? Are the people getting into order? Have they arms? Are they marching?"

While he was still hearing the answer of the man in yellow, there came an agitated messenger with news that an aëroplane was passing over Arawan.

"Arawan?" he said. "Where is that? But anyhow they are coming. They will be here. When?"

"Before night."

"Great God! In only a few hours. What news of the flying stages?" he asked.

"The people of the south-west wards are marching."

"Marching!"

He turned impatiently to the blank circles of the lenses again.

"I suppose it must be a sort of speech. Would to God I knew certainly the thing that should be said! And the people marching! The aëroplanes at Arawan!"

That imminence and the delay of Helen provoked an unreasonable irritation. His belief in his heroic quality and calling lost its assured conviction. The picture of a little strutting futility in a windy waste of incomprehensible destinies replaced it.

"What does it matter whether I speak well or ill?" he said, and felt the light grow brighter.

He had framed some vague sentence of democratic sentiment when suddenly doubts, those harpies of the soul, assailed him. Abruptly it was perfectly clear to him that his revolt against Ostrog was premature, foredoomed to failure, the impulse of passionate inadequacy against inevitable things. He thought of that swift flight of aëroplanes like the swoop of Fate towards him. His mind changed from phase to phase. In that final emergency he debated, thrust debate resolutely aside, determined at all costs to go through with the thing he had undertaken. And he could find no word to begin. Even as he stood, awkward, hesitating, with a foolish apology for his inability trembling on his lips, came the noise of many people crying out, the running to and fro of feet. "Wait," cried someone, and a door opened. "She is coming," said the voices. Graham turned, and the watching lights upon him waned.

His heart leapt. Through the open doorway he saw a slight grey figure advancing across a spacious hall. It was Helen Wotton. Behind and about her marched a riot of applause. The man in yellow came out of the nearer shadows into the circle of light.

"This is the girl who told us what Ostrog had done," he said.

Her face was aflame, and the heavy coils of her black hair fell about her shoulders. The folds of the soft silk robe she wore streamed from her and floated on the rhythm of her advance. How light and lithe her paces seemed! She drew nearer and nearer, and his heart was beating fast. The shadow of the doorway fell athwart her face and she was near him. He made one step to meet her. "You have not betrayed us?" she cried. "You are with us?"

"The people!" said Graham.

"I knew," she cried, "knew you were our leader. And it was I—it was I that told them. They have risen. All the world is rising. The people have awakened. You are Master still."

"You told them?" he said, and he saw that spite of her steady eyes her lips trembled and her throat rose and fell.

"I told them. I knew of the order. I was here. I heard that the negroes were to come to London to guard you and keep the people down—to keep you a prisoner.

"And I stopped them. I came out and told the people. You are Master still."

Graham glanced at the black lenses of the cameras, the vast listening ears, and back to her face. "I am Master still," he said slowly, and the swift rush of a fleet of aëroplanes passed across his thoughts. They are coming, coming.

"Master still," said a voice out of the shadows.

"And you did this? You, who are the niece of Ostrog."

"For you," she cried. "For you! That you for whom the world has waited should not be cheated of your power."

Graham stood for a space, wordless, regarding her. His doubts and questionings fled before her eyes. He remembered the thing that he had meant to say. He faced the cameras again and the light about him grew brighter. He turned again towards her.

"You have saved me," he said; "You have saved my power. And the battle is beginning. God knows what this night will see—but not dishonour."

He paused. He addressed himself now to the unseen multitudes who stared upon him through those grotesque black eyes. At first he spoke slowly.

"Men and women of the new age," he said, "you have arisen to do battle for the race. To do battle for the race! . . . There is no easy victory before us."

He stopped to gather words. The thoughts that had been in his mind before she came returned, but transfigured, no longer touched with a shadow of a possible irrelevance. "This night is a beginning," he cried. "This battle that is coming, this battle that rushes upon us to-night, is only a beginning. All your lives, it may

be, you must fight. Take no thought though I am beaten, though I am utterly overthrown."

He found the thing in his mind too vague for words. He paused momentarily, and broke into vague exhortations, and then a rush of speech came to him. Much that he said was but the humanitarian commonplace of a vanished age, but the conviction of his voice touched it to vitality. He stated the case of the old days to the people of the new age, to the woman at his side. "I come out of the past to you," he said, "with the memory of an age that hoped. My age was an age of dreams—or beginnings, an age of noble hopes; throughout the world we had made an end of slavery; throughout the world we had spread the desire and anticipation that wars might cease, that all men and women might live nobly, in freedom and peace . . . So we hoped in the days that are past. And what of those hopes? How is it with man after two hundred years?

"Great cities, vast powers, a collective greatness beyond our dreams. For that we did not work and that has come. But how is it with the little lives that make up this greater life? How is it with the common lives? As it has ever been—sorrow and labour, lives cramped and unfulfilled, lives tempted by power, tempted by wealth, and gone to waste and folly. The old faiths have faded and changed, the new faith—— Is there a new faith?"

Things that he had long wished to believe, he found that he believed. He plunged at belief and seized it, and clung for a time at her level. He spoke gustily, in broken, incomplete sentences, but with all his heart and strength of the halting new faith within him. He spoke of the greatness of self-abnegation, of that immortal life of humanity in which we live and move and have our being. His voice rose and fell, and the recording appliances hummed their hurried applause, dim attendants watched him out of the shadows. Through all those doubtful places the sense of that silent spectator beside him sustained his sincerity. For a few glorious moments he was carried away; he felt no doubt of his heroic quality, no doubt of his heroic words, he had it all straight and plain. His eloquence limped no longer. At last he made an end to speaking.

"Here and now," he cried, "I make my will. All that is mine in the world I give to the people of the world. All that is mine in the world I give to the people in the world. I give it to you, and myself I give to you. For as God wills I will live for men, or I will die."

He ended with a florid gesture and turned about. He found the light of his present exaltation reflected in the face of the girl. Their eyes

*Graham drew near the aëropile, marched into the
shadow of its tilting wing.*

met. The lights of the cameras flickered and fell, and the note of the armatures changed. They stood facing one another still, in the shadow.

CHAPTER XXIV.
WHILE THE AËROPLANES WERE COMING

ALL through the short winter afternoon that ineffectual fight for the flying stages went on. The first great movement of the people had been upon the Council House, an undisciplined convergence, without order, and in many cases without weapons, to clamour in astonished anger for the Master. The leaders and elected officers of the Clubs and Secret Societies and Sections knew no more than the common people of the state of affairs, and conceiving that the Sleeper was privy to Ostrog's designs, had made no organised attempts at revolt until Graham's reappearance and the escape of Ostrog. Then, however, the extraordinary tactical conditions of the struggle came to light, in the ease and rapidity with which the people were returned to their wards and factories, and marshalled there in their companies.

The people in the south-western wards of the city were the first in order, the first in motion towards the stages. They were perhaps the most homogeneous section of the workers. The director of their council of ward leaders was an Ostrogite, but he had so organised these subordinates that they were already accustomed to meet and consult. They gathered their people methodically, in exactly the sections and meeting places that had served for the Revolt of the Awakening. They placed their masses upon the ways, section by section, employing even in its details the order Ostrog had devised, and they were already pouring up through the galleries, and ascending ways beneath the Roehampton stage, before there was a hand raised to stop them. Then abruptly they were in collision with the details of the Ostrogites hastening all too late to their posts, and the battle was joined. And men grappled and died a hundred feet above the ground, where once the free air had blown over the tree-tops of Putney Hill.

The force Ostrog found at his disposal was smaller than he had counted upon, and he had hesitated whether to hold the Roehampton stage. The suddenness, the expertness, with which the Labour serfs had repeated the lesson he had taught them had done much to disorganise his designs. There were tens of thousands of people in the city that afternoon, officials, traders, aëronauts off duty, wind-vane policemen, members of the disbanded red police, wealthy shareholders and managers, footmen, pleasure dealers, aristocratic-minded people of various stations in life, who realised the seriousness of the uprising too late, who would have joined him had they dared to emerge from their chambers and rooms to attempt the journey of the public ways. As it was he had the bulk of the aëronauts with him, the aëropile company attendants, almost a thousand of the yellow labour police, several thousands of the wind-vane police, engineers whom he had concentrated at the stages overnight when the popular behaviour became threatening, and a disorderly multitude of several thousands of public officials and gentlemen volubly loyal to the existing social order but not remarkably efficient. There were arms for all these people but no ordered discipline for their concerted action, and when the levies of the South-Western Labour Societies were marching into the warren beneath the Roehampton stage, the bulk of the Ostrogites were still crowded and still imperfectly organised in the passages and halls of the basement below the central stages.

Ostrog, after his escape, had wasted a certain amount of time in telephonic communication with the flying stages of Paris and Berlin, only to learn that the news of the London rising had fired both these cities, that there the news from London roused the Labour serfs, and that in each the supporters of the existing order could scarcely hold their own for long unless reinforcements arrived. He immediately sent urgent messages for help to Say, Wadelai, Kimberley, and Stanley Falls, pressing the officers of the Consolidated African Companies to accelerate their despatch of the promised negro brigades. Even as he did this news of the attack on the Roehampton stage reached him.

The struggle for Roehampton lasted two hours. There was a temporary indecision on the part of the Ostrogites, a doubt how far the revolt had reached, and in that time the swarming blue canvas held the ends of the communicating ways and luggage slides. In spite of the distraction of a considerable proportion of their number in sacking the shops and houses of refreshment, a multitude of labourers were already pouring out among the sub-stage pillars and girders, and clambering up the staircase to the stage itself before Ostrog appeared on the next stage, the stage called Wimbledon. He saw at once that to attempt a recapture through the communicating ways was, at present, beyond his strength, and so the little band of Ostrogites in Roehampton were left to hold out as long as they could. He launched an aëropile to their assistance. It was speedily disabled. A chance shot from the roof spaces near killed the aëronaut as the machine was circling low, and it came down ingloriously athwart the Roehampton stage, smashing an Ostrogite in its descent.

And now the Labour Societies of Central and East London were in motion. Ostrog's ineffectual aëropile was still upon its carrier, when the attenuated sound of a nearer struggle, the roar and tumult of the fight that was beginning in the ways beneath the Streatham stage, came filtering up through a sponge of lifts, passages, and chambers to the ears of the aëronauts. A strange and unprecedented contest it was, fought out of sight of sky or sun under the electric glare, fought out in a vast confusion by multitudes untrained in arms, led chiefly by acclamation, multitudes dulled by mindless labour and enervated by the tradition of two hundred years of servile security against multitudes demoralised by lives of privilege and sensuous indulgence. They had no artillery, no differentiation into this force or that; the only weapon on either side was the little green metal carbine, whose secret manufacture and sudden distribution in enormous quantities had been one of Ostrog's most brilliant moves against the Council. Few had had any experience with this weapon, many had never discharged one, many who carried it came unprovided with ammunition; never was wilder firing in the history of warfare. It was a battle of amateurs, a hideous experimental warfare, armed rioters fighting armed rioters, armed rioters swept forward by the words and fury of a song, by the tramping sympathy of their numbers, pouring in countless myriads towards the smaller ways, the disabled lifts, the galleries slippery with blood, the halls and passages choked with smoke beneath the flying stages, to learn there when retreat was hopeless the ancient mysteries of warfare. Of all that happened out of sight of the sky through that terrible afternoon, when the soft clay of latter-day manhood went through the long-disused furnace of war, no history can be written. Here down a slant way, poured a host in the final degradation of panic; here, amidst the darkness of smashed electric cables and the broken debris of once seductive shops, men who had never seen one another grappled in the death struggle; here the blind fury of massacre wreaked itself on some wretched traders caught between the combatants among their commerce and hiding in vain; here masses of fomile aimlessly exploded, or, exploding accidentally, ripped and smashed, and opened huge pits of darkness, and here men who had been but a week ago the dull drudges of machines, fought grimly, steadily, intelligently, changed suddenly to heroes.

And while this fight went on, the two people whom fate had thrust to the central point of the struggle remained together in a little room opening into the Hall of the Atlas. Graham, glowing at first with the emotion of his eloquence, had proposed to lead the people in person, but the man in yellow had dissuaded him. There was no possibility of leading them effectually, he insisted, the battle was a fight in a warren, each passage, each lift had its own leaders, its own tide of success and failure, and here he was needed against the coming of the aëroplanes. Ever and again there was news of these, drawing nearer, from this Mediterranean post and then that, and presently from the south of France. There was indeed a perpetual coming and going with messages. But of the new guns that were known to be in the city came no news in spite of Graham's urgency, nor any report of successes from the dense felt of fighting strands about the flying stages. Section after section of the Labour Societies reported itself assembled, reported itself marching, and vanished from knowledge into the labyrinth of that warfare. What was happening? Even the ward leaders did not know. In spite of the opening and closing of doors, the hasty messengers, the ringing of bells and the perpetual clitter-clack of recording implements, Graham felt isolated, strangely inactive, inoperative. Indeed there was nothing to be done now, until those guns were found, or the people won a footing on the flying stages or the aëroplanes arrived. But it oppressed him that nothing was to be done; inactive he feared the slackening of his will, the return of his doubts, the rediscovery of his inadequacy.

Their intercourse was broken by countless interruptions, yet in the intervals they talked with a strange intimacy, touching on many matters. At first their mind was one of exalted confidence, a great pride possessed them, a pride in one another for the greatness of the issues they had challenged. But slowly uneasy intimations of a coming defeat touched Graham's spirits. At first he had walked the room eloquent with the solidarity and destiny of humanity, the providential nature of her intervention. There was an interval of fruitless inquiries, and then Graham recurred to the wonder of his sleep, spoke of the little life of his memories, remote yet minute and clear, like something seen through an inverted opera-glass, of all the brief play of desires and errors that had made his former life. He spoke more freely to her than he had ever done to any human being. She said little, but the emotion in her face followed the tones in his voice, and it seemed to him he had at last a perfect understanding. "And through it all, this destiny was before me," he said, "this vast inheritance of which I did not dream." Insensibly his heroic preoccupation with the revolutionary struggle passed to the question of their relationship. He began to question her. She told him of the days before his awakening, of the girlish dreams that had given a bias to her life, of the incredulous emotions his awakening had aroused. She told him, too, of a tragic circumstance of her girlhood that had darkened her life, quickened her sense of injustice, and opened her heart prematurely to the wider sorrows of the world.

There came messengers to tell that great aëroplanes were rushing between the sky and Avignon, coming Londonward in a mighty fleet. He went to the crystal dial in the corner and assured himself that the thing was so. He consulted a map to measure the distances of Avignon, Arawan, and London. He made swift calculations. He went out to the room of the ward leaders to ask for news of the fight for the stages—and there was no one there. After a time he came back to his pacing.

His face had changed. His consciousness had been occupied with the coming of a battle, with a long contest opening. Now it was dawning upon him that the struggle had already lasted more than an hour, was perhaps more than half over, that the arrival of the aëroplanes would mean a panic that might leave him helpless. Only two of the ward leaders returned, the Hall of the Atlas seemed empty, he fancied a change in the bearing of those about him. A sombre disillusionment crept into his mind, a revived perception of inadequate faith in the cause he had undertaken. But she gave no signs of doubt for all the shadow of these things, and he feared her astonishment if he should abandon his fear of greatness more than all the fears within him.

Presently came the report of the aëroplanes from Vichy, and soon they were over Orleans . . . Then they were passing Paris, and still the people under the flying stages fought and won no headway.

Graham continued the heroic strain she had imposed upon him with a dwindling zest. Ever and again came something like a twinge of exasperation at her headlong influence upon him. He was going to his destruction for her, and she did not even perceive it was for her. He could see his way to no personal interpretation of the attitude, though he searched his mind very eagerly.

"It may be," he said, "that we shall never rule. We gain no ground and the time goes by. But we have done the great thing; we have raised the banner of Humanity again, and all the world has heard us. That was our chief duty."

"That was our duty," she said.

He looked at her, envying the assurance of her virginal enthusiasm.

"The end may be near," he said. "The people make no headway, the aëroplanes are swift, and my use to Ostrog is at an end. I knew little. I acted in haste. My little empire of the world is about over. But I have known you—that is the great thing now. I have known you, and I am content."

She put her hand to her throat. "Content," she said. "Have we not done right? Have you not given your message? I would not change——" She stopped; she was smiling, her white lips smiling and her eyes were triumphant. She was so beautiful and so assured, so glorious in the face of their imminent overthrow that he, knowing the doubts he had from her, could have laughed aloud in the bitterness of his soul.

And suddenly came the man in yellow with wonderful news. "Victory!" he cried. "Victory! The people are winning! Ostrog's people have collapsed!"

She rose. "Victory?" she cried incredulously.

"What do you mean?" asked Graham.

"We have driven them out of the under galleries at Norwood, Streatham is afire, and Roehampton is ours—and an aëropile that lay thereon. The people win!"

Suddenly it seemed to Graham that Helen was human again. Their hearts were beating, they looked at one another. For one last moment there gleamed on Graham his dream of empire, of kingship with Helen by his side. It gleamed—and faded.

A shrill bell rang. An agitated grey-headed man appeared from the room of the ward leaders. "It is all over," he cried. "This glimpse of victory comes too late. The aëroplanes are crossing the Channel."

"The Channel!" said the man in yellow. He calculated swiftly. "Half an hour."

"Yes," said Graham, "It is too late."

"If only we could stop them another hour!" cried the old ward leader.

"Nothing can stop them now," said the man in yellow.

"Another hour?" asked Graham.

"It is a pity," said the ward leader. "We have found those guns. If once we could get them out upon the roof spaces——"

"Too late," cried the man in yellow, "too late."

"How long would that take?" asked Graham suddenly.

"One hour—certainly."

"Is it too late?" said Graham. "Even now——. An hour!"

He had suddenly perceived a terrible possibility. "There is one chance. Did you say there was an aëropile captured?"

"On the Roehampton stage, Sire."

"That . . . might give us time." His belief in this possibility faded as he spoke; yet he clung to it as a thing to be done.

He glanced at the two men and then at Helen. He spoke after a long pause.

"We have no aëronauts?"

"None."

"These aëroplanes are clumsy," he said, "compared with the aëropiles."

He turned suddenly to Helen. His decision was made. "I must do it."

"Do what?"

"Go to the flying stage—to this aëropile."

"What do you mean?"

"I am an aëronaut. After all——. Those days for which you reproached me, were not altogether wasted."

"What do you mean?"

"This aëropile. It is a chance——"

"You don't mean——"

"To fight—yes. To fight in the air. I have thought before——. An aëroplane is a clumsy thing. A resolute man——!"

With a gleam of triumph Graham saw the change in her face.

"But never, since flying began——" cried the man in yellow.

"There has been no need. But now the time has come."

Helen made a step towards him. Her face was white. "But—— How can one fight? You will be killed!"

"Perhaps. Yet not to do it—or to let someone else attempt it— —"

He stopped, he could speak no more, he swept the alternative aside by a gesture, and they stood looking at one another. Their faces said things their lips could never utter. For a moment her humanitarian inhumanity was swept aside, and he could triumph over her. For an instant there was nothing for her in the world but the man who stood before her. And then that moment of self discovery had passed, and her faith resumed its empire.

"You are right," she said in a low tone. "You are right. If it can be done . . . You must go."

He moved a step toward her, but she stood motionless. He did not dare to touch her. Her white face struggled against him, resisted him. "*Go*," she whispered, "*go now*." He turned quickly and walked out of the little room. The man in yellow hesitated and hurried after him. . . .

At first Graham could not look back. Then he looked back and saw her far off pale and steadfast with her hands clenched by her side. For an instant he could have cried aloud at the folly of this separation. For an instant the life of those latter days shone before his imagination, brilliant and seductive. Suppose even now he wished to crave for peace with Ostrog. She was still but a girl. After the shock of her disillusionment——.

He saw that life of surrender, a long vista of inglorious years. He saw, too, the infinite difficulty now of such an escape, even should he submit to seek it. "No," he cried aloud, "No. Death is better." He turned about and went towards the flying stages.

CHAPTER XXV.
THE COMING OF THE AËROPLANES

TWO men in pale blue were lying in the irregular line that stretched along the edge of the captured Roehampton stage from end to end, grasping their carbines and peering into the shadows of the stage called Wimbledon Park. Now and then they spoke to one another. They spoke the mutilated English of their class and period. The fire of the Ostrogites had dwindled and ceased, and few of the enemy had been seen for some time. But the echoes of the fight that was going on now far below in the lower galleries of that stage, came every now and then between the staccato of shots from the popular side. One of these men was describing to the other how he had seen a man down below there dodge behind a girder, and had aimed at a guess and hit him cleanly as he dodged too far. "He's down there still," said the marksman. "See that little patch. Yes. Between those bars." A few yards behind them lay a dead stranger, face upward to the sky, with the blue canvas of his jacket smouldering in a circle about the neat bullet hole on his chest. Close beside him a wounded man, with a leg swathed about, sat with an expressionless face and watched the progress of that burning. Athwart the carrier lay the captured aëropile.

"I can't see him *now*," said the second man in a tone of provocation.

The marksman became foul-mouthed and high-voiced in his earnest endeavour to make things plain. And suddenly, interrupting him, came a noisy shouting from the substage.

"What's going on now?" he said, and raised himself on one arm to stare at the stairheads in the central groove of the stage. A number of blue figures were coming up these, and swarming across the stage to the aëropile.

"We don't want all these fools," said his friend. "They only crowd up and spoil shots. What are they after?"

"Ssh!—they're shouting something."

The two men listened. The swarming newcomers crowded about the aëropile. Three ward leaders, conspicuous by their black mantles and badges, clambered into the body and appeared above it. The rank and file flung themselves upon the vans, gripping hold of the edges, until the entire outline of the thing was manned, in some places three deep. One of the marksmen knelt up. "They're putting it on the carrier— that's what they're after."

He rose to his feet, his friend rose also. "What's the good?" said his friend. "We've got no aëronauts."

"That's what they're doing, anyhow." He looked at his rifle, looked at the struggling crowd, and suddenly turned to the wounded man. "Mind these, mate," he said, handing his carbine and cartridge belt; and in a moment he was running toward the aëropile. For a quarter of an hour he was a perspiring Titan, lugging, thrusting, shouting and heeding shouts, and then the thing was done, and he stood with a multitude of others cheering their own achievement. By this time he knew, what everyone in the city knew, that the Master, raw learner though he was, intended to fly this machine himself, was coming even now to take control of it. And even as he cheered, and while the beads of sweat still chased one another from the disorder of his hair, he heard the thunder of a greater tumult, and in fitful snatches the beat and impulse of the revolutionary song. He saw through a gap in the people that a thick stream of heads still poured up the stairways. "The Master is coming!" shouted voices. "The Master is coming!" and the crowd about him grew denser and denser. He began to thrust himself towards the central groove. "The Master is coming!" "The Sleeper, the Master!" "God and the Master!" roared the growing storm of shouts.

And suddenly quite close to him were the black uniforms of the revolutionary guard, and for the first and last time in his life he saw Graham, saw him quite nearly. A tall, dark man in a flowing black robe, with a white, resolute face and eyes fixed steadfastly before him; a man who for all the little things about him had neither ears nor eyes nor thoughts. For all his days he remembered the passing of that bloodless face. In a moment it had gone, and he was fighting in the swaying crowd. A lad screaming with terror thrust against him, pressing towards the stairways, yelling "Clear for the aëropile!" The bell that clears the flying stage began a disorderly clanging.

With that clanging in his ears Graham drew near the aëropile, marched into the shadow of its tilting wing. He became aware that a number of people about him were offering to accompany him, and waved their offers aside. He wanted to think how one started the engine. The bell clanged faster and faster, and the feet of the retreating people roared faster and louder. The man in yellow was assisting him to mount through the ribs of the body. He clambered into the aëronaut's place, fixing himself very carefully and deliberately. What was it? The man in yellow was pointing to two aëropiles driving upward in the southern sky. That— presently—the thing to do now was to start. Things were being shouted at him, questions, warnings. They bothered him. He wanted to think about the aëropile, to recall every item of his previous experience. He waved the people from him, saw the man in yellow dropping off through the ribs, saw the crowd cleft down the line of the girders by his gesture.

For a moment he was motionless, staring at the levers, the wheel by which the engine shifted, and all the delicate appliances of which he knew so little. His eye caught a spirit level with the bubble towards him, and he spent a dozen seconds in swinging the engine forward until the bubble floated in the centre of the tube. He noticed the people were not shouting, knew they watched his deliberation. A bullet smashed on the bar above his head. Who fired? Was the line clear of people? He stood up to see and sat down again.

In another second the propeller was spinning, and he was rushing down the guides. He gripped the wheel and swung the engine back to lift the stem. Then it was the people shouted. In a moment he was throbbing with the quiver of the engine, and the shouts dwindled behind. The wind whistled over the edges of the screen, and the world sank away from him very swiftly.

Throb, throb, throb—throb, throb, throb; up he drove. He fancied himself free of all excitement, felt cool and deliberate. He lifted the stem still more, opened one valve on his left wing and swept round and up. He looked down with a steady head, and up. One of the Ostrogite aëropiles was driving across his course, so that he drove obliquely towards it and would pass below it at a steep angle. Its little aëronauts were peering down at him. What did they mean to do? One held a weapon pointing, seemed prepared to fire. What did they think he meant to do? In a moment he understood their tactics, and his resolution was taken. He opened two more valves to his left, swung round, end on to his hostile machine, closed his valves, and shot straight at it, stem and windscreen shielding him from the shot. They tilted a little as if to clear him. He flung up his stem.

Throb, throb, throb—pause—throb, throb—he set his teeth, contorted his face into an involuntary grimace, and crash! He struck it!

He struck upward beneath the nearer wing. Very slowly the wing of his antagonist seemed to broaden as the impetus of his blow turned it up.

He felt his stem going down, his hands tightened on the levers, whirled and rammed the engine back. He felt the jerk of a clearance, the nose of the machine jerked upward steeply, and for a moment he was helpless on his back. A vast bulk, as it seemed, had fallen from under him. He made a huge effort, hung for a moment on the levers, and slowly the engine came forward again. He drove upward, but no longer so steeply. He gasped for a moment and flung himself at the levers again. The wind whistled about him. One further effort and he was almost level. He could breathe. He turned his head for the first time to see what had become of his antagonists. Turned back to the levers for a moment and looked again. For a moment he could have believed they were annihilated. And then he saw between the two stages to the east was a chasm, and down this something, a slender edge, fell swiftly and vanished, as a sixpence falls down a crack.

At first he did not understand, and then a wild joy possessed him. He shouted at the top of his voice, an inarticulate shout, and drove higher and higher up the sky. "Where was the other aëropile?" he thought. "They too——" As he looked round the empty heavens he had a momentary fear that they had risen above him, and then he saw their machine alighting on the Norwood stage. They had meant shooting. To risk being rammed headlong two thousand feet in the air was beyond their latter-day courage. The combat was declined.

For a little while he circled, then swooped in a steep descent towards the westward stage. The twilight was creeping on apace, the smoke from the Streatham stage that had been so dense and dark, was now a pillar of fire, and all the laced curves of the moving ways and the translucent roofs and domes and the chasms between the buildings were glowing softly now, lit by the tempered radiance of the electric light that the glare of the day had overpowered. The three efficient stages that the Ostrogites held—for Wimbledon Park was useless because of the fire from Roehampton, and Streatham was a furnace—were glowing with guide lights for the coming aëroplanes. As he swept over the Roehampton stage he saw the dark masses of the people thereon. He heard a clap of frantic cheering, heard a bullet from the Wimbledon Park stage tweet through the air, and went beating up a long declivity above the Surrey wastes. He felt a breath of wind from the south-west, and lifted

his westward wing as he had learnt to do, and so drove upward heeling.

Up he drove and up, until the country beneath was blue and indistinct, and London spread like a little map, traced in light, like the mere model of a city, far behind him. The south-west was a sky of sapphire over the shadowy rim of the world, and ever as he drove upward the multitude of stars increased.

And behold! in the southward, low down and glittering swiftly nearer, were two little patches of nebulous light. And then two more, and then a nebulous glow of swiftly driving shapes. The whole south-west was soon as bright as moonrise with that multitude. The aëroplanes had come!

He swept round in a half-circle, staring at this advancing fleet flying in a wedge-like shape, a flight of phosphorescent birds through the lower air. He made a swift calculation of their pace, and spun the little wheel that brought the engine forward. He aimed at the apex of the wedge. He dropped like a stone through the whistling air. It seemed scarce a second from that soaring moment before he struck the foremost aëroplane.

No man of all that black multitude saw the coming of his fate, no man among them dreamt of the hawk that fell downward out of the sky. Those who were not limp in the agonies of air-sickness, were craning their black necks and staring to see the filmy city that was rising out of the haze, the rich and splendid city to which "Massa Boss" had brought their obedient muscles. Bright teeth gleamed and the glossy faces shone. They had heard of Paris. They knew they were to have fine times among the "poor white" trash. And suddenly Graham struck them.

He had aimed at the body of the aëroplane, but at the very last instant a better idea had flashed into his mind. He twisted about and struck near the edge of the starboard wing with all his accumulated weight. He was jerked back as he struck. His prow went gliding across its smooth expanse towards the rim. He felt the forward rush of a huge fabric sweeping him and his aëropile along with it, and for a moment that seemed an age he could not tell what was happening. He heard a thousand throats yelling, and perceived that his machine was balanced on the edge of the gigantic float, and driving down, down; glanced over his shoulder and saw the backbone of the aëroplane and the opposite float swaying up. He had a vision through the ribs of sliding chairs, staring faces, and hands clutching at the tilting guide bars. The fenestrations in the further float flashed open as the aëronaut tried to right her. Beyond he saw a second aëroplane leaping steeply to escape the whirl of its heeling

As he drew near he saw that the two aëropiles were still locked together even as they had fallen through the air. Free of the heap he came upon something—a heap of clothing and limbs, pallid under the night, a grey head, a dark clutching hand extended on the turf. Beyond, among the smashed vans, lay other human forms.

fellow. The broad area of swaying wings seemed to jerk upward. He felt his aëropile had dropped clear, that the monstrous fabric, clean overturned, hung like a sloping wall above him.

He did not clearly understand that he had struck the side float of the aëroplane and slipped off, but he perceived that he was flying free on the down glide and rapidly nearing the earth. What had he done? His heart throbbed like a noisy engine in his throat, and for an instant he could not move his levers because of the trembling of his hands. He wrenched the levers to throw his engine back, fought for two seconds against the weight of it, felt himself righting, driving horizontally.

He looked upward and saw two aëroplanes glide shouting overhead, looked back, and saw the main body of the fleet opening out and rushing upward and outward; then saw the one he had struck fall edgewise on and strike like a gigantic knife blade along the windwheels far away below. He put down his stern and looked again. He drove up heedless of his direction as he watched. He saw the wind-vanes give, saw the huge fabric strike the earth, saw its downward vans crumple with the weight of its descent, and then the whole mass turned over and smashed, upside down, upon the sloping wheels. Throb, throb, throb, pause. Suddenly, from the heaving wreckage a thin tongue of white fire licked up towards the zenith. And then he was aware of a huge mass flying through the air towards him, and turned upwards just in time to escape the charge—if it was a charge—of a second aëroplane. It whirled by below, sucked him down a fathom, and nearly turned him over in the gust of its close passage.

He became aware of three others rushing towards him, aware of the urgent necessity of beating above them. Aëroplanes were all about him, circling wildly to avoid him as it seemed. They drove past him, above, below, eastward and westward. Far away to the westward was the sound of a collision, and two falling flares. Steadily he beat upward as they passed. Presently they were all below him, but for a moment he doubted the height he had of them, and did not swoop again. And then he came down upon a second victim, and all its load of soldiers saw him coming. The big machine heeled and swayed as the fear-maddened men scrambled to the stern for their weapons. A score of bullets sang through the air, and there flashed a star in the thick glass wind-screen that protected him. The aëroplane slowed and dropped to foil his stroke, and dropped too low. Just in time he saw the wind-wheels of Bromley Hill rushing up

towards him, and spun about and up as the aëroplane crashed among them. The great fabric seemed to be standing on end for a second among its splintering ruins, and then to fly to pieces. A hot rush of flame shot overhead into the darkling sky.

"Two!" he cried, with a bomb from overhead bursting as it fell, and he was beating up intent upon a third victim. A glorious exhilaration possessed him now, a giant activity. Aëroplanes seemed radiating from him in every direction, intent only upon avoiding him. The yelling of their packed passengers came in short gusts as they swept by. He chose his third quarry, struck hastily, and did but turn it on edge. It escaped him, to smash against the tall cliff of London Wall. He skimmed the ground so nearly he could see a frightened rabbit bolting up a slope. He jerked up steeply, and found himself driving over South London with the air about him vacant. To the right of him a wild riot of signal rockets banged tumultuously in the sky. To the south the wreckage of half a dozen air ships flamed, and east and west and north the air ships fled before him. One had landed on the eastward stage, the stage called Shooter's Hill. None other had dared to slacken in his proximity. They circled about him like oxen about a wolf, trusting to their speed if he should charge upon them. He passed two hundred feet or so above the Roehampton stage. It was black with people and noisy with their frantic shouting. But why was the Wimbledon Park stage black and cheering too? The smoke and flame of Streatham now hid the three further stages. He curved about and rose to see them and the northern quarters. First came the square masses of Shooter's Hill into sight from behind the smoke, lit and orderly with its aëroplane and its disembarking negroes. Then came Blackheath, and then under the corner of the reek the Norwood stage. He wondered what time he had won for the people, how far they had progressed with the mounting of their guns.

On Blackheath an aëropile lay upon the guides. But Norwood was covered by a swarm of little figures running to and fro in a passionate confusion. Why? Abruptly he understood. The stubborn defence of the flying stages was over, the people were pouring into the underways of these last strongholds of the usurpation. "They win!" he shouted to the empty air; "the people win!" And then he saw the aëropile on Blackheath was running down its guides to launch. It lifted clean and rose. He knew that it came to fight him, to clear the way for the aëroplanes. Instantly he knew what he must do.

He shouted, and dropped towards his new antagonist. It rose steeply at his approach. He allowed for its velocity, and drove straight upon it. He saw it before him, saw the faces of the aëronauts growing swiftly distinct, saw with a strange tightening of the chest, the white face of Ostrog, resolute and calm.

The aëropile before him became a mere flat edge, and behold! he was past it, and driving headlong down with all the force of his futile blow.

He was furiously angry. He reeled the engine back along its shaft and went circling up. He saw Ostrog beating up a spiral before him not half a mile away. He rose straight towards him, won above him by virtue of the impetus of his swoop and by the advantage of the weight of a man. He dropped headlong and missed again. As he rushed past he saw the face of Ostrog's aëronaut confident and cool. He realised with a gleam of wrath how bungling his flight must be.

Right in front of his angry eyes appeared a strange thing. The eastward stage, the one on Shooter's Hill, appeared to lift; a flash changing to a tall grey shape, a cowled figure of smoke and dust, jerked into the air; this cowled figure stood for a moment motionless, dropping huge masses of metal from its shoulders, and then began to uncoil a dense head of smoke. For a moment he forgot the aëropile above in his astonishment. As suddenly a second flash and grey shape sprang up from the Norwood stage. And even as he stared at this came a dead report, and the air wave of the first explosion struck him. He was flung up and sideways.

For a moment the aëropile fell nearly edgewise with her nose down, and seemed to hesitate whether to overset altogether. He stood on his wind shield wrenching the wheel that swayed up over his head and she righted even as he shot down. And then the shock of the second explosion took her sideways, turned her on her edge.

Abruptly Ostrog's aëropile dropped and struck him. But it struck badly because of the second concussion. He did not know they were upon him until he reeled with the crash of the blow; they had dropped obliquely downward upon him as he came up the righting curve. He was thrown over sideways out of his stays, he saw the vans of their machine swooping through the air, saw their screws whirling upside down, saw Ostrog with open mouth and staring eyes, looking strangely rigid. He found himself clinging to one of the ribs of his machine, and the air was blowing past him and *upwards*. He seemed to be hanging quite still in the air, with the wind

blowing up past him. It occurred to him that he was falling. He knew next that the whole mass, the two locked aëropiles, was falling together. He could not look down.

He found himself recapitulating with incredible swiftness all that had happened since his awakening. His mind was clear and active. Chiefly he was sorry that he should never see Helen again. It seemed so unreasonable that he should not see her again.

CHAPTER XXVI.

FROM THE HILLSIDE

THE sun had set, the dusk was deepening, and above the city a couple of stars quivered on the verge of visibility. A man on horseback wrapped in a warm cloak rode towards the crest of the hill that had once been called Addiscombe. He was a tall, broad-shouldered man, one of the watches of the countless sheep that graze on the grassy solitudes under the wind-wheels along the hills of Surrey and Kent.

Over the vacant countryside—for all trees had been cleared to give the wind-wheels freedom—the hours were monotonous enough, and a man would sometimes pine for the city. His was a lonely life, for the whole country was given up to sheep, and when his duties kept him from sight of the swarming high roads that ran to the ferry-jetties at Dover, Portsmouth, and Clifton, he would sometimes ride for a day together without meeting a fellow-man. And his only companions during his time of duty were the engineers who came out to see after the windvanes and his rare fellow-watchers. On the hill the light and stir beneath the Norwood and Streatham stages shone very cheeringly across the valley. But to-night he had come to the ridge, the northern limit his regulations set him, for no simple longing of solitude. He had followed the phases of the revolt with some keenness, he had heard of the further troubles brewing between Ostrog and the people, the attempt at disarmament and the sudden interference of the Sleeper on the popular side; and now, as the night drew on, the London sky showed an unwonted red. He knew that a section of the negro police had come to Paris, that there were threats of their use in London. His blood grew hot at the thought of a negro control; but his discipline was strict; one must not quarrel with one's food, so that he was out on the hillside, one of that great host of men which counts for nothing in the world's affairs.

He rode his horse slowly up the hill towards the crest where the regiments of the wind-wheels were wont to groan and beat. But night, against the bright, deep blue of the north-east, came out black and clear cut, and, ominously, expectantly still. The clearness of the night promised a frost, and the horseman shivered as he rode.

Towards the crest the horse stumbled and the man spoke. In another moment, between the supports of two of the wheels, the flying stage of Norwood rose over the brow, with a greenish glare behind its lace of stays, and a red light on its westward side. He rode straight towards this, through the deep twilight between the supports. In a few minutes he was clear of the wheels on the further side, and the dense spire of flame-shot smoke that rose from the burning of Streatham came into view. He gave a startled exclamation, drew rein and sat watching. All about the stages London was red, and reeking with the smoke and steam of war. The small south-west wind-vanes came out black against the smoky glare of Streatham, the reflection, he judged, of an incandescence upon vast volumes of smoke or steam. He knit his brows, and presently dropped his bridle, and sat looking through the frame of his hands in order to concentrate his attention. He knew nothing of warfare, had never heard or read of the old days, knew indeed little of anything save the routine of his duties, but he could not but see these appearances indicated some vast struggle in the city.

"Still fighting," he said. "Still fighting. War—war. How will it end? How can it end? They are bound to win—bound to win."

"Bound to win," he repeated, after an interval. "They have flying. They can bring their damned niggers. I wonder how it will feel to take one's orders from a nigger? 'Git—ye white trash!'—I know 'em."

He cursed Ostrog with swift passion, shook his bridle and, turning eastward, rode through the stands and stays to a wide, vacant space, from which a southward view was obtainable. The afterglow of the southern sky above the crenellations of the downland wind-vanes was clear and empty.

Presently he came back to his original position, and scarcely had the city come up over the brow before he perceived something was happening on the flying stage at Roehampton. The twilight and a thin haze rendered everything doubtful, but that stage was brightly lit, and he was presently almost assured that an aëropile was being flung into the air. Then he was sure, for he saw the little speck soar clear of the hills against the brightness of the lower sky, and curve round upward and westward, dark and clear, and grow smaller and smaller, until at last it trembled out of sight.

His gaze returned to the city. Presently came a speck of light above the smoke, and for a moment he saw an aëropile whose wing had caught the light of the flames. It was flying with stiff wings as a rook flies down the south-west wind, and in a minute it had gone beyond the light. His eye, dazzled by the ridges and masses of glare, could not follow it into the dark. For a time he remained straining his eyes, and then came a little thing, a little oblong patch of black, that shot down very swiftly across the eastward glare of the city and vanished again. He dropped his hands. "That's an aëropile gone down," he said. "Edge down. Can it be——?"

He lifted his framing hands again.

"They would never dare——"

He looked long and earnestly, but he saw no more aëropiles.

The horseman remained motionless for a long time in the deepening twilight. It came into his mind that he could hear voices and the beat of engines. These aërial voices grew louder and louder. Suddenly the black bushes and dusky slopes before him jumped into a pallid clearness, almost as if a magnesium rocket had burst in mid-heaven. The voices rose to shouts. He looked up startled.

The first of Ostrog's air-ships, a vast and stately frame, brightly lit from stem to stern, so that it seemed an air-ship of woven moonshine came into view beyond the black contours of the wind-vanes and drove swiftly down the sky towards the distant city. It was flying very low, and all aboard were gesticulating and shouting. Then, like flames of lightning, another and another came into view, shining swift shapes, each crowded with multitudes of shouting men.

He groaned aloud, for he knew that with them they carried weapons and fomile and the destruction of all hopes of freedom for the beleaguered revolt. East and west came others, and their shouting fell in gusts.

He groaned aloud at the sight of them. "There they go," he said. "Yelling devils! There they go! They'll teach the fools who's master. They'll——"

He stopped in mid-sentence.

The sound was a shriek of fear and anguish from a thousand throats, that changed to a splintering crash and the thud of a near explosion. And all about him shone a glare that threw up the nearer wind-vanes as inky shapes and made the night suddenly very dark. And so low it scarcely cleared the wind-vanes that crested the hill, so close that he could hear the throb, throb, throb, pause, throb, throb, throb, pause, of its engine, like the beating heart of a living thing, rushed the dark shape of an aëropile overhead, passed like some busy twilight owl, and soared up into the sky among the whirling, unwieldly aëroplanes that now tore in a disorderly stream across the sky, clearing the stem of one, as it seemed, by a hair's breadth.

He saw nothing of the collision that flamed down the westward sky, of the strange beacons that were flaring up in the southward country. He stared at this ominous little shape, too astonished to think, until it had dwindled to a speck, and then looking back to the eastward whence that cry of headlong downfall had come, saw over the tops of the still windvanes a stream of fire pouring up into the twilight.

"But they are fighting," he cried; "fighting in the air."

He clapped spurs to his horse, and in a moment had come out upon a projecting headland along the hill brow, from which the base of the flame could be seen. It had seemed near because it was so great, but now he perceived that it was some miles off amidst the Bromley hills. Two of the three wind-wheels that capped that rise had been overthrown, and the third was spinning slowly. The aëroplane lay in a smashed heap, with the gaunt ribs of one broken van pointing heavenward, and the flames shining through the translucent material between the bars of its skeleton.

"No wonder," said the horseman. "No wonder the other poor devils were screaming and shouting."

He turned his eyes slowly back to the flying stages, and saw that only one of the aëroplanes had descended, that the others had swept across the city.

Suddenly he became aware of two little black shapes overhead, circling one above the other, and hardly had he seen them when the ground swayed and ten seconds after he heard a heavy report. His horse started, and as he quieted it came a second shock, and the thud of a nearer explosion, and a tower of smoke and flame flashed into being from out the Norwood stage that the people had destroyed.

It was ten seconds perhaps before he looked up again, and when he did so he cried out. Overhead was something that changed its shape rapidly and grew swiftly larger. Flap, flap, a thing that twisted over and over as it fell. In an instant he understood, clapped spurs to his restive horse, and went galloping down the slope. He heard the aëropiles smash behind him. He came round in a wide sweep and stopped. He sat for a moment staring at the flaring destruction upon the hill crest.

Then he slipped from his plunging horse, and, leaving him to gallop as he would, ran as fast as his boots and spurs would permit through the bracken up the hill again towards the black heap that had heaved and now lay still.

As he drew near he saw that the two aëropiles were still locked together even as they had fallen through the air. Free of the heap he came upon something—a heap of clothing and limbs, pallid under the night, a grey head, a dark clutching hand extended on the turf. Beyond, among the smashed vans, lay two other human forms.

He glanced at the first of these two men, a red-haired man lying face downward, hesitated a minute, and ran shivering to the other. This third victim lay across a rib of the broken van with his body twisted. Two little threads of blood ran from his nostrils into his grizzled moustache, but his upturned face had escaped injury, and in the white glare of the distant aëroplane it showed set and calm, and his eyes were open and steady. He was richly clad, and not in the black uniform of the Council aëronauts.

The shepherd stared at the man, not conceiving he could have survived this terrible downfall, and suddenly the mangled body writhed, and the expression of the face changed.

"Good God!" cried the shepherd. "The man is alive." He ran forward and knelt among the wreckage, ejaculating vague helpfulness, but fearing to touch the crushed body. He saw the lips of the man were moving and, suddenly motionless and intent, heard faint fragments of speech, heard a name he could not catch. Then the name was repeated, and he perceived that it was "Helen."

For a time the shepherd could distinguish nothing further because the accent was strange and because of the uproar from London that distracted his attention.

The aëroplanes were over the distant city now. They went to and fro above it like birds above a carcass, they curved down, and were hidden, and appeared again among the mounting white flames. Two more had overset, their glare blackened the night, and the leaden thudding of guns grew ever more frequent through that remote tumult of battle. The reflection of the burning aëroplanes flickered upon the livid face of this last straggler from a vanished age. Whether he saw, the shepherd could not tell, already it seemed his mind was wandering upon the borderland of death. "Weak men," he muttered, and again, "weak men."

"Weak men."

His breathing became laboured. His head nodded and fell forward, his eyes closed. His face softened and insensibly the touch of pain vanished from his lips. His doubts were at an end.

THE END

THE MAN
WHO COULD WORK MIRACLES

Originally published in *The Illustrated London News*
July 1898

The Man Who Could Work Miracles.

BY H.G. WELLS.

ILLUSTRATED BY A. FORESTIER.

IT is doubtful whether the gift was innate. For my own part, I think it came to him suddenly. Indeed, until he was thirty he was a sceptic, and did not believe in miraculous powers. And here, since it is the most convenient place, I must mention that he was a little man, and had eyes of hot brown, very erect red hair, a moustache like the German Emperor's, and freckles. His name was George McWhirter Fotheringay—not the sort of name by any means to lead to any expectation of miracles—and he was clerk at Gomshott's. He was greatly addicted to assertive argument. It was while he was asserting the impossibility of miracles that he had his first intimation of his extraordinary powers. This particular argument was being held in the bar of the Long Dragon, and Toddy Beamish was conducting the opposition by a monotonous but effective "So *you* say," that drove Mr. Fotheringay to the very limit of his patience.

There were present, besides these two, a very dusty cyclist, landlord Cox, and Miss Maybridge, the perfectly respectable and rather portly barmaid of the Dragon. Miss Maybridge was standing with her back to Mr. Fotheringay, washing glasses; the others were watching him, more or less amused by the present ineffectiveness of the assertive method. Goaded by the Torres Vedras tactics of Mr. Beamish, Mr. Fotheringay determined to make an unusual rhetorical effort. "Looky here, Mr. Beamish," said Mr. Fotheringay. "Let us clearly understand what a miracle is. It's something contrariwise to the course of nature done by power of Will, something what couldn't happen without being specially willed."

"So *you* say," said Mr. Beamish, repulsing him.

Mr. Fotheringay appealed to the cyclist, who had hitherto been a silent auditor, and received his assent—given with a hesitating cough and a glance at Mr. Beamish. The landlord would express no opinion, and Mr. Fotheringay, returning to Mr. Beamish, received the unexpected concession of a qualified assent to his definition of a miracle.

"For instance," said Mr. Fotheringay, greatly encouraged. "Here would be a miracle. That lamp, in the natural course of nature, couldn't burn like that upsy-down, could it, Beamish?"

"*You* say it couldn't," said Beamish.

"And you?" said Fotheringay. "You don't mean to say—eh?"

"No," said Beamish reluctantly. "No, it couldn't."

"Very well," said Mr. Fotheringay. "Then here comes someone, as it might be me, along here, and stands as it might be here, and says to that lamp, as I might do, collecting all my will—Turn upsy-down without breaking, and go on burning steady, and—Hullo!"

It was enough to make anyone say "Hullo!" The impossible, the incredible, was visible to them all. The lamp hung inverted in the air, burning quietly with its flame pointing down. It was as solid, as indisputable as ever a lamp was, the prosaic common lamp of the Long Dragon bar.

Mr. Fotheringay stood with an extended forefinger and the knitted brows of one anticipating a catastrophic smash. The cyclist, who was sitting next the lamp, ducked and jumped across the bar. Everybody jumped, more or less. Miss Maybridge turned and screamed. For nearly three seconds the lamp remained still. A faint cry of mental distress came from Mr. Fotheringay. "I can't keep it up," he said, "any longer." He staggered back, and the inverted lamp suddenly flared, fell against the corner of the bar, bounced aside, smashed upon the floor, and went out.

It was lucky it had a metal receiver, or the whole place would have been in a blaze. Mr. Cox was the first to speak, and his remark, shorn of needless excrescences, was to the effect that Fotheringay was a fool. Fotheringay was beyond disputing even so fundamental a proposition as that! He was astonished beyond measure at the thing that had occurred. The subsequent conversation threw absolutely no light on the matter so far as Fotheringay was concerned; the general opinion not only followed Mr. Cox very closely but very vehemently. Everyone accused Fotheringay of a silly trick, and presented him to himself as a foolish destroyer of comfort and security. His mind was in a tornado of perplexity, he was himself inclined to agree with them, and he made a remarkably ineffectual opposition to the proposal of his departure.

He went home flushed and heated, coat-collar

481

The lamp hung inverted in the air, burning quietly with its flame pointing down.

crumpled, eyes smarting and ears red. He watched each of the ten street lamps nervously as he passed it. It was only when he found himself alone in his little bed-room in Church Row that he was able to grapple seriously with his memories of the occurrence, and ask, "What on earth happened?"

He had removed his coat and boots, and was sitting on the bed with his hands in his pockets repeating the text of his defence for the seventeenth time, "*I* didn't want the confounded thing to upset," when it occurred to him that at the precise moment he had said the commanding words he had inadvertently willed the thing he said, and that when he had seen the lamp in the air he had felt that it depended on him to maintain it there without being clear how this was to be done. He had not a particularly complex mind, or he might have stuck for a time at that "inadvertently willed," embracing, as it does, the abstrusest problems of voluntary action; but as it was, the idea came to him with a quite acceptable haziness. And from that, following, as I must admit, no clear logical path, he came to the test of experiment.

He pointed resolutely to his candle and collected his mind, though he felt he did a foolish thing. "Be raised up," he said. But in a second that feeling vanished. The candle was raised, hung in the air one giddy moment, and as Mr. Fotheringay gasped, fell with a smash on his toilet-table, leaving him in darkness save for the expiring glow of its wick.

For a time Mr. Fotheringay sat in the darkness, perfectly still. "It did happen, after all," he said. "And 'ow *I'm* to explain it I *don't* know." He sighed heavily, and began feeling in his pockets for a match. He could find none, and he rose and groped about the toilet-table. "I wish I had a match," he said. He resorted to his coat, and there was none there, and then it dawned upon him that miracles were possible even with matches. He extended a hand and scowled at it in the dark. "Let there be a match in that hand," he said. He felt some light object fall across his palm, and his fingers closed upon a match.

After several ineffectual attempts to light this, he discovered it was a safety-match. He threw it down, and then it occured to him that he might have willed it lit. He did, and perceived it burning in the midst of his toilet-table mat. He caught it up hastily, and it went out. His perception of possibilities enlarged, and he felt for and replaced the candle in its candlestick. "Here! *you* be lit," said Mr. Fotheringay, and forthwith the candle was flaring, and he saw a little black hole in the toilet-cover, with a wisp

He made a remarkably ineffectual opposition to the proposal of his departure.

of smoke rising from it. For a time he stared from this to the little flame and back, and then looked up and met his own gaze in the looking glass. By this help he communed with himself in silence for a time.

"How about miracles now?" said Mr. Fotheringay at last, addressing his reflection.

The subsequent meditations of Mr. Fotheringay were of a severe, but confused description. So far, he could see it was a case of pure willing with him. The nature of his experiences so far disinclined him for any further experiments, at least until he had reconsidered them. But he lifted a sheet of paper, and turned a glass of water pink and then green, and he created a snail, which he miraculously annihilated, and got himself a miraculous new toothbrush. Somewhere in the small hours he had reached the fact that his will-power must be of a particularly rare and pungent quality, a fact of which he had certainly had inklings before, but no certain assurance. The scare and perplexity of his first discovery was now qualified by pride in this evidence of singularity and by vague intimations of advantage. He became aware that the church clock was striking one, and as it did not occur to him that his daily duties at Gomshott's might be miraculously dispensed with, he resumed undressing, in order to get to bed without further delay. As he struggled to get his shirt over his head, he was struck with a brilliant idea. "Let me be in bed," he said, and found himself so. "Undressed," he stipulated; and, finding the sheets cold, added hastily, "and in my nightshirt—no, in a nice soft woollen nightshirt. Ah!" he said with immense enjoyment. "And now let me be comfortably asleep.". . .

He awoke at his usual hour and was pensive all through breakfast-time, wondering whether his overnight experience might not be a particularly vivid dream. At length his mind turned again to cautious experiments. For instance, he had three eggs for breakfast; two his landlady had supplied, good, but shoppy, and one was a delicious fresh goose-egg, laid, cooked, and served by his extraordinary will. He hurried off to Gomshott's in a state of profound but carefully concealed excitement, and only remembered the shell of the third egg when his landlady spoke of it that night. All day he could do no work because of this astonishingly new self-knowledge, but this caused him no inconvenience, because he made up for it miraculously in his last ten minutes.

As the day wore on his state of mind passed from wonder to elation, albeit the circumstances of his dismissal from the Long Dragon were still disagreeable to recall, and a garbled account of the matter that had reached his colleagues led to some badinage. It was evident he must be careful how he lifted frangible articles, but in other ways his gift promised more and more as he turned it over in his mind. He intended among other things to increase his personal property by unostentatious acts of creation. He called into existence a pair of very splendid diamond studs, and hastily annihilated them again as young Gomshott came across the counting-house to his desk. He was afraid young Gomshott might wonder how he had come by them. He saw quite clearly the gift required caution and watchfulness in its exercise, but so far as he could judge the difficulties attending his mastery would be no greater than those he had already faced in the study of cycling. It was that analogy, perhaps, quite as much as the feeling that he would be welcome in the Long Dragon, that drove him out after supper into the lane beyond the gasworks, to rehearse a few miracles in private.

There was possibly a certain want of originality in his attempts, for apart from his will-power Mr. Fotheringay was not a very exceptional man. The miracle of Moses' rod came to his mind, but the night was dark and unfavourable to the proper control of large miraculous snakes. Then he recollected the story of "Tannhäuser" that he had read on the back of the Philharmonic programme. That seemed to him singularly attractive and harmless. He stuck his walking-stick—a very nice Poona-Penang lawyer—into the turf that edged the footpath, and commanded the dry wood to blossom. The air was immediately full of the scent of roses, and by means of a match he saw for himself that this beautiful miracle was indeed accomplished. His satisfaction was ended by advancing footsteps. Afraid of a premature discovery of his powers, he addressed the blossoming stick hastily: "Go back." What he meant was "Change back"; but of course he was confused. The stick receded at a considerable velocity, and incontinently came a cry of anger and a bad word from the approaching person. "Who are you throwing brambles at, you fool?" cried a voice. "That got me on the shin."

"I'm sorry, old chap," said Mr. Fotheringay, and then realising the awkward nature of the explanation, caught nervously at his moustache. He saw Winch, one of the three Immering constables, advancing.

"What d'yer mean by it?" asked the constable. "Hullo! It's you, is it? The gent that broke the lamp at the Long Dragon!"

"I don't mean anything by it," said Mr. Fotheringay. "Nothing at all."

"What d'yer do it for then?"

"Oh, bother!" said Mr. Fotheringay.

"Bother indeed! D'yer know that stick hurt? What d'yer do it for, eh?"

For the moment Mr. Fotheringay could not think what he had done it for. His silence seemed to irritate Mr. Winch. "You've been assaulting the police, young man, this time. That's what you done."

"Look here, Mr. Winch," said Mr. Fotheringay, annoyed and confused, "I'm very sorry. The fact is——"

"Well?"

He could think of no way but the truth. "I was working a miracle." He tried to speak in an off-hand way, but try as he would he couldn't.

"Working a——! 'Ere, don't you talk rot. Working a miracle, indeed! Miracle! Well, that's downright funny! Why, you's the chap that don't believe in miracles. . . . Fact is, this is another of yur silly conjuring tricks—that's what this is. Now, I tell you——"

By means of a match he saw for himself that this beautiful miracle was indeed accomplished.

"Go to Hades! Go, now!"

But Mr. Fotheringay never heard what Mr. Winch was going to tell him. He realised he had given himself away, flung his valuable secret to all the winds of heaven. A violent gust of irritation swept him to action. He turned on the constable swiftly and fiercely. "Here," he said, "I've had enough of this, I have! I'll show you a silly conjuring trick, I will! Go to Hades! Go, now!"

He was alone!

Mr. Fotheringay performed no more miracles that night, nor did he trouble to see what had become of his flowering stick. He returned to the town forthwith, scared and very quiet, and went to his bed-room. "Lord!" he said, "it's a powerful gift—an extremely powerful gift. I didn't hardly mean as much as that. Not really. . . . I wonder what Hades is like!"

He sat on the bed taking off his boots. Struck by a happy thought he transferred the constable to San Francisco, and without any more interference with normal causation went soberly to bed. In the night he dreamt of the anger of Winch.

The next day Mr. Fotheringay heard two interesting items of news. Someone had planted a most beautiful climbing rose against the elder Mr. Gomshott's private house in the Lullaborough Road, and the river as far as Rawling's Mill was to be dragged for Constable Winch.

Mr. Fotheringay was abstracted and thoughtful all that day, and performed no miracles either on that day or the next, except certain provisions for Winch, and the miracle of completing his day's work with punctual perfection in spite of

Struck by a happy thought, he transferred the constable to San Francisco.

all the bee-swarm of thoughts that hummed through his mind. And the extraordinary abstraction and meekness of his manner was remarked by several people, and made a matter for jesting. For the most part he was thinking of Winch.

On Sunday evening he went to chapel, and oddly enough, Mr. Maydig, who took a certain interest in occult matters, preached about "things that are not lawful." Mr. Fotheringay was not a regular chapel-goer, but the system of assertive scepticism, to which I have already alluded, was now very much shaken. The tenor of the sermon threw an entirely new light on these novel gifts, and he suddenly decided to consult Mr. Maydig immediately after the service. So soon as that was determined, he found himself wondering why he had not done so before.

Mr. Maydig, a lean, excitable man with quite remarkably long wrists and neck, was gratified at a request for a private conversation from a young man whose carelessness in religious matters was a subject for general remark in the town. After a few necessary delays, he conducted him to the study of the Manse, which was contiguous to the chapel, seated him comfortably, and, standing in front of a cheerful fire—his legs threw a Rhodian arch of shadow on the opposite wall—requested Mr. Fotheringay to state his business.

At first, Mr. Fotheringay was a little abashed, and found some difficulty in opening the matter. "You will scarcely believe me, Mr. Maydig, I am afraid"—and so forth for some time. He tried a question at last, and asked Mr. Maydig his opinion of miracles.

Mr. Maydig was still saying "Well" in an extremely judicial tone, when Mr. Fotheringay interrupted again: "You don't believe, I suppose, that some common sort of person—like myself, for instance—as it might be sitting here now, might have some sort of twist inside him that made him able to do things by his will."

"It's possible," said Mr. Maydig. "Something of the sort, perhaps, is possible."

"If I might make free with something here, I think I might show you by a sort of experiment," said Mr. Fotheringay. "Now, take that tobacco-jar on the table, for instance. What I want to know is whether what I am going to do with it is a miracle or not. Just half a minute, Mr. Maydig, please."

He knitted his brows, pointed to the tobacco-jar and said: "Be a bowl of vi'lets."

The tobacco-jar did as it was ordered.

Mr. Maydig started violently at the change, and stood looking from the thaumaturgist to the bowl of flowers. He said nothing. Presently he ventured to lean over the table and smell the violets; they were fresh-picked and very fine ones. Then he stared at Mr. Fotheringay again.

"How did you do that?" he asked.

Mr. Fotheringay pulled his moustache. "Just told it—and there you are. Is that a miracle, or is it black art, or what is it? And what do you think's the matter with me? That's what I want to ask."

"It's a most extraordinary occurrence."

"And this day last week I knew no more that I could do things like that than you did. It came quite sudden. It's something odd about my will, I suppose, and that's as far as I can see."

"Is that—the only thing. Could you do other things besides that?"

"Lord, yes!" said Mr. Fotheringay. "Just anything." He thought, and suddenly recalled a conjuring entertainment he had seen. "Here!" He pointed. "Change into a bowl of fish—no, not that—change into a glass bowl full of water with goldfish swimming in it. That's better! You see that, Mr. Maydig?"

"It's astonishing. It's incredible. You are either a most extraordinary . . . But no—"

"I could change it into anything," said Mr. Fotheringay. "Just anything. Here! be a pigeon, will you?"

In another moment a blue pigeon was fluttering round the room and making Mr. Maydig duck every time it came near him. "Stop there, will you," said Mr. Fotheringay; and the pigeon hung motionless in the air. "I could change it back to a bowl of flowers," he said, and after replacing the pigeon on the table worked that miracle. "I expect you will want your pipe presently," he said, and restored the tobacco-jar.

Mr. Maydig had followed all these later changes in a sort of ejaculatory silence. He stared at Mr. Fotheringay fearfully, and, in a very gingerly manner, picked up the tobacco-jar, examined it, replaced it on the table. "*Well!*" was the only expression of his feelings.

"Now, after that it's easier to explain what I came about," said Mr. Fotheringay; and proceeded to a lengthy and involved narrative of his strange experiences, beginning with the affair of the lamp in the Long Dragon and complicated by persistent allusions to Winch. As he went on, the transient pride Mr. Maydig's consternation had caused passed away; he became the very ordinary Mr. Fotheringay of everyday intercourse again. Mr. Maydig listened intently, the tobacco-jar in his hand, and his bearing changed also with the course of the narrative. Presently, while Mr. Fotheringay was dealing with the miracle of the third egg, the minister interrupted with a fluttering extended hand—

"It is possible," he said. "It is credible. It is amazing, of course, but it reconciles a number of amazing difficulties. The power to work miracles is a gift—a peculiar quality like genius or second sight—hitherto it has come very rarely and to exceptional people. But in this case . . . I have always wondered at the miracles of Mahomet, and at Yogi's miracles, and the miracles of Madame Blavatsky. But, of course! Yes, it is simply a gift! It carries out so beautifully the arguments of that great thinker"—Mr. Maydig's voice sank—"his Grace the Duke of Argyll. Here we plumb some profounder law—deeper than the ordinary laws of nature. Yes—yes. Go on. Go on!"

Mr. Fotheringay proceeded to tell of his misadventure with Winch, and Mr. Maydig, no longer overawed or scared, began to jerk his limbs about and interject astonishment. "It's this what troubled me most," proceeded Mr. Fotheringay; "it's this I'm most mijitly in want

He decided to consult Mr. Maydig immediately after the service.

of advice for; of course he's at San Francisco—wherever San Francisco may be—but of course it's awkward for both of us, as you'll see, Mr. Maydig. I don't see how he can understand what has happened, and I daresay he's scared and exasperated something tremendous, and trying to get at me. I daresay he keeps on starting off to come here. I send him back, by a miracle, every few hours, when I think of it. And, of course, that's a thing he won't be able to understand, and it's bound to annoy him; and, of course, if he takes a ticket every time it will cost him a lot of money. I done the best I could for him, but of course it's difficult for him to put himself in my place. I thought afterwards that his clothes might have got scorched, you know—if Hades is all it's supposed to be—before I shifted him. In that case I suppose they'd have locked him up in San Francisco. Of course I willed him a new suit of clothes on him directly I thought of it. But, you see, I'm already in a deuce of a tangle—"

Mr. Maydig looked serious. "I see you are in a tangle. Yes, it's a difficult position. How you are to end it . . ." He became diffuse and inconclusive.

"However, we'll leave Winch for a little and discuss the larger question. I don't think this is a case of the black art or anything of the sort. I don't think there is any taint of criminality about it at all, Mr. Fotheringay—none whatever, unless you are suppressing material facts. No, it's miracles—pure miracles—miracles, if I may say so, of the very highest class."

He began to pace the hearthrug and gesticulate, while Mr. Fotheringay sat with his arm on the table and his head on his arm, looking worried. "I don't see how I'm to manage about Winch," he said.

"A gift of working miracles—apparently a very powerful gift," said Mr. Maydig, "will find a way about Winch—never fear. My dear Sir, you are a most important man—a man of the most astonishing possibilities. As evidence, for example! And in other ways, the things you may do . . ."

"Yes, I've thought of a thing or two," said Mr. Fotheringay. "But—some of the things came a bit twisty. You saw that fish at first? Wrong sort of bowl and wrong sort of fish. And I thought I'd ask someone."

"A proper course," said Mr. Maydig, "a very proper course—altogether the proper course."

He stopped and looked at Mr. Fotheringay. "It's practically an unlimited gift. Let us test your powers, for instance. If they really are . . . If they really are all they seem to be."

And so, incredible as it may seem, in the study of the little house behind the Congregational Chapel, on the evening of Sunday, Nov. 10, 1896, Mr. Fotheringay, egged on and inspired by Mr. Maydig, began to work miracles. The reader's attention is specially and definitely called to the date. He will object, probably has already objected, that certain points in this story are improbable, that if any things of the sort already described had indeed occurred, they would have been in all the papers a year ago. The details immediately following he will find particularly hard to accept, because among other things they involve the conclusion that he or she, the reader in question, must have been killed in a violent and unprecedented manner more than a year ago. Now a miracle is nothing if not improbable, and as a matter of fact the reader *was* killed in a violent and unprecedented manner a year ago. In the subsequent course of this story that will become perfectly clear and credible, as every right-minded and reasonable reader will admit. But this is not the place for the end of the story, being but little beyond the hither side of the middle. And at first the miracles worked by Mr. Fotheringay were timid little miracles—little things with the cups and parlour fitments, as feeble as the miracles of Theosophists, and, feeble as they were, they were received with awe by his collaborator. He would have preferred to settle the Winch business out of hand, but Mr. Maydig would not let him. But after they had worked a dozen of these domestic trivialities, their sense of power grew, their imagination began to show signs of stimulation, and their ambition enlarged. Their first larger enterprise was due to hunger and the negligence of Mrs. Minchin, Mr. Maydig's housekeeper. The meal to which the minister conducted Mr. Fotheringay was certainly ill-laid and uninviting as refreshment for two industrious miracle-workers; but they were already seated, and Mr. Maydig was descanting in sorrow rather than in anger upon his housekeeper's shortcomings, before it occurred to Mr. Fotheringay that an opportunity lay before him. "Don't you think, Mr. Maydig," he said, "if it isn't a liberty, I—"

"My dear Mr. Fotheringay! Of course! No—I didn't think."

Mr. Fotheringay waved his hand. "What shall we have?" he said, in a large, inclusive spirit, and, at Mr. Maydig's order, revised the supper very thoroughly. "As for me," he said, eyeing Mr. Maydig's selection, "I'm always particularly fond of a tankard of stout and a nice Welsh rabbit, and I'll order that. I ain't much given to Burgundy," and forthwith stout and Welsh rab-

A blue pigeon was fluttering round the room and making Mr. Maydig duck every time it came near him.

Mr. Fotheringay, at Mr. Maydig's order, revised the supper very thoroughly.

bit promptly appeared at his command. They sat long at their supper, talking like equals, as Mr. Fotheringay presently perceived, with a glow of suprise and gratification, of all the miracles they would presently do. "And, by the bye, Mr. Maydig," said Mr. Fotheringay, "I might perhaps be able to help you—in the domestic way."

"Don't quite follow," said Mr. Maydig, pouring out a glass of miraculous old Burgundy.

Mr. Fotheringay helped himself to a second Welsh rabbit out of vacancy, and took a mouthful. "I was thinking," he said, "I might be able *(chum, chum)* to work *(chum, chum)* a miracle with Mrs. Minchin *(chum, chum)*—make her a better woman."

Mr. Maydig put down the glass and looked doubtful. "She's—She strongly objects to interference, you know, Mr. Fotheringay. And—as a matter of fact—it's well past eleven and she's probably in bed and asleep. Do you think, on the whole—"

Mr. Fotheringay considered these objections. "I don't see that it shouldn't be done in her sleep."

For a time Mr. Maydig opposed the idea, and then he yielded. Mr. Fotheringay issued his orders, and a little less at their ease, perhaps, the two gentlemen proceeded with their repast. Mr. Maydig was enlarging on the changes he might expect in his housekeeper next day, with an optimism that seemed even to Mr. Fotheringay's supper senses a little forced and hectic, when a series of confused noises from upstairs began. Their eyes exchanged interrogations, and Mr. Maydig left the room hastily. Mr. Fotheringay heard him calling up to his housekeeper and then his footsteps going softly up to her.

In a minute or so the minister returned, his step light, his face radiant. "Wonderful!" he said, "and touching! Most touching!"

He began pacing the hearth-rug. "A repentance—a most touching repentance—through the crack of the door. Poor woman! A most wonderful change! She had got up. She must have got up at once. She had got up out of her sleep to smash a private bottle of brandy in her box. And to confess it too! . . . But this gives us—it opens—a most amazing vista of possibilities. If we can work this miraculous change in *her*. . . ."

"The thing's unlimited seemingly," said Mr. Fotheringay. "And about Mr. Winch—"

"Altogether unlimited." And from the hearth-rug Mr. Maydig, waving the Winch difficulty aside, unfolded a series of wonderful proposals—proposals he invented as he went along.

She had got up out of her sleep to smash a private bottle of brandy in her box.

Now what those proposals were does not concern the essentials of this story. Suffice it that they were designed in a spirit of infinite benevolence, the sort of benevolence that used to be called post-prandial. Suffice it, too, that the problem of Winch remained unsolved. Nor is it necessary to describe how far that series got to its fulfillment. There were astonishing changes. The small hours found Mr. Maydig and Mr. Fotheringay careering across the chilly market-square under the still moon, in a sort of ectasy of thaumaturgy, Mr. Maydig all flap and gesture, Mr. Fotheringay short and bristling, and no longer abashed at his greatness. They had reformed every drunkard in the Parliamentary division, changed all the beer and alcohol to water (Mr. Maydig had overruled Mr. Fotheringay on this point); they had, further, greatly improved the railway communication of the place, drained Flinder's swamp, improved the soil of One Tree Hill, and cured the Vicar's wart. And they were going to see what could be done with the injured pier at South Bridge. "The place," gasped Mr. Maydig, "won't be the same place tomorrow. How surprised and thankful everyone will be!" And just at that moment the church clock struck three.

"I say," said Mr. Fotheringay, "that's three o'clock! I must be getting back. I've got to be at business by eight. And besides, Mrs. Wimms——"

"We're only beginning," said Mr. Maydig, full of the sweetness of unlimited power. "We're only beginning. Think of all the good we're doing. When people wake——"

"But——," said Mr. Fotheringay.

Mr. Maydig gripped his arm suddenly. His eyes were bright and wild. "My dear chap," he said, "there's no hurry. Look"—he pointed to the moon at the zenith—"Joshua!"

"Joshua?" said Mr. Fotheringay.

"Joshua," said Mr. Maydig. "Why not? Stop it."

Mr. Fotheringay looked at the moon.

"That's a bit tall," he said after a pause.

"Why not?" said Mr. Maydig. "Of course it doesn't stop. You stop the rotation of the earth, you know. Time stops. It isn't as if we were doing harm."

"H'm!" said Mr. Fotheringay. "Well." He sighed. "I'll try. Here——"

He buttoned up his jacket and addressed himself to the habitable globe, with as good an assumption of confidence as lay in his power. "Jest stop rotating, will you," said Mr. Fotheringay.

Incontinently he was flying head over heels through the air at the rate of dozens of miles a minute. In spite of the innumerable circles he was describing per second, he thought; for thought is wonderful—sometimes as sluggish as flowing pitch, sometimes as instantaneous as light. He thought in a second, and willed. "Let me come down safe and sound. Whatever else happens, let me down safe and sound."

He willed it only just in time, for his clothes, heated by his rapid flight through the air, were already beginning to singe. He came down with a forcible, but by no means injurious bump in what appeared to be a mound of fresh-turned earth. A large mass of metal and masonry, extraordinarily like the clock-tower in the middle of the market-square, hit the earth near him, richochetted over him, and flew into stonework, bricks, and masonry, like a bursting bomb. A hurtling cow hit one of the larger blocks and smashed like an egg. There was a crash that made all the most violent crashes of his past life seem like the sound of falling dust, and this was followed by a descending series of lesser crashes. A vast wind roared throughout earth and heaven, so that he could scarcely lift his head to look. For a while he was too breathless and astonished even to see where he was or what had happened. And his first movement was to feel his head and reassure himself that his streaming hair was still his own.

"Lord!" gasped Mr. Fotheringay, scarce able to speak for the gale, "I've had a squeak! What's gone wrong? Storms and thunder. And only a minute ago a fine night. It's Maydig set me on this sort of thing. *What* a wind! If I go on fooling in this way I'm bound to have a thundering accident! . . ."

"Where's Maydig?"

"What a confounded mess everything's in!"

He looked about him so far as his flapping jacket would permit. The appearance of things was really extremely strange. "The sky's all right anyhow," said Mr. Fotheringay. "And that's about all that is all right. And even there it looks like a terrific gale coming up. But there's the moon overhead. Just as it was just now. Bright as midday. But as for the rest—— Where's the village? Where's—where's anything? And what on earth set this wind a-blowing? *I* didn't order no wind."

Mr. Fotheringay struggled to get to his feet in vain, and after one failure, remained on all fours, holding on. He surveyed the moonlit world to leeward, with the tails of his jacket streaming over his head. "There's something seriously wrong," said Mr. Fotheringay. "And what it is—goodness knows."

Far and wide nothing was visible in the white glare through the haze of dust that drove before a screaming gale but tumbled masses of earth and heaps of inchoate ruins, no trees, no houses, no familiar shapes, only a wilderness of disorder vanishing at last into the darkness beneath the whirling columns and streamers, the lightnings and thunderings of a swiftly rising storm. Near him in the livid glare was something that might once have been an elm-tree, a smashed mass of splinters, shivered from boughs to base, and further a twisted mass of iron girders—only too evidently the viaduct—rose out of the piled confusion.

You see, when Mr. Fotheringay had arrested the rotation of the solid globe, he had made no stipulation concerning the trifling movables upon its surface. And the earth spins so fast that the surface at its equator is travelling at rather more than a thousand miles an hour, and in these latitudes at more than half that pace. So that the village, and Mr. Maydig, and Mr. Fotheringay, and everybody and everything had been jerked violently forward at about nine miles per second—that is to say, much more violently than if they had been fired out of a cannon. And every human being, every living creature, every house, and every tree—all the world as we know

Mr. Maydig gripped his arm suddenly. His eyes were bright and wild . . . He pointed at the moon at the zenith.

Incontinently he was flying head over heels through the air at the rate of dozens of miles a minute.

it—had been so jerked and smashed and utterly destroyed. That was all.

These things Mr. Fotheringay did not, of course, fully appreciate. But he perceived that his miracle had miscarried, and with that a great disgust of miracles came upon him. He was in darkness now, for the clouds had swept together and blotted out his momentary glimpse of the moon, and the air was full of fitful struggling tortured wraiths of hail. A great roaring of wind and waters filled earth and sky, and, peering under his hand through the dust and sleet to windward, he saw by the play of the lightnings a vast wall of water pouring towards him.

"Maydig!" screamed Mr. Fotheringay's feeble voice amid the elemental uproar. "Here!— Maydig!"

"Stop!" cried Mr. Fotheringay to the advancing water. "Oh, for goodness' sake, stop!"

"Jest a moment," said Mr. Fotheringay to the lightnings and thunder. "Stop jest a moment while I collect my thoughts. . . . And now what shall I do?" he said. "What *shall* I do? Lord! I wish Maydig was about."

"I know," said Mr. Fotheringay. "And for goodness' sake let's have it right *this* time."

He remained on all fours, leaning against the wind, very intent to have everything right.

"Ah!" he said. "Let nothing what I'm going to order happen until I say 'Off!' . . . Lord! I wish I'd thought of that before!"

He lifted his little voice against the whirlwind, shouting louder and louder in the vain desire to hear himself speak. "Now then!—here goes! Mind about that what I said just now. In the first place, when all I've got to say is done, let me lose my miraculous power, let my will become just like anybody else's will, and all these dangerous miracles be stopped. I don't like them. I'd rather I didn't work 'em. Ever so much. That's the first thing. And the second is—let me be back just before the miracles begin; let everybody be just as it was before that blessed lamp turned up. It's a big job, but it's the last. Have you got it? No more miracles, everything as it was—me back in the Long Dragon just before I drank my half-pint. That's it! Yes."

He dug his fingers into the mould, closed his eyes, and said "Off!"

Everything became perfectly still. He perceived that he was standing erect.

"So *you* say," said a voice.

He opened his eyes. He was in the bar of the Long Dragon, arguing about miracles with Toddy Beamish. He had a vague sense of some great thing forgotten that instantaneously passed. You see that, except for the loss of his miraculous powers, everything was back as it had been, his mind and memory therefore were now just as they had been at the time when this story began. So that he knew absolutely nothing of all that is told here, knows nothing of all that is told here to this day. And among other things, of course, he still did not believe in miracles.

"I tell you that miracles, properly speaking, can't possible happen," he said, "whatever you like to hold. And I'm prepared to prove it up to the hilt."

"That's what *you* think," said Toddy Beamish, and "Prove it if you can."

"Looky here, Mr. Beamish," said Mr. Fotheringay. "Let us clearly understand what a miracle is. It's something contrariwise to the course of nature done by power of Will. . . ."

He remained on all fours, leaning against the wind, very intent to have everything right.

THE LAND IRONCLADS

Originally published in *The Strand Magazine*
December 1903

The Land Ironclads.

By H. G. Wells.

I.

THE young lieutenant lay beside the war correspondent and admired the idyllic calm of the enemy's lines through his field-glass.

"So far as I can see," he said, at last, "one man."

"What's he doing?" asked the war correspondent.

"Field - glass at us," said the young lieutenant.

"And this is war!"

"No," said the young lieutenant; "it's Bloch."

"The game's a draw."

"No! They've got to win or else they lose. A draw's a win for our side."

They had discussed the political situation fifty times or so, and the war correspondent was weary of it. He stretched out his limbs. "Aaai s'pose it *is*!" he yawned.

"*Flut!*"

"What was that?"

"Shot at us."

The war correspondent shifted to a slightly lower position. "No one shot at him," he complained.

"I wonder if they think we shall get so bored we shall go home?"

The war correspondent made no reply.

"There's the harvest, of course . . ."

They had been there a month. Since the first brisk movements after the declaration of war things had gone slower and slower, until it seemed as though the whole machine of events must have run down. To begin with, they had had almost a scampering time; the invader had come across the frontier on the very dawn of the war in half-a-dozen parallel columns behind a cloud of cyclists and cavalry, with a general air of coming straight on the capital, and the defender-horsemen had held him up, and peppered him and forced him to open out to outflank, and had then bolted to the next position in the most approved style, for a couple of days, until in the afternoon, bump! they had the invader against their prepared lines of defence. He did not suffer so much as had been hoped and expected: he was coming on it seemed with his eyes open, his scouts winded the guns,

and down he sat at once without the shadow of an attack and began grubbing trenches for himself, as though he meant to sit down there to the very end of time. He was slow, but much more wary than the world had been led to expect, and he kept convoys tucked in and shielded his slow marching infantry sufficiently well, to prevent any heavy adverse scoring.

"But he ought to attack," the young lieutenant had insisted.

"He'll attack us at dawn, somewhere along the lines. You'll get the bayonets coming into the trenches just about when you can see," the war correspondent had held until a week ago.

The young lieutenant winked when he said that.

When one early morning the men the defenders sent to lie out five hundred yards before the trenches, with a view to the unexpected emptying of magazines into any night attack, gave way to causeless panic and blazed away at nothing for ten minutes, the war correspondent understood the meaning of that wink.

"What would you do if you were the enemy?" said the war correspondent, suddenly.

"If I had men like I've got now?"

"Yes."

"Take these trenches."

"How?"

"Oh—dodges! Crawl out half-way at night before moonrise and get into touch with the chaps we send out. Blaze at 'em if they tried to shift, and so bag some of 'em in the daylight. Learn that patch of ground by heart, lie all day in squatty holes, and come on nearer next night. There's a bit over there, lumpy ground, where they could get across to rushing distance—easy. In a night or so. It would be a mere game for our fellows; it's what they're made for. . . . Guns? Shrapnel and stuff wouldn't stop good men who meant business."

"Why don't *they* do that?"

"Their men aren't brutes enough; that's the trouble. They're a crowd of devitalized townsmen, and that's the truth of the matter. They're clerks, they're factory hands, they're students, they're civilized men. They **can** write, they can talk, they can make and **do** all sorts of things, but they're poor amateurs at war. They've got no physical staying power, and that's the whole thing. They've never slept in the open one night in their lives; they've never drunk anything but the purest water-company water; they've never gone short of three meals a day since they left their devitalizing feeding-bottles. Half their cavalry never cocked leg over horse till it enlisted six months ago. They ride their horses as though they were bicycles—you watch 'em! They're fools at the game, and they know it. Our boys of fourteen can give their grown men points. . . . . Very well——"

The war correspondent mused on his face with his nose between his knuckles.

"If a decent civilization," he said, "cannot produce better men for war than——"

He stopped with belated politeness. "I mean——"

"Than our open-air life," said the young lieutenant, politely.

"Exactly," said the war correspondent. "Then civilization has to stop."

"'BOOM!' CAME FROM SOMEWHERE FAR AWAY TO THE LEFT."

"It looks like it," the young lieutenant admitted.

"Civilization has science, you know," said the war correspondent. "It invented and it makes the rifles and guns and things you use."

"Which our nice healthy hunters and stockmen and so on, rowdy-dowdy cow-punchers and horse-whackers, can use ten times better than—— *What's that?*"

"What?" said the war correspondent, and then seeing his companion busy with his field-glass he produced his own. "Where?" said the war correspondent, sweeping the enemy's lines.

"It's nothing," said the young lieutenant, still looking.

"What's nothing?"

The young lieutenant put down his glass and pointed. "I thought I saw something there, behind the stems of those trees. Something black. What it was I don't know."

The war correspondent tried to get even by intense scrutiny.

"It wasn't anything," said the young lieutenant, rolling over to regard the darkling evening sky, and generalized: "There never will be anything any more for ever. Unless——"

The war correspondent looked inquiry.

"They may get their stomachs wrong, or something—living without proper drains."

A sound of bugles came from the tents behind. The war correspondent slid backward down the sand and stood up. "Boom!" came from somewhere far away to the left. "Halloa!" he said, hesitated, and crawled back to peer again. "Firing at this time is jolly bad manners."

The young lieutenant was incommunicative again for a space.

Then he pointed to the distant clump of trees again. "One of our big guns. They were firing at that," he said.

"The thing that wasn't anything?"

"Something over there, anyhow."

Both men were silent, peering through their glasses for a space. "Just when it's twilight," the lieutenant complained. He stood up.

"I might stay here a bit," said the war correspondent.

The lieutenant shook his head. "There's nothing to see," he apologized, and then went down to where his little squad of sun-brown, loose-limbed men had been yarning in the trench. The war correspondent stood up also, glanced for a moment at the business-like bustle below him, gave perhaps twenty seconds to those enigmatical trees again, then turned his face toward the camp.

He found himself wondering whether his editor would consider the story of how somebody thought he saw something black behind a clump of trees, and how a gun was fired at this illusion by somebody else, too trivial for public consumption.

"It's the only gleam of a shadow of interest," said the war correspondent, "for ten whole days."

"No," he said, presently; "I'll write that other article, 'Is War Played Out?'"

He surveyed the darkling lines in perspective, the tangle of trenches one behind another, one commanding another, which the defender had made ready. The shadows and mists swallowed up their receding contours, and here and there a lantern gleamed, and here and there knots of men were busy about small fires. "No troops on earth could do it," he said. . . .

He was depressed. He believed that there were other things in life better worth having than proficiency in war; he believed that in the heart of civilization, for all its stresses, its crushing concentrations of forces, its injustice and suffering, there lay something that might be the hope of the world, and the idea that any people by living in the open air, hunting perpetually, losing touch with books and art and all the things that intensify life, might hope to resist and break that great development to the end of time, jarred on his civilized soul.

Apt to his thought came a file of the defender soldiers and passed him in the gleam of a swinging lamp that marked the way.

He glanced at their red-lit faces, and one shone out for a moment, a common type of face in the defender's ranks : ill-shaped nose, sensuous lips, bright clear eyes full of alert cunning, slouch hat cocked on one side and adorned with the peacock's plume of the rustic Don Juan turned soldier, a hard brown skin, a sinewy frame, an open, tireless stride, and a master's grip on the rifle.

The war correspondent returned their salutations and went on his way.

"Louts," he whispered. "Cunning, elementary louts. And they are going to beat the townsmen at the game of war!"

From the red glow among the nearer tents came first one and then half-a-dozen hearty voices, bawling in a drawling unison the words of a particularly slab and sentimental patriotic song.

"Oh, *go* it!" muttered the war correspondent, bitterly.

II.

IT was opposite the trenches called after Hackbone's Hut that the battle began. There the ground stretched broad and level between the lines, with scarcely shelter for a lizard, and it seemed to the startled, just-awakened men who came crowding into the trenches that this was one more proof of that green inexperience of the enemy of which they had heard so much. The war correspondent would not believe his ears at first, and swore that he and the war artist, who, still imperfectly roused, was trying to put on his boots by the light of a match held in his hand, were the victims of a common illusion. Then, after putting his head in a bucket of cold water, his intelligence came back as he towelled. He listened. "Gollys !" he said ; "that's something more than scare firing this time. It's like ten thousand carts on a bridge of tin."

There came a sort of enrichment to that steady uproar. "Machine guns !"

Then, "Guns !"

The artist, with one boot on, thought to look at his watch, and went to it hopping.

"Half an hour from dawn," he said. "You were right about their attacking, after all. . . ."

The war correspondent came out of the tent, verifying the presence of chocolate in his pocket as he did so. He had to halt for a moment or so until his eyes were toned down to the night a little. "Pitch !" he said. He stood for a space to season his eyes before he felt justified in striking out for a black gap among the adjacent tents. The artist coming out behind him fell over a tent-rope. It was half-past two o'clock in the morning of the darkest night in time, and against a sky of dull black silk the enemy was talking searchlights, a wild jabber of searchlights. "He's trying to blind our riflemen," said the war correspondent with a flash, and waited for the artist and then set off with a sort of discreet haste again. "Whoa !" he said, presently. "Ditches !"

They stopped.

"It's the confounded searchlights," said the war correspondent.

They saw lanterns going to and fro, near by, and men falling in to march down to the trenches. They were for following them, and then the artist began to feel his night eyes. "If we scramble this," he said, "and it's only a drain, there's a clear run up to the ridge." And that way they took. Lights came and went in the tents behind, as the men turned out, and ever and again they came to broken ground and staggered and stumbled. But in a little while they drew near the crest. Something that sounded like the impact of a very important railway accident happened in the air above them, and the shrapnel bullets seethed about them like a sudden handful of hail. "Right-ho!" said the war correspondent, and soon they judged they had come to the crest and stood in the midst of a world of great darkness and frantic glares, whose principal fact was sound.

Right and left of them and all about them was the uproar, an army-full of magazine fire, at first chaotic and monstrous and then, eked out by little flashes and gleams and suggestions, taking the beginnings of a shape. It looked to the war correspondent as though the enemy must have attacked in line and with his whole force—in which case he was either being or was already annihilated.

"Dawn and the Dead," he said, with his instinct for headlines. He said this to himself, but afterwards, by means of shouting, he conveyed an idea to the artist. "They must have meant it for a surprise," he said.

It was remarkable how the firing kept on. After a time he began to perceive a sort of rhythm in this inferno of noise. It would decline—decline perceptibly, droop towards something that was comparatively a pause—a pause of inquiry. "Aren't you all dead yet?" this pause seemed to say. The flickering fringe of rifle-flashes would become attenuated and broken, and the whack-bang of the enemy's big guns two miles away there would come up out of

the deeps. Then suddenly, east or west of them, something would startle the rifles to a frantic outbreak again.

The war correspondent taxed his brain for some theory of conflict that would account for this, and was suddenly aware that the artist and he were vividly illuminated. He could see the ridge on which they stood, and before them in black outline a file of riflemen hurrying down towards the nearer trenches. It became visible that a light rain was falling, and farther away towards the enemy was a clear space with men—"our men?"—running across it in disorder. He saw one of those men throw up his hands and drop. And something else black and shining loomed up on the edge of the beam-coruscating flashes; and behind it and far away a calm, white eye regarded the world. "Whit, whit, whit," sang something in the air,

"SOMETHING ELSE BLACK AND SHINING LOOMED UP ON THE EDGE OF THE BEAM."

and then the artist was running for cover, with the war correspondent behind him. Bang came shrapnel, bursting close at hand as it seemed, and our two men were lying flat in a dip in the ground, and the light and everything had gone again, leaving a vast note of interrogation upon the night.

The war correspondent came within bawling range. "What the deuce was it? Shooting our men down!"

"Black," said the artist, "and like a fort. Not two hundred yards from the first trench."

And on its carcass the bullets must have been battering with more than the passionate violence of hail on a roof of tin.

Then in the twinkling of an eye the curtain of the dark had fallen again and the monster had vanished, but the crescendo of musketry marked its approach to the trenches.

They were beginning to talk about the thing to each other, when a flying bullet kicked dirt into the artist's face, and they decided abruptly to crawl down into the cover of the trenches. They had got down

" IT HAD THE EFFECT OF A LARGE AND CLUMSY BLACK INSECT."

He sought for comparisons in his mind. "Something between a big blockhouse and a giant's dish-cover," he said.

"And they were running!" said the war correspondent.

"*You'd* run if a thing like that, with a searchlight to help it, turned up like a prowling nightmare in the middle of the night."

They crawled to what they judged the edge of the dip and lay regarding the unfathomable dark. For a space they could distinguish nothing, and then a sudden convergence of the searchlights of both sides brought the strange thing out again.

In that flickering pallor it had the effect of a large and clumsy black insect, an insect the size of an ironclad cruiser, crawling obliquely to the first line of trenches and firing shots out of portholes in its back.

with an unobtrusive persistence into the second line, before the dawn had grown clear enough for anything to be seen. They found themselves in a crowd of expectant riflemen, all noisily arguing about the thing that would happen next. The enemy's contrivance had done execution upon the outlying men, it seemed, but they did not believe it would do any more. "Come the day and we'll capture the lot of them," said a burly soldier.

"Them?" said the war correspondent.

"They say there's a regular string of 'em, crawling along the front of our lines. . . . Who cares?"

The darkness filtered away so imperceptibly that at no moment could one declare decisively that one could see. The searchlights ceased to sweep hither and thither. The enemy's monsters were dubious patches of darkness upon the dark, and then no longer dubious, and so they crept out into distinctness. The war correspondent, munching chocolate absent-mindedly, beheld at last a spacious picture of battle under the cheerless sky, whose central focus was an array of fourteen or fifteen huge clumsy shapes lying in perspective on the very edge of the first line of trenches, at intervals of perhaps three hundred yards, and evidently firing down upon the crowded riflemen. They were so close in that the defender's guns had ceased, and only the first line of trenches was in action.

The second line commanded the first, and as the light grew the war correspondent could make out the riflemen who were fighting these monsters, crouched in knots and crowds behind the transverse banks that crossed the trenches against the eventuality of an enfilade. The trenches close to the big machines were empty save for the crumpled suggestions of dead and wounded men; the defenders had been driven right and left as soon as the prow of this land ironclad had loomed up over the front of the trench. He produced his field-glass, and was immediately a centre of inquiry from the soldiers about him.

They wanted to look, they asked questions, and after he had announced that the men across the traverses seemed unable to advance or retreat, and were crouching under cover rather than fighting, he found it advisable to loan his glasses to a burly and incredulous corporal. He heard a strident voice, and found a lean and sallow soldier at his back talking to the artist.

"There's chaps down there caught," the man was saying. "If they retreat they got to expose themselves, and the fire's too straight. . . ."

"They aren't firing much, but every shot's a hit."

"Who?"

"The chaps in that thing. The men who're coming up——"

"Coming up where?"

"We're evacuating them trenches where we can. Our chaps are coming back up the zigzags . . . . No end of 'em hit. . . . But when we get clear our turn'll come. Rather! Those things won't be able to cross a trench or get into it; and before they can get back our guns'll smash 'em up. Smash 'em right up. See?" A brightness came into his eyes. "Then we'll have a go at the beggar inside," he said. . . .

The war correspondent thought for a moment, trying to realize the idea. Then

he set himself to recover his field-glasses from the burly corporal. . . .

The daylight was getting clearer now. The clouds were lifting, and a gleam of lemon yellow amidst the level masses to the east portended sunrise. He looked again at the land ironclad. As he saw it in the bleak, grey dawn, lying obliquely upon the slope and on the very lip of the foremost trench, the suggestion of a stranded vessel was very great indeed. It might have been from eighty to a hundred feet long—it was about two hundred and fifty yards away—its vertical side was ten feet high or so, smooth for that height, and then with a complex patterning under the eaves of its flattish turtle cover. This patterning was a close interlacing of portholes, rifle barrels, and telescope tubes—sham and real—indistinguishable one from the other. The thing had come into such a position as to enfilade the trench, which was empty now, so far as he could see, except for two or three crouching knots of men and the tumbled-looking dead. Behind it, across the plain, it had scored the grass with a train of linked impressions, like the dotted tracings sea-things leave in sand. Left and right of that track dead men and wounded men were scattered—men it had picked off as they fled back from their advanced positions in the searchlight glare from the invader's lines. And now it lay with its head projecting a little over the trench it had won, as if it were a single sentient thing planning the next phase of its attack. . . .

He lowered his glasses and took a more comprehensive view of the situation. These creatures of the night had evidently won the first line of trenches and the fight had come to a pause. In the increasing light he could make out by a stray shot or a chance exposure that the defender's marksmen were lying thick in the second and third line of trenches up towards the low crest of the position, and in such of the zigzags as gave them a chance of a converging fire. The men about him were talking of guns. "We're in the line of the big guns at the crest, but they'll soon shift one to pepper them," the lean man said, reassuringly.

"Whup," said the corporal.

"Bang! bang! bang! Whir-r-r-r!" it was a sort of nervous jump, and all the rifles were going off by themselves. The war correspondent found himself and the artist, two idle men crouching behind a line of pre-occupied backs, of industrious men discharging magazines. The monster had moved. It continued to move regardless of the hail that splashed its skin with bright new specks of lead. It was singing a mechanical little ditty to itself, "Tuf-tuf, tuf-tuf, tuf-tuf," and squirting out little jets of steam behind. It had humped itself up, as a limpet does before it crawls ; it had lifted its skirt and displayed along the length of it—*feet !* They were thick, stumpy feet, between knobs and buttons in shape—flat, broad things, reminding one of the feet of elephants or the legs of caterpillars ; and then, as the skirt rose higher, the war correspondent, scrutinizing the thing through his glasses again, saw that these feet hung, as it were, on the rims of wheels. His thoughts whirled back to Victoria Street, Westminster, and he saw himself in the piping times of peace, seeking matter for an interview.

" Mr. — Mr. Diplock," he said ; "and he called them Pedrails . . . . Fancy meeting them here ! "

The marksman beside him raised his head and shoulders in a speculative mood to fire more certainly

"THE MEN ABOUT HIM STUCK TO THEIR POSITION AND FIRED FURIOUSLY."

—it seemed so natural to assume the attention of the monster must be distracted by this trench before it—and was suddenly knocked backwards by a bullet through his neck. His feet flew up, and he vanished out of the margin of the watcher's field of vision. The war correspondent grovelled tighter, but after a glance behind him at a painful little confusion, he resumed his field-glass, for the thing was putting down its feet one after the other, and hoisting itself farther and farther over the trench. Only a bullet in the head could have stopped him looking just then.

The lean man with the strident voice

ceased firing to turn and reiterate his point. "They can't possibly cross," he bawled. They——"

"Bang ! Bang ! Bang, bang !"—drowned everything.

The lean man continued speaking for a word or so, then gave it up, shook his head to enforce the impossibility of anything crossing a trench like the one below, and resumed business once more.

And all the while that great bulk was crossing. When the war correspondent turned his glass on it again it had bridged the trench, and its queer feet were rasping away at the farther bank, in the attempt to get a hold there. It got its hold. It continued to crawl until the greater bulk of it was over the trench — until it was all over. Then it paused for a moment, adjusted its skirt a little nearer the ground, gave an unnerving " toot, toot," and came on abruptly at a pace of, perhaps, six miles an hour straight up the gentle slope towards our observer.

The war correspondent raised himself on his elbow and looked a natural inquiry at the artist.

For a moment the men about him stuck to their position and fired furiously. Then the lean man in a mood of precipitancy slid backwards, and the war correspondent said "Come along" to the artist, and led the movement along the trench.

As they dropped down, the vision of a hillside of trench being rushed by a dozen vast cockroaches disappeared for a space, and instead was one of a narrow passage, crowded with men, for the most part receding, though one or two turned or halted. He never turned back to see the nose of the monster creep over the brow of the trench ; he never even troubled to keep in touch with the artist. He heard the "whit" of bullets about him soon enough, and saw a man before him stumble and drop, and then he was one of a furious crowd fighting to get into a transverse zigzag ditch that enabled the defenders to get under cover up and down the hill. It was like a theatre panic. He gathered from signs and fragmentary words that on ahead another of these monsters had also won to the second trench.

He lost his interest in the general course of the battle for a space altogether ; he became simply a modest egotist, in a mood of hasty circumspection, seeking the farthest rear, amidst a dispersed multitude of disconcerted riflemen similarly employed. He scrambled down through trenches, he took his courage in both hands and sprinted across the open, he had moments of panic when it seemed madness not to be quadrupedal, and moments of shame when he stood up and faced about to see how the fight was going. And he was one of many thousand very similar men that morning. On the ridge he halted in a knot of scrub, and was for a few minutes almost minded to stop and see things out.

The day was now fully come. The grey sky had changed to blue, and of all the cloudy masses of the dawn there remained only a few patches of dissolving fleeciness. The world below was bright and singularly clear. The ridge was not, perhaps,

more than a hundred feet or so above the general plain, but in this flat region it sufficed to give the effect of extensive view. Away on the north side of the ridge, little and far, were the camps, the ordered waggons, all the gear of a big army ; with officers galloping about and men doing aimless things. Here and there men were falling-in, however, and the cavalry was forming up on the plain beyond the tents. The bulk of men who had been in the trenches were still on the move to the rear, scattered like sheep without a shepherd over the farther slopes. Here and there were little rallies and attempts to wait and do—something vague ; but the general drift was away from any concentration. Then on the southern side was the elaborate lacework of trenches and defences, across which these iron turtles, fourteen of them spread out over a line of perhaps three miles, were now advancing as fast as a man could trot, and methodically shooting down and breaking up any persistent knots of resistance. Here and there stood little clumps of men, outflanked and unable to get away, showing the white flag, and the

"HERE AND THERE STOOD LITTLE CLUMPS OF MEN, OUTFLANKED AND UNABLE TO GET AWAY."

invader's cyclist infantry was advancing now across the open, in open order but unmolested, to complete the work of the machines. So far as the day went, the defenders already looked a beaten army. A mechanism that was effectually ironclad against bullets, that could at a pinch cross a thirty-foot trench, and that seemed able to shoot out rifle-bullets with unerring precision, was clearly an inevitable victor against anything but rivers, precipices, and guns.

He looked at his watch. " Half-past four ! Lord ! What things can happen in two hours. Here's the whole blessed army being walked over, and at half-past two——

" And even now our blessed louts haven't done a thing with their guns ! "

He scanned the ridge right and left of him with his glasses. He turned again to the nearest land ironclad, advancing now obliquely to him and not three hundred yards away, and then scanned the ground over which he must retreat if he was not to be captured.

" They'll do nothing," he said, and glanced again at the enemy.

And then from far away to the left came the thud of a gun, followed very rapidly by a rolling gun-fire.

He hesitated and decided to stay.

III.

THE defender had relied chiefly upon his rifles in the event of an assault. His guns he kept concealed at various points upon and behind the ridge ready to bring them into action against any artillery preparations for an attack on the part of his antagonist. The situation had rushed upon him with the dawn, and by the time the gunners had their guns ready for motion, the land ironclads were already in among the foremost trenches. There is a natural reluctance to fire into one's own broken men, and many of the guns, being intended simply to fight an advance of the enemy's artillery, were not in positions to hit anything in the second line of trenches. After that the advance of the land ironclads was swift. The defender-general found himself suddenly called upon to invent a new sort of warfare, in which guns were to fight alone amidst broken and retreating infantry. He had scarcely thirty minutes in which to think it out. He did not respond to the call, and what happened that morning was that the advance of the land ironclads forced the fight, and each gun and battery made what play its circumstances dictated. For the most part it was poor play.

Some of the guns got in two or three shots, some one or two, and the percentage of misses was unusually high. The howitzers, of course, did nothing. The land ironclads in each case followed much the same tactics. As soon as a gun came into play the monster turned itself almost end on, so as to get the biggest chance of a glancing hit, and made not for the gun, but for the nearest point on its flank from which the gunners could be shot down. Few of the hits scored were very effectual ; only one of the things was disabled, and that was the one that fought the three batteries attached to the brigade on the left wing. Three that were hit when close upon the guns were clean shot through without being put out of action. Our war correspondent did not see that one momentary arrest of the tide of victory on the left ; he saw only the very ineffectual fight of half-battery 96B close at hand upon his right. This he watched some time beyond the margin of safety.

Just after he heard the three batteries opening up upon his left he became aware of the thud of horses' hoofs from the sheltered side of the slope, and presently saw first one and then two other guns galloping into position along the north side of the ridge, well out of sight of the great bulk that was now creeping obliquely towards the crest and cutting up the lingering infantry beside it and below, as it came.

The half-battery swung round into line— each gun describing its curve—halted, un-limbered, and prepared for action. . . . .

" Bang ! "

The land ironclad had become visible over the brow of the hill, and just visible as a long black back to the gunners. It halted, as though it hesitated.

The two remaining guns fired, and then their big antagonist had swung round and was in full view, end on, against the sky, coming at a rush.

The gunners became frantic in their haste to fire again. They were so near the war correspondent could see the expression of their excited faces through his field-glass. As he looked he saw a man drop, and realized for the first time that the ironclad was shooting.

For a moment the big black monster crawled with an accelerated pace towards the furiously active gunners. Then, as if moved by a generous impulse, it turned its full broadside to their attack, and scarcely forty yards away from them. The war correspondent turned his field-glass back to the gunners and perceived it was now shooting down the men about the guns with the most deadly rapidity.

Just for a moment it seemed splendid and then it seemed horrible. The gunners were dropping in heaps about their guns. To lay a hand on a gun was death. "Bang!" went the gun on the left, a hopeless miss, and that was the only second shot the half-battery fired. In another moment half-a-dozen surviving artillerymen were holding up their hands amidst a scattered muddle of dead and wounded men, and the fight was done.

The war correspondent hesitated between stopping in his scrub and waiting for an opportunity to surrender decently, or taking to an adjacent gully he had discovered. If he surrendered it was certain he would get no copy off; while, if he escaped, there were all sorts of chances. He decided to follow the gully, and take the first offer in the confusion beyond the camp of picking up a horse.

IV.

SUBSEQUENT authorities have found fault with the first land ironclads in many particulars, but assuredly they served their purpose on the day of their appearance. They were essentially long, narrow, and very strong steel frameworks carrying the engines, and borne upon eight pairs of big pedrail wheels, each about ten feet in diameter, each a driving wheel and set upon long axles free to swivel round a common axis. This arrangement gave them the maximum of adaptability to the contours of the ground. They crawled level along the ground with one foot high upon a hillock and another deep in a depression, and they could hold themselves erect and steady sideways upon even a steep hillside. The engineers directed the engines under the command of the captain, who had look-out points at small ports all round the upper edge of the

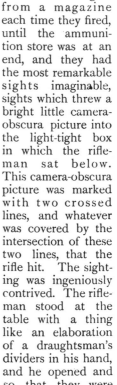

"HE DECIDED TO FOLLOW THE GULLY."

adjustable skirt of twelve-inch iron-plating which protected the whole affair, and who could also raise or depress a conning-tower set about the portholes through the centre of the iron top cover. The riflemen each occupied a small cabin of peculiar construction, and these cabins were slung along the sides of and before and behind the great main framework, in a manner suggestive of the slinging of the seats of an Irish jaunting-car. Their rifles, however, were very different pieces of apparatus from the simple mechanisms in the hands of their adversaries.

These were in the first place automatic, ejected their cartridges and loaded again from a magazine each time they fired, until the ammunition store was at an end, and they had the most remarkable sights imaginable, sights which threw a bright little camera-obscura picture into the light-tight box in which the rifleman sat below. This camera-obscura picture was marked with two crossed lines, and whatever was covered by the intersection of these two lines, that the rifle hit. The sighting was ingeniously contrived. The rifleman stood at the table with a thing like an elaboration of a draughtsman's dividers in his hand, and he opened and closed these dividers, so that they were always at the apparent height—if it was an ordinary-sized man—of the man he wanted to kill. A little twisted strand of wire like an electric-light wire ran from this implement up to the gun, and as the dividers opened and shut the sights went up or down. Changes in the clearness of the atmosphere, due to changes of moisture, were met by an ingenious use of that meteorologically sensitive substance, catgut, and when the land ironclad moved forward the sights got a compensatory deflection in the direction of its motion. The rifleman stood up in his pitch-dark chamber and watched the little picture before him. One hand held the dividers for judging distance, and the other grasped a big knob like a door-handle. As he pushed this knob about the rifle above swung to correspond, and the picture passed to and fro like an agitated panorama. When he saw a man he wanted to shoot he brought him up to the cross-lines, and then pressed a finger upon a little push like an electric bell-push, conveniently placed in the centre of the knob. Then the man was shot. If by any chance the rifleman missed his target he moved the knob a trifle, or readjusted his dividers, pressed the push, and got him the second time.

This rifle and its sights protruded from a porthole, exactly like a great number of other portholes that ran in a triple row under the eaves of

"THE PICTURE PASSED TO AND FRO LIKE AN AGITATED PANORAMA."

the cover of the land ironclad. Each porthole displayed a rifle and sight in dummy, so that the real ones could only be hit by a chance shot, and if one was, then the young man below said "Pshaw!" turned on an electric light, lowered the injured instrument into his camera, replaced the injured part, or put up a new rifle if the injury was considerable.

You must conceive these cabins as hung clear above the swing of the axles, and inside the big wheels upon which the great elephant-like feet were hung, and behind these cabins along the centre of the monster ran a central gallery into which they opened, and along which worked the big compact engines. It was like a long passage into which this throbbing machinery had been packed, and the captain stood about the middle, close to the ladder that led to his conning-tower, and directed the silent, alert

engineers—for the most part by signs. The throb and noise of the engines mingled with the reports of the rifles and the intermittent clangour of the bullet hail upon the armour. Ever and again he would touch the wheel that raised his conning-tower, step up his ladder until his engineers could see nothing of him above the waist, and then come down again with orders. Two small electric lights were all the illumination of this space — they were placed to make him most clearly visible to his subordinates; the air was thick with the smell of oil and petrol, and had the war correspondent been suddenly transferred from the spacious dawn outside to the bowels of this apparatus he would have thought himself fallen into another world.

The captain, of course, saw both sides of the battle. When he raised his head into his conning-tower there were the dewy sunrise, the amazed and disordered trenches, the flying and falling soldiers, the depressed-looking groups of prisoners, the beaten guns; when he bent down again to signal "Half speed," "Quarter speed," "Half circle round towards the right," or what not, he was in the oil-smelling twilight of the ill-lit engine-room. Close beside him on either side was the mouthpiece of a speaking-tube, and ever and again he would direct one side or other of his strange craft to "Concentrate fire forward on gunners," or to "Clear out trench about a hundred yards on our right front."

He was a young man, healthy enough but by no means sun-tanned, and of a type of feature and expression that prevails in His Majesty's Navy: alert, intelligent, quiet. He and his engineers and his riflemen all went about their work, calm and reasonable men. They had none of that flapping strenuousness of the half-wit in a hurry, that excessive strain upon the blood-vessels, that hysteria of effort which is so frequently regarded as the proper state of mind for heroic deeds. If their machine had demanded anything of the sort they would, of course, have improved their machine. They were all perfectly sober and in good training, and if any of them had begun to ejaculate nonsense or bawl patriotic airs, the others would probably have gagged him and tied him up as a dangerous, un-nerving sort of fool. And if they were free from hysteria they were equally free from that stupid affectation of nonchalance which is the refuge of the thoroughly incapable in danger. Death was abroad, and there were marginal possibilities of the unforeseen, but it is no good calculating upon the incalculable, and so beyond a certain unavoidable tighten-ing up of nerve and muscle, a certain firmness of the lips, this affected them not at all.

For the enemy these young engineers were defeating they felt a certain qualified pity and a quite unqualified contempt. They regarded these big, healthy men they were shooting down precisely as these same big, healthy men might regard some inferior kind of nigger. They despised them for making war ; despised their bawling patriotisms and their emotionality profoundly ; despised them, above all, for the petty cunning and the almost brutish want of imagination their method of fighting displayed. " If they *must* make war," these young men thought, " why in thunder don't they do it like sensible men ? " They resented the assump-tion that their own side was too stupid to do anything more than play their enemy's game, that they were going to play this costly folly according to the rules of unimagi-native men. They resented being forced to the trouble of making man-killing machinery ; resented the alternative of having to massacre these people or endure their truculent yappings ; resented the whole unfathomable imbecility of war.

Meanwhile, with something of the me-chanical precision of a good clerk posting a ledger, the riflemen moved their knobs and pressed their buttons. . . .

The captain of Land Ironclad Number Three had halted on the crest close to his captured half-battery. His lined-up prisoners stood hard by and waited for the cyclists behind to come for them. He surveyed the victorious morning through his conning-tower.

He read the general's signals. " Five and Four are to keep among the guns to the left and prevent any attempt to recover them. Seven and Eleven and Twelve, stick to the guns you have got ; Seven, get into position to command the guns taken by Three. Then we're to do something else, are we ? Six and One, quicken up to about ten miles an hour and walk round behind that camp to the levels near the river — we shall bag the whole crowd of them," interjected the young man. " Ah, here we are ! Two and Three, Eight and Nine, Thirteen and Fourteen, space out to a thousand yards, wait for the word, and then go slowly to cover the advance of the cyclist infantry against any charge of mounted troops. That's all right. But where's Ten ? Halloa ! Ten to repair and get movable as soon as possible. They've broken up Ten ! "

The discipline of the new war machines was business-like rather than pedantic, and the head of the captain came down out of the conning-tower to tell his men. " I say, you chaps there. They've broken up Ten. Not badly, I think ; but anyhow, he's stuck ! "

But that still left thirteen of the monsters in action to finish up the broken army.

The war correspondent stealing down his gully looked back and saw them all lying along the crest and talking fluttering con-gratulatory flags to one another. Their iron sides were shining golden in the light of the rising sun.

V.

THE private adventures of the war corre-spondent terminated in surrender about one o'clock in the afternoon, and by that time he had stolen a horse, pitched off it, and narrowly escaped being rolled upon ; found the brute had broken its leg, and shot it with his revolver. He had spent some hours in the company of a squad of dispirited rifle-men, who had commandeered his field-glass and whose pedestrianism was exemplary, and he had quarrelled with them about topography at last, and gone off by himself in a direction that should have brought him to the banks of the river and didn't. More-over, he had eaten all his chocolate and found nothing in the whole world to drink. Also, it had become extremely hot. From behind a broken, but attractive, stone wall he had seen far away in the distance the defender horsemen trying to charge cyclists in open order, with land ironclads outflanking them on either side. He had discovered that cyclists could retreat over open turf before horsemen with a sufficient margin of speed to allow of frequent dismounts and much terribly-effective sharpshooting; and he had a sufficient persuasion that those horsemen, having charged their hearts out, had halted just beyond his range of vision and surrendered. He had been urged to sudden activity by a forward movement of one of those machines that had threatened to enfilade his wall. He had discovered a fearful blister on his heel.

He was now in a scrubby gravelly place, sitting down and meditating on his pocket-handkerchief, which had in some extraordinary way become in the last twenty-four hours extremely ambiguous in hue. "It's the whitest thing I've got," he said.

He had known all along that the enemy was east, west, and south of him, but when he heard war ironclads Numbers One and Six talking in their measured, deadly way not half a mile to the north he decided to make his own little unconditional peace without any further risks. He was for hoisting his white flag to a bush and taking up a position of modest obscurity near it, until someone came along. He became aware of voices, clatter, and the distinctive noises of a body of horse, quite near, and he put his handkerchief in his pocket again and went to see what was going forward.

The sound of firing ceased, and then as he drew near he heard the deep sounds of many simple, coarse, but hearty and noble-hearted soldiers of the old school swearing with vigour.

He emerged from his scrub upon a big level plain, and far away a fringe of trees marked the banks of the river.

In the centre of the picture was a still intact road bridge, and a big railway bridge a little to the right. Two land ironclads

"HE HAD SPENT SOME HOURS IN THE COMPANY OF A SQUAD OF DISPIRITED RIFLEMEN."

rested, with a general air of being long, harmless sheds, in a pose of anticipatory peacefulness right and left of the picture, completely commanding two miles and more of the river levels. Emerged and halted a little from the scrub was the remainder of the defender's cavalry, dusty, a little disordered and obviously annoyed, but still a very fine show of men.

In the middle distance three or four men and horses were receiving medical attendance, and a little nearer a knot of officers regarded the distant novelties in mechanism with profound distaste. Everyone was very distinctly aware of the twelve other ironclads, and of the multitude of townsmen soldiers, on bicycles or afoot, encumbered now by prisoners and captured war-gear but otherwise thoroughly effective, who were sweeping like a great net in their rear.

"Checkmate," said the war correspondent, walking out into the open. "But I surrender in the best of company. Twenty-four hours ago I thought war was impossible—and these beggars have captured the whole blessed army! Well! Well!" He thought of his talk with the young lieutenant. "If there's no end to the surprises of science, the civilized people have it, of course. As long as their science keeps going they will necessarily be ahead of open-country men. Still. . . ."

He wondered for a space what might have happened to the young lieutenant.

The war correspondent was one of those inconsistent people who always want the beaten side to win. When he saw all these burly, sun-tanned horsemen, disarmed and dismounted and lined up; when he saw their horses unskilfully led away by the singularly not equestrian cyclists to whom they had surrendered; when he saw these truncated Paladins watching this scandalous sight, he forgot altogether that he had called these men "cunning louts" and wished them beaten not four-and-twenty hours ago. A month ago he had seen that regiment in its pride going forth to war, and had been told of its terrible prowess, how it could charge in open order with each man firing from his saddle, and sweep before it anything else that ever came out to battle in any sort of order, foot or horse. And it had had to fight a few score of young men in atrociously unfair machines !

"Manhood *versus* Machinery" occurred to him as a suitable headline. Journalism curdles all one's mind to phrases.

He strolled as near the lined-up prisoners as the sentinels seemed disposed to permit and surveyed them and compared their sturdy proportions with those of their lightly-built captors.

"Smart degenerates," he muttered. "Anæmic cockneydom."

The surrendered officers came quite close to him presently, and he could hear the colonel's high-pitched tenor. The poor gentleman had spent three years of arduous toil upon the best material in the world perfecting that shooting from the saddle charge, and he was inquiring with phrases of blasphemy, natural under the circumstances, what one could be expected to do against this suitably consigned ironmongery.

"Guns," said someone.

"Big guns they can walk round. You can't shift big guns to keep pace with them, and little guns in the open they rush. I saw 'em rushed. You might do a surprise now and then—assassinate the brutes, perhaps——"

"You might make things like 'em."

"What? *More* ironmongery? Us?..."

"I'll call my article," meditated the war correspondent, "'Mankind *versus* Iron-mongery,' and quote the old boy at the beginning."

And he was much too good a journalist to spoil his contrast by remarking that the half-dozen comparatively slender young men in blue pyjamas who were standing about their victorious land ironclad, drinking coffee and eating biscuits, had also in their eyes and carriage something not altogether degraded below the level of a man.

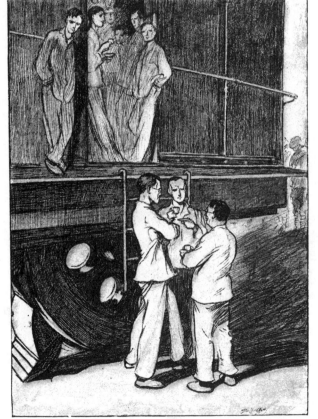

"SOMETHING NOT ALTOGETHER DEGRADED BELOW THE LEVEL OF A MAN."

BIBLIOGRAPHIC NOTE

For bibliographic details
about the work of H. G. Wells,
consult:

A Bibliography of the Works of H.G. Wells
(1893–1925)
by Geoffrey H. Wells
(Routledge, 1925)

H.G. Wells: A Comprehensive Bibliography
compiled by the H.G. Wells Society,
foreword by Kingsley Martin
(H. G. Wells Society, 1968)